Jan Holt was born in London in 1949 and grew up in Dartford and Greenwich. After completing an honours degree at Leicester University she worked as a librarian before moving to the Orkney Islands where she had a variety of jobs including milk delivery and air traffic control. Her ambition from the age of seven was to be a writer and she realised this after meeting David Milsted, then the single parent of two small children, in Orkney in 1983. After their marriage they moved to the island of Islay and then to the Isle of Skye where she achieved success with the publication of a number of pseudonymous novels. By now the mother of four, she began work on *Web of Innocence* in 1992. The family moved to Dorset the following year, during which she became ill. She died of cancer in November 1993.

David Milsted was born in 1954 in Sussex. After his teaching degree at Newcastle he worked in Carlisle where he was prospective parliamentary Liberal candidate for the city. He moved to Orkney in 1978 to teach and he became a full-time writer in 1985. Following Jan's sudden death he took over the unfinished manuscript of *Web of Innocence* and completed it from her notes the following year.

Web of Innocence

❖ JAN HOLT ❖

WARNER BOOKS

A *Warner* Book

First published in Great Britain
by Warner Books in 1995
Reprinted 1996 (twice), 1997

Copyright © David Milsted 1995

The moral right of the author has been asserted.

A CIP catalogue record for this book is
available from the British Library.

ISBN 0 7515 1336 9

Typeset by Palimpset Book Production Limited,
Polmont, Stirlingshire
Printed in England by Clays Ltd, St Ives plc

Warner Books
A Division of
Little, Brown and Company (UK)
Brettenham House
Lancaster Place
London WC2E 7EN

This book is dedicated to my family

❧ LONDON ❧

❖ One ❖

The red velvet curtains were a throwout from Marie's family home in Kent. After putting them up in place of the school issue the girls had renamed their dormitory The Velvet Room and the name had taken. They were The Velvet Girls. Now the westering sun shone full through the closed curtains. The Velvet Room was a glowing crimson womb, dim and exciting.

Three of the girls clustered round the table. The fourth lay on her bed turned to face the unnerving shrouded splendour of the setting sun. The curtains had a small hole in them. Her half-closed eyes saw it as a shining gold coin.

'Look at my naked lady,' said Jenny.

Marie squinted at the card. 'What's that frilly stuff round her?'

'She dances the dance of life in an egg,' said Jenny. 'Life comes and goes. See, she's got a bull, a lion, a sprite and a hawk. She's the Lady of the Dance. He is Rex Mundi.'

'He who?' asked Sam. There was no man on the card.

'Saturn. The planet. That's who the card is associated with.'

'Rex Mundi.' Marie giggled. 'He sounds like a 1940s rotter.'

'It looks a load of bull to me,' drawled Sam at her most Canadian. Her parents had wanted her educated at the best girls' school in the world. She would be going home to attend University when she was finished at Shaws.

'Tarot,' said Marie. Her small eyes sparkled. 'Will you tell my fortune, Jen?'

'I don't need to,' said Jenny rudely. 'Your future's all

eating. Chocolate bars and husbands, chomp chomp chomp, one after the other.'

'Phoo,' said Marie, not displeased. She didn't care if she was fat. 'You'll be slaughtered if you're caught,' she added gleefully. Fortune-telling was superstition and superstition was forbidden at Shaws.

Sam elevated her eyebrows and grinned. Shaws was high Anglican by tradition and in the circumstances Sam considered the ban on superstition something of an irony.

'So who will you do?' asked Gossamer from her bed.

'You. You're the mystery girl.'

'Oh no.'

'Why not, Goss?' asked Sam.

'I don't want to,' she said briefly.

There was a moment's silence. A fly buzzed, caught in the golden flood between the window and the curtain.

'You must want to know who your parents are.' There was a squeak of excitement in Marie's voice.

'Don't be silly.' Gossamer spoke dully. She always went stupid when people talked about her lack of parents. 'Tarot's just a silly game. It can't really say anything.'

'It can.' Jenny swept them up in her latest enthusiasm. 'I did big brother Peter in the hols and he's going to be frightfully rich. Canfield isn't though.' She chuckled. Johnny Canfield was or maybe was not a boyfriend. Jenny looked at life and love with a proper light-heartedness.

'I don't find it funny,' said Gossamer. They couldn't understand. It was all right being an orphan and all mysterious in theory but for her it was a fact. The reality of not knowing who she was or where she came from made her feel hollow inside.

'I know, darling.' Jenny was contrite. 'But we might really find something out.'

Marie looked over at Gossamer. 'It's so odd they didn't want you to know who they were,' she observed. Her tongue came out and licked round her lips.

'I don't want to know who they were,' said Gossamer.

'I shouldn't think they were murderers or anything,' drawled

Sam. Her long narrow eyes veiled a considerable intelligence. 'I mean, there's the money.'

'Or thieves or anything really bad,' cried Jenny. 'Oh, do go on and be a sport. I bet it's just that they weren't married or something and they thought it frightfully shame-making. It'll be something like that that doesn't matter tuppence now.'

'I was born in 1970,' said Gossamer, scarlet-faced. 'If what they say is true, it was all hippies and wife-swapping. It's more prudish now than then. I've told you, I don't want to know.'

'The world awaits us,' said Jenny dramatically. 'We will emerge from Shaws to find Life lurking sticky-fingered round the corner waiting to pounce. Sam the braindrain here goes home to the tundra and all those gorgeous lumberjacks.'

'Hey,' protested Sam mildly.

'Marie will be queen of the greatest soap opera in the world, West Enders. *Ci-devant* yuppies will dance with her at Frankie's between therapy sessions on how to live on less than a hundred thou per annum. Her lovers will lurch between stockmarket crashes while property goes boom-boom. Or doesn't. She'll toss her curls with a callous laugh as they tumble from Canary Wharf to Cannery Row.' Jenny laughed at her own cleverness.

Marie smiled.

Jenny went on: 'I'm for Montreux and Swiss finishing. So I've got simply de-luscious skiing in my future.'

'And de-luscious ski instructors,' observed Marie.

'And I'm attending a dance college in north London,' said Gossamer.

'Ducky, I'll do your future. That's safe enough, isn't it? No bogeymen there.' Without waiting for an answer she took up the pack and leafed through it. 'You're December twentieth, aren't you? That's Sagittarius. Your Tarot suit is Wands. Here, the Page of Wands. That's you. It's called your significator. If you were older you'd be the Queen. The Page, I'll have you know, is considered lively, intelligent, creative and energetic. Now, you shuffle the rest.'

She laid the pack face-down on the table, spreading the cards with a swirling motion. 'You do it,' she said.

Gossamer came from the bed reluctantly. Jenny had fun but no malice in her. Her future couldn't hurt her and truly she was nervous at the thought of leaving school and making her own way in life. Alone. Parentless. First there had been the orphanage. Then life as a boarder at Shaws. Next it would be college. She moved through life like a piece of property changing ownership. She wasn't a person at all.

She stirred the cards slowly. The rosy light made her friends' faces strange. When she was done she stood back. She could hear the trapped fly but a sudden languor made it impossible for her to free it.

Jenny cut the cards into three, putting them back together in a different order. She hesitated for a moment. 'Look,' she said awkwardly. 'You have to believe this while I'm doing it. I mean, I do. It really works.'

'You're doing my future,' said Gossamer. She sat down. She felt dull and heavy. Now she had given way the cards mesmerised her.

'Yes. I'm going to lay out the Horoscope. There are lots of layouts but it's the best for this, I think. I don't control the cards, Goss. You mustn't blame me for what they say.'

'Get on with it,' said Marie. She laughed nervously. The little rolls of fat round her deep-set eyes were pink in the swimming light.

Jenny put the Page of Wands on the table in front of her, face-up. She laid the first card from the shuffled pack to its left, in the nine o'clock position. 'The First House,' she said. 'Self.'

She hesitated a moment. Visibly she calmed herself and began to concentrate on the cards. The four girls fell very silent. Each card came off the top of the deck with a little slithering noise and then was laid with a small snap on the table. The second card went in the eight o'clock position. Jenny went on laying cards this way, anti-clockwise around the Page, until she had completed the circle of twelve cards.

'Each card is in a different House,' she said quietly. She looked directly at Gossamer as if the other two girls didn't exist. 'The card tells you about that House and you understand it in the terms of that House. The cards affect each other, too. You're Wands, Goss. It's your personal suit and it stands for fire, energy and heat. It's what they call an objective suit, full of action. Now, your layout.' Jenny touched the card at nine o'clock. 'The First House. Self. You have the three of Swords. This House is about you, how you feel. I have to look these up, I'm afraid. I can't remember it all.'

She thumbed through the book she had with her. She read for a moment and then she raised her eyes to meet her friend's again. When she spoke her voice was low.

'Heartache.'

'What?' said Sam.

'The card speaks about heartache. Tension. Inner conflict. Separations. There will be tears and trouble. Swords is the suit of aggression and struggle but it serves to strengthen your suit, Wands. So there is a suggestion that things will come right in the end.'

Gossamer said nothing. The room was a blood-tinged cave. Jenny's voice went steadily on. 'The Second House. This is to do with your financial resources, either how you feel about them or in the literal sense. You've got the four of Pentacles. Pentacles means you must take this card literally. It's telling you about money. It's good. It's very good. Nothing spectacular, but you're going to be financially stable and have material comfort. All right?'

Gossamer grinned uneasily.

'The Third House. Communications.'

'It's a moon and two little dogs,' said Marie. 'Upside-down.'

'Reversed,' said Jenny. 'This is from the Major Arcana and so is especially significant.' Her voice faltered. 'It's the card of ill-omen. You will be lied to. There will be insincere people around you. You've got hidden enemies.' She took a deep breath. 'It can be interpreted differently. It can mean that you are living in a world of lies and delusion which is self-inflicted. You might be resorting to drugs or alcohol. This meaning is less likely because you are Wands which is an objective suit. I think another person is being described. The Moon is always bad, whichever way up it comes. I'm sorry, Goss.' She bent her bright head and hurried on. 'The Fourth House. Home. The nine of Swords. This House is concerned with feelings, your reaction to what's about you.' Again she stopped. She bit her lip and when finally she spoke, her voice quivered. 'It's a card of anxiety and fear. You feel oppressed over matters to do with home. There might be a death. You're worried and you'll suffer.'

'You're not making this up, I hope.' Sam had an ominous note in her voice.

'No. I can't control the cards.' She stumbled on. 'The Fifth House. This concerns pleasure, love and creativity. You have the King of Cups.'

'He looks nice,' said Marie.

'He's OK.' Jenny relaxed and produced a brilliant smile. 'It's an older man for a start, and probably a real person. He'll be powerful, imaginative and very creative. He'll have a magnetic personality. He'll be charming and highly-sexed. I say, Goss, this is all right, even if Cups traditionally weakens Wands. It's romance, of course. There is a bad side, Cups can be very devious and manipulative and they make dangerous enemies because they're vengeful and unforgiving. But he doesn't have to be like that. He isn't reversed. He's exciting. He'll have charisma. He sounds gorgeous,' she said and laughed.

'You lucky beast,' said Marie. The sun slipped lower and suddenly the room was in shadow. Sam snapped a light on.

'She deserves something good. The Sixth House. Health and work. This is a fairly mundane House. I mean, it's about everyday stuff, nothing too significant. You've got the seven of Swords. This is a restless and variable card. You'll work hard for a bit and then take it easy. It's the card for writers and artists.' She grinned. 'It's also the card that denotes a thief. The Seventh House. Partnerships. This is a formal house, about marriage or business partnerships. It has a long-term meaning.' She stopped.

'It's another picture card,' said Marie. 'Why are some pictures and some suits?'

'The Major Arcana are pictures. There are twenty-two of them.' Jenny's voice was odd. 'They are very significant, carrying a lot of meaning. They indicate big changes, important affairs. They tell you about life's turning points. The suits are the Minor Arcana. They sort of extend meaning and help you sort things out on a more everyday level.'

'The Devil, upside-down,' said Sam.

Reversed.' Jenny's voice had steadied. 'This is a card of warning. If it applies to you, then you might be going to abuse power in some way, like with money or sex. Imagine being a corrupt business partner or an adulterous wife. It's the card of deviant or bizarre sex, or just excessive sex. It's the card for greedy people, greedy in the material sense. If it applies not to you but to someone in your life, then watch out. You will be abused, financially or sexually or in your work. It can be a symbolic card. You know, life is abusing you, but in this case I think it'll be a real person because it's in partnerships. You or your partner. It's the card of unequal relationships, one person in thrall to another.'

Her clear eyes were troubled. She looked at her friend.

'Go on,' said Gossamer. Her body still felt heavy and inert but inside she was thrumming. It wasn't nice.

'The Eighth House. Sex, death and money. The House of significant events in the big things in your life. You have the seven of Cups reversed. Remember Cups weakens Wands. Your element is fire, Cups is water.'

She read the page and looked at Gossamer again. 'You don't have to believe this,' she said.

'Tell me.'

'It's a card of delusions. Of danger. It's a second warning against retreating into drugs or drink. It's a card of fantasy and self-deceit.'

'Great,' said Sam bitterly. 'This was a terrific idea, Jenny.'

She went over to the window and pulled back the curtains, letting in the evening light.

'We must look back to the Moon. Maybe the Moon is the deceiver, and here you are warned about falling in with the deception. Maybe in both cases you are your own deceiver and the cards are warning you strongly to guard against this because it will harm you and lead you to make wrong decisions. The cards tell you your future, Goss, and here they warn of danger. But remember that the future is insubstantial and shadowy, like the cards themselves. The meanings can slide just when you think you've grasped them. You must interpret them and use them as a guide, as a help. They don't condemn, Goss. They forewarn because things can be changed, mistakes needn't be made. All right? Shall I go on?'

Gossamer nodded. Her face was drained and white.

'The Ninth House. Far horizons. This is a distant view. If it's practical, it tells you about travel. If it's symbolic, we have to work it out. The ten of Cups. Gossamer! Lasting spiritual happiness. That's what the cards predict for you. All this bad stuff about danger and warnings is short-lived. This card signifies permanence, lasting happiness. It's Cups, so it's foretelling emotional rather than financial success but you know you're OK for loot anyway. Your dreams will come true.' She grinned triumphantly at Gossamer. 'Isn't that a wow? Don't you think it's great?'

'Go on,' said Gossamer.

'The Tenth House. Career. Now then, the meaning's quite subtle here. It isn't just work. It needn't be how you earn your living at all. It's to do with how you see your life, what your ambitions are. It's more how you get on with what most concerns you, what you give most time to or most energy. You've got the seven of Pentacles. Pentacles are earthy, quite practical. Yes.' She thought for a moment. 'It says you'll find things tiring for a while and then they'll pay off. There's a sense of gestation, of casting your bread. You'll have to wait for your rewards, but they'll come. Taken with you being in Wands yourself, I'd say this did relate to a career in the normal sense. Pentacles and Swords strengthen Wands. The Eleventh House. We're nearly finished now. Friends and colleagues.'

She stared at the card in bewilderment. 'This isn't right. I can't interpret this at all. You've got the Emperor reversed. That's bad. I can't see what he's doing in this House.'

'What does it mean?' Sam was caught despite herself.

'Someone powerful, cold and calculating is using you for his ends. He's manipulating you. It isn't necessarily bad, he needn't actually wish you harm, it's just that he's not considering you at all. He's using you to serve his own ends. We've had dreams and delusions, insincere people and dangerous people. What's he doing in the House of Friends?'

'Perhaps he turns out to be a friend inadvertently,' said Sam.

'Perhaps he masquerades as a friend,' said Marie.

'Yes. That'll be it. We've had lots about deception. You'll have to watch out, Goss. Really.'

'Finish it,' said Gossamer.

'The Twelfth House. This tells what is hidden. You've got the King of Swords. An older man again. Clever. Emotionally cold or repressed. Quick-witted. Successful. A man who relishes a struggle and usually wins.'

'Is this the same man as the Emperor?' asked Sam.

Jenny was unhappy. 'I don't think so. What is hidden usually refers to the querist, to Gossamer in this case. It's what's hidden in her, her dreams and hopes, rather than what's hidden in her future. Usually you're meant to read court cards as real people, but this is a symbolic House. Swords is a less objective suit than Wands or Pentacles. Its element is air. It's more to do with feelings and subjective things, though it's a strong suit and relates to struggle and warfare. Sorry, I'm waffling. I've got something that should be read literally in a symbolic House. Perhaps this man exists only in Goss's dreams, he's what she hopes for. It need have nothing to do with reality.'

Jenny stopped and eyed her friend uneasily. 'I should

interpret the spread as a whole, too. It isn't just the individual cards and which House they fall in. They relate to each other as well. You've got three sevens, for example. Just having three sevens in a spread argues for a happy result despite all the doom and gloom. I think Goss should see her spread as containing warnings rather than real events. She can avoid trouble by not letting herself get taken in, either financially or in her love-life. There are lots of Cups and Swords. Cups are to do with romance and feelings. Swords are to do with struggling. Gossamer's own suit, Wands, is one of action. She's got to steer a path, keep her eyes open, not be gullible. Over money matters and in the long-term she'll be fine. The cards give her that. But there are stormy waters ahead. You've got to distinguish the King of Cups, who looks great, from that reversed Emperor who's using you in a cold-blooded way. He'll be the insincere one. He probably accounts for the Moon and the Devil. All your Major Arcana cards are reversed. That means the turning-points of your life are all threatened. There's danger. It might mean your hidden desire for a strong man in your life leads you astray. The trouble is, if the delusion and deception come from within you, perhaps from all this fear and anxiety, it might be that you fail to recognise your King of Cups and so risk losing him. You might be your own hidden enemy.'

She began to collect up the cards. Gossamer stayed ominously quiet.

'Do me,' begged Marie.

'No. I'm tired.' Jenny glanced swiftly round the group. When she spoke, her voice was gay. 'What can we do with our time to make a real impression? How can we get ourselves into the school record? Come on, some real mischief.'

'We could get pregnant,' said Marie and tittered.

'A Shaws girl is not at risk in society, whatever the dangers,' said Sam in a faithful and pompous rendition of their senior moral mistress. 'She can say no.'

'No,' shouted the other three in chorus. They collapsed with laughter, the tension draining out of them. Yet all three were virgins. It was what their parents had paid for and Shaws gave value for money.

But Gossamer had no parents.

It was the last day of her life at Shaws School. Gossamer awoke before dawn and lay thinking. She had hated Shaws. She had loved it. Having nowhere else, her school had been her home. It had protected her and stood between her and the world and now there was nothing. She had always been alone only it hadn't been obvious, hemmed in as she was by its grey, stony walls and grey, stony mistresses.

She remembered with discomfort a two-year passion for her music mistress. She had dreamt of leaving Shaws and setting up house with Miss Thrale. Life would be dedicated to art and music. It all made her squirm now and though such feelings were gone forever, she had little to replace them with.

She knew this coming summer would be different. Shaws and its certainties were behind her. She would be spending the summer with Jenny before Jenny went to Switzerland and she moved into her own flat in London. She might have no parents but she had lawyers and they were arranging things for her. Poised on the threshold of her future Gossamer was horribly aware of her own insufficiency. She had been decently educated at Shaws. She had been taught about dress and deportment, about manners and morals. She had been exposed to the staider elements of her literary heritage. But her reading and her television watching had been strictly censored. She had barely met a male and then only in outrageously strict circumstances. She realised she knew nothing of the world and she didn't know what to do about it.

She had spent her babyhood in a Catholic orphanage, but the settlement that controlled her fate specified she was not to be admitted to the Church of Rome. To Shaws she had gone at the appropriate age, feeling helpless and as lost as a feather blown on the wind. Yet here were no gorgons. The famous foundation charged magnificent fees for bestowing its unique character upon its students and its teachers were the best. They were firm but kind. Gossamer's housemother had helped her through her first period and taken her shopping for clothes, since there was no one else to perform this parental duty. It was an ordered, peaceful world.

Queasily Gossamer was aware that a normal upbringing with parents and siblings was different. Shaws did not allow for doubt. Its security, like its morality, was absolute. It didn't exactly say so, but everyone knew it accepted only virgins and whilst within its jurisdiction, virgins its students remained. As far as its Head was concerned, and she was a woman who was a friend of governments, it conferred standards in a society that had lost sight of its moral values. It was ineluctably, unstoppably gracious. The Shaws manner would see a girl through life, if she would but cleave to it.

Increasingly its graduates struggled with adultery, with or without divorce. They found themselves married to bankrupt or criminal husbands. Their offspring declared themselves to be homosexual. It made no difference to Shaws though whispers of unease occasionally penetrated the barrier of its certainty, unsettling the students. It stood for something more than an ephemeral collapse in morals. The world might spin, but at its still centre stood Shaws, dignified, sexually continent and possessed of a terrifying calm.

Gossamer had not one horror story from her youth. Always she had been met with kindness and care. Always someone had had time to talk with her. She remembered the nuns from the orphanage as kindly women, gentle to the little ones in their care.

She knew nothing of the moral compromises demanded by life yet she was aware nothing was as simple as she had been taught. She had had no balancing home life. Somehow she knew that whatever Shaws had given her, it wasn't enough. Especially where the other sex was concerned. She had seen the tip of the iceberg and didn't understand what might lurk below the surface.

It was mysterious, the world of the male. She had met

boys formally from other public schools for official dances, but she couldn't understand them. They all had access to some private store of knowledge that she was denied. Smutty references confused her. Her ignorant, sheltered friends, the products of high-church homes, were little better informed than she was. She had feelings which had changed from urgent passions over the music mistress to a frustrated desire to watch pop videos – Shaws banned videos brought from home. She knew just enough to know that her ignorance was a monster waiting to trip her up. Nervously aware she was different, Gossamer didn't feel she belonged and belonging was perhaps what she wanted more than anything in the world.

She thought Peter, Jenny's brother, de-luscious. It was fun to embark on her first real flirtation with an available male.

They had been playing tennis for most of the afternoon, she and Peter, Jenny and Canfield, Peter's friend from Amplethwaite. Jenny and Canfield had wandered off afterwards and Gossamer had taken herself to the flower garden.

Suddenly the world behaved as Jenny had predicted. It pounced.

Peter was there, on the path in front of her. His face was odd. Gossamer felt the tension in him. He stepped forward and literally grabbed her, pulling her body roughly into his. His breath came hot on her neck. 'Gossamer,' he whispered. His hand closed tight over one breast.

She had a dizzy moment of triumph. She had wanted him. His teasing calm had vanished. He wanted her. This whole scene was new to her.

But she didn't like it. He was too rough and she felt shocked. His body pressed heavily into hers. She tried to pull free but he had her pinned against the wall. She could feel the sun-warmed brick through her thin tennis clothes. She had seen it earlier, faded rose-red and cobwebbed, placidly guarding the flower garden in the Sussex sunshine.

They were in a very private place. Peter knew what he was

about. He pressed his lips against her skin and squeezed her breast more tightly. 'Come on,' he said thickly. 'The Laforge woman is coming to tea with her ghastly daughter. We've just got time if we're quick.'

She got his meaning. Outrage swelled in her. Her breast hurt and she wasn't a fast-food service. She struggled harder but he was a young ox, a blond, red-gold giant with his broad, rugby-playing shoulders and narrow blue eyes.

His hips thrust forward and with a jolt she felt the swollen thing inside his trousers.

'No,' she said hoarsely. She was afraid.

'Don't be silly. There isn't time for this. Ma keeps you too well guarded. Come on, Gossamer. Don't be so damned coy.'

'Let go of me. I don't have to.'

'You bitch.' He towered angrily between her and the sun. She could feel him panting and there was sweat in the creases on his forehead. 'What's the matter?' he jeered. 'Not romantic enough, is that it? You look the romantic type. Moonlight and bleeding roses.'

Tears stung her eyes. 'If you don't like me, why are you doing this? I don't want it.'

His lips thinned disdainfully. 'You like me all right. I've seen how you look at me. What are you, some kind of damned prick-teaser? Does Jenny know you're like this?'

'I'm not a, a what you say. I did like you. I didn't mean this, though.' She hated him forcing her to say it out loud. She felt sick and panicky.

'So just what did you mean?'

Gossamer floundered. 'Just friends. Not sex. Not like this.'

'You've got me going now. You'll have to do something about it.' He was deliberately cruel. All his life he had put blame onto other people. Now he fumbled with himself and she found to her horror he had taken a lump of flesh out from his clothes and put it in her hand. He began to move. 'Do it,' he mumbled. He shut his eyes and groaned softly to himself.

She had never seen the naked male sex. She knew little more than what was in a student biology text. She gave a cry of real horror and snatched her hand back, hurting her elbow on the wall.

'Jesus!' exploded Peter. He stood back from her, trembling, tucking himself away. His sweating face glittered with anger. Not only was it her first exposure to the naked male sex, it was her first exposure to naked male wrath.

Quite suddenly she got her bearings. She felt detached and cool. Unconsciously she straightened as confidence flowed back into her slim body. Her fingers pressed against the wall behind her. The brick was silk-smooth between the rough lines of mortar. Peter's thing had been smooth. She was rubbing the feeling of it away as she faced him, her head up now as she regained self-assurance. He was gross. She didn't have to put up with this.

He thrust a hand into his trouser pocket to find his cigarettes. He busied himself with lighting one for a moment. He looked at her again, pushing his blond hair back out of his eyes. His tennis whites suited him. He was the perfect young male, privileged, amusing, self-confident. He was not well-equipped to handle a refusal. 'I'll have to tell Jenny,' he said.

'Tell her what?' Gossamer was mystified. He was the one out of order, not her.

'What do you think she's doing right now?' Peter flicked ash, watching her, elaborately at his ease.

'I don't know.'

'She's fucking with Canfield.'

'No.' Gossamer knew he was trying to shock her.

'I mean, she's my sister. I can hardly fuck her myself.' His voice was drawling now. 'Not done, and all that. So Canfield has her and I get you.'

'No. No, it isn't like that.'

'Isn't it?'

The silence stretched. Peter smoked, watching her. Birds called from beyond the garden and somewhere a cricket trilled with asinine insistence. The fragrance of the flowers hung heavy in the sun-soaked air.

'I don't believe you,' said Gossamer desperately. 'She wouldn't be so daft. She likes him, that's all. I expect they kiss and that.' She sounded lame even to herself.

'Kissing is for kids whose balls haven't dropped.'

'Don't be so coarse,' she snapped.

'Don't be so prudish. I don't believe this act you're pulling, not for one moment. You've led me on. Now I want to collect. You're OK to look at. I told Jenny I was pleased she'd brought you. Now it's time to stop sodding around.'

He never swore when his parents were at hand. It was an act for her benefit, Gossamer thought chaotically. Had Jenny really set her up as bed-fodder for her brother? No, it was a lie, it had to be a lie.

'I'm going back to the others,' she said faintly.

'Frigid, are you?' The accusation was as unexpected as it was hurtful. 'Or are you a dildo-queen?'

She didn't understand him and went scarlet. She tried to move but his arm shot out and he was leaning into her again.

'I'm better than a candle, if that's what you play with,' he whispered. 'I'm much more fun. Come on, sweetie, relax and enjoy it. I can guarantee you a good time. I can't exactly produce testimonials but I assure you I've pleased in the past. The ladies like it with Peter.' His lips were on her neck again, more gentle now, but moving out along her shoulder. He drew back the collar of her shirt and kissed her throat. His other hand came up her bare thigh and under her short skirt. A moment later he was fumbling into her panties. Her resistance fuelled his excitement.

She fought hard. She cracked her own head against the wall but she had the satisfaction of hitting him in the face. Outrage gave her strength. Her inhibitions vanished in the face of her disgust. Peter swore and pulled back.

'You bloody cat,' he snarled.

Gossamer fled.

Not the house. There were maids and she shared Jenny's room. She was in no mood to be seen.

Not the lawn. The others would be gathering there for

tea. Gossamer got herself to the swimming pool and found it deserted. She burrowed into the rhododendrons at the back of it and sat in a dry earthy hide.

Peter's inept fumbles hardly indicated a vast sexual experience, she thought indignantly. She didn't know how men behaved in real life but she had read enough romances and seen enough films to know that the smash and grab approach was definitely not in fashion.

A tear of mortification trickled down her cheek. She had liked Peter, it was true. His elegant drawl, his self-assurance, his physical presence had all contributed to her enjoying a mild flirtation with him, her friend's brother. Could he really have been led to think she wanted sex, the whole thing? Heaven's sake, she was only seventeen, just down from school. He was only eighteen. She might fantasise deep kissing, tongue to tongue, but that was all. She didn't want that coarse clutching, that invasion of her body's privacy.

Her breast hurt, tingling faintly. She let her mind explore herself where he had come under her skirt. She felt odd there. A man's hands had gone inside her panties, touched her almost in her most intimate place. And she had touched him. It hadn't been slimy or damp. On the contrary, it had been firm and cool.

She shivered. One day she was going to love it. It would be inexpressibly romantic and right. She wouldn't be married. She might be convent-bred, but she had no desire to wait until after the knot was tied. Shaws had failed in that particular lesson. It was love, not the legal tie, that mattered. No, she would give herself pure and untouched to the first man she loved, the first man who loved her. It would be a consecration.

Careless of her white clothes, Gossamer lay back under the waxy leaves with her hands behind her head. She could see the soft blue sky above fragmented into a chaotic pattern, like a kaleidoscope. She was sensually aware of her warm body within the light crisp clothing. Her mind drifted pleasurable and slow over the insubstantial image of a man, a lover. It would be wonderful.

It wouldn't be Peter Kepesake, not now. Her mind had a
trick these days of imagining every nice-looking male in the
role, a kind of mental flirting. That was over. She knew him
for what he was.

There was the ordeal of tea to face. She had better wipe
her face and go into the house and tidy up. Perhaps she could
wash and change. It would give her the necessary time to
calm herself before seeing Peter again. And Jenny.

Jenny letting Johnny Canfield go the whole way with her.
She didn't know whether to be angry or appalled. No doubt
Peter was lying.

She crawled out of the bushes.

Gossamer need not have worried about tea. Peter took care
to station himself by Cynthis Laforge and startled his mother
by exerting his considerable charm to flatter the girl. She
was a large, heavy-faced girl whose dull blonde hair was
unattractively swept back from her face. Peter whispered
in her ear, stared frankly at her massive bosom and found
time to shoot the occasional malicious grin at Gossamer.

Sandings, the Kepesake home, stood high on the north
Downs facing south so that the view fell away into a
benign summery distance. It was Gossamer's second visit
in school holidays and Helen Kepesake was pleased with
her daughter's friend. She was also aware of tensions in this
supposedly tranquil scene. Her husband Geoffrey had not
turned up. Peter was becoming unkind to Cynthis Laforge
who was too dim to realise it yet. Jenny's manners seemed to
have vanished. Gossamer was pink and looked like a startled
fawn. Her friend Lydia, Cynthis's mother, was just waiting to
interrogate the girl and only Johnny Canfield by her own side
seemed to have retained his manners and the social graces. Of
course, it was bred in him, she thought absently. His people
were in the diplomatic corps.

Jenny and Gossamer were whispering.

'What's the matter with Pete?' Jenny had done her daugh-
terly duty of handing round sandwiches and was now
relaxed.

'He tried to touch me up. I resisted.'

'Poor old Pete. I thought you liked him.' Jenny seemed mildly surprised.

'For Heaven's sake, Jen. He came at me like a train. I mean, Gorilla-hands and all.' Gossamer could not help falling into school slang. It gave her feelings protection.

Jenny giggled. 'I thought he'd have more panache. I'll tell him next time he's horrid to me.'

'No!'

'So he's getting the Cynthis-creature all worked up to make you jealous. He is a cruel beast. She's hopeless, isn't she?'

'Jennifer.' Helen Kepesake's voice cut mildly across their whispering. They were being rude, of course. 'Could you take the cake round?'

Jenny grimaced and rose to obey.

'And how are you enjoying school?' Mrs Laforge was as formidable as her daughter threatened to be.

'It's fine, thank you,' said Gossamer. 'I've left now, though.'

'That's nice. And what will you be doing with yourself?'

'I'm going to college. In London.'

'Is that where your people live?'

Suddenly Gossamer was hot. 'I don't have any people,' she mumbled.

'I beg your pardon?' The high-bred neighing voice was insistent. Lydia Laforge had large china-blue eyes that protruded slightly. They had swivelled to focus on Gossamer properly now.

'Lydia.' Again the cool voice of Helen Kepesake cut across the tea table. 'I must show you the lily pond. Really, it's so attractive. The flowers are beautiful for once, big waxy things, absurdly Beatrix Potter.'

Gossamer turned her head away and stared into the blue tree-swimming distance.

It was being a bitch of an afternoon.

'Jenny's little friend,' said Lydia Laforge. She was not a woman to be deterred.

'Gossamer. A sweet child. Very unaffected. Shaws does

such wonders for their manners.' Privately Helen was having her doubts. She didn't think Gossamer was equipped to handle life in London.

'She told me the most extraordinary thing. She says she has no people.'

'No more she does. The child's an orphan, Lydia. I think she feels it, poor thing. She needs a mother now. You know, clothes, young men and all that.' Helen strolled with determined casualness down the paved way to the pond.

'No people at all? How Oscar Wilde. Was she found in a handbag?'

'I don't think she finds it funny. It must have been a lonely childhood. I'm glad Jennifer has befriended her. We like having her here.'

'She must have had people.' Lydia paused to admire a rockery. 'I mean, Shaws isn't cheap, is it? Or do they have charity children?'

'There's money,' said Jennifer's mother. 'A settlement, I think. Certainly her education is being paid for.'

'It must be quite considerable. So who were her people?'

'I really don't know.' Helen Kepesake had had enough. Geoff had come home at last with that tight excited look she dreaded. 'Harrods is having a sale next week in their household linen department. I thought I'd go up. Do you care to come?'

'She's very dark, isn't she? Quite an exotic.' Having achieved her object, Lydia settled to talk bed-linen and napery with her hostess.

Helen's sense of duty was strong. A couple of days later Gossamer found herself dead-heading roses with her. She liked the tall, thin, elegant blonde woman. She had squeaky eyes. Eyes with lots of crinkly lines radiating out from them. Mrs Kepesake probably hated them, but Jenny had told Gossamer about her mother's eyes that first awful night when they had wept, new babies at Shaws and both homesick for their old lives.

Jenny loved her mother's eyes because they were kind and Gossamer loved them for the same reason.

'Do you mind so very much?' Helen suddenly said.

Gossamer didn't pretend not to understand. 'I do rather. I know it's silly.'

'Hardly.' Helen's voice was dry. 'After all, I'm a parent myself. It's reassuring to be told one's necessary.'

'Jenny's lucky,' said Gossamer in a stifled voice.

'You must know something. Did no one ever bother to tell you what happened?'

'They don't know. Not at the orphanage nor at Shaws, I mean. There's this firm of solicitors that looks after my affairs.' Gossamer's voice flattened. 'You know, they organised my passport for the school trip. They've got me my provisional driving licence. I get a lump sum every birthday and Christmas, and money every term and every holidays. Very organised.'

'Who are they?' asked Helen, ignoring the bitterness in the girl's voice. It was hardly surprising that she was bitter. She had been treated disgracefully, to be left in such ignorance. Heaven only knew what she must think.

'Um, Chatteris Choate, they're called. Posh-sounding,' she added gloomily.

Helen was startled. 'Posh? My dear, they're the best. Well, the poshest. Frightfully expensive and used by all the most important people. You know, they get Cabinet ministers off the hook and things like that. Compared to them the Security Services shout their business in Hyde Park. Have you never asked them about your parents?'

'I've never met them.'

Helen was silent. Chatteris Choate. No wonder the child had money. If they were back a couple of centuries, her birth would be no mystery. She would be a bastard daughter of the aristocracy. But today? Who would care? Royalty?

Helen thought about this carefully but one look at Gossamer dispelled any belief she could be an illegitimate daughter of that lumpen red-faced Saxon line. She was quick and dark, slanting-eyed with beautifully modelled features, still a little unsettled with youth. Her slim frame seemed braced against the world despite her privileged upbringing. She had the faint air of one haunted, and Helen had no doubt that this was caused by the mystery of her parentage. The girl troubled her because she was clearly destined to be beautiful and yet she was so vulnerable, so ready to be hurt. She was a charming, gentle innocent and shortly she would be stepping into the world with nobody but a gang of over-priced well-bred jackals to help her on her way. Helen had no high opinion of lawyers. She thought they grew fat on the carrion of ruined lives.

She stopped what she was doing and looked at Gossamer. 'Jenny's off to Switzerland soon,' she said.

'She's looking forward to it.'

'I'll be lonely here. Geoffrey works all the time. Peter's going up to Oxford. If ever you feel like a weekend at home, or a few days keeping Jennifer's mother company, please phone me and come. You promise?'

'Thank you,' said Gossamer. Her voice trembled slightly.

'Good,' said Helen unemphatically. 'By the way, make an appointment to see those lawyers. Ask them some questions.'

'What if I don't like the answers?' The question was put casually but it hid a thousand and one nights of fearful imaginings and private horrors.

'With Chatteris Choate?' Helen was amused. 'My dear, they are top drawer. You won't find any monsters lurking behind their fastidious doors, I promise you. The truth is going to be painfully dull.'

His lips were on her belly. Her breath came ragged. He was going down and she adored it.

As always, he surprised her. He lay back now, apparently at his ease. 'Do something for me,' he said. He was smiling at her, offering a light challenge.

She was already naked because he liked her to undress in front of him while he still had his clothes on. Now she began to remove them for him, taking her time, investigating his body as it was revealed.

She adored his body. The touch of his skin against hers thrilled her. She pressed her lips to his throat, his nipples, the swell of muscle at his shoulders. She kissed the palm of his hand, his navel, his groin. She let her hair caress him. She placed her polished nails against his shoulders and dragged them slowly down, across his chest, across his belly and down his thighs.

She kissed his foot, the arching instep, the delicate place behind the ankle bone. She moved his thighs apart and kissed the silken skin there. She came back luxuriously to the quick of him. His manhood was powerful. The torpedo of flesh stood proud from the nest of hair. She inserted her fingers into his testicles and began to play with him, using all her skill to sense delicately the firm ovals within the soft bag, manipulating them, feeling his pleasure at what she did.

Her hand grasped the column of rigid flesh. As she slid her hand up and down with smooth gentle teasing movements, she kissed the exposed tip. She loved to taste his sex. He had taught her this and he was the only man she had ever done it with.

His head was back over the edge of the bed. He was surrendered to her. Carefully she came up over the body she adored. She knelt either side of his groin. She lifted herself on her knees. Carefully she held his sex so that it pointed up beneath her, beneath where her own body waited to be impaled on him. Carefully she lowered herself till her petalled flesh touched him. With her two hands she opened her sexual lips and allowed him between them so that they clung to his kiss-wet sex. A small moan of excitement escaped her lips. She pressed down on him. His hard strength began to enter her body, thrusting against the constricting ring of her entrance to seek the yielding cushioned place within. When he was barely inside her she stopped. She picked up his hands and carried them to her breasts. As he caressed her, she squeezed her sexual muscles on his sensitive tip. For long moments she masturbated him in this way, with him lodged just within her body. When she could bear it no longer she sank slowly down on him, feeling him open her inside and press against her thrilling nerves. Little ripples began immediately. He had the power to bring her like this to almost instant orgasm. Her flesh shivered and quivered. She moved up and down on him, gasping as her excitement rose to an unbearable pitch.

When she thought she could bear it no more, when the tension made her want to scream, he swept into action. He pushed up with harsh powerful movements that had her weeping with happiness. Her body shook to the attack. His swollen sex was close to explosion. Her own trembling flesh was melting, burning up in the heat. She began to cry out. His strength was enormous. He lifted her clear of the bed, filling her entirely, and she felt him come. He thrust up and up as he emptied himself into her. Her body was lava, hot and running everywhere. Her orgasm was total, torn from her body, erupting through her so that when it was all over she was limp and exhausted.

The satisfaction was total. He fulfilled her utterly. She lay bathed in peace afterwards, feeling him move and light himself a cigarette. When she opened her eyes to feast them on his loved face, she was overwhelmed at his physical beauty.

He laid a hand casually on her naked shoulder. She understood. Sex drained her, left her lethargic and content. But it supercharged him. He had to get up, roam about. He was restless with energy.

When she married she had had no intention of being unfaithful to her husband. Geoff Kepesake was not an exciting man, never had been, but in the wild days at the end of the sixties when he had courted her, he had been safe. The anarchy of the hippy movement in Britain, the rising tide of campus violence in America, May '68 in France had all terrified the sheltered Helen. She had been bred to marry money, to sell herself for an adequate security. She belonged to a class that regarded a working woman as someone on various charity committees. She had no resource, no ability to free herself when Geoffrey's nature became evident. She was high-church enough to despise the weasel escape of divorce, but she was frail enough when the opportunity offered to take a lover.

Not at first. She had schooled herself to accept her lot in life. Besides, her quiet charm had not aroused many men in the sexual maelstrom of the seventies. There was easier, more salacious game. Later they succumbed, as she approached the age of forty. Her looks had matured into something close to beauty. Her quiet dignity of manner suggested, wrongly as it happened, that she knew inner peace and certainty. In the new gutsy fearful world where earning a living increasingly resembled riding a rollercoaster, men found Helen's gentle passivity suddenly attractive.

She had one lover only throughout the eighties, an older man and gentle. This man was different. He was a magician. He could frighten her. She was spellbound.

She didn't care. So much of her life had been quiet and dull. She had waited. She had suffered. Now, briefly, in his arms, she knew happiness.

The really strange thing was that the two great sensual pleasures of her life were mutually incompatible. There was this here, of the flesh. There was also the lush hedonism of her church where she could kneel at the altar rail in an ecstasy of self-abandon, her mind a void save for the swelling sound of God's great music. There she could inhale incense in the dim crimson and lapis light to the ravishment of her senses. There peace alighted dove-like in her breast.

She had the lewd piercing excitement of her lover thrusting between her legs. She had the tranquil glory of her eternal church. She needed both.

They met rarely. She knew she was only a small part of his complex life.

It was a luxury to talk to him. 'Cal,' she said.

'Mmm?'

'Here's an odd story for you. It's about a friend of Jenny's from school.'

'Oh yes?' He didn't encourage her to talk about her family. The subject bored him.

She stroked the hair back from his forehead. 'The girl is being brought up by Chatteris Choate.'

He was silent a moment. 'The lawyers?'

'Yes. The poor child has no idea at all who her parents are.'

'I'm not with you.'

'She doesn't know a thing about them. Their names, what her father did or does, who her mother was, whether they are dead, anything.'

'Can't she ask one of the dinosaurs at Chatteris Choate?'

'They handle her money and they've seen her through school. She's been at Shaws with Jenny, so there's no lack of the stuff.'

'Her parents must be dead.'

'I should think so. But why the mystery? I actually wondered for an absurd moment if she were a bastard royal.'

'And is she?'

'No. She's gorgeous, all dark and romantic-looking. Tumbled locks over a marbled brow. And her eyes are pure gypsy. A most peculiar colour. She's only seventeen now but she's going to be a stunner. It's so sad. She needs a mother.'

'What's her name?'

'Gossamer Fane. The name doesn't mean anything to me. I don't know who gave her her Christian name. Nor does she.'

'What's she like?' His voice had gone lazy, almost uninterested.

'I told you. Exotic. There's a foreign touch to her.'

'No. In character.'

'She's a darling. Honestly, Shaws is quite a place. She's innocent and gentle and sweet as a summer's day.'

'It hardly sounds a suitable preparation for life.' He was laughing at her now, his eyes dancing with mischief.

'It would be if she had protection, if she had a mother. Don't you think that's sad?'

He came up on one elbow and looked down her so that her heart almost stopped, she loved him so. He laid a gentle finger over her lips. 'You softy,' he said. 'You're the one who needs protection.'

'Who from?'

'Men like me.' His lips were on hers and her arms wound round his neck. Her body arched up and she knew he would love her again.

For a moment he hesitated.

'What is it?' she whispered, feeling the tide in her take her up.

'You've been very lucky for me, Helen.'

'Have I? That's good.'

He was amused, the devil in him very apparent. 'I wonder if it is,' he said.

Jean-Luc Frémont sat on a desk corner in the typing pool and admired the cut of his trousers. His speciality was international law and he was a pupil at the great firm of Chatteris Choate who handled any branch of law that made money. He was mildly teasing Sasha because she had the wit to invent an amusing name for herself but not the ability to live up to it.

'What I love about you English girls is your romantic natures,' he said. He smiled into Sasha's eyes. She looked like a Pauline, he thought.

'I hope we're sensible as well.' Sasha was a shade tart. Just a shade. None of them had yet succeeded in being invited out by the gorgeous Jean-Luc. It would be a triumph if she was the first.

'You don't weigh up a man's possible income before going to bed with him as a French girl does. It's so refreshing.'

This was a bit barbed. 'We're not mercenary,' said Sasha doubtfully. There was always a feeling of shifting sand when you talked with Jean-Luc. Had she just accepted that going to bed with a man was the norm?

'You like to pay for yourselves in restaurants. You are such fierce *féministes*.'

Sasha was struggling with this when she saw she had lost his attention. He was watching a dark-haired girl dressed in a white silk shirt and a superbly-cut charcoal tailored suit going towards Germain's outer office. A silk square was knotted casually about her shoulders, its arrogant crimson counterpointing the severity of her clothes. She walked with a coltish grace, long-legged and slim with swaying hips.

'Mother of God,' murmured Jean-Luc. 'Who is that beauty?'

They saw Miss Sanderson, Germain's secretary, greet the girl and usher her in.

Jean-Luc turned back to Sasha. 'Who sees the great man himself?' he asked.

'I beg your pardon?' Sasha's mind seemed abruptly elsewhere.

'This little girl who is so lovely, so young and lovely. How come she is important enough to see Mr Germain himself?'

'I'm sure I don't know.'

Jean-Luc disentangled himself from her desk with an easy grace and flowed out of the pool and into the corridor. He looked at Miss Sanderson's closed door for a moment, his fertile brain working. Then he drifted elegantly away.

Inside the room Gossamer was not aware of the stir she was causing. She had asked for an appointment and been given one with a Mr Kevin Germain. She was becoming aware from various subtle signals that he was high up in the firm. Surely no one humble had such a formidable secretary, and no one insignificant would have produced quite the reaction from the receptionist downstairs. If she was to meet Mr Germain, in some way she was herself important.

She clutched her bag and smiled nervously at Miss Sanderson. The woman unbent enough to smile back. She was finding it frankly incredible that Mr Germain should have so young a client, one he might bother to see in person. She had never handled the file, Mr Germain kept it in his safe, but his daily life normally revolved around the great and the greater. This girl from nowhere was an enigma, one that Alison Sanderson would enjoy solving.

A light glowed on her desk. 'Mr Germain is free now,' she said. She went to his door and opened it.

Gossamer rose to her feet in one flowing movement as she had been taught at Shaws. She began to walk into the inner office.

He was on his feet to greet her, coming out from behind a desk that would have looked at home in an antique shop. She saw he was an immaculate man, barbered to a perfection she hadn't known existed. His clear, slightly full cheeks glowed a warm brown with a faintly orange-peel texture.

Gossamer pulled herself together and shook hands. She was led to two armchairs by an Adam fireplace in which a real fire glowed. There was a formidable dried flower arrangement to one side in the hearth, but on the mantelpiece and on his desk Mr Germain had blowsy bronze chrysanthemums.

They're out of season, she thought. Where does he get them from?

Alison Sanderson was speaking. 'I'll bring coffee, sir.'

'Thank you, Alison. Sit down, Miss Fane. What a cold, dull day it is. I trust you had no difficulty getting here.'

She gave him an automatic meaningless smile. He was silky, she thought. Like a big cat. She could almost see his fur rippling.

'It's very pleasant to meet you at last.'

'I've left Shaws. I felt I ought to see you.'

'Of course. At any time. Yes, I know you've left Shaws and now you are enrolled at the Ryder-Vail School of Dance and Design. How is your apartment?'

'Fine, thank you. You found it for me.'

'Miss Sanderson did. It's a bit of a jungle, property in London. We wanted you safely established.'

Gossamer took a deep breath. 'Why?' she asked. She leant forward intensely. She had to know.

'Pardon?'

'Why did you find me a flat? Why do you care? Who is paying you, Mr Germain? Why are you handling my affairs?'

Alison Sanderson came back at this point with a coffee tray and busied herself pouring. Kevin was glad of the opportunity to gather himself. It wasn't the girl's questions that troubled him, he had been prepared to answer them for years now. It was the girl herself.

She was frankly breathtaking. Her hair was raven's-wing and cut and curled to lift away from the flawless skin of her face and lie in a shining weight on her shoulders. Whoever had controlled her clothes' buying had shown marvellous taste, unless it was natural to the girl herself. Eighteen. Those cheekbones. Those extraordinary eyes. Those long silk-clad legs folded neatly to one side as she sat with a model's grace and stillness.

Whoever would have thought this might be the result of the union? She was a fabulous creature. Kevin felt rise within himself a slow rare excitement. This was no bit player. She would be centre-stage one day, she couldn't escape such a destiny with those looks, that heritage. He had a commodity here that no one else knew about. Her very existence was shrouded in mystery. He must tread carefully, and for the time-being he must keep this to himself. She was dynamite on a slow fuse and he, Kevin Germain, might be able to control the inevitable explosion if he made no mistakes now.

He was habitually cautious, a prerequisite for the successful lawyer. He set himself to wait for the inevitable disappointment, the first stupidity, the first vulgarity. He was misanthropist enough almost to take pleasure in the first sign of a coarse or selfish mind.

'The trust pays me, Miss Fane. You need have no fears on that score. The trust was set up to see you through school so that you could receive such education as was found to be desirable or necessary. I hope you were happy at Shaws. It was my choice.'

'Who set up the trust? How much is it for?'

'As to the second question, I have anticipated you, Miss Fane. I have on my desk the relevant documents for you to see. I hope they will make clear to you the terms and conditions of your financial resources. It's better you understand these things for yourself.'

'And my first question?'

Her directness was beautiful, the low-pitched slightly husky voice offsetting the challenge of those taut young shoulders. Kevin smiled. 'That is more easily answered. Your father set it up.'

Gossamer stared at him, her eyes huge in her white face.

'Your mother is dead, I'm sorry to say. She died around the time you were born.'

Gossamer's eyes slowly filled with tears. She looked down sharply and one fell clear into the coffee she held in her lap.

Kevin adjusted his posture. Jesus, what a creature.

'And my father?' Gossamer continued to look down, mechanically stirring her coffee.

'This is harder to explain. Your father set up the trust and placed it in our hands. He did it to protect you and help you. He didn't feel able to do this himself directly. He had his reasons, Miss Fane, and they were good ones, I can assure you. Moreover, having chosen to do things this way, he didn't wish for you to be involved in any vain pursuit of who he was or why he did what he did. I am here to protect his privacy, as much as I am here to ensure your well-being.'

'He's alive,' said Gossamer fiercely.

'I didn't say that. We lawyers are strange creatures, Miss Fane. We obey instructions. My instructions, and they are quite clear, are to tell you nothing of your father. Nor will I.'

'Why doesn't he want me?'

'You read into the situation what isn't there. He had his reasons. As it happens I agreed with them. He has done his best by you, Miss Fane, and it is more than many fathers would have done. My advice is that you rest content. It will do no good for you to pursue this. Indeed, it will do you active harm.'

'I don't understand.' She stared at him blindly. He found her vulnerability, her dependence on his words, intensely exciting. The exercise of power gave him a sexual charge at the best of times. With this innocent beautiful child it was almost out of control.

'You will,' he said. 'You see, it's part of the terms and conditions that I spoke of before. If you begin actively to trace your father, you negate the trust. It will be wound up and the money will stop. You will be on your own, Miss Fane. I might regret it, but as I told you, I obey instructions. That is my job, my responsibility to my client.'

'But I'm your client.'

'No. I'm afraid that's not so. Indeed, you are welcome to go to another firm of lawyers and instruct them to deal with me on your behalf. But don't instruct them to seek to reveal the identity of the man who set up the trust. You will bring trouble and grief upon yourself, even if you succeed, which frankly I doubt. The very act of making enquiries concerning your father will negate the trust, you understand.' He watched her for a moment. She was still close to tears but she was angry as well. 'You could look at this another way,' he said gently, modulating his voice until it was caressing and kind.

'Yes?' The word was dull.

'Your father, whoever he was, did not want his identity to be known. You could respect that wish. You could accept it. Simply because it was what he wanted, you could accept it, Miss Fane, and not fight it. You could allow him to know what was best. You could do him so much honour.'

She struggled with this for a moment. 'I don't seem to have much choice,' she said eventually.

'That's one way of looking at it.'

'There's another?'

'That you are looked after. Provision has been made for you, is being made for you. No one with whom Chatteris Choate is involved can honestly say that they are alone in the world.' He smiled and put his head on one side, lifting his eyebrows humorously.

'I'm not your client,' Gossamer pointed out.

'No indeed and you are always at liberty to seek advice elsewhere. I recommend it, if it will set your mind at rest. You can afford it, Miss Fane, to be absolutely frank with you. So, you are not our client. But we have your interests at heart and the provisions of the trust are wide. Come to us, to me, if you wish to ask about anything. You won't find us reluctant to help. I am aware of your age and your relative inexperience of London.'

She looked at papers, had things explained to her and signed something. Somehow she kept her mind working while her emotions whirled painfully. Finally she was free, in bondage to her ignorance and pierced by the pain of knowing to what extraordinary lengths the man who was her father had gone, to prevent her from knowing who he was. If she could not know him, it followed that he could not know her. He had left her to be alone.

Miss Sanderson showed her into the corridor. Gossamer walked blindly towards reception, towards the way out, seeing nothing but the dazzle of pain in her mind. She totally failed to notice the handsome Frenchman who materialised at the precise moment necessary for someone to open a door for her. At one moment smiling, debonair, full of a practised gallantry, he found himself the next staring after her retreating figure, ludicrously baffled.

Kevin Germain put through a private call when Gossamer was gone.

'Isabella?' he said. 'Germain here.'

'My dear. So nice to hear from you.'

'You mentioned a new property you had the last time I visited you.'

The silence was infinitesimal. 'Ah yes. But not to your taste, I think.'

'I might change my mind.'

'She can't oblige in the ways you have shown you enjoy. It's not her thing. She is not, how can I put it, sophisticated, Mr Germain. And you are such a very sophisticated man.' Isabella's voice was douce.

'She's young.'

'Very young. Adorably young. *Naïf, tu comprends*.'

'Tonight?'

'Nine thirty? *Bien*. And you will be gentle, Mr Germain.'

It was a command, not a request. A light sweat filmed his brow. 'I understand.'

She walked straight into a taxi, her brave scarf flying like a desolate flag. 'Hyde Park,' she said, fumbling in her purse. She was unfamiliar with London, it was all new territory, vast and alien. What had seemed exciting was now fretful and indifferent.

She began walking in the park in a vain attempt to control the cascade of her thoughts. It was almost the end of January and the weather had a malignant coldness. The grey polluted air pressed heavy as lead against her chest. She struggled to breathe against its suffocating weight. Her feet stumbled. Tears blinded her eyes. She began to run along the path, veering crazily between infrequent strollers, past the bag ladies on their benches, scattering sparrows and pigeons in her headlong rush.

There was freedom in her flight. She ran as fast as her heels permitted, her mouth open and gasping as she fought against the release of tears.

He came down a slight slope on her right from between the sad empty trees. He was running too, though more slowly than she was. She ran, he ran towards her and as they all but crashed he snatched her bag and fled along the path. She came to a halt, dismayed and shaking. The grubby thief with the pinched ferrety features was already disappearing into the distance.

There was a man in his way. Incredibly the man went for him, tackled him head on. The thief fell back. Gossamer began to run towards them. The thief was on the ground, whining. The next moment he had scrabbled to his feet and was running to the right, out of the park.

The man turned to face her, quite an old man, forty at least. Rather good-looking. He wasn't dishevelled at all by the violent encounter.

He held her bag, he was holding it out to her.

'Thank you so much,' said Gossamer. 'That was wonderful. He might have had a knife.'

'He did.' The voice was amused. She took her bag. A shiver ran through her. He was old in the sense that he was a generation up from her, that was all. He was astonishingly attractive.

'Are you a policeman or something?'

'Nothing so glamorous. I hope he didn't hurt you.'

'No. No. It was frightening for a moment. Then I was angry.'

They looked at each other. His eyes crinkled as he smiled. Squeaky eyes, like Helen Kepesake. Kind eyes. 'You're trembling,' he observed gently.

'Shock. Surprise.' She couldn't stop looking at him.

'I know what to do about that,' he said. 'Tea. The national resource at times of crisis. I shall buy you tea, Miss . . .'

'Fane, Gossamer Fane. That isn't fair. You've helped me. You got my bag back. I should do something for you, to thank you.'

'Allow me to buy you a cup of tea, then. There's a kiosk over there. It'll be orange, stewed and served in a disgusting polystyrene cup. We shall be able to sit on the bench nearby occupied by one tramp and two skinheads to enjoy the beverage and soothe our rattled nerves.'

Gossamer laughed. 'I'll buy the tea. It's lovely to have my purse still.' She began to adjust her crimson scarf.

'Safe from thieves, pickpockets and pooper-scoopers. Give me your arm, Miss Fane, and we shall totter over to the kiosk. No one half so nice has needed rescuing for days.'

If he was a knight, he had a considerable dose of self-mockery. And charm. 'Do you always talk like this?' she asked curiously.

'Only on Tuesdays. Why were you running?'

The change of tone was disconcerting. Her hand felt safe, tucked into his arm over the good tweed of his overcoat sleeve. He wore yellow leather gloves and his tanned, slightly craggy face was mobile and lively. He had very blue eyes. They seemed to be the only bright thing on this dull leaden day.

'It doesn't matter now,' said Gossamer. 'It's just that it seemed to, at the time.'

He gave her a look so odd and enigmatic that her heart did a flip. It was as if he knew and was telling her it would be all right.

She'd never met anyone so instantly reassuring. Her spirits rose mercurially.

Damn Chatteris Choate. Damn her father. She had a life to live and nothing was going to stop her.

❖ Two ❖

He offered her London.

He did it as a joke though she wasn't quite sure. He laughed into her eyes, teased her, all but chucked her under the chin, and he offered her London.

She didn't know anything about life. All of her years she had been cocooned away from the world and now she had come prepared to spread her wings in the sunlight of independence. Kevin Germain had denied her her heritage, her parentage. She felt like one of those toys on a heavy rounded base. If she was knocked she would fall over. She would come right again, Shaws had given her that much, but she would be sore and forever rocking.

Suddenly a laughing man in the park, young enough to flirt with, old enough to be sexually off-limits and safe, was saying he would show her a London the guide books didn't mention.

'Think of this city as a blowsy old whore spreading her rusty skirts,' he said. Gossamer felt saucy and charmed. 'She's got all sorts tucked away, the graceless old baggage. For those who know, you can lift the edge of her petticoats and peep under.' They sat on the bench drinking tea every bit as horrible as he had predicted.

'How do you know about it all?' she asked.

'From the vasty hall of experience.'

'The what?'

He grinned. 'The poet actually says the vasty hall of death, but I've always thought each experience in life is like a little death, the death of the old you.'

'That's terrible,' said Gossamer.

'And the birth of the new you. You can get to like moving on.'

She couldn't work out his age. He must be at least twice her own. More.

'Do you often run in the park?' he had asked when they first sat down.

'Never. I've only been in Hyde Park twice in my life before this.'

'Good Lord. You must come from Ealing or Dollis Hill. No one but a Londoner could be so unregenerate.'

'I'm just new to living in London. I only moved here a short while ago.'

'I don't believe it.'

'Why not?'

'A neophyte. A virgin. Someone who doesn't know this place. I suppose you're going to act like a tourist, visit St Paul's, Trafalgar Square and all that.'

'I haven't had time to do them all yet but I certainly intend to.' Gossamer was deliciously prim and nearly spoiled it all with a giggle.

That was when he said it.

'I'll show you London. I'm a Londoner. Let me be your guide.'

'Don't be silly. I don't need a guide. I can get everywhere by myself.'

'Not to the London I know,' he said slyly.

'What's that?'

'Tyburn. Newgate Prison. Foxtrotter's Lane, unchanged since Dickens's time. The Elephant Shop. The Venetian Bazaar. An eel house. A Roman Galley. Spitalfields.'

'You make it sound marvellous.'

'It is,' he said, suddenly sober. 'Look here, are you busy right now? Have you an urgent appointment?'

'No,' said Gossamer cautiously. It wasn't worth going back to college for what remained of the day.

'Will you trust me enough to come in a taxi with me? It's a couple of miles away, where I want to take you.'

'Why?'

'It needs eyes to see, this city. Let me show you a tiny gem, pure London. I promise faithfully I'm not in the white slave trade.'

She went with him out of curiosity and because he was so odd. It meant she didn't have to deal with that interview with Kevin Germain, the smooth face of Chatteris Choate. She really didn't feel able to deal with all that just yet.

It was off Kennington Park Road, not as far as the Oval but on that side of it. He paid the taxi to wait and she found its confident throb a reassurance as he took her through an arched passage into a court.

It opened into a very old London square, tucked decently out of sight of the main thoroughfare. It was sordid and sooty as a dead hearth. Around the square on all four sides were stumpy terraced houses presenting blank windows sly with dust and dirty lace to an incurious world. Their street doors wept old paint and small heaps of wind-blown rubbish had accumulated in their front areas. It was as sad a place as Gossamer had ever seen. She stood dismayed because what made everything worse was the centrepiece of the square.

In its day it must have been a monstrosity, a monument to the poverty of mind of a past religiosity. Now, in decay, partly ruinous, it was simply disgusting. The black filthy walls reared up retaining only their ugliness of line. Roofless, empty at its tall mean window slits, the desecrated church awaited only the blessing of demolition.

'It's horrible,' said Gossamer.

'I know. But look. This is what I brought you to see.'

He took her elbow gently and propelled her round the squat loathsome building. Now she could see that one whole outer wall was gone, leaving the interior gaping like a toothless mouth. Most of the plastered walls were cracked and chipped and covered in obscene graffiti. One wall was the exception.

Gossamer gasped, stared and smiled. 'Oh,' she said happily. 'Oh, I see. It's wonderful. And in this awful place.' She turned to him. 'You are clever,' she said impulsively. 'Fancy knowing it was here. Who did it?'

It was a fantasy scene out of a mediaeval past that existed nowhere but in the bright country of the imagination. Gorgeous castles absurdly turreted had high bright pennants floating against a clear sky. Hills heaped themselves in plump green pimples between which the sea swam serene and ship-dotted. Knights on white chargers cantered along forest paths. The corners were decorated with fire-wreathed dragons. Maidens with their hair plaited into fat flaxen ropes hung out of towery windows.

Gossamer was laughing, almost crying with delight. The whole scene was peopled and alive, full of strange beasts and intimate little scenes. It was bright, clean and nonsensically happy.

Her strange companion looked at it, his head on one side. 'A tramp did it,' he said presently.

'What do you mean, a tramp?'

'A derelict who lives in a hostel when he's not so drunk on meths that they won't let him in. He has lucid periods when he keeps off the poison. He begs, borrows and steals money for paint and comes here and paints this. You can see, if you look, he's planning to go around the corner and do a little archery contest there. He's a natural artist. He doesn't sketch. He rough paints and then fills in.'

'You know him?'

'I come here from time to time and watch.'

'You can't help him?'

He smiled, his eyes crinkling deliciously. 'He doesn't want help. He wants paint or meths. Clean him up and he'll die. He's dying anyway, but he's doing it his way, the way he's chosen.'

They left the square and its jewel set in filth. For a moment they stood by the taxi.

'You haven't told me your name,' said Gossamer shyly.

'Carey Lambert.'

She looked up hesitantly into his bright smiling eyes. 'Why?' she asked.

'Why what?' His voice was very gentle.

'Why were you so kind to me?'

Now it was his turn to hesitate. He put one gloved finger under her chin and lifted it slightly. 'That's better. A nice brave angle. All flags flying.'

Her brows drew together in puzzlement.

'I don't know where you come from,' he said. 'Or where you've been. But, my dear, in a corrupt and streetwise age your enthusiasm is as fresh and enticing as that fairytale world we've just been looking at. And every bit as lovely. Do you want to go back to Hyde Park or shall you take the taxi home? I can get another one.'

'I'll go home, thank you.' She had trouble controlling her voice. She gave her address to the driver and turned to Carey, holding out her hand. 'Thank you very much,' she said with the gravity of a polite child.

He shook her hand, his face lively with mockery. 'Farewell, Trafalgar Square.'

'Why do you call me that?'

'Because that's the sort of London you'll see from now on. The real London, the secret underplaces, you'll never know.'

'I wish I could.'

Suddenly they weren't joking. He waited a moment. Then he said slightly roughly: 'If you like, I'll take you somewhere again.'

'I, I don't know if I ought.'

'I never had a daughter. I always thought it would be fun. You're quite right, you shouldn't. Goodbye, my dear. Watch how you run in future.'

He was gone. In a swirl of coat-tails he had turned and disappeared into the anonymous crowd. Gossamer climbed into her taxi and went home.

Suddenly she was drowning. She was in at the deep end and she couldn't manage. The orphanage and her boarding school had been no preparation for this. She had known no other life barring a handful of weeks in the houses of friends. She knew nothing about people, about men. Who were the knights and who the brutes? How could you tell?

She became aware her looks were special. Among the winter-blotched faces of her urban contemporaries her tawny skin shone translucent and pure. Her wide mouth was vulnerable and appealing. Her winged face with its flying cheekbones gave her a gypsy air but her huge dark eyes were haunted.

He had called her lovely. At least, she thought he had.

She didn't know how to behave so she kept clear. Her shyness was taken as snobbery, as vanity. Everyone was so hard and aggressive she couldn't fight her way in. Having no weapons, she had no place with these people. So they thought her stand-offish. She worked.

The Ryder-Vail School had a modular system to cope with its restless clientèle. Each term taught a dance block. There was classical ballet, modern ballet and modern dance. You had to pass a test at the end of term. When you had three passes, you gained a graduation certificate. It was Gossamer's hard luck that she started in a classical term. Now she was finding modern ballet every bit as hard.

They were all too old for ballet. It served merely to give them grace and control, to strengthen their dancing muscles. It would be a help if they were going on to enter the acting profession, it was a skill they might need.

It was brutal. Every morning opened with half an hour's exercises at the *barre* which left them dripping with perspiration. They began with *pliés* and *ports de bras*. Gossamer discovered her body could speak to her. The *port de bras* forwards told her how stiff her legs were. The *port de bras* backwards told her about her back. It seemed always to be bad news. After that came the *battements tendus* where the foot slides along the ground.

It went on, getting worse. They circled legs on the floor, warming and loosening the hip. They bent and straightened their legs synchronously. They circled their legs in the air, an agony of muscular control. Then came the *adage*, the slow graceful movements that were the only part Gossamer enjoyed. They threw their legs about some more, then they stretched and contorted themselves with one leg on the *barre*, trying to touch their calves with their heads and that finished *barre* work. They went into the centre of the room and started over.

She worked. She found her body stirred in the dance but she wouldn't listen to it. The work wasn't impossible. She improved. It was a goal to set herself, to fill her time with. Her worldly ignorance paralysed her in everything else.

There was no one to trust. They all were too busy expressing themselves, forcing their personalities on each other. They shouted emotionally without stopping and the noise dinned in her ears and made her shrink.

She liked Trish. Trish came from the north and never spoke of her home or her parents. She was a thin gawky girl with a bony pale face and lank hair. She worked like a demon and already she had a quality that set her apart. Something of her spiky reserved personality came through when she danced. There was a passion, an anger in it that slightly frightened Gossamer. They had nothing in common except an ability to be quiet in each other's presence, and a refusal to chat about home.

She went back to Trish's digs one day. It was a bed-sitter and Gossamer was secretly appalled at the damp wallpaper and smelly shared lavatory.

'What are you going to do when you leave Ryder-Vail?' asked Trish. She was busy at the table with something.

'I don't know. I had vague ideas about modelling. I'd love to act, of course.'

'Your bust's too big for modelling. Men like it but the fashion magazines don't. Here, try this.'

'I don't smoke. I didn't think you did.'

'I don't. But we all need to relax. It's not cocaine, for Christ's sake.'

Gossamer took the fat joint and looked at it.

Trish was amused and her ugly monkey face twisted derisively. 'Think of life as a series of temptations,' she said. 'Some are safe to give way to. Some aren't. You have to learn which are which.'

'This is safe?'

'It's non-toxic, non-addictive and you're in safe company. I won't try to rape you while you're high.' She shrugged slightly. 'It's illegal, of course.'

Gossamer inhaled cautiously. 'Hold the smoke in your lungs as long as possible,' said Trish. She took the joint as Gossamer exhaled with a whoosh.

'I've never been with a man,' Gossamer observed presently. She felt philosophical and profound.

'I know.' Trish lay relaxed on her bed apparently examining the ceiling cracks. 'If you aim to stay that way for a while, keep clear of Woodley. He's waiting to get you alone and he's a grabber.'

'I was grabbed once by this brother of my friend. I'd just left school. It was horrible.'

'How far did he get?'

'His hand up my skirt.'

'You didn't like it, huh?'

'No.'

'You don't like the idea at all?'

'Oh yes.' Gossamer opened her eyes wide with surprise. 'But not fumbling around all hot and clumsy. I mean, I want to care for the man a bit, and I want him to care for me. I think I might prefer older men.'

'Or women,' said Trish softly.

'What?'

'Have you ever thought about women?'

'What? What d'you mean?' But she knew.

'I mean sex, lady. Girls together. Where have you been until now?'

'School. Boarding school. No, I haven't ever thought about women. Well, not since I got old enough to realise.' Gossamer stared at Trish in alarm. The older girl was sprawling back on her divan bed sucking in smoke from the last of the joint.

Trish chuckled. 'Don't look so scared: What do you say we get ourselves a pizza apiece, kiddo? I'm starved.'

She came back from Trish's with her head bent, deep in

thoughts chaotic and uncomfortable. It seemed to her that
sex surrounded her like vast jelly. Long sticky arms of
it kept reaching out to grasp her, to trap her. When
she thought back, school was all sex. Whispering in the
lavatories. Looking down each other's jumpers to see how
their breast buds were developing. Giggling about tampons
and riding horses. Stifled laughter about how babies were
made. Whispers about what men looked like, what men got
up to, what men wanted. The whole tense undercurrent of
ill-informed gossip was given importance and weight by the
warnings from their moral mistresses, those arch classroom
discussions about bodily integrity, the argument that a man
worth having was a man who valued one for oneself, not for
what he might get out of one.

Sex with women. She shouldn't have been surprised. She
remembered the girls who crept out of bed at night and slept
together. She had a kind of weary feeling that the school
had fostered rather than repressed such behaviour. Despite
endless warnings about men and their evil intentions, the
school had ignored the fact that girls openly soaped each
other in the showers, often with startling intimacy.

It had never occurred to her seriously that given the
choice in a normal society a woman might choose a woman
in preference to a man. She hadn't thought about what
went on at school at the time, accepting it as part of the
background noise of her life and having no home life with
which to compare it. But she had assumed that they were all
in training for men. They were being taught how to deal with
men. It hadn't occurred to her at the time that what she was
being taught was hopelessly unrealistic, hopelessly idealistic.
It had been so black and white. Life was shades between.

No, she didn't want sex with a woman. But the idea wasn't
frightening. Because it had a familiarity it was actually less
frightening than sex with a man. That was the jelly world
that threatened to engulf her. For all Shaws had gone on
about moral behaviour, it had in fact prepared her to handle
lesbian behaviour but not heterosexual behaviour. Now there
was an irony.

She was crossing the road near her block of flats deep in these thoughts when suddenly a car appeared from nowhere. She heard the engine scream and looked up in alarm. She didn't know whether to jump forward or back. It was swerving between the trees that lined either side of the road.

A huge buffet in her back threw her forward. She lay with her cheek in the grit, feeling her heart thud, wondering if she had been hit.

'Trafalgar Square,' said a shaky voice. 'You aren't safe to be out.'

It was the man from the park. Carey Lambert. He had appeared from nowhere and flung her to safety. With tyres screeching, the car disappeared at the end of the avenue.

She stared at him with her mouth open. 'I think we'd better get out of the road,' he said and helped her to her feet.

They walked uncertainly over to the pavement. She leant against a tree trunk, shaking. 'I never saw it,' she said.

'I was watching you. I'd recognised you. You were staring at your feet. You're some case, girl. I've never met anyone like you for getting into a mess.'

She looked at him. She could feel how drained her face must be. 'You saved my life,' she whispered. 'Don't tell me off.'

'Hey now. Do you live very far? I think you ought to go home and rest.'

'The block in the next street. Overlooking the park.' She lived at the western extremity of Hampstead Heath.

'I'll take you there. I don't trust you out alone.'

Once again her arm was in his. She leant on him, unashamedly glad of his support. She felt very shaky. She wanted to cling to him, he was so safe.

In the foyer of her building, the porter took one look at her and came hurrying across. Arthur was a big man, ex-army, grizzled with age. He was the building superintendent and guard, his presence justifying the high rental.

'Are you all right, Miss Fane?'

'A car just missed her. She's a bit shaken. Can we get her inside?'

'All right, sir. Up this way. Fifth floor.'

He left her at the door of her flat, with Arthur seeing her in. She was too upset even to thank him. Now he was gone.

Arthur busied himself making her tea. He approved of his young charge. He knew she was a nice girl. He could tell.

She sat shivering slightly, irritated by her own weakness. At last Arthur was done.

'Here's your tea, Miss Fane. I'll have to get back downstairs, now. If you'd like a taxi or a doctor or anything, give me a buzz. All right now?'

'Yes, thank you.' She nodded, wishing he was gone.

'Very nice gent, that. And lucky him being by. Now, don't think about it any more. Put the telly on. OK?'

Two days later Arthur called her across as she came in. 'A message for you, Miss Fane. Your friend of the other day.'

Gossamer took the envelope greedily. Arthur smiled, disposed for chat. 'How are you enjoying the weather, Miss? Cold enough for you?'

'Too cold.' She wanted to read the note, not make polite conversation.

'February's always the coldest month. I remember '47. That was a year, that was. We still had rationing and it was cold as a pig's belly. It really got to you, day after day. What snow we had, too. You don't get snow like that today.'

Gossamer nodded meaninglessly. She didn't know what he was talking about. Finally he released her. She turned away and opened the hand-addressed envelope. The single sheet of paper inside was thick and deckle-edged. It had a rich fat feel as she unfolded it. *Dear Trafalgar Square*, it read. *I think you owe me a cup of orange tea in the park. Why don't we meet so I can see if you're still alive in this dangerous city? Lunchtime tomorrow. Don't worry if you can't make it.*

He had signed it 'Carey Lambert'. Gossamer stood looking at it, her lips curving with secret pleasure. There was something uncomplicated about him with his funny way of talking to her. The thought of him was very pleasant in the unsatisfactory muddle of life at the School. Her teachers at Shaws would approve. She had never been back to the little square, fearing she might find only a leering furtive emptiness huddling between the blank windows of the silent houses.

She turned to Arthur. 'He was here?' she asked

'Yes. Very nice class of person.' And generous, he added mentally. The tip had been handsome.

She ran up the stairs, suddenly feeling too energetic for the lift. When she got into her flat, she looked at it severely. It was clean, of course. It was always clean, she had been taught to be tidy from birth and there was a cleaning service that operated in the building under Arthur's magisterial eye.

It was too clean. She must hunt round the junk shops and make it more personal. It needed clutter. It was her first home, the most space she had had in her life. She had allowed it to daunt her. That wouldn't do at all. She must make it her own, so that it reflected her personality.

Her personality. Sometimes she wondered if she had one. The city, her new life, overwhelmed her. She could feel herself shrinking, she didn't know how to assert herself or for what.

She was lonely.

In the afternoons at the School they took the part of the course labelled Design. This term it was art history. Next term it would be antiques. Gossamer found she had a certain natural taste and an ability to recognise what was considered good. It made it hard to buy junk for her apartment or to wear the sort of sloppy clothes affected by her companions. She had seen a T'ang porcelain horse in a gallery window that frankly she lusted after and she adored good clothes. The T'ang horse stayed where it was, but she acquired clothes that she despaired ever of having the opportunity to wear.

The cold grudging spring curtailed her choice for this

her third meeting with Carey Lambert. She wanted to impress him, to be chic, and yet she was frightened of over-dressing. She knew now her enthusiasm was gauche and despite his compliment she wanted him more aware of her sophistication. If she had any. She compromised on a beautiful handknitted sweater glowing with orange and red and crimson. Somehow its flamboyant colouring achieved a raucous harmony with the deep fruity purple of the matching scarf and hat. With black pants tucked into black ankle boots, black leather gloves and her own natural glossy black hair, she felt she could carry it off, the jewelled colours of her sweater emphasising the flawless clarity of her tawny skin.

It was windy and cold with a high bright sky. She skipped classes and saw him from a distance, waiting.

He was distinguished. Arthur had seen it and Arthur was a terrible old snob. Moreover, he was her secret. She had told no one at the School, hugging it to her.

At the last moment she was shy. She came up slowly and when he turned and saw her, she almost stopped.

'I'll always think of you now as the lilies of the field,' he said. No greeting, no commonplaces, no fumbling for words.

'Lilies of the field? Oh, you're being rude. You mean I toil not neither do I spin.'

'No, I don't mean that. Nor am I being rude. Didn't you know they were anemones?'

'Anemones? That's one of the words I almost can't say.' Why was it so easy to talk to him? He didn't talk like anyone she'd ever known yet it was so easy.

'Think of a bunch of them.'

'Oh. I see.' She blushed. 'My jumper.'

'I said I wasn't being rude.' He linked arms with her as naturally as if they had known each other a lifetime. They began to stroll along the path.

'How would you like a trip to the mysterious east? A journey into the sombre bowels of the Earth. An investigation into the fabulous denizens of the ocean deeps.' He had stopped walking and now was looking down at her with his head on one side, waiting.

'It would be mean to refuse.' She clasped her hands behind her back as if she was being told off and peeped roguishly up at him. 'Wouldn't it?' She felt breathless. She knew she should take care and she did, all the time, every day. But she had to indulge herself sometime, somewhere, or she wouldn't be alive.

He took her arm again. 'I'm glad they taught you manners, young lady. First we need a nice humdrum taxi. I'm afraid you'll have to imagine it's a magic carpet.'

'I like taxis,' she confided as they came out of the park onto Cumberland Gate. 'I love the leathery smell and the men who drive them. They remind me of Arthur.'

'Arthur?'

'You met him. He's awfully nice but a terrific old fusspot. He looks after our building. He says you're a gent.'

'He's got the rights of it, I'm afraid.' Carey hailed a taxi and handed her into it. 'Parliament Square,' he told the driver.

'Why? Are you sorry?'

'It limits what you can do. Think of the marvellous freedom of being a cad or a rotter. Think of the fun a bounder has. People who behave have a very dull time of it.'

'I find it hard to believe your life is dull.'

'Do you?' His voice was lazy for a moment. 'How is your life?'

He took her on the river, pewter-coloured and cold. The wind whipped white trails across its broken surface but they stayed outside on the river bus. When she felt cold he laid his arm across her shoulders to keep her warm and it warmed more than her body. She didn't believe they hardly knew each other. She felt so safe. He was such a good man.

They disembarked at Greenwich and he took her up through the famous park and onto Blackheath.

'They buried the dead from the Black Death here,' he said. 'They actually went black with it, you know. They haemorrhaged under the skin and that gave them the dark colour.'

She shivered. 'I never wanted to live in an earlier time,' she said. 'You know, doing without dentists, medicine, the whole thing.'

'That's very wise of you. Alarmingly practical.' He glanced down at her, hunched beside him. 'No hankering for knights and ladies? No desire to be a young lady at Almack's with lordlings sueing for your hand in the dance.'

'No,' she said, staring forward. 'No. I like my own time. Sort of.'

'Sort of?'

'It's so difficult. Everybody shouts. I mean, their characters shout. They're all so assertive, so right. And the things they do! Sometimes I don't know how to behave.' She stopped. In the heat of the moment she'd forgotten who she was with. It was hard to think there were things she shouldn't say, that he was a man. Yet he was so much older than her. He was her parents' generation. If she'd had any parents.

'Do you have a mother, Gossamer?' The question broke into her thoughts. He was uncanny. He could read her mind.

She looked up at him, huge-eyed and scared. 'No. How did you know?'

'You have a certain quality. An air of fragility. As if you've never been here before. Dear heavens!'

'What is it?'

'Your eyes. I hadn't realised.'

'What about them?'

'They're so dark. I thought they were hazel. Or brown. But they're blue. A deep dark smoky blue. Like pansies. Like velvet sapphires.'

She was mute. Her feelings were a great pressure inside her.

He linked arms with her as they walked. She liked this very much and was grateful to him for the ease of it, its naturalness. Shaws had made men sound threatening. She hadn't been warned about how protective they could be. 'A father?' she heard him ask. His voice had a sudden harshness.

'No. As it happens, no.' Tears trembled on her lashes. She had never had the luxury of sympathy.

'A guardian.'

'No.'

'Who looks after you, Gossamer?' His voice was very low.

'No one. I mean, I look after myself.' He had led her down by the river again to a most curious place, a building over a dank hole in the ground that they descended via steps. Now they walked along a dimly lit tunnel with curved walls tiled in stained brown and cream. It was surreal, a nowhere place of dreams and night terrors. 'There's a firm of solicitors,' she added. 'They handle my money.'

'Who are they?'

'Chatteris Choate.'

'I see.'

'What do you see?' she mumbled when he didn't say anything else.

'Can I give you some advice? Would you be angry with me?'

'I don't know. No, not angry.'

'Follow your heart.'

She was silent, thinking about this. Presently he said: 'I think you do know how to behave. You are just meeting situations new to your experience and you aren't sure what criteria to apply.' He shook his head impatiently. 'I'm not talking about morals here. You're beyond that.'

The tunnel began to slope up.

He went on. 'You have a gentle manner, unusual today. I suspect some people will assume you are weak and try to bully you. Don't let them. You aren't weak. And often you'll know better, even if they seem to have more life experience than you.' He stopped suddenly. Again there was that slight roughness in his voice. 'Do you know why I'm bothering with you? Jesus, that's crude. I mean, can you understand what it is about you that brings me here? I'm not one of your spotty louts at dance school, Gossamer. I don't want from you what they want. As you rightly surmised, my life isn't dull. Or empty. Or lacking in any way that there is, and you can damn well read into that what you please.'

He was facing her. Her heart fluttered and she stared at him, frightened by his sudden vehemence and desperate to respond properly, not to be too young.

When he spoke again, his voice was gentle. 'You have a beautiful quality of freshness, of youth. There's nothing stale in you.'

'I smoked a joint the other day.'

'Did you?' He was tranquil. 'As long as you wanted to and didn't do it to be one with the crowd.'

'Does nothing shock you?'

'Lots of things. The way people cheapen themselves. Yes, you've got it. They assert themselves all the time, shouting from the rooftops. But they don't value themselves. They have nothing inside, no touchstone.'

She felt wise. If she needed a father, he needed a daughter. They could help each other. Down under the river there she was happy.

She received a letter from Jenny.

Darling Goss,

How's life with you? I'm having a simply hideous time because I can't decide whether it's to be Pierre who has the sort of biceps you dream about or Calvin who's fearfully moody and elemental and has all of us in a sexual ferment. They both ski divinely and tell me I'm an ass on the pistes and will never manage to get off the nursery slopes. Sadie Oppenheimer who I room with is marvellous at everything including the culture we're being force-fed and she can't stand any of it because she's in love with a tribologist (I think she said that, not biologist) and wants to do nothing but have his babies and wipe his brow when he's tribolising. Or biologising but that sounds a bit dirty. You wouldn't believe this but I'm being made to read people like Gide and Mauriac in the French, godammit, and the only light relief we have is finding the dirty bits in Manon Lescaut. Honestly, what an ass the Chevalier Des whatsit was. Thank goodness men aren't like that today. I mean, should I be overwhelmed by Calvin (whom we've all nicknamed Heathcliffe) or seduced by Pierre who's sort of the Swiss equivalent to a surfer? Incidentally, I'm trying to persuade mother to let me go to California next summer but so far no go. I've got this lust to feel an earthquake. A girl needs to feel the earth move and I'm not sure the boys are up to it these days.

News from home is a bit grim. I think mother's lonely, poor wench, because father's being awful again and Peter seems intent on emptying the stock of every wine merchant in Oxford down his throat and sending daddy the bill. Poor old Canfield is having it rough, too. It seems his dear father has been caught out in quite the most disgusting and unfunny scandal and is absolutely persona non grata everywhere. He doesn't have a bean and it isn't something bearable like sex or spying which he could make money out of by spilling All to a Prurient Public. So Canfield has come home with his tail between his legs. His mother has left his father and gone off to Sweden to communicate with the trees in Nordic gloom and Johnny has nothing and no one. He's got himself into London Uni to do something useless like the history of uncials and I'm really very angry actually because if he did accountancy or finance or something sensible I'm sure daddy could wangle him into the firm. Johnny always was obstinate under those lovely manners. Meanwhile, if you see him around buy him a hamburger, darling, for old time's sake. He's terribly proud and won't beg and all that crew from Amplethwaite (Pete included) will drop him like a hot brick now Père Canfield has made himself de trop. Do you remember I said I did his fortune with the Tarot last Easter? It makes me feel all shivery because the cards said he would be poor and now he is.

On cheerier matters I see Marie is getting herself into the gossip columns. Do you ever come across her? She seems to be leading a high old life which just goes to show you don't need brains or beauty if you're loaded. Do you remember how she always said daddy has a yacht as if that settled everything? I guess she wasn't so far wrong.

We've all taken to drinking gin stingers here when they take the collars off our necks and allow us to indulge. Honestly, we're like those cormorants the Chinese fish with. Or is it the Greeks? Or was that octopuses? I must ask Sadie's biologist if I ever meet him. The point is, we thirst unsatisfied for most of the time. What we ain't like, now I reread that unfortunate last para, is shags. Nothing that is vulgar, dears. Remember the Shaws manner. I'll enclose the recipe for gin stingers. They'll amuse you.

Give mother a bell when you think of it. She's fond of you, can't think why. And remember that if you see Johnny he needs a dime.

Love in abundance, Jenny

So she had fallen for Johnny Canfield after all, thought Gossamer, well able to read between the lines of this massive letter. She was worried about him and trying to do what she could. Heaven alone knew, it would be little enough. Gossamer had never had much to do with him but she could easily imagine he would be too proud to take charity. And ashamed, too. What could his father have done?

She was unable to track down Johnny from the vague description given in Jenny's letter. Meanwhile she worked hard at the School and took to roaming through antique shops and art galleries, trying to fit what she was learning to the world around her. She kept herself to herself very much and watched as the class divided into those who took the course seriously and those who passed the time.

She began to wonder what she would do next, what she would do with the rest of her life. She was attracted to the stage but felt the hopelessness of trying to break into such an overstuffed profession. Meanwhile the buds fattened on the lime trees, the temperature rose above freezing and sometimes as often as once a week Carey took her out.

He delivered her home now, bringing her in to Arthur's benign approval and seeing her to the door of her flat. She asked him in once but he shook his head and she left it at that, content to allow him to manage things as he managed their excursions.

It was a delicious relaxation from the rigours of the week, from her guarded behaviour, from the cattiness of the other girls. Trish was never catty but she became more gaunt than ever and Gossamer was afraid for her.

The men were more assertive, too. She was asked out several times and when she found excuses, they looked sly. She overheard her nickname one day. They called her the Ice Maiden and it wasn't meant kindly in the least. Sex was a minefield she was afraid to enter, full of potentially lethal explosions. Or it was that jelly which would engulf her till she drowned. If she was honest, her fear came as much from within as from the men themselves. Something in her own nature scared her. She was poised on the top of a long slippery slope, afraid to let go. So she ignored the increasing clamour of her body, expressing herself only through the dance.

She talked to Carey, leaning on her elbows opposite him in little restaurants and coffee houses, in wine bars, on the walks they took through the strange London he knew so well. He listened sometimes gravely, sometimes with amusement, but he was never shocked nor censorious. It was a voluptuous thing, this spreading of her personality before him. He never trod on her, never snubbed her, and his rare comments gave her the confirmation she needed that somehow she was doing the right thing. He made her feel important, valued for what she was. She couldn't imagine being bored in his company. She found time to study him, to think about him as a person. She could see how time had marked him, she felt he must be all of forty, but his hair was a natural blond-streaked brown that the warming sun lit up and made to shine. His face was lined but he was slim and fit. When she first saw him without a winter coat on, wearing a dark business suit casually open over a coloured shirt, she saw how lithe and young his body was. If his arm was round her steering her across a busy road, or if he had caught her hand for a moment to help her out of a taxi, he was always warm and firm. He was a treasure-house, full of lively amusement, odd gobbets of knowledge, unshockable, experienced and somehow, wonderfully, concerned for her.

They stood one day together on the Albert Bridge, half-way across, looking east to a louring sky swollen and purple with cloud. A vast arc of rainbow trembled in the air.

'There's a lesser bow inside it,' said Gossamer, drowsy and content.

'There is.'

'Why is the sky a lighter grey inside the bow?'

'I don't know. Somehow investigating the physics of rainbows seems a bit like pulling the feathers out of angels' wings.'

She turned to lean against the iron rail with her elbows on it, facing him for the pleasure of looking at his face. He reached over and picked strands of her hair out of her eyes, brushing them gently back.

'Summer's coming,' she said happily.

'What will you do? Go off sunseeking somewhere with pals?'

'I don't know. I haven't thought about it. I guess the only ones I really like can't afford it.'

'Don't you get on so well?'

'They're a bit catty sometimes.'

He was silent for a long time. Then he said: 'I guess they're jealous.'

'Jealous? Of me? Why? There are better dancers than me and I'm not the only one who isn't hard up.'

'Because you're beautiful.'

It was a while before she raised her eyes. When she did he had his usual face on, the mocking, friendly face she knew so well. She saw it change suddenly and darken with alarm.

She turned her head and saw a heavy squat white dog was racing along the bridge. It had its jaws open and she could see the pink flag of its tongue. Behind it a man in shirt sleeves was running, shouting. The dog took no notice, running hard towards them.

Gossamer had not been brought up with pets and was unfamiliar with them, though she had liked Jenny's family spaniel. She felt instinctively the threat in the deep-chested beast hurtling towards them. She drew in against the rail, flattening herself to it. She wore heeled shoes and a short skirt, her legs unprotected by anything thicker than fine nylon.

The dog came close. She heard a horrible low growling roar from it. She saw the little eyes, the slobbering jaw. She gave a cry as its muscles bunched and suddenly there was a whirl of activity beside her.

Carey had bent to the dog even as it leapt. Somehow he had caught the open jaw with his two hands before the teeth sank into Gossamer's leg. He whirled the animal into the air and tossed it over the bridge. For a second its white naked-seeming body hung. Then it plunged into the water.

The running man pulled up short and stared after his dog. He was stubby and powerfully-built. His lips drew back in a snarl, twisting with rage.

"Ere, you,' he hissed at Carey. There was menace in every line of his body. 'You've murdered my dog. I'll fucking . . .'

He got no further. Carey had closed with him even as he spoke and now was chest to chest with him, the man's arm bent up hard behind his back. Carey jammed him against the iron rail of the bridge so that he was forced back over the black swirling water.

'Your dog nearly had this young lady.'

'You don't know that. Let me go, you bastard.'

'I'll have you over the bridge with the beast if you don't apologise.'

His red face went white. Gossamer heard his arm creak. 'Let me go.'

'When you apologise.'

'Jesus, you're mad. I'm sorry, aren't I? I was trying to catch 'im. You didn't 'ave to drown 'im.'

'I did. If you go down on the Embankment you'll probably get the filthy thing back. He didn't look that easy to kill, more's the pity.'

Carey released the man, standing back, watching him as he rubbed his arm. 'You bastard,' the man said sourly. 'You didn't know what he was going to do.'

Carey took a step in. The man ducked and ran past him, along the bridge, holding his arm.

Gossamer was shaking. Carey squatted down and ran his hand lightly up her leg. 'He didn't get you, did he?' he asked in an impersonal voice.

'No.' The gold-brown head was below her. 'Carey.'

He straightened up. 'Just as well or they might be hauling me off for murder.' He grinned at her. 'OK?'

'Carey.'

He opened his arms and she came to him. She felt his hard body pressing against her soft one. She felt his arms tight round her, holding her to him.

She hugged him as tightly as she could, as if she would force her body into his. He was warm through the fabric of his shirt and she felt his chin in her hair. She rubbed her cheek against him in an ecstasy of release and murmured his name.

He loosened his grip and reluctantly she let him go, turning her face away and groping for a tissue. A moment later she found a large handkerchief, snowy and starched, being pressed into her hand.

'I'm sorry,' she gulped. 'I didn't have time to be frightened.'

He put a finger under her chin and tilted her face up to his. He took his handkerchief back and used it to wipe the tears off her cheeks.

'Angry with me?' he asked lightly. 'Poor little dog, and all that.'

'No!' she blazed. 'I thought you were marvellous. The thought of its teeth in my leg, crunching through bone.' She

stopped, her voice trembling. It wasn't the pain she might
have suffered that was stirring her.

The rain swept over them unnoticed. The rainbow had
long since gone.

'Not while I'm by you,' he said in quiet voice. 'I won't let
anything hurt you while I'm near. You must know that by
now, Gossamer Fane.'

She woke the next morning in her big bed and wondered
sleepily why happiness engulfed her like a warm tide,
flowing into every nook and cranny of her body.

Her body. Her strong dancer's body. She remembered the
previous day, what he had said.

What he had not said. He had put her into a taxi and sent
her home after that intense moment.

She rolled over and closed her eyes, feeling the pressure
of his body as they stood crushed together, she in his arms
on the icing-sugar bridge.

She would never forget it. Never, she thought passionately.

Meanwhile, what should she do?

The answer was simple. Nothing. He had run things from
the start. It was right and proper, natural as the sun in
the sky. He was her father, her brother, her . . . Well, he
wasn't. Just as well, she reflected soberly. She was a little
girl compared to him. She had fantasised he was her father
often enough, the holder of some dark secret that he was
too ashamed to admit to her. He was her father and he was
finding out about his daughter, that was the fantasy. She
admitted it. One day he would realise he could trust her, she
would accept whatever it was that he had done and forgive
him and they could acknowledge their relationship and she
would have a family, she would belong.

Meanwhile, all she could do was show him the trust she felt
in his company, and not question him about his own life. She
didn't want lies between them. When he was ready, he would
reveal his identity. It was up to her to let him know that he
was safe with her, safe in her love. She must be patient.

Was it fantasy or was it fact? They were not physically alike, she knew. She had searched his face often enough when he was absorbed in something else. Her eyes were of so dark a blue they were almost black. His were the most beautiful sea-green, a blue-green slightly flecked with gold. Tiger's eyes. His hair was a warm reddish golden brown. Hers was midnight. His face was square and strong. Hers was wide at the top and pointed at her chin, her cheekbones like wings above her wide mouth.

No. If he was her father, she resembled her mother. Her dead mother. She no longer believed her father was dead. Kevin Germain had fudged when she asked. He had been quite clear about her mother, but about her father he had said neither the one thing nor the other. If her father was dead, it would hardly matter.

Her father was alive. He knew of her. They were linked by the cold formality of Chatteris Choate.

She must show him she cared. She must show him she was good. She must be what a father wanted from a daughter.

Then he would tell her the truth.

✸ **Three** ✸

Kevin Germain asked to meet her. He suggested she come to lunch with him one day. It was over Easter and so there was no school.

He took her to the The Cheese Trap in Wine Office Court, off Fleet Street. It was famed for its history of mad and mostly drunken poets.

He was delighted with her though he didn't let his satisfaction show. She had chosen to wear a dress and matching jacket with a high embroidered collar. The dress fitted her like a glove. She looked adorably chic, adorably young. She wore the silliest little pillbox hat with a tiny scrap of black lace veil. The joke was superb and his loins grew hot at the devastating combination of sinful clothes and youthful innocence.

He ordered oysters for them both. He had made a mistake bringing her here, he knew that now. It was too fashionable. There was a Cabinet minister and his secretary in one corner. Two senior hacks sat together in another. Now an actress had come in, rumoured to be having an affair with an MP. A female MP. She was accompanied by Malling Benedict.

He had just asked the girl about her dance school and she was explaining something to him. He wasn't listening to her, he was simply enjoying the sensuous rustle of her voice, low-pitched and husky. At the same time he watched her face, animated and sweet. He'd like to change the expression on it, make those eyes startle, flush that smooth skin. The mouth alone promised wine of a rare vintage.

He felt Malling see her, and himself, and knew the meeting

was unavoidable. He met Gossamer's eyes and interrupted. 'Watch out,' he said.

Her eyebrows rose dangerously. The poor little fool couldn't see the lecher in him but she knew all about bad manners. Then Benedict was by their table.

The man was lizard-like, stunted and yellow. His nickname amongst the cognoscenti was Pope. Pope Benedict. It was nothing to do with the Vatican though indeed he controlled a secret service. It referred to his legs, mean wizened things that had never grown properly. The great Alexander Pope had been similarly afflicted.

Now Benedict's eyes flickered between them. 'It is the lawyer and his lass,' he said and snickered.

Gossamer looked at Kevin, puzzled.

'How d'ye do,' said Germain easily. 'Gloria, meet the famous Malling Benedict. You're honoured, my dear.'

The little man's eyes pierced her. She had no idea what to do or say. She knew Malling Benedict was the leading gossip writer of the day, famed for his spite.

She felt Kevin's hand close over hers. His silky voice was continuing. 'Gloria is my niece from South Africa, Malling. She's over for the shops and a little London gloss.'

'Is that right, Miss . . . ?'

'Gee, Harrods takes the pip out of anything in Jo'burg,' Gossamer said, clipping her syllables. 'Uncle Kevin says . . .'

She felt Kevin squeeze her hand gratefully. At the same time Benedict's eyes released her. His interest was gone. She was a colonial nobody however stunning her looks, and he had no interest in what her uncle Kevin might have said. He had wanted something juicy about Chatteris Choate and under-age nymphets. This girl was no good to him.

When he was gone Gossamer raised eyes brimming with mischief to Kevin's. They shared a moment of absolute harmony. 'What was that about?' she asked.

He released her hand. 'He's filth,' he said genially. He was extraordinarily pleased with her. It was like watching a client turn out a good performance in court. 'He'd have had a little para about us next week, something to make you blush and me want to issue a writ. It's my job to protect you, not expose you to gossip.'

During the rest of the meal he seriously wondered if he should take a chance. Was she the one to marry? She was beautiful and would get better. She was innocent and he would enjoy removing that quality from her. She was doe-like and loving. That would make a pleasant change.

The fantasy was enticing. He could continue to enjoy more esoteric pleasures at, for example, Isabella's, and have this child's innocence to come home to. She had a shining quality. She was a gem of the finest water.

If he took her, he would be snatching her out from under the nose of a London who didn't realise she existed yet. She was too important to remain an unknown for much longer. She was going to be a player in the game, whether she knew it or not. With her looks and her background . . . her background. Ah, there was the rub. He would be furious. He would sack Chatteris Choate when he finally knew. It would cost the firm millions, millions every year. Chatteris Choate specialised in the legal requirements of city dealing and in this respect alone he was a very valuable client. Their absolute discretion was a commodity they charged highly for. If he wasn't so bloody-minded and intractable, Kevin would have told him about her by now, but his instructions were clear. He was to say nothing, ever, unless the trust was broken and needed winding up. The man was a brute and had never forgiven an enemy. His hatreds were legendary.

That was the joke, of course. This sweet thing had been sired by a monster. She didn't know it. No one did.

Only he did, Kevin Germain. There had to be a profit in it. He was a lawyer. He had patience. He would work out what was best to do.

Then he would act.

Carey was so tender it hurt. All that spring she felt fat with happiness like the buds burst open on the trees, sticky things with wet bright leaves hanging rag-like until their strength developed. The School, when it restarted, was both easier and less important to her now. The ballet term was over with its gruelling *barre* work and agonising exercises. Now they were doing contemporary dance and though she might have found it hard had she done it before the ballet, it seemed easy the other way round.

Life was perfect, full of anticipation yet marvellous in itself. Summer was coming but each day was heralded by a cool pearl-misted dawn.

Gossamer often went to bed very early. She almost never went out in the evening because she was uninterested in the men she met. Of the girls, her closest friend was Trish. She went to bed early and so she rose early and would lean on her balcony in a sweet satisfaction watching the mist rise over the little park she lived by and the larger expanses of the Heath beyond. At that time of day even London seemed blessed with clean thrilling air.

Trish was strange these days. She had come back after the Easter break looking both plumper and more hawk-like, as if a terrible tragedy was shaking her life. If Gossamer spoke to her she smiled and spoke back, but it was as if she had to make an effort. Gossamer found that Trish watched her covertly. She remembered the curious questioning in Trish's bedsit that time and felt her interpretation of it justified. Trish never went out with the boys. Indeed, if she said anything about men it was caustic and bitter.

Gossamer's flat was her womb at this time and she felt it around her, protective in the muddling world. It was very small. It had one large L-shaped room. Her bed was at one end, round the corner for privacy. The rest of the room had a table and four chairs and a three-piece suite, opening through glass patio doors onto a broad balcony where she had tubs of flowers. Apart from this one room she had a tiny bathroom and an even tinier kitchen. The enormous rent, which sucked up a large proportion of her trust income, was for the address, the view and the facilities of the building, which included Arthur.

She was happy. Like a canary in a cage, she wanted to sing.

And Carey was unbelievably sweet. Gossamer was now certain he was her father. She had no fears, no reserve with him any longer. Her trust in him was absolute and she made herself into the daughter she believed he wanted her to be. Her sexual innocence therefore did not trouble her, except that her body felt strange so often. There was time after she was established in his care for her to make her first adventures with men.

The only problem lay in her dreams. Increasingly, they were hot. She woke covered in perspiration and shame at the thoughts and images that jostled in her unconscious mind. She dreamed of naked men. She remembered the feel of Peter's sex in her hand as if it was still there. His lips, his hand on her thigh, his sex, all were sensory stigmata. He had been heavy, firm, silken and cool. She hated him for his brutish attack, and yet she understood better his desperation, the screaming need of his body.

It wasn't that one or two of the boys at Ryder-Vail weren't good-looking or that they lacked the friendly approach. She was flattered when some of the older students took an interest in her. But she couldn't cross the Rubicon. Something held her back, intruded between her and the reality of a man in her life. She was locked in her fantasy world of fairy castles and *preux chevaliers*. And she knew that once she had lain in a man's arms, allowed him into her bed and her body, there was no going back.

She was frightened. There was something inside herself that frightened her, a kraken half-sensed slumbering deep in her hidden nature and she dared do nothing to release it.

Carey invited her to go to Frankie's with him.

Frankie's was the current ultra-fashionable venue for the rich darlings of London. Pope Benedict haunted it, himself a celeb as he hunted celebrities. A restaurant and night-club offering cabaret, it was the place the more thrusting glitterati adored more than anywhere for the moment. It had cachet. It conferred grace. You could swank there.

It was lusciously, obscenely expensive. It was decadent. It

was fun. Every girl at Shaws had wanted to be escorted to Frankie's and Marie had certainly made it. Now Gossamer was going to go and she could not have asked for a happier introduction. She was to go on Carey's arm. She could imagine no greater bliss.

Most of the money she had available after her rent and college fees went on clothes which she loved with a guilty passion. For Frankie's she bought a special dress, having it altered in the shop until it was perfect.

The satin was marbled ice-green. Cut low at the bosom and strapless, it was stiffened at the breast to cup and flaunt the flesh it cradled. It came tight over the ribs to a low waist and then the skirt was stiffened once more into an absurd puff, a tulip-shape, the petals of the bell ending above the knee.

Only someone with a rich skin and flawless figure could wear it, and Gossamer had both. Her black hair, black brows and smoke-blue eyes over hollow cheeks gave her a ballet dancer's haunting beauty. The bones of her naked shoulders stood out fragile as a bird's. Her breasts were those of a girl still, but sweetly rounded and firm, promising a ripeness to come. Her slender waist told also of her youth, but her long slim legs had acquired a woman's grace from her formal training.

She had been taught to apply make-up as part of her course and she did it with professional skill. Jewellery was a problem. She had some junk jewellery, but somehow it didn't go with the sensual perfection of her dress. She left her ears and throat and wrists bare therefore, having nothing to wear.

Carey called for her. Arthur buzzed from the foyer that he was on his way, and so she was ready for him, choking in her excitement, when he arrived at her door.

He came in to her flat for the first time. She caught her breath.

She had known he was a good-looking man. She hadn't realised how stunningly handsome he was. The heavy white shirt and utter blackness of his evening clothes brought into high relief his blond-brown hair, his sea-green eyes, his tanned rugged skin. His body had a marvellous and utterly masculine grace.

He stood now, just inside her sitting room, leaning against the wall as he opened his gold case and lit himself a cigarette.

'Turn round,' he said.

He watched her pirouette, her face anxious and absurdly young as she waited for his opinion. He came over to her and bent to kiss her brow. 'Any man would be proud to be with you,' he said.

Gossamer's heart sang so it hurt, she was so happy.

'I have something for you,' he said.

'You do?'

'I'm glad you're wearing no jewellery.'

'I don't have anything that goes.'

'How about this?'

He took a little box from his pocket and opened it for her. It was a pair of earrings, pearl drops set in twisted filigreed gold. Her eyes lifted to his, huge and misted with unshed tears. 'They're beautiful,' she said, her voice breaking slightly.

'I'll put them on for you, shall I?'

'Please.'

His hands were putting aside the tendrils she had allowed artfully to escape from her piled hair. She felt his bare skin against her own, at her neck and shoulder, at her ears. 'You must always let a man buy your jewellery for you,' he said.

'Must I?' Her voice quivered.

'Fine jewellery is special. It acquires a patina, like good furniture. It carries feeling. It should be a present, given with meaning. A woman who buys her own jewellery is a lost soul. Incidentally, these pearls are real so they won't last forever. Meanwhile your skin will polish them and bring out their lustre.'

He stood back and smiled at his handiwork. She nodded her head slightly and felt them shake.

'Thank you,' she said.

He took her hand and turned it palm-up in his own. He carried it to his lips and kissed it gently. 'Thank you,' he said, emphasising the second word.

For the first time she consciously wondered what he would be like as a lover. He would be charming, she knew it. He would be wonderful. He was the ideal man, beautiful, strong, protective, full of charm and intelligence. Whatever he did for a living, he was obviously successful in it. Why wasn't he married?

She knew. It was because there was some tragedy concerning her mother. That was why he had cast her off. Did she remind him unbearably of her mother? Were they like? Had these pearl drops once belonged to that sad shadowy figure haunting her past?

'Shall we go? Do you have a wrap?'

Unable to afford an evening cloak, she had bought a vast length from a bolt of white silk, sewn up the ends and now was using it as a wide scarf to wrap over her shoulders.

They went down to the foyer and out to the waiting taxi in style.

He was known. The head waiter murmured 'Mr Lambert' as he led them to their table. Heads turned and acquaintances nodded. Gossamer felt a surge of jealousy at this life of his hitherto closed to her. Then she remembered where she was. He had brought her along. He was showing her off.

It was quiet yet, comparatively early, and they ate together saying little. Occasionally he pointed out some celebrity and as the noise slowly rose around them she felt cocooned in his company, utterly at peace.

The band was playing and it was Frankie's malicious pleasure to concentrate on real dances, the waltz, the foxtrot, the quickstep, and these had come back into fashion so that the girls scrambled to learn them, not to be forced to sit out at Frankie's. Carey asked her to dance.

She stood up as if in a dream. She felt like Cinderella. She gave Carey her hand and he led her onto the dance floor. It was half full, just right. There was a faint stir through the room and Pope Benedict who had just come in saw her, and made a note to score off Kevin Germain. He recognised Gossamer instantly, partly because it was his job to remember faces and partly because her combination of innocence and beauty was unique in his experience. She must be a whore, he concluded instantly. Trust Lambert to break Frankie's rules. Few men would dare. He would phone Isabella in the morning and see if the girl was one of hers.

Carey drew Gossamer into his body and without perceptible hesitation they flowed into the waltz, effortlessly picking up the step.

As they danced, the floor cleared around them a little. Gossamer was professionally-taught in addition to her natural grace in the dance. Carey was superb, unlike any of the boys at the School. His light guiding hand was at once a support and an extension of her own body. Gossamer let go. She relaxed utterly into the music and she felt her body and his join and move as one. She was ravished.

'Wake up.' It was said gently but she blinked and saw that they were standing still, Carey clapping slightly as the band had stopped playing.

'Don't look like that,' he said equally lightly.

'Like what?'

'If I kiss you, we'll be thrown out. It isn't done here.'

She laughed and coloured. The band began to play again. She moved serenely into his arms and again she entered heaven.

She was more aware now. She felt the cloth of his jacket. Very faintly she smelt his skin. The light dry clasp of his hand made her heart flutter. Every part of her body was coordinated. She felt his movements before he made them and so was with him, a liquid perfection of grace. This time when the music stopped they were by the bandstand. She turned to face the orchestra to clap politely and found that the conductor was kissing his fingers to her. She laughed hesitantly and looked up at Carey. His smile was enigmatic. 'I think he appreciates how well you dance,' he said. He took her elbow and guided her back to their table.

A waiter brought a magnum of champagne. Carey looked at it and then raised cool eyes to the man's expressionless face. 'I didn't order this,' he said lazily.

'No, Mr Lambert. It's from Mr Wollstein. He's over there with his party, sir.'

Gossamer looked across. A short fat man with a short fat cigar was waving genially in their direction. Carey indicated for him to come across and join them.

There were three of them, Solly Wollstein, his wife Andrina and their son David. Solly was as Jewish-looking as his name, complete with thick glasses and a vast nose, but his wife was a tall plump Anglo-Saxon and the boy a lissom dark youth aged about twenty.

'Meet Gossamer Fane,' said Carey. 'Gossamer, this is my good friend and occasional business associate Sol Wollstein. Andrina, his wife, the most charming woman I know, and David. How do you do, Davie? How's life treating you?'

'Fine,' said David, his eyes on Gossamer.

'Call me Andy, dear,' said Andrina in pure East London cockney. She folded Gossamer to her ample and stiffly-corseted bosom. 'My dear, it makes me cry to see how beautifully you dance. I didn't think girls could do it any more. What a dream. Where did you find her, Carey?'

'Don't ask stupid questions,' said Solly. He looked benignly at Gossamer. 'You must call me Solly because I love it when beautiful girls do and you're the most beautiful girl I've ever seen. Isn't she a stunner, David?'

The boy went scarlet and mumbled.

She drank champagne. She answered when she was spoken to. She danced with Solly who was very good and with David who was very bad. She longed to dance with Carey again but she was separated from him now at their table and though she was pleased to be introduced to his friends, she missed their earlier intimacy.

The nightclub was very full now. The cabaret had started but Gossamer used the dark and the distraction to study Carey. She had never realised how unbelievably good-looking he was as she did here, set against his peers, men of his class and age. He must have had many women as lovers. He must have someone now. Perhaps he had brought her here.

She shut down her mind.

The cabaret stopped. People came over to Carey and were introduced to her. For the first time in his company she wondered what others thought of their relationship. Did they think they were lovers? Would Carey bother with someone as young as her? Yet everyone was so nice to her.

A voice she knew swam out of the crowd. Marie, square, plump and bejewelled came up to her with two fathful swains.

'Gossamer,' she squealed. 'I didn't know you came here.'

'My first time,' said Gossamer. She stood up to kiss Marie on the cheek.

'Meet Barmy and Collywobbles. They take me everywhere. Not a brain cell between them but such a shriek. You don't have to remember which is which.'

The two young men were in immaculate evening clothes very slightly askew. They were flushed with drink but still steady on their feet.

'Barny,' said one, shaking her hand. 'Lovely to meet you. Any friend of Marie's and all that.'

'Colin. Isn't she frightful?' said the other. 'Super to see you. You must have lunch with us sometime.'

Gossamer introduced Carey and the Wollsteins. She saw that Marie's surname, Horden-Smith, was not lost on Solly. Marie was the daughter of a shipping magnate, hence her crack about daddy having a yacht. Daddy had a fleet, actually.

'Ask the young lady to dance, Davie,' urged Solly aimiably. 'Young men have no manners these days.'

Awkwardly David invited Marie and they went off together.

Barny looked at the table, plainly deduced that David Wollstein was her escort and therefore unavailable to ask, and requested Gossamer's hand.

She looked across at Carey. He nodded. She went off to the dance.

Barny might be half-way drunk but he was no social fool and he had seen the little interchange. 'I say,' he said pleasantly, clumping with heavy accuracy round the floor, 'are you here with Carey Lambert?'

'Yes.' Gossamer was breathless, concentrating on not getting her feet trodden on.

'Goodness,' said Barny simply and didn't utter another word.

They were suddenly interrupted. A tall fair youth was swaying right beside them. 'Gossamer,' he said thickly. 'Where have you been hiding yourself?'

Barny stopped and Gossamer turned to face Peter Kepesake. He had never looked more like a rugby player. 'Gonna dance with me now?'

Barny stepped forward, short, slender and impeccably polite.

'I'll see Miss Fane back to her table, don't you know. Her party's over there.'

'She'll dance with me, won't you, Goss? For old times' sake. Are you with this person?'

'She's with Carey Lambert,' said Barny. 'Don't be a fool.'

'But we're old friends.' Peter grabbed her and pulled her roughly onto the floor.

'Let go. You're drunk,' she hissed. She desperately didn't want a scene. She didn't see Barny making his way back to her table.

'Still the virgin queen?' Peter was openly jeering. 'Little Jenny's forging a path in the land of the cuckoo clock. Why aren't you?'

'Let go, Peter. You're making a scene. Stop it.'

Peter stopped and she bumped into him. She could have wept with exasperation. Then she saw why he had stopped.

Carey was shorter than Peter who was well over six feet and wide to match. But there was no doubting who was master and who was fool. Carey's hand was on her shoulder and he faced the drunken youth.

'You drunken scum,' he said quietly. 'You are bothering

Miss Fane and you deserve to have your balls cut off. I'd gladly do it but I see a waiter is coming to do it for me.'

Peter was open-mouthed at the smooth obscenity. A waiter was suddenly there, murmuring he had to leave.

'I don't know what this place is coming to,' said Carey. 'I thought you didn't admit drunks.'

'No, sir. I'm sorry, Mr Lambert.' The waiter was submissive with Carey and aggressive to Peter simultaneously.

Carey steered Gossamer back to their table. 'I'm sorry about causing trouble,' she said miserably. She looked up at him woefully and suddenly, in the crowd beyond, she met a pair of sharp dark knowing eyes. Spiteful eyes, in a wizened face. Malling Benedict was watching her.

Carey changed course abruptly and took her into the bar. He stood very close to her in the chattering crush.

'My poor child,' he said caressingly. 'Who was that lout?'

'Peter Kepesake. He's the brother of a friend of mine, Jenny. We were at school together and I went to her house in the holidays sometimes.'

Carey was silent for a moment, his face closed. 'Is he an old flame?' he said eventually.

'No! He tried, he tried . . .'

'What did he try?'

'To force himself on me once. When I was seventeen.'

'He didn't succeed?'

'No! You know he didn't. You know . . .'

'I know.' His voice was very low. She could hardly hear him in the crowd. His body was pressed to hers. 'I know all about you, Gossamer, don't I? You keep nothing back.'

'I belong to you,' she whispered. 'You know that.'

'Body and soul?'

Her face was directly under his, turned up, her lips parted, trembling slightly. Her whole body trembled slightly, pressed against his.

'Is that what you want?' she whispered. This was ecstatic.

'It's the only way with me. Nothing less.'

'I couldn't keep anything from you. I only wish I had

something to give you. Something precious. I'd give you anything. Everything.'

His face twisted slightly. 'I believe you would.'

'You think I'm a child. You think I don't know what I'm saying. I do. I mean it. I'd do anything for you.' The champagne bubbled in her brain. He had to believe her. There might never be another chance to tell him and she passionately wanted him to know.

'No, I don't think you're a child, Gossamer. Can't you see, that's the trouble.'

She took his hand, holding it fiercely with her own. She bowed her head and in the privacy of the space between their two bodies, she kissed it.

He freed it without saying another word. He took her back to their table, arranging it somehow so that she sat next to him.

She drank champagne and watched the swirling beautiful crowd. Perfume hung in the air. Diamonds sparkled. She caught Andy Wollstein watching her with concern and she lifted her head proudly in response.

She saw faces in the crowd, mostly men's faces, turned towards her, then turned away. Carey took her up to dance again and she floated against his breast, resting her cheek against the cloth of his shirt. She was supremely happy.

Afterwards he said, 'I'm going to take you home now.'

'Yes.' She was deliciously submissive.

'You know, I think you might be a little drunk.'

'Yes,' she said happily. She was drunk on him.

She made her goodbyes. Andy held her tightly so that Gossamer heard her corset creak and smelled her expensive powder. She was whispering urgently. 'My dear, you're so young. Do you know what you're doing? If you need any help . . .'

Gossamer, released, turned round. Carey was watching Andy with a curious glint in his eye. The plump woman grew confused and fumbled with her wrap, with her drink.

They came out into the night air and waited while the doorman called a taxi. The air rushed to Gossamer's head and she stumbled as she came into the leathery interior.

They sat in silence. Her head whirled with the fumes of the alcohol and with the emotions she had experienced that night. She felt she must burst.

Carey paid the taxi to wait at her flat. Silvio was on duty in the foyer, he was the usual night porter. Carey took her to the lift and she leant dreamily against him as they ascended.

He found her key in her little purse and let them both in. They went through her tiny hallway. A sidelight had been left burning and the room was a soft creamy cavern of pale fabric and dim light. He half carried her to the sofa and let her subside onto it.

He lifted her legs so she could lie comfortably with her head on one end and her ankles on the other. He removed her shoes and held one of her feet for the moment.

'I've made you drunk,' he said. The sound of his voice made her spin. 'That's very bad of me.'

He massaged her foot, sitting on the edge of the sofa. 'Will you be all right? Perhaps I should make you some coffee.'

'Could you help me out of my dress? I love it, but it's terrible to manage in and out of.'

'I love it too. You have marvellous taste, Gossamer.'

He sat her up by main force so that her head nestled into his shoulder. He felt at the back of the dress and found the zip. He began to slide it down.

She wore nothing under the top of the dress, indeed, it was made to support her without help. Carey allowed her to slip back onto the sofa but now the bodice of her dress was folded down.

Her young firm breasts lay exposed to his eyes. Sweetly rounded, they proclaimed at once her youth and her maturity. Her skin was its most tawny and her nipples were *café-au-lait* in colour, soft and snubby in repose.

Gossamer sat herself up with some difficulty and reached to the low tight waist of the dress. The puff of the belled skirt made it difficult. 'It's here somewhere,' she said.

His hands were round her waist, his shoulder brushing her bare breasts. She rested her cheek on his arm while he released the dress.

'I have to stand up,' she said, 'and work it up over my head.'

They stood up, her breasts touching his shirt front. He grasped the bell of the skirt and lifted the material up.

She gave a wiggle, raising her arms in the air. He lifted the dress with its stiffnesses and softnesses up over her head and off her arms. She fell back onto the sofa and looked up at him.

Her hair was still up, soft tendrils framing her delicately flushed face. Her eyes were dark luminous pools. Her naked breasts were like the pearls at her ears, translucent and pure. She wore a tiny scrap of amber satin lace at her groin. She wore also a garter belt in amber lace that supported her cobweb stockings.

She looked up at the man standing over her, his face dark above the nimbus of light in which she lay.

'I love you,' she said.

'I know.'

She smiled up at him. 'I love you so much.'

She reached up her arms and he bent to her. He picked her up in one liquid flow of muscle and carried her round the corner into the shadows where her bed was.

He laid her on the bed, folded back the covers and moved her so that he could cover her up.

'Carey,' she said.

He bent down and let his lips touch hers for one infinitesimal moment of time. Then he stood up again.

'I want you to . . .'

'I know what you want. I know all about you. Too much.'

'No!'

'Goodnight, darling child. I'll contact you tomorrow. Sleep well, pretty. You were a princess tonight. You still are.'

He was gone. She wept the easy tears of alcohol and slept.

* * *

Saturday. If she had a hangover, it was unnoticeable in her sea of grief. She loved him. She loved him utterly, she had told him she loved him, she had offered herself to him and he had rejected her. Kindly, but it was a rejection.

She felt too awful to cry. She was dry inside, so dry she felt herself curling up. The pain was terrible.

He had taken her out, out into the grown-up world to which she thought she belonged. His world. She had made a scene, caused trouble, got drunk and thrown herself at him like a tart. He must despise her. She was a silly little drunken tarty girl and now he knew.

She hadn't realised she had pride. His rejection hurt simply because it was that, a rejection. It was the first time she had invited a man to make love to her, offering what she held dear, and he had passed up on the chance. It probably hadn't been difficult.

True, her hurt pride was nothing to her sense of loss and her shame at her behaviour, but she was aware of it all the same.

She felt cheap. She had thrown away something so valuable it broke her heart.

It was some time before she pulled herself together enough to face the other problem.

She believed he was her father. She had tried to get him to make love to her.

She sobbed in her terrible grief. She couldn't resolve it. She had no answers, only the enormity of her feelings.

Arthur buzzed her from the foyer. She wiped her eyes and stumbled over to the speaker. Dear God, if he came and found her like this.

'Florist's boy on his way up, Miss Fane.'

'Thank you, Arthur.' She blew her nose and tightened her wrapper round her. She must wash and dress, fix her face.

It was a basket of flowers, roses and pinks. Eagerly she tore at the wrapping to find the card.

The scribbled handwriting was uncertain and childish.

Dreadfully sorry for last night. Phoned Jenny for your address. How about dinner tonight? I'll phone.

It was signed Peter. Gossamer screwed it angrily into a ball and threw it in the bin. Damn him, she thought fiercely. Couldn't he leave her alone?

An hour later the second bunch of flowers arrived. She was sitting superficially calm on her balcony in the thin sunshine.

It was a bunch of anemones in a box. The card said simply: *for Trafalgar Square.*

She was still puzzling over it when Peter phoned.

'I say, Gossamer, I am sorry I was such an ass. We drove over from Oxford and I was tanked up, I'm afraid. I'll have to go back tomorrow, too. Shouldn't be here at all.'

'You were very embarrassing, Peter. It wasn't nice.'

'Look, I've said I'm sorry. You did look terrific, Gossamer. Hows about some grub tonight? They do an awfully decent steak . . .'

She was ruthless. 'Look, no. I'm sorry, Peter, but you don't behave when we're together and I don't like it. It isn't fair of you to use Jenny to get to me. Leave me alone. That's what I want from you. Leave me alone.'

She slammed the phone down. She was shaking. She blamed him for part of the evening's fiasco. How childish he was, and he had embroiled her in it. She hated him.

She suddenly realised what Carey's card meant. It was a farewell. She had begun as Trafalgar Square. Now it was over.

She touched the pearls at her ears. Abruptly she couldn't bear her flat any more. Grabbing her bag she ran out.

She spent the day walking, dry-eyed because there was nothing left to cry for. She had lost the man she adored and in some way she couldn't understand, her adoration wasn't allowed. It was sick. She had felt so right and good but the truth was, it was sick. If he was her father. Perhaps her only salvation lay in the fact that he couldn't know she had guessed. She was spared that last exquisite twist of horror.

How could she love him in this way, knowing what she thought she knew? Why didn't her genes forbid it?

Was this some clue to her mother, that mysterious death, her own abandonment? Had her mother had unnatural urges also?

Shaking with horror she walked and walked, praying for exhaustion.

Images came to her. Helen Kepesake, asking her to come down to Sandings. When she felt better she would go. Maybe she would even be able to tell Helen when the pain had eased a little, and accept help.

Andy Wollstein. She had tried to warn her last night, as if Carey was dangerous.

Dangerous. It was a word to apply to him, now she thought about it. She remembered how swift he was at times of crisis. How he saved her. She remembered Barny, hissing at Peter that she was with Carey Lambert. What did he mean? They made Carey sound like a monster. He wasn't. He wasn't. She knew him better than anyone and she knew he was tender and gentle and true.

She had spoiled it. Soiled it. She wasn't good enough for him. He was doing the right thing, to cast her off.

It was evening. Like dirty water the shadows flowed from corners and alleyways. Car lights were on. Shop fronts were lit up or closed at the end of the working day.

Youths were out getting ready for an evening's heavy drinking. She drifted helplessly. Her legs ached with tiredness. Her will was gone, she didn't know what she was doing.

She turned into a cinema and watched a dreadful film about someone killing everyone. Arnold Schwarzenegger. Of course.

Out again she reeled like a drunk, only it was exhaustion. She hadn't eaten all day. She must find a taxi and go home.

She saw a face she knew. Hope leapt in her. Here was help, someone who would help her come to terms with what she had done, what she was. Trish was strolling along apparently by herself, not in a hurry, and Gossamer rushed up to her.

'Trish. Trish,' she called.

Heads turned and looked away after a moment, full of sly amusement.

'Trish!'

The girl stopped and looked round. Gossamer ran up to her. 'I'm so glad to see you,' she said breathlessly. 'I've done something so awful. Trish, if I don't talk to someone I'll die. Are you going anywhere? Please, can I come to your place and talk?'

For the first time she noticed how oddly Trish was dressed. She wore a tight cheap-looking red leather skirt. It was very short. She wore very high heels and black stockings. On her top she had a little tight blouse that revealed her upper breasts. The jacket she wore over it was blue denim.

She looked terrible. Her hair was fluffed out and her face heavily made up.

'Oh,' said Gossamer unhappily. 'Are you going to a party? I'm sorry.'

For the first time Trish spoke. She tried once and then cleared her throat and tried again. 'Fuck off,' she said.

Gossamer fell back a pace. 'Trish?'

'Fuck off, Gossamer. Can't you see I'm working?'

'Working? I don't understand.'

'Well, you wouldn't, would you? The last of the innocents, you. This is reality, kiddo. This is what it's like.'

'What is? I don't understand.'

'I'm a whore, duckie. This is my patch. I had to fight for it so you bugger off and let me cruise.'

'No. I don't believe you.'

'Your privilege. Meanwhile I'm missing out on the punters. Forty smackers for ten minutes. You're costing me.'

'You aren't serious?'

'How do you think I live? I don't have private means like some I can mention. Morality's as long as your purse, sister. If you haven't learnt that you're a fool.'

She reeled away from the harsh face, the ugly words. She remembered how poor Trish had been, how latterly she had dressed better and yet had had a ravaged look. In her innocence she had wondered about drugs. It wasn't drugs. It was prostitution.

She found a taxi and managed to blurt out her address. When she arrived and was fumbling in her purse for some money, she saw a heavy dark sports car in gunmetal grey squatting in front of the building. Arthur was standing at the passenger door, bending over and talking to whoever was inside.

If she could get in without Arthur seeing her, it would be wonderful. Life would be like this now. She would take it small steps at a time. She stuffed a fiver into the taxi-man's hand and ran for the steps.

Arthur straightened up. 'Here she is,' he said cheerfully. 'Miss Fane. Miss Fane! Your gentleman to see you.'

She thought she would faint. It would be Peter in some borrowed car. She couldn't face him.

Arthur was looking at her. She stood as if at bay, one foot on the wide steps that led up to the glass doors of the foyer. Above her was her flat, sanctuary.

'Uh,' she said. 'I don't feel . . .' She stopped. The driver was getting out of the car. He came across to her in swift strides.

'Gossamer.'

'Carey,' she said faintly. The darkness sucked upwards and swallowed her. She fell.

❊ Four ❊

She came round in her flat, lying on her bed. For a moment she couldn't think why anyone else should be there. She thought she was waking from sleep.

She saw Carey sitting on the bed by her, his face cool and remote. Waves of love and relief flowed through her. She had had such awful nightmares.

'I think she's better now, Arthur,' he said. His voice was loud and a little harsh. It wasn't like him to get the pitch of the thing wrong.

Arthur's genial face loomed over her. 'Feeling more the thing now, Miss Fane? I can get a doctor if you like.'

'No. No doctor.' It was an effort to speak. 'I'm fine now. And, and Mr Lambert's here.'

'Right you are. Just call down if you want me to get anyone, sir.'

Blessedly he went. She lay there looking up at him. He stroked her hair back from her face.

'What is it?' he asked presently.

'I thought you weren't coming back.' Her need was naked. He smiled faintly. 'You underestimate yourself.'

She remembered. 'Trish,' she said, agony in her voice.

'I beg your pardon.'

'I saw, I saw a girl I knew. I know. She's at the School. I met her on the street. The Marylebone Road. She looked awful. Really awful. Ghastly clothes and make-up. She said she was a . . .'

'Prostitute,' he finished gently.

She lay letting the pain seep out of her. 'How did you know?' she asked after a while.

'It's not so unusual. There are a lot of students on the game. They can't live, otherwise.'

'How can she? Oh, I sound like a prig. That isn't what I mean at all.'

'You mean, how can she let just any man at her. How can she let fat dirty old men fumble with her body. How can she let strangers puff away on top of her. How can she touch their bodies. Do things for them.' He paused. 'She does it for money, Gossamer. It drives people to do many things.'

'Nothing shocks you.'

'I know the way of the world. I might not like it, but I know about it.'

'I'm so ignorant.'

'Yes. It's probably time you grew up. You've been so lovely in your innocence.'

'Carey, I'm sorry about last night.'

'Are you?'

'Getting drunk.' Her voice tailed off.

'Saying what you said.'

'No,' she whispered.

He bent his head to light a cigarette. The sudden flare from his lighter threw his face into sharp relief. She ached with love for him.

He inhaled and blew the smoke slowly out of his lungs. 'You offered yourself to me,' he said.

'Yes,' she whispered. His voice was so cold. He made it filthy. She cringed inside, waiting for the whiplash of his contempt.

'We should be straight here. We're talking about sex.'

'Yes.'

'You're a virgin.'

She nodded, dumb.

'I'm forty-two. You're eighteen and a virgin. You have no parents. I take you out and get you drunk, then I bring you home and you offer sex to me. If I had taken advantage of your offer, Gossamer, what kind of a man would that make me?'

'I don't know,' she whimpered.

'I do.' His voice was brutal. 'It would make me a shit, that's what it would do. You're young. You're beautiful. You're absurdly trusting. You're the sweetest thing I've ever known. And you want me to take you drunk. Fuck you when you're drunk. It seems to me you and Trish have the same sort of ideas about sex. About men.'

She rolled onto her side, turning her back on him. Inside her head was filled with screaming. Perhaps it was better not to care. Then people couldn't do this to you.

'Don't think I don't know what Andy Wollstein was up to last night, telling you what a big bad wolf I was and how I eat little girls like you. What did you think, Gossamer?' His voice jeered. 'I have a trail of virgins in my past. Is that the sort of man you think I am?'

She turned back to him and sat up, her eyes blazing in the white exhaustion of her face. 'I know what you are,' she said, struggling to keep the tears at bay. 'You're the best thing that's ever happened to me. You've brought the sun into my life. You've shown me things. You've made me happy. You helped me and saved me when I was in danger and you've been strong and . . .' She broke off, willing him to understand.

'And?'

'Loving.' Her voice broke in a sob. 'You've been loving with me. No one's ever been like you in my life. Aren't I allowed to fall in love with you? Why do I have to care what people think? I know you aren't like that. Doesn't how I feel count for anything?' Tears trickled unheeded down her cheeks.

'You're a child.' It was a murmur. 'How can I take advantage of you?'

She wore a jacket over her shirt. They must have undone it when she was unconscious. Now she came up on her knees on the bed facing him.

'I'm not a child,' she said intensely. 'I want you. I don't know if you want me. If you'll have me, I'm yours. Do you understand? I'm yours. Whether you'll have me or not.'

Time was suspended. She stared at him, fierce in her grief, knowing she was about to lose him.

The dark face had never told her less. She had never understood him so little. She saw his mouth begin to move. Her own lips hurt because he didn't kiss her. The emptiness in her heart was bursting with pain. When he spoke, it was queer and strained. 'I'll have you.' His voice shook. 'Jesus, I'll have you. You don't know what it's all about.'

'Teach me.'

He took a handful of her hair and pulled her head back. He brought up his other hand and held her face for a long moment. 'You fool,' he said.

His harsh face was like a hawk's stooping for the kill. She felt his mouth close on hers.

It was brutal. The strong body that had shielded her offered no protection now. It demanded. His mouth was hot and urgent. His lips bruised hers, she caught the slight roughness of his chin, and as he opened her mouth with his she felt the urgency in him, his strength, and she was afraid.

He released her suddenly and she fell back on the bed. His face was stone as he looked down at her. She brought up her hand and slapped him hard round the face.

He jerked slightly. 'What was that for?' His voice was as cold as his eyes.

She undid the buttons of her shirt. When she spoke her voice was trembling. 'You insult me, trying to scare me off. You think I don't mean this thing. You want me to draw back. I won't do it, Carey. I love you and I want you to make love to me. Now I think I ought to shower and brush my hair. I want you to find me beautiful if you can. I want it to be good for you.'

She saw the tension leave his face and the dark, bitter look go with it. He bent over her and kissed her naked breast where she had exposed it. His lips were so tender on her skin that she wanted to die.

He stood up and removed his jacket. She came off the bed and undressed completely in front of him. She blushed as she shed her panties but she didn't let it stop her. She walked past him and through to the bathroom. She showered carefully and then she brushed her hair and applied a very faint make-up. She cleaned her teeth. She was trembling so hard she found it difficult to control her movements now.

She let the towel drop. She looked at herself in the long bathroom mirror. Her legs were long and shapely. Her belly was flat. Her breasts were taut and beautifully shaped, standing proudly forward from her body as it swooped inwards to her slender waist. Her black hair shone as it caressed her sloping shoulders. She could find no mark, no blemish on her skin.

She walked out of the bathroom, the blood throbbing in her veins.

The light in the sitting room was very low. He stood in his shirt sleeves over by the glass doors to the balcony. Beyond them the city sprawled, an immensity of straight and looping lights, high glittering buildings, dark parks. Through it all the river snaked.

She came over to him, her reflection faint in the black window glass.

He looked at her, head to toe, for a long moment. Then he looked over the city again. 'It's quite a view,' he said.

She controlled her voice. 'Nearly all my life has been in the north. I couldn't wait to get away from school. But I miss that border country, the huge skyscapes, the high blowing cold air, the great rolling grassy hills. This apartment has stopped me feeling claustrophobic in London. I'm glad I'm high up.'

He turned back to her. 'You are the loveliest thing I've ever seen,' he said without changing his tone of voice.

'I'm so glad you think that. I want there to be compensations for you.'

'Compensations?'

'For my youth. My ignorance.' Her voice broke. 'I won't be very good to begin with. You'll give me a chance, won't you?'

She was in his arms. She could feel the powerful throb of his heart against her naked breast. She put her arms up round his neck and looked into his face. 'I love you,' she said and pulled his head down to hers.

This time his lips were tender. As he kissed her, deeply, lingeringly, his hands slid down her body. His thumbs came over the swell of her breasts. Round her waist his fingers almost met, she was so slim. He went on down, over the swell of her hips. She trembled and pressed herself into him. She was almost fainting with the luxury of his kiss. She felt his hands over her buttocks, pulling her against him. She strained on tip toe, kissing him, rubbing herself into him, feeling his hair and his neck.

She could feel his sex.

He was kissing her neck, her shoulders. His lion-gold head bent lower and he kissed her breasts. Something exquisite was happening to her, something that reminded her of those dreams. His lips were at her nipples. He was kissing them, sucking them, and she stood there in her flaunting nakedness with her head thrown back, offering her body to him to do with as he pleased. He kissed the underside of her breasts, the nipples again, and then he sank to his knees.

She saw them reflected in the window, the kneeling man at her naked body. He kissed the silky tangle at her sex. He kissed her thighs. Pride filled her. She blazed with it, glorying in him, in his surrender to her body. There would never be a moment like this in her life again. She was suspended between two states, in bliss.

He stood up.

'I'm glad I'm the first,' he said and swept her up. He carried her to her bed and laid her on the rumpled clothes, smoothing them back so he could see the naked length of her.

'Last night you lay in beauty,' he said. 'You said I could take you and, by Christ, I nearly did. That first sight of you would have moved mountains, Gossamer, let alone a mortal man.'

The dark fire was in her. She had a power over him. He really wanted her, he really thought she was beautiful.

'You'll have to tell me what to do,' she said huskily. Being naked under his eyes was so erotic she felt stirred low inside.

His face twisted. 'Undo my shirt.'

She took her time. She slid his tie from him in one long sensuous movement. She undid one button, then the next, one at a time until all were undone. She opened the fine white material, letting her hands caress his chest as she did so. She saw his throat. She saw his bright eyes blazing. His hair caught a thread of light and shone red-gold. Her hands were palm-flat to his chest, feeling him, the light dusting of hair, the flat hard nipples, his ribs, the muscles in his shoulders. Her hands were greedy to learn. *Licence my roving hands* . . .

He kissed her. She felt his bare chest against her sensitive breast. Again she had that ripple of feeling deep inside her, as though something stirred.

Something else struggled. A memory. Something important.

Her teeth began to chatter with nerves. Would she hurt him? Would she be clumsy? She wanted to be so good for him.

She cried out. He had slid his hand between her thighs and he was touching her sex.

'Open your legs.'

She had to force them apart. He began to caress her vulva. She felt his fingers in at her. She shut her eyes, aware that she was blushing scarlet.

She was so sensitive and jumpy that the whole area was alive and writhing under his probing fingers. Her back arched helplessly and her breathing became short and jagged. She cried out suddenly. A thin sharp pain had pierced her.

'Did that hurt?'

His voice was a life-raft in her sea of emotion. 'Yes. No. It doesn't matter. Go on.'

She felt his hand caress her cheek. She opened her eyes and stared at him. His other hand was still between her thighs.

He was smiling. 'Try not to grit your teeth quite so obviously.'

'What? Oh. I see. I'm sorry.' She was rigid with tension.

He released her and stood up. He took off the rest of his clothes. Then he laid himself on the bed beside her.

She hadn't known it was so big. She was furious with her own ignorance. Peter had seemed big but Carey was a man in his maturity.

'Play with me,' he said.

'Aren't you, aren't you going to come into me?'

'Eventually. Anyone ever tell you it hurts to begin with?'

'Yes. No. Sort of.'

'Make me come, Gossamer. Then I'll be better able to loosen you up.'

'How?' She reached for him, up on one elbow, fascinated as she overcame her embarrassment. It was certainly a peculiar sight.

He put his hands behind his head and relaxed. 'Hold it,' he said.

She took a hold of him, firm and alive in her grasp. She felt it kick a little.

'Slide your hand down. That's it. Hold him. He likes a little firmness.'

Slowly she revealed what lay beneath the foreskin.

'That's enough. You can see where the skin's attached.'

'Yes.'

'It's very sensitive there. Kiss it.'

'What?' Momentarily she was appalled. But this was what she had asked for. She had said she would do anything. She had wanted her ignorance to come to an end.

Her hair fell in a heavy cascade over his groin. It flowered over his thighs and belly. She put her lips to the red bloated tip of his penis and kissed it.

'Again.' His voice was harsh.

She kissed it several times. Hesitantly she put out her tongue and touched it.

'Move your hand. Up and down. For Christ's sake.'

She began to masturbate him. She concentrated fearfully. She felt him begin to move.

He rolled sharply onto his side, pushing her back off him. He came on top of her and put his urgent sex between her thighs. 'Open them,' he said hoarsely.

She felt the blunt throbbing thing against her vulva. He

was making queer little jerks. She began to cry out, sobbing, calling his name, moaning at the half-pleasurable pain.

Like a knife bright and double-edged her memory came back. 'Oh God,' she cried in agony. 'You aren't my father?'

'No,' he grunted and came.

He didn't leave her for long. His own semen smeared her thighs, her vulva. He began to rub it gently into her, using it as a lubricant.

'That was a hell of a thing to say,' he observed presently.

She lay with her legs open, her eyes shut. 'I didn't know,' she said. 'I loved you so much. I just didn't know.'

'Do you like what I'm doing?'

'I want you in me,' she said faintly.

He slid fingers into her. Again that thin pain pierced her. He stirred round inside her, loosening her, easing her, lubricating her.

He began to kiss her breasts. All the time he invaded her with his fingers, waking her up inside, bringing her long sleep to a close. The only difference was that in this version she endured the piercing thorn, not him.

He kissed her belly. He slid an arm under the arch of her back and lifted her, speared on his fingers, and kissed her. She stuffed her fist into her mouth as he let her back onto the bed, holding her thighs apart, looking into her sex. He bent low over her and kissed her there, where he had felt her. She felt ripples of tension inside her. She thought she would burst. His mouth, his fingers were everywhere.

Then he was round at her again, over her and his face was above hers. She felt him probing. He pushed her legs impatiently. He was driving into her, firm again and ready for sex. She lifted as he came into her, her mouth open in a soundless scream.

He pushed hard. Her mind tore in two, coruscating with pain. Her body jerked sharply up into his, beyond her control. He was fighting to stay in her. Her body bucked under him, she felt herself rift. Fire flamed inside her.

His own hips pushed into hers. He had penetrated her

fully. Her shuddering flesh clenched his tightly. He came awkwardly, she was painfully tight on him, but the second he began to ejaculate he felt his own softening flesh ease in her damp clasping heat. He drove into her again. She was tight and wet and hot. On his elbows, he drove again, ignoring the noises she was making, caught up in his own dark pleasure.

Afterwards he lay relaxed against her pillows, smoking. She lay beside him, gazing up at him with eyes drowning in adoration.

'Does it hurt?' he asked presently.

She shook her head drowsily, smiling at him. 'Not worth a damn,' she said. 'I feel wonderful.'

'You'll bleed a little,' he said.

'Yes. It'll be good to get this over. I so want to do things for you. You must teach me.'

His eyes slid over her. 'I guess we'd better dress and go out and eat.'

'We could send out for something.'

'Could we hell.' He looked at his watch, suddenly restless. 'Look here,' he said. 'The truth is I never meant for this to happen. I'm flying to the States tomorrow and I have to check in at Heathrow at 4.30 in the morning. I've a drawerful of documents to read.'

'You need to go home and work. I understand,' she said immediately. 'It's all right. You won't find me demanding like that.' She would make it true, she thought.

He kissed her, rolling her over on the bed and ending on top of her, laughing. 'You beautiful witch, I want to stay all night and make endless love to you. But I'm too old and you're too new to the game. Look, I'll be gone several days, maybe a week. You'll have time to sort things out.'

'Sort things out?'

'Darling, what happens when a man and a woman make love?'

'Oh.' She blushed. 'Babies.'

'Right now you go and wash yourself out as thoroughly as possible. I mean thoroughly. I've taken a chance tonight but if we're unlucky you'll have to take that pill the French have been using for ages. But anyway you go to the doctor or the clinic while I'm away and get some permanent protection. When I come back . . .' he stopped.

'What when you come back?'

'I'll make you enjoy it too. I'll teach you the arts of love so you'll enjoy it all your life. Whoever you are with.'

She put her arms round his neck. 'I only want it with you.'

'For now. Till someone younger comes along. Someone who'll give you half his life, like you deserve.'

'What do you mean?' She was puzzled and looked into his face trying to see his meaning.

'That's the problem with the older man, Gossamer. Didn't you realise? I have a life and it's full. I want you in it. But I don't want to lose anything else. I'm too used to independence.'

She stroked his cheek and reached up to kiss his mouth. The taste of him made her feel drunk. 'I don't want to own you,' she said. 'I can't stop you owning me and that's all I ask. To belong to you. I don't ask you to belong to me. I know that won't happen.'

He kissed her and reached for his shirt. 'Order some food,' he said roughly. 'And remember I'll be back.'

Darling Goss,

Mummy came out for Easter. I met her at Lausanne and she looked frightful. Have you any idea what's been going on over there? Is it Peter? Is it daddy? She won't admit to anything and now I'm frightened she's got cancer and won't tell me. She says she hasn't and will be fine shortly, she's just tired, but I feel isolated over here and I think I might come home early.

It's got boring here since the skiing ended. Sadie has gone off to the Canaries to get some sun and it feels like a nunnery all of a sudden. My French has got better at last but I don't see the point. I don't feel very European and frankly I suppose I'm missing England. It would be

*good to see some friends again, including you even if
you don't bother to write much.*

*How's the school? Do you dance like an angel now?
Pete phoned for your address and I gave it to him.
You're a big girl and no doubt you can shoo him off
if you aren't interested. I think he's a total waste of
space of course and he doesn't have anything between
the ears, but he is my brother and if you did like him,
you'd be a bonus in the family. And mummy likes you
so much.*

*How is the boyfriend scene? You never say anything,
you slyboots. Are there too many to list or are you
playing Liz I, virgin queen? Incidentally, you say you
can't track poor Canfield down. Thanks for trying,
petal. It's more than some others have done, naming
no brother's name.*

*I'm kind of tired so I'll stop this here. I guess I'll
be home in a month or so. I don't see me staying on
any longer.*

Best love, Jenny

She was going to be ready for his return. She bought a piece
of soft white plastic. She sewed it tight and filled it with
cotton wool. Lying on her back she penetrated herself after
greasing it with vaseline. She penetrated herself again and
again, finding that she had muscles she could use.

She would use them for Carey. He was her heart's
delight.

She spoke to Trish at the School. She caught her in the
canteen when she was eating, so she couldn't escape.

'I'm sorry about the other night,' she said. 'I was stupid.'

She sat down opposite and began to eat in silence.
After a while Trish said: 'What was wrong? Why were
you so upset?'

'I've met someone. I thought he didn't want me.'

'What do you think now?'

Gossamer's face broke into a radiant smile. 'He does,' she said. 'It's all OK. It's perfect.'

Trish grinned reluctantly. 'I don't believe you,' she said. 'I don't believe anything about you. You have this fairy-tale existence. So who's Prince Charming?'

'Old enough to be my father. I adore him.'

The monkey face opposite narrowed. 'You've slept with this bozo?'

'Yes.'

'It's not so good at your age if they're much older.'

'It's good, Trish. Honest. He was very worried about my age too. I hope I've convinced him it doesn't matter.'

'If you have, he's a fool. Of course it matters. It just depends how much.'

Marie sent her an invitation to a party. The address was in York Mansions, the Horden-Smith London home. When she phoned, Marie was insistent she come.

'Do you go around with Carey Lambert much?' she asked curiously.

'A bit.'

'How did you meet him? Who introduced you?'

'No one. We met by accident and liked each other.'

Marie laughed. 'You don't meet men like him by accident.'

'I don't understand. What do you mean, men like him?'

'Important men. Don't play this naïve game with me, Goss. I mean, are you lovers?'

'Does it matter?' Gossamer was struggling.

'Darling, he's the original big bad wolf and he likes all his little piggies slick and rich. His ladies are the sort who file their teeth, and that's the acceptable side of his sex-life. They only whisper about what else he gets up to. He's unattainable as far as good little girls are concerned. I'd adore to be added to his stable but they say he likes it cruel. The velvet claw and then crunch, gobble.' Marie gave a shivery laugh. 'I mean, he sounds fantastic. I always thought you were so pure. Do you really go to bed with him? What's he like?'

'He's a friend,' said Gossamer stiffly.

'You prude.' Marie was delighted. 'Bring him if you can. Mummy will be furious, he's such a bad man. He's the sort Barmy and Collywobbles protect me from.'

'Look, I can't make it,' said Gossamer.

'I'm sorry. I'm only teasing you. I mean, he is exciting. I expect it's all rot what they say, and he looks absolutely de-luscious. Loaded with boodle, too, though they say he came from nothing.'

She couldn't control the question. 'What does he do?'

'What does he do? Are you serious?'

'Stop it, Marie. I said I met him by accident. I don't know anything about him.'

'Oh I see. You really don't know him well. Come to the party. I'll tell you what I know. There's bound to be a lot of rubbish in it, though. You know, gossip, slander, malice. He's too successful for his own good.'

So she went to the party. She wore tight black trousers and a sequinned strappy top that left her shoulders bare. She hated going alone but when she went in through the discreet entrance she saw it didn't matter.

Marie's parents must be away. The party goers were young, beautiful and very loud. Music roared from the drawing room. It was the Stones, *I – can't get – no – sa – tis fa – ction*. A drink was thrust into her hands and it took her ten minutes to find Marie.

She was introduced to several people. Barny took her through to dance and for a while she forgot her worries as she gave herself to the sexual thunder of the music. The room was dark with lights swirling on the walls. She danced with someone else but when he closed with her, to hold her and press himself against her, she sheared off.

Food was laid out in the dining room. It must have been beautiful. Lobster shells were ripped apart. Dips were smeared across the cloth. Crab claws looked like broken weapons. A whole salmon was reduced to a pink crumble where people had torn into its flesh. Stubs of cigarettes protruded obscenely from oyster patties.

She went to find a bathroom. A girl was in it, tall and elegantly blonde wearing a backless dress. She half turned as Gossamer entered. Her hair was a sheet of swinging silk. 'Fuck off,' she said, and turned back to her silver box, her silver straw.

Gossamer went down the stairs. Someone grabbed her, pulled her down with him and began kissing her, feeling her breasts. 'I love you,' he mumbled. 'I love you. I love you all.'

She broke free. The music was harshly up-to-date now. It roared and swept around her. A girl had stripped and was dancing naked on the dining-room table among broken plates and glasses. The lights drifted over her, bubbles of pink and green and purple.

She began to search for Marie. There were figures everywhere, drinking, kissing, winding together. She ignored the offered ecstasy. She opened a door and saw it was a bedroom. Marie was in bed, propped up on her pillows.

'Marie.'

'Gossamer. Climb aboard, darling.'

'Thank you for inviting me. I have to leave now.' She had been stupid to think she would learn anything here.

She had approached the bed. She suddenly saw Marie's breasts were naked, huge and flubbery. The bed heaved. Marie flung back the covers.

She had two men with her, the three of them naked in the bed. One man had his face buried between her legs. Marie grabbed her, pulling her down onto her naked flesh. 'Join in,' she said thickly. 'There's room for another. Barny fancies you like anything. I fancy you. Can I tickle you there, Goss? I like playing with women.'

Gossamer pulled free. White hairy buttocks wobbled in front of her. She could see his hard sex swinging between his legs. She turned for the door. She heard Marie laughing from the bed. 'This is nothing,' she called. 'Nothing. If you go with Lambert, he'll want more than this. He likes it hot.'

'Who is he?' she said desperately.

'OffWorld. Satellite TV. He runs it, sweetie, it's his bag.

You're playing with the bigtime. The thing is, can you afford it? Can you go the distance? It's an apple in the mouth and an onion up the bum with him.' Marie spluttered with laughter.

Somehow she got herself out onto the street. She began to run. She'd left her bag behind but she couldn't go back.

It was late. The streets were rowdy as she worked her way north. She hurried through the crowd unseeingly. She was blinded by the images from Marie's party.

Suddenly she stopped. OffWorld TV. Satellite. She scanned her mind.

There were two competing companies. The giant Dayfield Corporation owned one. That was called DayStar. The other was run by a consortium. That must be what Carey did. Marie said he ran OffWorld. It was Luxembourg-based, unregulated because it was telecommunications rather than British TV and it was made up from Eurocrap and US offal. DayStar and OffWorld were both cabled into her flat from rooftop dishes. OffWorld didn't make programmes itself. It was buy 'em and beam it, Italian housewives stripping on camera, old American game shows, dubbed Spanish soaps.

Shaws taught its girls basic business studies. Most of them were the daughters of businessmen and would marry into the business world. Some of them might even run parts of it themselves. If Carey ran OffWorld he was mega. He was one of the star players.

Was anything Marie said true? Did it matter? All that mattered was what Carey was with her. Loving. Gentle. Beautiful. If he was a man of passion, maybe he had lived wildly. She knew he was passionate, it was that he hadn't loved before. Not like he was going to love her.

She went on. Her feet hurt. She was going north up the Finchley Road. If she took her time, she'd make it home.

The streets were quieter again. She heard noises. She came up, keeping in the shadows.

Two youths were beating up a third. He was down on the pavement, being kicked. He had bent into a foetal ball but the heavy boots were remorseless. He did nothing to defend himself.

It was the noise. The soft thumps. The wet grunts. The snickers of laughter as flesh split.

Anger soared insanely in her. She slipped off her shoes and ran forward. 'Stop that,' she screamed at the top of her voice. 'Stop it. Police! Police!'

They stopped and turned to her. She saw the feral faces caught in orange streetlight. Their bodies were hunched, ready to jump. She heard a dog-like low growling roar coming from human mouths. She opened her lungs and ran at them.

Screaming, she hit the first one with the spiked heel of her shoe. A window went up and somewhere a siren started. The two youths looked at each other, falling back. They weren't used to being attacked. They took to their heels.

Sobbing, Gossamer bent over the youth on the ground. She forced his hands off his face. She saw the bruises, the split cheek, the blood. 'They've gone,' she sobbed. 'It's all right.'

He was terrified. His face was so thin it hurt her. 'Shall I get an ambulance?' she said. 'Can you stand up?'

She helped him to his feet. He stood half-bent, wheezing air. 'I think I'm OK,' he said. His voice was high-pitched. 'No ribs gone.' He looked at her. 'That was very brave.'

She wiped her nose. 'There's blood on your face. Your shirt's all torn. Why were they doing it?'

'Don't you know? They just like it. Oh, my knee hurts.'

'Let me get an ambulance.'

'No. Look, where do you live? Can you get a taxi home? They might be waiting round the corner. Don't let them get you.'

'I'm nearly home. I lost my bag earlier at this awful party I was at. I've been walking home.'

'Let me come with you as far as the door.' He grinned painfully. 'Not that I'll be able to help you much.'

They walked together. He limped, so she got him to put his arm round her shoulders and lean on her. Two waifs, she thought. They were in the avenue, each tall tree standing sentinel over its patch of blackness. It was illogical but she found his presence reassuring.

'What's your name?' he said presently.

'Gossamer.'

'That's lovely. I'm Anthony.'

They stopped. 'I live here,' she said. 'I'll get a taxi to take you home. Really you ought to come in and get cleaned up, but I shouldn't, I mean, I oughtn't . . .'

'No one else is in?' His comprehension was swift. He laughed bitterly. 'You don't understand, do you?'

'Understand what?'

'Why I was being beaten up. I'm no danger to you, darling. Don't you see? I'm gay. I'm out. They don't like it, the macho types. It threatens them, I don't know why.'

'Come in,' said Gossamer. 'I'll make you some coffee, Anthony.'

Silvio was asleep at the desk. They went up in the lift and for the first time Gossamer got a sight of her waif.

He was distressingly thin. His hair flopped dismally except for a gay and pathetic plait on one side. His lipstick was smeared and his jeans had holes in them. She hid him at the fire escape and went back down and woke Silvio so he could let her into her flat. Her key was at Marie's.

After Silvio was gone she collected Anthony who was shivering nervously despite the warmth of the building. She took him into her bathroom and made him remove his tattered shirt. Gently she bathed his wounds. She cleaned his ugly, damaged face. Tenderly she washed his hair for him under the shower, getting the grit and the broken glass out of it. Every gesture, every action, calmed the turmoil inflicted on her by Marie.

He took off his shoes and sat in his jeans. His narrow bruised chest was bare. She knelt by him and dabbed witch-hazel on his cuts and bruises. He sat passively all the while, terrifying in his gentleness. She had never met anyone so childlike and weak.

She made coffee and put a couple of pizzas in the

microwave. When she came back he had found some Dave Brubeck in her music and put it on.

They sat companionably. After a while Gossamer fetched a couple of thick fluffy blankets. She left him snuggled down on the sofa and took herself round the corner to bed.

Someone was at her flat door. She hadn't been buzzed from the foyer, or else she hadn't heard. Gossamer stirred sleepily and pulled herself reluctantly from her sheets. She put on a wrapper, remembering Anthony. She came round the corner and saw he was sitting up, rubbing his head and smiling at her, a bit bewildered. Sunlight streamed in. She rarely pulled the curtains, no one could see in, and she hadn't thought to the previous night.

She went out through her tiny lobby and opened the front door.

He was there. Her heart lifted and she gasped, falling forward into his arms.

'Hey,' he protested, laughing. 'What's this? Not dressed yet, you lazy creature?'

'I was late last night.' She looked at him, her happiness a great flood in her. 'Oh, Carey.'

They went into her living room. Carey saw Anthony and stopped.

Anthony was in his underpants, pulling on his jeans. His thin ugly face flushed. The bruises stood out stark. His cheeks were grazed and one eye was swollen. He looked appalling. His skinny hairless chest was covered with purple and yellow bruising.

'Who's this?' Carey's voice was tight.

'Anthony. Anthony, this is Carey Lambert.' She turned to Carey. Warm indignation grew in her as she remembered. 'I met him last night. He was being beaten up. I brought him here to clean up and then it got too late so he bunked down on the sofa.' Gossamer's voice tailed off. Carey was staring at Anthony, his face harsh. Anthony looked frightened.

'Look, I'll go, Gossamer,' he said nervously. 'Your friend doesn't want to meet me.'

'No. You haven't had breakfast. I'll send out for something.'

'Get out,' said Carey.

'What?' Gossamer was startled. 'No. You don't understand.'

'I do. Get out. Don't ever come back.'

'No. I'm sorry.' Anthony was scuttling round looking for his shirt in terror. Carey's anger blazed so that the room was suddenly stiflingly small.

'Carey! He's my guest. He's hurt. He hasn't harmed me.'

'Yet. Go.'

She couldn't stop him. The youth was cringing with fear. He got past Carey and was out through the door before Gossamer could do anything to prevent it.

They turned to each other, both pale with anger.

'Don't ever do that again,' said Carey. 'Don't ever pick up street scum and bring it home. You stupid cow.'

'Don't ever do that again,' said Gossamer immediately. Her voice trembled. 'I invited him here. He was harmless.'

'And HIV positive, no doubt. You touched his blood. A fucking little queer boy. You stupid tart.'

'You bastard!' she said. Her voice rose dangerously.

'You do as I say.'

He advanced towards her. She saw his anger suddenly separate, from himself and from her. She saw the naked man, glittering, powerful, enraged. She gave a queer moan and fell on her knees. He stopped dead. She put her face against his groin. She smelt him, smelt his arousal, and rubbed her cheek on him. 'Carey,' she whispered drunkenly. Her body flamed.

He took her hair and hauled her to her feet. 'You obey me in this,' he said.

She laughed.

He shook her violently and threw her across the room. She landed on the sofa with its tumble of blankets. She came up in a superb flow of movement and standing on the couch she launched herself at him.

He went down under her weight. She felt him struggle to

free his arms and then he had hers bent back. His mouth was over hers. He was kissing her passionately. He rolled on top of her, pulling her robe off. 'I love you, I love you,' she cried ecstatically. She was naked, still warm from her sleep. He kissed her breasts, nuzzling into them. His hands pulled his clothes apart. He hooked one of her legs up so violently she was lifted off the floor. He was kneeling, about to enter her. She saw his face harsh and blazing. As he thrust into her body she cried out in pain and exultation.

The pleasure was gross. Everything inside her was molten. Her body had its own agenda, it was obeying rules she knew nothing about. Something huge was carrying her and every time Carey thrust into her she hit a mountain peak. Her body writhed. Her mind was spinning out of control. She was faintly aware of noise, her mouth was open and she was shouting. He was thrusting harder. The sensation was utterly novel and primaeval as life itself. She had known this without knowing it, known to hold back. Until now. Body and mind were fusing. She was this. This was her wholeness. The veil of the temple split and she saw the inner secret and took her place there, finally at one with herself and her true deep nature.

He was done. She lay slumped on the floor, her misted eyes glowing with a dark soft fire. He had come away from her and was adjusting the disorder of his clothes.

'You crazy bitch,' he said queerly. 'You've really got it.'

I've got you, she thought in silent ecstasy. Already she had the sexual wisdom not to say it.

A bubble of guilty laughter rose in her throat. 'I don't know what happened,' she said. She stretched herself luxuriously there on her white carpet and saw with pure joy the effect of her naked body on the man kneeling by her.

He put a hand on her flat belly sunk between the twin ridges of her hip bones. He bent and kissed her breast. His mouth was warm and gentle and she saw his brown-gold head through a mist of sudden tears. Her body jerked. She gasped. She felt split inside. She went warm and runny as though something had burst. A spasm took her body, an intense ripple of pleasure. There was a terrific heat. Her body burned, flushing a deep red. She stared into Carey's eyes, embarrassed and frightened. A lassitude flooded her and she whimpered.

'What was that? Oh, Carey.'

'You're something special,' he said. He muffled his face in her hair.

'I am?'

'Not many girls orgasm from the outset.'

'That was . . .' she hesitated. He was right. 'Oh,' she said.

He stood up and she pulled herself to a sitting position. She felt shaken and strange. She needed to absorb her new knowledge and become acquainted with this person that she now was. Carey was speaking to her.

'Now take a shower and I'll make some coffee,' he said. 'For future reference, I like Java best.'

'Yes.'

'You did as I said? You went to the doctor?'

'Yes.'

'What else did you do while I was away?'

'Nothing. Nothing unusual. I went to a party but it was horrible. That was last night.'

She was on her feet now. She remembered Anthony. Was Carey right about him? It seemed very wrong to her but she had no street wisdom, it was true. Perhaps she could ask Trish.

Her mind jumped away from that. Trish might be offended, with some justice.

Meanwhile Carey was here. In the flesh.

'Was America fine?'

'I made the deal.'

'Carey,' she said. 'Are you something in OffWorld?'

He came through from her kitchen and looked at her. 'Has someone been talking?' His voice was genial but Gossamer felt the temperature drop.

'Marie said so. She was at Frankie's, the fat girl. It was her party I went to.'

'The Horden-Smith girl.'

'Yes. Is it true?'

'Yes. That's my job. I'm chief executive.'

She looked at him helplessly. 'It's a big job.'

His mouth curved at the corners. 'It is. I was in the States signing films for first showing. Specifically for next Christmas. We've got the video release down to six months. That's very good. I spent maybe half a million bucks.'

'Carey, what do you see in me? You could have had anyone.'

'Maybe I already have. Anyone else been talking to you about me?'

'Anyone else? No.'

He smiled. 'Go shower, sweetheart. You look like a whore.'

Jenny came home from Switzerland. She came to see Gossamer at her flat. She was thin and restless, very tanned with her bright gold hair.

The two girls spoke awkwardly. It was as though they were both loaded with things unsaid. Gossamer found it hard to mention Carey. She didn't know how to introduce the subject. It wasn't as if the relationship was exactly easy to explain. She asked if Jenny had seen anything of Johnny Canfield.

'Come out with me.'

Gossamer was startled. 'Sure. Where to?'

'Just come, huh? Do you have a car?'

'I'm taking lessons but I haven't passed my test yet.'

'We can walk. There's time.'

They talked idly. Jenny knew something of Marie's carrying on. She mentioned having had a letter from her.

'She's really odd, Jen.'

'How d'you mean?'

'I went to her party. I mean, it was sick. Most of them were doping.' Gossamer choked slightly. 'Marie was in bed with two men.'

'Two men!' Jenny turned startled blue eyes on her friend. 'Really?'

'Mmm.' They eyed each other in horror. Suddenly they burst out laughing. 'I had to phone her the next day. I'd left my bag with her. I think she was a bit embarrassed. I mean, she's been to Shaws like us. The full vice thing seemed a bit strong in the circumstances. She said something about her father. I didn't understand it.'

'What was it?'

'Along the lines of doing to him what he'd done to her.'

Jenny thought about this. 'No,' she said, shaking her flying blonde hair. 'I don't get it. What a muddle people are. Don't you think?'

This was so loaded that Gossamer was forced to protest. 'Where are we going? Come on, Jen, spill the beans.'

And they arrived. It was a squalid block of tenement flats in Bianca Road, the Victorian building sagging and battered. Jenny picked her way through the rubbish at the entrance and they went into the hallway. It stank of urine and stale cooking oil. They went up smelly stairs getting narrower and meaner as they ascended. Jenny stopped in front of a door. She pushed it. It wasn't locked. The two girls went in.

He looked up and when he saw who it was, his face twisted with pain.

'Johnny,' said Gossamer.

Jenny started to cry. 'Tell him,' she cried. 'Tell him, Goss. He's not to stay here. I won't have it. Tell him.'

She was snivelling. She wiped her nose on her sleeve. Johnny had backed across the room. His thin face was dead white.

'This is cruel,' he said huskily.

Gossamer looked at Jenny helplessly. She was staring at Canfield. 'You can't stay here,' she cried. 'It's terrible.'

'Don't be silly. Lots of people live here. If they can, so can I.' He was thin and restless, his quick dark gaze anxious and strained.

'Make him take some money, Goss. He doesn't have to be here. I've got money. He has to take it.'

'No. Don't do this, Jen. And I don't like you bringing Gossamer here.'

Gossamer went over to him then. She put her hands on his shoulders. He was shaking slightly, his eyes sliding with shame at his predicament. 'Johnny,' she said. 'Don't be so damned proud.' She hugged him, hearing Jenny sniffle behind her. 'Let's go out and get some food.'

They went to a working men's caff near Euston Station and ate pie, beans and chips with mugs of hot tea. After that they walked to Trafalgar Square and sat together on the steps of the National Gallery. They didn't talk much but somehow things were decided. Jenny would move into a flat. Unknown to her mother, Canfield would move in with her. If Helen came to visit her daughter, Johnny's stuff would be temporarily lodged at Gossamer's.

They grinned uneasily. They were three conspirators, trying to outwit the sea of fate they drifted on.

After they had left Canfield, Jenny said: 'You've got someone, haven't you?'

'A man, you mean.'

'Yes. A man.'

'How do you know?'

'Canfield saw it. He says you're different. More grown up.' Jenny blushed. 'Sexually aware.'

'It didn't take us long to stop being virgins, did it?'

'No. I guess even Shaws isn't proof against what it's really like.'

'Did you know you loved Johnny before?'

'Oh yes. I thought Switzerland might cure me. I wanted to play around. I wanted to have fun. Suddenly it's all deadly serious. I don't feel ready for it, Goss. It isn't fair.'

'You could move in with me. You don't have to live with Johnny. It's a terrific commitment.'

'The commitment's made. Don't you see that? I needn't honour it if I don't mind being miserable, but he's the man for me whether I like it or not. Poor Canfield. Isn't life a bitch, Goss? Isn't it?' She started to cry again.

But Gossamer was so happy.

He came at intervals to her flat as the weather moved into

full summer. Term would end soon and she neither knew
nor cared what her future might be. It was enough for now
that she had this precious thing.

Sometimes he was gentle. He would sit with his tie loosened, his shirt-sleeves turned up over his strong forearms,
watching her as she undressed. He liked this very much, her
being naked while he was still dressed. She would walk up
and down like a naughty kitten displaying herself to him.
She delighted in it. She had not been taught to think of
her own good looks and her all-female school had allowed
little opportunity for her to understand the effect she might
have on others. Discovering her own beauty even as she
discovered Carey meant only one thing to her. It was a gift
for him. So with delight but no vanity she showed her body
to him as he asked.

Their relationship was so unequal – she neither knew nor
asked where he lived – that it was delicious to exercise what
small power she had. Her power was sexual. She could not
make him love her but she could make him aroused. She
believed that if she was patient, love would come. Her
goodness would be enough for them both. His dark past
could be left behind him because she would be sufficient.

So she aroused him. He would sit while she played naughty
games to tease him, laughing at her parody of how she
thought a whore behaved. Having aroused him, she would
satisfy him. She would open his clothing and find his erect
sex. She made love to it. She made him make love to her.

His maleness was endlessly exciting. She adored each part
of him that was so different from herself. His muscled arms
and legs with their virile dusting of hair. His strong broad
chest and compact powerful hips. His hard tight buttocks.
He was a very clean man, immaculate in his clothing and
personal care. She loved this too because it added to his
masculinity for her. She found his strength thrilling. The
sense she had of latent power, even latent cruelty in him,
was an erotic force acting on her.

When his loving was gentle she nearly swooned with it.
She orgasmed readily now. Her whole nature responded

ecstatically to her active sex life. Her body was fluent and quick to learn. She adored love. She was consumed with lust.

At other times and increasingly he was hard with her. He would come tired and late and not stay long. He took her so violently she felt rattled and shaken afterwards. Then he would go.

She had trouble managing this aspect of him emotionally. She liked to lie dreamily in his arms after congress and his abrupt abandonment of her bed left her almost traumatised. She told herself to grow up, to act like an adult. He was a busy man. That he felt she could cope with such behaviour was an indication of his respect for her maturity.

They didn't go out together at all.

She did other things. Jenny told her mother she was enrolling at the East London University to study Post-Modern Culture and the New Gender. This subject caused much hilarity between the girls. It provided an excuse for Jenny to move into town and get Canfield out of his slum. The three of them went about a lot together, to concerts, to see a film, or just to walk together. Johnny was studying mediaeval history and he was taking it completely seriously. Jenny had long since stopped telling him off about it.

Gossamer took up ice-skating. There was a rink in north London near to her apartment and she went regularly. She enjoyed hard physical exercise. There was an added bonus. She met Anthony again.

She saw him one day. He wore a black turtle-neck sweater and tight black jeans. He skated well, his body less clumsy on the hissing ice than she would have expected. She herself was in a crimson suit. She ignored the stir she made when she skated. She was already more than competent at the sport and she looked beautiful flushed with exertion.

She came up to him and skated alongside. He wobbled alarmingly when he recognised her.

'Hello, partner,' she said gaily. She grinned as they powered side by side across the ice.

He spun. She took his hands and they began to ice

dance. He was good, he had natural flair and she was gifted herself.

Afterwards they drank coke together and talked in the café. She made it plain he was welcome in her flat. Neither of them said anything about Carey. She knew instinctively Anthony was a friend and would remain one. She had been too lonely all her life to cast such treasure away, even for her beautiful predatory lover.

⚹ Five ⚹

Her bust was deeper and richer. She had gone up a size at her hips though her belly stayed flat and her waist was as slim. She told Carey with indignation she was getting fat.

He stood in front of her, laughing. If he squeezed he could still span her waist with his hands. 'Darling,' he said. 'You've become a woman.'

It was true. Embarrassingly she glowed from the sex she enjoyed. Her body had a slow lush ripeness. Despite the fragility of her bones and the vulnerable hollows at her cheeks she was developing a sleek patina that told its own story. Her smoky eyes became smouldering as Carey banked fires of passion in her soul.

It was June and time to finish at Ryder-Vail. Gossamer was almost sorry. She had relaxed and become more easy with the other students. She enjoyed herself now and felt she belonged. Her awkward time was over though she was still quiet and hard-working.

It was the climax of the year. The students would exhibit their talents to those of the entertainment and media world as could be persuaded to come and watch. It was their chance for employment. Otherwise the dreary round of the agencies was all that lay in store.

Madame Emmeline Naveurs had been beautiful herself some fifty years ago. She had run away from her bourgeois upbringing in provincial France and joined the Bolshoi at a young age. Later she fled to England where Sadlers Wells embraced her. She had worked as a principal with Ballet Rambert. Now she ran Ryder-Vail with an iron hand, still managing to attract enough students of excellence to cause this little stir once a year. She had friends in astonishing places for such an elderly and autocratic woman. No one knew how she did it.

They all prepared nervously for the end-of-term concert therefore. It held their future in its hands.

Gossamer spent a weekend down at Sandings with Jenny and Canfield. They lay on the lawn while Helen fed them strawberries and cream. Gossamer was a bit shocked at the change in Helen Kepesake. She had aged, acquiring a papery transparent look. Her eyes had become pale and remote though her manner remained loving and gentle. Privately Gossamer decided she was ill. If she chose not to tell Jenny, it was her own affair. Jenny was so absorbed in Canfield that nothing short of a bomb under her nose would focus her attention elsewhere. Gossamer said nothing.

Carey invited her out. They hadn't been out together in a long time. Now he invited her to go with him to a musical evening at the French Embassy. His business connections made him an important man. Gossamer didn't understand it but she was deeply grateful.

She chose a pencil-slim dress in crushed velvet. It was a deep glowing royal blue that made her black hair glint blue and her eyes look like sapphires. The exposed flesh of her bosom and shoulders was covered with royal blue netting lace. She wore long gloves to match.

Carey came early, before she was ready. He was excited. His eyes glittered. She hadn't seen him in such a mood and she didn't know what it meant.

He looked marvellous in his evening clothes, a sleek panther of a man.

She was in her brief underwear when he arrived. She had slipped on a wrapper but he made her take it off.

'Put on your shoes,' he said.

She slipped her feet into her high heels. She wore brief blue lace panties and blue stockings. That was all.

'Come here,' he said throatily.

She came to him gladly.

He held her lightly by her waist and kissed along her shoulder until he reached her throat. Her eyelids drooped and she hung her head back. Who else had a man like hers? Triumph glowed in her.

'I've bought you a present.'

'Have you?'

'Parisian perfume. The best. *Indécence*.'

She unstoppered the little cut glass flagon. She touched her skin with it. It was in truth indecent. Short of the act itself it was the sexiest thing she had ever smelt. 'Oh,' she said guiltily. 'It's gorgeous.'

'And another present.'

'Carey. I love you so much.'

'Here. You've outgrown pearls, my girl. I think you can carry diamonds.'

He fitted them to her ears. This time he kissed her skin as he did so. Her hand fluttered over the front of his trousers. She could be as greedy as he was for sex.

He caressed her naked breast. 'I like you like this,' he murmured in her hair.

'May I kiss you?'

He shook faintly with laughter. He knew what she meant. 'I want a favour first.'

She opened her eyes wide. She denied him nothing, he knew that.

'Let me take a picture of you. You're heartbreakingly lovely, my dear. I can't often be with you. Let me have a remembrance for when we are apart.'

As an idea and expressed in that particular way, it was lovely. The practice of it made her feel uncomfortable. Carey took out a camera and began to snap her as she walked up and down in her underwear. He began to make love to her, kissing her skin and touching her, but he kept breaking off to photograph her again.

She had no powers of resistance where he was concerned. He knew her sexual nature now and could easily arouse it. His fingers scratched lightly over the outside of her panties.

He bit gently at her buttocks. He sucked her nipples. Her flesh seemed to swim in a daze of sexual heat. He took her hand and slid it beneath her panties, then signed her to slip them down. He photographed all this.

She felt the warm caress of his tongue, the velvet muscle of it sliding into her.

Involuntarily she began to move on it. He withdrew his tongue, then forced it against another place. Gasping, she pitched forward and wheeled round, wet and splayed.

He was facing her, photographing her again. She became very red-faced. She felt dirty. His eyes were brilliant and hard. He brought his face close to hers as he crouched by her. His fingers explored between her thighs, and she impaled herself on them. He felt with his fingers as they slid within her body.

It wasn't unpleasant. It was sexy. But she felt bad about it. They didn't need soft-porn sex games. She didn't feel such things had a place in their relationship.

She didn't protest. She knew she couldn't withstand him in matters such as this and for all she knew this was absolutely normal behaviour among mature adults where sex was concerned. She wanted to belong to his world. If this was the price it was a small one to pay.

So she knelt and he took pictures while she blushed and tried to laugh. She had so looked forward to this evening.

Afterwards he stood up and opened his clothing. He held her upturned face in his hands, she smelt her musk on them. 'You can kiss me now, Gossamer Fane,' he said. She kissed him where he wanted, and he subsided with her to the floor. She knew he wanted to have her in this way and she was willing to let him. The camera clicked and whirred.

The diamonds sparkled at her ears. They were matched by the sparkle of tears on her cheeks.

She was nervous and slightly scared by the time they arrived. Carey had provided a chauffeur-driven car. He addressed the driver by name and so Gossamer concluded it was his personal car or part of the perks from his job.

She wasn't in the mood to support so outrageous a perfume. It proclaimed her *une femme scandaleuse*. On the contrary, she wanted to observe the proprieties and seem quiet and cultured.

The room where they gathered was vast and glittering. The women rustled in their silks and satins. The men were black and white brushstrokes. Waiters moved among them serving champagne and canapés. They were announced, formally greeted, and then Carey begged to be excused for a moment.

She stood alone, very beautiful and quite forlorn in her sensuous dress and sinful perfume.

Jean-Luc Frémont had been destined for the *diplomatique* by his patrician family. To this end he had studied history at the Sorbonne but he had then confounded his family by switching to law. Now, at a time when he should have been moving up through the lower ranks of embassy staff, he was instead a pupil lawyer at Chatteris Choate. International law was hardly the stuff of youthful rebellion and his family had long since come to terms with his choice of profession. Meanwhile he had an uncle who was an attaché at the French Embassy in London.

Marc Frémont found his nephew very presentable. Here was a young compatriot, single, exquisitely bred and clearly destined to have a place in the world. He was an asset to the subdued and formal festivities conducted within Embassy walls. He was therefore the frequent recipient of august invitations and it pleased his superiors at Chatteris Choate that he accepted.

He saw her, blue and alone. He recognised her with an effort. The beautiful young girl had changed in half a year to a beautiful young woman. A surpassingly beautiful young woman. She made his heart knock, she was so lovely. The vulnerable line of her cheek invited the caressing hand. Her slim loins had an opulence about them that spoke volumes for her experience. Jean-Luc found himself almost trembling and with an effort he pulled himself together.

What had happened to her? Who had brought her here? She looked like a very high-class tart.

He watched with narrowed eyes as she walked across to a picture hanging on the wall and began to stare at it. Several men turned their heads as she went by. Jean-Luc continued his effortless flow of conversation with the dowager he attended while he cast his mind back.

Carey Lambert. She had come with Carey Lambert. A bubble of laughter rose in his throat. The man had a magnificent nerve to bring such a girl here. He was truly outrageous. By abandoning her he had subtly underlined his offence. She stood alone. He had brought her not as his companion but as a small poke in the eye to the oh-so-formal French. It was like referring to one's private parts in the middle of an elegant conversation.

Why had she been at Chatteris Choate that day? Presumably she was a client. In that case he had a duty to explore this strange situation. Jean-Luc extricated himself with grace and went to join Gossamer.

He came up softly behind her. He had rarely seen a back he so longed to stroke. She was a dangerous piece.

If she was nothing to Chatteris Choate and was in fact the whore she appeared to be, it would delight him to take her from Carey Lambert. The man was known to be vicious. He had his own tastes that way but he could be kind when he chose. He would take a wife soon and it was beneath his dignity not to be kind and civil to the woman he married. There were standards to observe, always. The likes of Carey Lambert did not appreciate that of course, with his dreadful television company and publicly licentious behaviour. Yes. He thought he could take a woman off Carey Lambert, especially one as young as this.

'You admire Renoir?' he asked silkily over Gossamer's shoulder.

Her head went on one side as if she seriously considered the matter. 'He's a bit soft and sweet,' she said. 'He makes a very superior Christmas card.'

Jean-Luc gave a gasp of laughter. At the same time he found her husky voice quite thrilling. His ear was acute. She was educated.

He was pleased. The mystery deepened. It was always hard to keep an interest in the world. Its ways were boringly simple. This was better.

'Let us move on,' he said. 'Tell me your opinion of this work.'

'I've often wondered what he would have done if there had been no waterlilies at Giverny.'

She was showing off. How delicious.

'You've seen one, you've seen them all?' he enquired gravely.

'Something like that.' She looked over her shoulder, her eyes dancing.

His heart lurched painfully. He knew a sudden surge of real anger. *Cet homme vil.* This was no whore. She was a young girl corrupted and she didn't know it yet.

'And this one.' They stopped before a tiny dark canvas.

'Ah,' she said softly. 'It's a La Tour.'

He was astonished. She must have read the little brass plate.

'I love them,' she continued. 'The candles. The hands. The light and shadow. They're so tender they make you hurt. And tranquil. If I had my choice on that desert island, I'd want one of them with me.'

'Your favourite?'

She turned to him. Her eyes were extraordinary, a very dark soft blue. 'It's obscene to talk about favourites with a master,' she said. 'But I suppose I love *The New-Born* best. One day I'll go to Rennes. It's in the Musée des Beaux-Arts there.'

'I know. Rennes is my home town. Permit me. I am Jean-Luc Frémont. We met once but I think you will not remember.'

She crinkled her brow adorably. Very faintly he caught her perfume.

He recognised it. It was a man's gift explicitly for favours received. *Vraiment, un homme sale.*

Nonetheless she was of a beauty quite extraordinary. Her youth, she must be barely of age, those eyes *comme pensées*, that grace of manner that was profound to her nature – it was sensually exciting. She was innocently sexual, prettily experienced in vice. She had seen and done things too young. Where had Lambert found her?

She shook her head ruefully as she failed to remember him.

'It was at Chatteris Choate,' he said gently. 'I am a lawyer.'

Her face closed. 'Oh,' she said flatly. 'My name is Gossamer Fane.'

'You saw Mr Germain, I think.'

'He administers my trust.'

He knew all he needed to know. He must speak to Germain immediately. The girl was in danger.

'Miss Fane, the music is about to begin. Will you do me the honour of allowing me to take you through?'

She smiled roguishly. 'I feel I should snap my fan open and peep over it at you,' she confided. 'Something vulgar with black feathers, *comme une coquette*.'

'And blush and giggle?'

'*Naturellement*.'

'Gossamer.'

The tone was lazy. All colour fled from her face and her eyes came up, frightened and pleading. 'Carey.'

'Are you going to introduce us?' He was very much at his ease. Even Jean-Luc who prided himself on being imperturbable felt a shiver go up his spine.

'Jean-Luc Frémont. He's a lawyer with Chatteris Choate. He met me there once.' She smiled suddenly at Jean-Luc and he saw she was relaxing. She put one lace-gloved hand on Carey's arm and looked up at him with such love that she shone. 'Carey Lambert,' she said. She stood smiling, looking up at her lover, at peace.

Carey met Jean-Luc's eyes. The Frenchman was smaller than himself. 'It was so kind of you to look after her,' he murmured.

'It was all pleasure, I assure you. Her taste in art is excellent.'

'As it is in everything.' Carey looked steadily at the Frenchman. Gossamer appeared to be in a happy world of her own. 'Chatteris Choate?'

'That is correct.'

'Give my regards to Kevin Germain.'

'You may be quite sure that I will.'

They went through to the music.

In rapid succession Carey took her to Frankie's, Ma Belle and the ZigZag Club. They dined at Casolini's, La Guerre Humaine and Dorlaine's. It seemed to Gossamer that she drank and danced and ate and danced all her days and nights in his arms. He made love with surpassing sweetness, employing none of the little tricks and novelties that she had come to dislike so much. She felt winged by her happiness, soaring through the air.

They made the gossip columns. Pope Benedict still didn't know who she was. He pondered the matter in print.

Kevin Germain asked to see her in the office.

Gossamer assumed she had overspent. She had money in her account but it had to last the quarter. No doubt Mr Germain would wag a fatherly finger at her.

She didn't care. She had needed clothes for her whirlwind of social activity with Carey and that was more important than anything.

She chose a fawn silk suit and arrogantly high heels to wear to Chatteris Choate. Let him see she had grown up. Let him feel her independence.

Alison Sanderson showed her through. It was high summer and the air conditioning gently susurrated. The office was full of cream and yellow roses.

Kevin shook her hand and offered her pale dry sherry which she accepted. They sat as before though now no fire burned in the hearth.

He had been prepared but his heart sank. The girl was beyond his grasp. He could see it at once. Jean-Luc had done his best but it was too late.

She was deeply, shiningly lovely. It was as though the

summer day caught and cupped itself within her glowing skin. Added to this was the sense of promise, of experience. Those eyes knew things now. He felt himself weighed as a man, as a male. She had crossed the Rubicon and it suited her.

Damn it for being Carey Lambert. He could hardly believe it was coincidence. The vicious bastard knew, he always knew what he was about.

For a moment even his atrophied lawyer's soul was touched. That such a child should be brought to this. She should have been woken slowly, with care, with tenderness. He would have done it that way though he was himself, he acknowledged it, a depraved man. It was as Jean-Luc had said. There were limits.

They talked about her college, what she might do afterwards. He could not baulk forever. He mentioned her appearance in the papers.

She shrugged. 'I met Malling Benedict in your company,' she said. 'He's a fly. He buzzes. It doesn't matter. When the royals start up again he'll ignore me.'

'He writes that you are in the company of Carey Lambert.'

She stiffened dangerously.

'Miss Fane, I'm going to make you very angry. I stand *in loco parentis*. Please forgive this intrusion into your private affairs.'

'You need make no intrusion. My private affairs are fine.'

Kevin looked down at his hands. They were beautifully manicured. He had had a teacher at school who had warts on his hands. Such a thing would make him physically sick now.

'You cannot understand what sort of man Carey Lambert is,' he said quietly.

'Perhaps,' she said icily, 'I understand him better than you do.'

'I understand that he can be most charming to women. Dangerously charming. Even his evil reputation is superficially attractive. Women think they can reform him. They can't.'

'You go too far.' She was hissing with rage.

He raised his eyes to her. His voice was low. 'He has caused at least one suicide,' he said steadily. 'He has destroyed several marriages and abandoned the women concerned. There is a story concerning a sixteen-year-old who had an abortion that went wrong. She is in an institution now. He is a man who delights in whores and . . .'

'Shut up. Stop it.' She was standing, her eyes bright with tears, hectic spots on her cheeks.

He looked down. 'It's true, Miss Fane. We are none of us saints but he, he is genuinely evil.'

'We're not talking about the same man.'

'Don't you see?' Now it was his turn to be hard. 'If he wasn't so charming it wouldn't be true. What you see in him is what they all see. Till he unmasks himself. Till he tires of you and throws you away. Or more likely, passes you on as a business favour. I can't have that.'

'You!' she spat. 'You filth. You oily filth protecting my father and denying me my right to know.'

He was on his feet pale with outrage. 'Your father . . .' he said.

'Don't talk to me about my father. He doesn't care enough to acknowledge me, the minimum right a child has.' Her voice shook dangerously. 'What do you think my childhood has been like? I'm a property. A property on the books to be sold on. First the orphanage. Then Shaws. Now you. Well, Mr Germain, I'll have you know I'm of age. I control my own affairs now. You administer my trust as per instructions and you keep the hell out of my private life. You aren't paid to involve yourself in it and I won't have it. I . . . I . . . I . . .'

She stopped, unable to go on. Her shoulders shook. She turned on her heel and made for the door. As she reached it Alison Sanderson came in, her face rigid with shock. Gossamer had been shouting. Now the girl blundered through, her eyes filled with tears. She ran unseeingly along the corridor, secretaries open-mouthed at her passing.

Alison Sanderson stared. That most urbane man, her boss,

looked shattered. He sat down shakily. 'Dear God, what have I done?' he said blankly. 'What have I done?'

She shut the whole business out of her mind. She had work to do. She was preparing her exhibition pieces for the Ryder-Vail display. No one would say she had thrown away her college experience. She might be in love but she was serious about her work.

Jenny and Canfield were coming to watch. The display was open to the public and Gossamer arranged tickets. Helen said she would come too. It was heart-warming to have friends, almost family, in the audience, like the other students.

Except Trish. No one was coming to watch Trish.

Marie said she would come and bring Barny and Colin. Gossamer refused to remember what she had said about their duties as minders, as protectors. It had been said in connection with Carey.

He was lazily kind. He watched her with amusement, waiting. She said nothing about that beastly interview. She would not go back to Chatteris Choate. It was an outrage.

Carey said: 'What do you want to do, darling?'

'Modelling or acting. Acting's so hard to get into, though.'

'Would you allow me to help?'

'Help?'

'You're very brave, Gossamer. I know that. You're a fighter, too. It's one of the things I love in you.'

Her heart turned over. It was a word he never used. The L word. She felt so dizzy she hardly heard what he said next.

'But the world is unfair. There are many good people who never achieve recognition while many very ordinary untalented people go to great heights.'

'Yes.' What was he talking about?

'I have many connections. I used to be in advertising. I was a media buyer after that. I know many programme-makers though now I'm in OffWorld I don't deal with them directly. You know we buy in, we don't make. But that makes it easier. If I help you, OffWorld can't benefit. So my advice is disinterested.'

'Your advice?' She wished she could follow his meaning. She seemed very stupid all of a sudden.

'I can introduce you to people. Recommend you.'

She stared. She swallowed suddenly. 'What if I'm no good?'

'Are you no good?'

'No. I don't think so.'

'Shall I come to this concert of yours and see?'

Her mouth fell inelegantly open. He had shown no desire for involvement in her life at all and she had humbly accepted this. His circles were so different. 'Oh Carey. Would you?'

'Don't look like that, child,' he said softly. 'Like I'd offered you Christmas.'

'But you have,' she said. 'You must know that. Carey, I love you so much. I don't care what anyone says.'

His eyes narrowed but he said nothing. She was transfigured with happiness.

On the morning of the display Gossamer lay late in bed reading the papers. She saw the news item low on page three. Lawyer in serious accident.

She read it. She read it again. A sickness invaded her. She lay against her pillows and trembled.

It was a judgment. He shouldn't have spoken to her the way he did. He was being punished.

The thoughts turned in her mind. She didn't like them. She reached shakily for the phone.

She was put through to Alison Sanderson. She could hear the woman was crying.

'It's Gossamer Fane,' she said unhappily. 'I've just seen about Mr Germain in the papers. Is it true?'

'Yes, it's true. Oh, Miss Fane, I can't believe it.'

'How bad is he?'

'Very bad. Very bad indeed. The vehicle struck his head. He may never recover. If he does he'll be paralysed. It broke his back, too. He's in a coma, Miss Fane. They think he'll die.'

She put the phone down. She felt freezing. She climbed

out of bed and went through to bath. After her bath she dressed in very sober clothes. She had Arthur call her a taxi. When she arrived at her destination she dismissed it and went in alone.

She sat for a long time allowing the scent of old wood and incense to permeate her soul. It was a big church and constantly filled with mild clerical comings and goings. The stained glass cast jewelled patterns on the stone flags of the aisle. The incised figures on the stones naming those long gone and at rest below made Death a tranquil friend, no enemy to be feared and resisted. Here in this cool company one could find peace.

After a while Gossamer returned to her flat to prepare.

Strangely she had forgotten by the afternoon. The day was too full of events and she couldn't comprehend the awfulness of the accident. She laid it to one side and concentrated on the here and now.

They were to rehearse in the afternoon. Then they would rest. The display began at eight. It would be a large audience, part friends and family, part general public and part professional talent seekers. For some of the students it would be the most vital night of their lives.

The dress rehearsal was terrible, sloppy, ragged and stumbling. Their timing went to pieces, several girls cried and the lighting was all wrong though they had had the technical rehearsal the day before.

Madame Naveurs was scathing. They were her worst students ever. She was ashamed of them. She would retire in disgrace. They had shown potential, it was true. She had had her hopes. At one time they were promising. Now it was all for nothing. *Pouffe*! She washed her hands of them. They had bloomed too soon. They were the ejaculation premature. Useless.

The startling vulgarity soothed their nerves. She was putting them on. They'd be fine.

Nick Woodley caught Gossamer in an empty classroom.

She was staring at the view, on her points, gently rotating one leg to warm the hip.

'Hi, Goss.'

'Hello, Nick. How're you feeling?'

'Like an unwanted dog-turd. Is it worth it for this?'

'Performance nerves are supposed to be good,' said Gossamer doubtfully. She swapped legs.

'Do you have any plans?'

'So so. I'd like to get into advertising. I mean modelling. On TV.'

'Wouldn't we all. You might make it though. You can really move and with those looks . . .'

She glanced at him. 'Thanks, Nick. But you're good, you know. The best man of our year.'

He moved over towards her. 'You've changed,' he murmured.

'I came here straight from boarding school. It's hardly surprising.'

'You mind if I ask you something?'

'What?'

'Why d'you hang round with Trish all the time? You're not a dyke.'

'I don't think she is.'

'She is, honey, believe me.'

Gossamer shrugged. 'I like her. Her sex life is her own affair.'

'Who's your man, Gossamer?'

She relaxed. Most people never looked at the gossip columns. They didn't matter.

'That's my affair and nothing to do with you, Nick Woodley.'

He came right up to her. 'You're sensational,' he said quietly. 'I know you're going to the top. Give me one, Goss. When I'm old I can say I made it once with the great Gossamer Fane.'

I could do without this, she thought wearily. 'No, Nick. Don't be stupid.'

'We'll both dance better tonight. No one will ever know,

just us two. Till I publish my memoirs. Come on, Goss. It'll be fun. I've wanted you for the whole year.'

'No. Stop it, Nick.'

'Oh, darling,' he said and kissed her hair. His hands were on her body.

She was disgusted. Her gorge rose. Kevin Germain had told her off and been awful but he was the nearest thing she had to a father. Now he was a vegetable in hospital, like to die. She wanted to vomit.

She hit Nick hard. He swore and jumped back. 'Stupid cow,' he said raggedly. 'There was no need for that. Christ, have you marked me?'

She started to laugh. 'Nick, you're terrible. I'm not giving you a quickie. I'm sorry I hit you. It's been a hell of day. Someone I know has been knocked down in a hit-and-run and he's probably going to die. I can't cope, see.' Her laughing was becoming hysterical. Nick backed off in alarm.

'I'm sorry,' he muttered. 'Oh Jesus. Will you be OK tonight?'

His single-track mind calmed her. He couldn't see what mattered most.

'I'll be all right,' she said, turning back to look out of the window again. Tears trickled down her cheeks. Nick left her alone.

By the time they gathered in the green room to change she was sick, really sick. She fled to the lavatories and emptied the lunch she had forced herself to eat. She came back white and trembling.

Trish looked at her steadily. 'You want help?' she asked.

'Help?'

'Mmm. Something illegal. To tide you over.'

'No thanks. I'll make it alone or not at all.'

'Thanks,' said Trish wryly.

'I won't let you down. I promise. I mean, I promise I'll try.'

Trish laughed good-naturedly. 'Stop it, petal. You'll wind me up as well as yourself and then where would we be?'

Madame Naveurs came through to see them, a caricature

in floor-length glittering black satin. She rapped on the floor with her ebony cane. Her legendary diamonds, supposedly the gift of a prince, flashed. It was almost time to begin.

'I wish you all achieve what you want to achieve from this night,' she said. 'You have been taught well. It would be nice if you could show it. I must tell you, *mes enfants*, we have an arts producer from Channel Four, some advertising executives, Marcelle Cateneau from the Royal Festival and Michelle Cordova from the London Contemporary Dance. And many more. I have done my best for you. Now you will do your best for me. Be *magnifique*, as I know you can.'

She swept out. The girls looked at each other and grinned uneasily through their make-up. The starters moved out to the wings where the men already waited. Madame made her presentation speech, the opening music rolled. They were on.

Gossamer had two pieces. One was a solo tap which she had choreographed herself. It told a quaint little story where she hung around bored with motionless vapid friends. She scraped her feet, slurring her steps and then mooched off alone. Gradually she began to dance, working herself up into a frenzy of happiness and exploding joy. Then she rejoined her friends, the other students slouching statue-still, smoking, loitering, hanging around. All the fire and passion went out of her. Once more, she was one of a crowd.

She danced this piece about a third of the way through the first half. Her nerves had become excruciating but as her scenery went into place and the students acting her friends stationed themselves, she felt a kind of uplift. This was what she was about. She had striven for this. Whatever happened, it was part of her, the desire to perform. She must accept the consequences of failure, of public humiliation.

She wanted to do it. She walked onto the stage and felt the miracle enfold her. She was not herself. The dazzling blackness that hid the hot rustling audience was necessary. She became the character she had created.

Afterwards she felt limp. She stood in the wings and

watched the next two pieces. Then she retired to the girls' green room. She began to change and make-up for her second piece.

The interval passed in a dream. Some of the students went to talk with people who had come to see them. Gossamer sat with Trish who had taken to smoking small cigarillos. They were to dance the finale together.

She wore a lavender blue dress tight round the bodice and exposing her shoulders. The skirt was frou-frou, a series of deep frills crisp and rustling. Carey's diamonds were at her ears. Her make-up was lavish, harsh red lips and brilliant blackened eyes.

She was to dance with Trish as her partner. Trish had recently shaved her head completely. The hard lines of her cheek bones were accentuated. She had made up her face almost white, her lips red and her eyes black but without the exaggeration Gossamer had used. She wore a man's perfect evening suit complete with tails, cut to emphasise her slim height. She had on a black fedora also. Her white shirt front was dazzling. The two of them sat silently until at last it was their turn. Gossamer was aware of every part of her body to its very extremities. Hands, wrists, fingertips – everything must be placed precisely. Piercingly, almost as a homesickness, she was also aware of the grubby green room, the dusty wings, the bare slightly splintery boards of the stage. All this was nearly over. The family she had lived in was about to eject her once more. Whatever her problems, she had settled here and become a part of the School. It had shaped her day, structured her life. She would be drifting soon.

A kind of panic had her. She didn't want to be alone again.

Her thoughts flew to Carey and she shivered. She was aware that if he was the sole anchor in her life, she was frightened.

She had never had such thoughts before. It wasn't life that was frightening her. It was Carey.

'Break a leg,' whispered Trish. They were on.

They had a *mélange* of dances prepared, the waltz, foxtrot, quickstep and so on. As the music changed so they flowed effortlessly from one step to the next. Their dancing was cold and technically perfect. Trish's visual oddity and sexual ambivalence seemed to grow as the dance developed. There was a harshness in the partnership. One could sense deviance, cruelty, corruption.

It was a long piece. It began so simply and became so extraordinary that gradually the audience began to shift on their seats with the sheer discomfort of the thing. Evil came from the dance. The two dancers were puppets. The dance was the thing, it had them in its grip and it controlled them. Snapping, sliding, twisting and turning; coming close breast to breast, moving apart, the two girls were living robots.

Gradually it came to a climax. The tension grew. Their postures became more extreme till their bodies must hurt, they contorted them so. At last the crescendo came. It was electrifying. The music thundered to its close, the girls leapt into the air and crashed simultaneously to the floor, both doing the splits.

They bowed over their extended leg. They stood up and held each other's hand high in the air.

Gossamer hadn't heard the applause after her tap piece. Now she felt the animal roar of the audience come at them as a great hot breath. She turned to look at Trish. It was as though the sea was about to crash over them.

Trish looked at her. Gossamer saw tears on her make-up. Trish swept off her hat. They bowed once more and ran off.

There was champagne in the dressing room. The doors were open and there were people everywhere. Mothers, aunts, embarrassed fathers and unknown men in suits to whom everyone was extremely deferential, all flowed round the students.

Jenny came in with Canfield and Helen behind her. She squealed and rushed over to Gossamer, kissing and hugging her. She wrinkled her nose and stood back.

'You stink, Goss. Yuck.'

'It makes me sweat. I haven't had time to change. There's a

room through there with a buffet supper. We're all supposed
to go there.'

'You were great, darling. Terrifying.'

Canfield was there, shaking her hand, congratulating her.
Her eyes went over his shoulder. She looked anxiously
towards the door.

Helen embraced her and congratulated her. Then Gossamer lit like a flame.

She did nothing. She stood there profoundly happy among
her friends. The noise buzzed excitedly around her. People
yelped and squealed. Some of the girls were trying to change.
Gossamer felt enormously peaceful. He had come.

Helen Kepesake turned and saw who was at the door.

Gossamer saw her face. She saw every drop of colour
vanish. Helen went almost green, she was so white. Her
lips turned blue even under their lipstick. She swayed and
put out a hand to steady herself. Her whole body had gone
lifelessly slack. You could see the skeleton supporting her
by its rigidity alone. The will was gone. The muscles were
slack. The flesh hung.

Carey moved towards them. He had two men with him.
Gossamer saw him see Helen. She saw his eyebrows elevate
themselves. His whole loved beautiful face was alive with
mocking amusement. The corners of his mouth curved. His
bright blue eyes pierced the core of the joke. He came right
up to Helen and stopped.

Gossamer saw his lips move. He had a hand held out.
Helen moved with a small lurch and managed to put her
hand in his.

Carey put his arm gently round her shoulders and turned
her to face Jenny and Gossamer and Canfield. Marie was
pushing over towards them.

She heard Carey's voice. 'Aren't you going to introduce
us, my dear?'

'You know Helen already?'

'Helen and I are old friends. Aren't we?' He looked warmly
down into Helen's face. It was a deathmask. Very lightly he
dropped a kiss on her cheek.

'Jenny. Jenny Kepesake. And Johnny Canfield. Carey Lambert.'

They shook hands. Jenny had noticed her mother and was looking at her worriedly. Marie came closer, pushing through the crowd.

'I'd like you to meet Gareth Hart-Mason and Jerry Laslo. Gossamer Fane.'

'That was most impressive tonight, Miss Fane.'

'Thank you. Thank you so much.'

'Goss!' Marie was shrieking at her. 'You were marvellous. Fantastic. So decadent, darling. I didn't know you had it in you.'

'Marie Horden-Smith,' said Gossamer quietly. She introduced Marie all round. She saw Marie's name register with the men. She wondered dully who they were.

Carey almost never made any public display of affection. Now he bent towards her, laying a possessive hand on her so that he touched her breast. He kissed her neck, a light lingering kiss. A lover's kiss. He stood back from her, smiling.

'I have to go, darling. You were wonderful.'

'Thank you.'

'I'll be in touch.'

'Yes.'

He went with his two friends. Marie was breathing in her ear. 'Yummy. He's so yummy. Gosh, I'd do anything for a man like that. Even go on a diet. Gossamer, you are lucky.'

Gossamer took a step towards Helen. She saw life come back into her face. For a moment Helen blazed with hate for her. Gossamer stood back, shocked. She sat down and began to remove her stage make-up.

'There's food through next door,' she said, busily applying cold cream. 'I'll just be with you. I must get out of this dress.'

Trish was offered a place with Danse Macabre, a small independent dance troupe based in Brighton. They made a speciality of modern pieces and were known for the erotic quality of their productions.

Gossamer did nothing. She met Anthony and went skating on Saturday. She attended a church service on Sunday and prayed for Kevin Germain. She walked in the park and on the Heath.

She phoned Jenny.

'I thought your mother didn't seem well,' she said carefully.

'No.' Jenny sounded puzzled. 'She seems better now. She's been to the doc, that I do know. I think she's been having trouble sleeping. We've done up our new flat, honeybun. As soon as Johnny's exams are over come to the official flat-warming.'

'How's Johnny?'

'Deep in his Part Ones. If it isn't in a book, he doesn't see it. Most chastening.'

Gossamer giggled. 'I trust you soothe his brow and don't make unreasonable demands on him?'

'As if I dared. I thought sin was supposed to be fun. It's remarkably like cleaning the lavatory at the moment, earnest and worthy.'

'Do you good,' said Gossamer rudely.

'Any word on the job front?'

'No.'

'Wait and see. That man of yours didn't look like one who forgot things.'

'I know you only met him for a moment . . .'

'He's not one to ignore, though, is he? I suppose you want my opinion.'

'Well, er, . . .'

'Frightening. I thought he was frightening. Absolutely shatteringly gorgeous but he made me feel about thirteen and as though I was wearing white socks and school sandals. Can you handle this relationship, Goss?'

'Of course.'

'Goss.'

'Yes?'

'Don't play too near the edge.'

'It's image, Jenny. He's not like they say.'

'Darling, if it's shaped like a cone, smells of sulphur and rumbles, don't be surprised if it erupts.'

She felt the anger growing in her. 'Your mother knows him.'

'She says he was a friend once. She asked me how much time I spent in your company.'

'He's not a disease.' Her voice throbbed with emotion. 'He has a bad reputation. I know that. I'm not saying he's been a saint.'

'Goss,' said Jenny strangely.

'Yes.'

'Don't snap at me. You know, I get the creeps about that older generation. Canfield makes me feel safe.'

'I don't understand.'

'Canfield's father, for one. He was part of a paedophile ring, you know. They took little children and did things to them. I think Marie's father was naughty with her when she was young, that's why she was shoved off to Shaws. Even my pops is a bit odd sometimes and I don't think all's well between him and Mummy. Are they all corrupt, Goss? What happens to them? What goes wrong?'

'I don't know. I don't understand. Don't ask me, Jenny. My father won't even acknowledge me, remember? What am I? A child of incest? What's the secret, Jenny? I can't handle other people's grief. I've got too much of my own.'

She slammed the phone down. It rang almost immediately.

'Darling?'

'Carey.' She sobbed his name gratefully.

'What is it?'

'Nothing. I've been speaking to Jenny. Her mother isn't well.' Gossamer waited with thumping heart. Now she had said it she would have given anything to take it back.

'Helen always lived on her nerves. A lovely woman. Jenny's very pretty. You were friends at Shaws?'

'How did you know I went to Shaws?'

'Don't be silly, Gossamer. You told me.'

'I always said boarding school. I never said Shaws.

It was deliberate. I didn't want you to know I'd been there.'

'Why not?'

'Because, because . . .' Gossamer faltered. She took breath, holding the receiver tightly. 'Because I went through that time believing you were my father. Half-believing it. I was falling in love with you. I kept trying to hold the day at bay when we had to admit it. So I spoke generally. I wanted to give you room, not tie you down.'

There was a silence. 'It sounds silly,' she said flatly. 'It was silly. But I was very confused.'

'I think you're a bit confused now.'

'Carey. Were you and Helen Kepesake lovers once?'

His tone was silky. 'Is my past becoming a problem to you, Gossamer?'

'No. Yes. I don't know.'

'I can't change what's past and gone. It's only now or in the future I can change things. Do you understand?'

'Yes.' She spoke humbly. She had frightened herself. She had too much at risk.

'As it happens, I phoned about your future.'

'You did?'

'I did. Jerry Laslo wants you to audition for a job.'

'He does? What sort of job?'

'He's an adman. He has a new product to handle. They want a new face.'

'Gosh.'

'There'll be competition. The client will have the final say.'

'I understand.'

'The studio's near the Elephant and Castle. It's set up for Thursday. Wear something sexy.'

'Carey, I'm so grateful.'

'Tell me tonight. I'll pick you up at seven.'

'Tonight. I love you.'

He chuckled and broke the connection.

Kevin Germain was conscious but completely paralysed. He

lay in his private room in the private hospital and the minutes of his life ticked by. They would not know for some time how permanent his condition might be. His eyelids could flicker. People had been taught to communicate with less.

For the time-being he could communicate with no one. The nurses and the doctors did everything for him. He was utterly without power over his own life in any personal or intimate matter. Yet the whole man, his thoughts, his dreams, his wishes, lay locked within the barrier of his damaged brain.

He had a visitor. He lay inert on his bed. His eyes were open and apparently focussed. The room was full of flowers and barred sunlight.

'Hello,' said Carey. He smiled down at the man on the bed. Then he sat down.

'You're her trustee,' he said. 'I bet you thought you were the only one who knew. You were wrong, weren't you? Because I know. Of all people, I know.'

He continued to smile at the man on the bed. Their eyes met.

'You haven't told him yet, have you?' Carey went on. 'I made enough splash. I made it easy for you. I put us in the papers. I didn't hide anything. I was content to put the ball in your court. And you dropped it. Oh dear. You waited too long.'

He sat peacefully for a while. 'She's quite something, isn't she?' he said presently. 'It's funny, but I've nearly got caught in my own snare.' He leant forward. 'In case you're wondering, she's fantastic in bed. She's as hot as you can imagine. She's everything she looks to be. She doesn't even realise herself how extraordinary she is because she's only had me. I take some credit, of course. I pressed her on-button. I fired her up. But she had the hardware in place, Kevin. From birth. As we both know.' He dropped his voice to a whisper. 'Her cunt is like warm velvet. It's alive. It wriggles.' He chuckled.

He was silent again for a while. His eyes were very bright. 'What did you tell her, eh? That was very naughty of you. You made me angry. You told her bad things about me.'

He snickered. 'It must have been hard sifting the evidence to give her a suitably toned-down version. It didn't work, though. She thinks she can reform me.'

The sunlight fell in bars across the bed where the venetian blind filtered it.

'Maybe she can. That's the risk I run. She's really something special.'

He got up and walked across to the window and looked out, parting the slats to do so. 'I expect they'll move you soon. The view's very nice and it's completely wasted on you, isn't it? You'll get the room that looks out over the laundry block or the incinerator. It's not as though you'll be able to complain.' He turned round and looked at the bed. The sun behind him made him a dark thing, a man-shaped emptiness in the sunshine.

'Sometimes it frightens me,' he said quietly. 'I've tried to do things right in my life. You might not believe me but it's true. Always they've gone wrong. They've turned sour. That's an exaggeration. Almost always they've gone wrong.' He stretched luxuriously, his arms outflung. The light rayed from his fingertips. He relaxed and put his hands in his pockets. 'It's when I've been bad that things have really worked out,' he whispered confidingly. 'The more bad I am, the easier it gets. Isn't that scary, Kevin? I may call you Kevin, mayn't I? I know we've never formally met before this, but I feel we're old friends. It comes of sharing an old secret, I suppose.'

He walked over to the bed. 'I wouldn't have wished this on you. God knows, I'm not that far gone. It isn't that I'm not above arranging little accidents. All sorts of terribly romantic things happened early in my acquaintance with our mutual friend. Once I knew she existed I got myself a mole in Chatteris Choate. She never knew I pulled the strings. I even arranged a near-miss for her with me conveniently at hand. But I wouldn't arrange this, Kevin, what's happened to you. I wouldn't put a man, a fellow-sufferer, where you are. Not deliberately.'

He bent over the bed. 'I'd use the situation if it was given to me, though. That's the kind of man I am. I'm going to use this one. You're here. The line of communication is broken. So we can play madder games, can't we, till someone stops us. Stops me.'

He looked up. Someone was coming into the room. It was a middle-aged woman, her face grooved with grief. She carried a great armload of flowers and for a moment the smell of summer was stronger than the smell of treachery.

'Hello,' she said to Carey, looking at the man on the bed. 'I didn't know Mr Germain had anyone with him. I've brought fresh flowers.'

'They're very lovely.'

She pushed her hair back out of her eyes as if she didn't know what it was. She had been so immaculately groomed before. 'I'm Alison Sanderson. I'm Mr Germain's personal secretary.' She put down the flowers and went over to the bed.

'I'll leave you now,' said Carey softly. 'Say goodbye for me, won't you.'

'Yes. Yes, of course. You'll come again? Visitors are good for him, you know. He needs stimulation.'

'We all do what we can,' said Carey.

Half-way along the corridor towards the exit he put his hands in his pockets and executed a skittish dance step. He was whistling as he left the hospital and made his way back into the world of the living.

❋ Six ❋

Gossamer turned up at her job audition with almost no idea of what to expect. Weakly she wished Carey was with her. The fine summer weather had turned thundery and a yellow rancid sky hung heavily over the city. It was an effort not to get sticky. It was also an effort to find where she was going, so much so that she was very nearly late. She didn't know south of the river at all and the upper end of the New Kent Road was all shops. Many of them were very sleazy shops. When she found it, the street door to the studios was a wooden panelled door so discreet as to be almost invisible. A small brass plaque to one side announced Dayfield Promotions, Elephant Studios. On either side of the door was a newsagent and a florist's. Gossamer rang, announced herself and was admitted.

She didn't properly understand the advertising agency she had come to audition for. She knew by now that Tring Laslo was a small creative hotshop. It wasn't independent, though. Somehow it was associated with or owned by Rimer Dayfield, the biggest advertising agency in the world. Dayfield Promotions, another part of the corporate empire owned by Alec Dayfield, owned the studio she would be in and they made ads and pop videos, doing promotional work of all kinds. Alec Dayfield also owned and ran DayStar, the other satellite TV network, the one that directly competed with Carey's OffWorld TV. Alec Dayfield was a fairly legendary city figure reputed to be personally worth $500 million. He lived mostly in New York. His reputation as a ferocious corporate raider meant that the standard cartoon caricature of him usually had him as a wolf, slavering as he gobbled up little independent businesses.

Gossamer was almost amused at herself. She had an itch to know, to understand all this. Her business course at Shaws had not been entirely wasted. There was a kind of jigsaw about the whole thing, it all fitted a larger pattern. The bits looked muddly on their own but once you grasped what the whole thing was about, how the city worked, it was really rather neat. At least, that was what she suspected.

If there was another implication she ignored it. A woman who had a good understanding of the financial sector would make a good wife – for a businessman.

The new product she had come to model for was yet another brand of jeans. These were French jeans, made in France, and they wanted to break into the massive British market. They needed something to make them distinctive if they were to chip away at the monster companies at the top end of the market and the cheap and nasty fly-by-nights at the bottom. Tring Laslo said they could do it. The campaign was drawn up and approved. Now all they needed was the Girl.

The company was branded as Jeans de Nîmes. They were in fact based in Nîmes and the word denim was derived from de Nîmes. However, this was considered too subtle to be a marketing point. Instead, the pitch was going to be 'nothing more'. They were going to play it in French and English. The idea was that each in a series of adverts stated '*rien de plus*', nothing more. A girl needed nothing more. The brand name would be read straight off the jeans, sexily taken in close up on the model's arse. Underneath would be 'All a girl needs'.

That was it. *Rien de plus*. Jeans de Nîmes. All a girl needs. The image was to be provided by the girl and she had to be as sexy as possible. That was the link. It was the jeans that made you sexy. If you had the jeans, you came fully equipped.

They wanted to get as near the line as possible. The image had to be hot but attractive. They wanted to buck the whole

health and responsibility trend by reminding people that if
sex wasn't fun, it wasn't sex.

The girl had to be beautiful. Her body had to be perfect.
And she had to smoulder. They didn't want a snooty girl,
though. This girl had to look attainable and unfrightening.
The idea was that men got hot between the legs seeing her,
and the girls picked up the message. Wear these jeans, you'll
give this message.

A little of this was explained to the roomful of girls.
Gossamer was shattered. About forty girls from her own
age to over thirty were gathered together and herded like
cattle. She was staggered by the onslaught of delectable
flesh. The other models were putting out so hard she
felt she had Sunday School tattooed on her forehead.
She shrank inside herself and knew she would fail. She
felt gauche and young. The clean bare minimally-furnished
rooms were cattle-sheds.

A woman took them in charge. She wore a hard red suit
with padded shoulders. Her glasses had *diamanté* frames
and hung on a chain round her neck. She held a clipboard
and ticked off each girl in a bored irritated manner. In a
high nagging voice she bullied the girls into some sort of
order. The combination of the pouting smouldering models
exhibiting leg and breast, and the schoolmarmish cross
woman began to get to Gossamer's sense of humour. It
was revolting. This was grotesque. Since she personally
didn't have a chance against these sophisticated charmers,
she might as well relax and take it all in. It would make
a funny story for Anthony over their next hamburger and
coke after skating.

They were told to parade in line through the next room
where the ad executives and client all sat. The 'client' was
four Frenchmen and one French woman. They looked aloof
and unimpressed as though the girls had a bad smell.

Gossamer dutifully shuffled in the line like a glamorous
prisoner in a chain gang. She wore a short straight skirt and
a closefitting top that emphasised her bust. Some of the girls
wore shorts. Others wore dresses. Some wore jeans. They all

smiled and gazed confidently at the men and women who watched them. Up until the last moment they had all been talking hard to each other, mostly a combination of bitching and bragging. Now they fell suddenly silent as they paraded. Gossamer herself was ignored, the new kid on the block. She found it funnier and funnier. She saw Jerry Laslo watching her and gave him a friendly grin.

Back in the room they had started in, the red-suited woman told some of them they could go. There was much disgusted grumbling and cursing at this. The rejected girls flung out down the stairs. Gossamer was left with twelve other girls. She grinned at them uneasily but mostly they disdained eye contact. One or two were bragging about their agencies and the other ads they had done.

Redsuit told them that next they would be going into the studio that had been hired for the day. The girls would be on camera. They were told they had to walk onto the set, slip the jeans on with their back to camera, look over their shoulder and smile, and then walk off the set.

The other girls now stripped to panties and nothing else.

Redsuit looked at Gossamer standing staring at the others. 'Hurry up,' she snapped.

'I didn't know. I mean, I didn't know we had to get undressed.'

'All the agencies were warned. What agency are you with?'

'I'm not.'

The woman looked down her list and sniffed. 'No. I see. Well, it's up to you. All they want is the jeans. If you can't take your bra off, go home, dear, and stop wasting everyone's time.'

One of the girls said suddenly: 'We're all together, ducks. We're meat. They don't matter. It's a laugh, see.' She grinned at Gossamer. She had long pointed breasts with amazing coloured nipples. Gossamer tried not to stare at them. They were lipstick red. She grinned uneasily. Another girl had one nipple pierced. They all wore briefs but the girl with a pierced nipple had on a G-string. As she turned and Gossamer saw her back, she looked almost totally nude.

She was also beautiful. The long silky smooth tanned flesh was perfect. She stood and stretched and shook her hair slightly. She might have been a Siamese cat, aristocratic and purring.

Gossamer took off her top. It had tiny pearl buttons all down the front. Her hands fumbled and were sweaty.

She stepped out of her skirt and slipped her stockings off and her garter belt. Now she wore plain black seamless briefs, very decent actually. She had chosen them for the smoothness of line. She could thank her lucky stars for that.

The girl beside her was absorbed, flicking her nipples erect. Redsuit made them all go through to the studio.

Now it wasn't just the client. There were cameramen and technicians. Gossamer stood among the girls in the cable-strewn gloom and felt sick. She was also angry with herself. Everyone was working. She was being juvenile. Sex wasn't involved here.

The set was white and naked except for the jeans. They were all trying on the same pair for this rough run-through. They were reminded the product was supposed to be sexy and then each girl went in turn and slid into the jeans, smiled back over her shoulder, and walked off. She had to strip and hand the jeans over then.

There was no buzz doing it. Gossamer's walk was from Shaws rather than her professional training. The School had always insisted that they use their bodies gracefully and move flowingly. When she came to look over her shoulder she imagined Carey was there and they were sharing a joke. She walked off the set and took the jeans off.

Back in the room she tried to get dressed but she was told to wait. When all the girls were back Redsuit read out three names.

One was the girl wearing the G-string. One was a girl with straight red hair down to the small of her back. The third was Gossamer.

The other girls began to get dressed. The friendly girl winked at Gossamer. 'Do your best, sweetie,' she said. 'Don't let them get to you.'

Redsuit unbent. 'I'm Claire, girls. You are Julie, Candice and Gossamer. That's right, is it?'

They murmured assent.

'Right. I'll organise coffee in a minute, girls. Meanwhile they want to make sure you have no blemishes. So it's a slow walk in close-up in your panties with a couple of turns for good measure. They'll still be looking at hair and eyes and expression, so keep putting out, dears. Then there'll be a camera close-up and they'll watch the monitor.' She looked up from her clipboard and smiled. 'After that I couldn't say. It depends on the client. You can all ride?'

Candice sniggered.

'Horses, dear, horses.'

They all could.

They paraded almost nude in front of the men and women. They were watched with the objectivity of a buyer at Tattersalls. Gossamer wouldn't have been surprised to feel a hand run over her hocks. She felt the eyes on her body as something remote. She knew she was getting closer to getting the job but she refused to think about it. It was a game. It wasn't an awfully nice game, either.

She remembered parading nude for Carey. He liked to have her around him without any clothes on. She was so anxious to please him she had never felt anything but a humble gratification that her body pleased his aesthetic senses.

It was strange to think of herself as genuinely beautiful. It was strange to think other men might hunger for her, just because of how she looked. She felt she would never understand. She would never be like other girls, taking it for granted. Men were so mysterious.

She had forgotten where she was. She had walked and turned lost in her own thoughts.

Later she sat in front of a camera. Still she was almost naked. She was to speak, to say something about herself.

'My name is Gossamer Fane,' she began politely. 'I've just

graduated from a dance school in north London. I've never done any professional work before. I live in London now but much of my life has been spent in the far north, on the Scottish border.' She smiled at the camera as though it was a friend. This was truly absurd. 'I go skating every Saturday,' she confided. 'I find London quite amazing. The streets are scary after dark but there is so much here, so much happening. I haven't travelled much and I'd like to. Especially Greece. I'd love to go to Greece.' She laughed. The camera was like a confessional, easy to talk to. Nothing she said mattered. They only wanted her expressions and to see if she filmed well. What she said was irrelevant. 'Greece for the scenery and the Classical remains. But I'd love even more to go to Venice. All that art. I've done some art history and I'm hooked.'

'Thank you, Miss Fane,' called a distant voice. Gossamer stood up and walked off. As she went by, the cameraman straightened and smiled at her. 'I hope you get this one,' he whispered. 'You're a darling.'

He must have been fifty and he had a face like an elephant's hide. Gossamer felt she was exploding with laughter. Never had she spent so futile and ridiculous a day. She began to get dressed. She rather thought G-string would get it. The girl dripped sex and that was what they wanted. She herself had been Angela Brazil.

When they were all three together again it was clear G-string, Julie, thought she had the job too. She spent some time perfecting her make-up as they sat together. Then Claire came through.

'The client likes you all, dears. Only one can do it though. Candice, Julie, thank you very much. Another time, perhaps. Can you come through, Gossamer?'

She felt dizzy walking through. Suddenly she wasn't a hunk of flesh any more. She shook hands all round and they addressed her deferentially as Miss Fane. A bottle of champagne was opened.

Jerry Laslo took her to one side. 'Star quality,' he said, smiling down at her.

'You're very kind. I was sure Julie would get it.'

'Too close to the bordello. We want the naughty but nice. These jeans are going to make ordinary girls feel like you look.'

'What do I do now, Mr Laslo?'

'Jerry. Have you got a business manager?'

'No.'

He considered a moment. 'I'll give Carey a bell. We'll get you sorted out. We're planning a run of six adverts initially. We'll see how they go. You ever been to Paris, Miss Fane?'

'Please call me Gossamer. You're a friend of Carey's, aren't you? I went once on a school trip.'

Jerry looked enigmatic. 'I wouldn't exactly call myself a friend. I used to work for him when he had his own agency. Rimer Dayfield sucked us in and spat him out.'

'Is Tring Laslo independent?'

'Is the government honest?' He grinned. 'We get along. We're allowed our own name and to generate our own business. Meantime we use Rimer Dayfield for financial and other services. The lead is long, Miss Fane. Gossamer. It serves to keep client clashes at a minimum. But it's there.'

'Client clashes?'

'The problem of a big agency is that it might have two clients with competing brands. You can't have Unilever and Proctor and Gamble. You can't do BP and Esso. But Rimer Dayfield have this associate structure and they kid the client we little agencies have autonomy.'

'And you don't?'

'Maybe we do. Anyway, there's you, Gossamer. We'll be working quite closely together. I'll show you the boards next week and let you know what will be happening. The first ad's in Paris. I'll try and get you some money upfront so you have something to spend. OK?'

'OK,' said Gossamer warmly. She smiled happily. Sometimes life could be really sweet.

They handmade her ten pairs of jeans to wear on camera.

To go with the TV campaign they prepared a billboard ad. This had Gossamer in close up from the back, so that most of the vast area of the ad was her jeans-clad backside. She was standing twisted round at her naked torso but only her waist and lower ribs were shown. Her hands were slotted into her back pockets. The label could clearly be read. Across the top in huge print was '*Rien de plus*'. Then you saw her backside with the label, Jeans de Nîmes. Underneath it said: All a girl needs.

Seeing the boards, the roughs for the campaign, was great fun. All Gossamer had to do for the first ad was to walk down the middle of the Champs-Elysées with the Arc de Triomphe in the background. She wore only the jeans, being otherwise barefoot and barebreasted though the latter would not be directly shown. She would walk serenely and with a swing through the traffic as it careered into accidents and crashes. There would be close-ups of bemused drivers, of men on bikes in berets and all the other standard French imagery. At a pavement café a young successful-looking gorgeous businessman type would see her coming. He would stand up. She would come closer with the sunset, the Arc de Triomphe and the traffic mayhem behind her. He would hand her a sheaf of flowers which would cunningly serve to cover her breasts just at the moment you thought you must finally see them. They would kiss. She would look over his shoulder and smile into the camera that soon-to-be-famous smile. All a girl needs.

Naturally she would not actually walk semi-nude down the Avenue des Champs-Elysées. It would be filmed and she would be filmed but the traffic crashes and all the bystanders and drivers would be cut in from other sources. The walk could be done anywhere. It was the café scene that had to be done for real.

'Carey,' she said. She was lying full-length on her sofa. She was nude, her head in Carey's lap. He was fully dressed watching the late news. One hand was casually resting on her breast. He had a cigarette in the other.

'Mmm?'

'Do you know I'll have to be topless?'

'You sound like a bunnygirl. What are you talking about?'

'These advertisements. For the jeans. Did Jerry Laslo tell you?'

'Jerry? I don't see him about. I gave him a call when I thought you needed a leg up. He came up with the rest, honey. I don't bother with detail when I give someone a job to do.'

This was unpleasant. 'You don't mind me being bare-breasted?' she said doggedly.

He squeezed the one he held. 'I like it.'

'I mean on camera. You're teasing me.'

'I don't give a shit when I'm not around.' The casual brutality was shocking. 'If I catch you with someone, there's an end to it, of course. Perhaps we should start using condoms.'

She sat up sharply. He caught her round the waist and pulled her so hard she thought she would bruise. 'I'm teasing,' he said into her hair. 'Of course I care.'

She felt knocked about. 'Why do you do this? You know how I feel. It really hurts me.' She was breathless.

'Let's say I need to make sure occasionally. You're a lovely thing and now very many people are going to know it.'

She screwed round to face him. 'You aren't serious? You know no other man compares with you.'

He grinned. 'That's just fine. Keep thinking that and you'll be OK. No, I don't mind other men seeing your breasts. Just as long as that's all. Seeing is one thing, baby. This is another.'

He kissed her hard. His hand went down between her legs. She felt the fire leap in her. Her guts trembled and weakened. She didn't like what he had done but he said it was from weakness, from jealousy. She wouldn't let him be jealous. He owned her, body and soul. It was her constant delight to prove this.

He was kissing her belly. 'I have to kiss someone in each

ad,' she said. She writhed and groaned at the pleasure he gave her.

He slid a finger into her. 'There's kissing and kissing,' he said. 'Make sure you keep them sorted out.'

Half an hour later she came out of the shower. He was standing up, preparing to go. He never stayed the night though sometimes he brought a change of clothes. He said it was to protect her, to observe the decencies. Gossamer thought this was mad but accepted that he knew more of the world than she did.

'Jerry Laslo said he used to work for you,' she said.

'That's right.'

'Tring Laslo is owned by Rimer Dayfield.'

'Associated with. It's an odd structure. Dayfield uses it a lot. He keeps space between himself and his satellites. He owns it all right, though.'

'Isn't DayStar your competitor?'

'For satellite TV? Not really. They're upmarket, BBC in the air. OffWorld serves the out-of-work steelworker, the part-time checkout girl. They don't want finance programmes, in-depth documentaries, interviews with politicians. They want it cheap and cheerful. That's what we give them. Friendly wallpaper. Nothing demanding.'

'Jerry said something about Dayfield buying up a firm of yours.'

Carey looked at her blandly. 'Blabby, our Jerry.'

'He's very nice to me. I mean,' Gossamer blushed. 'Nothing like that. You know.'

'I know. Jerry isn't suicidal.' Carey walked over to the glass doors onto the balcony. They stood open to the humid night air. London roared quietly in the distance like a beast consumed by an endless mindless anger.

'I used to be an adman,' said Carey. 'I was a media broker afterwards. I had my own consultancy. Mediad, I called it. We were hot.'

'What's a media broker?'

He turned round and leant against the doorframe so that she saw him against the night. The liquid ease of the man, the light amused manner were very much in evidence. She accepted he had a black dog in him somewhere. It was where his cruelty came from. It would be her job to exorcise it. It would be love's job.

'Let's say a thirty second slot half way through News at Ten costs seventy grand. That's about right. The TV company charges the ad agency 85 per cent of that. The agency passes on the full cost to the client. It's in that 15 per cent that the agency makes its profits. So the guy who negotiates the slots in the papers and on TV is an important man in the agency. He's the media buyer. Now back in the seventies it seemed to me there was a lot of nonsense talked about media slots. For example, the back page was scorned. I happened to think people looked at the back page, it carried sport and it was on the outside. For a glossy it was part of the cover. I had all sorts of other fancy ideas, too.'

He turned back and looked out of the windows again. Gossamer grew nicotiana in pots on her balcony and the air was scented with them.

'So I set up my own company. We would be media buyers for the agencies, they didn't need an in-house buyer any more. We were cost-effective for that alone. And we would get a better deal.'

'Were you successful?'

'For a while. But during the seventies Alec Dayfield began to create what was to become Rimer Dayfield. They grew exponentially. That guy practically invented corporate raiding. He couldn't leave anything alone. By the eighties they were so big they were hurting my business.'

'They didn't use you?'

'Did they hell. Everything was in-house. Dayfield would buy up a little company, restructure it financially, then make it use all his increasingly global facilities, marketing, sales-promotion, management consultancy, PR and so on and so forth. And media buying. So I had to move to survive.'

'What did you do?'

'I decided to go back into advertising directly. The bigger

Rimer Dayfield got, the more problems they had with client competition. There was room for an independent. The blue chips were uncomfortable. But there were problems.'

He smoked, staring into the night again. Gossamer realised suddenly that this was pillow talk. He hardly knew she was there. He was talking to himself. 'I wasn't listed. I had no stock market quotation. I'd been lazy and I was paying for it now. I was cautious, too. I could feel it in my water, what was happening in the eighties. It was a bubble. When it burst, I wasn't going to get caught with my pants down. I had to move fast and I didn't need debt. So I didn't go to the banks, though God knows they were throwing money at you then. I even had an asset I could raise money on. I'd bought a long lease on my premises and as property exploded in value throughout the eighties, this had become worth serious money.'

He paused again. They heard a siren wailing in the night.

'I decided my move had to be equity funded. To go public quickly I looked round for a defunct company. I found it soon enough. Slough Freezers. They were just the job. They had a quotation, they were public and they weren't in business any more. They were three industrial freezers in a lock-up in Slough.' Carey snorted with laughter. 'I bought them, flogged the freezers the same day, backed Mediad into them and changed the name. Zowee, I was a public company listed on the market. Then I set about a rights issue to raise the money to buy the agency I wanted.'

He was silent for so long that Gossamer felt she had to speak.

'What happened?'

'My fault. I used a Dayfield business research company to find Slough Freezers. I thought it was funny, using Alec's own business to steal a march on him. I intended to compete directly. I thought I could do it. He was over-extended. I knew a crash was coming and he was busy junk-bonding his way into Madison Avenue. I was going to be in place to pick up the pieces. And I wasn't going to be in hock to a damned bank, either. Rimer Dayfield had made advertising equity glamour stock. I would get my own agency and ride their backs to expand it, constantly issuing shares to buy on. So I made my rights issue after the city analysts picked me over and declared me fit to go.'

'What happened?'

'I thought he was too busy. I didn't think he would see what the corners of his empire were up to. The bastard turned round and made a hostile bid. He junk-bonded me. He bought me up, lock, stock and barrel.'

'What's a junk-bond?'

'Illegal in this country. Alec used the States. He borrowed money on a high-risk high-return basis. He pledged the assets of the company, my company, that he was taking over. I had that damned lease, you see. That damned valuable lease.'

'You couldn't stop him buying your company?'

'Not once it was public. He had me by the balls. The Take-Over Panel won't even let you buy your own fucking shares. He said he was leaving me as chairman but that was a nonsense and we both knew it. He bought out the contract the Board made him sign with me and I got £3 million out of it. Peanuts. That bastard bounced me out on the street and the whole city knew it. And he survived the crash when it finally came in '86.'

'I don't understand. Why didn't he keep you on? You were good at your job.'

Carey turned to face her again. His face was smooth and untroubled despite the bitter tone he had been using. 'The guy sacked me in '70. He bounced me in '86. He knew I wanted to play up with the big boys. I wasn't content with second fiddle. I'm no Jerry Laslo.'

'Then you went into satellite. But he did that too.'

'Yes, he did. Only we'll break him. When they looked around for someone mean enough in play to take on DayStar, there I was. The whole city knew I wouldn't merge with that bastard, I'd fight to the death. Or take him over. And I've come out on top. We're in profit already. Daystar loses £3

million a week. He can't carry it forever. He's like a tree
rotting from the inside. He's poured in £400 million's worth
of cement, but the tree is going to go over anyway.'

'Carey, if you hate him so why did you send me to
Tring Laslo?'

'Hate him? That's *Girl's Own Paper* language. That guy
is sitting at the pinnacle of a tumbling empire. He's probably
financing DayStar from the pension funds. He could be in
prison in a year. Me, I'm earning four grand plus per week
and another in corporate perks. I'll be here to pick out the
plums when his companies crash. He's not that much older
than me, Gossamer. He's almost at the end of his time.
Mine's just about to arrive.'

'I still don't understand why you used Tring Laslo.'

'Firstly Jerry Laslo owes me one. He could get you in on
the floor. Secondly I did it for you, lamebrain. There's no
vendetta here. Alec Dayfield and I are perfectly ordinary
business rivals and what has gone on between us goes on
all the time. The financial community is limited, Gossamer.
We all tend to know each other. We're all fighting in the
same arena. This Jeans de Nîmes promotion. I like it. It'll be
good for you. We'll get you a business manager but you're
started, sweetheart, if Jerry pulls this off. I think he will.
Your face is going to be big. You'll have to decide which
way to go.'

'Which way to go?'

'You'll get offered work. Marcus'll guide you but if for
example you accept a *Playboy* centrefold, you won't get to
do a Mothercare ad. You get me?'

'Of course. I wouldn't do centrefolds anyway. Who's
Marcus?'

'I'll introduce you. I think he's just the guy. If you want
to do centrefolds, if that's the way you want things to go,
fine. Fine by me, anyway. Your career is your career and
I don't muddle it with your private life.'

'You're my private life, Carey.' She came up to him
and stood against him. She could feel his clothes against
her flesh.

He kissed her shoulder and ran a hand down her back and into its hollow. 'I'm sorry you're not all of mine,' he said.

She could feel his hair on her cheek. He continued to kiss her shoulder. 'What do you mean?' she said. Her voice wobbled. Was he proposing? At last?

'I'm a bad man, Gossamer. I have tastes I can't throw. There are things I don't ask you to do. So I go elsewhere. Can you understand that?'

'No,' she cried. 'What can't you ask me to do? I'll do anything for you.'

She had pulled back. He held her lightly at her waist, his expression calm. 'I can't ask,' he said softly.

'It can't be that bad. Will it hurt me? Is that it?'

He smiled gently. 'It'll hurt you, yes. I'm not asking.'

'I'm offering. I don't want you to go elsewhere. I can't stop you, but I don't want it. You must know that.'

He stroked her back. 'You're so sweet, child. You know, I think I'm bad for you, just like all those friends of yours tell you. I think I ought to go away and leave you in peace now. You can find a nice boy your own age.'

She fell to her knees so that his hands were on her head. She pressed her face into him, then she turned it so that her cheek was against him.

'I beg you not to leave me for my sake,' she said hoarsely. 'I won't listen to other people. They're jealous of me because you make love to me and they wish you wanted them. Or they wish they had me. I could understand what was going on in Kevin Germain's mind. He was hot for me himself. He didn't like you being where you are. He didn't like you being between my legs, in my bed. He was a dirty old man and I found him disgusting. I'm sorry he's so badly hurt but he was horrible to me, and to you.' She gulped. 'I know you've done bad things, Carey. I want that to stop. I love you regardless, whatever you've done. That's real love, darling. No strings. Nothing held back. I want to be everything for you, everything a woman can be.'

'But that's the problem, my sweet.' His voice was cool and far above her.

She looked up. 'I don't understand.'

He lifted her to her feet. His eyes were dancing. 'You can be everything a woman can be, and very lovely with it. But it isn't what a woman can do that I'm talking about. It isn't about being a woman at all.'

He was right. It hurt. It hurt a lot. He used a condom and he used a lot of grease but it hurt so bad she wanted to die for a while.

When he was gone she lay awake a long time. It was cruel, this. Not Carey, not him. No, it was Fate that was cruel. She was so prepared to love and be loved. Why must she be constantly tested like this? Why did she have to prove to herself over and over again that her love was boundless?

Was it always like this? You just wanted to relax and be happy but always you had to go that one step further. When you had got used to that step and it had stopped seeming odd or disgusting, when you had adjusted to it and managed it and incorporated it into you, you had to start out over with something new, something even more extreme. Something damnably painful.

She had hated it. It was as simple as that. Even when constant use loosened her and made it painfree she couldn't ever imagine liking it. She would do it for him to save him going elsewhere. But it was a penance.

Was this the nature of love? Now she thought about it, it was very like the sort of love God demanded in the Old Testament. It was blasphemous to muddle that up with sex, of course, but her experience was a kind of shadow of poor Abraham's. What had he gone through, after he understood God wanted him to murder his own son Isaac? What terrible suffering had that good man endured as his love for God was tested in this terrible way? And look at all the others. Job. Even Jesus, suffering in the wilderness. Were love and suffering inextricably bound up? Did you have to prove the one by enduring the other?

Was it like this for Jenny and Canfield? Jenny had been made for pleasure and she longed innocently for fun. But she fell in love with Johnny Canfield and he fell on hard times and now Jenny was down there with him, practically living on baked beans and never going out anywhere.

Maybe Marie had the rights of it. She went hard at getting pleasure and she had two good companions to help her.

Gossamer shivered. She didn't want that. She didn't want what Marie had. What Jenny had was better. If she loved a Canfield, her own money would help immensely if he wasn't too proud to lean on her for a while before he got going himself.

But she didn't love a boy at University. She loved a man, a grown man with a history and a complicated, tortured soul. And he loved her, she was sure. Otherwise he would have become bored with her by now. She could give him no intellectual stimulation and she was ignorant of his world. All she could offer was her body. The service it supplied was one he could get readily elsewhere from some other girl. And her love. She could offer her love. That was the unique thing about her. That was why he wanted her. She might hate what had happened tonight, she might dread having to do it again, but if she could be steadfast in her love and yielding and faithful, he would be freed from his malignant past and able to escape from the perversions of his present.

Love would set him free. It would set her free also.

She fell asleep.

She liked Marcus Wainwright. He was cheerful, vulgar, goodhearted, earnest and he listened to her. He was excitable, childish and very sharp about money. He was in love with his job and its jargon and he found both endlessly fascinating. He was a fresh draught of water to Gossamer and she felt safer with someone between her and her new world. She signed a contract under his tender loving care and a large sum of money was duly deposited in her account. Marcus recommended a financial adviser and Carey dropped his nose in to make sure she was in safe hands here, too.

It occurred to her she could do without her trust money.

She could afford the risk of chasing up the real identity of her father and mother. She didn't do it. She was more than ever convinced the incest explanation was the right one. She would rather not know for sure. There were other explanations though they were far weaker. For example, she could be the offspring of a married man and his mistress. The mistress had died. If the man admitted to his wife about the daughter, his own marriage would be bust. He wouldn't take that risk, which was bad of him, but he had provided for her.

She had a day in the East End with a photographer doing still shots of her. She had a day in Docklands filming the billboard ads. Then they all flew to Paris and she had two cheerful hard-working days there.

She admitted to herself she found it quite thrilling. The man chosen to be the lover she met in the advert world was really very attractive. He was in his thirties, devastatingly handsome and not at all snooty with her. He was also married with three children. He took her home to meet his wife and they all ate cassoulet together. It was odd kissing him with her bare breasts against his jacket, and then laughing with his wife and children, but she was living an odd life. She liked it. She was busy, involved and she felt successful in her own right, even if Carey had helped her to get started.

Marcus and she had long giggling phone calls about the offers she would receive. She issued ridiculous instructions about what she would and wouldn't accept, sort of 'cancel Madonna and pencil in Di' stuff. It was fairytalesville and she loved it. Everyone was so nice to her, from the cameramen to the client to Jerry Laslo to Philippe, her on-set 'lover'.

Back in London they all gathered to see the rushes. As the edited ad appeared out of the cutting room mess, Gossamer was astonished. She was gorgeous. She was simply gorgeous. She was warm and saucy and sparkling and naughty – everything that was fun about youth and sex and success. She was so enticing she was edible. She watched in amazement at how she turned men on.

It was like she had a button. She could make men want her sexually.

She had power. She had spent most of her life wanting a man who had comprehensively rejected her. Now she had the whole world in her hand.

❧ Seven ❧

They brought Philippe over for the second advertisement which was to be filmed in Britain. He looked so good with her they decided he was worth keeping. Gossamer found herself arranged on a stone catafalque. It was made of plastic which was a mercy because they were filming in a wood and the weather had gone unseasonably cold. Goose-bumps wouldn't do. She had to lie with her eyes shut on the simulated stone. They wove flowers in her hair.

She looked so lovely she was naïvely astonished. Her black hair was tumbled loosely and then artfully bound with woodland flowers. Once she was in position on her pedestal, her arms slack at her sides, they covered her bare breasts with thousands of rose petals. Their red velvet softness reminded her of that other life, so long ago. The Velvet Girls. They had been the Velvet Girls in their Velvet Room.

Look at them now.

A fan was set up to lift and very gently blow the petals. Someone stood with more to hand, letting them into the airstream to waft over her as she lay.

It took a long time to get this right and tempers were fraying by the time the desired effect was achieved. Gossamer lay apparently asleep, or dead, covered in rose petals in the midst of a wood with more blowing about her like thistledown.

They began filming. Gossamer lay still. Philippe approached her. He was wearing a dress shirt undone at the neck, a bow-tie hanging loose. Looking impossibly handsome and rich, he knelt by the catafalque and began to kiss her.

They took this three times before Gossamer got herself

under control. She had to lie with her eyes shut and when Philippe first touched her she jumped. She couldn't help it. Then she giggled and upset the rose petals.

She settled down. Philippe approached. The director was talking him through it.

'Kiss her arm. Her shoulder. Really sexy. Put some hunger into it. Keep it stylish. Now her cheek. Open your eyes, Goss. Lie still, no expression, eyes open.'

She lay as she was told. All this was in close-up. Philippe was already out of shot.

'Now. Sit up. Let the petals fall. We'll air brush the tits, don't worry. Look over to the arch. No hair shaking. Stand up.'

They had set up a trellis arch among the trees hung with muslin which lifted and blew softly. Gossamer stood and faced it. The jeans could now be seen, all she wore.

'Walk now. Slowly does it. One look over the shoulder, the look, the smile. Give it to us. Lovely. Lovely. Cut.'

When Gossamer saw the edited ad she loved it. They had used filters and so the wood was hazy and mysterious, full of pale gold sunlight. She herself was a dream, a dream in jeans. Philippe was the perfect male, the lover, the successful man. He looked so ardent as he kissed her still body it was hard to believe they weren't lovers in real life.

Her eyes were wonderful. The close-up when she opened them from her dream sleep came straight after a close-up of the rose petals. Her eyes had that same velvet quality, a deep rich pansy-soft blue.

She took Philippe as her escort to Marie's nineteenth birthday party.

This was no hole-in-the-corner affair as Marie's last party had been. The Horden-Smiths were celebrating their only child's birthday and it was being done in style. Gossamer received her formal invitation. Tentatively she asked Carey if he would come with her. She was not surprised when he said no. She was even faintly relieved. She knew the best society disapproved of him and Marie's mother was of the best there was. Philippe was still in London for another day or two and so she took him.

A red carpet had been rolled out across the pavement in front of York Mansions. The guests arrived in state. Gossamer had her photograph taken by the paparazzi as she walked on Philippe's arm up to the open front door. The orchestra could only dimly be heard, playing in the garden which was strung with lanterns. Gossamer shed her wrapper and entered the glittering throng.

She had a lovely time. Philippe was a charming companion, droll and friendly. They attracted admiring glances because they were both so very good-looking. Gossamer found this funny. Philippe was sufficiently older than herself to lend her a certain cachet. That they were professional colleagues rather than lovers was not evident to those who didn't know her.

Even Jenny, there with a very smart Canfield, asked excitedly who Philippe was. Gurgling with laughter Gossamer admitted he was her TV lover for the ads she was filming.

'He's married with three children,' she added. 'I've stayed with him in Paris. His wife is lovely. We're just friends.' She twinkled at Jenny.

'Ooof. With friends like him, who needs lovers,' said Jenny. 'Introduce us, darling. Then I can waft on his arm.'

Jenny wore a bright blue satin dress and was so obviously delighted to be out having fun that Gossamer's heart sank. Canfield was too bright not to see the effect of the evening on her. She hungered for this sort of life. He was still very presentable, he had all the clothes of his former life before his father fell from grace, but they would wear out, become unfashionable, and then he would not be able to come to occasions like this until he was finished as a student and earning.

She herself was absurd in long red silky feathers, a dress that would have been high fashion in the twenties. They flowed and fluttered as she danced, bits fell off and stuck to Philippe's evening clothes and he pointed out how a detective could trace her movements all evening because she moulted as she moved.

Peter Kepesake was there, behaving himself. He had invited Gossamer to the Commem. Ball at the end of the Oxford term but she had refused. Now he seemed determined to put his bad behaviour behind him.

She danced with him. 'Do you see much of Jen?' he asked.

'Some. Not as much as I'd like.'

'Does she seem happy?'

'Peter, she's chosen where she is. Johnny won't be poor forever. He's bright. He'll get on. She'll be OK.'

'It's not the life for her.' Peter was restless.

'No. But then things aren't always as we plan, are they?'

'Things are bad at home,' he said abruptly.

'Oh.' Her heart sank.

'I suppose they always have been only I was too young to notice.'

This was said so pompously she had a sudden unforgiveable desire to laugh.

'Jenny's got enough to bear,' he went on. 'I can't help, stuck away in Oxford. You see, I've found out what's wrong between ma and pa.'

Dear God, she thought faintly. Does he realise about Carey? Does he know what he's saying?

'She has the patience of a saint,' said Peter gruffly. 'It's pulled me up in my tracks, I can tell you.'

Gossamer felt that perhaps she preferred the old Peter.

'You've been about the world now. I can see that. You go with Carey Lambert so you're no innocent. I saw him, you know.'

'Carey?' She was getting angry.

'No. My father. I was coming from Trafalgar Square. I'd had a few, you know. Some of the boys were with me. It'd been quite an evening. But I know what I saw.'

Gossamer danced patiently. 'Should you be telling me?' she asked.

'It's in case Jen ever finds out. She'll need you. You'd better be prepared. After Canfield senior it's a bit much.'

'For God's sake, Peter. What are you talking about?'

'Pa. I saw him. It was by Charing Cross where the all-night chemists and the arcades are. Where the runaway kids hang out playing for hire. My father, my father you understand, was picking up a nice young lad. I saw our car. Dad got the boy into the car and drove off. I'm not pretending I don't know what it meant. No wonder mother has looked awful all summer. She must have found out.'

'Peter, I'm so very sorry.'

'I don't want Jenny to know.'

'No. I understand.'

Her heart ached. Why did they all have to grow up?

Yet she enjoyed the evening. She danced with Johnny Canfield and with Barmy and Collywobbles both. She danced with Philippe and went to supper with him. She introduced him to Marie.

In return Marie introduced her companion. He was an immaculate young man in his late twenties, very attentive to Marie. His name was Ivor Spence.

Later Marie became confidential. She was a little drunk and Gossamer suspected she had taken something. 'How do you like Ivor?' she asked.

'He looks eminently respectable. Is he nice?'

'Darling, so nice you'd die of boredom. He's an investment banker. I call him Ivor door.' She giggled.

'Why?' They were in one of the ladies' cloakrooms tidying their hair and touching up their make-up.

'Ivor door out of what I'm going to do. He's it.'

'I'm not with you, you drunken besom.'

'I can handle the juice, sweetie. You know what I asked daddy for, for my birthday?'

'No.' Gossamer was patient.

'He wanted to give me a car. A Ferrari. But I said I wanted stock.'

'Stock?'

'Equity, sweetie. Voting stock in the company.'

'Good Lord.'

'I'm on this road, see.' Marie was dreamy. 'It's a wide road. Barmy and Collywobbles are gambolling like spring lambs along by my side, picking flowers and things. They can't see the fatstock man with his little cleaver just up ahead. In the distance is Horden-Smith. The firm. The business. The shipping line.'

'I'm with you so far.' Gossamer's voice was dry. She could feel the rehearsal.

'That's where I'm going, clutching my equity. I'm going to accumulate shares and take daddy over. It'll take some time. It's going to be lonely too. And the sun will stop shining quite soon. Down one side of the road there's a wall. There's a door in the wall. If I go through the door there are sunny meadows forever. Specifically, there's a double-fronted mock Tudor pad in Hampstead Garden Suburb, a Volvo saloon for nanny and the children and Ivor Spence coming home every night from the city.'

'I gather you don't want to marry him.'

'Well I do, in a way. Dull but dependable. He could do with the leg up the marriage settlement would give him, too. Sir and Lady "call me Davinia" Spence are so nice it isn't true. Really nice. Honestly good fairly rich people. Not like daddy. Not like *père* Canfield. Not like your naughty Carey Lambert. Not a skeleton in the cupboard, unless I enter the family, and I'm so rich they'll forgive me. I guess I ought to go for it.'

'So why don't you?'

Marie sighed. 'I pretended to be dumb at Shaws but I can remember Miss Manningtree in science. Flanders and Swan do that hilarious song about it. *Heat can't go from a colder to a hotter*. Thermodynamics. You remember?'

'Vaguely. Very vaguely.'

'I think badness is like that. Badness is hot. Goodness is cold. Goodness doesn't flow out from good people and infect bad people, Goss. It's the other way round. Bad people are contagious. Look at you. You were the biggest prude ever and so innocent it was comical. Now look at you after months with Carey Lambert. Honey, you look wicked. I'm talking about real naughties here. You look like you know things and you act like you don't. No wonder the men have their hair on end when you go by. I reckon poor old Ivor wouldn't be able to withstand me. You see? He's good. He's also pompous, dull and twenty-eight going on forty-nine. I don't sleep with him but I bet he has the sexual panache of blancmange.'

'You're exaggerating.' Gossamer kept her voice steady. Marie liked to do things for effect. She liked to shock. You couldn't take her seriously.

Marie linked arms and they headed back to the party. 'Am I? I never was nice, you know, though it isn't all my fault. But at least I didn't delude myself. You have to know what you are, Goss. Else it's all a nonsense.'

She drank champagne, floating in Philippe's arms, and finally they left.

The doorman offered to call a taxi but they decided to walk and cool their heads. Philippe was staying in a hotel near Hyde Park. Gossamer could get a taxi from there.

They went down by the river and walked along the Embankment. Gossamer made Philippe go onto Hungerford Bridge with her. She liked being on it when the trains came over but it was too late for that now and too late for the beggars. The night was moving towards dawn.

They stood looking through the girders at the quiet flowing river.

'Would you care to come back to my 'otel with me?' asked Philippe.

'Let's keep it friends, huh?'

'I was suggesting nozzing more. I am an 'appily married man. But as friends, might we not like to enjoy ourselves together a little? You are a ver' beautiful girl, Gossamer. I would like to do more than kiss you. I think we could enjoy it, wizzout hurting anyone. No one would know, just us two.'

'No, darling. I have a lover.'

'This I know, my dear. It is ver' evident. Why is he not wiz you tonight?'

'He's a very important businessman. I don't get to see him very often. But we've been together a while. There can be no other man for me.'

'He feels zis way too?'

She shrugged. The Royal Festival Hall shone quietly. She had grown to love this city.

'You want to marry him?'

'I think so.'

'But he does not?'

'I don't know. I don't ask.'

'Oh Gossamer. Is he married already?'

'No. Please, Philippe. I don't want to talk about him.'

They left the bridge and began to walk to Hyde Park. *'Ma petite fille de La Vierge,'* he said presently.

'Why do you say that?'

'It is your name in my language. Gossamer. *Tu es une fille de La Vierge.'*

'That's very pretty.'

'I pray She looks over you, *petite*. I think you need Her.'

The jeans ad was placed in magazines, on billboards and the first TV commercial was run. Marcus Wainwright took Gossamer out to dinner to celebrate. He gave off the sexual vibes of a potted plant and this made him very relaxing company. Pope Benedict spotted them and phoned Marcus the next day. Marcus ran a small stable of minor celebs and was known on the gossip circuit as a source. Marcus explained to Gossamer they should have a story. If she didn't want the tabloids sniffing out the truth about her ignorance of her parents, then she must have something to give them. She could be an orphan but they must invent respectable parents as boring as possible, and hope no one ever bothered to check.

Gossamer was revolted by this but agreed. She saw the sense of it. She would have discussed it with Kevin Germain but he lay silent and motionless in his hospital bed. So Marcus drew her up the most banal background he could think of. Since it had to include her going to Shaws, they had to account for some money. They invented a smaller trust than her real one and the wish in a will that she should attend the school. Her father had been the branch manager of a small National Provincial Bank, they decided. Since the National Provincial had vanished, swallowed by larger banks, they felt this was safe. Her mother was a housewife. They died in a traffic accident when she was very young.

Gossamer forgot Malling Benedict had seen her with Kevin Germain and she forgot the pretence about her being his niece.

Malling Benedict didn't forget. He knew she went with Carey Lambert. He bided his time. The girl was going to get a far higher profile shortly, he was sure. If she did, he would get his paper to employ a private detective. That background could do with someone sniffing about in it. It was too good to be true.

Johnny Canfield had got a job as nightwatchman for the long vac. He had to guard a small shopping precinct in Neasden and when he wasn't working he was either travelling to or from work or sleeping. All pretence that he didn't live with Jenny had long since vanished. Helen seemed not to mind and she visited her daughter often. She gave the couple things from Sandings to make their flat nicer and helped unobtrusively with their finances. But Johnny's job tied him and so it was Jenny, Gossamer and Anthony who met at Victoria one evening to travel to Brighton together. They were going to see Trish opening in the latest production of Danse Macabre.

Gossamer had passed her driving test that morning and was in a mood to celebrate. She bought champagne for the train and to the disapproval of the other travellers they drank it on the journey.

She wore a black silk shirt, floppy black trousers and a black wide-brimmed hat. Anthony wore a red shiny shirt, red jeans and a black wide-brimmed hat. He also wore a long earring and lipstick. Jenny was in blue jeans and a white silk shirt with huge red polka dots on it. The jeans were Jeans de Nîmes. The first advert had been showing for a fortnight and was being well received. Guiltily Gossamer had taped it and watched it with fascination by herself. Every time it was shown on TV she received a repeat fee. It was mysterious and marvellous and absurd. She was earning lots of money, she had plenty anyway, and far from being glamorous, Marcus was making her invest it in building societies and pension plans. She wanted a share portfolio and a stockbroker but Marcus said no, not until she made it onto television proper.

Forewarned by Gossamer, Jenny had on a black wide-brimmed hat too. They bundled off the train at Brighton and headed down the hill to the sea-front. They bought chips and candyfloss and, feeling a bit green, went to see Trish.

Danse Macabre was always odd and this production was no different. Gossamer never picked up the story, if there was one, but the images certainly haunted her. It was all about ambiguity. The black dancers had whitened their faces. The white dancers had blackened theirs. They all looked naked though they wore some sort of close-fitting invisible stocking material. This had the effect of flattening the girls' breasts and the mens' sex organs. Since the men were subtly padded at the breast and the women equally padded at their groins, it was hard to tell which sex anyone was. This made for alarming theatre.

It was professional and dramatic. They collected Trish afterwards and went for a wander along the sea-front.

The sea crashed to their right. The pier was ahead with the funfair at its end, a monstrous carbuncle of fun. Gossamer had promised to take Anthony on the ghost train. Trish seemed happy. Her hair was growing and she had a gorgeous silky fuzz of uniform depth all over her head.

It was a good evening.

Carey came four nights in succession to Gossamer's flat and stayed for about two hours each time. This time was spent in bed. On the fifth night he didn't come and Gossamer lay awake sobbing. She loved him so dearly and she was so grateful he wasn't there.

Jenny lived with Canfield. At the moment he worked nights but they had lived together for weeks and weeks now. Jenny never looked drawn and rattled. Yet that was how she looked after a session with Carey. Was there something wrong with her? Some flaw in her make-up that made her weak in bed?

Perhaps this was so, if she was the child of incest.

She went back to the little square Carey had taken her to that first time. It wasn't far from the Elephant Studios. She wished she hadn't. It was all gone, the ugly church, the silent houses, the fantasy scene. It was a site for development now. The wind blew gustily and she smelt autumn, dull and sooty.

The second ad was out, the woodland scene, and they filmed the third. The client was happy. The response was good. The end of summer and the campaign were combining to drive a real wedge into the market. Some shops had sold out already and were ordering more.

It was nice seeing Philippe again except that he was unpleasant about Carey, whom he had never met. He said he must be a man who enjoyed taking innocents, being the age he was and the age Gossamer was. She was angry and he didn't mention it again. She thought of Helen, Helen Kepesake.

Heat don't go from a colder to a hotter.

Carey invited her to a party at OffWorld. They had been in profit for twelve months and they were going to celebrate. Gossamer was open-mouthed with delight. This was straight into his world from which she had been hitherto excluded. It seemed to give her relationship with Carey the significance she longed for. Perhaps if they had a more conventional life together, their behaviour together might be more conventional. Unless it was. Unless this was the norm. How could she know? She knew no other man intimately and it was hardly something you discussed with anyone.

She pulled herself together. She had friends. She had money. She had a burgeoning career. She was meeting new people all the time. It was her lack of background that made her jumpy, not Carey. She should be moving into all this from some solid suburban home with a proud mum and a cautious dad at her back. There should be envious siblings, a cat and a dog, aunts and uncles. All her life was floated on the surface. She had nothing to keep her up save her own abilities and her nerve. It was as if she poised herself over a chasm, black and empty. She was wrong to blame Carey.

I don't blame him, she thought guiltily. *Why did I think the word blame? No, I tend to focus my worries on him because he is the most important thing in my life. So he frightens me most though he helps me most and he matters most. I've invested too much in him and I know it. I've no safety blanket. Perhaps that's why he stays clear sometimes. Perhaps that's why he's kept the involvement limited. It's damage limitation. He knows I care too much. I have no fall-back. I have no family.*

I might have had Helen Kepesake, she thought. But I can't. Because my lover and my friend's mother were lovers once. Not so long ago. Just before I came on the scene.

What an extraordinary coincidence, her mind said. And how odd and horrible that Carey should have done with her what he does with me. She obviously didn't mind. She took it for normal. It's me. There's something wrong with me. I'm flawed.

Her mind said: *I wonder if Carey knows?*

When he picked her up she felt exhilarated and happy. She wore black because she wanted to look as sophisticated as possible. The dress was sewn with glitter thread and sparkled and shone as she moved.

He brought her a diamond bracelet. He clasped it onto her wrist and kissed her.

'Carey,' she whispered.

'To go with the earrings.'

'Oh, you darling.' She flung her arms round his neck and

kissed his cheek. His smell, the look of him, his sleek rich appearance, excited her. She held back and touched his face. 'You look so handsome,' she said. 'I am lucky.'

'We'd better go.'

They were chauffeur-driven to the OffWorld premises, an extraordinary Art Deco building between Golden Square and Regent Street. It was a haunt of the adworld and small TV companies wanting prestige addresses. Gossamer felt she was swimming in important waters. It didn't matter, it didn't signify, but it was such fun.

As she climbed out of the car her wrist caught fire. She stopped and waited for Carey. 'Should I insure it?' she said. 'It's so fabulous.'

'I've insured it, sweetheart. You don't have to think about that.'

'I love you,' she whispered as they went into the building.

It was his place. The roost he ruled, the dungheap he crowed on, this was it. Everyone here was hired or fired at his command. He had absolute authority.

It didn't show. They were a noisy drunken bunch remarkably lacking in deference. Carey obviously didn't mind. Gossamer realised he had been built in her mind as a monster. Demonstrably it wasn't true.

Damn everyone. She would be fine with Carey if they all kept their noses out of it.

She met the Channel execs, the Finance Director, the programming consultants, the PR men, the secretaries. There was a huge buffet laid out, tables heavy with bottles and cans of drink. There were balloons and party hats for everyone. They were in the atrium of the strange building which grew round them like glass Lego. The lifts were glass and it was like seeing into someone's stomach, the way they went up and down with you able to see the occupants.

Gossamer felt herself looked at. She didn't care. She was looking good, she was making out. She had a right to be Carey's companion.

The wives and husbands of the OffWorld team were readily identifiable. They had saucer eyes. They looked at her too.

Carey was warmly affectionate. There was no abandoning here as he had done at the French Embassy. She went round on his arm and he involved her in his conversations. When the music started he danced with her a couple of times, but it was pop and disco music and he dropped out fairly quickly. The noise got louder, bouncing between the glass walls. The team were certainly having a good time at the firm's expense.

Carey's arm was across her front. She leant back against his chest, very happy. His hand was on her breast. He squeezed it gently. Her eyes were heavy, she adored him, but she felt watched.

She opened her eyes more fully. A square man was watching her intently through the cigarette smoke and swirling lights. He sat there, solidly watching.

She felt embarrassed. It was bit gross, actually, Carey fondling her like this in public. He wasn't drunk, he never got drunk, and she felt a little cheapened. Yet it was thrilling to be so obviously his, his chosen companion.

'Who's that man?' she asked.

'What man, my dear?'

'The one watching me.'

'You can't blame him. You knock spots off every other girl present.'

'Who is he?'

'Ah. Jake Carrington. He's over from the States. You should meet him'

'Why?'

'He's a programming executive. It helps to know people in this game, child. I'll introduce you.' He lifted a finger and Jake stood up and came over.

He sat next to them. 'Jake,' said Carey.

'Good party,' grunted the American. His suit looked a little shiny. He had faintly the air of an ex-cop. In British terms, he looked thuggy.

'This little lady here is Gossamer Fane.'

'Pleased to meet you, Miss Fane.' He put out a hand like a ham and shook hands.

'Miss Fane is in a commercial on TV at the moment. It's making a minor stir.'

'What do you sell?'

'Jeans. French jeans.'

'Hey, is that you? I saw that ad. It's a good ad. You looked terrific.'

He spoke in short spurts without any inflection. He might have been reading from a script.

'Class,' he said and shook his head thoughtfully.

'Miss Fane is just starting her career, of course. She's looking for new directions.'

'I get you.' Now he was nodding. 'You been across the pond, Miss Fane?'

'No. I'd like to.'

'It's pretty good over there. They mince you up good but I guess it's fun, too. You could make out. With those looks, honey, that I'd guarantee.'

She took it he meant to compliment her though she didn't like it.

They were silent for several minutes. She felt a certain tension. Then Jake spoke. 'Sugar,' he said and waited.

'Um, yes?'

'Go powder your nose a moment, huh? I gotta have a word with Mr Lambert here. You give me that?'

'Of course,' said Gossamer stiffly. Really, he was straight out of prohibition. He wasn't real.

She circulated a little and one or two people spoke to her. She ate some prawns and a breaded chicken leg. She saw that Jake and Carey were in earnest conversation.

After a while she drifted back. It would be embarrassing if they sent her off again. And rude of them.

She felt Carey's hand lightly on her shoulder after she sat down. Again she felt the tension between the men. Mostly it came from Jake.

'Gossamer,' said Carey.

'Yes?'

'Mr Carrington would like a word with you. He might be able to help your career. I've said he can use an office upstairs. Is that all right with you?'

'Of course,' she said. She bit her lip. It couldn't be helped. Carey wasn't to know she wasn't interested. Nor was that fair on him. He had introduced her to Jerry Laslo and look where that had taken her. She was being childish.

They went up in one of the glass lifts. Jake had taken her arm which she didn't like but she could hardly do anything about it. She saw the party below them. White faces swam as people looked up. She felt sleazy, going up like this in full view. These lifts were indecent.

In the soft maroon corridor Jake kept a hold of her elbow. 'Along here,' he said. 'We should find one unlocked.'

'It's really very kind of you to trouble, Mr Carrington. My business manager, Marcus . . .'

'We don't need none of that. This is between friends, huh? You, me and Lambert.'

'If you say so.'

He tried a doorhandle. When it opened he slipped inside like a burglar, taking her with him.

There was a table down the centre and chairs drawn up along each side. The large windows faced the back of a hospital covered in fire escapes and scaffolding. Jake didn't put the lights on which was strange but quite a lot of light came in from outside.

'Come over here, sugar.'

She went reluctantly over to the window.

'You are the most succulent piece of tail I've seen in a long time.' He waited.

'Look,' she said hesitantly. Whatever he meant, his manner was offensive. It was more like a proposition than an offer of work.

'I love that cool British look, too. You're some lady. If Lambert hadn't put me on to you, I would never have believed this.'

His hand settled on her arm. Gossamer tried to step back.

'I think you've got the wrong idea,' she said. Her voice rose and wobbled. She was frightened.

'Don't worry,' he said. 'I'm gonna see you right workwise.' His other hand landed on her thigh and moved swiftly up under her dress. He clamped her bottom. He pulled her in to his body and fastened his lips on hers.

She began to fight. He picked her up bodily and dropped her on the carpet. He was down over her instantly. He had his hand up the front of her skirt now, over her sex.

She cried out, struggling hard. His arm flattened her. It was like having an iron bar hold her down. The more she fought, the more he got access to her underparts.

'Not so much noise, baby,' he panted. 'We don't want the troops in.'

She drew breath and screamed. She could hear the noise of the party thundering from the atrium. The music was very loud.

She clawed out for his face. He had torn her panties off now. He had his trousers open and she felt his weight coming on her.

She screamed and screamed. Dizziness overcame her. There was brutality at her groin. The lights came on and suddenly the pressure was off and she was scrabbling frantically backwards.

It was Carey. She turned into his arms on her knees, sobbing and gulping hysterically.

The two men were arguing. She couldn't really hear what they said. 'Get the police,' she gulped. 'It was rape. Get the police.'

Carey had her head pulled in to his shoulder. 'He's gone. It's all right. He's gone. Gossamer, it's all right. Nothing happened.'

She couldn't get air into her lungs. She heaved and wheezed. 'He tried, he tried . . .'

'I know. It's over now, sweetheart. Stop this. Calm down. You're safe.'

She began to cry properly, long shuddering sobs. She tried to get her clothes back together. All the time she cried she kept trying to feel how far he had got when he was interrupted.

Carey knelt holding her. He had her face into his shoulder and he stroked her constantly, soothing her like she was a child. When her crying had calmed to small hiccups he drew her away from him and looked into her face.

She was snivelling, trying to wipe her nose. Her hair was stuck across her face in long damp strands. The diamond bracelet caught in her hair and Carey had to untangle it.

He gave her his handkerchief. His face was bright, his eyes glittery and clear.

'Tell me what happened?'

She hooked a strap back into her shoulder. It was broken and it fell off. She didn't notice, she just kept hooking it back up. In between she blew her nose and gulped down sobs. 'He just grabbed. He hardly said anything. He seemed to think it was OK. He thought I wanted it.'

'But you told him?'

'I fought. Really hard. He held me down. I started screaming. Why didn't he stop?'

'Some men like resistance. He made a mistake. He thought you were playing. This is my fault, Gossamer.'

'Your fault!' She stared at him, aghast.

'We talked about your prospects. I said you were very good, waiting to be discovered. He must have thought you were after the casting couch. Of course, it doesn't work like that over here. For some actresses in the States, it's how they get on.'

She stared at him. 'But I was with you.'

He reached forward and wiped under one eye where her make-up was smudged and running. 'Oh my poor innocent love.'

Her brows drew together. She was panting as if she had run a great race. 'I see,' she said. 'Executive perks. He thought I was house entertainment.'

'Something like that.' Carey gave her a look of guilty amusement. 'He doesn't think it now, pussycat.'

'Tell me, Carey.' She wasn't having humour. 'Is it me

who looks like a tart or is it the tarts who look like me?'

'Baby, it's the same difference. No one can tell them apart these days, not the high class ones.'

'You would know, of course.'

'Oi, oi, oi,' he protested mildly. 'I didn't make the mistake, remember.'

'Mistake, huh. The man tried to rape me. You got here just in time. He wasn't going to stop, Carey.'

'But I did get here in time. He hasn't raped you. It's OK. You've had an ugly experience but there's no real damage done.'

She was profoundly angry. 'I want the police.'

He was silent.

'I want the police, I said.'

'OK. Of course. Whatever you say. May I say something first?'

'Like what?'

'You're very young and not very wise to the world. You're just starting out in a career where image is everything. You project a certain image on TV.'

'Carey!'

'Let me finish. We all know that's acting, that's not the real you. But a complaint to the police is the real you. Go ahead, report Jake Carrington. Doctors will shove things into your vagina. Policemen will ask you how much you led him on, why you came into this room with him. He will lie and say you gave him the go-ahead. I wasn't here at first. I'll say what I saw, that he had attacked you and you were fighting him off, but what happened before that is between the two of you. He's not a stupid man despite this mistake with you. He'll bluff it out. You'll feel terrible and it'll get you nothing except grief. He didn't succeed because I stopped him. There's no material evidence.'

'Look at me,' she whispered. Her dress was torn, her stockings laddered and her arms were bruised. Make-up smeared her face.

'I've let you down,' he said. 'The truth is, I'm not used

to protecting someone so young. I forget. I forget you need looking after.'

She stared at him, unable to pinpoint what was wrong in what he said. 'I'd like to go home,' she said. Her voice shook.

'Listen to me. I'm going to phone for help. We've got to get you out of here without anyone realising what's happened. You must keep a clean reputation at this point.'

'Me?'

'Yes, you. I know it's unfair but that's how these things work, once the sniggering starts. We won't let it. I won't let it. Trust me in this. I'll get someone to bring some clothes and get you out of here. I can't leave, see. It's my party. We must avoid scandal.'

'Why do I feel guilty?'

'Oh love, women usually do. Of course you aren't guilty. Don't feel like that. It isn't your fault at all.'

He took her to his office after first checking the corridor was empty. They went up the fire stairs since they could hardly use the lift to the top floor. He unlocked his office and let her in to his private bathroom. She was barely aware how sumptuous it all was.

Her appearance shocked her. Mechanically she began to repair her face, washing away the traces of her tears. She pinned her dress as best she could. She found the more respectable she made herself look, the worse she felt inside. It was a denial of reality. She didn't want to keep this thing in. She wanted to scream she had been abused, see the man suffer for what he had done and receive proper sympathy for her plight. Instead she was going to be smuggled out of the building like she was a bad smell.

A woman appeared. She was in her fifties, carefully dressed and very smart.

'Miranda. Miss Fane has been attacked. I want you to take her home.'

'Yes, Mr Lambert. You poor dear.'

'Miranda's my personal assistant, Gossamer. She's totally discreet.'

Gossamer's head swivelled between them.

'That's right, my dear. Don't you worry. No one's going to know.'

I want them to know, thought Gossamer. Can't you see, I want everyone to know. I haven't done anything wrong.

A large trenchcoat was put on over her clothes. It came down to her ankles and hid her tattered stockings.

'Look after her,' said Carey. 'She's precious cargo, Miranda.'

'Certainly, Mr Lambert. I'll go right the way home with her. She'll be quite safe with me.'

Gossamer looked back as she was led out of the door. Miranda had an arm firmly across her shoulders. She was shivering inside the borrowed coat.

Carey stood in the middle of his beautiful office, at ease. He was lighting a cigarette. At his back the city glowed jewel-like in the night. He was smiling.

Gossamer suffered herself to be led away.

Miranda took her into her flat. She said she wouldn't leave until Gossamer was in bed. Gossamer had to change in her bathroom, she was damned if she'd get undressed before the woman.

Miranda made her hot milk and put the electric blanket on. 'You'll feel cold,' she said. 'You've had a shock. Now take this pill.'

'What is it?'

'Aspirin. Come on, be a good girl.'

She took it. She slid down on her pillows. In truth, Miranda had made everything warm and comfortable.

Exhaustion came over her in waves. Miranda was still there. 'You work for Carey,' she said weakly.

'The finest boss I've ever had. A real gentleman. Not like s . . .'

She was asleep.

She stayed in bed the next day as though she had 'flu. She lay and shivered and let her mind wander strangely. The Tarot game. Not a game. The cards had told her fortune.

Had they warned how bruising it would all be? Had they told her Fate would knock her about till she was sore and shaking? Was the great voyage of discovery that Shaws had taught her life should be a blind sailing in uncharted waters full of reefs and skerries?

She was making a success of things. She had a man. She had a job. She had friends. She had her health. Why did she feel queer and oppressed, as though now and again someone reached into her life and stirred it, in case it got too calm?

She might look fine but she felt on the edge of the abyss. There were whirlpools ahead. Mother, she said silently. My poor dead mother. Help me. I've ignored you. Always I've called on my father. Forgive me. You died near to when I was born. I hope it wasn't my fault, mother. If it was, forgive me. Please forgive me. Help me now. I feel lost in a maze that everyone says doesn't exist. Am I mad, mother? Is it all my fault?

Tears trickled down her face. Was it all her fault?

Carey phoned. He asked how she was. She knelt on the floor shivering though the central heating was turned fully up. 'I'm all right,' she said through chattering teeth. 'I'm fine. Just dandy. Super.'

'I'll come round. Just let me cancel my appointments.'

'Don't cancel those appointments. I'm fine. Terrific. Really.'

He came half an hour later. She was remorseful. 'I feel so bad,' she whispered.

'He's gone. He's left the country. I told him to get on a damned plane or I'd personally reshape his face.'

'Wow. Really brave. But he looked a slugger, Carey. He might have reshaped yours.'

He looked at her gravely. 'I fight battles to win. Usually I do.'

'Good,' she said at once. She grinned, baring her teeth.

'You're in shock.'

'Never a bit of it. A Shaws girl is in no danger. She can always say no.' Gossamer tittered.

He went away and came back with hot milk and a pill. 'I did this last night,' she confided.

'Miranda told me.'

'Does she often have to rescue hysterical teenagers from your business associates?'

'No. You're the first.'

'I don't like hot milk.'

'It's this or sweet tea.'

'Bully.'

He sat there watching her. The tide lapped higher up the beach. 'Why do I love you, Carey?' she asked presently.

'Because I reveal you to yourself. I've freed your true nature.'

She was asleep.

They didn't make the fourth ad for Jeans de Nîmes. The company was sold out. It was the most successful small campaign ever, one for the record books. Gossamer signed a retainer promising to come back for more ads when they had restocked. The client held a party one afternoon before flying back to Paris.

Jerry Laslo spoke to Gossamer. 'You were terrific,' he said. 'You have real quality. You're so beautiful, so young, so fragile-looking. Yet you have real punch, real sex-appeal. Go carefully, sweetheart. You could get to the top. Don't be greedy now. It's a minefield, this profession. Take care and have good luck. I hope we do business again. You've been good for Tring Laslo.'

Peter Tring was at the party. Privately both he and Jerry thought Gossamer's appeal came from her youth and her experience. That would be Carey Lambert's doing. How she fared would depend on him. If he cut her up as he usually did when he was done with a woman she would be useless.

'I don't know the man at all,' said Peter quietly.

'You don't need to. He's OK with men, actually. With anyone where no sex is involved. Not a bad employer. Remembers favours and repays. He also demands repayment where he thinks it's due. A bad enemy but he doesn't look to make many. It's as though he knows he doesn't have the time to fight on too many fronts. A hard bastard but fair in his way.'

'I take it he's bad to the women he gets involved with.'

'They won't learn, the stupid cows. Look at this little girl. She's illuminated. That's his doing. But he can't leave them intact. He has to spoil them for the next man. So he hurts them. Badly. One woman topped herself.'

'Jesus.'

'This one's looking wobbly. Have you looked into her eyes?'

'Only on screen. Gorgeous. Like a butterfly's wing.'

'She's a knock-out, isn't she. And a sweetheart, too. Heart of gold. A dream to work with. The technical boys love her. Even the client loves her. Very sunny and good-tempered. But she's getting that punch-drunk look Lambert's women get.'

'This isn't physical, is it? Christ, we see her body all the time.'

'No. It's emotional. I don't know what he does but if he tried to get my daughter in his clutches, I'd kill him. Bare hands. I'd rather swing for it than let him have one of mine.'

'Can you warn her?'

'She's been warned. Again and again. You can tell because if anyone mentions him she goes all defensive. You can see her bracing herself. I think it gives him an extra buzz, swimming against the tide.'

'What about mum?'

'I told you. She's an orphan. Little orphan Annie.'

'It's a mess, then.'

'It's a mess.'

❈ Eight ❈

He scooped her up and took her to Xantos for four days. They inhabited a luxury villa loaned to him by a business friend and every day they swam in the silk-warm Aegean, lazed on sandy beaches, went scuba diving, riding and walking. And they ate. Every memory was jewelled and precious. Galloping along a beach side by side, Carey on a great black horse and herself on a smaller chestnut, she felt the world could spin to its end and not hold more bliss than this.

They were sun-drugged and slow, letting each lazy day trickle through their fingers like fine sand. It was a time of cheap wine, fat peaches, whitebait lemony fresh from the sea, coarse brandy, lobster, swordfish and star-thick nights cool and secret with the doings of man and his gods.

She saw ruins old as the volcano on which they played. She ambled up narrow, steep-stepped streets dazzling with sun-tired crumbling stucco and brilliant geranium-red flowers.

She ate grapes misted straight from the vine.

She stood in a church of sonorous sombre glory and knew that its magnificence was in part due to the poverty and simplicity of its people. No wonder then that in green and lawnmowered England the Church had become a shabby furtive thing whining feebly to a God of garden gnomes and family saloons. The dark glory of the Greek Orthodox was foil to the harsh unyielding sun, the stark blaze of Mediterranean light that hurt your eyes and dazzled your mind. Greece ravished you, soul and body.

She slept the languorous nights with limbs heavy from much loving. Carey was gentle, slow, sweet with her. His patient tenderness brought her to starbursts of pleasure.

There was no room for fear in his caresses. Though still he said nothing, no man could have been more loving in his behaviour. He treated her body as something precious and frangible, to be wooed and softly enticed into webs of pleasure. She was holy and it was both his will and his art to worship her.

They flew home to London in the grip of autumn, yellow fogs, acid air and the sour chill from dank gurgling drains. Carey kissed her goodbye and she took a taxi home.

She was unpacking when the phone rang.

'Goss?'

'Yes.'

'It's Jenny. Look, hon, I feel bad. Can you come and get me?'

'What? Now? What do you mean, you feel bad?'

'Sweetie, I'm not up to arguing. I'm on the Embankment just short of Blackfriars Bridge. Bring a taxi. Please. Straightaway.'

She abandoned her cases and ran downstairs. Arthur ordered a taxi and she hopped with impatience out on the steps until it came.

Jenny was sitting looking oddly huddled when Gossamer finally saw her. She was watching the river and Gossamer had to get out of the taxi to attract her attention.

She was deadly white in the face. It was early October but very cold, especially down by the river here. Gossamer found that she wouldn't stand upright but crept across to the taxi and crawled in like a sick beast.

'Should we go to a hospital? For God's sake, Jen, what's wrong?'

'Take me to your place. I'll be fine. I'm just so sore and so tired. I can't go home, Johnny's asleep there and he needs his sleep. Just take me to your place, Goss. A little sleep and sympathy and I'll be fine. Hold my hand.'

To Gossamer's horror she rested her head on her friend's shoulder and wept silently all the way back.

She dragged herself upright to get past Arthur and Gossamer helped her once they were in the lift. Inside,

Jenny leant against the wall of the sitting room, trembling.

'Could you help me to bed, Goss? I swear I'll be all right. I just need to lie down and be warm. I can't get warm. Can you turn the heating up here? Our flat's so cold and I can't get warm.'

Gossamer slung her cases off the bed and smoothed it. She put extra blankets over the duvet and switched on the electric blanket. She helped Jenny off with her coat and shoes and led her over to the bed.

'This is a terrible thing to do to you.' Tears rolled down Jenny's cheeks.

'If you don't tell me what's wrong I'm calling a doctor.'

Jenny lay in the bed with the covers heaped over her. Her white skin looked tight and stretched over the bones of her face. Her hair was damp and dirty.

'I couldn't tell him,' she whispered hoarsely. 'You do understand?'

'Tell him what? Can I get you something? A hot drink? An aspirin?'

'Not aspirin.' Jenny tittered. 'Brandy. Do you have any brandy? And paracetamol. Not aspirin.'

Gossamer did as she asked. Jenny sipped the brandy eagerly and then screwed up her face. 'Christ, it hurts.' She gave Gossamer a sly twisted look. 'I'm being punished.'

'Tell me. Or it's the doctor. Maybe it's the doctor anyway.'

'No. Not necessary despite appearances. Goss, I got pregnant.'

'Oh God.'

'We take precautions. I wasn't on the pill but we always took precautions. Not good enough. I guessed, see. Obviously. So I bought a kit for testing myself. Positive. Then I sent off to one of those labs. Positive. I couldn't tell Johnny. I couldn't tell anyone.'

'Why not? He loves you. Look what you've done for him.'

'Because he'd leave the Uni. He'd feel he had to. He'd

marry me and get a job. A proper job. A proper awful job that goes nowhere. We couldn't have that, now. He's going to be a professor, Goss. Perhaps in America. We'll have a good life, you see. But he has to have his chance. So I didn't tell him.'

'What have you done?'

'You know what I've done. They said it would hurt and it does. Just for a while. They told me to take paracetamol and it would all be over.'

'Backstreet? They could kill you. You stupid cow!'

'Don't be silly. £400 and Harley Street. One horrid doc with fat clean fingers and dreadful hard shiny metal things. Such a cold business, Goss. The cold's inside me now. I'll never be warm in there again. And a nurse who swallows starch. So clean. So quick. In and out, pop goes the weasel. But the pain! I can't stand it.' She whimpered and the tears slid down her cheeks again. 'Let me rest here,' she whispered. 'When I can hide it I'll go home to Johnny. He mustn't know. Promise you won't tell him?'

She heard Arthur buzzing her. She went slowly to answer. She didn't know what to do. It was too much responsibility. She was ignorant.

It was Carey. Gossamer felt a flood of simple relief. When he came in she caught him by his lapels in her tiny hall.

'What is it?' He was tanned from their brief holiday. His eyes glowed brightly.

'Jenny's here. She's had an abortion. She's in a terrible state. I don't know what to do. She doesn't want Johnny to know. She's done it for him, see.'

His face went shuttered and calm. He slipped his coat off and came into the sitting room.

'In my bed.'

They went round the angle of the room to where the bed was. Jenny lay burrowed under the covers.

Carey went up and sat on the edge of the bed. He laid a hand on Jenny's brow. It was white and oily. She stared up at him, her blue eyes dull in the bruised sockets.

He felt her pulse, saying nothing.

'Jennifer.' When he did speak, his voice was unexpectedly commanding. It wasn't rough or harsh. It was filled with authority. Gossamer felt the knots beginning to untie in her stomach. He was coping. It would be all right. The correct decision would be made.

'I'm going to take a look.'

'No.'

'Yes. Where was this?'

'Harley Street. A Doctor Fitchley.'

'How long did he take?'

'Ten minutes. They gave me a cup of tea afterwards but I sicked it up.'

'Then you were out?'

'They called me a taxi.'

'How long ago?'

'At three. I don't know what the time is now.'

While he spoke he rolled the covers back, prised Jenny's legs apart and took a quick look. Gossamer turned away. There was blood on Jenny's thighs.

Carey covered the girl again. 'I'm going to put you in a clinic.'

'No.' Terror came over Jenny's face. 'Johnny. And mother. They mustn't know.'

'They won't. We'll have a story. Don't worry about that just now. I'm going to phone. Gossamer, sort her out some night things and a toothbrush and so on.'

'Yes.'

He took a card out of his wallet and dialled. He spoke quickly and clearly. Then he came back to the girls. 'Gossamer, tell Arthur an ambulance is coming for your friend. They'll need a stretcher. Collect anything you want. We must go with her.'

'They said I'd be all right.' Jenny was crying weakly. 'Don't do this.'

'Listen.' Carey leant over her and stared down into the drained exhausted face. 'I'll make it all right. You must have proper medical attention or you'll never have those babies you and Johnny want one day. Think of that. It's a gynaecological clinic. They fix anything in that region and there are a dozen other things we can say this is. No one will doubt us. Now tell me what painkillers you've had so I can tell the doctors when we arrive.'

He took her hand and held it. Jenny looked up into his face and smiled weakly. 'Thank you,' she whispered. She shut her eyes and lay there till the ambulance came, holding his hand, trusting him.

They went together in the ambulance, Carey holding Jenny's hand and Gossamer carrying her things. When they arrived they were shown into a private room and then Gossamer and Carey were shooed out. Nurses closed round Jenny and the door shut.

Carey had a long talk to a doctor who then went into the room. Gossamer and Carey went to sit in a waiting room. It had large leather armchairs and heaps of glossy fat magazines. Carey went off to phone to cancel his appointments. Then he came back.

They waited quietly together for an hour. The doctor came and talked to Carey out of Gossamer's hearing. They went together to an office where Carey signed some documents.

'She'll sleep for several hours now,' said the doctor, leaning back. 'Is there a number where we can reach you for when she comes round? She'll appreciate company.'

Gossamer gave him her phone number and he wrote this down. 'You want flowers?' he asked, looking up.

'Flowers?'

'For her room.' He was patient.

'Yes. Yes, of course.' Numbly Gossamer handed over her credit card. She signed a receipt for £50.

The doctor's eyes flickered. 'She's in to have two venereal warts removed. Unpleasant but not serious. We make a speciality of turning our ladies out looking pretty. She'll appreciate friends, fruit, chocs, flowers, books, magazines and so on. A little pampering at this stage does wonders for the recovery. We'll keep her in for a couple of days, I think. All the pretty things you can bring her.' His lizard eyes settled on Gossamer again. She nodded. He was young and looked terrifyingly competent. 'Who's the boyfriend?' he asked. 'Will he come?'

'Oh yes,' said Gossamer huskily. 'He doesn't know.'

'No,' said the doctor. He looked at Carey. 'Well, make him come.'

'Yes.'

They left together. Carey hired a taxi and took her to Bambino's. He bought her a brandy.

'I should be home for when they ring.'

'Just get yourself calmed down first.'

'Yes. Carey, thank you so much.'

He grinned and lit a cigarette. 'But how unpleasant of me to know what to do.'

'I'm glad you know what to do.' Her voice was still husky. She looked solemnly into his eyes.

'You realise it's another nail in the coffin of my reputation.'

'I don't understand.'

'They'll do what they're being paid to do. Nothing will cling to Jenny of this. But the whisper will go round. I've got another girl into trouble and then ditched her.'

She stared. 'Is this how it is? All of the stories?'

'Of course not. Don't be naïve. These things happen and they happen to me. No one tells me the stories, you see. So they get exaggerated. They have little unpleasant frills added on. Things nothing to do with me are blamed on me. I'm the fall guy, hadn't you realised?'

'Why?'

'Gossip. Innuendo. Jealousy.' He bared his teeth. 'Women like me, Gossamer. I can't serve them all. I don't want to. Some of them get a little angry. A little malicious. It's easy to believe what you want to believe in circumstances like that.'

'I'm glad you knew what to do today,' said Gossamer steadily. 'Will you let me field the bill for the clinic?'

He gave a shout of laughter. 'Will I hell. I know your resources are good, darling, but believe me this would stretch them. Such service comes dear. Let's say it's a present to a friend, and the daughter of a friend.'

* * *

Carolyn Carstairs was a casting director with DayStar. The DayStar *Friends* channel was going to launch a soap. It had been scripted and Carolyn was appointed to cast it.

Carolyn was a tough lady used to the TV world and adept at making out in Medialand. She enjoyed her job and was fairly ruthless at it. She knew it was early days for satellite TV. She saw it as a nineties phenomenon, in the sense that TV had taken Britain by storm in the sixties, then colour TV had replaced monochrome in the seventies. The eighties had seen the video take command. Now it was time to move forward again. She could see a day coming when viewers made their own channels by accessing a 'programme bank' so that they could enjoy their chosen soaps, game shows, drama and documentaries as and when it suited them. Already 'smart' TVs were being designed that 'learnt' their owner's tastes. Meanwhile they had to channel-hop to choose and choice was the buzzword.

The first satellite soap was going to be set in a commuter village to give a nice mix of rural locals and whizzkid urban business types. For the snob appeal there would also be the big house and its inhabitants. The execs had dubbed it Alice in Agaland but the official title was *Dragon Hurst*. It was ambiguously set in Surrex. Or Sussey.

Carolyn had had an ongoing relationship with John Carleton for four years. They shared a mortgage in Kensal Green. Carolyn came in daily to the DayStar offices in Wapping. John travelled south of the river to the Elephant Studios in the New Kent Road. These were owned by Dayfield Promotions so that in the end both John and Carolyn worked for the same boss, but it didn't feel like that.

It was John who told Carolyn about Gossamer. He had directed the Jeans de Nîmes ads. He had been very taken with the good-humoured hard-working model. She made no fuss, she sported no airs and graces and she was a darling to look at. They'd all liked her. She had a good voice, though the ad hadn't used it.

Carolyn was having trouble casting Cresta, the daughter of

the big house. The role was small as written at present, they had made the pilots without it, but if they got someone good and it went over well it would be expanded. She was to create sexual havoc in the village so she had to be a looker.

Gossamer sounded ideal. She was the right age. She was a newcomer. She was unknown. She looked good. All that remained was to see whether she had enough acting ability in her.

Carolyn rapidly found out Marcus Wainwright was the man to contact. She asked him to wheel the girl along for an audition. She made sure she sounded very disparaging. There was no point in raising false hopes if the girl didn't come across well, and there was no point in needlessly upping the price if the girl did come over as well as she had in the ads. She checked the girl wasn't tied up. But Gossamer was free.

Marcus got on to Gossamer and told her what he'd fixed. He was quite a kindly man and he told her not to get her hopes up too high. It was nice to have them sniffing round you, he'd expected the ad to produce work, but not everything came off first time. The thing was, she would be on the books. Even if she didn't get this part she might find she came to the top of the list for something else later on.

Gossamer had no professional acting training and didn't set her hopes very high either. DayStar was non-Equity so that was no problem. Regardless of how she got on it was nice to be asked and even moving on the fringes of TV was exciting.

It was very different from the audition for the ad. There was no one else. She appeared to have been asked alone. She waited in the reception area for a hair-raising fifteen minutes before a smart young woman appeared. She approached Gossamer who stood up nervously.

'Gossamer Fane?'

'Yes. Are you Ms Carstairs?'

'I'm Trudi, her PA. Can you come with me now?'

They walked upstairs, Gossamer following meekly after Trudi who had nothing to say to her. They went along a corridor. She had a momentary thrill when she recognised a man pushing past her as the main evening newsreader. DayStar devoted a whole channel to news and news-related programmes. *Friends*, the channel that was going to make the soap, was all about comfort TV, light escapist drama and sit-com. It aimed to be cheerful and just a shade cosy. It was marketed for the viewer who might instead have read a thriller or a crime novel. It wasn't stupid but it wasn't demanding.

There was also a movie channel but all the films were bought in.

Trudi bustled into a room and gestured Gossamer to sit down. She sat down. There was a table with three chairs along one side next to a wall. There was a window with a fire escape going across it. There were two armchairs, one of which Gossamer sat on. There was an empty tea trolley behind the door.

Gossamer waited. She decided she preferred the adland approach. It was cheerier. Her stomach was in knots and she was beginning to want the loo.

Three people swept importantly into the room followed by Trudi. A short woman with narrow shoulders and a big bust seemed to be in charge. 'Trudi,' she roared over her shoulder. 'Coffee for four. That OK for you, Miss Fane?'

'Yes, thank you.'

'I'm Carolyn Carstairs. This is Piers Roebuck and Jeremy St John. Has Trudi given you a script?'

'Er, no.'

'Take mine,' said Piers and unexpectedly smiled. He had a gold tooth.

The script was enormous. Gossamer sat limply with it.

'Page 74,' said Carolyn. 'Cresta. Has anyone explained?'

'Not really.'

'She's eighteen. Posh, good school, mummy and daddy own the big house in the village and a small estate attached to it. A bit of a wild one, rebellious, likes a bit of rough, not above getting it in the village. No Sloane Ranger, darling. It's *passé*.'

'Right.' Gossamer was bewildered. She waited for her
sense of humour to assert itself. It didn't. She wanted
the part.

'Daddy's a businessman. Venture capitalist. There might
have been hankypanky between him and Cresta when she
was young, if we think the viewers will take it. Where's that
damned coffee?'

'It's coming, Caro.' This was Jeremy.

'Thank God. I'm dry as Thatcher's knickers. Are you
a prude?'

Gossamer was startled. Carolyn was a tricky one. 'I'm not
likely to admit to it if I am,' she said.

'You looked torrid in those jeans. Can you do it again?'

'Look torrid? Of course.'

'Look torrid with Jeremy. No. Piers. You might find
it easier.'

Gossamer stood up and put down her bag and the script.
She slid out of her coat. She wore a short-sleeved black
mohair cardigan buttoned up across her front and black
denim knee-length shorts. Piers came over to her loosening
his tie. For a moment he stood in front of her.

She looked at his neck. She opened her nostrils and inhaled
the man-smell of him. She thought about wanting him. She
remembered wanting Carey. Then she had got him. She had
got him. She felt the triumph of the thing blaze in her. She
looked up, her eyes slightly narrowed, smiling at Piers. She
hardly saw him. Her chest was heaving slightly. Her lips
parted. She felt his hands come gently on her arms. They
ran down the soft fluffy mohair and onto her bare forearms.
He stroked her gently.

She lifted her face, letting her lips curve. She moved into
him and very gently brushed against his groin. His hands
came up and onto her shoulders as she clasped his waist
lightly under his jacket. She could feel his body through
his shirt.

Her head went back. Her eyelids half closed. She felt him
press against her as he held her more firmly. He bent his
head to kiss her.

'Cut.' Carolyn was amused. 'Ten out of ten, children, but no exchange of body fluids. You know the rules.'

Gossamer stepped back. Piers was grinning, tightening his tie. She sat down.

Jeremy handed round the coffee. 'Now,' said Carolyn, putting on her glasses. 'Page seventy-four. From the top. Piers, you read Jimmy. I'll read Sandra. Jerry, do Phelps, there's a sweetie.'

They read it three times. Gossamer knew sharply that this was what she wanted to do. She wanted to act. When Carolyn told them to stop, she felt exhausted.

Carolyn looked at her watch. 'OK, love. Thanks for coming in. We'll be in touch. I'll get Trudi to show you out.' She swept out of the room with the men behind her. Gossamer still had the script. She didn't know whether that meant anything or not.

A week later Marcus phoned and congratulated her.

She had had no idea of the work involved. They read scripts in the morning, rehearsed in the afternoon and went for a take the next day. Everything was out of sequence but they were expected to know all their lines at all times. They did outside scenes with everybody in a frightful temper and they did studio scenes to a background of barely controlled rage.

She bought a car, a white XR2 convertible, so she could get quickly to and from work. She learnt her lines at all hours of the night and day. She made mistakes, got bawled out and carried on. Much of the time she hadn't the least idea what the scene was about. She was sure it was awful. The meal breaks were an enormous relief, the food was stupendously good and it was only at these breaks she had a chance to get to know the rest of the cast.

They worked too hard to throw tantrums. On Sundays she slept and learnt lines. Marcus handled all the money side of it and she was assured she had sold herself into slavery. Her contract had her tied so tight she had to ask permission to breathe. Marcus told her not to worry, it was the usual thing.

She surfaced at Christmas with a week off. They had twelve episodes in the can and twelve to go. Initially it was planned as a bi-weekly and they wanted three months in hand.

Her part was small. They had rewritten ahead of her and increased it, as they had one or two other parts which came over well. When Gossamer saw the finished product she could hardly believe it. It didn't look bad at all. She already respected many in the cast for their dedication and tireless hard work. Now she saw how professional they were.

She went out with Carey maybe once a week or every ten days. He would normally accompany her home and make love to her. He still wouldn't stay the night. Jenny looked much better and with term restarted, she and Johnny came out once or twice in the evening. Jenny was a student herself now though she said her course was nonsense. Gossamer spent a weekend with them once. She also took to going to the specialist movie-houses in London with Anthony. They were looking for the world's worst dubbed movie and had several hot contenders.

The Times announced the engagement of Miss Marie Horden-Smith, only daughter of Charles and Teresa Horden-Smith, to Ivor Peter Gaynsford Spence, second son of Sir Cecil and Lady Davinia Spence.

They all went to the party.

Carey took her to Florida for Christmas. She won £1,000 in the hotel casino. She bought him a set of Scarfe originals for Christmas and had them framed. He bought her a diamond collar.

She came home to the drizzling misery of London in January and caught a stupendous cold. The studio was furious and unable to do a thing. She couldn't be Cresta with a big red nose.

Operation Desert Storm was launched.

She recovered. They filmed all her bits to catch up. Now they had eighteen episodes in the can.

In February the director called them all together, the whole cast at once.

'You've been fantastic, boys and girls,' he said. 'We're on a winner here and we all know it. I know you're tired but you can have a rest soon, when we start screening. I've got the date for that. March the fifth, that's a Tuesday. We'll be screening Tuesdays and Thursdays. Forever, or until they get tired of us or we drop dead.'

Everyone dutifully laughed.

'So we have something to celebrate. DayStar are going to do us proud. We're their first soap and we need to be successful. So there'll be a big launch party here at the studios shortly. I'll give you the firm date as soon as I have it. Wives and husbands, boyfriends and girlfriends welcome, no one else, darlings. Don't drive to it unless you're teetotal. Alec Dayfield might come himself to pat you on the head. Asbestos wigs will not be regarded as funny.'

They had two days off before the launch party. Gossamer arranged to meet some of the cast in town first. They would have a preliminary few drinks and then move on to Wapping. They all felt a need to fortify themselves. As the initial screening got closer, they became more and more nervous. It was so easy to pan soaps. No one knew how long Alec Dayfield would continue to fund them if they were badly received. His reputation was that he was ruthless with lossmakers. He tolerated them for so long and then he cut the lifeline. His whole satellite operation was a lossmaker but the amount of loss per week was gradually declining. The financial projections were good, if he could carry the debt that long.

He was not a predictable man.

She wore a deep cherry dress in soft seductive velvet. It clung to her curves and emphasised every aspect of her femininity. She had a creamy feather boa to drape over her shoulders. She didn't wear Carey's bracelet or collar. They seemed too ostentatious for such an occasion. Essentially it was fun, not formality, that would set the keynote.

She wore the diamond earrings though. She loved these

with a guilty passion and they seemed truly hers in a way the other jewellery did not.

She had passed her nineteenth birthday in December. She was surprised Carey knew it. She didn't think she had ever told him. But he did know it and he remembered.

He bought her a fur. She protested it wasn't done anymore, the environmentalists made so much fuss. He laughed and said it was ranched not wild mink and she wore leather shoes, didn't she?

The fur was heavenly. Life was heavenly. Everyone was happy. It was like the Tarot, it had all worked out. Her bad times were behind her. She had not allowed anyone to put her off Carey and he was more charming and attentive than ever.

Mostly. Just once or twice the devil got into him and his love-making became almost abusive, so that she shook afterwards and felt violated. He was capable of an extreme emotional violence and now and again he lashed out with it. Each time she rocked and came back upright again. She could only hope the occasions were getting fewer and shorter. She was so busy in the Wapping studios it was easy not to think about it when it happened. Yet one or two of the cast noticed and commented the next day, as if she was ill. It showed when he hurt her. It took time to recover.

They met in Bambino's and drank pink gins. There were five of them, Piers, Gossamer herself, two girls who played sisters in the village and the man who played the publican of the Dragon Arms. For some reason he was always known as General Lee.

They shared a taxi out to DayStar. Gossamer felt on top of the world. They were held up by a bomb scare and when they arrived they were told by the doorman to go through to Studio Three.

It was the *Dragon Hurst* set. Space had been cleared and all the technical stuff pulled back. The food was laid out. Music had been hired and because the bomb had made them late it was already in full swing. General Lee, who admitted to fifty, swept Gossamer into the crowd and they danced together.

A lot of the execs were there, huddled anxiously in corners talking. Being big in Medialand was perpetually exhausting as they fought and jostled for position. They listened to gossip, read the runes, gazed listlessly at their teabags and all but eviscerated chickens. Alec Dayfield was a great hirer and firer and he believed in creative conflict among the higher echelons of his staff. He was a surprisingly hands-on man for one at the top of such a vast empire. He took a childlike delight in his businesses and would go among them and play if he felt like it. A bow-wave of anxiety greeted these forays and sacked execs bobbed about like debris in his wake.

None of this concerned Gossamer, the lowest of the low. She danced, chattered, ate and drank. She fended off a few passes but she wasn't overly troubled. She had made her stance clear weeks ago and the rovers had turned to more rewarding game.

She became aware of a ripple through the party. A man had come in, not very tall, wide at the shoulder, with a flock of execs fluttering round him.

He was smoking a cigar. He seemed not to mind the obsequious bobbings of his underlings. She was surprised at how young he was. Carey had said there was not much difference in their ages. This man looked mid-forties, that was all. He looked well on it, too.

He was accompanied by a languid beauty who looked as if she had left New Orleans the day before. Gossamer recognised her from the newspapers. Her name was Carlotta Natchez and she had been seen in the company of MPs and Cabinet Ministers.

General Lee was at her shoulder. 'The Biloxi Babe, they call her,' he hissed. 'They say you can smell the mangroves when she opens her legs.'

'Stop it,' she chided, but she was amused. Cottontails and Spanish Moss, the lady looked too good to be true. 'I bet she's from Birmingham really.'

The General snorted with laughter. 'I gather you don't mean Birmingham, Alabama.'

The party got rowdier. Alec Dayfield danced with his

southern beauty and one or two of the senior female executives. Photographers and gossip columnists had come in with his entourage. There were occasional bright flashes as they snapped couples. This party would pay for itself. It was good advance publicity for the launch.

Gossamer shimmied, tangoed and all but break-danced. She had long stopped drinking and was now sweating the booze off. She felt marvellous.

Malling Benedict was there, talking to Alec Dayfield. Their heads were together, Alec stooping to come down to the height of the little man with the wizened legs. Alec looked up and clicked his fingers. Carlotta wafted over and took the Pope off to dance.

It was funny to think this man had sacked Carey. Then he had stolen his business. Now she worked for him, though the chain of command was huge between her humble position and his eminence.

He had something in his hand. Not a drink. He was leafing through something. The media writer from the *Mail* was looking over his arm. The men were laughing. Another one joined them. Alec straightened up and passed what was in his hand.

The men crowded, looking.

Now Alec was looking up, looking around. He signalled the *Dragon Hurst* director over. The music thundered and shuddered off the huge walls.

Gossamer was standing sipping a mineral water. Her hair was wet underneath, she had been dancing so hard. She held it up from her neck and drank her water.

Micky Grossman, the director, wasn't finding whatever it was funny. He staggered slightly and eased his collar. He stared round the studio as though he'd just been told he had a month to live.

Alec spoke to him. Micky licked his lips, jerking with nerves.

What was wrong? Was he being sacked? Was this how the legendary wolf picked off his sheep?

Someone fetched Carolyn. She came over with her man,

John Carleton. Gossamer knew that this was the man who had suggested her name to Carolyn.

They talked with Alec Dayfield. Caro was angry and standing upright, defending herself. Dear heavens, were they all being sacked? Alec Dayfield hadn't stopped smiling the whole time.

Carlotta came back with Pope Benedict. Whatever it was was given to her. She looked at it with Pope Benedict smiling beside her.

Clear across the room Gossamer heard her shriek of laughter. The tall dark girl turned round. Her sloe eyes searched the room. Then she pointed.

Almost everyone not terminally drunk knew something was happening now. Even the music became slightly uncertain. Carlotta had stopped pointing but Gossamer felt turned to stone. There was a clear line of sight between her and Alec Dayfield. He was looking at her.

Alec spoke to Micky. Then he took back whatever it was and slipped it in his pocket. He turned on his heel and left the studio. Micky, the director, came over to Gossamer.

She was aware of people looking at her, of titters, of broad looks. She stood with her heart thumping, wondering what on earth it could all be about.

Micky reached her. 'Gossamer,' he said roughly.

'Micky?' The man was shaking. He looked shocked and livid.

'Dayfield wants to see you. Right now. He's in my office. Go now.'

She felt a slow anger burn. 'And if I don't?'

'Don't be stupid. You cow, how could you do this to me? Go and see him. He told me to tell you.'

'Not until you tell me what this is about.'

'Oh fuck off, darling. I've had all the grief I'm going to take from you.'

He turned away. Gossamer stood there alone.

Piers came over. He took her elbow. 'Nice and simple, dearie,' he said. 'Just straight through the crowd and don't look to your right or your left.'

'What's going on, Piers?'

'They found it funny at first till the implications sank in. We might all be for it, darling, all because of you being naughty. So chin up and let's go see the bossman. Try to save the rest of us, Gossamer. We've all worked very hard on this.'

He steered her through the crowd. They were staring now, not laughing. There was a rumble of anger.

She stumbled. Piers was setting a fast pace and she was in high heels. They got across the studio at last and she came out through the soundproof doors.

'That's as far as I go,' said Piers. 'On you go like a good girlie. Go and see the boss like he says.'

She went up in the lift alone. She knew where Micky's office was though she had hardly ever been there. By the time she reached his door she had combed her hair and tidied her face. She lifted her chin. She didn't know what was ahead of her but she would face it with dignity.

Micky's office was full. There was an angry argument going on. It stopped abruptly as she appeared. They parted like the Red Sea. She saw Alec Dayfield. He had lit another cigar.

He looked at her framed in the doorway. 'I tell you what,' he said. They were the first words she had heard him say. Everyone else was silent.

He had a deep voice. 'I'll see the little lady somewhere else. Get me a decent office. I can't sit down in this rathole. Spending money usually makes me feel good. Tonight for some reason it makes me feel tired.'

She was hustled along the corridor. She went up in the lift with him and two of his entourage whom she didn't know. No one said anything. They had a building guard with them and he hurried ahead, the keys clinking at his waist. He unlocked a senior executive office, not belonging to DayStar but part of the parent company itself, the Dayfield Corporation. It was Marty Louvine's. He was the finance director, a very important man and not known to Gossamer at all.

She found herself suddenly alone with Alec Dayfield. The

office was a sea of pale grey carpet. The desk was vast and very neatly organised. The windows gave onto the river. There was no fire escape across them.

Alec Dayfield sat down. He swivelled in Marty Louvine's chair thoughtfully. He blew cigar smoke.

Gossamer stood there. She had no idea what to do or say. She could feel the man's power. She felt like a day-old chick between the cat's paws.

He reached out and showed a claw. 'You got much money, Miss Fane?'

'Some.' She was startled.

'Good. Because I'm having the boys pull your contract. There's a penalty clause for what you've done. I think I'll invoke it.'

'I don't know what I've done,' she said stiffly.

He studied her. He had very dark blue eyes, cold as steel. 'You got an agent?'

'A business manager.'

'Did he give you any advice about this game? I gather from Caro Carstairs this is your first job in TV.'

'I don't know what you're talking about.'

He stood up and reached into his jacket pocket. He took out something. It was what they had all been looking at. He put it down on the empty clean desk top and gestured for Gossamer to take a look.

They were photographs. Curiously she moved forward. She picked them up.

They were warm and soft from much handling. Her face jerked unpleasantly when she saw the subject of them. She couldn't control her sensation of disgust and shock, though she knew he wanted her to feel these feelings.

Was this a lead-up to some line? What the hell was going on?

The pictures showed a woman and man together. They were explicit. They were very lewd. The woman lay on her back with her legs drawn up and wide open, exposing herself to the camera. Another showed her face in close-up with the man's sex in her mouth. One showed her from the back, kneeling, holding herself open. Again the man was there, poised to accept her open invitation.

Gossamer began to shake. She felt her blood drain. Something hammered in her ears. Her hands were palsied. Mechanically she shuffled through them.

They were pornography, and she was the woman in them. She was the one lewdly exposing herself, engaging in unnatural practices. The man's face was never shown. He was merely a penis on camera, entering or about to enter her, above and below, before and behind.

The filthy things slid from her hands onto the lovely chinchilla carpet. She fell forward and stopped herself, her arms stiff, her hands on the edge of the desk. She lifted her face slowly and stared open-mouthed at Alec Dayfield. She was aware her nose was running. She couldn't do anything about it. She just leant, propped on the desk. She stared at him aghast, her nose dribbling.

He spoke quite gently. 'Chickens come home to roost, sweetheart?'

She couldn't speak.

'No one explain to you there are things you can and can't do, if you want to be on TV? Were you that hard-up, darling? Jeeze, it's gonna cost you some.'

Suddenly her silence irritated him. 'You been dropping something? Why don't you speak? Wipe your fucking nose.'

He meant drugs. There had been tabs downstairs but she always steered clear of all that. Gossamer groped in her bag and found a tissue. She wiped her nose.

He leant forward. The light caught the planes of his face. He looked hard and angry.

'You've jeopardised the whole show. We might have to pull it. I've spent frigging millions on this. All those good people downstairs who've worked so hard will be out on their arses. Because of you. Jesus! We've got the whole fucking media here tonight. They've all seen.'

She found her voice. 'They can't print this,' she whispered.

'No.' He shook his head irritably. 'They can write about it

though. You're out, lady. Forever. You can be a whore like Carlotta. Maybe you already are. But you can't work legit. No way, sister. And you've screwed me. You've screwed me good. That's an achievement, by the way. There's not many do that and certainly there ain't no other nineteen-year-old whore who's done it.'

'I'm not a whore.'

'No?' He wasn't interested. 'Tomorrow Micky will come in here with the writers and the editors and they'll see what they can do. They'll cut you right out. Caro's gonna see if she can get someone new. They'll have to reshoot every scene you've been in. You bitch. If they can't do it, the whole show's off the road. Because of you, you horny bitch.'

'I'm not a whore. I didn't know these pictures existed.'

'You didn't see the camera? I know you've screwed me, but don't make me out to be stupid too.' He laughed. 'You'll get to recognise cameras, no bother. They'll come mob-handed tomorrow. You'll be monstered by the tabloids, sweetie. Make what you can out of them. I'm going to take it all off you for the damage you've done to the production. We have a personal behaviour clause, you know. Maybe you didn't read the fine print.'

'I'm not a whore. My lover took these. I thought they were for him alone.'

He looked at her steadily. After a while he said: 'If that's true, you're some unlucky. You've got to learn to pick them better.'

She gasped suddenly and looked round blindly. She needed to sit down.

He stood up and came round the desk. He sat on one corner and smoked his cigar peacefully.

'There is one way out of it,' he observed.

She stared at him. If she didn't cry she would burst. But she couldn't. She was dry. And empty.

'You look a mess now but I've seen your ads. I've seen some of what you've done in this crappy soap. I saw you earlier tonight before I got the snaps.' He paused. His face was cold, his tone level. 'You've made your choice now whether you meant to or not. There's no going back. You've dropped a lot of good people in the shit. But you have something. You're a lovely piece. Not too bright, that's obvious, but dim women never troubled me. Look at Carlotta.' He grinned. He looked quite different. Then it was gone. 'You're very young. You've got one hell of a lot of tread in your tyres yet you're nicely run in. Jeeze!' he snorted suddenly with laughter. 'You can't be that ignorant. The tricks this guy's had you play put you up with the big league, baby. I only play this naughty once in a blue moon myself. It's not really my taste. You knew what you were doing, all right. This wasn't the boyfriend you took home to mama. No girlie your age does these things with a man unless she's being paid good for it. Much older than you, was he?'

She nodded wordlessly.

'You crazy dame. Do you understand what I'm saying?'

'No,' she said huskily. She couldn't take much more of this.

'I'll take you on. I can ride out the gossip. I don't give two shits about what the papers say. I live mostly in New York anyway.'

'Take me on. What d'you mean?' She was bewildered. He was going to sue her for endangering the production. Was that what he meant by taking her on?

He stared at her coldly. 'I'm a very rich man,' he said. 'I'm not married. Contrary to popular belief I'm rather nice to my lady friends.' He snickered. 'It's my soft underbelly, you might say. I'm not too demanding. I don't expect you to perform shit like this. All I ask is that you don't go with anyone else while we have a thing going. I'm astonishingly faithful. You play right by me and you can come out of this mess OK on a personal level. I'm noted for generous redundancy pay.'

'You mean sex,' she said blankly.

She stood up. She lurched over to him. The photos lay face up on the floor. She looked down at them. Then she hit him across the face.

He caught her wrist after the blow. For a long moment they faced each other, him sitting on the desk, her standing by him. One side of his face reddened slowly.

'You get it wrong all the way down the line,' he said.

'Let me go.'

'You hell-cat. Christ, you're beautiful.' He let her go. She rubbed her wrist and backed off, watching him.

'You can have everything,' she said. 'I've got quite a lot of money. You can have it all. I've got some very expensive diamonds, too. You can have them.' She groped suddenly at her ears. She began unscrewing her earrings. She got impatient and tore at them. Her lobes began to bleed. She threw the earrings across the room. They made a hard sound hitting the window.

A red drop appeared on the silver carpet at her feet. It was as though her dress had turned to liquid and was dripping.

'I'll instruct my business manager accordingly. And my lawyers. I'm sorry about the cast. I cared about them. I'm sorry I've let them down.'

She turned and blundered over to the door. The tears were coming at last.

Somehow he was at the door before her. 'Tell Micky I'm sorry,' she said huskily. Tears and blood fell from her face.

'Look here.' His tone was quite different. 'Are you putting me on?'

'Get out of my way before I spit in your face,' she said. 'You foul-mouthed scum.'

She had the door open. She stumbled out into the corridor.

Beyond the building it was night. It was all night. Gossamer ran into it and the night swallowed her up.

Grief was a luxury. There was no time now for its seductive embrace. Gossamer took a taxi home. There was a lot to do.

Her mind was working curiously well. It was already three in the morning so she was safe for some hours yet. This wouldn't be in the papers yet.

She began to strip her flat. She had a trunk from her schooldays and all her lovely clothes and personal things went in that. Her practical everyday clothes, jeans, shirts, jumpers, she put in a suitcase. Rapidly she sorted her documentation. It came to her how lightly she travelled through life, how uncluttered by the past she was.

She showered and changed, throwing the cherry velvet dress in the bin.

She sat down to write the letter to Chatteris Choate. She made her instructions very clear. They were to cancel the flat and have someone clear it out. They should put her things in store and deal with DayStar. She accepted her guilt and that her personal behaviour had endangered the production and they were to act accordingly. She gave them full power of attorney. The mink coat and the diamond jewellery were to be sold against the settlement with DayStar. She considered that a moment and then crossed out the bit about the diamond jewellery.

She left a message on Marcus Wainwright's answerphone. She said simply she was sorry and he should contact Chatteris Choate. She was in breach of her contract with DayStar and accepted her guilt in the matter.

She wrapped up the diamond collar and bracelet in brown paper and parcel-taped it firm. She addressed it to Alec Dayfield personally at Dayfield Promotions, using the Wapping address.

At six in the morning she carried her one lightly packed case downstairs. Silvio fetched her car for her. For the first time she saw he had books spread out everywhere. It seemed he was studying for a law degree.

She hadn't known.

London was already awake. She drove till she saw the first post box and posted the letter with her apartment key in it to Chatteris Choate. She shoved the parcel in too. She had bought stamps from Silvio.

She drove to her bank and drew out money in cash. Then she deposited her luggage. The drive back into town took a long time because she was tangled with the rush hour now.

She drove to Lincoln's Inn. Here she slowed, cruising. When she saw what she wanted she stopped on the double yellow line and got out. She ignored the angry horns behind her.

They were a couple. They were pinched with cold and lethargically busy packing up their cardboard and sheet-plastic home.

'Here, you,' she said roughly.

They turned to look her, immediately hostile.

'Has either of you got a driving licence?' She was fumbling in her bag.

'What's it to you?'

'Have you?'

The girl answered. 'Yeah. He has.'

'Right. The white car. It's yours. Here's the papers. Tell me your name and I'll sign it over to you.'

'Why?'

'My affair.'

A policeman was strolling towards them. 'Good,' said Gossamer. 'He can be a witness you aren't stealing it. Put your stuff in it quick so you don't start by being done for parking.'

Again it was the girl who reacted first. The man seemed dumbfounded.

The policeman reached them. Gossamer wrote down his number.

'What's happening?' he asked. 'This your car?'

'It's mine. You're a witness. I'm giving it to this couple of my own free will. Here, see, I've got all the papers, the insurance, everything. They can do what they like with it. It's worth a lot.'

'I think you'd better come along to the station.'

'No. I'm doing nothing illegal except parking and I'm going now.' She bundled the couple and herself into the car.

'Wait a minute,' said the policeman.

'You'll have to arrest me. I'm not committing a crime. It's my property and I can give it away.' She pulled out into the traffic.

The first place she could, she stopped. Hastily she completed the registration document and signed it. She gave the man permission to drive on her insurance. 'I should sell it today,' she said. 'Don't get robbed.' She still had the receipt from buying the car and she gave this to him.

'Why?' he said. 'And why us?'

'Why not?' she responded. 'Life's not fair, is it? You have to take it when it kicks you in the teeth. This is a drop in the ocean as far as you're concerned. Life'll go on being bloody, don't you worry.'

They stared at her as she walked away, her bag over her shoulder.

'Thank you,' the girl suddenly shouted. 'And bless you.'

She lifted a hand. She didn't bother looking back.

She sat in a café drinking coffee and writing postcards. Trish. Jenny. Anthony. Just to say goodbye.

Then she took a taxi to OffWorld.

The receptionist wasn't having any. Strange girls off the street didn't get an appointment with the chief executive just for asking.

'Contact Miranda, his secretary,' said Gossamer patiently. 'Tell her it's Miss Fane. And it's very urgent.'

He was in a meeting. She waited. The building hummed around her, warm and bright. People came and went. The morning wore on.

Finally she was told she could go upstairs.

She felt very calm now. She felt transparent, too. People couldn't see her, she was sure. She was insubstantial, floating by them, not of their world at all.

Her own reality had gone.

It took an achingly long time but at last she was in Carey's gorgeous office facing him.

'This is a pleasure,' he said genially. He sat at his desk. He hadn't come round to greet her. 'I can only give you ten minutes, Gossamer. I'm keeping my next one waiting.'

'I don't know where to start,' she said.

'The beginning?'

'A year ago? No. Why do you do it?'

'Do what?'

'Maim things.'

'I'm not with you.'

'Yes, you are. What is it in you that makes you destroy good things? Why can't you be happy? Are you what's called a sadist?'

He was tense now, very alert and bright-eyed. 'What's brought this on?' he asked.

'I think the time for games has passed. Which of the journalists did you give the photos to, Carey? And why? What have I done to you? Why do you hate me?'

'I don't hate you. On the contrary. I'd never have gone this far if you hadn't been so delectable. Sadist I might be, but I'm no masochist.'

It should have been a relief that he confessed so easily. That it wasn't meant she had been hoping somehow it wasn't true. He would explain things. He had yet the power to make everything right.

But of course he was guilty. There was no escape. Things were as they looked to be.

'I knew you had the devil in you,' she said slowly. 'I didn't know you were the devil.'

'Huh!' He was delighted. 'Lucifer himself? I think not. But I take the compliment.'

'You're sick,' she said queerly.

'Actually no. My motives were really quite pedestrian and very logical. You don't understand that, of course. You see yourself as the important thing, naturally enough. You are a pawn, my dear. You aren't the business at all.'

'The pawn in what? What were your motives?'

'I didn't choose you. Fate did that, sweetie. You are who you are and that can't be bucked. Helen told me about you. Jenny's poor little friend. We were in bed together at the time, I seem to remember. Mind you, that's the only place I ever went with Helen. Not much between the ears. All that patient suffering because of naughty old Geoff. We call him Peter Pan, you know.'

'Peter Pan?'

'He collects lost boys.' Carey smiled, inviting her to share the joke.

'Who am I?'

'That would be telling. The joke isn't over yet. What are you going to do?'

'I've been sacked. They're reshooting my bits with a new actress.'

'Dammit. I've been hasty. I thought they were too far on.'

'You wanted to hurt the production, not me? You mean this is business games?'

He had his head on one side, watching her like a bird. It occurred to her he was enjoying himself.

'You mean you sacrificed me for some trivial business advantage?' She stared at him, puzzled. 'Wait a minute. You're getting tired of me. You wanted shot of me. You thought you'd put it to good use.'

'Bravo. Well done.'

'What if I hadn't got a job with a rival? Would you have smashed my career then?'

'Probably not. I get bored, Gossamer. People are so gullible. It staggers me how easily you can push them around. You had ample evidence I was rotten. People kept telling you to keep clear of me. You were constantly warned and told to take care. And I hurt you. In little ways but I hurt you. Still you took no notice. You wouldn't believe it. You wouldn't accept they were right, you were wrong and I was bad. I am bad, Gossamer. But you invited it. Women usually do.'

'You're saying this is my fault?'

'I have my nature, Gossamer, and you have yours. Mine is sadistic. Yours is very sexual. I satisfied that in you. Instead of some callow fumbling boy you had an expert. I gave you a very good time in bed. Now if you enjoyed that so much you were prepared to put up with all the shit I gave you, then I have to say yes, it was your fault.'

'I loved you! I truly loved you. I hoped you would change.'

He got up and came round the desk. 'You kid yourself. You don't know me. You're just a little slut, don't you know that? A damn good one, to be sure. A really classy piece of ass, once you'd worked out what to do with it. Thanks to me, since we're talking about using people. Because that's what you did, of course, you liked me being someone in the world, you liked showing me off to your feeble friends. You got a kick out of being with me and why don't you just admit it? Let's have some honesty here. I've treated you badly because you liked it. It made you feel holy. I was a cause. You're made for it, Gossamer. You're sex in a wimple. All that dewy-eyed freshness on the surface and hotter'n hell underneath. It's a magic combination. Accept you're a whore and go out and enjoy it. I've liberated you, sweetheart. I've broken you from that bloody school, that bloody prissy upbringing. You'll make far more as a lady of the town than you'll ever make on lousy TV soaps.'

She gasped. 'Alec Dayfield offered to take me to America. He said I could be his mistress.'

She had brought him up cold. He stood stock still, staring at her. The golden mask slipped and she saw the raw man, thinking.

'Sweet charity,' he whispered. 'I never anticipated that. Of course. Even I can forget just what a piece you are. I'm used to you. You're very special, Gossamer and you mustn't forget it. Don't undervalue yourself. I've given you a terrific start. You accepted?'

With a kind of joy she finally felt the anger surge in her. It had been missing all this time. She needed its strength.

'No,' she said, exulting. 'You've had me dancing in hoops, Carey, but no more. I don't accept what you say. I'm not what you accuse me of. You're handing me a line, passing the blame to me. Don't elevate this into our true natures and all that crap. You're a very nasty man who likes to hurt women. There's nothing more to it than that. I'm young and I was gullible. But you played me like a fish. You were lovely to me for months. Then every time you were nasty, you were extra nice afterwards. You are scum, you really are. You aren't clever, you're just spiteful, like a child who knows no better. You've got something missing the rest of us have and you can't bear it. You have to make us out to be wrong but in your heart of hearts, you know it's you. Heart of darkness, Carey. Oh yes. A rotten mess of a man, a—'

'That's enough.'

He reached her with two swift strides. He grabbed her hair and yanked it back so hard she thought her neck was broken. He rammed a handkerchief in her mouth. He spun her round and put his arm across her neck. She gurgled and choked, unable to breathe with the gag and the pressure on her windpipe. His hand fumbled at her belt. She fought to get her airways free. He yanked her jeans down and thrust her savagely forward. Her face landed in an armchair.

She knew what he intended and it was too late. Her hands flailed helplessly. She felt his flesh enter hers. She couldn't scream, she couldn't breathe, she couldn't fight his strength.

The rape was quick. She felt herself released. She slid to her knees, pulling the gag out, tears streaking her cheeks. She stood up with her back to him, pulling her trousers into place.

She turned round. Her voice wouldn't work properly. 'I'm going to the police,' she rasped. 'I've got the evidence in me.'

'You do that. You do that, you stupid whore. You've been my companion for months. There are those photographs. I added to them, by the way. And good ol' Jake Carrington will testify how you led him on and slapped him back at the last moment. You're a prick teaser. Don't think you can catch me, darling. I'm just a bit ahead of you in this game.'

'I hate you,' she said.

He straightened up and smiled. He smoothed his hair back and checked his watch. 'I really have to go,' he said with mock apology in his voice. 'It's really been fun.'

She wiped her face. She picked up her bag. She struggled to control her breathing. 'But most of all I pity you,' she said.

'Hah! That's an exit line. I admire you for coming up

with one in the circumstances. Goodbye, darling. Hang loose.'

She stumbled over to the door.

'I should take up Dayfield's offer,' he called.

She went out. She made her way unseeingly downstairs. She walked out of the building. She hailed the first empty taxi she saw.

'Where to, miss?' The cab driver looked at her blearily.

'Heathrow,' she said. 'Take me to Heathrow.'

❖ AFRICA ❖

✴ Nine ✴

Each morning for a week she came out onto her balcony at sunrise. The vast inverted bowl of light above her shimmered with a soft brilliance, a mother-of-pearl purity that was both beneficent and cleansing.

Below her mists rose from the heated earth into the cool morning air. Shapes loomed in the mist, exotic and mysterious. Mud hovels and minarets, hotel towers and church domes reared skywards and between them, like inverted feather dusters, tree tops hung limp feathered fronds in the damp air.

The birds were first. Shrill indignant squeals, low chirring chuck-chuck-chucks and echoing piercing shrieks came seemingly at random through the shivery-still hollow air of dawn.

East of the town were low breast-shaped hills. Between them the sky glowed. Gradually it stained a pale red as though an artist's wet brush wiped softly across it. The silhouetted hill-slopes were tree-frilled, delicate as lace. Into the red-swimming space rose the shimmering gold coin of the sun.

Memory tugged for Gossamer, gold against red. So long ago. So far away.

Now there were human sounds as the city awoke and scratched its armpits. Roosters crowed. Chickens clucked. Donkeys honked indignantly. Clanking bicycles made a surreal passage through the mist-veiled streets. A car revved noisily expressing its importance, its value. The street boys laughed under her window and she smelled a thousand cooking fires. Goats baa-ed, their bells clonking disdainfully.

The sun swelled higher, hardening and firming the uncertain sky into its customary blue. The mist turned to faint wisps and vanished puffily upwards. The sun flooded warm everywhere. Noise and chatter and traffic filled the streets and piazzas below.

Gossamer turned into her hotel bedroom to get dressed before breakfasting. This was her holiday, a week in the north before she flew back to Addis and from there made her way on south to the village where she was working. She had wanted to come to Gondar and see the palaces and the castles. She had found the ruins to be inhabited only by the ghosts of past kings and one last sad caged lion. She had roamed silent and absorbed with tourists, through the ceremonial gates and on into the royal compound between the basalt walls. It was strangely European, this one-time abode of Ethiopian emperors, and it was very old. The other tourists had cast curious eyes at her, young and so self-contained, but she ignored them, refusing to swap confidences, entire of herself and alone.

Being there pressed like a weight on her shoulders. The past was so mysterious. They had taught her it was primitive and they were so utterly wrong. She walked with thick curtains obscuring her vision of how things had been. The dazzle of modern life blinded her in her own country. In Africa a wind of truth lifted the corner of the curtain sometimes, to afford her tantalising glimpses of that shared, infinitely complex heritage.

They were Christians, these Ethiopians. Yet it was their Church that she found so incomprehensibly alien. So many people came. There was so much noise and bustle. Worship was so emotional and public. Her English soul shuddered and shrank. She had been bred to a religion that was personal, essentially private and potentially embarrassing. This communal display of emotion was akin to using a lavatory in public.

She could enjoy it as a spectacle, though. The kneeling crowds shouted and wept. The priests bawled and swung censers. It was like witnessing a mystery play done on the grand scale with lots of feeling. Mediaeval Europe must have been like this, colourful and entertaining, before Lutheran gloom had cast its pall and taken the zest out of life and worship.

It was all very strange, very exotic. Yet the longer she stayed the more she saw that these people were Londoners like the ones she had left behind. They were certainly poorer, they were friendlier and they were noisier, but she was sure they had exactly the same propensities for thieving, for cruelty and for goodness as did the people she had lived among at home.

It had taken her a long time to get here. She hadn't known where she was going when she had left London blindly, in such pain. She had travelled slowly and as she gradually made Africa her destination, she had had to arrange visas and vaccinations. Latterly she had had to have work permits. But that was good. She was finding her feet. She had made a new life for herself and given herself time to recover.

She was sorry to be leaving Gondar and she wanted to go north but there was political trouble in Tigre and Eritrea and it wasn't permitted. She took a taxi to the airport, it took a day and half by road to get to Addis, and she was driven past the itinerant priests who patrolled the all-weather roads begging for alms. There were vast numbers of them in the country dressed in their leather hats and full-length robes. They wore heavy ornate crosses and all carried gorgeous great fly whisks. It was not a rich church, the Ethiopian Orthodox, and she was used now to the upturned umbrellas held out to catch money flung by passing motorists.

The plane carried not only passengers but an alarming amount of livestock crammed protestingly into bags and sacks. It was a relief to arrive safely. The heat in Addis hit her with physical force. The air was thin so high above sea-level, and she found it hard to breathe. Her heart thumped unpleasantly in her chest. The rains still hadn't come, they were over a month late, and people were becoming scratchy and ill-tempered.

She could book her hotel from just by where she collected

her luggage. She was tired now. She got one of the cheap blue taxis but despite her coming in from an internal flight the driver treated her like a tourist, taking her up Menelik Avenue and past the Grand Palace before delivering her to her hotel in the Piazza. She sat in the corner of the back seat idly fanning herself with her hat while he chattered on about the sights they passed. The cracked leather seats sweated and stank. She wasn't very fond of Addis.

Yet it was good to see the blue-green groves of eucalyptus again, planted everywhere to provide a city with firewood. She would remember the smell of them forever, she thought, and it would be an affectionate memory.

Ethiopia! Getting here had been quite an achievement. She could laugh at herself for feeling proud that she had done it. She still had a curl of excitement at being in this extraordinary and amazing corner of the world. The trouble with London was that it made you feel nowhere else mattered. Here life was friendly, battered and grubby. It was cluttered with its own past. The future trembled excitingly like a new day about to dawn. It was all so alive, so brightly coloured.

They came to the modern heart of the city. Here were the hotels and office blocks and supermarkets. It was as familiar and tasteless as any city centre at home so that grotesquely, even though she didn't like it, she was moved. Only the sun was foreign.

Most of the time she was fine. She tried to keep busy. But at other times a great loneliness swept over her like a vast sea and she felt she was drowning. Unable to bear London, she had left, running away if truth be told, but in so doing she had left her friends behind.

She had an urge to belong, natural enough in anyone but exacerbated for her by her orphaned upbringing. It distorted her judgment and made her vulnerable. She must learn to manage for herself, emotionally. She must learn not to depend on other people.

It was a bitter lesson. It was cruel that she had to learn it so young. She had never had a family. Was she never to have the security of acceptance either?

Above all she must not feel sorry for herself. Self-pity was annihilation of the soul. She must not succumb. This war-torn, drought-damaged country with its endemic problems of poverty, disease, the need for education, it would bring her own petty problems into perspective. Disaster here had a scope and a majesty that was breathtakingly awful. It did her good to work in such an environment.

She had a day or so of luxury left before going back to her village. She had a little shopping to do, to restock her medical supplies and to buy another shirt and pair of trousers as well as humble necessities like soap, washing powder, chlorine tablets and salt tablets, but that was all easy and familiar stuff. She would be able to get some novels here in English, it was the main language of the country though Amharic was widely spoken, and that would be a great luxury too.

She was too tired to notice anything odd that evening, going to bed soon after her evening meal of roast veal, cabbage and *crème caramel*. She had already grown to prefer the local dish of *wott* and *injera*, the hot pepper stew and sour-batter pancake, but it would be insulting to tell the hotel staff so. They were proud of their European cuisine.

It was over breakfast she first heard the tense mutterings between people and saw how heads gathered over the newspapers. She ignored it, going out about her business, but it was brought home to her that something was wrong when she heard distant shots at lunchtime.

The centre of Addis was full of tiny iridescent beetles that day, their wing cases open as they found footing on the dazzling concrete walls of the modern buildings. It was as though the building material was impregnated with emerald chips, brilliant spots of green fire.

The man in the pharmacy selling her toothpaste told her the students were demonstrating again and the government was tired of it. There was word of riots. He would barricade his shop windows soon. It was all very bad for business.

She would be leaving Addis tomorrow. She had nothing to worry about. It was just sad, that was all, sad and violent.

In the night she heard dull thumps and explosions.

The hotel staff were definitely jumpy the next morning. Outside on the pavements it was uncanny. All the street boys were gone. The roads were quiet, even the angry buzzing of the taxis temporarily stilled.

Gossamer considered what to do. She could phone the British Embassy for advice, or even go there. It was a nice enough walk past the Cathedral and onto Fikre Mariam where the eucalyptus gave a scented shade as you passed. But it hardly seemed necessary. She was leaving Addis. The trouble was with University students. She would be safe once she was outside the city.

She packed up and settled her bill. As she was doing this, a man approached her.

'Excuse me.' His voice was civil and educated. Gossamer turned to look at him. She had just been going to ask the receptionist to get her a taxi to take her to the bus station.

He was English, about thirty she thought. He wore the usual safari shirt and bush trousers that most Europeans wore travelling in Africa, that she herself was wearing.

'Are you Miss Fane?'

She almost physically reared back from him. A kind of dreadful sick fear invaded her and she knew quite sharply that her instinct to flee had been good. She could not have borne to stay in England.

'Why?' she asked coldly. She was sure he was a journalist.

'I was in Jinka last week. I had to come up to Addis and they told me to stay in this hotel. I said I'd be back and they suggested I look out for you, if you are Miss Fane. You'd be returning from up-country about now. I've got a Landrover and they said the bus wasn't a great deal, not if you could avoid it.

Gossamer relaxed, feeling almost dizzy. She smiled dazzlingly to make up for her coldness. 'You were in Jinka? That's some coincidence.'

'But a happy one, it seems. If you'd like a lift, you're welcome. This city feels distinctly uncomfortable to me.'

'Yes. I gather the students are rioting. Was it Father Berhanu who said I'd be here?'

'It was the Oxfam lady. Jean Tennant. She said you wouldn't enjoy the bus. Once was an experience, she said, but any more was unnecessary.' He grinned.

He had good white teeth. He wasn't very tanned, he couldn't have been in the country long, but with his brown hair and brown eyes he should take the sun quite easily. He had a stocky competent look about him. If he lacked experience driving in this country, he looked as though he would be a quick learner. Jean had thought him safe enough and it was true, she would be very glad of a lift back to Jinka. It was a marvellous piece of luck.

'Well, the truth is I'd be more than grateful,' she said. 'When do you want to leave? I'm ready whenever you are, but I can get my room back if you aren't finished here yet.'

'I'd like fine to go. I would have stayed but I don't like places where the police are shooting their guns off on the street.'

'No,' agreed Gossamer and shuddered.

'Give me an hour. OK? I'll meet you here.'

'Yes. Look, what about food? Do you want me to get something in? And some beer, maybe.'

'I'll see to that. And I'll see you later.'

Abruptly he was gone.

Gossamer ordered tea and settled in the foyer. Not an exciting man but he had an aura of toughness about him that was reassuring. He carried that faint indefinable air of success, too. Whatever he was, a journalist, a safari organiser, a UN official, he was on his way upwards. She couldn't imagine him trailing a wife and children either. He looked too independent for that.

They had two days coming up confined in a vehicle together. She would know if her guesses were right or wrong soon enough.

Leaving Addis Ababa was frightening. Normally the dual carriageway cut a swathe through the busy markets but on

this morning everything was silent with no crowds in sight.
Traffic crawled nose-to-tail. There wasn't that much of it but
there was some kind of obstruction ahead. Police occasionally
appeared, several of them at a time in open jeeps carrying
rifles, driving past the long line of lorries and cars on the
Bole Road.

His name was Mike. 'How long you been in this country?'
he said quietly after ten minutes of slow crawling. The big
Mercedes lorry ahead of them was driven by an Italian who
kept shouting out of his window in Amharic. It didn't seem
to make any difference.

'A few months.'

'Is it always like this?'

'I've been here several times. The place was packed,
everyone going about their business. The traffic ran fine
except for the occasional goat or donkey getting raffled up
in it.' They were passing a huge petrol depot. Its compound
was empty and the big wire fence around it was obviously
padlocked shut. Even the bars were closed, and the *duka*
groceries. The sun shone down balefully. Heat shimmered on
the tarmac. The air was uneasy and crackled with tension.

'You haven't been here long yourself, then?' It was the
obvious conclusion to draw from his question to her.

'Newly arrived.'

'Do you mind my asking why you went to Jinka?'

'I'm a writer. I roam about.'

She had thought of him in some tougher occupation.
He might be an engineer, for example. Or, she suddenly
thought, a smuggler. A gun-runner. He might be ignorant
of their current circumstances but his air of self-sufficiency
was unimpaired.

It was a road-block set up by the police. In Jinka the local
police were friendly to a fault, amiable card-playing men
always happy to extend official business to include a beer
or three. Here there was a sense of threat.

'Where are you going?' asked the man at Mike's open
window. His voice was rough and contemptuous.

'Soddu.'

'Lemme see your papers.'

In silence Mike handed over his passport and authorisations.

'This lady your wife?'

'She's a friend. I'm giving her a lift.'

'Where to?'

'Soddu.'

Gossamer handed over her passport and travel authorisation. 'I'm helping in a school in Jinka,' she said quietly. She smiled at the stone-faced policeman. 'I've had a holiday in Gondar. I'm on my way back to the school. This gentleman offered me a lift because he's going the same way. Or I would have been on the bus.'

'No bus,' said the policeman with an air of finality.

'Mike,' said Gossamer with an air of friendliness. 'See if the policeman would like a can of beer. It's hot work for a day like this.'

Mike's head swung slowly and she met his eyes. She smiled into them, willing him to understand. He mustn't offend the policeman's dignity. There was no room for anger or pride here, except on the part of the man whose country it was. They were the intruders, not he.

'Sure,' said Mike easily. He fished in his breast pocket and took out a packet of Gauloises. He tapped two out and lit them both, offering one to the policeman. It was accepted in stony silence as he continued to check their papers. Mike then pulled some beer forward. He put it on the dash and opened a couple of cans. The policeman reached in without seeming to lift his eyes, put a can to his mouth and with an apparently open throat emptied the entire contents down. Still without looking he put the can back in the cab.

Two vehicles behind them, someone honked impatiently. With magisterial slowness their policeman looked up. They had a lorry behind them and couldn't see what the vehicle was, but now its driver descended and strode forward.

'*Qu'est-ce qui se passe?*' he demanded. 'Why are we stopped.'

'I don't know,' said Mike.

'You are English?'

'Yes.'

'I am Swiss. There are five of us. We wish to proceed. Why do they hold us up?'

Several brusque sentences in Amharic from the policeman had an utterly clear meaning. He followed them up by prodding the Swiss overlander in the chest, signalling him back to his vehicle.

'I've done nothing wrong,' said the Swiss angrily. 'Does he not speak English?'

Gossamer leant across Mike. 'Calm down,' she said. 'He does speak English. Your behaviour is offensive and you are causing trouble. You must have patience.'

The Swiss stared at her, his blue eyes popping slightly. Gossamer remembered that it wasn't so long ago that Swiss women couldn't vote. He didn't like the policeman and he didn't like being told off by her. The situation was ridiculous.

Another policeman had swaggered up. Their man closed their papers and handed them back to Mike. 'You go now,' he said. 'The hotel in Soddu is very good.'

Mike switched on and engaged first gear. A third policeman had come across from the jeep and the little Swiss confronted them like a Bantam cockerel. The lorry behind them was waved through with complete indifference. At the last moment their policeman looked up and met their eyes. A broad grin split his face and he winked.

In Mike's mirror they could see the police had moved the Swiss overlanders to one side and were preparing to make them empty their crowded vehicle of its entire contents for a detailed and leisurely search. Then the road straightened again and they could see only the vehicle behind them.

Gossamer said nothing. They were passing clusters of false bananas, the giant leaves split and tattered and covered with road dust. They looked like a small child's attempt to draw giant turnips. Between them and the omnipresent eucalyptus were crazy wooden shacks of varying sizes and shapes with improbable names like Shanghai Suzy and Hotel de Romance. In one or two the upstairs shutters were open and heavy-eyed girls peered out.

'They won't get much trade today,' observed Mike.

Gossamer gave a guilty giggle. 'That Swiss did us a good turn,' she said.

Mike shrugged. 'You tried to warn him. You obviously know how to behave here.'

It was strange being the one who knew how to behave. 'Up to a point,' said Gossamer. She fell silent. Now they were driving through fields of parched barley. The rains were late and urgently needed. Usually June to September this area ran with liquid mud, she had been told. It was bad news that it was so dry.

In the distance was a line of blue mountains. On their right rose a lonely volcano, a pimple in a flat plain with a church on the top. The immediate area was flattish descending into the rift from the high plateau. The air was crystal clear. The dun plains shimmered faintly. The traffic had spread out to its customary sparseness and they were making good time, the Landrover running smoothly. There was an atmosphere of customary calm. Gradually the neurotic air of the city fell away from them.

Mike drove silently for some time. Once or twice he looked at her but that was the only uncomfortable thing. He seemed to be relaxed. Gossamer watched the road, the scenery, the occasional village and Mike's forearm, steady on the wheel by her side. He had turned back his shirt sleeves and she could see the dark springing hair over the pale skin. He certainly hadn't been in Africa long.

As they descended further into the rift valley it grew hotter and hotter. They took the fork in the road to Shashamanne. It was still a tarmac all-weather road and when they came close to the waters of Lake Zwai, Mike pulled up. Thorn acacia and msasa trees provided roadside shade. He climbed out of the cab with relief and wiped his neck. 'You mind if we take a break?' he asked.

They ate fresh fruit, being hungry for nothing else. Flies buzzed and they flapped them drowsily away. A herd boy driving cattle to water in the lake came by, his stick balanced across his shoulders and his hands dangling nonchalantly over each end. Further along the road a man lay in the shade like themselves, by a stack of charcoal which was for sale. They had just passed a straggling village with donkeys, chickens, goats and Coca Cola signs. Further along the road would be another one. Yet it was peaceful. The tensions of Addis were hard to recall in this rural somnolence.

Mike chewed a grass stem. 'You like this place?' he asked.

Gossamer looked upwards through her closed eyelids. They swam veined and purplish. 'I needed a change,' she said easily. She opened her eyes and found he was looking at her again.

She was used to men looking at her. She was sufficiently exotic to appeal across national borders, to more than one cultural type. It was easy to believe that at least one of her parents had not been English. Even here where tribal custom had ritualised women's beauty into something quite specific, she knew she aroused speculative glances. Strolling in the Mercato in Addis where tribespeople came from all over the country wearing their local dress, she still found it easier to wear a shawl over her head. It diminished her western arrogance somehow. She became at once less individual, more integrated.

Mike wasn't looking at her like that. There was nothing lascivious or sexual in his look. Rather it was as if he was considering her. She was a specimen. She was worthy of a certain cool interest as an oddity, but nothing more. And nothing personal.

'Say when you want to go,' she said. She heard her own voice, husky and low. She rose to her feet and found the water. She took off the cap and wiped the rim. She handed it to Mike.

He took a long drink, wiped it and gave it back to her. She decided that he had the most neutral face she had ever seen.

They got back into the Landrover. The cab was sweltering

and Gossamer eased her shirt from where it stuck to her body. The hotel in Soddu was good, she knew. She could shower tonight and change.

They were stopped again in Shashamanne, among the shacks, shanties and the stink of poor sanitation. Jean had warned Gossamer that this town had a reputation for squalor almost unparalleled in the country, and it was true. It was curious because they were near to a spa with natural hot springs traditionally enjoyed by the ruling family. Now they were held up here while the police searched the Landrover.

They made no objection, squatting quietly in the dust and drinking beer while they waited. Rastafarians went by, they were settled locally, so that bizarrely she thought of Notting Hill. On her way north Gossamer had seen a street market in full swing so that one barely noticed the town for women gay in beads, decorated headdresses and elaborate colourful necklaces. These were Galla people, darker and broader of feature than the Amhar to the north. The whole place had been bustling with colour and life, squealing animals, heaps of produce, people laughing and drinking.

Opposite the police compound, a tin balanced on the end of a stick indicated a bar. The sign was broken and a reek of paraffin floated out into the stifling air droning with flies. Further along a butcher had a street stall with lumps of meat hanging on big hooks. They were black with flies. Now and again he negligently whisked at them.

They were released and went on through heavily populated farmland in ominous silence. After a while Gossamer said: 'I don't understand it. I haven't been in the country long but it hasn't been like this at all. I wish I'd phoned the Embassy in Addis. You'd almost think something was going on.'

'Wouldn't you,' Mike agreed. 'Can you phone these people you're going to, in Jinka?'

'No. The school has no phone. Probably the only phone in the village is the one the police have, unless they still use radio. I don't know.'

'You teach at the school?'

She was used to his laconic questions now. 'I'm no teacher,' she said. 'Father Berhanu does that. I help out. You know, I sharpen the pencils, clean the blackboard, listen to the little ones read.'

'How d'you get the job?'

'It's not a job in that sense. I don't get paid though I get somewhere to stay. I met Jean Tennant in Assab. That's on the Red Sea. She was coming to work here for Oxfam and she told me there'd be something to do. I came on with her. I wanted to stay in the country for a while and it seemed a good idea.'

'You're just drifting?' Again he gave her that sideways look.

She was annoyed suddenly. He had offered almost no information about himself and she had had the courtesy not to ask. 'I'm working,' she said stonily. 'Like you.'

'Right.' He fell silent again.

It was at the hotel in Soddu that they had their first real information. The hilltop town was shrouded in a damp mist. Mike took the Landrover to refuel after dropping Gossamer to book their rooms. She had offered to contribute to his fuel costs and been politely rejected.

She had stayed here before. Tadessa, an Amhar in this Galla region, was a friendly man who remembered her. He was inclined to chat.

'It is the Ogaden,' he said. 'The Somali have crossed our border and the nomads are roused. Even those Danakil brigands are sharpening their knives. The government is upset.' He clicked his tongue and smiled at Gossamer roguishly. 'As are we all,' he added. 'War is not good for business, unless your business is war.'

'There was trouble with the students in Addis Ababa,' she said.

'There is always trouble with the students. Young men are young men the world over.'

'Do you know how serious all this is?' asked Gossamer.

For a moment his face was hard. 'For foreigners, you mean.'

She had the grace to feel ashamed. 'For everyone.'

He shrugged. 'Time will tell,' he said. 'It is in God's hands.'

She passed this information on to Mike and they listened to the BBC Africa Service that night but nothing was said beyond a mention of the police firing on students in Addis.

They ate in silence. Soon after the meal Gossamer excused herself and went to bed.

A cold man. Pleasant manners but nothing more. He was one of the most contained people she had ever met, in stark contrast to the Africans she had become friendly with since staying in Jinka. Whatever went on in his head he kept there, unwilling or unable to let it out.

Maybe he filed all the information that came his way in some mental filofax, to be reproduced as local colour in a piece of future work. She didn't know and she didn't care. She would be seeing Jean tomorrow evening, busy kindly uninquisitive Jean who was running a local health programme in Jinka. And Father Berhanu. He would be glad to see her back.

It was good knowing she was useful, knowing she helped. As medicine for a broken heart, it was the best.

She woke in the night hearing the rain. It fell in heavy sheets, solid water that rattled on the tin roof and gurgled down past her window. The temperature plummeted and she felt cold. The whole world seemed turned to rain and she lay in the cold damp darkness hearing the deluge. Africa had such mightiness. The sheer scale of life here was so different. Curiously it comforted her. She was an ant scurrying on the surface of the world, busy about her affairs. But her affairs were only important in ant terms. She must remember that when the misery came on her again, when the bleakness descended and froze her soul.

It was a hundred and fifty miles to Jinka from here and there was no all-weather road. If the rains persisted it would take closer to two days than one. She would be finding out quite a lot about Mike, how well he could drive, how he behaved under adversity. Mud was a great leveller. This thought made her grin and despite her shivers she fell asleep again.

The morning brought a sky of palest blue, a demure curtseying colour so meek and sweet you felt sure butter wouldn't melt in its mouth. Black kites wheeled in it. Gossamer had seen them in Addis. Here they were gilded in the soft melting air.

'I hope the road's all right,' said Mike at breakfast. 'It seemed mostly dry earth to me on the way north.'

'I believe it can be difficult,' said Gossamer carefully. Father Berhanu had told her hair-raising stories of hours spent slopping around in a slithering mud soup.

'It might have been local rain,' said Mike optimistically. 'And it's sunny enough now.'

Gossamer had her doubts. It didn't feel like the hard hot African sun to her. It was more like a warm English spring day. Indeed, she felt homesick as she saw the brilliant green of the soaked vegetation after they set off. The world steamed faintly in the insect-humming air.

The road wasn't too bad to begin with. Gradually the ruts became deeper and the Landrover started to slither on the fine black clay. The road went up and down and looped round corners. On their left the land rose to a mountain range. On their right, to the west, lay a network of lush river valleys intersecting high areas of dry bush, white in the sunlight. Occasionally it was possible to glimpse movement. Gossamer had been told there were kudu, hartebeest, Grant's gazelle, even ostrich out here, but she didn't know how to tell one from the other. She reckoned she'd have a sporting chance with an ostrich, but that was about it.

Mike pulled up. 'That river wasn't there on the way up.' He sounded aggrieved. It crossed their road in a turbulent brown flow. They would have to ford it.

'It'll be a shingle bottom, won't it? I remember seeing fans of stones across the road. This must be how they get there.'

'You'd better be right.'

Mike pushed the vehicle at the water. It sloshed through throwing up a large bow-wave. But the tyres gripped and then they were up and out of the water slithering on their way.

They had a long, goodish stretch. The villages they drove through now were poor. She became aware Mike was tiring. The Landrover shuddered and jumped and the steering wheel must be hurting the muscles of his arms unless he was used to this. She didn't think he was. He was concentrating grimly, his dark hair pushed back and his eyes narrowed. There was no need for sunglasses. The sun was veiled and soft.

They rounded a bend. The wheels sank and span. They began to slide sideways down the hill. Mike wrestled futilely with the steering. They slid gracefully into a set of deep ruts and ended up resting on their axles.

Gossamer sat at the side of the road and slapped biting insects off her skin while Mike walked round the vehicle inspecting it. A cigarette hung from one corner of his mouth and he squinted as blue smoke rose from it. Then he began to root around in the back. After some effort he hauled out two very long ladder-like objects. They were much his own height and about a foot wide. He placed one of these in front of each of the two front wheels, ramming them under as best he could. He used a spade to dig them in as far as he could go. Then he began to dig the axle out.

He got the Landrover mobile again after half an hour. Gossamer watched him vanish along the track. She walked over to the things he had used to drive out of the mess. They were clotted deeply with wet mud. She plucked each one out of the gloop and dragged it over the grass where she wiped it on the ground. Then she hoisted them both together on her shoulder and set off to plod after the Landrover.

They were too heavy. She had to abandon one. She walked on with the other digging uncomfortably into her shoulder.

In due course Mike appeared on foot. For the first time since the road got bad that day, she saw him smile.

'Good girl,' he said genially.

'The other's back a bit, at the side of the road. I'm sorry I couldn't manage both.'

He had streaks of mud across his trousers and shirt. 'Keep going,' he said. 'I'll catch you up. She isn't far. I just took her to the first hard standing.'

It didn't take him long. Soon he was by her side balancing his easily.

'What are these things?' she asked. 'They're terrific.'

'Sand ladders. I was told I'd need them. Seems I was told right.'

Several hours later he said: 'We aren't going to make Jinka tonight.'

She had known this for some time. 'I don't think there are many villages near here,' she said. 'There's tsetse fly down this way so they can't keep cattle. That's why it's so underdeveloped.'

'Frankly I think I'd rather sleep in the Landrover than in village accommodation.'

'Have you got mosquito nets on board?'

'Yup.'

'We'll be all right, then. Not very comfortable, of course. You needn't be too much of a gentleman. I realise the driving is very heavy and I've lost count how often you've dug us out.'

'I'm not a gentleman at all. How would you have made this trip if I hadn't offered a lift? I can't believe a bus comes this way.'

'Unless their route is entirely on all-weather roads the buses run when conditions permit. I'd probably have sat in Soddu for a day or so until a truck went through and hitched a lift.'

'You're resourceful.'

'No. It's normal here. It isn't unsafe the same way it is back home in England. I wouldn't hitch there.'

'Speaking as one of the boys from back home, that crack about not being a gent wasn't meant to imply anything. I can assure you your virtue will be entirely safe with me.'

She stared at him. 'I didn't think anything different,' she said.

What on earth was eating him? The bitterness in his voice

sounded uncommonly like loathing. Why should he dislike her so much, unless he disliked all women and she hadn't thought him that unintelligent. She hadn't made any play for him, she hadn't been putting out or behaving in the least flirtatiously. There had been no buzz between them at all, he was absolutely not a warm friendly man and they had retained the stiffness of strangers in their relations together. How could she have offended him so?

Mentally she shrugged. He had some hang-up, she was daft to blame herself.

It began to rain. She became very cold but she said nothing. He was wrestling with the driving, no doubt that kept him warm enough, but she was simply the battered passenger. It was really a most unpleasant journey. With anyone the least bit friendly she would have simply said she was cold and got something from the back to keep her warm. She had the feeling he had a sleeping bag and all sorts with him though he hadn't mentioned a tent. But the man was a morose misogynistic pig and she wasn't admitting to anything fallible like coldness. Heaven only knew why he had offered her the lift. She could be with one of the jolly Italian drivers that came this way, having an entertaining time, or with a local who would have asked her about England and found her answers very funny.

They became stuck so profoundly that even the sand ladders couldn't free them. Finally he rigged up a winch to a wayside tree and only then did the Landrover come free from its sticky bed. For a long moment it looked as though it might go over on its side. Mike got under the side and pushed up so that Gossamer found herself afraid that if it did tip, he would be trapped underneath it.

In the late afternoon the rain stopped and the sun shone steadily again. She was so tired herself she didn't know how he kept going.

They hit a good stretch. 'How far have we come?' she asked weakly.

'About seventy miles. In eight hours,' he said bitterly.

'This bit's good. Why don't we stop for the night? Then we'll have a good start in the morning.'

'I'll say this for you,' he said, startling her. 'You don't whine.'

'I will if you play tricks like trying to hold up the side of the Landrover again.'

'A risk can be worth taking.' He shrugged.

'And if it had fallen on you?' Her voice rose dangerously. To her horror she could hear hysteria creeping in. 'What should I do? Sit with your bleeding broken body till you die or trot off down the road and hope to find a hospital or a helicopter?'

'We can stop here,' he said and did so.

They ate corned beef and bread rolls and fruit. He brewed horrible coffee on a little primus stove.

'You can have the sleeping bag across the bench seats,' he said casually. 'You're shorter than me. I'll take the back.'

'Have you got blankets? It'll get cold tonight.'

'I've got spare stuff knocking about. There's a tarpaulin thing somewhere.'

As though the words were dragged out of her she said: 'Your neck and shoulder muscles must be tired. I've got some oil in my case. If you like I'll massage them for you and try to ease the muscles a bit.'

It came out very ungraciously. He raised his eyebrows and stared at her.

'I'm not making a pass at you,' she snarled.

He produced a big infectious grin. 'I know. Sure. Go right ahead. I'll take my shirt off, yeah?'

So that was it, she thought grimly, digging her fingers viciously into his neck. He couldn't bear women to make any sort of sexual approach to him. Either he hated them or he was a total chauvinist. Maybe, she thought, spitefully cheering up, he was a sexual failure. All this dour macho stuff was sublimation.

The thought made her positively sunny. He was sitting on a stone hunched forward while she worked on him, grunting occasionally as she assaulted his battered muscles especially

fiercely. 'Put that tarp thing on the ground,' she ordered. 'I'll
do a better job if you're lying down and properly relaxed.'

He obeyed. 'You really know how to make this unpleasant,'
he marvelled.

'You know perfectly well that unless it hurts it doesn't do
any good,' she said primly.

He had a good back, broad, narrowing slightly to a
muscled waist. She had only had experience of one adult
male in her life. She pushed that thought out of her mind.
This was clinical stuff. He was hairless on his back and had
two small moles.

She did his shoulders, his upper arms and his neck,
reaching right up till her fingers explored his skull under
his longish hair. When she was done she sat back on her
heels screwing up the perfumed oil she had been using.
'Right,' she said coldly. 'That's you. I hope it helps.'

He rolled over and lay on his back. 'Don't you want to
work off your spleen on my front as well as my back?' he
asked. He had a faint cross of almost black hair on his chest
and his nipples were ringed with it.

'Don't kid yourself,' said Gossamer and went to bed.

She woke in the night and lay stiffly, listening. Mike was
snoring slightly in his sleep, more a nasal heavy breathing
than anything. She was glad now he didn't like her. It made for
an absence of complications in their situation. She couldn't
have stood it if he had made any sort of a pass at her. She
couldn't bear the thought of a man handling her sexually. Her
mind jumped away from any future involving this. Maybe
such a frame of mind wouldn't last. She didn't know. But
for the time being she would rather lose all her physical
pleasures than risk the emotional pain they would make
her vulnerable to. It was hard even to remember there was
physical pleasure involved. She had to be careful not to think
too much or it would make her vomit.

It wasn't raining. The evening had been clear when she
went to bed and if she squinted through the dirty windscreen
she could see stars. She knew the night would be busy. The
African night was charged, full of life and death. Something

coughed, lion probably rather than leopard which was so rare now.

Kudu. Oryx. Water buck. Buffalo. She couldn't tell them apart. They were just names, individual raindrops in the drought of her ignorance. Some were gone, wiped out by war and overhunting. Yet they resonated in her mind. She was the alien creature here. It did them good as westerners to experience this diminishing of their status in the natural world. How long would she survive out there in the lion-haunted dark? One night? Two? She knew nothing, nothing that would preserve her life. She was most profoundly ignorant.

They made coffee in a pearl-soaked dawn. Neither of them said much. Mike hunched his shoulders and looked grey with pain. Gossamer felt as though she had been beaten up. Every part of her was bruised.

The road got drier. The land either side lightened in colour and changed from broadleaf tree to acacia. A scrubby savanna opened out to the right. They made twenty miles in the first hour and stopped for breakfast.

The sun was hot. Mike leant against the side of the Landrover soaking it into his stiff body. He had his face tilted up and his eyes screwed shut. 'What's that noise?' he enquired lazily.

Gossamer had taken off her boots and socks and was wriggling her toes to air them. 'What noise?' She'd have liked to nod off.

'That.'

In the far distance something coughed. They both sat silent, drowsing. They heard a high snap followed by several more.

Gossamer turned to look at Mike, puzzled. He was staring at her. 'It couldn't be gunfire, could it?' he asked hesitantly.

'I haven't heard anything like it since I've been here. Perhaps there's a safari party out somewhere. They do come down this way, I believe. They fly to Baco and go on from there.'

'Baco?'

'It's beyond Jinka. It has an airstrip.'

'We're fifty miles from Jinka. Maybe more.'

She listened. 'I can't hear anything now.'

They went on. The good stretch was over. They were back to floundering along through rutted mud, splashing their way through rivers and digging or winching themselves out.

They rounded a corner. On one side a riot of creeper-hung vegetation like a green wall came close to the road. They had seen the river that ran almost parallel to them. On the other was a steep bank of reddish mud impregnated with huge stones. Mike started to slide for the hundredth time. They were brought to a jarring halt by the wheel hitting a large stone squatting with almost visible malevolence in the track. If they had hit it at speed it would have ripped out the underneath of their vehicle despite the sump guards fitted.

'Christ,' said Mike wearily. He rubbed his jarred arms.

'Look.' Gossamer's voice was full of a sudden fear.

Two men had been sitting smoking at the side of the road. Now they stood up and approached the Landrover. Both carried rifles, a familiar enough sight except that these were held in a way that suggested they might be used. Both men had bandoliers of cartridges across their chests.

They wore camouflage jackets and twill trousers like it was a uniform. They had berets pulled sideways across their heads.

They looked like soldiers.

Mike opened his window slowly. One of the men came up to it. The other stood back holding his rifle loosely, directly in front of the vehicle.

'Out,' said the soldier. He gestured unmistakably with his rifle. Then he stood back.

Mike opened his door and very carefully got out of the Landrover. The soldier ducked his head and looked in. 'You too,' he said.

Gossamer slid across the seats slowly. She climbed out of Mike's door and stood beside him.

She felt very short. Mike himself was maybe just under six foot. The soldier was taller again.

The other man came round and again stood with both of them in view, his rifle held ready. It looked very professional, the way he kept his distance and covered his companion. The one by them spat at their feet. Then he ran one large hand up and down Mike's body.

'We're foreign visitors,' said Mike quietly. 'We aren't armed. We mean no harm. Do you want us to turn back?'

He was ignored. Now it was Gossamer's turn. The hand came on her body and ran over her breasts as though she might be carrying a revolver there. She went rigid.

The one covering them said something. Gossamer couldn't follow it, she only had a dozen or so words of Amharic and she didn't even know if this was what they spoke.

The man feeling her grinned. So it had been a dirty joke. He squatted in front of her, grinning maliciously, and began to run his hand slowly up the inside of her leg.

She trembled with tension. The last time a man had touched her properly it was to rape her. She felt her lips draw back in a kind of snarl.

'Stop it,' said Mike tensely. 'There's no need for that. I tell you, we aren't armed. We bring no trouble.'

'You are trouble,' said the man covering them. His tone was contemptuous.

'Are you the government?' asked Mike. 'I'll report you to your authorities. You mustn't behave like this.'

His hand was in her crotch. Gossamer was so stiff she thought she would fall over. In slow motion she saw Mike reach out. She tried to say no but she couldn't frame the words. The other soldier moved in and casually hit Mike with his rifle. Mike fell over in the mud. The big hand in her crotch tightened and he stood up.

She stepped back off his hand. Her own were up, she had no memory of putting them there. She looked down at Mike and back up at the soldier. He handed his rifle to his companion and undid his belt.

'No,' she screamed shrilly. She turned and began to run. The trees before her were solid, impenetrable. She crashed at them feeling thorns tear her. She spun round.

He was laughing, coming at her in almost leisurely strides. He reached out immense arms and gripped her shirt, tearing all the buttons off. Her back hit a tree trunk and she slid down it, struggling with feeble hands to tear him off her.

He came down on top of her, pulling her flat. She rolled and fought and bit, kicking and wriggling violently. His weight was impossible. His body crushed hers to stillness. He pulled her shirt open so that her breasts spilled out. She screamed hard, screaming again and again trying to punch him in the face. One of his hands was scrabbling at her waist. He had her trousers open. His upper body pressed hers flat while he lifted his lower to free their clothes. He was laughing all the time.

She could hear herself making harsh coughing noises as she sobbed. Suddenly his body jarred horribly. It went stiff and then collapsed.

She began frantically to pull herself out from under him. His weight was enormous and unyielding. Her head bumped the tree and she hauled herself up.

A hand came under her arm and helped. She stood up, tottering and blinking.

Mike stood there looking very strange. His chest heaved. There was blood spattered on him. She looked past him and back up to the road and the Landrover. It stood there unchanged, canted sideways slightly where it had slewed into the boulder.

'Where's the other one?' she whispered. Her voice croaked. The first pain she felt was from her throat.

'He was watching you. I knocked him back. He struck his head. I got one of the rifles and shot him.'

'You shot him,' she rasped slowly.

'I couldn't shoot this one. You were underneath. I hit his head in.'

She cranked her head to look down. The back of the man's head was a raw concave bloody mess, his woolly hair oozing red-black. A fly settled in it and began to feed.

She could feel her lips move but no sound came out. Mike stared at her. She realised his eyes were dilated with shock. He had just killed two men.

There was blood on her. Her naked breasts projected from her shirt. She thought suddenly of Arthur. What would he say, seeing her like this?

'It must be civil war,' she said jerkily. 'We mustn't stay here. No one must know what we've done.'

'We'll go back to Soddu. We'll say we couldn't get through, the rain was too bad.' Mike was whispering like a conspirator.

'They won't be alone,' said Gossamer desperately.

'No. Right. I'll turn the Landrover. We'll change our clothes and dump these. And we'll have to hide them. Bury them.'

'In the bush. Only till tonight. There'll be lions. Hyaenas. We mustn't leave them where vultures will show where they are. They'll have to be under cover.'

'Oh Christ,' said Mike. 'You find somewhere. I'll turn.'

'Yes. Yes. Quick, though. They must have friends down the road. We haven't got long.'

Through the nightmare that followed Gossamer had one thought strongly in her mind, more to keep out other thoughts than because it had special validity. Mike, though barely known, was as civilised as she was. The experience they were going through was as traumatic for him as it was for herself. Maybe it was more so. He had killed two men, wiped out two lives in a violent bloody assault.

It had been necessary. It had been justified. She was quite sure that after both men had raped her, Mike and she would have been despatched quite coldly, as if they were game animals. They had neither provoked nor invited the attack. Now it behoved her to help clear up the mess, to help protect them both from the consequences. This was a thing they had to do together. Nothing could make it all right, but it would be better for their working together. That way they both shared the responsibility. She was demonstrating that she knew Mike had done the only possible thing.

Only after they were jolting back the way they had come did she lay a hand on Mike's arm.

'What is it?' His eyes were fixed on the track ahead. The less time they spent stuck, the better.

'Thank you.'

'Don't remind me. I want a safe hotel and a bottle or two of whisky and case of beer. Let's wave goodbye at the airport and never see each other again, yeah?'

'Yes,' she said dully. Perhaps it was best to repress horrors. Maybe he had the rights of it.

They got stuck. Mike freed them in a slow agony of impatience. They splashed through water courses. They rumbled over rocks. They slithered through mud. The sun shone with a harsh brightness. The treacherous rains might never have been, save for the chewed up slop of the road.

They changed on the move. Gossamer sat with a cloth and wiped the muck off Mike, helping him into clean clothes as he drove one-handed. He wriggled out of his trousers unselfconsciously, driven by the fear of what followed them up the road. She too took off her torn shirt and trousers without thinking about modesty. The need was to appear normal. She had no idea whether he took a sideways look at her nearly naked body. She didn't care if he did. She doubted he did since he kept his eyes glued on the road.

They came to the good section. At the far end of this was one of the rare villages. 'We have to warn them,' said Gossamer.

'Then we'll be admitting we met trouble.'

'We can't leave these people vulnerable.'

'Maybe they know already. What if the police hold us up? You thought about that? We could hit a mulish bureaucracy and go down with the ship.'

'There are women and children involved.'

'We'll tell someone on the way out. Then we'll rush off. Something vague like we heard gunfire. Or saw bodies. No, they might make us come back and identify them.'

The village was called Fiké according to a drunken board at each end. It had been simply a double line of *chika* houses, square tin-roofed dwellings with walls made of mud and straw over a wooden lattice. A couple of buildings were wooden shacks, also with tin roofs. There was a verminous looking bar and the usual children, starved dogs, donkeys, goats and chickens wandering about. The African children looked cheerful and interested. They had been waved at as they went by the previous day. It was a very poor region because of the absence of cattle, but it made for lusher vegetation because it was not overgrazed as elsewhere in the country.

They entered the village slowly, knowing immediately something was wrong. It lay too quiet under the glare of sunlight.

'Oh God,' whispered Gossamer. Mike braked hard. A body lay sprawled in the road, its head towards them as it lay face-down in the dust.

'Don't get out. Shut your window,' said Mike. He reached behind him and picked up one of the rifles they had stolen from the soldiers. It might be evidence of what they had done, but he was prepared to take that risk until they reached safety again. Then they could dump the weapons.

They sat with the engine throbbing noisily. The heat was intense. The sun blazed down. Flies crawled over the body like a gently heaving black carpet. He had been shot, Gossamer thought, in the back.

Mike licked his lips. 'They're ahead of us,' he said. 'And behind.'

'If it's the army perhaps they have officers here. We'll be safe with officers, surely?'

'And if it isn't the army?'

'Somali raiders? Afar tribesmen? They're traditional enemies, I think, of the Galla people. I suppose they just use a conflict to get at each other.'

'Not a very profound analysis.'

'I didn't think I needed to know. Oh God, what about Jean? And Father Berhanu. All my friends in Jinka.'

'Oxfam are pretty bright. Maybe they've got a plane in,' mumbled Mike. Sweat poured off his forehead and stained his shirt under the armpits and between his shoulder blades.

A line of five men wearing khaki uniforms came into view. They each held a rifle. When they saw the Landrover they lifted their guns and fired.

'Jesus!' exploded Mike. He crashed into reverse and shot backwards. The windscreen starred.

He backed crazily until they were out of the village. Then he crashed into forward gear. He turned the wheel savagely to the left. A moment later they shot off the road down a small dust track that led into the bush.

They crashed through a brake of young birch-like trees and found themselves in tall *Hyparrhenia* grass. Once free of this they came to some poor millet fields which Mike drove straight across. Then they were into more high grass, elephant high, so that they thrust between yellow-green waving walls along a track no wider than their vehicle.

'Which side is the army?' he bawled. They were jolting and lurching so badly Gossamer wondered how long the Landrover could take the strain.

'I don't know.'

'One lot were happy to rape you. The other lot are happy to slaughter their own people. And us. I don't know if it's worth trying to get close up to ask who the good guys are.'

'What are we going to do?' Her voice rose unpleasantly.

'I'm going to stop and look at the map soon. I'll see if we can get round this lot and up to Soddu any other way. Assuming Soddu is OK.'

'We were only there yesterday morning.'

'Yesterday was years ago,' said Mike and stopped.

He had a revised War Office map, scale 1:500,000. The Italians had done most of the mapping of the country when it was owned by them after they invaded in 1935. They had stayed until 1941 when they were evicted with help from the British.

The map was hopeless, with nowhere near enough detail. Gossamer couldn't help. Though she had been in Jinka for several months she had never gone into the interior.

'You know,' said Mike in a conversational tone, 'compared to the official road this is a damned good track.'

'Not big enough for lorries,' said Gossamer. Talking was a wearisome strain. Fear was steadily numbing her.

'I get you. Most of the road traffic is lorries transporting goods.'

'Yes.'

'I find it hard to believe this road doesn't go anywhere,' Mike resumed.

'There's nothing in the south-west. There's rainforest, I think, over towards Sudan. We're going west now, aren't we? Soddu is north and east a bit.' She concentrated. 'Perhaps we ought to dump the Landrover and walk east over the mountains. Then we'll reach Arba Minch in the Rift Valley. It's quite big. There'll be some sort of order there. We can shelter with the police if necessary. We could be smack in the centre of something very localised.'

'With very localised uniforms,' said Mike.

'I'm trying not to think about that,' said Gossamer weakly.

'This country is run by a military dictatorship,' said Mike quietly. 'It's very wobbly. It's close to cracking up. That's what I was told before I came here. I did some research, you know.'

'That's more than I did. Except for what jabs I needed.'

'I'm going to drive on for a bit. OK? I want to see where this goes.'

'Whatever you like.' Gossamer shut her eyes and leant her head back. She felt very sick. She wanted a giant hand to come out of the sky and pluck her out of this.

Mike was absolutely right. The road did lead somewhere.

❧ Ten ❧

She had lost count of time this terrible day. The sun
blazed steadily. They bumped through tall grasses, through
woodland that was almost English with its bracken and
bramble-filled clearings, and so, rising by degrees, they
came up onto the plateau. She was glad when they did. The
soft mosses and velvet glooms of the wood were oppressive
and the raucous calls of the hornbills were peculiarly wrong
among the home-like trees.

The country opened up with acacia thorn and crotal bushes.
They could see tyre marks on the ground where the flattened
grass made a double silvery trail leading ahead. Over everything hung a vast ominous silence that Gossamer told herself
was only her jumping nerves. Then they saw it ahead of them,
the circle of mud *tukul* huts, the thorn-fenced compound. The
cluster of conical thatched roofs had a jolly gingerbread air.

'What's that overhead?' asked Gossamer faintly.

Mike pulled up and switched off. The damp English wood
might never have been, it was so dryly hot. The horizon
swam so that flat-topped trees shifted their position as you
looked at them in an eerie unwelcoming dance. At intervals,
quite unreal, termite mounds reared like miniature red ochre
castles, doorless, windowless.

All the time the cooling engine ticked.

'Can you drive?' he asked presently.

'Yes.'

'This?'

'I don't know about four-wheel drive.'

'I keep it in all the time unless we're on the all-weather
road.'

He was silent again. 'I'll tell you what,' he said eventually.
'I'll walk up. I'll take one of the rifles. It'll be OK. You
stay here in the driver's seat. Turn it round, there's a
good girl.'

'No.'

'What?'

'I'm coming with you.'

'Look.' He was reasonable. 'We both know something's
wrong. Those are vultures. So let me go and look, yeah?
There's been trouble here but maybe someone can tell me
what to do, where to go. We might even be able to pick
up a guide and go across country. We have rifles. They'll
know we can protect them.'

'I'm coming with you.'

His voice turned ugly. 'And if there are horrors? I can't
have you all hysterical.'

'The horror is being left alone.'

They bumped slowly forward. It was quite hard to see
through the windscreen. The wipers had made a clear arc
in the encrusted dirt and mud, but this was spattered
with bright sulphur yellow or lime green streaks. No need
of massy pyramids or wrought gold artefacts, thought
Gossamer crazily. The jewelled blood of insects paved their
way to the halls of the dead.

The bullet holes, there were two of them, had drilled
straight through starring the laminated glass opaque around
them. There was little clear glass left.

The village was busy but not with human life. With that
queer inconsiderateness for humanity and its concerns that
she felt symbolised Africa, Gossamer saw that the mess
was being mopped up. Around two hundred vultures were
present either on the job or waiting to fight their way in.
Mike drove in and they scattered in a vast clumsy rattle of
feather and bone, screaming and hissing their indignation.

There were bodies everywhere. The women wore long
skirts but little else save for necklaces and arm bands on
their naked upper bodies. The babies were naked and many
of the children too, though some wore shorts and torn shirts.

The men wore the traditional *shamma*, the short robe of so much of rural Ethiopia.

They were all dead.

Gossamer, huge-eyed with horror, climbed out of the cab. She ignored the vast naked-headed entrail-gobbling birds with their scimitar beaks. She walked unsteadily over to one of the children.

It was a boy with a neat curly head of hair. He had spindle legs in giant shorts. He was maybe eight years old. She took his head into her lap, sinking down onto her knees. She hunched forward over the thin little body and began to cry.

Mike came over to her and watched for a moment as she rocked and sobbed in her grief. He turned away. He began to walk through the village. At one end he found a soldier dead from a knife wound. His weapons had been removed but otherwise he had been left among the villagers as carrion by his erstwhile companions. He wore the khaki Mike had seen in Fiké.

He walked back to Gossamer. The heat throbbed in his brain. He couldn't tell if he was dizzy with it or if flies swam in his vision. He was glad she had stopped the terrible noise she had been making. Now she rocked to a low keening noise, still holding the dead child. He had a bullet wound, Mike saw. These people had all been shot.

Why?

Then he saw that there were no animals. So the livestock, meagre as it must have been, had been taken. An army needs to eat, of course, and it is easier to kill your neighbour if your affinities are tribal rather than national. Clan, urban gang, ethnic enclave; all were tribes by another name. All were blood-soaked.

Mechanically he began to search the huts. Whatever their own dilemma, if anything was left alive here they had a duty to it.

Nothing was. A baby had been shot on its mother's breast.

He came back to Gossamer. 'We must go,' he said. His

words were strange and metallic-tasting to his mouth.
Behind him the air crashed violently as feather-covered
scrap metal hit the ground. He could see clearly the
sugar-pink scrotal skin of its naked head. It hopped heavily
away gobbling in outrage at his interference in its feast.

He bent down and began to manhandle Gossamer to her
feet. He had to pull the child out of her arms. She was
boneless, a dead weight, and he was surprised at how light
she was. She was very thin.

Her eyes were open. They had lightened and were almost
amethyst, the colour of a bruise. Her cheeks were streaked
with tears and dust.

He held her by her upper arms. She sagged in his grasp,
her head lolling with the inadequate support of her neck. He
shook her slightly trying to get her eyes to focus on him.
'Snap out of it,' he said roughly. 'I can't manage with you
like this.'

He saw sense returning to her. Almost he was sorry. Her
eyes darkened in front of him with pain. He had never seen
anything like it in a human being. It was as though he looked
straight into her and saw the horror that filled her. 'My fault,'
she whispered. 'You told me not to come.'

Her lips were the colour of her skin, pale coffee brown,
dusty and dry. Despite everything he had time to feel regret
at what was happening to her looks. She had had such
perfect beauty, those velvet eyes, that Etruscan face.

'We'll go back to the Landrover,' he said gently.

He held her as they walked over to it. Another vulture
cannoned onto the street and provoked a chorus of angry
gobbling and croaking. She pulled abruptly out of his arms
and dropped on her knees in the dust. She began to retch.
Her body heaved and shuddered for a moment and then
she was sick, again and again, jerking out of her the
contents of her stomach till there was nothing solid left,
then nothing liquid.

Still her body shuddered. She hung over the filth under
her, hulping and gulping. Her hair hung in dank tangles.

Slowly she straightened, wiping her mouth on the back

of her hand. She was trembling violently. He hauled her to her feet and propped her against the Landrover. He pushed a cloth into her hands so she could wipe her face. She seemed hardly to have the strength to do this. He tipped water out of his jerry can and despairing of her aid, he splashed it into her face.

She lifted her face then and shut her eyes. He splashed more water onto her, washing her face with his hands. Then he held a cup of water to her lips. She drank greedily but it made her hiccup with pain and for a dreadful moment he thought she was going to throw up again.

He made a kind of nest for her in the back of the Landrover. She crawled into his sleeping bag and curled up. She was ghost-white under her tan, limp as an exhausted child.

She woke up two hours later. They were still. A terrible lethargy gripped her. She knew where she was and vaguely what had happened. There had been a village, a poor lonely village. There had been a massacre. She and Mike were trapped between warring factions.

A very old war, she thought drowsily. A cauldron of hate brought to the boil now and again over tens of thousands of years.

Her stomach rumbled painfully. Her throat felt sand-papered and she was so dry her mouth felt stuck together. She thought she ought to rouse up and find Mike but she couldn't. She was too tired.

He wasn't so bad. He was rude, he was unfriendly, but when it came to the crunch he made the right moves. She could have done worse, stuck out here suddenly naked in a violent world. She could have done worse for a companion.

She had a nagging feeling of having been here before. That was impossible. Yet this feeling of having the world torn out from under her feet, she knew it. Once before she had suffered this sort of emotional violence.

Carey.

The back door of the Landrover opened and it rocked

slightly. She felt the cooler air on her heated cheeks. The light was dim, it must be about sunset.

'You're awake,' he said.

'Yes.' Her mouth was foul and gluey.

'How do you feel?'

'Tired. Thirsty.'

'That's not surprising.'

'Not very fair on you, though.'

'Me? I'm all right.' His voice was cool like the night air.

'Why won't you use my name?' she asked.

'What?'

'You've never once called me by my name.'

'It's a bloody stupid name.'

She closed her eyes. It didn't matter what he thought of her name yet his reply hurt her. She felt attacked. Her eyes prickled drily. She had no tears left.

'Do you want a drink?'

'I'd better get up. Where are we?' She spoke very gently as if sound was a measured quantity. She had never known such exhaustion.

'Hidden in the bush about five miles from that village.'

With agonising slowness she pulled herself from the bag. She was so shaky she couldn't lace her boots. He performed this simple act for her, her feet dangling out of the back of the Landrover.

She drank slowly, taking salt tablets with it. She sat there afterwards letting her body soak up the water.

'You ought to eat,' he said gruffly.

'I'll just go into the bushes for a moment.'

'Be careful.'

'Yes.'

They spoke woodenly to each other, turn and turn about like strangers. But then, they were strangers. Only the massacre tied them together.

When she came back he gave her bread. She sat with her back against a wheel of the Landrover. She drank more water. 'I'd make coffee,' he said apologetically, 'but I don't like to make any light.'

Afterwards he gave her glucose tablets. She couldn't face tinned meat but the glucose was a great relief. She began to feel some energy flowing into her drained body.

'Mike.'

'Yes.'

'What are we going to do?'

'I've had some thoughts about that. But I'd rather discuss it in the morning.'

She slept heavily all night long and woke feeling convalescent. For the first time the indifferent life of the bush held no fears for her. Almost she was part of it.

Mike crawled out through their sheltering bushes and began to sweep their surroundings with his binoculars. He saw no human movement in the pink trembling air and came back to Gossamer. He lit his Primus and made coffee for them.

She drank it very sweet and felt it put life into her like air in a limp balloon. They ate the last of the bread and some tinned meat. Gossamer felt stupefied with food. It was very good.

'It's decision time,' said Mike. 'We can't stay here.'

'Have you made up your mind?'

'I'm asking what you think first.'

'If we can get across the road I think we should walk to Arba Minch over the mountains. I don't think they're high. The only thing is that they'll be inhabited. Or we can make our way north roughly parallel to the road but keeping off it and see how Soddu is. Obviously I want to get to Addis Ababa, we'll be safe there, but it's so far away.'

'I think we ought to ditch the Landrover and go south.' Mike looked at her. 'We're only about a hundred miles from Kenya. That's where we'll be really safe, across the border.'

She stared at him. 'I knew we'd have to give up the Landrover some time,' she said huskily. 'I didn't think you'd let it go this easily. It must represent a lot of money to you.'

He looked away restlessly for a moment and then turned his dark gaze back on her.

Her mind was like the sky, empty and piercingly clear. Her thoughts came singly, each one the reverberant shriek of a bird.

'There are no other considerations but survival,' she said. She understood about the Landrover now. Then: 'I'm a liability. You're frightened I'll collapse again like I did in that village.'

Mike didn't reply but she saw some of the tension come out of his shoulders. 'I understand,' she said. 'It's kill or be killed, like it was yesterday. We must pass through the bush unseen, unheard. If they don't know we're here, we might make it.'

She shut her eyes. 'I won't collapse again.' She achieved a pathetic dignity. 'You can always dump me. If I get out alive I won't say anything. I'm not that kind.'

'Don't be melodramatic,' he said bitingly. 'Let's get the gear sorted. We're going to have to backpack the lot.'

She stared at him. In a high whining voice she said: 'I'm not leaving my jewels. And I need a proper supply of clean clothes.'

His face darkened angrily. She grinned, her face creasing stiffly. 'Don't be so damned pompous,' she said.

He laid it out in neat heaps so that she was irrepressibly reminded of boy scouting. Salt, and chlorine tablets for sterilising water. Mosquito nets. Antibiotics and antiseptics. Chloroquine against malaria and sterile dressings to treat wounds. He stacked the tinned food, there was far too much of it to carry. They must take as much as they could but it would go in last. Water was more important. There were the rifles and ammunition to be carried as well.

Gossamer washed all over and put on clean clothes. She would be dirty enough by the end of one day, let alone a week, but it might be nice to start clean. She regretted not being able to wash her hair. Instead she bound it back and pulled her hat down over her face.

Mike took shaving gear and allowed her to pack a spare

pair of socks. Their feet would need looking after. They were depending on them.

It was an hour before they were ready to leave. Each wore a haversack and each carried a large army issue water bottle. And each carried a rifle, Mike having shown Gossamer how to use hers.

It was like acting a part. She was the girl guerrilla now. She knew she had to take it seriously and she knew that she would, but for the time-being it was surreal.

It was a vile day. The sun blazed serenely down. The great grassy plain they had looked upon turned out to have large areas of ankle-turning lava boulders hidden in the undergrowth. The walking was hard and slow. Her legs began to scream with pain. Periodically Mike rested, checking the horizon with his field glasses. As soon as Gossamer caught up he would set off again so that she never had a rest. Determined not to whine she grimly kept going. Sweat dribbled in her eyes. Little black flies kept trying to land in them and drink. She had a constant acute thirst.

Her load bounced on her back and dug into her. Her neck ached from the weight pulling back. The tops of her shoulders became sore where the straps rubbed. Her strong skating ankles felt rubbery and weak. When they stopped to eat, the shrilling of the cicadas was like an electric drill piercing her brain.

They saw no wild animals though occasionally they disturbed birds in their passing. Dragonflies floated like jewelled twiglets about their legs eating the insects they dislodged. Sticky brown blobs of tick larvae stuck to their trousers and hatched, crawling into their clothes if they weren't quick enough to brush them off.

That evening Gossamer thought of her other life. She forgot Carey, she didn't think of television studios nor did the diamonds she had thrown away enter her mind.

She thought of take-away food, French cinema, dancing on stage and wandering through clothes shops. She thought of art galleries and red buses. She thought of a T'ang horse. She didn't think of all this with longing or with regret. It was an utterly other life, so other that the girl who had experienced all those things, though known to her, was not her.

She thought with affection of buying a newspaper, entering a taxi, joking with a fruit-seller on the street.

She thought of Silvio, studying law at night. She thought of the glossy luscious feel of a magazine, fat with proffered luxury.

She was too tired to be hungry but when Mike gave her food, she ate it obediently. They had barely exchanged a word since setting off that morning. If it was to be like this all the time she would be spending a week or ten days in the company of a man, another human being, about whom she would learn nothing. She didn't care. Let him keep his distance. It was preferable to the other thing.

Heat. Ticks. Thirst. Muscular agony. It was the last peaceful day.

On the following day Mike saw people on the move. After careful watching he decided they were villagers. Gossamer lay flat on the ground uncomplainingly. They had already been going for an hour and she was tired out.

'They look herded,' he said.

'Can you see who's herding them?'

'No.'

He waited a further half hour. Gossamer dozed. He tapped her shoulder. 'I think we'd better get on,' he said. 'There's cover ahead. We're exposed here.'

'Aren't we going towards what they're coming away from?'

'Yes. But we have no choice.'

'We can join them.' She had a moment's illumination. 'They must be refugees.'

'Yeah, we look local.'

The ground was smoother and firmer. It was mostly made up of a thick tussocky grass filled with growing thorn. Against the tick-swarming lava of the previous day it was positively pleasant.

They were not able to enjoy it. They crept and scuttled

from one piece of cover to another. Gossamer did not borrow Mike's glasses but she saw a faint brown dust raised in the lower land to their left. The whole country was fleeing, it seemed. She heard distant gunfire and suddenly a piercing fear entered her. She knew their situation was horribly dangerous.

They ate sheltering among boulders on a small kopje. Added to their other troubles was the urgent need to find water. They had to refill their bottles. There was water down to their left, so much was obvious by the change in vegetation, but that was where there were people also.

In the afternoon Gossamer heard the fleeing people. She heard wails and cries, the bleating of goats and the baa-ing of bewildered sheep. There were few donkeys, it was so poor in this cattle-free region, and people had large loads slung on their backs.

Then there was a more sinister noise. They heard it droning from afar. As it grew louder Mike made her lie as flat as she could.

It was a helicopter, vast and ugly as a giant locust. It crossed the great range of country with insolent ease. Then, as the clattering obscenity of its engine noise began to fade slightly, Gossamer heard gunfire.

She heard Mike swear softly beside her. He wriggled till he could see and levelled the field glasses.

He kept swearing, the same word over and over in a horrified monotone.

'What is it?' Gossamer wished he would lie still. They must make no movement.

'They're firing on the people. On those poor people. On those families. Dear Jesus God, what's happening here?'

'We've got to get out. We've got to get out and tell people. Tell the world. They'll listen to you. You're a writer, aren't you? They'll take notice of you.' She whispered urgently. The noise of death rattled clear and sharp as the gunship raked the unarmed refugees, up and down, up and down. 'What's the day, what's the time?' she added. 'This is a war crime. Can you see a number on the helicopter? Write it down.'

She said all this but she wouldn't look. Not again.

'I'm not thinking properly.' Mike's voice was harsh with self-condemnation. 'This is an excellent vantage point. We'll have to look out. The boyos who ordered this might be sitting around here with their damned uniforms and fly whisks, watching.'

'If they run to helicopter gunships, maybe they take before and after pictures like we do. Like we did in the Gulf War.'

'Don't let your rifle barrel reflect,' said Mike suddenly. 'I'd better use the glasses less. I wish we had better cover. I wish we had a better map,' he added bitterly.

'South. We can't go wrong. Nobody's taken Kenya away.'

'Maybe we've gone wrong already. There's an army ahead of us, you know that?'

'There was one the other side, too, remember? We made our decision, Mike.'

'I wish this bloody country had a decent God-fearing dusk,' he grumbled absurdly. 'The bloody sun switches off like a bloody light every night.'

After thirty minutes the gunship wheeled abruptly and turned away. It flew east into the Ogaden. 'They must have been checking this side of things when they arrived,' said Mike. 'Surely they'll have gone back to base.'

'Let's go,' said Gossamer. 'Let's get away from this awful place.'

Almost unconsciously they worked towards the west as they made their way south for the rest of that day. Their instinct to put distance between themselves and the atrocity they had witnessed was beyond rational control. They could not dare get too far to the west or they would end up in war-torn Sudan instead of peaceful Kenya. Yet the threat was from the east.

Late in the day they came quite suddenly to a broad valley. It was flat-bottomed, twice as long as it was wide. It was a vast low-lying plain scored by dry gullies that might have been river beds at a wetter time. There was a permanent water course there, they could see the solid line of thick green running roughly along the middle of the valley.

They began to descend into a cauldron of heat. There were spaced out umbrella thorns, giraffe country though there were none to be seen, and low scrubby thickets. The termite mounds stood sentinel over an empty land. Everything that grew apart from the grass seemed to be covered in thorns.

They were short of water, very tired and frightened. They moved slowly, stumbling a little, aware that from a distance they would fade into the surrounding tawny countryside and be lost in the shimmer of heat. For the first time they saw distant game, reddish-coated big-eared deer-like creatures with long etiolated necks. They passed a dry wallow, the mud cracked into neat hexagons. The skeleton of an elephant lay there, shreds of grey skin in tatters on parts of the ribs.

All around, the bush shrilled with insects. Underlying the demonic insistent high-pitched whine was the slow low cooing of doves, infinitely restful.

The first gully they came to was full of thicket. They tried to chop their way in with Mike's knife. Then they tried to wriggle their way in and both tore their shirts. Finally they slogged along parallel to it till they found a little sinuous path.

With tortuous slowness they penetrated the thorn. They had to pick their clothes free all the time or have them shredded on their bodies. Suddenly Mike screamed.

Gossamer pushed ruthlessly forward. Thorns tore her malevolently. Mike was hunched on the ground, his back to her, bent over hard.

As she touched him he lifted his head and looked up at her. His face was a greasy grey under the flush of sunburn.

'My leg,' he whispered.

She looked past him. His leg was caught in a steel gin-trap. Her mind began to scream.

She shut it off with a snap. There was work to do. She

ran her eyes over the trap to see how it worked. 'That spring,' she said.

'You'll need a lever.' The words dribbled through his lips. His trouser leg was stained red.

His strength weakened her. She had to pull herself together again.

'The rifle,' she said calmly. 'I'll need to lever against something.'

'Try that tree.'

It forked into subterranean roots just above the ground making a kind of Norman arch at ground level. If she could get the barrel end into this, she could use her weight on the butt to depress the spring. Then the jaws would be opened.

First Mike had to be moved. He got his arm over her shoulders and stood up. As he did so he grunted and she felt him sway. His eyes were shut. She bent to pick up the trap. He opened his eyes and watched her, resting on her bent back. As she lifted the trap, he hopped forward. The air hissed between his cracking lips. He was green and faint with the pain.

They had only a foot or so to go. She let him sink to the ground and she edged the trap slightly round. Now she could ram the barrel into the tree root.

He moaned slightly, the sound bubbling out from deep within him.

She positioned the gun over the spring. She bore down on the butt feeling the close-grained wood slippery under her palms. She knelt on it then and the steel jaws opened.

Mike lifted his maimed leg out.

Gossamer released the spring. The trap snapped violently shut. She pushed it to one side and helped Mike so that his back was resting against the tree. His eyes were shut and he was trembling.

Carefully she unpacked her haversack. The medical stores were lighter than the tinned food and she carried most of them. When they were laid out, looking pathetic in the extreme, she turned back to the injured man.

She gave him a salt tablet and some of their precious reserve of water. Then she gave him two painkillers. Then, unable to put it off any more, she began to unlace his boot.

Again he made that low grunting noise as she took off his boot. She worked the sock down. His foot was white and wet, ribbed with red streaks where the pattern of his sock had pressed into the swollen hot flesh. She took scissors and began to cut his trouser leg.

The blood welled fresh and richly crimson, a deep glowing colour that made her think momentarily of those insect splashes on the windscreen of the abandoned Landrover. Their own blood was beautiful too. She poured water into the cap of her drinking bottle. It was the size of a cup, deliberately so. She added TCP in a liberal dosage.

'Hold on,' she warned. Then she doused the wound.

He whimpered, his head snapping back to hit the tree as the flesh burned above and below. Hastily she began to wrap the mess in sterile bandages. It was horrible. It was bloody. It was on both sides of the leg. But she didn't think it was deep. The meat of him was ravaged, but not his bone nor his sinew. He had plenty of meat, she thought, light-headed with relief. It was all the difference between damaging a car wing or having a bit drop off the engine.

'You'd better start the tetracycline,' she said. 'Here, have two to start you off.'

'Cold-hearted cow,' he said.

Her eyes flew up, startled. He grinned weakly at her. His chest heaved up and down. She smiled suddenly and taking the slack of her sleeve, she wiped his brow. Then she held his head against her breast, putting the antibiotics on his tongue and holding the cup to his lips.

For a moment she stayed like this, kneeling by him and holding him. When she felt him try to pull away she released him and stood back.

'You stay here,' she said cheerfully. 'Drink the rest of the water. I'll take both the bottles and get them filled. We know we're getting closer to the river.'

He considered. 'All right,' he said reluctantly. 'But take the compass. Do you know how to take a bearing?'

'No. I'll mark where I come out of this horrible spiky stuff. Why is Africa all spines?'

'Why is there a trap in the bush miles from anywhere?'

'Poachers. After leopard,' she said knowledgeably. 'I was told about them.'

'You mean,' he said faintly, 'a leopard comes this way?'

'Only at night. They cough. Lions roar.'

'Oh.'

'Hyenas do both. I'll be back before dark.'

'If you aren't I'll come looking for you.'

'No. Stay here. If I get stuck, really stuck, I'll wait till daybreak. I'm not a fool. I'll find you.'

'I know you're not a fool,' he said.

It was the first nice thing he had said to her. Feeling deliciously light without her pack, Gossamer went to find water.

Suddenly it was easy. She came clear of the thorn and onto a pleasant open grassy sward. Carefully she marked her exit point with an elaborate decoration of sticks. As long as she worked her way along the edge of the gully's denser vegetation she would find it.

The soil was light and sandy. Birds chirped as the heat of the day began to wane. Ahead of her was a lush green strip. She reached it in under half an hour. Thrusting into a tangled undergrowth of lianas and creepers that even smelled wet, she came suddenly to the bank of the river.

Broad and clear it ran over a shingle bed of fine white pebbles. Better still, it was edged with what could only be called sandy beaches. She ran forward with a cry and knelt in the water at its edge. She plunged her face and head in, again and again, allowing her clothes to soak as water cascaded off her. Her skin seemed to suck the water in. Almost unbearably she did not drink. Instead she rinsed out and filled the two heavy water bottles. She dropped chlorine tablets in. It would be foul-tasting but fit to drink by the time she was back with Mike.

She knew she had to get back but she could not resist swiftly stripping her shirt. She dunked it in the water after emptying the pockets and banged it with stones. She sloshed water all over her upper body, relishing the feel of it dripping over her naked breasts. She washed her loosened hair free of dust and sweat. Then she put the wet shirt on and headed back to Mike.

He was so plainly relieved to see her that she felt guilty for her self-indulgence. She also felt enormously revitalised. She described the place she had found.

'Tomorrow. We go there tomorrow and you can wash and rest in comfort while your leg heals,' she said. 'Perhaps we could even swim.'

'No crocodiles?' he asked. 'I thought all the rivers here had them.'

She gasped. Her hand flew to her mouth like a guilty child's. 'I forgot,' she said. 'I remembered not to drink it and I didn't paddle in it though I think you don't get bilharzia in running water. But I plain forgot about crocodiles. I've never seen one. It was so lovely there.'

They passed an itching uncomfortable night. It was clear his wound ached. Gossamer cut sticks and arranged their mosquito nets like tents over them but the heat stayed trapped in the dense undergrowth and made sleep difficult. Moreover, the undergrowth moved. It rustled. It growled. It coughed. It made chuck-chuck-chuck noises. It whirred and occasionally it even shrieked.

The night was very long and very dark. They greeted the dawn with heartfelt relief, gummy-eyed and tense.

Getting out of the gully was the worst. By the time they were on the plain Mike's stiffness had eased and he moved quite well with a swinging limp and a crutch. Gossamer carried both packs and staggered along behind him. The longer they travelled, the less food they carried and the lighter their packs got. There was an end-point to this process they did not discuss. Already they knew their estimation of the time needed to travel had been wildly optimistic. Now they were losing more time. They had seen some game only from an extreme distance. Mike made no pretence to be even an adequate shot though he had handled a rifle. And they were frightened of the noise hunting would involve. They needed to preserve the secrecy of their passing, if they could.

They spent the rest of that day and the next night by the river. Wary of crocodiles they found a clear space in the riotous undergrowth and rigged the mosquito nets. Gossamer washed all of her own clothes and put them back on wet. She washed Mike's clothes as well, helping him out of his socks and trousers but leaving him to remove the remainder for himself. He wore the blanket to cover his nakedness while his clothes dried. She didn't tell him she found his modesty funny in the circumstances.

They might almost have been tempted to stay despite their dwindling food supply, so idyllic seemed their surroundings, but for what happened at dawn.

Gossamer had woken to listen in comfort and unfearfully to the shrieking birds of the new day. She loved the dawn, whether here or at home in London, and for some reason she felt terribly safe.

She eased herself out from under her mosquito net. Mike was a grey-shrouded heap, spiders spinning small webs over the bumpy terrain of his net. Perhaps they thought Mike some vast and God-like spider under his webby net, she thought with amusement, and went to find herself a private place. A real plumbed-in lavatory was a wistful thought.

She was crouched inelegantly when she heard voices.

She kept absolutely still. The poachers, maybe, looking for whoever had disturbed their trap.

Maybe not. She began to work her clothes noiselessly back together.

The voices were sharp on the cool morning air. She heard crashing feet. She eased herself forward and began very quietly to burrow under the foliage. She found herself face to face with something long and segmented with a great many legs. She stared at it dumbstruck. Close to her men moved impatiently, talking loudly and with arrogance.

The bird-shrieks stopped. The whole riverside animal web fell silent. They held their breath, waiting for the invader to go.

An ant walked over the back of Gossamer's hand. It bit her. She saw another one like it just behind. Delicately she moved her hand. It stung sharply.

The men talked and moved on. She heard more men. Moving a leaf from in front of one of her eyes, she tried to see them.

She found she was looking at a soldier's boot. He was so close she could have breathed on him. If he stepped back he would kick her in the face.

Her heart thundered irregularly. She was surprised he couldn't hear it. She smelled tobacco and a cigarette end was dropped near her nose, glowing dull red.

She retracted her neck like a tortoise. Sure enough his heel came back. He trod on the cigarette end and ground it into the leaf-matter.

A small iridescent beetle waddled past her nose. She saw some more ants. They were very pale. Perhaps they were termites.

He said something. For a wild moment she thought he was speaking to her. But then he turned and with another man, who had just come into view, he went off after his friends.

There was a long silence after they had gone. Very slowly, as shy as any gazelle, she raised her head and began to check that her surroundings were safe again.

How could she ever have feared insects? Man was the enemy.

She began to work her way back towards Mike. She had not thought of him all this time. She could only pray he had stayed under his netting and made no noise.

When she saw the undisturbed net she felt a rush of relief. Her prayers had been answered. This was followed illogically by anger. How could he sleep so deeply?

She woke him by touching his arm. His eyes came open and turned slowly to focus on her. She was keeping close to warn him as soon as he was awake to make no noise.

She saw his face change. It was such a small play of muscles. She saw the skin tighten, the mouth harden, the eyes grow cold.

He deeply disliked her. Loathing might not be too strong a word. For some reason she couldn't fathom, she disgusted him.

She ignored the knowledge, filing it away. 'We have company,' she breathed. 'The camouflage and green beret boys.'

'Close?'

'Mmm.'

'Can we move?'

'Very quietly.'

They finished their water. Gossamer crept to the river and checking no one was in sight, she filled both bottles and put chlorine tablets in. She felt safer with a full supply of water on them, even if it was heavy to carry. The weight went down all too fast.

There was nothing they could do about crocodiles except pray that the poachers had neither been single-minded in their choice of prey nor unsuccessful. They waded the shallow river. On the far side when they were in cover again Gossamer changed Mike's dressing.

His wound was very clean and smelt fresh. He continued to take his antibiotics. The only problem was that she didn't have many dressings left.

They worked their way out of the band of soft lush growth and used the compass to orient themselves. They had to bear slightly left and make for the hills ahead of them. They picked a notch in the skyline on the right bearing and began to make their way towards it.

They felt horribly exposed. They tried to keep in cover but it made moving in one direction very difficult.

The heat of the day began to build. Gossamer was grateful. The combination of the glare and heat shimmer made things hard to see which was just how she wanted it to be.

Mike kept nervously scanning round them every time they stopped. This was as much to rest his leg as to let Gossamer have some relief. She was carrying a disproportionate share of the load now but such was her anxiety to be out this valley that she would willingly have kept going.

Mike sat on a stone, his bad leg stretched straight ahead. 'We've got company,' he said softly. Neither of them had raised their voices since his scream of pain in the leopard trap.

Gossamer said nothing. She shrugged into the haversack, the straps settling into their familiar sore places on her shoulders.

She helped Mike into his haversack and he hefted the rifle. They began to creep back away from the men he had seen, moving along the valley parallel to its edges to a denser cluster of trees and scrub.

They went very slowly keeping low. Once in the thicket Mike stuffed their haversacks as deep into the thickest part as he could, pulling thorn back into place despite his scratched and torn hands.

'I think they're coming this way,' he breathed.

There was no tree fit to climb. They had been lucky not to startle any beast from out of such a shady spot. The absence of game might be an ecological tragedy but currently it was saving their lives.

For the moment.

Mike cast with urgent silence all about them. Gossamer crawled to see if there was some low-down run into which they could wriggle.

She felt her shirt pulled. She rose silently to her feet. He pulled her arm and drew them both round a tree trunk.

It was hollow. Like a cowrie shell it had a folded gummy mouth running vertically down one side. By squeezing against a thorn they were able to slide within the tree itself.

Immediately they were in a dim microworld. Underfoot it

was incredibly soft. A fine ammonia-smelling dust rose to irritate their nostrils. The inside of the tree was grey and crumbling, full of tiny crawling things that had no idea of their gigantic presence.

Gossamer looked up, to alleviate the smell as much as anything. She could see little. Other trees in full leaf hung over their patch of sky. The branches were heavy with vast pouches hanging from them. Weaver birds' nests? Some form of tree infestation? She didn't know.

Mike had his arms around her. The space was very confined. He had his back to the opening into the tree so that she faced it, his body solid and comforting between her and the source of danger.

She clasped him lightly. She could feel her heart hammer with an odd syncopated rhythm. She could smell him, a fresh strong male smell. They were still both clean from the river, Mike smooth-shaven again.

She faced the open vee at his neck. One or two wiry hairs came up. She knew what his chest looked like. She had seen him shirtless.

She must keep her mind busy. She mustn't think about what might be happening outside. She was in a tree with a man. He had his arms round her but that was for practical reasons. He was a man who didn't like her.

She didn't like it. She didn't like being forced against a man who hated her, though his hatred was inexplicable to her. She didn't like being this close to him when she knew he didn't like being with her at all.

She wondered what kind of a writer he was. She hadn't asked. It wasn't that she hadn't been interested but he had been so offputting she hadn't felt he wanted her to ask personal questions.

She set herself to decide whether she would dare to use all the dressings they had on his leg, or whether she should keep one in reserve.

She could hear his watch ticking. Quite suddenly she heard voices. She heard an engine roaring and spluttering. The noise swelled.

They were surrounded. There might have been twenty men only a few feet from them. She felt her skin prickle and knew she was starting to sweat with fear. Her heart hammered jaggedly. She realised she could feel Mike's heart as well as her own, their chests pressed against each other. Had he squeezed her tighter as they heard the enemy? Or had she clung harder to him?

They stood locked together. His chin was in her hair. They might have been lovers, frozen like this.

There were shrill calls, deeper shouts and much cheerful banter going on outside. Whichever side it was, they felt safe. To her horror Gossamer smelled smoke. Then she smelled the familiar hot peppery smell of *wott*.

It was principally an Amhar dish, of the north and of the central plateau. If they were down to fight the invading Somali then they were being incredibly casual about their presence in this area which would be largely sympathetic to the Moslem invader. Indeed, it was probably government forces who had had that helicopter gunship, used so cruelly on fleeing locals.

Mike moved slightly. It would hurt him to stand this still on his bad leg. His movement released another noxious cloud of ammonia. Gossamer wrinkled her nose and tilted her head back.

Her eyes had adjusted to the gloom within the tree. What she saw was so terrifying she found her breathing had stopped. Her whole body froze rigid. She could feel her blood congeal.

Mike moved faintly, knowing something was wrong but not what it was.

A great racketing started in Gossamer's head. Nineteen years. All for this moment. All leading inexorably towards this moment, in a hollow tree, caught in a foreign war.

Her tongue had stuck to the roof of her mouth. Her hands had clenched Mike so tightly she must be hurting him. With an enormous effort of will she unclasped one hand and began to slide it up his back.

Loverlike. Slow and smooth. Against his shirt.

She could smell her own sweat.

His head was moving. His lips were at her ear. She felt his breath warm.

Loverlike.

'What?' he breathed. Her clean hair stirred gently.

She had forgotten the danger from outside. She twisted her neck slightly keeping her eyes fixed on the nightmare within. She lifted herself against him till her lips were up to his ear. 'Snake,' she said.

He vibrated. She moved enough to allow him to turn his head. When he saw it he turned back and laid his face in her shoulder. She heard the tiny noise he made in his throat.

Her hand slid up, pink and vulnerable, like a featherless chicken wing. The snake was slithering very slowly down from the open top of the hollow tree. She could hear the rustle of its scales. Almost she could hear the contraction and release of its muscles. Its tongue flickered in and out.

She had her left arm up now, along his shoulder, the hand spread to protect the back of his neck. Her elbow wrapped round his shoulder. Her torn short flapped so that, pink and juicy, the meat of her lay exposed to the approaching fangs.

Her right hand was well up. He couldn't stop her without jerking, without reaching behind him. She was giving him no choice.

Her right hand was in his hair now, covering his right ear.

They were cheek to cheek. She forced the man's face against hers, his pointing down into her shoulder. Hers pointed up. She watched the snake as she might look on the face of God.

With great fear.

She felt pressure. He was trying to twist her round. 'No,' she sighed.

They were tight to each other, both trembling so that she didn't know whose body was whose.

She entertained a kind of delirious hope that it was full and was coming out of curiosity rather than the desire to feed. It was hugely fat, a bloated tube of squamous horror, endlessly long. Its body, barely tapering to indicate any sort of a tail, disappeared unendingly above them for some four or five feet unless fear was distorting her perceptions. Further up she could see alternating white and dark bands, the dark bands with white spots on them. Nearer the pattern seemed more complex. It had u and v shapes in white, so pretty across the gross tubular body.

As it looked at her she saw that what she had perceived as dark colouring was actually nearer to orange and brown. Chestnut, she thought. Rust. And chocolate.

She never ate chocolate in Africa. It was too hot. She liked chocolate from the fridge.

Her mind felt very clear and cool. Thoughts ran tinkling through it like water over a stony bed. She thought she had an idea of what it was. Few snakes were so large, unless they were pythons and strangling snakes. She had a feeling that what she was looking at was a puff adder.

It started to swell, confirming her thoughts. She had heard that before they struck they puffed up.

The thing was, she told herself confidentially, she didn't think she could survive without Mike's help. He, on the other hand, would actually be helped by not having her around. Now that his leg was healing nicely he would be far better off without her. True, she had helped him over the business of the trap, but if she hadn't been around he would have levered himself free. She wouldn't have had the strength herself, not if it had been her with one leg stuck in the thing.

She told herself quite chattily that she was sure there were more horrors to come on this dreadful flight through warring factions. She simply couldn't cope. She had collapsed in the village where everyone had been massacred. She couldn't look at the slaughter of the refugees. There were different sorts of bravery and that kind of emotional toughness was beyond her.

Besides, who would care if she were dead? Jenny would be sorry but Jenny had Canfield. Anthony would miss her but he would find solace in the arms of some male lover.

Nobody cared about her in all the world. As for the man she was trying to protect, he loathed her.

Her body pressed against his, bowing in to his protective curve. She needed the comfort of human contact. This wasn't going to be a pleasant death. There would be terrible pain. Maybe there would be paralysis. Maybe it would be haemorrhaging. But it would be over in hours. If she was captured and raped they might keep her alive for days until they tired of her.

It occurred to her that Marie might genuinely grieve. She was in some way Marie's alter ego. She was the prude, the moral one. This was funny in the circumstances.

In the circumstances of Carey Lambert.

He was a puff adder. They didn't just inhabit the African bush. They walked the streets of London and she had already been bitten and done her internal bleeding. She had suffered the pain once. Could it hurt so much the second time around?

Were all human relations just an analogy for real life, like this?

She whimpered very quietly deep in her throat. Mike twisted her sharply away from the snake. Above them the bats that had filled the tree with their droppings fell off their roosts in alarm. They clattered out of the tree. Someone outside shouted. A brown arm came momentarily into view and the snake opened its great mouth and struck.

She saw the fangs. For one photographic split second she saw the two curving half-inch fangs like bone-white needles. They sank into the arm and she knew the venom would be pumped straight into the victim's bloodstream.

Mike had his hand over her head. Outside there was pandemonium. The victim was screaming continuously. The snake had been pulled outside the tree attached to his arm. There was a rattle of machine-gun fire. Voices shouted and they heard footsteps crashing about. The man went on and on screaming. Suddenly his voice was cut off, mid-scream.

They heard authoritative tones. They heard a pleading voice. Orders were issued. The jeep's engine revved. There was a cacophony of hurried noises. They held each other trembling violently and all the time the racket went on and on outside. A voice started to wail. There were more gunshots.

Then there was silence. Lovely, beautiful, blessed, perfect silence.

Slowly. Mike released himself. He edged to the gap in the tree. He eased himself round and looked out.

He was gone for a moment. Then he came back. 'They shot him,' he said oddly. 'He's here with the snake. Do you mind coming out?'

'No.' Her voice grated drily, barely above a whisper.

She came out into the sweet-smelling air. The man lay quiet, his skin blue-black and misted like a grape. The snake, cut almost in half by bullets, lay beside him. The victor and the vanquished shared the same fate.

The skin was beautiful, glowing chestnut to a rich deep chocolate brown, with brilliant white markings.

'We must move on,' said Mike hoarsely. 'I'd like to get out of this valley. Can you retrieve the haversacks while I take a look around?'

As they left the thicket, noise exploded from the river. They heard the rattle of gunfire, short sharp cracks and long blasts. They slunk across the grassland keeping to any cover that they could.

Behind them the noise of the battle continued intermittently until nightfall.

❋ Eleven ❋

They kept going till long past dark, stumbling up stony broken slopes until they felt there was sufficient distance between themselves and the enemy behind them. Mike laid the blanket in a depression between boulders and they rigged the mosquito nets over themselves, pulling branches and twigs over the top of the whole. They burrowed into all this with the haversacks.

Mike worked some food free. They spooned cold Irish stew down with crumbling digestive biscuits and warm chlorine-tainted water.

When they were finished they lay quietly side by side, shuffling slightly to fit their bodies together like two prawns so that they could sleep.

'How's the leg?' she asked. He was certainly no complainer.

'Gossamer,' he said.

She was silent.

'What went on in that tree?'

'Leave it. We all act oddly under stress.'

'You tried to protect me.' His voice was a deep soft buzz in her ear.

'You've been doing the same for me for days.' She had a sudden urge to cry. She couldn't handle an emotional scene.

'I haven't put myself between a venomous snake and you.'

'You tried. I felt you try.'

'Only because I couldn't have stood it. Knowing that you set yourself to die for me. You being what you are. You knew how dangerous it was, didn't you?'

'It was a puff adder, I'm almost sure.' She gave a sudden horrified squawk. 'I saw it puff, ready to strike.' She quivered at the memory. 'That man put his arm in. I saw its fangs.' Her eyes were wide open in the claustrophobic dark and she stuffed her fist into her mouth.

'I don't understand you.'

'Leave me alone.' Her voice rose dangerously. He must be able to hear how close she was to tears.

'Tell me why.'

It was brutality. He lay against her in the dark knowing she was deep in the horror of the thing but he wouldn't leave her alone. She wanted comfort, not this beastly interrogation. She hated him. She hated him for insisting she speak. She hated him for bullying her when she was so distraught.

She swallowed drily, fighting not to break down. 'Don't be silly,' she said unevenly. 'I can't do this alone. I have to have you. I'd have been dead twice over, more, without you. But you, you'd be better off without me. I know you hate me but you still look after me. So it was simple, see. Either I died quickly with the snake or slowly in the bush, captured and raped.' She closed her eyes and thought about breathing. In. Out.

He was silent for a moment. Then he said: 'You don't die quickly. I think it takes hours.'

'That is quick compared to some deaths.' In. Out.

'I don't hate you.'

She began to shake. 'Oh, dear God,' she cried. 'I can't bear this.'

He put a hand on her shoulder. She lay on her side with her back to him and his body followed the pattern of hers as he faced her.

She felt his face muffled in her hair. 'I'm sorry,' he said.

'For saving my life?' Her voice was high and ragged.

'I'm no James Bond. No buccaneer. No adventurer. I'm just a very frightened man more used to a board room squabble than a bush war. I'm out of my depth.'

'I thought you were a writer.' She would not cry. She would not give way. In. Out.

'Yeah, that too.'

She fell silent. After a while sleep washed over her and she gave way, sinking through the great currents of being until she was rocked numb and unknowing on the deep ocean floor of life.

The whole of the next day they slowly climbed higher and higher. At first the coolness and the smoother ground were a great relief. They had a sense of entering a peculiar emptiness where they would be safe from the attacking factions. They had trouble over one large section of bog finding they had to step from tussock to tussock, but their loads were lighter now and they themselves had gained a certain stringy toughness.

They came to a high ground of coarse yellow grass dotted with huge circular succulents. It was a science fantasy world, the plants alien and unearthly. Some four feet across and two feet high, they were vast rosettes of fleshy pointed leaves that were pale and whitish underneath and a cold blue-green on top. As the day began to end they closed up and the air came very cold.

Cloud rolled down and Mike squatted, shivering. 'I wish we could drop down out of this,' he said.

'It isn't nice. I suppose it's safe though. No one can see us.'

They went on. Now uncannily there loomed tall cottony cactus-like things, fat six-foot spikes covered in coarse white hair. They trudged past these ghostly plants unable to see where they were going.

Mike was restless. 'I can't tell if we're keeping in the right direction,' he fretted. 'What if we're going too high? We could find ourselves in mountains, unable to get through.'

'I didn't think there was anything very high this far south,' said Gossamer. 'I know there are mountains north of Gondar, but nothing serious down here.'

They were dropping already but they hadn't realised it. The cloud thinned, the air lightened and it grew warmer. The ground became firm again. Suddenly they were in a lovely high valley full of something remarkably like heather. The landscape was dotted with small stumpy trees, bonsai trees like woody branching cacti. Clumps of improbable green vegetation sat in fat spikes absurdly wiglike on the ends of the branches.

They had very little food left. They ate a tin of sardines each, their bellies rumbling with hunger. The cold sharpened their appetites unpleasantly.

Mike's leg was dry and scabbed hard. Gossamer was very proud of it. She kept him on the tetracycline though. They both rattled, what with salt tablets, vitamin pills, chloroquine and Mike's antibiotics. All they lacked was good filling food.

They dropped back into the heat the next day. Immediately they felt they were not alone. They passed an empty village, its huts burned and desecrated. There were no people in it. Soon afterwards they found the man on the poison tree.

It was a large tree with a fat bifurcated trunk and a great mass of spreading branches. Apart from its relative leaflessness there was nothing special about it.

The man had been tied to the tree and he was dead. He wore khaki. His clothes had been torn and his back was lacerated so that the congealed wounds were against the bark of the tree.

Mike licked his lips. 'Poor sod,' he muttered. 'I suppose this is their idea of fun and games. He can't have been here long or the hyenas would have got him.' He thought of themselves in the picture-book valley while this man suffered and endured the final agony of being tortured to death.

Gossamer stared into the distance. 'It's a poison tree,' she said.

'A what?'

'The bark, roots and flowers all contain poison. Strychnine, I think. See, they've broken his skin and tied him against it.' Her voice was carefully calm.

Mike took her hand. They went on like this for a while. His hand was dry and hard and slowly her urge to cry and the weak feeling in her knees passed.

That afternoon they found themselves walking across a level sandy plain only sparsely covered in vegetation and very hot. The ground winked at them occasionally as though it hid chips of diamond. They saw zebra at an extreme distance. They felt very exposed.

Gossamer stumbled and screamed. Mike was there instantly. 'What is it?' he cried.

Wordlessly she pointed. She had knocked a stone aside as she tripped. Squatting under it was a huge hairy spider-like creature, the span of Mike's hand. It lifted two hairy arms and waved them in the air. They could see the jaws. It emitted a small twittering noise.

'Oh God.' Gossamer's teeth chattered. She clung to Mike's shirt. 'Oh God, what is it?'

She felt him start to shake. She turned to stare at him and found he was laughing. She shook him. 'Stop it,' she said. 'Stop it!' Her voice rose hysterically.

He put his arms round her and held her tightly. 'You silly cow,' he said. 'You poor silly cow. All the dangers we've been through and it's this thing that breaks your nerve.'

She started to cry, rubbing her face in his shoulder. 'I said I wouldn't do this,' she sobbed. 'I said I wouldn't break down.'

'No. I know. You can't help it. You've been frightened too long and you're hungry.'

'That's it,' she sobbed. 'It's gone on so long.'

'We can't be far. Despite everything we have to have done most of the distance. We'll be safe in Kenya, I promise. We'll be safe soon.'

She pulled away from him and wiped her eyes, sniffing. She turned and looked the way they were headed. 'What's that?' she said. She sniffed again and wiped her nose on her sleeve. Her clothes were stiff with dried sweat.

'What?'

'Is it a dust storm? Are we heading into a desert?'

Mike put the field-glasses onto the distant blur. 'Christ,' he said. 'Oh Christ.' He looked wildly round them. In all directions the ground spread relatively flat with very little cover. The surface was broken by innumerable little stony outcrops in the brown sandy earth, but few of these were more than a couple of feet high. They were at least three miles into the depression and the only vegetation was a sparse straggling grass with the occasional almost white dry bush.

Gossamer stared at him. 'It's fire we can see,' he said. 'I can see the flames. There are some jeeps. People are running too. I think it's a battle. I think we're about to meet both sides of the enemy.'

She looked wildly round. 'We must hide.'

'Where? We can hardly sink into the ground.'

She stared at him. 'OK,' he said. 'Here, in the stones.' He began to dig with his bare hands. 'You bury the haversacks,' he said. 'Quickly. Under a bush if you can.'

They both had knives. They dug rapidly. It was very easy after they had broken through the compacted surface. Gossamer tumbled the rucksacks into her hole and covered them up. She spread the spare earth as far round her as she could. She broke off a branch and wiped the ground to make it look more natural. She could hear gunfire now and smell the burning land.

Mike was working savagely digging at the edge of a rock. 'Get in,' he said.

She pushed herself under the rock into the shallow depression he had made. He began to heap the cinnamon-coloured earth back over her body.

'What about you?'

'In a minute. I'll do me in a minute. Shut up and keep still.'

Her face was under the rock. He partly tore and partly cut a bush free and wedged it over her face. Then he vanished.

She knew her covering was very shallow. She must not twitch. For a while she could hear him scrabbling away near at hand. She said nothing, concentrating on keeping still. One hand was up by her face. The other was buried parallel to her body.

Time passed. The noise stopped. Apart from the occasional slip and squeak of earth, she heard nothing.

She put an immensity of effort into keeping still. She had done yoga at one time and now she practised relaxation, shutting down each of her muscles one by one until she had reached a state of complete limpness.

She had to start at her left toes over and over. She worked up her left leg and then up her right. She began to win. Her muscles went slack one by one. Now she was trying to reduce the rigidity of her abdomen. She mustn't think. She mustn't let fear in. She had a dancer's trained body and an exceptional awareness of her edges. Now she must use that awareness and use the self-control she had been taught.

Her life depended on it. Maybe Mike's did as well. If he heard her captured, would he lie still? Would he have that much sense?

Her nose itched but she ignored it. She was working on her chest muscles now. A kind of dimness filled her mind as though the world slipped and removed itself from her, like an ebbing wave. Was it drawing back from her, or was she shrinking away from it? It didn't matter. Nothing mattered.

There was an acrid smell in her nostrils. The atavistic fear of fire thrilled sharply through her, waking her up. She had a mental vision of little desert creatures fleeing for their lives, lizards, scorpions, those monstrous hairy spider-like things, little voles and shrews. Snakes. All fleeing.

Carefully, persistently, she began to force herself to relax again, starting with the toes of her left foot. There was no time to feel afraid. There was time only to relax, to be still, to be one with the brown earth, part of its texture and being.

Think of something.

*He who would valiant be
'Gainst all disaster.*

Good. Think of schooldays. Life that was cool, calm and collected. Even, regular days.

There were people. She could hear drumming feet, hear the throb of an engine.

*Let him in constancy
Follow the Master.*

School. Boarding school. Long summer days out by the tennis courts. Walks with friends talking of all the world. School trips, giggling in uniform.

There's no discouragement—

Holidays. Twenty girls still at school. Daughters of servicemen stationed in Brunei. Daughters of diplomats in Costa Rica. Daughters of oilmen, of archaeologists, of wayward botanists employed by American Universities to find the plant that would cure AIDS. Herself, the orphan.

Shall make him once relent,

Talking about boys. About sex. Her humiliation in not knowing. She had nothing to do with boys, she hardly ever spoke to a member of the male sex, men were excitingly mysterious.

His first avowed intent

She knew what sex was. She didn't know what men were. School had been right. Men were the danger, the enemy. They were not to be trusted. You had to be on guard. They used sex without kindness.

She felt a rush of bitterness. King sodding Arthur and the sodding knights. Oh yeah, and the rest. Bastards. Carey the bloodsucker. Mike the cold-hearted. They must hate women.

Why?

Why had she done what she did with Carey?

To be a pilgrim.

Why had she done what she did with Carey?

Who so beset him round
With dismal stories—

She was hot with shame at what she had done. She hadn't liked it. Why had she done it?

Because he was King Arthur. He was Lancelot. He was her *preux chevalier*. Her King of Cups.

Do but themselves confound
His strength the more is.

Because she was a stupid gullible little girl who adulated a grown man and allowed him to corrupt her. Because it had pleased her to abase herself, to give herself voluptuously up to him, to wallow in him so that she was beyond thought, beyond sense. Beyond decency.

She had been confounded. His strength was the more. She had made a compact with the devil, selling her conscience for somewhere to belong. Someone to belong to.

He had been so brightly beautiful. She had gazed on him with love and foolishness. She had become an idiot in her love. Nothing had discouraged her and if Carey hadn't tired of her she'd probably be hanging around King's Cross earning him a bob or two. Her stupidity had been bottomless.

She could smell burning. Little flightless beetles would go pop as their chitin exploded.

Then fancies flee away—

He had relented. He had grown tired of her. Cruelly, with savagery, he had released her. She was free.

I'll fear not what men say.

But she did. She was terrified of people knowing about those photographs, about her humiliation at DayStar. Mike had said something that frightened her though he probably meant nothing by it. What had it been? It was when he was going on about her inferiority in the matter of saving his life. She wasn't good enough, had been his idea. It would embarrass him to be saved by something like her. *You being what you are.* That was what he had said. You being what you are. Female. Young. Weak. Of no account. That must be what he meant. But her sore humiliated soul was reminded of Alec Dayfield's assumption. She was a whore, she groped men for money.

I'll labour night and day
To be a pilgrim.

She had walked through the wilderness of the world. She had dwelled in the city of Destruction and that city was a man. So had she entered the valley of Humiliation and she still lived there between its steep walls hard by the slough of Despond.

Carey had let her go, poor maimed thing that she was, and now she was free.

She was buried alive. She was free.

Don't think about it.

All her friends, even the ones who had shared school holidays with her occasionally, had had homes to go to. All had had one foot in school and one in the outside world. So when it came time to leave the safe haven of Shaws, they had walked free. Balanced.

She had pogo-sticked into the world. She had hopped. She only had one foot and she had lurched into the world a cripple.

Someone was right by her.

She could hear him. He was breathing heavily and muttering occasionally under his breath. One of his knees was on her arm with only two inches of sandy soil separating them. He was kneeling resting his gun probably on the rock she lay under. She could hear the metal scrape. She could hear him work the bolt.

Inside she quietly screamed. I want this to end. I want this to end. I want this to end. She said it to herself, over and over and over. She had had enough. She had lost track of how many days she and Mike had fled through the war-torn bush. The blood-soaked bush. The bush filled with secret atrocities, private torturings, casual premature death.

This was mankind brought down with a vengeance. Here in this war he was no more than a dogfox, than a little brown bird, than an insect. The forces of nature were too great and surely it was man's nature that unleashed this killing. The forces of nature in man.

Her body gave an uncontrollable shudder. Behind her eyes Fear woke up and danced madly with his partner Panic. She jolted because the man kneeling on her fired his gun.

She could smell him. She could smell the gun.

She had been so brave with the snake. Why couldn't she be brave now?

Because Carey had taught her to be terrified of men, of what they could do. Nature was impassive, impersonal, but a man would deliberately hurt her and gain pleasure from her pain. Carey had taught her that. Mike was the closest she had come to a man since Carey, for her relationship with Father Berhanu in Jinka was dignified and restrained, most soothing. But Mike was nasty. He did his duty by her but it was like she was a dog.

Why? Was it something in herself?

A flaw?

She was so frightened. If this went on much longer she

would give herself up simply to put herself out of her misery.

Breathing was difficult. Fear tightened her chest. Her throat felt bruised. She heard the man on her cough and spit. He fired his gun again. Then his weight came off and she heard the drumbeat of his running feet fade away.

Breathing was very difficult. Her eyes watered. It was smoke. It was fire. A tiny sob welled in her throat and Gossamer released the bush that covered her face and pushed it out from the crack under the rock. She twisted her face away till she faced into the rock. She shut her eyes and felt her chest heave painfully as she stifled her coughing.

As in a nightmare there were noises, cryings out, shoutings, shootings, drivings. The world thudded, squeaked, twittered and roared. She was seared, the tongue of flame passing over her and licking her sweetly. She heard dull roarings and still the smoke rolled in hot choking clouds. She sobbed drily and lay still.

To be a pilgrim.

You had to be brave to be a pilgrim and you had to know where you were going and why. She was lost and lonely and afraid and unloved. She couldn't manage it. The burden was too heavy.

Unloved. That was it. She had believed Carey loved her and she had believed love supreme. Love forgave all. Love countenanced all.

So. It wasn't true. Like Santa Claus and the Tooth Fairy, it wasn't true.

To love was to be vulnerable. She was better as she was, her fancies flown away. Unloving and unloved. If she was unloving, it was because her love had been torn from her living body and thrown away, so that inside she had a bleeding emptiness.

'Gossamer.'

Unloved. *Mother*.

'Gossamer. They've gone.'

He stroked the sandy earth off her. Her cheek was tender where the fire had hurt her. He had lost part of his eyebrows. He squatted patiently by the silent girl getting the grit out of her clothes as best he could.

She said and did nothing, her eyes tragic in her dirty face. He poured some precious water into the cap and gave it to her. He had to hold it to her lips. Still she said nothing.

'Gossamer,' he said desperately. 'What's happened? Why are you like this? You were so brave.'

She jerked suddenly and swallowed. She smiled. 'You could call me Sam,' she said.

'What?'

'Sam. It's sort of from my name. Then you wouldn't have to say it.'

With the back of his hand he gently touched her cheek. 'I'm sorry,' he whispered. 'I'm sorry I said that.'

'The truth,' she said with difficulty.

He knelt by her where she sat. He put his arms round her and held the stiff unhappy body against his own. The sky lost its soft lightness and became a brilliant peacock blue. Gradually the brightness dimmed as if sucked into the vacuum of space. Its colour deepened and darkened. Foot of the Day, the evening star, shone out low on the flat horizon. The moon became visible and hung drunkenly on its back, a thin diamond-bright crescent. One by one the first stars appeared. They massed in fistfuls till they pricked the entire moth-black sky. The Milky Way made a web across the sky, it was gauze on the wound of the weeping planet.

The sky trembled under its weight of stars sagging earthwards. Gossamer sat in the circle of Mike's arms with her soul weeping and he held her, stroking her, saying nothing, offering a wordless comfort.

They came out of the depression the next day. They climbed up almost able to smell water, their senses so finely attuned. They climbed steadily into a pale blue sky wisped by white clouds. There was a breeze. It was very pleasant except that they were tired and frightened and hungry and thirsty.

Gossamer said nothing all day. She ate the little Mike gave her. She drank sparingly, taking advantage of the cooler day to conserve their water. She had developed a slight limp but she made no complaint.

He had stopped to adjust a strap on his haversack. It worked loose and tangled with the rifle strap and every so often he had to take it off and pull the thing tight again.

Gossamer was just ahead. He watched her with troubled eyes. She limped steadily forwards as though she would walk to the ends of the earth if he said so.

Damn her. Damn her for what was happening to her.

Suddenly she stopped. She stood for a moment and then awkwardly she turned and looked back.

He couldn't see her face, the light was behind her. Her arms went up so that she stood against the sky as though crucified. For a moment she was frozen in silhouette. Then she fell.

He grabbed his haversack and ran. He felt the pain in his injured leg fierce suddenly as he pounded up the stony slope. The sky was the softest blue he had seen since entering the continent of Africa, English in its softness.

He stopped abruptly. He was on a precipice. Below him, far below, a river wound in a peaceful blue ribbon between banks of dazzling white sand edging a lush greenery. It was a fairytale vision. The river flowed through a wide gorge so that level with his eyes far across it the dry savanna grassland started again.

Of Gossamer there was no sign.

He stared down. The cliff face was a steep broken descent from which trees and bushes grew in profusion. A tumble of scree footed it. He could see no outflung broken body.

'Gossamer,' he shouted. The gorge caught his voice and threw it back. The sound reverberated, bouncing between the stony walls until it was swallowed by their indifference.

Mike swung the haversack onto his back. He turned round and stepped over the edge.

Concentrating hard he began to climb down.

She was on a ledge. He saw the dull dusty grey of the haversack first. It was hooked on a bush, cradled in the leaves.

The girl lay on her back, one knee slighly raised and her arms outflung. Her eyes were closed. He jumped down beside her, shrugged off his haversack and knelt over her.

He saw her breast rise and felt weak with relief. This was followed immediately by a profound fear concerning broken bones.

A broken back.

She had grazed one cheek. He leant over her and brushed her hair back where it had come loose. Her hat was tied on her haversack, she had been unable to keep it on in the breeze that had blown all day.

Her cheekbones were high and winged, her face slanting with an exotic beauty that showed through the dirt, the exhaustion, the hollowness of deprivation.

A numbing anger filled him. He was terrified of what hurt she must have sustained. He fumbled in her haversack and found the antiseptic ointment. He knew he was behaving crazily but still he squeezed out a little of the white cream and dabbed it on the torn cheek.

Her eyes fluttered and opened. Her lips parted and he caught a glimpse of white teeth. There was a light puzzled crease on her brow as she frowned up at him.

He was lying along the ledge beside her, lying half across her body resting on his elbow.

'Gossamer,' he whispered.

The dark blue eyes cleared and focussed. She smiled, a real full happy smile straight into his face just above hers.

'It's all right,' she said. 'It's all right now.'

'Are you hurt?'

'No.' She grinned saucily. 'We're safe now.'

He felt her try to move. 'Careful,' he said. He touched her face again.

'Mike.'

'Yes.'

'Look.'

He turned his head. The cliff face was obscured by hanging greenery. 'What is it?' he said gently. He could feel the coldness growing inside himself, clutching at his heart. She had hit her head.

She laughed. 'Look again.'

This time he reached out. He saw a break in the warm reddish stone. He moved aside some foliage.

Petra. A rose-red city.

Gossamer continued to look up quizzically into his face. 'See?' she said.

'What is it?'

'A safe haven. You can go in.'

He sat up. She then sat up proving she hadn't broken her spine. 'You've banged your head,' he said.

'I'll say.' She fingered the back of her head and yelped slightly.

'Let me look.'

She twisted round. 'Don't hurt me,' she said.

His fingers investigated her skull carefully. He could feel the lump but there didn't seem to be any broken skin.

He stood up and helped her up. She stood against him, leaning away from the edge. 'I'm glad I didn't go over there,' she said.

'So am I,' said Mike carefully.

She hunkered down and went on to her hands and knees. 'I'm going in,' she said. She dropped onto her belly and wriggled into the face of the cliff.

Mike wiped his face with a shaking hand, grasped his haversack and followed.

He thought he had gone mad himself. It was green inside, a wonderful watery green that was all dancing light and soft delicate air. Gossamer sat on a stone and watched. The waterfall fell out of the cave roof and tumbled down into a pool from which it appeared to drain away down into the cliff itself.

Further up and along there were cracks to the outside that
admitted a green-dappled sunlight and a delicate lacework of
hanging foliage. The whole air of the cave was that of diffuse
watery light, as though they were merfolk in some subsea
kingdom. The light was constantly on the move and a soft
flicker teased the edge of Mike's eyesight.

'How did you know it was here?' he asked helplessly. He
had a feeling of things being out of his control.

'When I woke up. When I was on that ledge. I just
knew.' She looked very comfortable. 'There's lots of it,'
she added.

'It's beautiful.' He didn't know what else to say.

'There's so much of it. They used to live here. But now
I'm thirsty and I'm filthy and I'm famished. Let's drink what
we have left and fill the water bottles. Then I'm going to
take a shower.'

'We don't have much food left,' he said nervously. Her
fey mood was frightening him.

'That'll be all right, too,' she said.

A kind of expectant trembling filled him. Her certainty
was hypnotic after all the days of struggle. He wanted to
accede to her oddness yet he felt he had to cling to the
rational.

She'd been right about the cave, though.

'Leave the haversacks here,' she said firmly. 'Go and find
the food. It's hereabouts somewhere. You can climb down
the cliff.'

He left without a word. She was scarier and scarier.

It was easy climbing down. There were innumerable
ledges and green stuff grew everywhere providing lavish
handholds. He was aware of other entrances to the city in
the cliff. He soon reached the floor of the ravine.

Fine white pebbles fringed the river which was wide and
deep. The air smelled glancingly clean. Tall slender trees
had silvery trunks like birches but they hung feathery heads
over the water like soft palms. It was a slice of paradise
set in the dusty plateau above and suddenly Mike knew
that Africa was like this, all over. It was full of sudden

contrasts, pearls of beauty, and if a man wasn't careful it would get to him and he would have to stay. Africa would own him.

The shingle scrunched under his feet. He caught movement out of the corner of his eye. He heard a bleating noise.

His heart smote him. It was a kid, a wild goat kid, and it was caught in a bramble on the cliff.

He hated this. He was going to have to kill it. He might be hungry but he had never butchered his own food and the young feebly struggling thing awoke compassion rather than bloodlust in his breast.

He took a hesitant step forward. Then his heart froze.

The inert piece of wood lying below the kid resolved itself. It was a crocodile.

He ran forward. He might hate to kill the little beast but he was damned if a mobile handbag was going to pinch his dinner out from under his very eyes.

The terrible saurian head came round and he saw the ghastly comic-book smile of the thing. It waddled a step forward. Mike bent down and picked up a big rock. He threw it and it landed square on the thing's head. It made a grunting noise and waddled abruptly back into the water. There it lay almost entirely submerged, its eyes up and its nostrils clear of the water, watching.

Mike scrambled up the cliff, slit the kid's throat and cut it free from the brambles. He took it along the river a short way and keeping a wary eye on the edge of the water he decapitated the little corpse and skinned it. He slung all this into the river. It sank slowly, whirling down on the stream and then abruptly it disappeared. Mike quickly rinsed his hands and the knife. He removed his shirt, emptied the pockets and dipped it in the water. Then he washed the carcase and gutted it. By the time he was ready to retreat up the cliff he had eyes watching him with silent malevolence from several parts of the stream.

He picked up his wet shirt, stuffed his papers into his

trousers pocket, took up the pathetic remains of the kid and climbed swiftly back up to the cave.

It took him a moment to find the right place. He thought of calling out but didn't. Finally he found Gossamer's haversack. He ducked down and wriggled in to the cave.

He stopped and licked his lips. He was a sophisticated man and he had led a full life. But what he saw took his breath away.

It was the slimness of her. The long pale flanks, the slender haunches, the sucked-in belly, the exquisite full pointed breasts: all yielded a supple grace and vulnerable fragility that literally took his breath away.

She was standing in the pool singing to herself. Water streamed over her, through her hair, down her body, cleansing her skin and washing away her terrible numbing fatigue.

Just so might a nereid have been in Arcady.

He stood staring at her. He was aware of a perfectly crude and entirely natural feeling. He stood transfixed and inevitably she turned and saw him.

'I'm sorry. I couldn't bear to wait. I'm not showing you anything you haven't seen elsewhere before so just ignore me.'

He found his voice. 'Ignore you?'

She had turned her back. 'I'm embarrassing you,' she said calmly. How comically prudish he was. 'I'll just go out and sit in the sun for a moment to get dry. I promise to leave you in peace while you get clean. I'll wash our clothes in the river if you like.'

'There are crocodiles. Don't go down.'

'I'll manage here then. When you're done call me in. You can retreat decorously while I clean our things up.'

He had deposited the carcase on a shelf of rock. He stood barechested holding the knife, aware of the fatuity of the situation. She glanced round at him from under her long dark lashes. He saw her breasts in profile again. She stepped out of the water and shook herself slightly.

'I'm sorry,' she repeated. 'I didn't think you'd care. I won't do it again.'

He caught her arm as she made to go by him to the exit. He felt it, wet and cool in his hand. He took her other arm unaware he still held the knife.

He looked into her face unable to find the words. She was puzzled but unafraid. Then he lifted her arms slightly, holding her away from him, looking down her body.

Droplets of water ran slowly over the satin texture of her skin. The green-dappled light confused him. Her breasts were tipped a pale café-au-lait colour. Her wet black hair was pushed back from her face. He could see the graze on her cheek, water standing on the greasy remnants of the antiseptic cream.

She had wet black hair below, too, water caught in its curls and dripping down her thighs. Her thighs were very slim.

He felt the flame in him. Slowly he pulled her towards him, in against his own naked chest.

He saw her face. 'Why do you do this?' she whispered.

He felt his mouth open. He felt her nipples brush his chest. He felt the long cool body of her. 'Gossamer,' he said unsteadily.

'Let me go, Mike. I'm sorry. I didn't think you'd be like this.'

His lips were at her ear, his face questing at her. His hands were in the small of her back. He pressed her body gently into his own. 'Like what?'

'You don't like me.'

'You fool,' he breathed. His lips trailed round from her ear across her cheek. For a moment he touched her eye. He kissed the lid, feeling it flutter under his lips.

Now he was kissing by the side of her nose. His lips touched hers. He touched her mouth gently several times, as though asking, as though seeking entry.

She could feel her heart pounding. She had been sure she was safe from this. Yet he held her so gently. His caress, his lips were so tender. Her pent-up desire to be wanted spilled out. She wanted to arch her back and press into him, invite him on. Invite him in.

Whore. He wanted sex. This wasn't comfort. This wasn't kindness. This wasn't tenderness. He wanted sex and so did she. The truth was, she wanted him.

She got her hands against his chest and pushed. 'No,' she said.

He caught her lips again with his own. This time he opened her mouth. She tasted him. She felt the rub of his stubble. She felt his chest warm and dry against her breasts.

He pulled her sharply and kissed her neck. Her head fell back and she gasped. He drew his head back a little. 'If you mean to stop me, do it now,' he said huskily.

She brought her head up and faced him. 'I don't understand,' she said.

'I want you. What's to understand?'

'I didn't mean to rouse you.'

He put a hand in her wet hair and held her head. He kissed her brow, her eye, her cheek. 'I want to make love to you,' he said. 'Are you going to let me?'

He looked into her face for a moment. Then he held her head and kissed her mouth deeply, opening it and tasting her and stirring her until she could no more pull back than he could.

She woke up naked in Mike's arms. He was kissing her. He was bare-chested and he smelled of the sun. She herself was quite naked and she was wet and cool.

They were in a cave. The rock was warm and pale in the filtered sunlight. The air was deliciously soft and moist. It was the first time she hadn't felt thirsty in many long days.

A sensation of panic flooded her. Yet stronger than it and in command of her body was her desire to submit to Mike's caresses. The feel of their naked skin, touching. His hands holding her. His thudding heart. The sweetness and intoxication of his mouth. Everything in her yearned to respond.

Where were they? How had she got here? What had changed between herself and Mike? Demonstrably he had been a man who disliked her, right from the start.

There was no mistaking what he was feeling now. He was kissing her more deeply, using his mouth, hands and body to arouse her so that her longing matched the force of his.

His skill was enchanting. But she was eager as well. She had suppressed her desire for him, knowing it was inappropriate and out of place. Knowing he had no desire for her.

They had seen the battle. He had dug her grave. She couldn't remember anything since seeing the shallow hole under the rock and knowing she had to get in it.

If this was a dream she would give herself up to it utterly. She moved her body sensuously against Mike's and for the first time kissed him properly back. Her hands slid over his naked back and one explored his neck and up into his hair.

He bent to kiss one breast, holding under it with his cupped hand while he kissed its upper contour. Then he pulled free. He took the blanket from his haversack and spread it on the dry sandy floor. He unbuckled his belt.

She stood numbly while he stripped. When his hands were free he caught her face between them and twisted her so that she lay on the blanket with him over her.

'Darling,' he whispered.

'Yes?'

'I want you very badly but I mustn't make you pregnant. Have you any protection?'

She reached up a hand and touched his unshaven cheek. 'It's fine,' she said.

He hesitated a moment, his eyes searching hers. Then he kissed her. She felt the tension in his body and her own thrilled. He would enter her soon.

How strange.

Half a year. No man for half a year. She had thought no man ever.

She gasped. Her body had its own rules. She felt her

velvet flesh split. She was tight but moist. All the time he tried to come into her he kissed her. When he was right in he hesitated.

He was a very tender lover. He was so strange, so different. The man was conducting an orchestra with her body and occasionally he waited for her.

She was slow on the uptake. She missed her cue several times. How odd to make love like this, not with one to command and one to serve, but as partners, both playing together. Taking turns. Teaching each other things. Having patience for one another's pace. Savouring the act. Exploring its emotional potential. Strolling in the garden of sexual delight and softly calling to each other, *see this, see this*.

He came to climax fiercely when he was sure she was ready. Her body was flooded with peace. He continued to lie beside her, shifting his weight but cradling her in the aftermath. He kissed her ear.

She was unable to keep quiet. 'I felt like a novice,' she said, marvelling. 'You're wonderful.'

He laughed. 'Dreadful girl. I owe you an apology.'

'You do?'

'I didn't shower first.'

She was lying on her back with her head pillowed on his arm. Now she turned it to look at him. They were almost nose to nose. She kissed the tip of his. 'I've been away, Mike.'

'What do you mean?'

'We hid in the desert. What happened?'

'What?'

'Mike, I can't remember. There was the fire and the battle. We hid. You buried me, didn't you? What happened after that? How did we get here?'

'My God.' He stared at her. She began to feel afraid. As he saw her expression change he drew her in to his body. 'You were very upset when I got you out,' he said to her hair. 'You cried for a bit and we spent the night there. Then we walked the next day. You didn't say anything. You fell off the cliff here and banged your head. You told me the cave was here. You knew it was here. You told me I'd find food. I did. I came back and found you naked and you were so beautiful and I was so hungry for you.'

'Yes,' she said. 'It's like a film I once saw. It's as though I've seen it and mostly forgotten it. It's not like it happened to me. Yesterday. Today.'

'You're remembering?'

'I'm remembering. Except that it doesn't seem to belong to me.'

'How did you know about the cave? Have you been here before?'

'No. I don't know where we are. I've only been in this country since the end of March.'

His brown eyes looked into hers. 'And when we made love?' he said lightly. 'Was that you or someone else?'

She shut her eyes and sensed her body. She smiled. 'That was me,' she said softly. 'That was definitely me.'

They collected dry kindling from outside, scrambling like goats from ledge to ledge both in their nakedness. Back in the cave Mike built a fire and used his lighter to start it with dry grass. He rigged up a spit and they began to roast the kid.

While it was cooking he showered. Gossamer stood with him and used her hands to wash him clean. It was astonishingly wonderful to touch his hard naked body. He sat between her legs, his back to her, whilst he shaved with his stump of soap, brush and razor.

The meat sizzled. Mike washed his face and turned to her.

She was surprised at the passion in him despite having been teasing him. She was more active this time, kissing him, exploring his body, giving way to her desire to please herself even as she gave herself to please him. He was less gentle but she was more assured. They came to a climax that was almost blinding and she knew he was moved even as she was.

He was different with her afterwards. She no longer had

the feeling that all his doors were shut and locked against her. For all that, he volunteered no personal information and she asked for none. Yet they were companions now, real companions, not mere voyagers trapped unwillingly on the same journey.

They ate as much meat as they wanted. Then they ate the last of the raisins. Afterwards they lay flat, spreadeagled on the blanket side by side, groaning with full bellies.

Later, in the dark, they made love again.

He took his time. She enjoyed every moment of it. They meshed now, engaging emotionally as though machined for the purpose. It was almost frightening. She both responded and was responsible. She hadn't known the act of love could be like this, funny, tender, frighteningly intense, blindingly beautiful. She was astonished at her own virtuosity and yet she knew she needed him, and his. It was a two-handed achievement. For two bodies. Two partners.

Afterwards he lay on his back. She lay half across him, her head on his shoulder, his arm comfortingly across her body. Fulfilment cradled her and she was at peace.

'Mike,' she said dreamily.

'Yes, darling.'

'You're a wonderful lover.'

He gave a snort of laughter. She rolled over onto her elbows and rubbed noses with him. Then she kissed his mouth. He stroked her hair and she could feel his lips smiling up into her face.

'I've only . . . I mean, I'm not very old and . . .'

'I know,' he said roughly. 'Don't say it. You can't help it, you poor silly bitch. You might learn something though, if it's not too late.'

She had wanted to say something. Not a lot. Just something to the effect that she had only loved one man and he had been a brute and she hadn't realised till things had got out of hand. That was all. But his response astonished her.

He was too complex for her to understand. She had been aware of his dislike, he hadn't troubled to hide it. Then he had craved her naked body. She could understand that. She knew she was beautiful and that she could stir men and rouse them with her looks alone. But she hadn't expected all his dislike to vanish, as it apparently had. He was simply lovely to her. He made love tenderly, superbly, kindly. He drew her into equality through their love-making. He laughed with her, obviously happy and satisfied.

Trusting him now, she had wanted to probe. She had wanted to get another man's opinion as to Carey, in fact. She wouldn't have said as much, but she had a crying need to know if men tended more to be like Carey or more to be like Mike, when they were naked with a woman. Naked in the fullest sense.

Thinking it through, she had been silly to try. She would never have told Mike enough for him to give her the response she actually wanted. That Carey was a freak. But she had never got that far because Mike had stopped her.

'Too late? I'm only nineteen.'

'It isn't years, it's experience.'

'I know. I can't help being so young but it can't be too late as well.'

'Some experience gets in the way of other experience. Learning some things stops you learning others.'

She cried out: 'What can you know about what I know?'

He sat up and held her tightly, pressing her face against him. 'I've walked through hell with you by my side,' he said. 'And I've made love to you. What else need a man know?'

For some terrible moments she had thought he knew of that other life. 'I'm sorry,' she gasped. 'I'm so sorry. You've made me happy yet you're so strange to me.'

'Strange to you?' he murmured.

'Such a stranger.' She pulled free of him and looked into his face. The embers of the dead fire showed the contours of him but they shadowed his expression. 'I know you're brave,' she said shyly. 'You have a sense of responsibility. You never complain. You can be kind. You think quickly. You can handle strange situations. You have self-restraint. You have compassion. And as a lover you are perfect.'

There was a charged silence. The embers settled slightly, making a small noise.

'All I know about you is your name. I don't know where you live, how old you are, whether your parents are alive, how you were educated, even if you are married.' She gave a little gasp. 'You might have children. I don't know about your job, your friends, or anything about you. Yet I suppose I know all that's important to know about another human being.'

'I'm not married. I have no children.' His voice was cool.

'I've not had a good time,' she said deliberately. 'I've found people difficult. If we get out of this alive, perhaps it'll have done me good.'

'I hope so.' The neutral voice seemed to come from so far away.

She felt tears prick her eyes. 'I'm young,' she repeated, keeping her voice steady. 'I can learn. It's just that I've a long way to go.'

But not with you, it seems, her mind added silently.

'Your looks get in the way.'

'What?'

'You're so beautiful. You're incredible to look at. It's hard to think straight, even when you're filthy and starving. I'm not a particularly susceptible man, I learnt long ago what bitches most lovely women are, but I couldn't withstand you. Then again, you're very young, as we both keep saying. You're starting out. Short of plastic surgery, you're going to have to live with the problem.'

'The problem?' She was groping to follow his meaning.

'Of your looks. I know what you are yet to have held you in my arms, to have made love with you feels like an honour.'

'I'm just a human being,' she whispered. 'I have feelings. I need things.'

'You'll get whatever you want.' His voice was brutal. 'But you need to be clear what it is you want or you might not like what you get.'

'Mike,' she cried blindly.

In a second he had his arms round her. He crushed her to him. After a moment he said: 'Yeah. Like this. Be like this.' Abruptly he kissed her and she knew he wasn't acting. He had a hunger for her that wasn't appeased. 'Perhaps I should call you Sam,' he said. 'The other one, she's got the fancy name. I'm in the dark with Sam.'

She was bewildered. 'I don't mind,' she said helplessly.

He lay down, pulling her on top of him. 'Sam,' he whispered. 'Darling. Each time we make love I want you more.'

'Yes,' she agreed. 'Yes, I know. I mean, it's like that for me. I want you more.'

'You haven't made love for some time, have you?'

'No. Six months. Do I hurt you?' Her voice was piteous.

'Oh, my sweet love. I'm frightened of hurting you.'

She moved on his body. There was some terrifying muddle going on. The minute they spoke, she knew she wasn't understanding. But their bodies could speak and did speak. Whatever it was, it was true for them both. He felt it as strongly as she did.

They were in this cave half as old as time. The cliff was riddled with caves, moulded and wrought by ancient human hands. It was Petra again, hidden, unknown, lost in the ancient Empire of Ethiopia.

Their bodies could and did speak. They made love. They slept. They woke and ate and drank and they made love again.

But they had nothing to say to each other. They were out of the world but they were of it.

Now they must go back.

❊ Twelve ❊

He stood before them as if from nowhere. Mike gasped and stood still.

They had been approaching for some time a vast rock lying like a whale in front of them. The terrain was both beautiful and almost consciously primitive. Huge boulders the size of a house lay scattered in genial profusion. Leafy trees grew between them but there was enough firm dusty ground to walk with ease through this natural playground that with a little art would make so spectacular a garden.

A sort of strawy grass grew. They had seen nothing and no one all day. Both of them had the feeling of an empty land, a kindly land, untouched by the war.

They didn't trouble to speak. They had a harmony between them and they didn't interfere with it or try to shape it with language.

Sometimes Mike held her hand. He smiled at her and his manner was gentle and friendly. Gossamer felt an enormous and undemanding affection for him and she felt it went both ways.

They were happy.

Now, suddenly, this man stood before them. Even as they faced him, other men appeared silently from the landscape around them, till twenty men faced them, silently.

They wore traditional costume, a sort of blue tunic wrap-around. On their arms and ankles they wore strings of beads. The skin of their foreheads had lines of decorative scars.

They carried spears. Some of them held rifles.

Very slowly Mike squatted before the first man who confronted them. He was not young and his hair had gone a dignified grey. Mike unslung his rifle and laid it on the ground. Then he shrugged off the bandolier with the bullets and laid it by the gun.

'Do the same,' he said to Gossamer without turning his head away from the old man. 'Move slowly. Let them see what you are doing.' He stood up and stepped back.

She put her rifle on the ground with Mike's. They had agreed she must only use it *in extremis*. Not only had she probably bent the barrel using it as a lever to free Mike from the gin trap, but when Mike had buried her they had forgotten to plug the barrel, though he had done so with his own. The combination of dirt and possibly being out of line made it more dangerous to the one who held it than the one it was pointed at. Nevertheless, they had kept it for possible bluffing purposes.

She put down her cartridge belt. Now she stood by Mike.

'We mean no harm,' he said clearly. He held out his empty hands. 'We wish to pass.'

The bush chirped and squeaked, untroubled by the presence of humans.

'*Parlez-vous Français?*' asked Gossamer. '*Tenaystelegn,*' she added tentatively.

The old man turned to her and spoke. 'I do not speak Amharic well enough to converse in that language,' he said. 'I certainly do speak a little French but I suspect that we would be more comfortable in English.'

Mike said: 'We're trying to escape from the war.'

'Aren't we all?' He clapped his hands softly. Women appeared as silently as the men, some with babies and small children. Slowly the tribe gathered. There was an atmosphere of interest and friendliness.

Some of the women wore tunics. Some wore just loin cloths. All wore beads and all had fat swags of blue beads hung over and under their ears. A thin leather thong supported these, worn around the forehead.

'We are Murlé,' said the old man. He squatted in the dust and the tribe settled round him. 'Since our lands are partly in Sudan and partly in Ethiopia, we have lived with war about us for many years. Why do you come here?'

'We had come south from Soddu the first day we met trouble. My companion, Miss Fane, was heading for Jinka where she assists in a school. We never got there. I decided after we were forced off the road that we were closer to Kenya than Addis Ababa and we have been making our way south ever since.'

The old man turned to Gossamer and smiled. 'I myself received my education in a school such as that at Jinka. Later I went to your country, to the University in Oxford. I came back and taught the students in Addis Ababa all about Miss Austen with her tales of wise and foolish virgins in English country villages that had remarkable similarities to rural villages in my home country.'

'What happened?' asked Mike quietly.

'I grew old. I wanted to see my people. Because of the wars there was no school any more in my village. I came home to start one. There were wars. There was drought. There were more wars. I decided to stay with my people. I am after all more Murlé than Professor of English Literature, perhaps.'

They were handed bowls of a porridge-like substance. The old man looked into his and smiled at them. 'I know how you like meat,' he said. 'We have very little meat and then I do not think you enjoy our custom of eating it almost raw.'

Gossamer said earnestly: 'We're very grateful for the food. I am starving for bread or potatoes or cereal. We've been carrying tinned meat though it's nearly gone. We hope we're not far from Kenya.'

'Not far indeed. Go to the crest of those hills and you will see where you are going.'

Mike sighed. 'May I give you our meat, then,' he said. He was trying not to wolf his porridge. Like Gossamer he craved carbohydrates.

'You have had no trouble on your journey?'

'Some,' said Mike. He smiled faintly. 'We don't understand

which side is which and both frighten us. We've thought it better not to be seen.'

'This is a local thing,' said the old man. 'It is, ah, serendipity. The real war is in the north. The people of Eritrea and Tigre have come together. They are boys, only boys. But they have brought Mengistu down.'

'Mengistu!'

'It is hard to mourn the passing of a dictator,' said the old man and his eyes twinkled. 'When Addis settles down, this local eruption will be calmed. I think our land is ready for peace. We have drought to fight, and ignorance, and the World Bank, and our foreign debt. I do not think we need to fight among ourselves as well.'

They spent altogether just over an hour with the tribe. They handed over their rifles and ammunition with a warning about Gossamer's. In exchange they received some baked cakes made from millet, and fried yams. Handing over their remaining corned beef and a tin opener seemed like a good swap.

They walked on in silence. They climbed the low range but they were not fast enough. At about seven the sun dropped below the horizon and they made what they hoped would be their last camp.

'I suppose we all have the capacity to lead entirely different lives,' said Mike. He sat resting his back against a rock looking at the aching beauty of the stars. The waxing moon was a little fatter but it looked just as drunken to northern eyes.

'Professor of English Literature and tribal father?'

'Something like that.' He reached up and pulled her down beside him. She came gladly. She needed the reassurance that he felt emotion for her, more than just lust.

'You've got your passport safe,' he said prosaically.

She patted her breast pocket. 'All the time,' she said.

'There might be trouble at the border.'

'They can hardly keep us out.'

'No,' he agreed.

'Though I wasn't planning on being able to exchange my Birr for Kenyan shillings.'

'I've got traveller's cheques on me,' said Mike.

'It seems funny to sit here talking about trivialities like money when we've been so afraid for our lives.'

'It's been a time for basics,' said Mike. He kissed her. Ignoring the possibilities of mosquitos he made love to her under the thundering silence of the stars. His body was strong and firm. As he held her afterwards, in silence, she knew that to see your lover by starlight was dangerous. The stars weighed down so that the dark was filled with a web of magic and they were contained within it.

She felt the sadness in him and marvelled that each time his love-making was so different.

The next morning they stood on the crest of the hill and looked into Kenya. Lake Turkana, the Jade Sea, spread south as far as the eye could determine. They walked down through dry thornbrush and termite castles and so they came safe and their terrible journey was over.

There was a moment of pure farce as they moved from Ethiopia's solar calendar back onto the Gregorian, used by the rest of the world. The end of November 1983 became at a stroke August 1991. Even the hours of the day fitted differently: the Ethiopian day starts at dawn and runs with a six hour difference, so they had to alter their watches.

They stepped forward in time and left the horror behind them, locked in the past.

Nothing could irritate them. Nothing could touch them. They spent hours at the border getting permission to enter, but their papers were in order, they carried money, and the nervous border guards knew perfectly well what was happening to their north. They drank tea like camels.

They were given three-month visitor passes. There was no bus for two days but a lorry, turned back from crossing the border, agreed to take them in the direction of Nairobi.

They arranged themselves on the back, nestling on the goods. They found to their horror that sacks of fertiliser and sacks of maize were carried muddled together. There were truck tyres and bananas. In all this they made themselves comfortable. Gossamer slept.

She came to at intervals. Sometimes there were tribespeople at the side of the road, tall, blanketed, carrying spears. She saw wattle trees and groves of palms beside the Lake where they passed a tourist resort. Further south the Lake had shallow muddy margins with clumps of dark-green algae growing. Once Mike caught her arm and they stared at elephants, a family of them, an unbelievable sight.

The lorry stopped in Nakuru, only sixty miles from Nairobi. They walked in their tattered clothes like hippies along suburban roads pink with jacaranda blossom. Mike found a bank and to strange looks he managed to change money. They went to a clothing mart and Gossamer bought a dress and some sandals and underwear.

'I'll pay you back,' she said.

'Don't worry.'

She found the proximity of people almost oppressive. The town was claustrophobic. Mike booked them into a hotel and while she went to bath he made telephone calls.

She was lying on the bed when he came back. The sheets were very white, very clean. Her body smelled of soap, her hair of shampoo. She had dried it and now it shone blue-black, full of health.

'Did you get through?' she asked. He hadn't explained who he was calling.

'Yes.'

He was remote, like the man she had first met. However, he had booked them one room and now he bathed himself and then he came to her.

'You OK?' he said.

'Yes.'

'In Nairobi, you know what to do?'

'I want to find out what happened to Jean. What happened in Jinka. I'll have to get onto the Embassy about money. My bank should wire some here so I have funds. I've got money in Addis but that's no good just now.'

'What will you do then?'

'I don't know, Mike. I've never thought, all this time. It seemed unlucky. I just wanted to live.'

He touched her brow. 'That time has passed. You need to forget it. You need to get on with your own life.'

'Yes.'

He drew back the sheet and looked at her clean sweet-smelling body. His face was almost grim.

He was miles away from her. He looked at her like she was meat. The whole enigma was there, confronting her. It was like the beginning, when they first met. He didn't like her.

His eyes were on her nakedness.

Slowly, unwillingly, she spoke. 'What is it about me?'

It was unbearable, his coldness. It gave the lie to everything they had been through, fighting to keep each other alive, safe.

'You're nineteen,' he said.

She kept silent. She felt an anger in herself.

He sat down on the edge of the bed and reached out to one of her breasts.

'Don't touch me.' Her voice was cold and low.

He was startled. His eyes flew to meet hers.

She came up on her elbows. She was hissingly angry. 'What we've been through,' she said. 'You made love to me. Love. You didn't screw me because I was there. We had something. It was good. Right. Now we're back in civilisation and we aren't in fear of our lives. You go cold as ice and treat me as if I was a reptile. As if you were being forced to do this.'

She sat up properly. Her voice was shaking with passion. She was trying not to shout. 'No one's forcing you, Mike. No one's making you do anything. You don't owe anything. I'm not asking for anything. I'm not expecting anything. I don't owe you any apologies and I don't need favours, especially sexual favours.'

Outside her open window in the gardens of the hotel the bell-birds were calling their twin insistent note.

'Do you want me to pay for it?' said Mike.

She stared at him open-mouthed. Then she began to back very carefully away from him, to the other side of the bed.

'I've never paid for it,' he said harshly. 'But you, you're worth anything. You're superb. The best.'

She got off the bed and backed against the wall. His eyes rested on her nakedness. 'You're mad,' she whispered. She was genuinely frightened.

'Mad?' He gave an ugly laugh. 'You don't realise what you are. You will, of course. Give it a year or so and you won't think me mad.'

'What am I? What do you think I am?'

He came across to her. Her eyes widened in fear and she held her breath.

Not rape. Please, not rape.

'You don't have to be afraid.' His voice was curiously husky. 'I couldn't hurt you. I've never wanted to make love to a woman more. And you aren't a woman. You're a child.'

'Why do you behave like this? It was so simple before.'

He stood in front of her. 'Sam,' he said gently. 'I like that. A special name. For a special occasion.'

'I liked you. I admired you.' She was whispering. 'We were equals, weren't we? We both wanted it. We both wanted this thing.'

He touched her cheek with the back of his hand. Then he bent and kissed her shoulder.

'Why do you suddenly treat me this way? You frighten me.'

He stood against her. His body was very solid. She could feel herself shaking where she touched him.

'It's whatever you want,' he murmured. 'Separate rooms, or here together. I want to make love to you. It's up to you.'

'I've been raped,' she said on a high note. 'I'm frightened of men. You're the first since . . .'

'I wondered why. I wondered why you'd gone so long. Gossamer. Sam, darling Sam. Oh my love, oh darling . . .'

He was kissing her, kissing her cheek, her neck, her shoulder. One hand had come up and he clasped her waist. She could feel his sex, risen and firm against her belly. Now his other hand came up and he took her head and drew her away from the wall. He kissed her with an ardent passion that was so sweet it was unbearable to make him stop. She knew she should. Something was horribly wrong with him. But she was passionately aroused herself.

He laid her on the bed and knelt over her kissing her body, her breasts, her belly and her thighs.

She was enormously stirred. She knew that desire overwhelmed him. Though he hated women he was a wonderful lover. It was astonishing. It was unbelievable. Had some woman taught him how to behave in bed and then abandoned him? Was that the source of his tormented character?

Meanwhile she could not think. She could only respond. She caught at him, too moved to be passive. They came together on the bed writhing in an agony of desire, wanting to touch their bodies all their length, touch and be touched.

He entered her like fire. Her body shuddered greedily holding his. She cried out, savagely taking what she needed. He was the same, ferocious in his appetite:

> *And tear our Pleasures with rough strife*
> *Through the Iron gates of Life.*

Yes. That's what they had done. They had passed through the Iron gates with a vengeance and they deserved this now, they deserved anything they could get after the pain and the fear and horror of the past days.

He came hard in her and then she was there too. It was the first time he hadn't waited for her to climax but now he continued to move in her as her body shook and shuddered in orgasm.

He held her tightly, crushed almost painfully against his body. She felt her cheeks wet. His face was against her own and she didn't know who wept, nor why.

They went to Nairobi by *matutu*, a sort of cheap minibus general to Kenya. They drove high through a green country neat and bright as an alpine pasture. They came down through fields of millet, grazing cattle and busy townships. Here was none of the poverty she had grown accustomed to. Children wore neat school uniforms. Little donkey carts cluttered the highway. Mimosa scented the air. All the time Mike said nothing.

He had hardly spoken after his strange outburst the previous day. They had eaten that evening in silence and then gone to bed together. She didn't understand why but she accepted it now. They had no language but sex.

She had fallen asleep in his arms without him making love again, as though he needed to prove he could control himself, he wasn't an animal on heat. But deep in the night she had woken to his caresses and he had entered her gently and made love with a lingering slow passion so that once again she marvelled at his skill, at his knowledge as a lover.

He took her to the Hotel Jomo Kenyatta on Tom Mboya Street. It was quite grand. It fronted a very busy street teeming with cafés and street vendors, but it was built round an inner court in which was a flame tree and trellises of bougainvillaea.

'I've paid in advance for three days,' he said.

'I should have some money by then and I'll be able to repay you. I want to find out what happened to Jean. I'll go to the Embassy tomorrow.'

'You'd better carry some cash. You'll need it for taxis.'

She was silent.

'I've paid full board,' he said awkwardly.

She stayed silent.

'So, goodbye.'

'Goodbye?'

'You'll be going back to England.'

'You're leaving now?' she said idiotically.

'Yeah. That's right. I've got a flight, actually.' He fumbled for cigarettes and busied himself lighting one. 'The thing is to forget all this. It's a bad memory, nothing more.'

She simply stood there, unable to believe her ears.

'Are you sure you have enough money?' he said. He licked his lips nervously.

She found her voice. 'How do I repay you?' She was very calm.

'It's nothing. Don't think about it.'

She drew on her store of pride. She straightened her back. She faced him quietly. 'I don't need your address,' she said. 'I can send it to your bank if you like. Or your publishers.'

'Publishers?'

She looked away, controlling her anger. If he had to lie to her, he could make the effort to remember what he had said.

She looked back. 'Thank you for looking after me. For taking care of me. For protecting me. I know what you did for me and I won't forget.'

'But you should.' His voice was rough. 'That's the thing to do.'

He had killed two men. He needed to forget. 'Yes,' she said at once. 'Bad memories.'

'Goodbye, then.'

'You're going now.'

'Yeah. My flight, you know.'

'Your flight.' She held out her hand. He hesitated a moment, then he took her slim tanned hand in his. 'The boy done good,' she said and smiled.

'What?'

'No James Bond, you said. You did pretty well. You did fine by me.'

He drew her to him quite slowly and kissed her on the mouth. Then he went away.

She only knew his name, Mike Andersen. She didn't know where he was going. She didn't know anything about him at all, except that he had some terrible twist in him where women were concerned. He must have been hurt very badly, she thought tenderly, to be so frightened of her.

He had liked her, she was sure. He had fought against it continuously, but he had liked her.

Poor silly man. What a waste.

There were moonflowers on her balcony, shaped like bells with pale sweet-scented yellow petals. She had her evening meal in the courtyard under the flame tree. Blue starlings with bright orange-yellow breasts came to drink at the fountain. A liquid bubbling filled the air, bottle birds, her waiter told her.

She didn't like the jacarandas any more. They smelled musty close to and she saw vultures in them.

It was the flame tree that she remembered best, flawless, beautiful.

❖ LONDON ❖

⚓ Thirteen ⚓

Gossamer straightened the picture and then stepped back, quietly drinking it in. A girl with a piece of sewing, but she was inattentive to it. Her attention was held elsewhere, beyond the frame but not by the viewer. She was thoughtful, abstracted, still and serene. The candle and the hands, light and luminous like the face that was also lit from within, and the shadow that enclosed them, all spoke of tranquillity and repose. Yet the girl looked out, looked beyond, her lips slightly parted, her eyes clear and untroubled.

A girl, Gossamer supposed, of about her own age.

It was not an original La Tour, of course. Idly Gossamer wondered if she could afford one and just as idly decided that she did not need to know. It was an honest print, honestly framed, and did not pretend otherwise. She had chosen it as much for that reason, for its integrity, as for anything else, although the fact of its being a La Tour set the seal on its rightness for her. There was an assurance in its tenderness that was balm to her soul. *For if I do hurt, I do it but in healing* ... Where did that come from? It didn't matter. What mattered was that it was perfect for her and that it connected with her in ways that had to do with more than mere artistic taste.

I chose you, she told the picture. She turned slowly around, addressing the whole room: I chose you all, she silently told it. Not a bunch of lawyers or interior decorators, and not ... not anyone else. You are all *my* choice. And I chose this place. I found it, and saw that it was right. I choose to be me. My name is Gossamer Fane and this is my home.

She hugged the knowledge deliciously close. Welcome home, she told herself. She held fast to it.

The writ of Chatteris Choate had run even in the land of flame trees and moonflowers. The man who dealt with her at the British Embassy came from the same mould as Barmy and Collywobbles, but something supercilious had been poured into it, and he had been inclined to treat her as though an invisible brush and shovel were part of his diplomatic equipment. At first. Then, suddenly, he was enormously flattered to be of service and Gossamer was hilariously aware that if they had been dancing he would have been at excruciating pains not to tread on her toes.

He'd asked how long she had been staying in Nairobi and she'd told him, two days.

'And before that, Miss Fane?'

'Addis. I came by Landrover, to begin with. With a friend. Then it got stuck, and we had to travel on foot. We had a bit of trouble on the way, but we made the border eventually. He was able to fly out straight away as he had funds here.' And she had smiled at him, and he had all but buckled at the knees. He'd gooped at her with saucer eyes.

'Gosh,' he'd said.

'It was rather hairy, actually,' she'd admitted frivolously, playing her part in this suddenly amusing charade. 'We had to dig ourselves graves at one point. Because of the gunfire, you know. And then there was a nasty incident with a puff adder, while we were hiding in a hollow tree. Fortunately it decided to bite someone else. So here I am.' It was like acting, she realised. She was playing to him as to a receptive, credulous audience.

'Of course, er, yes. Well, I'll just, er . . .'

'Thank you,' she'd said. 'You're very kind.'

It was all a fraud, of course, but hugely enjoyable. She'd imagined Marie was with her and they had exchanged comradely grins behind the back of this particular gambolling lamb.

And damn you, Mike, she'd thought. Damn you, and

thank you, and maybe one day you'll come clean and tell me what your problem is. Or even, maybe, why you felt you had to lie to me, in spite of everything we shared. In spite of what we almost had, and could have had, if you'd only let it happen.

But, damn you, you didn't, wouldn't, couldn't. With the result that we are both a little less than we could have been. Well, I can live with that. I won't let it be my loss. *Ave atque vale* . . . I am a Shaws girl, I'll have you know. A Shaws girl knows her Latin, and she is never put out. A Shaws girl is in no danger, it's not allowed. She comports herself.

So then that nice young man at the embassy, a very minor spider in the great web of interconnected influence, had tweaked the invisible threads and smoothly organised for her money, credit, a through ticket to Heathrow and a reservation at Brown's Hotel.

And she had never given him cause to suspect that she was a bewildered gilded fly, caught in its intricate geometry. After all, hadn't she once been a very promising actress? She could act her way out of it.

Play your part hard enough, she told herself, and one day you may become it. And then there will be no pain, no questioning, no yearning. Nobody knows who you really are. Including you. Therefore you have the right – the duty – to invent yourself. Starting now.

You're very special, Gossamer, and you mustn't forget it. He had said that: Carey Lambert. Very well then, she thought, I won't. But I will forget you. You taught me a lot of things, and one of them was how to be angry. I will become the product of that anger, I will find myself and be myself. For me, alone.

I will shortly be twenty years old, she told herself. In some ways I feel hideously mature, in others I am just starting, starting from scratch. It is up to me to synthesise. I must define myself and be myself, it is the most important thing to do. I must get wisdom. Nobody else can possibly know what it is to be me, so it's time I faced up to it. I seem all along to have been the invention of other people. Now is the time to write my own script. I must stop floating.

Thirty thousand feet above the turning earth, connected to nothing but herself, she planned her life. Several time zones and uncountable hours later she hit the ground, running.

London simmered in a late summer stew of stone and tarmac and traffic, but Brown's Hotel was the ideal setting for the long working weekend she had allowed herself. Life within its precincts seemed to move at its own leisurely and well-organised pace, like a country house without the eccentricities. The routines she lived in allowed her the feeling that she was dictating them herself, and with this to sustain her she voyaged out, safely adventurous, on her quest to find a home.

Hampstead was out, of course. She did not want anything to do with any of that. For all that Chatteris Choate would be paying the rent, it was her money and she was determined not to spend a single penny of it on something that might echo in her false past. No doubt they had already found some other pretty bird to fill that particular gilded penthouse cage. Perhaps even now Carey Lambert was charming her and teaching her the special tricks he liked best of all ... She wrenched her mind away from the thought. She would miss Arthur, though, good old solid, kind, dependable, normal, decent Arthur. And Silvio, propping his eyelids open to earn the money to see him through his degree. She blushed to remember that it was only at the very end that she had seen him as a person, a creature of hopes and plans just as she was, and not as a mere functionary, a servant, a piece of property just as she had allowed herself to become. She built the thought into the foundations of her new life.

I'll be OK, she'd said. *I'll survive. I've learnt from all this mess.* Now was her chance to prove it.

She went to Chatteris Choate, by appointment. She had wanted to ask after Kevin Germain but she restrained herself, feeling that to do so would be somehow gross of her, over the telephone to an unseen secretary. She remembered, too, that her last leave-taking of the man had been in tears and anger, and although she could convince herself that she had been fully justified in her rage the memory of it gave her some embarrassment. Upset as she had been then, upset and outraged, she had been aware of the effect her words had had on the man. Her last memory was of a white face, shocked, as if crumbling from within. She had left him a stricken man. And then he had had his terrible accident.

Of course she knew that was not her fault. Somehow, that made it more difficult. Where there was fault there could be apology and atonement, as the nuns at the orphanage had taught her. Confess your sins and be healed of them, released: that was what Rome taught, and it was true. It reached down deep into universal human experience and resonated there eternally. But regret, the mere unfocused wish that things could in some indefinable and impossible way have worked out otherwise, remained like an open wound whose pain could always be revived. Like a lost soul, it could never be laid to rest.

She blessed the urge that had prompted her, afterwards, to pray for her unknown father's man of law.

She was also aware that she had done a lot of growing up, and was healthily and happily glad of the knowledge. She had outgrown Little Miss Innocent, she had shed her like a skin in another continent, another world, another life that was part of her continuing story, a part of her that began to reach down below the brittle surface of fleeting experience, began to fill the aching void that had come so close to swallowing and annihilating her. She felt she had earned the right to tune her voice to the Song of Experience.

London felt sluggishly warm after the naked honesty of the African sun. As on her first visit she dressed with some calculation, as much to say what she was not as to assert what she was. The powder-blue suit, well but not severely cut in crispy-cool cotton, spoke of ease and natural elegance and accentuated the piercing blue of her eyes. Her white silk blouse was dazzlingly cool against the rich and deep tanned gold of her skin. She wore a pair of tiny ruby stud earrings that glowed beneath her darkly lambent waterfall of hair, but no other jewellery. She wound a silk square of blazing ochre around her neck, letting it flow down one shoulder, and chose shoes and handbag to match it.

Dressed in the colours of earth and sky she arrived at Chatteris Choate, happily aware that she was turning heads in pleasure. The receptionist rose to greet her and led her off straightaway, past the typing room, but not to Miss Sanderson's door. Instead they continued a little way further, past a right-angled bend in the corridor where the decorations were a little less opulent and the office doors, it seemed to Gossamer, a little less highly polished. Her guide paused outside the third door along, knocked, and opened it to announce the visitor.

Jean-Luc Frémont flowed up from behind his desk to greet her.

He had not changed at all – or if he had, thought Gossamer, it was only in the sense that he was every bit as he had been, only more so. Here was a handsome, cultured and charming man perfectly aware of his attributes and perfectly at ease with them. He was feline in his acceptance of himself. He took her hand and clasped it briefly.

'You bring the breath of summer to the dusty lawyer, Miss Fane,' he smiled. 'It is so good to see you.'

He spoke truly. As on the last occasion, he felt his heart lurch and beat faster. He felt his senses sharpened in the presence of this woman – for so, indeed, she now was. She was unique, exotic. He saw that she had passed through the threshold of womanhood and none, he felt sure, would ever pass again through the particular door that fortune had chosen for her.

Or perhaps, he reminded himself, Fate. Again he cursed the vile serpent Lambert in his heart. Carey Lambert, *homme méchant et sale*, user and abuser of women. The worm that flies in the night, the father of lies and the begetter of corruption.

All this passed through his mind as his eyes drank in the gloriousness that stood before him. She thrilled and – he acknowledged it – awed him. Chatteris Choate's lines of communication passed through many spheres of influence, and he had learned something of her recent adventures. His uncle Marc had hastened to impart the intelligence to him, but not before he'd heard it from other sources. Was it possible that she had the innate gift not merely to overcome the trials of her life but to grow from them? If so, she was indeed a rare and precious creature. Yet she had also the capacity to be the focus of great and terrible danger. Her mystery, like her beauty, had deepened and intensified.

She held his eye and smiled back as she took her seat. 'You don't look at all cobwebby to me,' she said. 'And I'm quite sure dust is not allowed on the premises.'

He laughed. '*C'est vrai*! It is forbidden, absolutely. Also we are searched regularly for watch-chains, half-moon glasses, and snuff.'

He saw the unspoken question in her eyes and became at once professionally attentive. 'Tell me how it is that we can be of service to you, Miss Fane.'

'Is Mr Germain . . . ?'

'His condition is unchanged. Which is to say that there can now be only one change, and that the final one.'

She felt the prick of tears and blinked them back, rebuking herself for them. 'Is there nothing they can do?' she asked.

'All that can be done has been attempted. Now they say only that he is 'comfortable'. Also that they are managing his condition.' The words hung between them like a sentence of death.

'I am so sorry,' she said. 'He—' she swallowed. 'He tried to help me, and I behaved badly, and I regret it. I – I was under a misapprehension at the time.'

'I know it.' He spoke softly. 'And I too will confess to playing a part in that sorry drama.'

She started. 'Oh?'

'*Oui, vraiment*. You see, Miss Fane, it was I who first spoke to Kevin Germain concerning, let us say, what appeared to me to be the perilous nature of that misapprehension.' He continued, sparing her the necessity to reply. 'I must be honest with you. When we met at the Embassy – you recall the occasion?' She nodded, numbly. 'At first I was amused by you – no, that is not correct to say – I found amusement in what you seemed at first to be. Which was, forgive me, *une coquette*. Lambert had brought you, Lambert displayed you, and having done so he abandoned you. It seemed to proclaim that you were, let us say, of a certain type. I beg your pardon for my own misapprehension.'

'No,' she whispered. 'There's no need to. It never occurred to me, you see. I didn't ... understand.'

'*Vraiment*, you did not understand. That quickly became clear to me.' He produced a tissue from the box in his desk drawer. The lawyer in him was prepared for tearful female clients, but the man in him was dizzy with desire and tenderness for this creature. Her superlative beauty, her physical poise aroused him. At the same time he was assailed by her vulnerability, her ingenuousness. Together, in this woman, they were a potent combination, unimaginably volatile. He acknowledged the effect of it on himself, he saw with revelatory insight the danger it threatened. To herself most of all.

He forced himself to continue. '*Alors*, you were not a hired ornament. We spoke, and I was instantly cured of that gross delusion. I was – I ask you to accept this as a compliment, not as a piece of flattery – I was *interested* in you. And then, as swiftly, I saw that you were also no courtesan. You told me of the trust adminstered by Kevin Germain, and then I knew.' His voice dropped and grew hoarse. 'And I felt fear. And also anger, and the instinct to protect.'

She looked at him. His recollection had altered him, she saw. He could indeed be the gallant knight, hastening to her rescue on his milk-white steed. She felt a sudden gratitude, and her heart went out to him as her mind regarded this image, and all that it suggested, with detachment, resolving never to risk playing such a part again.

She realised he was speaking. 'I was leading you into the dancing, do you remember? And he spoke your name. He pulled you up, controlled you, as surely as if you had been on a leash. And it was then that my oh so noble impulses turned to hatred, Miss Fane. Also to revenge. *Ah, oui:* I claim in all sincerity that I was motivated to speak to Monsieur Germain by the desire to save you from such a fate, but I also admit to that. I wanted to hurt him. The thought of doing so gave me great gratification.'

She spoke levelly. 'I understand that, too. Now.'

'I acknowledge it. In the event I failed, my scheme did not carry. And I think perhaps it was as well that it did not – for he told me himself, after your interview, that he knew from the outset that he had lost the battle. It is better that you should have made the discovery for yourself, since you have proved you had the strength to do so.'

She shook her head, and looked away. She would not tell him the price that had been paid for it. She had hurt people. Her friends at *Dragon Hurst* had been a family to her and she had betrayed them. The fact that she had done so in all innocence only made it worse. Innocence hurt people, and if Lambert had preyed on it, that was only because she herself had connived at it.

The bleating of the kid excites the tiger – Kipling, was it? Something they'd read at school. She had been an accessory to that slaughter.

There was a question she had to ask, and she asked it now although the name seemed to stick in her throat: 'Do you know if Alec Dayfield has decided whether to sue me?'

'Yes I do, and no he is not. Your instructions in the matter of – of certain items of jewellery – were followed, and so the matter was closed. I should add that we were – instructed is not the correct term – allowed to make it known to you that nothing remains in dispute between you and DayStar. Also – permit me to quote him – that he has an open mind, concerning you. Those were his words to me, exactly. There, now I have passed them on.'

'I see. Well, that was generous of him.'

'You think so?'

'Yes. In the circumstances. All the circumstances.'

'Without knowing precisely what those circumstances were, I cannot pass opinion.' He raised his hand, although she had not been about to interrupt. 'Nor do I wish to know. You are in no dispute which could concern us. *Ça suffice.*'

'You do not stand *in loco parentis*, then?' She flushed at the phrase, remembering how it had hurt her when Germain had used it.

'I agree,' said Jean-Luc softly. 'It was an unfortunate phrase, and he regretted it. He meant merely that he was concerned for you, deeply concerned. And I would have to say, rightly so. But it upset him to think that you would see him as taunting you with a piece of knowledge he was not permitted to share with you. Such was not the case.'

'Yes. I see that now. And he gave me fair warning.' *What you see is what they all see, till he tires of you and throws you away. Or passes you on as a business favour . . .*

She shivered, though the room was pleasantly warm. 'And you, Monsieur Frémont? You too are not permitted to tell me who my father is, I suppose.'

'The question of permission does not arise in my case, Miss Fane. I do not know. That is the truth.'

She felt sure he was telling the truth. It made a sort of sense, after all. 'I suppose that's why you've been given the job of . . . dealing with me. Assuming you have?'

Jean-Luc nodded. 'I am happy to say so, yes. I am here to give you all the help you may require, and to keep you informed of the state of your financial affairs – which, as you may see for yourself, is a very healthy one. Unless I receive other instructions, that is my only involvement in your life on behalf of Chatteris Choate. For my own part I should like to offer you friendship, also, if you will accept it.' He flashed her a dazzling smile. 'There can at least be no question of my assuming any sort of parental role.'

Gossamer allowed herself to appear charmed by this but she did not respond in kind. She had once been happily and meaninglessly flirtatious in the company of this attractive and amusing man. She had felt secure and at peace. It seemed a lifetime away.

'I should be very happy to have your friendship,' she said. 'Meanwhile, I should like to draw some money until I find myself work, and I need to find myself somewhere to live.'

His eyes registered amusement. 'I think we can manage a small allowance without too much difficulty. You do not wish us to find some suitable accommodation for you, as before?'

'No. No, thank you. I don't want things to be as they were before.'

He met her eyes. 'I understand. *Bon.* In that case, unless you decide to buy a large house in Mayfair I think it is safe to say that you may exercise a completely free hand in your choice.'

He explained her finances to her, briefly but fully enough to let her understand that it was as he had said. She could afford to reinvent herself in the image of her choice. No wonder Jean-Luc had been amused by her request.

He closed her file and tidied it away. 'I look forward to hearing that you have been successful. And your occupation, what is it to be? Shall you return to modelling, perhaps? Or acting?'

She caught her breath. He had said he did not know all the circumstances of her breach with *Dragon Hurst*, but how much did he know? There was no suggestion of sarcasm about him.

'No,' she replied levelly. 'I should prefer to take up some sort of charity work, I think. I was very impressed with the work I became involved with in Africa, and I'd like to do more at this end if I can. One of my colleagues out there suggested I could.' Her face clouded as she remembered that clear-headed and kindly woman.

'I am sure that your talents would be greatly appreciated,

Miss Fane.' Again there was no hint of any other meaning in his words. 'The school where you were working, it has I hope survived these disturbances?'

'I don't know. I asked at the embassy in Nairobi if they had any news of the Englishwoman I worked with there – a Miss Tarrant, Jean Tarrant – and they did make enquiries in Addis, but they couldn't help me. She – the mission – was right in the middle of the fighting and it was – it was a terrible situation to be in.' She saw again the mutilated bodies and knew, briefly, the sickness of pure terror. And remembered Mike. She felt again the prickle of tears and blinked them back.

'*Eh bien.* So I understand. I have heard, too, something of your own experiences. Perhaps I may be of some assistance in finding out for you if your friend is safe?'

'Oh, could you? It would be wonderful to know she was all right, and Father Berhanu too of course.'

'I shall do my very best, Miss Fane.'

'Thank you.' They shook hands warmly and in friendship.

As she turned to leave she caught sight of a picture on the wall she had not noticed before. It was of a cathedral, but the artist had depicted it as if it were rather a work of nature than something built by man. An unseen sun burned away the mist that still clung about the spire, making it look a little a like a mountain peak, and the surrounding buildings too were invested with the same suggestion of landscape rather than mere architecture. The figures in the street put the whole into perspective though they were not dwarfed by their surroundings.

Jean-Luc joined her. 'You admire my little extravagance?'

'I think it's very beautiful. It makes me want to be there inside it. It makes me want to join in.'

He caught his breath, remembering other pictures, another time. He felt the stirring of a strong feeling for this woman. It was not just desire, or even admiration. There was an urge to fellowship, for she had spoken his own thoughts and shared his pleasure in the picture, and there was affection in it too. And, yes, there was fear. There was still so much of the *ingénue* about her, and such guilelessness could be so perilous. Suddenly he longed to embrace and protect her.

He spoke slowly and carefully. 'It is by Jean Béraud. Rennes cathedral, a morning scene. It is often so, soft and misty like that, and very lovely. Do you see, though, how he has expressed the integrity of all he has portrayed? It is not only the buildings but the people also: see how they all go about their business. The men of affairs, the tradesmen, the nursemaids, the *concièrges*, even those two whores by the doorway there, see?'

'Yes,' she said. 'They are all of a piece with it, aren't they? They are individuals but they all belong. It is a lovely picture.'

'I love it,' he said simply. 'And of course, it is my home.'

'And so you belong, too.'

'Yes. As you say, I belong.'

'That must be a wonderful feeling.' Their eyes met, and understood, and then she left.

Outside in the corridor she almost bumped into a woman of about her own age hurrying along with a bundle of files under her arm. They apologised to each other and then, as the woman focused on Gossamer, she seemed startled. Momentarily the colour drained from her face then she flushed as if confused, suddenly like a naughty schoolgirl caught out in something.

Then, just as swiftly, the woman composed herself. 'I'm glad to see you're back with us, Miss Fane,' she said.

Gossamer said thank-you to the woman's slim and rapidly retreating back. She searched her mind for some memory of her, but could find none. Presumably she was some sort of secretary, but Kevin Germain had been looked after entirely by Alison Sanderson on all Gossamer's visits here. There was something else, too, something that struck a chord of memory but she couldn't place it.

It came back to her when she was in the street: it was the woman's perfume.

Parisian perfume. *Indécence*. A little cut glass flagon.
Carey, I love you so much.

The memory was painful and humiliating, and she flicked
it away. It was just coincidence. All that must have nothing
to do with her now.

She was rich. She realised it had never properly struck her
before, but she knew it now. It was her money, not an
allowance that depended on her being what other people
– Kevin Germain, her unknown father, anybody – wanted
her to be and doing what they expected her to do. Her
own judgement, not guilt or gratitude, would decide how
she chose to use it.

A lot had altered in a few months. She had trusted
and been betrayed. She had loved and been abused. She
had given, and been rejected. She had looked on evil and
named it to its face, and she had acknowledged goodness.
She had emerged, unquestioning, from the protective shelter
of Shaws and had undergone a swift and shattering course
in the getting of wisdom.

Or at any rate the beginnings of it.

She had discovered in sex her own intensely erotic nature,
and she feared it in all its grossness and glory. Carey
Lambert had awakened it but the man she thought existed,
the adored and trusted master of her body and soul, was a
carapace. Inside it lurked a creature who had all but lured
her to self-destruction, and she had been blind to it. Mike
Andersen had rekindled it and she had given to him as an
equal, and he had taken it and then repelled her, shut her
out, leaving her bewildered and confused.

She yearned to trust, and to be accepted, and to belong.
Sex offered a bridge across the abyss to that longed-for
haven, and then lit the fire that destroyed it, turning the
dream into a nightmare.

She must stay awake and keep alert. She must go
carefully, resist the wild dance of desire. She could not
help her beauty, her attractiveness to men, and it would
be pointless to deny or resent it. It was enjoyable. Nor could

she drive out or destroy her sexuality. It was compulsive, woven into the fabric of her being. She knew herself to be addicted, but she told herself that an addiction could be diverted, channelled into something that did not end in self-elimination.

She wanted what she yearned for to descend as a white dove, warm and whole, not as a destroyer that devoured where it desired.

One thing, one aspect of her old life remained, and that was friendship. That was what she must nurture: that, and self-control. The ravenous beast of sex must go hungry.

A handwritten note on Chatteris Choate's headed paper came to her by messenger the following morning. Gossamer suppressed the desire to giggle as the leather-clad figure passed it over, behaving as if urgent dispatches by courier were an entirely unremarkable part of her daily routine. Her fellow guests remained impassive behind their teapots and *Daily Telegraph*s and affected not to notice anything at all.

It was from Jean-Luc Frémont.

Chère Mademoiselle,

Please excuse this apparent intrusion into your personal affairs. If you have not already found the sort of occupation you seek you may perhaps care to contact the Hon. Miss Ida Spenlowe-Humfrey (who is known to me) of the Project Aid Foundation in Kensington. This is a relatively small organisation raising money through various social events in London for specific projects in the Third World, including some in the area you were working in. These are administered by the bigger charities, but although it has no workers in the field it keeps closely in touch with all the actvities it assists in this way. I think they may be looking for someone such as yourself who can help organise its social events in London. Your experience of Africa – to mention but one of your many attributes – will surely be of assistance to you should you care to telephone them for an appointment.

I fear I have no news yet of your friend Mme. Tarrant but I will continue to ask and if I hear anything I will contact you at Brown's Hotel until I hear that you have found a place that you like. There are I believe some quite attractive apartements *in that area of Kensington, so you may like to look at them while you are there. Of course you may already have suited yourself in both respects! – in which case I merely remain,*

Votre ami,
J-L.

The address and telephone number of the Project Aid Foundation were written underneath.

At first Gossamer was inclined to be wary, remembering other times when paths had been smoothed for her. But then she told herself it would be ridiculous to behave as though Jean-Luc Frémont were another Carey Lambert. It had, after all, been part of that wicked man's intention to spoil her for any other sort of relationship – however 'merely amicable' – with any other man. She recalled the night at the embassy when, snake-like, he had struck venom into the heart of a happy conversation. She saw herself as she had been then: craven, fawningly subservient. If she were to purge herself clean of Lambert's poison, she had better make sure she didn't unwittingly do his dirty work for him. To be true to herself was to be open and trusting when she chose. Her mind gave her an image of her own strong hand, throttling the serpent of suspicion and self-delusion.

And besides, she thought, what dark corrupting tides could possibly run in anyone with such a reassuringly tweedy name as the Hon. Miss Ida Spenlowe-Humfrey?

She dialled the number, and a strong female voice, a sort of fruity bark, identified itself as the Project Aid Foundation.

'Good morning,' she said. 'I should like to speak to Miss Spenlowe-Humfrey please, if that's possible.'

'It is, and you are. And *you* are?'

She warmed instantly to this direct and confident woman. 'Gossamer Fane. I heard about the Project Aid Foundation through a mutual acquaintance.'

'Ah! The admirable Monsieur Frémont, I presume. A very *well-finished* young man, don't you think?'

'Er – yes,' said Gossamer, blinking. 'Very.'

'Quite. Oh yes, he's told me all about you, Miss Fane.'

'Oh?'

'Hah! Quite so, my dear, of course he hasn't. I doubt if even you could do that. But he told me enough to make me hope you're on your way to see us.'

'Well, yes – I mean if that's—'

'Jolly good! Where are you?'

'Brown's Hotel.' She had to resist the urge to say exactly whereabouts in the building. Even over the telephone Miss Spenlowe-Humfrey had an almost irresistibly commanding presence.

'Oh, *very* good! Splendid place. In that case we'll say about half an hour, shall we? Holland Park tube, turn right outside, right again at the off-licence, then third left after that. Clear as mud?'

'Oh, absolutely,' said Gossamer, hoping it didn't sound like parody.

'Jolly good.' The line went dead.

Miss Spenlowe-Humfrey's directions were completely reliable, as Gossamer had been sure they would be. She found herself in one of London's quieter places, a little world of squares and gardens whose streets led nowhere in particular once they had left behind the busy life of Holland Park Avenue. A middle-aged businessman sat with a pint of beer at a table outside the Addison Arms reading *Bluff Your Way in Management* and, apparently, taking notes. A shop called Annabelinda's displayed one very expensive dress that looked as though it had recently emerged, unrefurbished, from a trunk in someone's attic. Trees erupted at intervals from the pavement, ivy and clematis wound up from tiny basement courtyards, bright-eyed lobelia and dusty-blue aubretia foamed in wooden tubs, and the stifling sourness of traffic fumes gave way to the elusive subtlety of sun-warm stone and railing, of leaf and bark and geraniums in hanging baskets.

For Gossamer it felt like a home-coming to a place, a way of being, that had always been hers. She stopped to stroke a plumped-up tabby cat sunning itself on a wall and the animal chirruped and butted its head against her knuckles, rising on its haunches like a benign weasel before settling down again to doze. Gossamer's spirit rejoiced, empowered by the glorious ordinariness of it all. She felt utterly at ease.

From the outside the premises of the Project Aid Foundation in St James' Gardens looked like any of the other attractive early Victorian buildings in this leafy square, its function betrayed by a discreet brass plaque which could not be read until the building was closely approached. Offices here, evidently, lived in happy proximity to private flats and houses.

Gossamer rang the bell, and an already familiar voice squawked through the intercom: 'Is that Miss Fane?'

'Yes.'

'Jolly good. Push hard when the buzzer goes off, and I'm first on the left.'

Miss Spenlowe-Humfrey rose to greet her from behind a large desk in a small room that overlooked what might have been a country garden. Box files lined two walls, while the third was largely taken up with a world map in which several coloured and number-coded flags were stuck. A utilitarian grey filing cabinet stood in one corner, in another a small sink and working surface. A computer winked on the desk, next to a telephone and an ashtray containing a burning cheroot.

'Glamorous it ain't,' she said, extending a square-fingered hand. Gossamer shook it, noting its firmness. She saw a woman in late middle age, an intelligent characterful face beneath a neat frizz of untinted grey hair, and a pair of solid shoulders that owed nothing to any padding in its wearer's worsted jacket. Her overwhelming impression was of a woman without an ounce of flab on her, either physical or mental.

'It doesn't need to be, does it?' said Gossamer, and her hostess grunted approval.

'Quite. Now shove that cat off the chair behind you, so we can talk.'

Gossamer hadn't noticed the cat, a huge bundle of fur that took up most of the only other chair, much as if it had been dropped there from a great height. It opened both yellow eyes as she approached and lumbered haughtily to the floor.

'It seems to have attached itself to one of the young men who drift in and out of the place. Don't know which one, they all look the same to me. Unlike cats. Now then, let me have a look at you.'

Gossamer sat neatly, the way a Shaws girl should, and allowed herself to be looked at.

The older woman reached for her cheroot and drew on it, to cover her thoughts. Jean-Luc Frémont had told her what to expect yet the reality still came almost as a shocking surprise, and besides the man's description had nowhere done justice to the reality. Yes, she told herself, here was a young woman who had supped on horrors and knew at first hand what most of her age could only guess at. Yet there was an apparent innocence also, an unworldliness that left even her obvious intelligence terrifyingly unprepared for life's other dark trials.

How had such a creature been formed? There must be mystery here, and indeed Jean-Luc had so hinted before clamming up behind the armour of the professionally reticent lawyer. The girl's beauty, her spiritual as well as physical radiance, blazed like a young sun. Yet she seemed unaware of its potential either for paradise or for torment. She could have everything or have everything taken from her. This Gossamer Fane, this girl-woman, would excite in those she met the instinct to cherish and protect – or provoke the lust to wound and spoil.

Suddenly she knew instinctively that such had already

been the case – and, just as surely, knew that the girl had failed utterly to distinguish one from the other. She was like some beautiful and exotic animal that had been reared in captivity and released into the wild lacking a vital instinct for survival. And the wild was full of raptors.

Ida Spenlowe-Humfrey suppressed a shudder of pity and fear. Slowly, carefully, she began to interview Gossamer. The girl spoke freely and fully of her African experiences. She sketched the outline of a male companion in her adventures but did not fill the picture in. She told of her modelling work and her acting, but left the tale unfinished. Her *curriculum vitae* included a full account of Ryder-Vail and Shaws, but went no further back in history. All these things suggested the almost palpable absence of something, yet it eluded even Miss Spenlowe-Humfrey's shrewd attempts to grasp it and hold it up for examination.

At length, exasperated, she asked: 'Tell me, my dear, who do you turn to for advice, for guidance, when you feel the need of it?'

'Chatteris Choate are my trustees and advisers, Miss Spenlowe-Humfrey. Before his accident I used to consult Kevin Germain, now it's Monsieur Frémont.' You can't be blamed for not telling the truth, Gossamer reminded herself, if you yourself don't know it. She was determined not to tell any more stupid stories about herself: that must be past and done with.

Miss Spenlowe-Humfrey smiled, and gave up. If the girl was determined to be taken at face value, then so be it. She would be a fool to turn the offer down. There could be a thousand reasons for it: life was short, and there was work to be done.

'And of course,' she said, 'no one with whom Chatteris Choate is involved can ever be alone in the world – eh?' She grinned.

Gossamer grinned back in recognition of the phrase. 'Is that what they tell everybody?'

'Oh, I should think so, Lord knows I've heard it often enough. I expect they all have to repeat it like a mantra, three times before breakfast. It's probably why their fees are three times more than the going rate. Now if you'll come and look at the map with me, I'll tell you all about our work here.'

Her examination over, Gossamer felt a knot of anxiety dissolve inside her. She had skimmed over the deep and shark-infested waters of her past and come safely to shore.

Miss Spenlowe-Humfrey spoke briskly, and with simple enthusiasm. 'The whole point of the thing, from my point of view, is that I can't stand committees and I'm hopeless at bureaucracy, but I do want to do a bit of useful good.'

It was simple enough. The Project Aid Foundation – this remarkable woman and her helpers – organised social events, mostly in London, to raise money for various highly specific schemes and projects in the Third World. 'All small-scale stuff,' she explained. 'A clinic here, a water purification plant there, and so on.'

Gossamer nodded eagerly, thinking of the school, and Jean Tennant. The projects themselves were organised by the bigger charities – 'Lots of bumf and committees, you see, all very good and necessary but not my cup of poison' – who also provided the expertise and personnel to run them, and reported back on their progress. 'We're a sort of sponsorship charity, you see? We give the *noblesse* a chance to obleege, as it were. Not to mention the *richesse*, when it comes to business patronage and so on. All enlightened self-interest, needless to say; I suspect it's a sort of each-way bet against giving money to the Tories. As for the bright, or not-so-bright, young things of my own class, it gives them somewhere else to go in the evenings. How does it strike you?'

'It obviously works,' said Gossamer, 'and that's the main thing, isn't it?'

'Quite. It's all money, as they say, going straight to where it's needed. Most of my helpers don't get paid, and the few who do – you for instance – get paid very little for working very hard in short bursts. Does that bother you?'

Gossamer shook her head. 'The money doesn't matter,' she said. She hoped it didn't sound crass or arrogant. 'I mean, it's not the most important thing, for me.'

'Just as well, my dear. Good!' The older woman fancied she might know what the important thing was, but she reminded herself that it remained none of her business. 'Now go on, let me show off a bit. Pick out some of these little flags and ask me to tell you about them, from memory.'

There were scores of them. Gossamer picked a few at random, and heard about an agricultural co-operative in Mali, a fish farm in Bangladesh, a rehabilitation clinic in Cambodia, an orphanage in Peru. 'One of our newest, that one. Village caught in the middle of the war between the army and the Shining Path guerrillas. We pay to have the orphans looked after and cross our fingers both lots leave us alone on the grounds that we're not worth encouraging. Go on, one more.'

Gossamer pointed to a flag just inside the Ethiopian border with Kenya.

'School, clinic, agricultural co-op, you name it. All organised by one man, a Murlé tribal chief who also happens to have been a post-grad when I was up at Oxford many years ago. A very remarkable man.'

'Yes,' said Gossamer softly. 'I know. I met him. I gave him my gun, and he gave me some food, and we talked about Jane Austen.' Memories returned with aching poignancy, remote and strange and yet forever a part of her.

'It's a very small world, my dear.' Gossamer felt a hand laid kindly on her arm. 'Let's lock up here and have a drink down the road, shall we? Then we can talk about what you'll be doing when you start work for us.'

They sat in the blissful sunshine outside The Garnett Arms on the corner of Penzance Street and Princedale Road. Gossamer drank a dry Martini and Miss Spenlowe-Humfrey a pint of draught Guinness.

'This is one of the few places outside Ireland where they don't chill the stuff,' she explained. She took a long swallow.

'Aah! Genghis is goon for you, as Mr Joyce so memorably put it.' She lit a cheroot, blew a long plume of blue smoke into the drowsy air, and asked: 'Does this bother you, at all?'

Gossamer shook her head. 'Oh no, Miss Spenlowe-Humfrey. I don't smoke, but I like the smell of tobacco. It's a friendly sort of smell.' It evoked a brief, intense memory of Mike Andersen. An enchanted pool, a waterfall.

Her companion took another puff and continued: 'And for God's sake call me Ida if you feel you have to call me anything. After sixty-odd years in this vale of tears I've learned to live with being named after a Gilbert and Sullivan opera. Now then, to business.'

Gossamer's job, she learned, was to help Ida with what she called 'all the bloody bumf' in the office and to be on hand to organise and, where appropriate, participate in the various 'thrashes' the Project Aid Foundation laid on to raise funds, as Ida put it, 'to enable decent ordinary people of the sort I wish I was to do what they're good at'.

'It'll suit me completely,' said Gossamer.

'Thank God for that,' said Ida. 'Let's have the other one, shall we?'

Their eyes met. 'Thank you,' said Gossamer.

'My pleasure, believe me,' said Ida Spenlowe-Humfrey.

Later that afternoon she found a home.

It was pure serendipity, and she did not question it. Ida knew of a flat five minutes' walk away in Addison Place that she thought 'might be the sort of thing you have in mind'. Gossamer could not have described what she was looking for, but she knew it when she saw it. So absolute was her knowledge of this that the estate agent who showed her round (while Ida kept a discreetly low profile two steps behind them) seemed at some pains to point out its defects.

'Of course you realise this isn't double glazing, Miss Fane?'

'No, it's lovely.' The big, crescent, fan-lighted window looked out on communal gardens blazing with late summer flowers and shaggy at the edges with overhanging trees. The wobble in the glass was beautiful, and Gossamer imagined all the people who had lived here in the past and looked pleasurably through it.

'And the rental does not include services of any sort.'

'Good, I don't want servants. I had those at boarding school.'

'Er, ah, um, yes, ha-ha, of course. And although the cracks in the plasterwork are of course merely superficial—'

'Are they?' she said happily. 'Oh good, I'll paint over them. How much did you say the rent was?'

He named a figure and, while Gossamer was registering the amount, reduced it by £50 a month. She accepted.

Afterwards, Ida said: 'Well done, my dear, you discomfited him in such a nice way he was positively grateful for it. I take my hat off to you, I've always had to work much harder to achieve that effect.'

That evening, Gossamer faxed Jean-Luc:

Job landed and flat hunted – 22B Addison Place, Kensington, W11. Moving in Friday. Many thanks again.
Love, Gossamer.

Ida, too, wrote the lawyer a note:

Mon jeune vieux,
You were quite right, she is a joy and an asset. She flies without apparent effort but, as you said, there are times when she will need a safety net. Curse you for not telling me where and when to have it ready, but I will do all that I can. I note that she appears to have sprung from nowhere.

                                                    Yours, Ida.

So it was that Gossamer Fane, who had never known a home, came to find one. She played hard at it, arranging and building until at last, on the Sunday morning, she allowed herself to hang the La Tour that stated, simply and beautifully: this is my place, here I belong.

She stepped back, and drank it all in.

Her place. Her belonging.

Voices gibbered in her mind ...

Precious cargo.

I reveal you to yourself.

La petite fille de la Vierge.

A succulent piece of tail.

No, she shouted silently. No, no. Wrong, all wrong.

And then: *I know who you are.*

But you didn't, she told it. You can't. I did not exist, then. This is me, now, here.

A tremendous calm descended on her, wrapped her round and strengthened her from within. She was ready to begin the world again.

The phone rang shatteringly, shockingly. She had not given out the number to anybody yet.

'Hello?'

'Hello Gossamer, it is Jean-Luc. Forgive my intrusion, I discovered your number. I have something to give you and something to tell you, and I hope that you will permit me to call on you if it is convenient.'

He arrived a little over half an hour later, handsome and immaculate in carefully tailored casual clothing on a sleepy Sunday London afternoon. 'Am I the first to greet Gossamer Fane in her new home?' he asked.

'You are. And you are welcome in it.'

She led him in; he was impressed by what she showed him. 'It is a good place for you,' he said.

'Yes. Yes, it is. A very good place.' She twinkled at him. 'Would you like a cup of tea?'

'Ah, now I know that I am welcome!' He gave a stiff little mocking bow.

'Excuse me while I organise the servants,' she said, and tripped off to her kitchen – *her* kitchen – to see about it.

She found him in the sitting room, absorbed in the picture. He turned and smiled at her as she brought the tea tray in. 'How very unlike the variously-sized lilies of Monsieur Monet,' he said.

'Oh, you remember!'

'Oh yes, I remember. I remember having my breath taken away.' He sat down and she passed him a cup. He was holding a parcel in his lap, and he set his tea down to give it to her.

'For you,' he said. 'For the home of Gossamer.'

She opened it. It was a picture, a quietly busy, uniquely ordinary townscape. 'Oh, it's so beautiful,' she gasped. 'Béraud?'

'*Oui*, Béraud. Do you wish to know where it is?'

She decided swiftly. 'No. No I don't, because it doesn't matter. In fact it matters not to know. I'd rather just belong in it.'

'As I thought.' He smiled warmly, understandingly. 'Where shall you put it?'

Gossamer considered. 'I should like it in my bedroom,' she replied, 'so I can wake up to it.'

'*Bon*. There it shall be, to greet you. I am so glad that you appreciate it.'

'I do,' she said simply. 'I do, very much. Thank you, Jean-Luc.'

They talked of domestic matters, and he smiled and nodded as she prattled happily on, defining for both of them her new life here. Gossamer knew how amused he must be by her enthusiasm for domesticity, but she felt no embarrassment or awkwardness. He seemed to rejoice in her own happiness, to be pleased to share it with her. She told him about her interview with Ida Spenlowe-Humfrey and he grinned.

'*C'est une femme formidable, non*? A woman of character.'

'Oh yes, absolutely. And not at all *formidable*, really, more sort of – robust and invigorating.'

They laughed freely together.

'But also,' said Jean-Luc, suddenly serious, 'a woman of great integrity. A most tremendously good person, yes?'

'Oh yes. Good through and through. Good for me.'

'Good for all she meets, I think. She has courage and humanity, Miss Spenlowe-Humfrey. She has come to terms with much in her own life, I believe. As must we all, sometimes.'

She sensed his need to prepare himself for what he had to say next. She let him take his own time to say it.

'My dear Gossamer, I know that Ida is not the first splendid woman you have known to have those admirable qualities. And I am afriad I have terrible news to tell you.'

She looked at him, pitying his distress. She was sure she knew what it would be.

'It is that your friend Jean Tennant has been killed. I am so sorry.'

The silence spoke between them. 'How – how was she killed.'

'Horribly and with great brutality,' he said simply. 'But let us hope swiftly. She and Father Berhanu got all the children safely out of the way before the soldiers came, but there was no opportunity to organise their own escape. They were hacked to death, and then the school was set on fire. It was a senseless destruction.'

This is a local thing – it is serendipity.

'Yes,' said Gossamer, quietly and steadily. 'I know how it must have been. I saw something – something—'

He was sitting next to her, his arm around her shoulder, and she sobbed freely into his chest.

'I'm sorry,' she said at length.

'Do not be. Promise me you are not.'

'All right then.' She smiled weakly. 'Thank you.'

They parted later, Jean-Luc reminding her that he was always at her service. Their eyes met. They kissed briefly and chastely, and she closed the door.

Returning, she took down the fly-whisk she had brought back from Ethiopia and hung on the wall, remembering those strange men of that religion and Jean's simple and selfless devotion to hers.

'May your God bless you,' she whispered. 'May you be at peace.'

She slept safely.

*   *   *

The man cradled the receiver against his ear and wrote down names, addresses, phone numbers. He smiled in satisfaction and anticipation. He felt the surge of power, the challenge of it, the potency of excitement and risk. He was like a cat that is about to spring.

'Thank you, my dear. You have done superbly, as always. And, as always, you will be rewarded for it.'

A question was asked. His tiger-eyes flickered and his mouth twisted in a slow, considered smile. 'In my own time and in my own way,' he said. 'Again, as always. You have never yet had cause to complain, I believe. I take great pains to reward loyalty. As you know.'

He replaced the receiver and sat, his fingertips pressed lightly together, thinking, planning, gathering himself. His eyes narrowed. His face was a suave mask of concentration and desire.

At length he lifted the receiver and pressed a coded call button. The line rang out twice and then was answered with a single word:

'Isabella.'

'Lambert.'

A tiny pause, and then: 'An unexpected pleasure, Mr Lambert. It has been some time.'

'I have been much occupied with business. I hear you have some young wines newly in for tasting.'

'Indeed so. A most interesting collection. You wish to sample soon?'

'I feel the need of a little refreshment tonight.'

'That is possible, for such an honoured client. Your pleasure is perhaps for something fresh and firmly rounded, a light-bodied little vintage with perhaps the hint of ripeness yet to come? Yours would be the first palate to consider it, *vous comprenez.*'

'You know my tastes exactly, Isabella.'

'I know you have the means to indulge them, Mr Lambert. Shall we say, at ten o'clock?'

'At ten o'clock.'

He prepared himself for pleasure as an athlete who paces

himself against the race to come, as a cat that cuffs and paws where it will later claw and tear. His body responded to the apprehension of it. He began to know how he would bring all his will to focus on the prey that had come once again within his grasp. The knowledge thrilled him.

Still Gossamer slept safely on.

⚜ Fourteen ⚜

Ida had promised hard work in small doses and Gossamer at once found herself working very hard indeed. During the first few weeks of her new life she was plunged so deeply into the activities of Project Aid that she had virtually no time to catch her breath. She felt sure this was all to the good.

Her job was to assist Ida with organising a fundraising Fashion Extravaganza to be held at BAFTA in mid December. 'Also you can help me to organise our Young Things,' added Ida.

Gossamer met a succession of Ida Spenlowe-Humfrey's Young Things during the following days. According to Ida the secret of organising the Young Things was to find each one of them one thing to do, something they liked doing anyway, and send them off to do it untroubled by thoughts of anything else.

'That's the absolutely fatal thing, you see,' she explained. 'One thing drives out another, because there isn't room in their poor little heads for both. On the other hand they are extremely well-connected to people who can smoke and read at the same time, as my father used to say. So their real job is to act as a sort of, what-d'ye-call-it, something to do with chemistry?'

'Catalyst?' Gossamer suggested.

'That's it! Trivial little substance that lets two really important chemicals get together and do something worthwhile. Take dear Zara, for instance. Sweet girl, pots of money and a head full of fluff. Zara Moberly-Mabbs, name mean anything to you?'

'I don't think so, no, though it sounds as if it ought to.'

'Went to Shaws I believe, bit older than you. Definitely not one for the academic honours board, however. Dear Zara likes messing about with cameras, you see. Went on a photography course and took ever such a lot of super snaps of all her friends who went on it with her, that sort of thing. The point there is that she knows quite a lot of photographers who are much better at it than she is and actually get their snaps in papers and magazines and so on. So we wind up her clockwork, point her in the right direction, and off she toddles to do her catalysing for the greater good of Project Aid. Ditto all the others.'

Ida assured her that she would soon get the hang of it. The other part of Gossamer's job seemed altogether more daunting. It involved matching up potential wealth donors, as Ida called them, with projects most in need of the funds the Fashion Extravaganza hoped to raise.

'They'll only open their wallets for something specific, you see,' Ida explained, 'something they can feel has their name written on it. That's where I really need your help. It's easy enough to get funding for an orphanage, say, or a famine relief centre, they've got what those awful marketing types call sex appeal. But getting people to cough up for a fish hatchery in Bangladesh is another matter. *Who's Who* can come in handy for that sort of thing of course, but what you've got to do is make some of our rather less appealing projects look attractive. Turn yourself into a one-woman advertising agency and sell the product. Awful, isn't it? And I've been doing it now for so long I feel I'm starting to get cynical about it, which is dreadful. So, over to you.'

She took down a box file and rummaged inside it. 'This is where I keep our really big moneybags. I think I'll label it 'Milk With Care'. Ah, here we are. What'll we match this one up with, for instance?'

Ida produced a document and passed it across. Gossamer read the name at the top, and her head swam. She felt the blood drain away from her face, but Ida seemed not to notice.

'Of course it's thanks to him we've got the use of BAFTA,' she continued, 'which doesn't come cheap and of course we're very grateful, though from his point of view he's getting a free television programme out of it. But there's more where that came from or I'm not a Spenlowe-Humfrey, so how about it my dear? What do you suggest we use to loosen the purse-strings of Mister Dayfield Corporation?'

There was a photograph, a publicity shot, attached to the sheet. She could not tear her eyes away from it. The man's hard, almost brutal features stared back at her. She saw them distort in condemnation and disgust. She saw again the lips move to call her bitch and whore but it was still Ida's voice that washed over her.

'... orphanages would seem the obvious ones to go for, given the man has no offspring so it's safe to assume a complete ignorance of children and consequently a romantic attitude to them. What do you suggest?'

Gossamer opened her mouth but no sound would come out. *I'm not a whore, I'm not a whore*, she screamed silently.

You bitch. You horny bitch.

And then: *Are you putting me on?* The paper face fell from her nerveless fingers as once before, on a terrible night of humiliation and betrayal, a set of photographs had fluttered to a silver-carpeted floor.

No!

Had she said it out loud? Her eyes met Ida's.

'Are you feeling unwell, my dear? What is it?'

Gossamer gulped, swallowed, moved her lips. But still no sound would come out. She looked down at the photograph.

'It's him, isn't it? Alec Dayfield. You know him.'

'Yes,' she croaked. She felt a little control come back. She coughed and swallowed again. 'I met him once. It wasn't that we ... I mean I wasn't ... I'd rather not—'

They heard the front door open, the chatter of carefree voices. The Young Things were arriving, and the terrible enchantment was broken.

'Then you shan't.' Ida gently squeezed Gossamer's wrist. 'He'll have to deal with me instead, and serve him right. Not another word.'

She released her kindly grip. 'Now then, here are some completely untroubling people to meet,' she murmured. 'Nice big puppies with no sharp teeth.' Ida went to the door, tactfully shielding Gossamer while she composed herself for introductions.

'My dears, welcome back to the dragon's lair. I've someone for you to meet who's going to give you all sorts of very useful things to do.'

Then she stood aside and Gossamer, outwardly restored, stood up. 'Gossamer dear, meet Davina and Nicholas, and Zara, and the one with the wretched cat wrapped round his ankles is called Benjamin.'

'Nice to meet you, Benjamin.' Gossamer shook the limply proffered hand while its owner gawped and gulped. She greeted the rest, remembering now that the blonde with the horsey face had been one of the 'Occupational Sixth' at Shaws when she and her friends were juniors. Presumably the 'occupation' had been photography.

'You must be Zara,' she said. 'A Shaws Girl is instantly recognisable.'

'Oh, right, by her, oh gosh I can't remember it, poise and something.'

'By the quiet self-assurance of her poise and demeanour,' Gossamer quoted. 'Which is at all times second nature to her.'

'Oh horrors, yes! Gosh, Gossamer Fane, it's really you! I say, haven't you, um ... oh Lord!'

They laughed freely. Gossamer relaxed, and Ida smiled benignly at them. 'Nicholas is very good at making coffee,' she said. 'Aren't you, Nicholas? Then we can assign you all to your duties.'

'Oh, right, yes,' said Nicholas, obeying orders. Davina went with him. Ida, busying herself at the desk, tidied away the DayStar papers. Benjamin sat with Sebastian the cat on his lap.

'I'm surprised you remember me, Zara' said Gossamer. 'I don't think I'd know anybody who was a Junior Bug when I was in the Sixth.'

'Oh, but we all envied you like mad, of course. I should think we'd all remember you.'

Gossamer reeled. She must have been thirteen at the time, quite physically mature for her age, yes, but gawky and childish in thick knickers and a bra like a crêpe bandage. How could a sophisticated seventeen-year-old possibly envy that?

Zara sensed her incredulity. 'Oh, but absolutely! You were incredibly pretty even then. Half of us were mad with jealousy and the rest had a crush on you, didn't you know? Oh you *must* have known!' she squealed.

Gossamer was wide-eyed with astonishment. 'No,' she said. 'Honestly, I hadn't a clue.' She saw Ida's shrewd eyes register understanding.

So, even then she had been unaware of the effect she had on people. Marie's words came back to her: *You look like you know things and you act like you don't. No wonder the men have their hair on end when you go by.* It wasn't just attractiveness or even sexiness, there was something else, something that made every experience, every contact, somehow off-key. And it was closed to her, she couldn't apprehend it.

Was this how it always had been and always would be, and she never seeing it – or else getting it wrong, responding with all the passion and generosity of her nature when it was least appropriate and most dangerous, or else most likely to meet with cold, incomprehensible rejection?

You have to know who you are, Goss. But I don't, she cried out inside herself, I'm not allowed to, it's forbidden me. And whenever I try to I get it wrong and it brings misery and disaster.

They all knew who they were, Ida's gambolling puppies. They all seemed thoroughly at ease with the knowledge. Was that really only because Ida was correct in her hilarious estimation of them as simple organisms incapable of mental or spiritual complexity?

Zara, she realised, was speaking again. 'And as if that wasn't enough, there was your Great Mystery.' The schoolgirlish capital letters were clearly audible. 'You know, your origins and all that. None of us knew who you were or where you came from.'

'No,' said Gossamer levelly. 'Neither did I.'

'Oh gosh no, that must have been awful for you actually. Still, you must have found out since.'

'No,' she replied as before. 'No, I haven't. I can't.'

'Oh gosh. Oh how awful. Gosh.'

Nicholas and Davina came in with the coffee.

The Extravaganza was to be a cross between a fashion show, a concert and an auction. Each outfit modelled was to be assigned to a funded project and sold to the highest bidder on the night, it being understood that nothing should be left unsold at the end.

Ida's network of Young Things assured a ready supply of volunteer designers and models eager either simply to have fun or to advance their careers through exposure on peak-time satellite TV.

Annabelinda of Princedale Road donated the voluminous crumpled thing in her shop window and a statuesque blonde model – who turned out to be her daughter – willing to be engulfed by it. Rumour had it that it was a wedding dress uncollected since the groom's discovery that he was gay. They took to calling it the Marquee.

Organising the concert element enabled Gossamer to get in touch again with Trish. She suggested that Danse Macabre's programme of bizarrely exciting and erotic performance would be ideally suited to the occasion and Ida agreed with enthusiasm, saying it sounded just the thing to give safe sex a good name.

Gossamer contacted their agent, Dirk Dolenz. He was lukewarm at the prospect of a charity event and froze her out altogether when he realised there would be no fee. In a disparaging Midlands accent he assured her that his artistes would have no interest in anything that did not pay.

'It's obvious you don't know what the real world is like out there, for artistes,' he said.

'I do have some idea, Mr Dolenz. I was at Ryder-Vail with one of them, Trish Temple.'

'Oh yeah? Well you ought to know better then, darling. How do you think you'd be earning a living now, if you was still an artiste?'

'I think I'd be agreeing that exposure to a peak-time audience on DayStar television was something worth going for, Mr Dolenz, fee or no fee.'

After that he agreed to put the proposition to them. But he was unwilling to give her Trish's address, presumably suspecting she would go behind his back and arrange something he couldn't get a percentage of.

'All I can tell you at this moment in time is, they're at the Festival.'

'I see. And which festival is that, Mr Dolenz.'

'You're asking me which festival? You never heard of Edinburgh, darling? Jesus! Where've you just come from, then?'

'Ethiopia,' said Gossamer. He had no answer to that.

In fact, as Gossamer discovered, the Festival was over and Danse Macabre had embarked on an extensive Scottish tour. She tracked them down to an Arts Centre on the Isle of Skye. Later that day she heard Trish's familiar caustic tones:

'Hi there, voice from the past, how's things? How did Mister Right turn out?'

'Wrong,' said Gossamer crisply.

Trish chuckled vigorously. 'All men are bad news, honey-child, even when they're trying not to be. Some gays excepted, of course. Believe it. So, to what do I owe the pleasure, then?'

Gossamer explained briefly. 'Yeah, sounds great,' said Trish. 'You spoken to Dummkopf about this?'

'Dummkopf being Dirk Dolenz, yes. He said he'd pass the proposition on.'

'He'd bloody better. Anyway, listen, we'll be through with this tour in a couple of weeks, let's meet after that, okay?'

'Lovely, yes. I'll look forward to that.' She gave Trish her address. It was good to hear her again, good to be in touch with this part of the past. 'How's Skye?' she asked.

'Fucking incredible! I found this amazing bit of mountain this afternoon, just low enough to be out of the cloud and just high enough to be out of the midges. One day I'll buy it and live on it, build a commune for Hebridean dykes, starting with the couple who run this place. I'll keep a room free for when you come to your senses, okay?'

Gossamer laughed. 'See you soon, Trish.'

'You bet.'

She chuckled again and hung up.

On her first free afternoon she returned to the ice rink near her old apartment in north London. She was tempted to look in and see Arthur, if he was still there. Then she visualised herself taking the lift, approaching the door, and – what? Giving the new occupant some terrible warning? She shook the idea off as absurd and theatrical.

She had half hoped to meet Anthony again and was not surprised to see him. He was skating alone, utterly absorbed, as if his blades and his body were an extension of his imagination and his will.

She watched as the music finished and Anthony, detached, poised himself for the next piece. Gossamer recognised the opening bars of the first of Erik Satie's *Gnossiènnes*, a supernaturally plangent piece for solo piano played here with a haunting string accompaniment.

She slid out onto the ice and worked across it towards him, allowing her body to become an instrument in the music, a complement to his. As she approached him the other people seemed to fall away on either side to leave them space to perform, content to watch.

He saw her then, and recognised her. She put a finger to her lips and skated close to him in time with a swell in the music. Their eyes met and made an unspoken agreement. They began to dance together.

He was vastly her superior in technique, and she was out of practice. But the music and his presence seemed to raise her above mere competence so that they moved and spun and swooped in harmony. He was wearing black as before, turtle neck and jeans, while her suit was white with ice-blue flashings. She knew they made a breathtaking spectacle, a duet of grace and beauty and she saw that he, too, was glorying in it. There was applause, warm and genuine appreciation, when it was over.

They skated off the ice together and embraced. 'Hello, partner,' said Anthony, grinning.

She kissed him. 'That's my line,' she said happily.

'In about ten minutes' time they're due to play a lot of rock'n'roll and sixties stuff,' he said. 'We can have ourselves a really good bop.'

They sat it out till then, and brought each other up to date on what they had been doing. Anthony was currently working in a gay seafood restaurant in Shepherd Market.

'Go on,' he said, 'think of a really full-frontal camp name for a gay seafood joint.'

'Um, how about The Pink Lobster?'

'Not bad, but wrong. It's called The Queer Fish.'

'Of course,' Gossamer laughed, 'it should have been obvious! What do you do there?' She hoped it wasn't something horrible like washing-up.

'I wait. They also serve who only walk about a lot, and wait. Also a spot of song-and-dance, believe it or not.'

'Really?'

'Yeah, really. Our speciality is a really naughty cabaret version of "Molly Malone". You know. Cockles and mussels,' he sang, 'with innuendo.'

She laughed, squeezing his arm. 'And you skate here in your free time. Don't you ever get tired?'

'Ah, but I do sleep in till about one in the afternoon, usually. I live in a rat's second-best broom cupboard, so there's not much else to do anyway.'

He picked up on what she told him, briefly, about her escape to Kenya. She had not dwelt on any particular incident but could not avoid conveying something of the danger and the horror of it. She had to mention Mike Anderson but only referred to him as a sort of freelance journalist who had given her a lift. 'Did you think you were going to die?' he asked, suddenly serious.

'Yes. Twice. Once when I was trapped inside a hollow tree and there was a snake, a puff adder. And again when we got caught in crossfire and had to literally dig ourselves into the ground.'

'What did you think about, can you remember?'

'Oh yes, quite clearly. I realised I could cease to exist very soon and I thought how silly it was, and how I'd never know how the story ended. Why do you ask, particularly?'

'Oh,' he said lightly, glancing away. 'I just wondered, really.' He looked back. 'I remember thinking, that time I was getting beaten up, that they'd quite likely go on doing it until I was dead and I sort of switched off worrying about it. I just kept thinking, isn't this stupid? And then I started coming over all sleepy, and you came along.'

'I remember looking back on my past,' Gossamer said carefully. 'Scenes from it. A bit like watching bits of my own past life on television. Did that happen to you?'

'Yeah, a bit.' He grinned suddenly. 'But I kept wanting to change channels.'

Just then the loudspeakers erupted into 'Tutti Frutti' Anthony leaped up and hauled her onto the ice. Afterwards Gossamer glowed with exertion and simple happiness.

They drank coke in the café, and Gossamer had an idea. She told him about the Fashion Extravaganza and asked him if he would like to take part in it.

'Sure,' he said. 'I could change my evening off if it didn't fit. What do you mean, as a model?'

'Well yes, I expect so. There is going to be a dance performance, we think we've got that organised. We're

getting Danse Macabre, you remember Trish's lot we went
to see down in Brighton don't you?'

'How could I forget! So what do I do?'

'I'll put you in touch with the Sloane who's sort of in
charge of recruitment in that department.'

They left arm in arm. Gossamer slipped her arm in his
because it felt the natural thing to do, just as she had known
from the first he would be a treasured friend. They made a
couple, and people took an interest in them.

Anthony smiled and said out of the corner of his mouth:
'You'll be getting yourself a reputation as a fag-hag at
this rate.'

Gossamer was wide-eyed. 'A what?'

'Don't you know? Oh dear!' He bent closer and whispered:
'A fag-hag is a straight woman who goes about with a gay
man. What you might call a selective camp-follower.'

'Oh!' She felt herself blush although she didn't see any
reason to. 'Well, I don't mind if you don't.'

She held him a little closer, and they walked on. He had
said nothing about Carey Lambert, had never mentioned him
again after that first time. It was one of the things she loved
him for.

As they parted Anthony told her to be sure to bring
Trish along to the The Queer Fish for a meal if she had
the chance.

'It'll be great fun watching the entire restaurant trying
to size you up and work out just what you are, Goss.' He
grinned and kissed her back. 'Cheers.'

Anthony's lighthearted words lodged in her mind and gave
new tongue to the words of others.

What was she? Mike had said he knew, and the knowledge
turned his desire to loathing. Lambert had defined it, cruelly
and appallingly, when he took her gift to him and defiled it
and flung it in her face. Then he had proved it to himself
by raping her.

Again she asked herself if there was something wrong
with her, something that invited abuse and violation. Jeff

Carrington had treated her as a procurable favour, Alec Dayfield as a commodity on offer to the highest bidder. And Philippe, whom she liked and trusted, who had called her *la petite fille de la Vierge*, had blithely assumed she would be his partner in a meaningless betrayal.

Whom should she distrust, herself or all the men who became involved with her? She knew she could trust Anthony, of course. She realised that, ironically, together they presented an image of ideal love, Platonic love unpolluted by lust and jealousy and anger. It was a precious thing, a flame that did not burn or falter.

But she knew also that it was not enough, for her, or at any rate that she could only cherish it the way she wanted to by denying that other aspect of herself, the dark flame that consumed and destroyed, and threw deep, deceiving shadows.

She found nothing to kindle dangerous flames among any of the men she had become acquainted with lately. They were pleasant, attractive and conversible, and she felt absolutely nothing for them at all, one way or the other. She had taken to going sometimes to the pub, at lunchtime or in the early evening, with a party of the most regular of Ida's helpers, many of whom were (as Ida herself privately admitted) by no means as gormless as she made them out to be. Nicholas was not often among them and when he did come it was always in close company with Davina, who seemed to confirm Gossamer's earlier suspicions by paying him a lot of very obvious attention. It was more pleasant when they did not come, although she was sure Nicholas himself would never have been anything more than ordinarily attentive to her on his own. She wished, for his sake, she could convey to Davina that she did not feel the merest tingle of interest in him. She gloomily suspected that Davina would take that completely the wrong way, too.

She had bloomed into full maturity, a classic English loveliness suffused with the exotic, alluring to herself as well as to others. She knew herself to be admirable and desirable, her own sexuality could delight and arouse as well as appal her. She knew to that extent what it was that men saw, and that it could be dizzyingly seductive.

Her desired régime of continence was never under threat, however. The personalities of the men she met seemed to present a set of smooth surfaces with no snags or crannies for her own psyche to engage with, no complexities or hidden strata. Being with them was like existing on a diet of carefully chosen, perfectly balanced, vitamin-enriched nursery food: she couldn't fault it, except that it was insufferably bland.

She seemed only to want what was bad for her.

She found herself thinking of Jean-Luc. He was a very attractive man, kind and courteous and attentive. He had a highly polished surface but she was sure there was cragginess and complexity beneath it. She could feel relaxed in his company, and knew he had the power to awaken warmth and fun in her as he had done, lightly and momentarily, at the embassy party long ago. He was interesting and he made her feel interesting, a valued intellectual companion. He had never been anything but chaste towards her, nor she towards him. For her part she suspected that could change in an instant, if he invited it and she allowed herself to respond. She told herself it would be unwise to speculate on that possibility.

A man of Jean-Luc Frémont's background would surely have an eminently suitable proto-fiancée stowed away somewhere, like an investment policy waiting to mature. Besides, he was her lawyer. She had imbibed the unwritten code of Shaws, and she was sure it had a very definite clause in it forbidding emotional entanglements with one's legal or financial advisers. *It simply doesn't do to mix one sort of business with another*, she quoted to herself, and giggled. What lovely nonsense.

She missed having Jenny to share it with. The first decent patch of free time she had, she must get in touch again. Jenny had a way of helping things make sense.

She missed her especially the night she went to Frankie's with some of the Young Things. They made a sextet:

Gossamer with Benjamin, Zara and her boyfriend whom everybody called Humpers, and Davina and Nicholas.

The floor was crowded, it was Friday night and the frenetic energy of the place made her wilt. She told herself she had had a hard week, but that was not good enough: so had almost everybody there. Even the people who enjoyed lives of leisure led them at a hectic pace. Less than three years ago she had thought of this place, this life, as Nirvana, and while she might have grown up a little that was no reason to grow old.

She danced with Benjamin and later with Humpers, but not Nicholas. The noise and beat of the music, the laser show that stabbed and flashed all around them and the sheer physical pleasure of her body in motion acted as a sort of anaesthetic. Thinking was impossible, life a continuous sensual experience, so long as she was dancing.

They left the floor, exhausted, laughing, and found themselves a table, Davina allowing Nicholas to escort her across as soon as she saw the others were no longer dancing. What a stupid little cow, she thought venomously. If she wanted something on a collar and lead she should get herself a dog that would roll over to order. This, when she considered it, was in fact a pretty fair description of Nicholas himself. They probably deserved each other.

The sourness of her thoughts depressed her again. She surveyed the dancers instead. The men mostly wore an approximation to City chic: the same narrow range of dark trousers, bow-ties, blue and red braces, red and blue pinstriped shirts. The same haircuts, the same shoes, the same designer faces. It was like the human equivalent of buffet food, you got the same sort of plateful however many times you went round.

It was the women, the girls as Gossamer found herself regarding them, who were the garnish. Some were elegant in long slit skirts or loose trousers, and some startlingly attractive in clothes made to enhance and adorn. She herself had chosen a dark crimson dress that fitted closely yet allowed her freedom to move but she had not, like so many of the dancers, set out to present herself so blatantly. These were women pretending to be girls got up as women. They were setting out their wares, touting for pleasure. And why shouldn't they? she asked herself sternly. They were young, they looked good, they were having fun: really it was all quite innocent.

But that, she realised, was what made her so uneasy. Sex wasn't safe, wasn't just playing, it wasn't just having a mindless good time and then making sure the penis was safely sheathed in latex.

Perhaps she was the one who wasn't real. Perhaps these were all healthy, normal human specimens whereas she was diseased. Few if any of these girls, she told herself bitterly, had ever been as self-destructively stupid as she had.

A wave of melancholia swept over her and she suddenly loathed herself. A moment earlier she had presumed to pass judgement on Nicholas and Davina, who very probably did love each other. Davina was right to protect the object of her love against such a toxic substance. Oh Jenny, she thought, if you were here, you and Canfield, it wouldn't be like this, it would be fun. You could show me how to find what I've lost, how to be properly young and optimistic again.

She made a conscious effort to pull herself together before she ruined the evening for her friends. She heard her name shouted over the din of the music and this jerked her from her reverie. It was Zara with her hand on the pinstriped arm of a male in blue braces.

'Goss? You were miles away! Meet Giles, Giles this is Gossamer Fane. Giles is an ace reporter, Goss, he's going to make a big splash for Project Aid and get our photo in the papers.'

'Zara's talking nonsense, as usual. Hi, Gossamer, nice to meet you.' He held out a hand as he slid smoothly into a seat next to her. 'Giles Bamburgh. I write up the odd piece for the comics from time to time, that's all. But I'd be very happy to do something for this big event I've been hearing about, and I gather you're pretty well in charge of it.'

He was very pleasant and seemed genuinely interested,

and soon Gossamer found herself deep in shouted conversation with him. He asked her if she would mind his taking notes and she said no, of course not. She told him in detail about the work of Project Aid as well as all the plans for the Fashion Extravaganza. He said he got the impression she herself had first-hand experience of conditions in the Third World and she told him about that, too, about the school and the civil war and the Oxonian Murlé tribesman. She was tempted to ask him if he knew a writer called Mike Andersen, but she held back.

'Look,' he said finally, 'I must come properly clean about old Zara's nonsense, I'm not a serious journalist. I do the odd bit of freelance scribbling, that's all. The stuff I write ends up on the Social page or in the diaries usually, when it gets in at all. But I'll do everything I can to get this in, I promise. I mean, apart from the fact that it'll make a good saleable story I'd really like to help you, you know?'

Gossamer smiled and nodded, warming to him. They got up and danced together and her spirits lifted. Something in her past was at last connecting to something in the present, free of all that old poison. She began to feel properly happy. He danced well, and she danced with him rather than opposite him. She wasn't surprised when he asked if they could see each other again, soon, and she agreed that they very probably would. 'I mean, you could do a follow-up story,' she said, twinkling. 'Couldn't you?'

'Oh yes,' he agreed, 'I very probably could.' He handed her to Benjamin, smiling.

He photographed the six of them, flushed and laughing at their table when they came off the floor. He had to ask the girls to sit on the men's laps to get them all in, apologising with a sheepish grin for the low-tech backwardness of his camera. He took several shots, including one by mistake just as they were all getting up again.

Zara clapped her hands. 'I do *love* getting my piccie in the papers!' she squealed. 'I haven't had one in for simply *ages.*'

Ida had been entirely accurate, Gossamer noted, in her

assessment of Zara's interest in photography. She met Giles's eyes and they shared their amusement.

She returned home in a happier frame of mind, her previous dark brooding seeming like a brief bout of 'flu. Next time, if there was a next time, she must make sure to see it coming and take the appropriate precautions.

Now she felt she could visit Jenny simply for the sake of good, close friendship and not as a wretched sickly parasite.

She fell asleep promising herself a late lie-in and a day's contented domestic pottering. It felt good to be home.

Malling Benedict scanned his rivals' columns in the morning papers. This was a daily ritual, partly to remind himself how superior his own product was and partly to pick up anything of deeper interest that they might have missed.

Very, very rarely it happened that someone stole a march on him, and then there would be trouble for somebody. The paper allowed him a generous supply of 'legmen' who were supposed to be nothing more than unthinking instruments of their master's will – except when he had them fired for not thinking on his behalf.

This morning's crop, so far, was a particularly dire collection of PR handouts and the tedious doings and sayings of unentertainingly well-known people. Pope Benedict was pleased with that, of course. He had a rather nice little goose – a Junior Minister whose uses for rubberwear were said to extend greatly beyond the practical – cooking in one of his slow ovens, and it was reassuring to confirm that no one else had opened the door first.

He turned to the *Telegraph* last of all, expecting to find nothing of interest to him. A Duke obliged to sell one of his family's residences after taking a loss in the market on Black Monday, dear dear. The nephew of a long-forgotten Socialist minister discovered standing as a Tory in a Council by-election. His eye flicked up to the main photograph, saw the usual collection of B-list *Country Life* fluff, and flicked away. Then he looked again, and rapidly checked the accompanying para.

Yes, it was her. Gossamer Fane, 19, escorted by the Hon. Benjamin Sturminster, elder son of Lord Marnhull, at Frankie's, seen here with, blah blah. So, the little fish had swum into his nets again. How very amusing, especially as she appeared to be swimming in such an interesting pool. If the report was reliable she might well be mixing in some very newsworthy company quite soon.

He had not forgiven her for giving him the slip last time. He took that sort of thing as a personal affront. Well, now he could afford to wait and watch, for a little while.

The Pope occupied an office on the ground floor, one with four walls, a window, and a door that shut. It was his special privilege as an institution and a law unto himself, never mind the official line about it being a concession to his disability. Now he summoned a gofer from the open-plan hells on an upper floor.

He circled the item and tossed the *Telegraph* over. 'Find out who they got this from,' he said, 'and bring me his telephone number on a platter. Get hold of him before anyone else does.'

The minion checked the story. 'Oh her again, Carey Lambert's ex, the one that got away. Well, well. I could do the legwork on this little beauty for you.'

'No thank you.' Pope's mouth opened and shut like a trap. He looked up. 'Don't worry, dear boy, your position in this firm is secure. For the present.'

He gazed at the closing door with satisfaction. This would need very careful, very delicate handling. He allowed himself a slow reptilian smile that bared his little yellow teeth, then he lidded his eyes and plotted his possible ways forward.

After a few minutes he focused his attention on the Junior Minister. It would be Guy Fawkes day soon, a suitable date for the burning of a Member of Parliament.

Malling Benedict enjoyed a very great measure of job satisfaction.

*   *   *

Gossamer had a lovely time with Jenny.

Johnny was at the University most of the day, either in tutorials or else in the library. 'It's either doing exams or working up to them,' Jenny said. 'I've lost sight of the things I play second fiddle to, I think the latest one is the Plantaganet exchequer. It's terribly exciting, apparently.'

She looked well on it, though, and she wasn't complaining. Her eyes shone when she spoke about him. 'He's doing well, Goss. He's going to be big, I just *feel* it. Things are really going to work out. We're going to have those good times.'

It was a fine crisp November day, the air still and dry and the sun shining. They walked through Greenwich Park and across Romney Road to the pier and the *Cutty Sark*. Gossamer bought tickets for the ferry and they sailed up to London Bridge and back, playing at being tourists. They bought ice creams and Jenny treated her to a hideous Royal Family tea towel for her kitchen. Gossamer got her own back by buying a Houses of Parliament snowstorm for Johnny to put on his desk when he became a professor in the States.

'Are they really going to want a professor of Mediaeval English History in the USA, Jen?'

'Of course they are,' she replied, lapsing into a very bad imitation of a Southern drawl. 'Lawks-a-mussy, all that stuff is just so gorgeously *old*, y'know?'

'Perhaps they'll think he came over on the *Mayflower*,' said Gossamer, and they giggled like schoolgirls. An American couple nearby began a very careful conversation about the substandard hygiene facilities in their hotel, and they nearly choked on their ice creams. They had a competition to find the silliest use for Canary Wharf and Jenny won it by suggesting a King Kong theme park to compete with EuroDisney.

They talked. To begin with, Gossamer gave her a simple narrative of her time in Africa, including Mike as a companion. She tried to make the whole thing as matter-of-fact as she could, but even so she could hear it sounded a bit Indiana Jones. There would be time later to tell her the other things, but for now it was a case of catching up on news.

'Well I can't compete with that, I'm afraid. Living in sin with a scholar and a genius seems very tame in comparison.' Jenny was doing temping work to supplement Johnny's grant and the occasional contributions Helen Kepesake persuaded them to accept on the strict understanding that it wasn't housekeeping money. Gossamer reminded her that she had intended to enrol at University herself. The story they'd made up about her doing Post-Modern Culture and the New Gender hadn't been all nonsense.

'I know, Goss, and I will. But I can wait. We've got all the time in the world, the rest of our lives together to take turns. I can enjoy having lovely things like that to look forward to.'

Gossamer's heart turned over. She was so happy for her friend, and so poignantly aware of the great emptiness in her own life. Jenny might be slogging away at pointless jobs just to keep them both in baked beans but her life had direction, enrichment, purpose. *We've got the rest of our lives together*. She knew it was true, for them, and she wasn't jealous. It was just that it gave shape and definition to so much of her own yearning.

'Like children,' Jenny said. Gossamer was startled out of her reverie and must have looked blank. 'Babies, Goss, you know? I ache to have Johnny's babies, God I feel I could burst sometimes, it's so powerful. I fantasise about getting a dud packet of the Pill so I can fall accidentally pregnant. And sue the manufacturers for billions of pounds, of course, so we can afford to have it.'

Gossamer responded by teasing. 'And there's you saying there's plenty of time and you're getting a big buzz off deferred gratification. You're nothing but a fraud, Jennifer Kepesake.'

'Oh I know! It must be me 'ormones, ducks, on account of I'm a woman.'

Gossamer was serious after that. 'I know what you mean, though,' she said levelly. 'It's because you love each other.'

'Yes.' Jenny put her arm round her. 'Oh my poor Goss.'

'You were quite right, Jen. It was cone-shaped and it rumbled, remember?'

'Yes. One of my more unforgiveably priggish remarks. I remember. I also remember how I felt when he took me under his wing that time I had the abortion. It was overwhelming, I just knew I could let go and he would catch me. And he turned it full on you, didn't he Goss. He took you up to a high place and showed you all the world. Christ, no wonder you banged the phone down on me.'

'It wasn't because I didn't think what you said about him was true.' Suddenly the importance of saying this became urgent. 'I knew he could be dangerous. He could hurt, he had a cruel streak and he enjoyed the power of using it. I knew that was a part of him, a thing he did, I knew he had this dark place in his soul and I wanted to meet him there. I loved him, Jenny. And it was like being tested, not by him but by it, by love itself, and the only way I could pass the test, drive the darkness out, was through my love. I didn't hold back, Jenny, I didn't keep anything in reserve. I gave everything, *everything*. I didn't dare listen to any of you, it would be like Orpheus looking back or something, I had to have absolute faith in it, suffer for it so that we could both come through on the other side.'

Jenny held her with her eyes. 'That's nun's talk, Gossamer. It's putting gravel in your shoes so you'll enjoy going round on your knees. That's not love, it's perversion. It corrupts.'

'But what is, then? What is love, if it's not yielding and letting go and making yourself completely vulnerable and risking everything? You do, you and Johnny. You can't say you don't believe in it.'

'*Amor omnia vincit*, you mean.' Gossamer nodded numbly. 'Yes. Without saying anything more because it would sound smug, yes it does. It's mutual, it's us. It's not one-way traffic. The point is, you don't have to think about it. It's just something you're in, a place where you feel you've always belonged. Both of you.'

Gossamer spoke about Mike after that. Jenny listened wonderingly.

'One minute we could see everything, the next minute everything went dark. I tried to say something, and suddenly there was nothing either of us could say, except as polite strangers. It was like a sort of bereavement. Or a homesickness for a place that's been destroyed so completely you begin to wonder if you were just dreaming it.'

Jenny was silent for some time. At last she said, 'I could be brutal, Goss.'

Gossamer smiled weakly. 'Go on then. I can take it from you.'

'I could say, my gawd you don't half pick 'em.'

Gossamer's head fell forward and she spoke very quietly. 'You could be right.'

'Oh come on Goss, I was only—'

'No. Really. It's this terrible feeling I've got that it's me, I'm the trouble that makes the bad things happen. I send out all these signals without knowing it, all the time I think I'm doing one thing, saying one thing, they're picking up something quite different and I don't understand what they're sending back. I find myself attracted to complex men, older men with dark histories and complicated past lives. Men like Carey Lambert and Mike Andersen. But they frighten me, Jen, and perhaps it's because they bring out something in me which attracts them and then repels them. And all the time I'm still here saying, What's gone wrong, what did I do, please tell me somebody.'

She was very close to the wreckage of weeping now. 'Something in me gets in touch with something monstrous and cruel in them, and that's where we meet. All the time I was with Carey I half thought, more than half thought he could be my father. Can you imagine that? Or, get this, I've wondered lately if Mike might be my half-brother or something. What's the matter with me, Jenny? What am I?'

The tears came now. Jenny took her in her arms and to hell with what the other passengers thought they were watching. 'Oh Gossamer, oh darling, nothing's the matter with you. It's them, that's all, you've been unlucky, you've been unlucky twice and it's horrible for you but that's it, that's all.' They rocked to and fro, Jenny holding her like a mother, soothing, loving it all away.

'Twice unlucky, my poor darling. Carey was and is a bastard, no two ways. He used you, and people get used by other people, men and women, it happens and it's horrible and it's over. And Mike's screwed up, he's a man with a history like you said and somewhere in it there's something that got twisted right up and you triggered it somehow and you got hurt, both of you got hurt by the sound of it. But that's his problem, Goss, his problem to sort out and maybe you've helped him make a start on that and maybe when he's over it he'll find you again. But if he doesn't sooner or later you'll be with someone and find peace and love and sharing. I know it. Believe it and never doubt yourself, never never give way to despair.'

Gossamer's racking sobs had subsided and now she breathed a long relaxing sigh. She emerged from the embrace, her face messy from crying, and smiled lopsidedly. Jenny smiled broadly back and said: 'I, Madame Jenny, Reader of the Tarot and Stupendous Mistress of the Velvet Room, have spoken. So mote it be. You've put nasty stuff on my best coat, you besom.'

'And you,' Gossamer said, 'have got ice cream on your nose.'

'I know. I've been holding back from wiping it off out of consideration for you because I'm wonderful.'

'Of course.'

'So let's go and make a steamy threesome with Professor-elect Canfield, shall we?'

They stopped to rest on a bench in Greenwich Park and when they got up to go Jenny winced with pain. 'Ouch, my poor bloody back.'

'Oh Jen, what is it?'

'Well I'm glad you asked me that, it's what medical experts call badbackitis actually. Caused by too many crappy office chairs and lousily-sited VDUs. Cured by not working as a secretary and having pots of money so you can afford to keep an osteopath in the cupboard. There's a lot of it about, you know.'

Johnny arrived home shortly after they got back. He still looked absurdly young to Gossamer, but interesting with it. She began to see what Jenny had noticed in him all along. They hugged and kissed warmly, and Jenny gave him a swift résumé of her doings.

'But the Shaws Spirit saw you through,' he grinned. 'A Shaws Girl never perspires under pressure.'

'Of course not,' said Gossamer brightly. 'We simply glow.'

Johnny made tea and called through, 'How's yer back, Jen?'

'Boring,' she called back.

'She should see an osteopath, shouldn't she Goss?'

'Yes she should.'

'Can't afford it out of what you give me for the housekeeping, you brute.'

'Use mummy's money, I can do without my bit on the side for a week or two.'

'Oh all right then. Just to keep you out of that hussy's clutches.'

They were in love. It informed everything they did, every word and every action. It was a partnership. It was good to be with. It gave hope.

Johnny wondered aloud if they should go up the chippy or down the boozer and Gossamer said that as it was going to be her treat they should do both.

A few days later Giles Bamburgh called her at Project Aid and asked her if she'd mind meeting him to do a little research for a follow-up story.

'I thought perhaps we could meet in the Cheese Trap in Wine Office Court, do you know it?'

After only a fractional pause she said that yes, she knew it, and they fixed a date.

Dirk Dolenz confirmed Danse Macabre's booking for the Extravaganza but reserved the right to do deals for the future with DayStar, and Gossamer replied that, speaking on behalf of Project Aid, she had never supposed otherwise. Trish got in touch to arrange an evening with her.

'We're sort of mostly based in Brighton still and it'd be great to pop up to London so long as you don't mind me staying over. I can't bear rushing off to last trains.'

'No, that'd be lovely, I've got a spare room. Trish, do you remember Anthony that time we came down to see you in Brighton?'

'Acceptable Y-chromosome bearer, blond hair, nice body, yes of course I do. Definitely one of the good guys.'

Gossamer told her about The Queer Fish and she said it sounded a great place and she looked forward to eating one. 'You're turning into quite a bohemian in your old age, Gossamer Fane. Good for you. See yer.'

Gossamer supposed she was, in a mild sort of way. It was a little like a calmer, saner re-run of her previous life in London, this time with nobody pulling her strings.

It was rather pleasant, to be going on with. And it was good to put down these meetings in her diary. They stopped her feeling adrift while she waited to catch the wind and discover which way she was going to make her longer voyages.

⋇ **Fifteen** ⋇

'It still doesn't look as though there are any mad poets here.'

They had made their order for lunch and now sat with their drinks, gently testing each other out. Gossamer had schooled herself to treat this as just a normal, pleasant meeting with a normal, pleasant man.

Jenny had jollied her out of her paranoia by telling her not to go round like a cartoon character with a big black cloud over her head labelled 'Psychosexual Hangups'. 'Next time you meet a nice ordinary brightish sort of bloke, leave it parked outside, okay? Preferably somewhere it'll get permanently clamped.' She had promised she would.

Giles Bamburgh, for his part, had resolved to play it straight and play it clean. Pope Benedict had shown some of his hand, had given some of his reasons for regarding the girl as 'someone it would be decidedly worthwhile to draw a bead on'. Whatever his other reasons were, they were his own affair. Giles knew there was a mystery here, though not necessarily a deliberate mystification. She certainly didn't look like the sort of girl who needed to go round throwing dust in men's eyes. She could be an assistant branch librarian and still be bewitchingly fascinating.

He had made a resolution: he must not tell her any lies about himself or about what he was doing. If asked straight out he must admit that Pope was paying him a very useful retainer for being her marker.

He had two reasons for wanting to see this girl again, his need to earn money and his desire to get to know her better. He told himself he could handle balancing one against the other.

'Mad poets?'

'Mmm. The first time I was here was for lunch with my lawyer. He said it was supposed to be a haunt of mad poets.'

'Oh, I don't think they breed mad poets any more. Either that or they all go South for the winter. I wish I had such a generous lawyer. Perhaps you could give me an introduction.'

Her face clouded. 'I'm afraid I can't, Giles. He had a terrible accident. He'll never recover, that is if he's still alive.'

'My God, you've got to be talking about Kevin Germain!'

'Yes, that's right. Do you know him?'

'Of him, only. I lack the disposable assets to know him any other way. It's one of the reasons I'm not a Lloyds Name.'

He looked into his drink rather than meet Gossamer's eyes. Of course he'd known she was not South African but there had been a lingering hope that this part of what Pope had told him might have a perfectly quotidian explanation. A niece of Kevin Germain would surely not fail to know whether he was still alive, far less forget to call him 'Uncle Kevin'.

'I feel guilty about not asking, since I came back to England,' she continued. 'You don't happen to know, do you?'

'I hear there's no change,' he said. Which was true; Pope had told him. 'How long were you away?'

'Only about six weeks. I was supposed to be having a short holiday from the school but the war stopped me going back. There was nowhere else to go but home again.'

'Home being?'

Just perceptibly, she faltered. 'Here. England, London. I gave up my flat when I went to Ethiopia.'

'Oh, right. A bold move.'

'I wanted a change anyway.'

The hors d'oeuvre arrived. They had both chosen oysters and the ritual of dealing with them required a decent silence and a tacit understanding that it wasn't done to watch.

'And before that?' he asked, after they'd finished with their napkins. 'I mean, before England, London. Where you came from.'

'Oh, a little place in the Borders, Heronsburn. Nobody I know has ever heard of it.'

'Including me, I'm afraid. And then Shaws, of course.'

She tensed. 'Yes,' she said shortly. 'How did you know that?'

'Zara.'

He saw her relax. So much for dead parents in the Midlands, then. But why the mystery? Why the look of panic when he asked a perfectly neutral question about her school? Why should any educated, accomplished and sociable young woman feel any sort of reserve about that? The parts didn't add up to the whole.

'I have a confession to make,' he said, and saw her tense again. 'I did a little research of my own, got a cuttings agency to do a search. To save putting my foot in it as much as anything. Hack's perks, you could say.'

'Oh. I see.' She braced herself for what was coming.

'And I saw that your name was once linked, as they say, with that of Carey Lambert. That's right, isn't it?'

'Yes, that's right, it was. And then it stopped being. By mutual consent.'

'I see. I'm sorry.'

'There's no need to be. It was a perfectly reasonable question.'

She felt a dread rising in her. It was all going wrong, that long rancid shadow was falling across them and she must drive it away somehow before it infected anything.

'I was in love with him, Giles. But not he with me. And so we parted.'

'And you, er, went to Ethiopia.'

'Yes, that's right. A complete change.'

'It must have been all of that.'

Gradually the atmosphere between them grew less tense.

They chatted through the entrée, talk of Africa leading back to her time at Ryder-Vail and the Jeans de Nîmes campaign. 'I'm ashamed to say I didn't recognise you. I had to have it pointed out to me.' He did not say who by.

'That would rather depend which bit of me you failed to recognise, wouldn't it?' she asked, coquettishly. 'I think even Frankie's might draw the line at that kind of exposure.'

Laughing, he poured more wine. 'You wouldn't mind if that got used, would you? The connection with the adverts, I mean. I have to say I don't get to call the shots on what actually gets printed.'

She seemed to be considering it carefully. 'No, I don't mind. It's all in a good cause after all.'

When they finished talking, Giles paid, they exchanged phone numbers and parted. He checked his notes on all that she had told him about the people she was meeting and working with in the run-up to the Extravaganza. A lot of them were very definitely News Names.

She had given him a lot of copy, but he felt he knew rather less about her than he did before.

Gossamer felt absurdly let down and was cross with herself for it. It was a silly schoolgirl reaction, pathetic and ridiculous.

It became suddenly clear to her what she should do. If trying to hide from the past had this debilitating effect on her she should simply stop doing it. She should face it down instead, and bring it out into the open so she could watch it squirm and wither. Ida had yet to interview Alec Dayfield. Very well, then: she would do it.

Ida did not ask Gossamer's reason for wishing to see Alec Dayfield. She merely inhaled deeply on her cheroot, smiled broadly and said: 'Certainly my dear. Shall I just tell his secretary that I am indisposed and will be sending my representative?'

'Thank you,' Gossamer replied simply.

'Good luck, my dear. And good for you.'

She wore a dark trouser suit and a white shirt and carried

a briefcase. The cinnamon silk scarf at her throat was her only concession to femininity. In the taxi she checked through her papers to be sure of mastering her brief.

DayStar and OffWorld were contenders for a market the experts said could not support both for much longer. Each strove to undercut the other with sign-up deals to hook the public in, each to outbid the other for exclusive rights to the things the public wanted to watch. Each had gambled to the limit if not beyond, and something had to give. The analysts pored over the rivals' six-monthly accounts; proponents of public service broadcasting rubbed their hands with lugubrious glee and stood by to pick up the tastiest morsels from the inevitable wreckage.

A cartoon in *Business Week* showed two satellites cut away to reveal Alec Dayfield and Carey Lambert inside, sweat pouring down their faces as they pedalled furiously to keep themselves in orbit. The caption read: Two Driven Men Attempt To Defy Gravity.

It was nothing less than the truth. By temperament Lambert and Dayfield were leaders, ruthless and absolute, the business equivalent of military dictators with OffWorld and DayStar two nation states locked in a war that could end only in conquest or mutual destruction. Their combat had become almost an end in itself, the business of broadcasting merely one of several means towards it. Of course there were civilities to be conformed to, neutral zones in which a cease-fire might be observed. They belonged to the same clubs, moved in the same circles, appeared together in the same public arenas, were mutually supportive under hostile questioning from the House of Commons Select Committee on Broadcasting.

There were deals to be done, too, across the front line; it was well known, to insiders, that Dayfield used Lambert's revived media broking agency to promote DayStar in the press and on terrestrial TV. Dayfield had sold off his own agencies, partly to raise capital but also to satisfy the British television regulators, always alert for breaches of the rules concerning conflicts of business interest. Since

OffWorld was part of a Luxembourg-based consortium no such regulations applied to Lambert.

But the war proceeded on innumerable battlefronts both public and private. There were skirmishes, guerrilla raids, reprisals, covert operations, defections. Hostages were taken and traded, agents turned and put in place. Decoys were dispatched, wittingly or not, to compromise the enemy.

How many, Gossamer wondered, were brave enough or foolish enough to risk once again being caught in the cross-fire? She paid off her taxi and shivered suddenly in the biting wind that blew off the river. This part of Wapping was an unlovely place on such a deadly-grey November day. Her boat trip with Jenny, all that redemption of tears and laughter, seemed a world away.

The huge glass doors sighed open as she approached them. She crossed the threshold, half expecting to be cut down as she entered. Innocent parties, too, could make themselves mortal enemies. She remembered the look of bewildered anger on the faces of her friends that terrible night of the *Dragon Hurst* party.

She remembered her confrontation with Alec Dayfield, the horror and the shame of it. Now she was to meet him again. Her knuckles whitened on the briefcase. She put on a neutral half-smile and made her legs carry her forward.

The contrast between this place and OffWorld could not have been starker. Each was a statement of its presiding genius, equal and opposite. OffWorld's atrium was a pleasure-dome, a place of glamour and beguilement. The cynosure of its age, it spoke of the enchantment of power.

DayStar House had a reception area, not an atrium. It spoke bluntly of power through efficiency. It was a place of work. A uniformed guard stood by the desk, walkie-talkie in hand. The woman who sat behind bared her teeth in a switched-on smile as Gossamer approached.

'I represent Ida Spenlowe-Humfrey of Project Aid, I have an appointment with Mr Dayfield at eleven.' She checked the time on the simple clock above the desk. She was early by the five minutes required to be processed and transported to an upper floor.

The receptionist's badge proclaimed her as Alessandra. Gossamer distracted her mind with the thought that the first two syllables were probably her own addition.

'I'm afraid we don't have a note of your name,' she said, as though this were an oversight on their part.

'Fane,' Gossamer said.

'Is that Fane, er?'

'Miss Fane.' Gossamer smiled back. The woman wrote on a badge and handed it over. 'Could you just sign in here please?' Gossamer wrote her initials against Ida's appointment.

'Eleventh floor, Ms Fane. I'll tell them you've arrived.'

Gossamer rode the lift. It was a grey steel box, not an observation car. By the third floor there were five other people in it but none that she recognised. They affected not to look at her. After the ninth floor she had the lift to herself.

She breathed deeply. She brushed brisk fingers over her suit, adjusted her scarf, checked her earrings. There was a vanity mirror in the lift. It reflected the image of the sort of glamorous female executive Medialand itself would have been proud to invent. All she had to do was act the part, make it hers.

Or be herself.

Alec Dayfield's secretary, a superbly handsome woman in early middle age, greeted her and showed her straight in. It was a relief to have no waiting. It was a large office, almost bare save for the big desk at one end and the man silhouetted at the window, looking out over the autumn Thames.

And this also, her memory spoke to her, *has been one of the dark places of the earth.* She all but gasped. Why should that come back to her now? 'A' level English at Shaws: the book, a slim paperback, the feel of it, the smell of it. Reading it had been like a bomb going off inside her.

Heart of Darkness.

Why now?

He turned. He was huge against the blank bright greyness of the window. Did she hear him draw breath? Did he, too, have some apprehension of this terrible immanence?

Words came. 'I thought it would be you,' he said.

'Why?' she asked.

He crossed to the desk, sat down, looked at her. 'You tell me,' he said.

She regarded him coolly. 'It's my job,' she said.

A smile came and vanished. 'It's my job, she tells me. Ida Spenlowe-Humfrey made the appointment, you turn up. Whose idea was that?'

'Mine,' she said.

'So. Tell me. Why?'

'To prove I am not what you thought. To show you were mistaken.'

He laughed harshly. 'What makes you assume it matters two fishes' tits to me what you are, Gossamer Fane?'

She coloured, but it was not shame or embarrassment that she felt, it was the kindling of a controllable and creative anger. 'I don't recall saying it mattered to me what *you* thought, Mr Dayfield. It seems to me that I'm not the one making assumptions.'

His laughter now seemed genuinely appreciative. 'Bravo,' he beamed. 'So who does it matter to?'

'Me,' she said. 'It matters to me. It matters to me to remind myself that I was deceived and betrayed. It matters to me to demonstrate in front of you that I am not a whore, yours or Carey Lambert's or anyone else's. It matters to me to tell you that the man I loved, the only man I had ever made love with, used me as an instrument to harm you. It matters to me to overcome that humiliation.'

His eyes kindled pale fire. He leaned forward, his hands gripping the edge of the desk. Ignoring her last sentence he asked: 'He told you this? That he used you for that?'

She almost flinched from the naked intensity of his question. She nodded.

'Tell me what he said.' It was an order.

This was not at all how she had imagined things would

be. She had hoped to rise above the past, not to revive it and dissect it, but she made herself answer as calmly, as flatly and matter-of-factly as she could.

'He said he was bored with me, he'd had all the fun he wanted out of me but he'd found a useful way of getting rid of me, by wrecking your production. He was annoyed with himself for moving too soon. He'd reckoned on it being too far down the road to re-shoot.'

He grinned savagely, his big features suffused with glee. 'Had he now! Poor Carey must be getting old, he came too soon.' His next words were a direct question: 'Anything else?'

She looked him straight in the eyes. 'I told him about your offer. You remember your offer, Mr Dayfield?' A shadow passed, very briefly, across his face and she saw that she had proved him wrong, that this was something that did matter to him even if he could not admit it to himself. She continued:

'I watched him think about that. It was like watching a clock in a glass case, I actually saw all his works going round. It was something else he hadn't taken into account.'

'And when the clock struck?'

'He said I should accept your offer. I said no.'

'Thank you for that.'

'I didn't do it for you.'

He smiled again. 'Two palpable hits. Well done. My God, this sounds like it must have been quite a conversation. Anything else?'

'I told him what I thought of him. I told him what he was.'

'Don't tell me, I can guess. You had some ripe words for me too, I recall. "Foul-mouthed scum", wasn't it?'

'I withdraw that,' she said.

His eyes sparkled mischievously. 'All of it?'

She grinned back, 'You are quite foul-mouthed some-times.'

His head went back and he barked with laughter. 'Yeah,

you're quite right. I can be a crude bloody bastard at times.'
He stopped laughing. 'Try living through my life and not
being, Gossamer Fane.'

It was almost an appeal, a reaching out to connect with
her. She responded carefully: 'We all have pain in our lives
at times, I think.'

'Oh yes, we all have pain.' His voice was suddenly altered:
deeper, huskier. 'Great pain. Unendurable pain.'

She thought he might collapse under the burden of this
sudden intensity. Instincively she reached forward as if to
catch him. His eyes fixed on her but it was as if he was
staring through her at someone else.

Then, as suddenly, he rapped the desk and straightened
himself. 'So. End of story, yes? You gave him a full
description of himself and walked out of his life.'

'Yes!' She wasn't going to tell him how Carey Lambert
had stopped her mouth.

'A sound move. Now, apart from showing me how
devastating you look in a business suit, what else have
you got to show me and is it in that very serious-looking
briefcase, and if so how much is it going to cost?'

She laid her case on the desk and opened it. 'Yes it is,'
she said brightly, 'and it's going to cost you lots. And
it's fish.'

'Fish.'

'That's right.'

'DayStar Television is going to sponsor fish. Why?'

He hadn't offered her a seat so she took one. And then she
told him why, her presentation organised and immaculate.

And all the time she was aware of an attraction, a
gravitational pull towards this man. She knew he could
crush her with one blow of his huge paw. Yet there it was,
undeniable and unnamable, a force that would draw her to
him if she let it.

And all the time one part of her mind, detached, was
revolving all this, another part was getting sponsorship
for a fish farm in Bangladesh. It was eerie, this parallel
operation of consciousness. It could be useful, certainly,

but she wasn't at all sure she liked the idea of having it.

In fact she wanted very badly to have its antithesis, to focus her whole self on one point only. She had had it once but it had been broken, raped away. There was no point in wanting it back again.

He rose and gripped her hand, tiny in his big warm fist. He was barely taller then she was yet she knew he could make her appear to herself as a child if he wanted to.

In the instant their hands clasped she knew, too, that he possessed a powerful sexual urge for her. There was something else, she thought, to acknowledge and beware.

'I shall look forward to seeing you again, Gossamer Fane. At BAFTA.'

It had not occurred to her that he would be there himself, though of course he would have to be. He was himself a celebrity. 'How strange to be on your own television,' she smiled.

'It'll be stranger still for Lambert.'

Her heart seemed to stop. 'He'll be there too?'

'Oh yes. Your friend Ida has something we both want.' He opened a desk drawer and took out a folded-back copy of *Business Week*. 'The original of this.' It was the cartoon, Two Driven Men.

'The artist is related to a cousin of hers, it seems. So she swooped and got it, and put it up for auction. Knowing, of course, that we'd both want to own it. A redoubtable lady, your friend Ida. I shouldn't want her as an enemy.'

'I can't imagine she has any. In her own sort of way she seems to love everybody.'

His face was hard. 'Then she must have enemies. You can't love without making enemies. Where there's love there is always hate, Gossamer Fane. You'd do well to remember that.'

She was dismissed.

She was almost out of the building, almost safe, when a voice hailed her. She froze, her heart lurching. A man's voice, raised in recognition and surprise.

Slowly she turned and forced herself to face it. 'By all that's holy and wonderful, it is you. Goss Fane! A good deed in a naughty world if ever there was one. Come and have a cup of coffee and tell me where you've been.'

It was General Lee, the barman of *Dragon Hurst*. Beaming, he took her in his arms and kissed her. 'By God,' he said, 'if I was twenty years younger we could raise a few eyebrows. Come on, I'm buying and a refusal always offends.' He swept her off.

They sat sipping their coffee. It was very hot, which helped to offset its nastiness. They passed comment on it, and on their surroundings. Gossamer's uneasiness communicated itself to him and he leaned forward and said softly:

'Relax my pet, I'm the only one of the old gang here today. Not that that needs to trouble you at all.'

'No? I've never stopped feeling bad about it.'

'Then stop now. Oh, there was a lot of feather-spitting to begin with, of course. They're actors, right? They felt threatened, which is hardly surprising really when you consider what a precarious business acting is. But it soon wore off once the little grey men announced a re-shoot. Eighteen scenes all over again and ditto the money, imagine it! You've no idea how many maintenance payments were kept up out of all that lovely extra moolah.'

She laughed in spite of herself. 'So much for them,' she said. 'What about you?'

'Me? Oh, I've never quite got round to acquiring an ex-wife. I spent all mine on fast women and slow horses.'

'I don't believe a word of it! And that's not what I meant, as you very well know.'

'No, I know. Well of course, speaking personally I've never forgiven you. That's why I'm trying to poison you with cups of hot toxic waste.'

She spoke to him with her eyes and he put his hand, warm and dry and soft, on hers and squeezed it gently. 'Speaking as a fully qualified Heavy Breather, you mean? In my capacity as the Don Giovanni of the dubbing suite.'

'I'm sorry, I don't understand.'

There was a silence. His expression altered. Then, 'No, I see you don't. Well, the least I can say is I wasn't the only one, we all thought we knew the score and we were all wrong.'

'Please explain it to me. Is all this something to do with – with . . .'

'Yes, my dear, it is. Well, you see, it's like this: when they make sex videos, blue movies as we used to call them in the days when people still had to go out to watch what they couldn't get at home, the one thing they can't do *in situ*, as it were, is the noise. One can't really call it 'dialogue', can one? There's nowhere to pin the microphones, you see. And they're too mean to hire a proper sound studio. So they film it silent and add a bit of humpy disco music afterwards. Along with the odd resting actor, off camera, to do the panting and grunting. And so forth.' He spread his arms out and grinned apologetically. 'Behold a superstud,' he said.

She didn't know whether to laugh or cry. 'Oh, no!' was what she said.

'Oh yes, I'm afraid. I was very young and very broke, of course. The last time I did it must have been, ooh, all of eighteen months ago, at least.'

She goggled. 'Just before *Dragon Hurst*?'

'That's right. When everything else starts to conk out, one finds one can still pant like an eighteen-year-old. I found I got quite worn out just watching it.' His eyes danced with silent laughter.

Now she was able to laugh, and did so freely. Then she asked: 'And the others . . . they all thought the same?'

'Oh yes. A lot of them have, as they say, been there and done that. The consensus was you'd just been bloody unlucky. Only we all got it wrong, didn't we, Gossamer? It was much, much worse than that, wasn't it?'

She nodded.

'And I suppose he said it was a private thing, just between yourselves.'

She nodded again.

'And I think you loved him. The old suspension of disbelief.'

It was like knots untying themselves inside her. It was so liberating, to be understood. 'Yes,' she breathed.

'The bastard,' he said simply. 'You must introduce us some time so I can kill him face to face. Unless you can think of something nastier.'

'I think,' she said slowly, 'the worst thing you could do would be to ignore him. It's what I'm going to do.'

'Attagirl.'

He had to leave to go to rehearsal. He told her he'd come up in the world since *Dragon Hurst*: now he was playing a Chief Steward on a cruise ship. 'If I can hang on till I'm eighty I might get my own wine bar,' he said.

They embraced warmly. 'So long, my sweet. Be brave, be splendid. You're a very lovely woman.'

'And you're a lovely, lovely man,' she said, and meant it.

'Oh, I know. It's being so wonderful keeps me going, don't you know.' He waved, and left. It seemed a very long time since she had felt so simply, unashamedly happy.

As she turned from handing in her badge at the reception desk she saw Alec Dayfield emerge from the lift and cross the floor to the doors. He had not noticed her. He was deep in low-voiced conversation with another man, taller than him, who bent his head away from her to hear what his companion was saying.

She could not see his face but she felt sure she knew who he was. She could feel the man's aura across the room filling her senses. The world seemed to stop. She was poised, trembling, out of time.

Their murmured conclave continued as they passed outside. Rain had begun to fall. The man unfurled an umbrella; as he raised his face to open it and hold it above them both, she saw that she was right.

It was Mike Andersen.

She was glad there were no taxis. She walked in the cold rain through the brave new bleakness of Docklands to Shadwell station, needing to feel the earth beneath her feet.

She saw his face. She saw it set in concentration behind the wheel of a Land Rover. She saw it grim with resolution under gunfire. She saw it dissolve into hers by a waterfall in an enchanted place.

She saw it shut up tight against her, and turned away.

The rain slanted down, and she paid no heed to it. Her clothes grew sodden, her hair clung icily to her scalp, the hand that gripped her briefcase grew numb. It was as though all belonged in another place, another world, another time.

Perhaps she wasn't up to this business of being herself. Perhaps she should just let herself be invented by someone else. Then she would know who she was, what she was, what she had to do. Then she could live.

Round and round and round and round . . .

Somehow she had arrived. Outside the station someone approached her with magazines and she found she was holding one in her hand. She bought a ticket, found the platform and was soon rattling off to Cannon Street on an absurd little fairground tramcar of the Docklands Light Railway.

Slowly, reality seeped back in. She flicked through the pages of the magazine. It was *Town Talk*, a flimsy, glossy, garish thing given away free on the streets and in the subways.

Her glance was hooked by the sight of her own name.

There was a photograph. A photograph of two bottoms. Hers. One wore Jeans de Nîmes, the other a dress that clung. Benjamin's lap was just visible under it.

She heard Zara's laughter, Zara's happily squealing voice: *We're going to get our piccie in the papers!*

The headline was SPOT THE BOT.

She made herself read the text.

Stop drooling guys, this one's way out of your league!
All four cheeky curves above belong to lovely Gossamer Fane (19) currently putting it about in the good cause of

Project Aid, the charity for the beautiful people. Gorgeous Gossamer is to host a Fashion Extravaganza at BAFTA in December, and the snap on the right was taken during a recent working party at Frankie's.

We last saw Gossamer being squired by satellite media magnate Carey Lambert, the 43-year-old supremo of OffWorld TV. Like they say: that was then, this is now . . .

Believe it or not there is more to Ms Fane than meets the eye. Something of a mystery, this gal. The first time she came at us from Medialand, last time it was from the heart of war-torn Africa where she escaped by the skin of her denims. Where's she gonna come from next? Nobody seems to know, and if they do they're not telling . . .

Still, those of you with long memories and an eye for beauty may recognise her from the left-hand pic as the model for Jeans de Nîmes in a campaign that last year ran all the other denim cowboys right off the range.

'Course, back in those days there were certain other points of comparison 'sides a tasty ass. Back then, boys, Goluptious Goss was also wearing . . . nothing else at all. Hey! Whoa up! Forget it, pardner! Like we said, she's way out of our league . . . Still, we could always try buying a ticket for that li'l ole extravanganza, if'n she wuz ter be one of those there models . . .

Filth.

The page was headed: MALLING ABOUT.

Malling Benedict.

She threw the thing on the floor.

Putting it about.

Pope Benedict was just a man who slimed everything he touched. Everyone knew that. She should take no notice of it.

The thing is, I have no control over what actually goes in . . .

She wanted so badly to believe it.

She had to believe it. The alternative was called paranoia.

She was back on the rollercoaster.

Everyone seemed to have seen *Town Talk*. Zara thought it was a hoot, was gushingly jealous of Gossamer for having once done modelling work and couldn't understand why anyone should want to give it up.

Davina said she supposed the extra publicity for Project Aid couldn't be a bad thing, and Nicholas agreed with her.

Benjamin was shame-faced, as if apologising for being the owner of the knees she was sitting on. Gossamer ruffled his hair and told him not to be silly, it didn't matter a bit, and she didn't suppose anyone took Malling Benedict seriously. Everyone agreed with that.

Ida, privately, said the man was a horrid little shit.

'And he's put me in an awkward situation, which of course is what I really find unforgiveable. You see my dear, the Vane-Venables girl asked me if you might be available to model one or two of the more gorgeous creations and I'm rather afraid I may have led her to believe you might be. She knew about the jeans thing, which I'm ashamed to say I didn't, and she's got contacts at Ryder-Vail where it seems they still speak highly of you. So she was really rather importunate.'

'It's all right,' said Gossamer. She spoke almost automatically. She hated to see Ida embarrassed and her first instinct was to stop her feeling bad. Pope Benedict's nasty little piece wasn't her fault, any more than it was Benjamin's. Or even Giles's, probably. It shouldn't be allowed to spoil things.

A resolution grew swiftly in her. 'I'd love to model Annouska's gorgeous creations, and of course I'll do it. It'll be fun.'

'Oh, I'm so glad you said that! For all sorts of reasons, one of which is very selfish. It'll make me feel a bit happier about treading the catwalk myself.'

Gossamer goggled. 'I know,' Ida snorted. 'My first reaction precisely: I must say it never occurred to me to raise funds by holding an auction to get the model to leave the stage. Apparently I'm down to model something called The Mature

Executive Look. God only knows what that is: personally I thought I was already wearing it, but there you are. I can't wait to see what bloody Benedict makes of *that*!'

It was only later Gossamer realised that Ida's last words probably meant that Benedict would be there.

Jean-Luc Frémont rang her at home a few days later and invited her to accompany him at a reception at the French Embassy.

'It is I am afraid a poor substitute for what I should like to do, which is to take you out on your birthday, but alas I must be out of the country at that time on business.'

She had all but forgotten about her birthday, now only a few weeks distant. She would be twenty years old.

'Oh dear,' she said, 'what is it?'

'Well, if I tell you that it is a complex matter of European Law regarding the manufacture, distribution, inter-Community transportation and sale of liqueur chocolates you will begin to feel sleepy. And if I add that it will take a team of lawyers many days of examination and deliberation to produce a precisely legal and thoroughly European definition of the words 'liqueur' and 'chocolate', you will need a very handsome prince to wake you up again. *Eh bien*, it is my job and somebody has to do it, no?'

'You could always eat the evidence,' Gossamer suggested, thinking of the tarts in *Alice in Wonderland*. 'You might find you all agree very quickly.'

'Ah, such a very practical and very English solution is not possible for it might do away with the need for lawyers, and that of course would be terrible. Would you have me beg on the streets?' Laughingly, she allowed him not to.

'So,' he continued, 'if you will accept, I will arrange for you a formal invitation.'

She accepted gladly and began happily planning what she would wear. No diamonds, no sinful perfume, the collar and lead of ownership. She would be her own woman in equal company.

Her birthday was approaching, and afterwards Christmas.

Furs and Florida belonged to last year, another woman in another world. She had changed since then, subtly perhaps but irrevocably. Realising that, she told herself, was what being twenty should mean for her.

Could it be that the last twelve months had been a loop in time, a digression from the mainstream of her life?

As the days passed until the reception she began to hope fervently that this could be true.

She wore no diamonds, but she glowed.

Jean-Luc had a present for her when he called. 'You do not have to open it now,' he said, 'if you would prefer to wait until it is truly your birthday.'

But she did not want to wait, and not only because it would seem churlish. Whatever he gave her would be something that defined her for him, and just as she was sure he was a man without darkness in his soul so she knew it must be something she would rejoice in, without corruption.

The price of diamonds had been high and it had almost broken her to pay it.

Her ringless fingers picked carefully at the gold wrapping paper and revealed a jewel box covered in soft leather. Inside was a pair of earrings, sapphires set in delicate pendants of honey gold. There was no grossness of display about them, they did not speak of a man's proprietorship. They were, simply and wholly, a gift. They complemented her perfectly.

She gasped, and felt her eyes brim. 'Oh they're beautiful, Jean-Luc. They're so beautiful.' He smiled, knowing that they were. 'Thank you,' she breathed.

'I hope that you will wear them. They will suit, I think.'

She had chosen a black sleeveless tuxedo suit, elegant and stunningly sensual, that subtly accentuated the strength and suppleness of her mature young body. Jean-Luc's gift picked up the pure blue of her eyes, the deep-tanned bloom of her flawless skin. They were what she would have chosen for herself.

He was crisply splendid in evening dress. She kissed him lightly, savouring the scent of his hair and skin. The glossy raven's wing of her hair caressed his face as his lips brushed her cheek in return. 'You are beautiful,' he said. 'A very beautiful person.'

She could have cried at that. Her eyes widened. 'I believe I may be,' she said.

'What you believe is true,' he replied softly. 'It is what we believe of ourselves that truly shapes us.'

An Embassy car was waiting for them outside in the still cold air and the driver shimmered round to open the door for her. 'With the compliments of my Uncle Marcel,' Jean-Luc explained. 'I think he does it to remind me of what I am missing by not joining the *corps diplomatique*.'

'Then so long as he goes on doing it,' she said as they settled into ample luxury, 'you need not miss it.'

He laughed delightedly. 'That is an aspect that has escaped him so far, I am glad to say. I think I neglected to tell you that tonight's reception is held to further the exchange between our countries of *la culture*. That is to say, the Arts, not agriculture.'

They purred effortlessly through the London traffic as though transported in their own special pocket of inviolable space. Gossamer could not recall when she had last felt so untroubled and Jean-Luc beside her observed her sense of happy ease as one who knows he is giving pleasure.

They exchanged smiles as the car smoothly sped them on. She almost wished they would never arrive. It was as if this was something too uncomplicatedly lovely to last.

They were among the first to arrive, deliberately so, for Jean-Luc wished for an opportunity to re-acquaint her with his Uncle Marcel. The diplomat bent over her hand to kiss it and pronounced himself *bien enchanté*.

'I had the pleasure of your brief acquaintance on an earlier occasion, *mademoiselle*, and I am so happy to renew it. It is good to see that my nephew does not squander all his time on the worthless trivialities of confectionery.'

'Surely nothing that engages the attention of so many lawyers can be trivial, Monsieur Frémont?' Gossamer teased.

'Precisely, *mon oncle*. And how can it be worthless when we all charge so much?'

'*Mon dieu*, do you hear him Miss Fane? He speaks like a tradesman! He would sell opinion by the kilo and judgement by the metre! I ask you, will a *liqueur au chocolat* become suddenly more delectable for being defined by a panel of lawyers? Pronounce for me, please: I appeal to you.'

'Oh, I'm sure it cannot suffer for it,' Gossamer replied, smiling. 'Any more than Culture can be harmed by being exchanged in an Embassy.'

'Ah *bon, vraiment*! I see you are a born diplomat, *mademoiselle*. My felicitations.'

He kissed Gossamer's hand again, beamed at his nephew, and excused himself to greet the wife of the Junior Minister for the Arts, chortling softly as he went.

Gossamer caught Jean-Luc's eye and he bent to her. 'I'm having such a lovely time,' she murmured. 'Thank you.' He kissed her hair lightly by way of acknowledgment.

'Come,' he said. 'It is time to begin the circulation.'

She danced, she floated, she was faultless. Her clothes, let alone her beauty, set her visually apart from the other women yet she knew she roused no hostility. She met only with acceptance, both in her own right and as the pleasant and charming companion of Marcel Frémont's nephew.

She realised, with a pleasant thrill of understanding, that it felt like being welcomed into a family.

Jean-Luc was attentive but not confining. She moved with him from group to group with spellbound, seamless ease. She conversed with the Ambassador's wife, who was donating a hat to the Extravaganza, on the subject of Ida Spenlowe-Humfrey and was complimented on her observation that their mutual friend's motto in life was not so much *noblesse oblige* as *noblesse ne s'excuse pas*. She discussed with the *directeur* of the Paris Opera the difficulties of staging *La Bohème* in contemporary dress in an age when the contemporary became passé halfway through rehearsal. She listened to a disquisition from the Junior Minister for the Arts on the importance he attached to having what he called 'a broad remit of outlook' on his reponsibilities, and drew cheerfully self-deprecating laughter from him by agreeing that what really mattered was a knowledge of what one liked.

All her fears, all her loneliness seemed to fall away from her. She shone with her own light.

Music began, and Jean-Luc offered his arm. 'No fan?' he smiled. 'No vulgar feathers?'

'And no blushing or giggling. I promise.'

'Bien sûr,' he murmured. *'Parce-que tu n'es pas une coquette, non?'*

'Bien sûr,' she whispered back. She joined the dance. *Yes*, said her mind; *yes*, sang her soul. Yes.

They changed partners. Jean-Luc danced with the Ambassador's wife, the Opposition Spokesperson on the Arts and Broadcasting, and the fiancée of the French cultural attaché. Gossamer was partnered by Marcel Frémont, the Assistant Head of BBC Radio Three, and Lord Melsetter, Liberal Democrat Spokesman on the Arts, Leisure, Sport, Science and the Media, whose area of expertise (he informed her sadly) was aquaculture.

Finally they were in each others' arms again for a waltz. They flowed around the ballroom basking in admiration. As the music ended there was applause, much of it directed to them. Jean-Luc bowed to her and she gave him a little curtsey, and there was kindly laughter.

As they moved off the floor an attendant appeared at Jean-Luc's elbow. *'Excusez-moi, Monsieur Frémont: le téléphone.*

Jean-Luc frowned in surprise. 'Excuse me, Gossamer, I can only believe it is a matter of some urgency.'

'I expect it's those liqueurs,' she smiled. 'I promise I won't tell Uncle Marcel.'

She turned away, and saw that she was standing before the La Tour. A candle, hands, tranquillity of light and shadow. The sweet poignancy of it, the sureness, the completeness, the enduring tender strength of it. All this was hers.

She would never lose this moment. It could never be taken away from her. It was rooted in her deepest being and would stand fast against all adversity.

She felt him first as a movement of bodied air.

Then as a crawling between her shoulder blades. Then an icy prickling at the nape of her neck. She knew the smell of him.

She turned, and saw him. This was no hallucination, then. The colour drained from her face, then returned. Beyond him she saw faces half turned towards where they stood facing each other. Her mind registered that there had been a tiny faltering in the bumble of voices in the room. She turned back to the picture, standing a little to one side of it. Whatever happened next it must appear as though they were having a conversation about it. She would be calm. She would carry it off.

'Thank you for that,' he said, stepping forward alongside her. They were both regarding the La Tour now. 'You are lovelier than ever, Gossamer Fane.'

'And you are still Carey Lambert,' she said.

His gaze did not waver. 'It is a very long time since I gave up trying to be anyone else. To know thyself is the beginning of wisdom, after all.'

'Congratulations,' said Gossamer drily.

She heard him give a little gasp. Good, she had made a wound. 'Do you find you can live with the knowledge?' she added. She might as well rub some dirt in it while she could. Still they did not look at each other. Lambert raised an open hand to the picture as if to make some point about it.

'With very great difficulty, yes.'

She took stock of this. Pity. He was asking for pity. A very old trick. It was in all the books.

'If you look very closely you can see the *craqueleure*,' she replied coolly, fixing her eyes on the wash of painted candle-light. 'Isn't it sad that true connoisseurship should consist only in a minute examination of the surfaces of things? It misses all the truth. Why are you here?'

'I hope to speak to one of the directors of the French television service. I have only just arrived. I had no prior knowledge of tonight's guest list.'

'I see. And why are you here?' She indicated the space around them.

'Partly to spare you the experience of bumping into me later on. But mostly for my own purposes.'

'Oh, but of course.'

'As you say, of course.'

He wanted her to ask him what his purposes were. Good. She wouldn't.

'I hoped you would choose not to ask,' he said, and a shiver ran swiftly through her. Always he had seemed to read her inmost thoughts. 'It was to let you know that I wish to apologise. And to make atonement.'

'You apologise, then,' she said flatly.

'Yes.'

'And you crave atonement.'

'Yes.'

'It is granted. Now go away.'

It didn't work. He was still there, a presence at her side. 'You know, Gossamer, that it is not like that. You know that full atonement can only be granted after full confession.'

Her lips moved very slightly to frame her whispered 'yes'.

He did not reply. The urge to speak was hers.

'But I am not a priest,' she said.

'True forgiveness may only be granted by the person wronged. Only then may the sinner know true humility. You know that.'

Her lips moved again but this time the word was unspoken.

His voice was low, husky: broken. 'I would be healed,' he said. 'And I seek to offer healing. Not here, not now. If it is not wanted I will not intrude with it.'

Now she could not keep the passion from her voice, though he alone should hear it.

'*You* seek to offer *me* what you call "healing"?'

'I seek to offer you an explanation.'

'Ah, I see. A self-justification, I should have guessed.'

'A *mea culpa*. But you should know that *mea culpa* must necessarily involve *apologia*. And that may rightly be called self-justification. I should be playing false if I denied it.'

'My God,' she said. 'My God. Carey Lambert has a horror of playing false!'

Now his voice was stronger, the voice of the old Carey. 'I have never told you a lie, Gossamer. Never have I lied to you about myself. And you must confess – I'm sorry, that was unfortunate – you must *admit*, Gossamer, that I have told you a lot about myself. All of it was true. But it was not the whole truth. I did not dare and could not trust to tell you the whole truth. I hope you are listening to these words as you concentrate on the brushwork of this painting for the sake of others who may be watching us, I hope you hear what they are telling you. They come straight from the hell to which I have condemned myself, and from which only your understanding can set me free.'

She reminded herself that this was the same man who had once taught her to commit the act of sodomy. He had meant it then. And of her own free will she had complied.

Where was Jean-Luc? She played for time. She turned to him, her face a mask of conversational brightness. She saw him as if for the first time: she saw his laughing eyes that now showed what looked like pain, saw his mouth twisted as if in a grimace of agony. She looked quickly away again.

'You want to explain. You want me to understand.'

'There has been misunderstanding, Gossamer. Terrible misunderstanding.'

'It seems to me that the last time we spoke you explained yourself very thoroughly and in great detail. I understood then, all right. And I remember every word of it.'

He spoke rapidly, urgently. 'So do I, Gossamer. I would give anything to forget those words, but I cannot. They crucify me. If I could re-live my life, erase one part of it, it would be that part. The words were true, Gossamer,

but they were not intended for you. They were intended
for someone I believed was you. I was wrong. I did you
wrong, great wrong.'

Let it be said. Let the saying of it be observed as if it
were lightsome party chatter. Her body language said, *Oh
really, how fascinating, do tell me more*. Her voice, sleek as
a stiletto, said:

'You sought me out, Carey Lambert.'

He was very still. His eyes stared straight ahead, his voice
was a whispered croak: 'Yes.'

'And then you charmed me. Oh, how you charmed me.
You focused on me, to delight me. You bent your will to
make me yours entirely.'

'Yes.'

'And then you took me, you plucked me like a carefully
tended fruit.'

'Yes.'

'And then you made me love you.'

Despairingly: 'I know.'

Rage was in her voice. 'And when you'd got my love,
when you could be sure of it, you abused it. You abused
me.' Why should she stop at that? She fought down self-pity.
Strength took its place. 'No, let's be specific. This has all
the classic elements of La Tour's painterly sensibility, don't
you think? You made me masturbate myself while you took
photographs. Observe the shading of the eyelids. You made
me masturbate you so you could come over me, over my
face, my breasts, in my hair and in my eyes and down my
throat. You defiled me while your camera clicked. And then
the crowning glory, the ultimate defilement, the thing you'd
always had to pay for before. My pain and humiliation. Or
do you think that cleaning would alter our interpretation of
mood of the painting? Oh, and you made me willing, that
was what you truly savoured, that was what really got you
up. You indulged all your fantasies with me. I was the object
of your darkest perversions. Restoration can be something
of a poisoned chalice, don't you think? You made me your
slave. A fucking-machine, tight and warm and wet whenever

you wanted to use it. One waits with some trepidation to see what they have done to the ceiling of the Sistine Chapel, does one not? Your very own one-man teenage whore with all her holes at your disposal, day and night.'

She heard him swallow and catch his breath. 'Gossamer.'

'But you knew I loved you. You knew you had it, all of it, pure and simple. So then you used me. You knew you could. You could do it, you could get away with anything. And so you did. You set me up and then you sat back and waited for the result, licking your lips and preening yourself.'

His voice was a whispered scream: 'Oh Christ.'

'But it didn't come off. I did the business for you in all innocence but you miscalculated. You botched it. Didn't you, Carey Lambert?'

Now she could smell his sweat, sense the dry constriction of his throat as he spoke. 'There is a point at which restoration becomes vandalism. Go on.'

'But you didn't just botch it. You had to suffer my knowledge that you'd botched it. Oh, and that was intolerable, wasn't it! You couldn't live with that, it would destroy you. You were brought face to face with the truth about yourself, and it was unbearable, and there was only one way you could shut it up. So, you raped me.'

Silence.

'There is such tenderness in those parted lips, isn't there, those hands that ache to be unfolded, those eyes that widen in hoped-for adoration? You raped me, Carey Lambert. You pushed me onto my knees on the floor and stuffed a gag in my mouth and pulled my jeans down and wrenched my pants to one side. It was the one game I'd never let you play voluntarily so now you did it for real. Look at the picture while I tell you about it, Carey Lambert.'

He obeyed, and she lowered her voice to a penetrating whisper that only he could hear, unbearably loud and clear.

'Of course it was better than taking my virginity because I didn't want you, I didn't want it at all, I was tight and dry and miserable and it was your will against mine and you won, you made up for your big failure, you proved you were stronger in the only way you know how and it worked, Carey Lambert, oh yes it worked, I have never known such pain as I knew then, and do you know why? Because up to a few seconds before I'd hoped it was all a mistake and that I'd got everything wrong and you'd explain it all away and everything would be lovely again but this was your way of really telling me how wrong I'd been and how completely you'd fooled me all along. But not anymore.'

Power surged through her. Her eyes blazed, her lips smiled, her voice was penetratingly soft as she continued remorselessly: 'Hear this, Carey Lambert, hear this because it's the one thing you really taught me and I'll never forget it. You said you'd turned on my body, and it's true, you turned it on and there's no way I can turn it off. Sometimes I burn with sex, I ache and scream with the remembrance of it. But love is dead in me. You killed it. I have made what I can of what you made me, and it's mine, mine only. It hears what you say, it understands the clever words you use, it even admires them, but it doesn't respond any more, it doesn't give anything back. So make an appointment Mr Lambert, say what you want to say to me, it won't mean anything. Show me that little dried-up thing you call your soul and I'll look at it and pass on.'

He took a very deep breath and slowly let it out through his nostrils. Let him take his time, she thought. If Jean-Luc returns now he won't be able to say it, and I will have crushed him forever.

'I shall make an appointment to speak to you, as you ask,' he said, evenly and pleasantly. 'I shall use whatever time you spare me to explain and apologise in full. Also I have something to tell you about yourself. Then, after I have spoken you will know whether or not it has changed anything. Once again I say: thank you.' She saw him put on a sudden public smile.

'Ah, Monsieur Frémont. I was just saying to Miss Fane how fortunate your countrymen in Rennes must be to have so many of this master's finest works to contemplate.'

Jean-Luc's face was a mask of politeness barely concealing shock and anger. He spoke to Gossamer. 'Forgive me, Gossamer. It was a matter of some importance, I am afraid. Good evening, Monsieur Lambert. I did not know we were to have the pleasure of your company.'

Carey smiled easily. 'My presence is something of a last-minute arrangement, Monsieur Frémont. I must admit I came largely to have the opportunity of speaking to Marcel Briouze of RTF; unfortunately I was delayed in arriving. And indeed,' he checked his watch, 'I cannot stay much longer, I'm afraid. I hope it was not bad news, your matter of importance?' His expression was one of interested concern.

Gossamer had known this man intimately. She felt a buzz of excitement off him, a sense of glorying expectation like that of a card player who knows he holds the winning trick.

She realised that Jean-Luc knew this, too. She saw the two men's eyes meet like emissaries on a piece of contended territory. He spoke quite calmly:

'It was indeed bad news, Monsieur Lambert. And as it will be in the later editions of tomorrow's papers there is no reason why it should not be told now. Kevin Germain is dead.'

A spark of triumph blazed in Lambert's tiger eyes and, in a blink, was gone. 'That is very tragic news,' he said with every evidence of sincerity. 'Even though the facts ruled out any chance of recovery it was always impossible not to hope. Please pass on my condolences to your colleagues.'

'Thank you, I will. It is true, I do not think that any of us had quite ceased to hope.'

'Hope may be frail,' Lambert replied, 'but it can endure when all else has fallen by the wayside.' He caught Gossamer's eye. 'You must excuse me. Thank you again, Gossamer. Monsieur Frémont.' He departed.

Jean-Luc drew to Gossamer's side. 'Forgive me, Gossamer, I had no idea that man would be here tonight.'

'No, I know.' She squeezed his arm. 'There's nothing to forgive, honestly. I am so sorry about Kevin Germain.'

'Yes, it is a sad end to a sad story. Gossamer, if I am not allowed to ask your forgiveness I must instead say "pardon me" for this next intrusion: what did he mean by thanking you? Perhaps I should not ask . . .'

'It's all right. He had something to say to me. I let him say it. That's all. It was nothing. Believe me, Jean-Luc.' She believed it herself, though a wave of what felt like exhaustion swept suddenly over her as she spoke.

He relaxed. 'I do. And very gladly.'

'It was . . . It was a shock to see him, of course. I was terrified I wouldn't know what to say.' She smiled. 'But it turned out I did. I just feel a little tired now, that's all.'

'Do you wish to go home?'

'Yes. Yes please, Jean-Luc if that's all – oh, but I'm being stupid and horrible! All I'm thinking is that I feel a bit tired and I don't feel hungry, but what about you?' This was his birthday present to her, and she was spoiling it for him, letting Lambert spoil it for both of them.

He smiled ruefully. 'Well, it is true I had booked a table, but . . .' he shrugged.

'Oh, Jean-Luc! But then—'

'But then a table is just that, a table. A piece of wood with legs. Gossamer Fane is a person, with feelings which are of greater importance to me than the *amour propre* of a restaurateur.' He grinned boyishly. 'Or even of a lawyer.'

He gave her his arm and she held it gratefully.

They stood close, facing each other in front of the picture Jean-Luc had given her. The air emptied between them. Their lips met. They kissed, slowly, lingeringly and beautifully.

Their contours merged. She felt him harden against her belly. She knew the beat of his pulse and her passion rose to join it. His fingers brushed across her breasts and the thrill of him shot and shuddered through her.

They moved to her bedroom hand in hand, like children, and kissed again with gentle urgency. He moved behind her. She felt him lift her hair, and then the melting tenderness of his mouth upon her neck.

He was all tenderness. Her jacket slipped away and her breasts rose free, firm and tingling and splendid. Adoringly, he cupped and moulded them. She breathed his name aloud. His strong, sure fingers flexed and rippled.

Wordlessly they helped each other to full nakedness. He was beautiful. Through the rising flames of her desire she saw his beauty, saw it and considered it as a thing of sheer delight, the strength and sweetly sculpted masculinity of it. She moved her hand to his risen sex and touched the wetness there with her finger's tip, and heard him sigh.

Together they were on the bed. His hands played grace-notes on her body as she thrilled against the warmth and strength of his. Her hands slid over him, exploring him as he adored her to a bursting ache of delight and desire.

They kissed deeply, kneeling, his strong flanks clamping her firmly, their mouths mingling, his lovely sex beating against her. He raked his fingers lightly down her back and she flung herself backwards, pushing her aching breasts against the hard roughness of his chest. His hands cupped and parted her below and she groaned aloud. He released her and she fell back, arching and spreading for him.

She began to burn with a liquid velvet fire. Through the flames of her arousal she saw him kneel between her outspread thighs and regard her with pleasure and appreciation. He moved forward, she saw the hugeness of his sex poised to enter her and she opened wide to take him into the rippling wetness of her furnace flesh. His long lithe body came over her and she lifted, borne by flame-waves, to receive him.

She heard the breathing of him and smelt the sweat of him and saw the desire of him as she felt his hungering hugeness beat between the parted lips of her vagina.

She froze and felt it close against him.

Fire turned to ice as he lifted to enter her, and she slammed shut.

He pushed against her and she thrust up, straining, groaning, her hands screwed into fists. He reared again, and pushed again, and she was sealed, locked fast. He descended on her. His penis, forced down by the sudden rejection, thrust between her buttocks and even before he pulled away with a strangled apology she had screamed aloud and twisted away from him onto her side, her thighs clamped together.

She heard and felt herself begin to sob, scoured by arctic winds.

He lay beside her. She knew his chest was pressed close to her back and that his heart was beating against her but she could not feel his warmth. She recognised how considerate he was being to her by not touching her with his sex. She knew that she had invited him to enter her body with his and make love to her and that she had wanted him to and that if he used his strength to open her now and take her it would not be rape. She knew it as surely as she knew he would not, could not, do it.

She had no explanation to offer him. She could not explain it to herself. Misery began to grip her, and she shivered.

'My darling,' he murmured. He drew the duvet over them and she waited to feel warmth return. 'Shh, shh, it's all right, it's all right.'

Tears started then. He stroked her back. His hands were full of loving affection, and a little warmth seeped back. Her thighs relaxed a little against his and she felt his sex, soft now and wet against her.

'Shh, shh,' he said again, anticipating her apology and forbidding her to utter it. But she felt so sorry, so sorry for him.

He soothed her with his hands, his warmth, his kindness.

She turned over on her back, and he kissed her lips, and then her breasts. Her nipples hardened between his lips, between his tongue and his lip, hardened on his tongue as he lightly rolled them against his teeth.

Her thighs parted and his tongue stroked down across her belly.

His head dipped down, below, between. His tongue moved against her and she began to open, and he eased it in and gently, very gently, worked it there. She began again to ripple. She closed her eyes.

He licked her softly, up and down. She began to move under him, with him.

His tongue found her clitoris and rolled against it, flicking its retreating cowl of flesh. She shuddered and, moaning with appreciation turning to pleasure, began to thrust.

His tongue flicked harder, up and down and in and out. Waves of sexual pleasure rolled up her body and crashed inside her head. She wanted to want him. She wanted to ascend to the highest plane and meet him there.

She stroked his hair, and lifted. She was so nearly ready for him, so very nearly there.

But it was suddenly unbearable and hideous. She yelled despairingly and pulled up the bed, shrinking and turning from him, crunched over on her side in a foetal ball. Ice possessed her again.

She watched as if through another person's eyes as he left the bed and pulled on underpants. She watched as he picked the duvet up where it had slipped off, a long cold season ago, and put it over the girl on the bed. She felt him stroke the girl's hair and call her his poor darling. She felt the girl's lips move and heard, as if from a very long way off, her sad uncomprehending little voice:

'I don't know why. I'm sorry, I'm so sorry.'

'Don't worry about it,' she heard him tell her. 'It's not your fault. It happens and is to be regretted, but it is not a matter of blame.'

He heard her tell the girl, with kindly laughter in his voice, that it happened to men as well, sometimes.

A few seconds, or minutes, or hours later she asked him if he had to leave, and he said yes, there was much he must now do before departing for Brussels. Her bent over her where she lay, her eyes and the tip of her nose above the duvet. 'I'm sorry,' he said.

'Don't say sorry,' she whispered.

'*Eh bien: je regrette.*'

'That's not fair,' she murmured, 'doing it in French.'

They kissed, and she heard the latch on the outer door click behind him, and she cried herself to sleep.

Was all happiness now forbidden her? Her very soul infected?

She wept without control until exhaustion overtook her. Hovering over the abyss of sleep she heard a voice:

I have something to tell you about yourself.

She let herself fall into oblivion.

❧ Sixteen ❧

A few days later she received a letter.

My dear Gossamer,
I write this note in haste before my departure for Brussels.

Following the sad death of Kevin Germain I have taken the liberty of enquiring into matters which I know to be of your particular concern, and I have to tell you that I cannot discover anything which you do not already know. Administration of the trust which was established at the time of your birth now passes to the firm of Chatteris Choate, on whose behalf I am now privileged to act until the date of your twenty-first birthday, after which control of all funds passes absolutely to you, to dispose as you wish.

It would appear that all other matters relating to the establishment of the trust were confided only to Mr Germain and were not recorded by him in any form that I have been able to retrieve. I can only assume that the instructions received by Mr Germain in 1971 were absolute and for all time.

I am so sorry I cannot be of more help to you in this. Should you desire it I shall be happy to impart this information to you in a more formal way on my return. In the meanwhile may I assure you that all the assistance I can give you, both as a lawyer and a friend, is yours for the asking. I shall pass Christmas at the home of my family in Rennes, so

*the New Year will find me once again brooding in my
dusty web.
A bientôt,
Ton ami,
Jean-Luc F.*

The news, so kindly and thoughtfully broken, fell like a
numbing blow on the back of her neck. *Absolute and for all
time*. It was as if a sentence of death had been pronounced
and enacted in one unthinkably swift and terrible instant.
She felt no desire to have the information imparted in a more
formal way any more than she would wish to watch a TV
report of a fatal accident to which she had been a witness.

She behaved as one bereaved, as one shocked beyond
endurance or even belief. She became two people.

One was a wealthy and beautiful young woman whom
it pleased the world to call Gossamer Fane. She worked,
ate, drank, slept, laughed even, talked and was spoken to,
the fully functional shell of a human being, moving in the
autumn light of Kensington.

The other was a little girl, cold and lonely in the
cloistered shadows, enclosed by the comfortless stones of
an orphanage. The little girl stretched out her hand for
reassurance and clutched at black and empty air. Ahead
lay the fearful unknown like the empty space on an old
map. Time past and time future were unknowable. They
belonged to other people, like the kings and queens in the
pictures in her History book. She could not be like those
people. She was a stranger in their country. Alone, she
escaped into the bright country of her own imagination.

The little girl, arrested in history, peered out through the
eyes of the woman she inhabited and wondered helplessly
at what she heard and saw, at what the woman said and
did, in the company of all these strangers, this strange world
which she alone could not belong in. She knew she ought to
be grateful that she was tolerated in it. She had been well
trained to the habit of gratitude.

At night they lay down together, the girl and the woman,

and slept without dreaming. They had been through so much together, but still there was no connection. The key to it, their own special key that would unlock the box of history, was lost.

Perhaps something would happen. Perhaps it would be tomorrow. Perhaps there would be no more tomorrows but, one day, simply nothing. Meanwhile, one day went on succeeding another.

It was a very busy time at Project Aid. Nobody noticed anything out of the ordinary about Gossamer. And of course she was grateful for that, too. What could she say to them, if they asked her what was wrong?

Trish came, a week before the Extravaganza.

She had become a strikingly, almost terrifyingly hand-some woman, a living sculpture of the atheletic female form. Her eyes regarded Gossamer knowingly above the prominent angles of her cheek bones and below the strong sweep of her brow, which was topped with a soft fuzz of dark hair that showed the line of her skull.

Gossamer told her about Project Aid, about the Extrava-ganza, about Ida, about Anthony. Trish sat still, cross-legged on the sofa, taking it all in. Gossamer fell silent.

'So tell me,' Trish said with gentle but incisive coolness, 'how's Gossamer Fane? You haven't mentioned her.'

'Oh, all right,' said Gossamer lightly. 'Busy, you know.'

'Really? Well, do give her my regards, won't you, next time you see her. Tell her I'd like to meet her again.'

'What do you mean, Trish?' Gossamer asked, her voice threatening to crack. Trish looked at her, sardonic and clear-eyed. 'I'm here.'

'Bollocks,' said Trish. 'You're not Gossamer Fane. You're a telephone answering machine, so sorry but I'm not available at the moment, please leave a message. Or one of those circular letters I get from my sister every Christmas. Like, I'm waiting for you to tell me about the twins' pony club and wish me a happy and prosperous new year.'

'I never knew you had a sister,' Gossamer said blankly.

'Oh, yeah. Three years older. We both grew up together

in a little crooked high-rise flat. One of us ran away from it to
the land of wall-to-wall pregnancy, the other one decided to
face it all down. Now tell me about Gossamer Fane, orphan
of this parish.'

'There's nothing to tell,' Gossamer heard herself saying.
'I still am. The solicitor who ran my trust has died and it
turns out he was the only one who knew who my father
was. So now I'll never know.'

'That matters?' said Trish. 'What about your mother?'

'She died when I was born. And yes, it does matter.'

Trish snorted gently.

'Oh, I know what you're thinking,' Gossamer said with
sudden vehemence. 'But it matters to me and I don't care what
you think. It matters to me because now I'll never know where
I've come from, or why, or how. I shan't know who I am.'

Trish grinned warmly and reached a hand out to her. 'Hi,
Goss,' she said. 'Good to see you. Are we going to have fun
tonight?'

Gossamer felt something like warm life begin to return.
'Yes,' she said. 'I think we are.'

They did have fun.

Trish had come prepared for the occasion. She was
stunning, a spectacular feat of alluring androgyny. She
gelled her hair and brushed it close to her scalp, with a
razor-sharp parting. She highlighted her cheekbones and
made her mouth sensual with a light brushing of plush
peony. She wore male evening dress, severely cut to her
spare form. A thick white cotton shirt hid her shallow
breasts and was topped by a tightly knotted bow-tie. Her
shoes were black, leather soled and very shiny. She had
perfected the arches of her eyebrows with stage make-up,
and drawn in a pencil moustache.

She stood in the doorway of Gossamer's bedroom: elegant,
languid and excitingly, enticingly dangerous, one hand in her
trouser pocket, the other perched lightly on the sharp point
of her hip, her slim calves crossed with one foot resting on
the toe. The image had all the breathtaking ambivalence of

fin de siècle decadence captured in the jewelled delicacy of a Renaissance miniature.

'Well,' she said, 'go on. Do I look wonderful or do I look wonderful?'

Gossamer gasped and stared. 'It's amazing,' she said. Trish arched one eyebrow. 'You're sensational.'

Trish moved across the floor with little dancing steps. 'And all tax-deductible,' she said. 'My costume for a little number called *Aspects of Lust*. Raised quite a storm in the Outer Hebrides, that one. Especially the guy who played the nun. What are you wearing, darling? Or is that it, just bra and pants?'

Gossamer had been undecided, but there could be no question now.

She looked towards the back of her wardrobe, took a dress off its hanger, found the gloves. Crushed velvet, soft and blue, superb and simple. A drift of lace over the gorgeous swell of her breasts, a long sheer plunge of bare back below her softly sculpted shoulders.

No diamonds, no perfume, no lover's tokens. She was not a girl being taken out and romanced but a partner, a complement, to a dear friend. And this was going to be fun. She wore the little sapphire earrings Jean-Luc had given her, a gift of warm friendship. Warm life was there, she could connect with it, if only she could accept it, accept herself.

She took Trish's arm as they left the flat. Trish carried a long and tightly rolled umbrella. It was a darkly overcast November night and the sodium lamps cast deep hard shadows. The taxi driver looked to Trish to say where he was to take them and when she had got the address from Gossamer and huskily passed it on he said, 'Righto, squire,' and, rubber-necked, ogled Gossamer's cleavage as she stooped to board the taxi.

Giggling, they were borne away.

The Queer Fish was busy but their table was reserved in what Anthony, greeting them with delight and admiration, said was the No Moustache Area. 'Yours doesn't count,' he told Trish, 'because you're not wearing earrings.'

The restaurant had quickly acquired a reputation as a fun place to be and a smart place to be seen in. There was a single concentration of black leather jackets and earrings whose owners jingled when they moved, keys dangling from their belts.

Many of the parties were gay or bi and a couple, according to Anthony, were transvestites though they were not there as a couple. But there were many straights among the patrons, too, some there for the ambience and others simply for the food, which was excellent. The menu was hilariously self-referential: Gossamer had *Soupe de moules André Gide* and *Sole Bonne Significant Other*. Trish devoured *Plat d'Aphrodite*, which of course was oysters, and *Tourte du Matelôt Butch*, which she said was deliciously variegated, like the clientèle. Urged on by Gossamer and Anthony, she had some more. Trish's leanness was not entirely a matter of aesthetic choice, Gossamer realised.

Trish leaned back and gave her a smile of simple happiness. 'What a lovely place,' she said. 'Full of gaiety in every sense. Thank you.'

'Thank you for coming,' Gossamer replied. They clasped hands across the table and ordered another bottle of crisp chilled Muscadet.

Gossamer sipped her wine and gazed around. She saw that many people were looking at them in frank admiration, and it didn't matter. It wasn't threatening, it was just lovely. She supposed she might be a little bit drunk but that didn't matter either. She felt safe.

Then she saw someone she knew, sitting with a female companion at a table in the opposite corner. He caught her eye almost immediately, smiled, leaned forward to murmur an explanation to his partner and then came across.

'Gossamer,' he said, 'how good to see you.'

'And it's good to see you, Giles. Trish, meet Giles Bamburgh, ace reporter. Trish is an old friend from Ryder-Vail, Giles. She's going to dance with Danse Macabre at the Extravaganza.'

'In that case I shall make an extra special effort to

be there,' he said. 'That is if I'm given a press pass. Hello, Trish.'

Trish shook his hand, and then kissed it. 'You ought to be a wicked squire with a name like Giles,' she said.

'I'm afraid the last wicked squire in my family was five generations ago,' Giles replied swiftly. 'He probably wasn't wicked enough.'

'Perhaps you'll make up for it,' Trish said, lazily and levelly.

Giles responded with small talk about the Extravaganza. He asked about the clothes Gossamer would be modelling and she told him, truthfully, that she hadn't been told yet what they were. After a little while he excused himself, smiling. His partner was talking into a mobile phone, Gossamer noticed.

She looked at Trish, who seemed deep in thought. 'What do you make of him?' she asked.

Trish gave a little shrug. 'What do *you* make of him?'

'He seems pleasant enough, really. Wouldn't you say?'

'I'd say he was a poisonous little prick. I'd say not with a bargepole, Gossamer Fane.'

'Oh come on, Trish! What makes you say that?'

'I don't waste words, that's what makes me say it. And I've been around more pricks than you have, sweetie, yeah? I mean, metaphorically speaking, screw him and you risk a life-threatening disease. He's a carrier.' She fixed Gossamer with her glittering eyes and spoke intently. 'Listen: I say what I say because of what he said when I gave him that wicked squire shit. Right? Now there are various responses you can expect to that. If he's a dork, he gawps at you with his mouth open. If he's an okay sort of bastard he laughs a bit. If he's ditto and a bit bright he laughs and says something like, Oh yeah I know, I keep meaning to get round to a bit of ravishing but somehow there never seems to be time for it.' Gossamer thought Trish must be a bit drunk, too. She went on:

'And if he's a stuffed shirt or a prick in aspic he goes all snotty on you and says it's been a family name since the Conquest and who do you think you are. But what he

doesn't do, not in Real Life, is cap you with a well-turned
aphorism like that prick just came out with.'

'He looks quite real to me, Trish.'

'Yeah, doesn't he just. Which means he's inventing himself
for the occasion. It means he's putting on a show, a bit of
glamour. I don't like people – okay, men – who do that. Nor
will you if you've any sense.'

'I'm not sure that I do have,' Gossamer said.

'Then stick around me, kid, and with a bit of luck some
of it'll rub off.'

She broke into laughter, seeing Gossamer's look of sad
confusion. 'Aw shit, Goss! Be like the Mind of God, kiddo.
Stop regarding him and he'll go away just like Bishop
Berkeley said, you know?'

Gossamer knew. She had taken a General Studies course
in Philosophy in the sixth form at Shaws. She could not
keep the surprise from her face.

'Oh yeah, I've been around some of that stuff too. Like
I say, I've been around, poppet. Live my life, you get to
pick things up. Like knowing that faking an aphorism
doesn't mean yelling your head off in ecstasy when some
bastard's shooting his wad up you. Now fuck him, let's
have some more wine, it looks like cabaret time at the Ol'
Queer Fish.'

The Cabaret was performed on a slightly raised stage in
one corner. To begin with some of the waiters sang in close
harmony to the accompaniment of a banjo and a kazoo. The
songs were ordinary enough but sung in such a way as to
be sprinkled with allusions and *double entendres*, most of
which passed Gossamer by. Trish, in common with most
of the audience, found them hilarious. Sometimes Anthony
and one of the other waiters, a bespectacled Harold Lloyd
lookalike, performed a graceful little dance which was witty
in itself. The evening was well advanced, the audience had
dined and wined well, and the applause was generous and
warmly appreciative. Gossamer drank dry white port and
enjoyed it all hugely.

Then some of the clientèle joined the artistes, performing

mimes and dances. The mood grew ever more mellow. Giles and his partner performed an outrageous mockery of a tango to the ludicrous accompaniment of the banjo and kazoo, and were justly rewarded with a storm of applause.

Trish leaned across. 'Goss,' she shouted intimately against the merry hubbub. 'Your piece for the Ryder-Vail performance, remember? The moochy loner, yeah? Let's do it, sister.'

'But it needs lots of other people to know what they're doing,' Gossamer protested.

'Fine, Ant and I'll select some and clue them up. Aw, go on!'

'And look what I'm wearing, Trish! It's a jeans and plimsolls thing.'

'Bet you there's a waiter or somebody roughly your size who comes to work in 'em. Well, trainers anyway. And if not, so what? They can use their imagination can't they? Right, that's agreed then.'

Gossamer's mind whirled. Part of her resented being landed with this and was planning ways of ducking out. The rest of her was going through the old routine, working out the moves, the steps, the attitudes.

And she remembered how she had melted at the thought that Carey, her beloved and adored Carey, would be there to see her do it that first and only time. That was what, after a little while, propelled her onto the stage. Carey was not there. So she would do it, do it for these appreciative, ordinarily extraordinary people.

The jeans were not forthcoming but the trainers were. She practised a few steps and it was like thinking on her feet. All the old magic returned with a force that empowered her, that made her soar.

Trish had assumed the mantle of director and gave instructions. A selection of people, equally male and female, were placed in three groups of four about the stage. Trish was at the fringe of one, Anthony at another. There was to be no music for this, only the rhythms and plangencies that flowed from the dance itself.

So it began. The three groups began to move, excludingly, to an unheard disco beat. Trish and Anthony faded to the background. Gossamer moved from group to group, dancing to a different music, ignored and unimpressed. She went off by herself and, little by little, began to make her own dance, that she had always called to herself the Dance of Joyous Life. She never knew where the name had come from, only that this was what it represented to her, then and now. It was a simple thing, deceptively complex. She sensed the appreciation of her audience like a tightening in the air.

Her dance began to grow and make space for itself at centre stage. It seemed to cry out to be joined. She took it around the groups and, like satellites drawn from their dreary orbits, first Anthony and then Trish made connection with it and it became a dance for partners.

One by one the others followed like the undead brought to life, until all had joined in. A few came up from the audience and became assimilated. Still it went on in near silence but for the sound of feet and the strong urgings of the music in her head. The stage was crowded but not congested. Faces and bodies glided by, moving with her.

An inconspicuous little man and his pretty blonde partner moved as one entity and made the dance between them. It was his partner who choreographed it, and a detached part of Gossamer's mind wondered if she was trained. She had a dancer's body, neat and slim with small firm breasts beneath a black roll-neck and strong trouser-suited legs. He was competent but she was good, and her creative skill was enough for them both.

It occured to Gossamer that Trish had said nothing about how to end this. Perhaps she would lead them all down onto the floor and get the Dance of Life going with everybody there. Most of them looked ready to do it, she thought: she spotted a few who were resolutely determined merely to observe and enjoy, and Giles's girlfriend, if that was what she was, was talking into a Vodafone. But the rest seemed on the brink of rising up and joining in, if the dancing should come to them.

But the end of the Dance made itself. The door of the restaurant was flung open and two ugly crop-haired young men burst in. Flashlights seared her eyes and blinded her, and she faltered. The lightnings flared again and again and she blundered to a standstill. The Dance ended, and all was uproar. Red and green lights bobbed and pulsed in her vision and she staggered off the stage, found a chair, and sank down on it. Suddenly she was exhausted. She let the babble of confusion and outrage surge round her, a world away from it.

A white-faced man staggered to her table and collapsed into the chair opposite, looking as though Death itself had grinned and blown its killing breath into his face. It took a while for Gossamer to recognise him as the male half of the dancing partnership. His blonde companion sought to comfort him with a look and he returned it wordlessly. Their hands touched, and parted. For Gossamer it was as though a Greek tragic cycle had just been played before her. Uncomprehending, she understood the pain and sadness of it and was stricken. Then Anthony came and spoke to them, and led them away through the service door into the kitchens.

Trish came over, kissed her lightly, and helped her back into her shoes. She had forgotten she was still wearing trainers. Trish knelt at her feet and looked up at her. Her lips moved and Gossamer tuned in.

'. . . magnificent. You were so splendid. Forget the shit, honey. Only taste the sweet. You're excused shit, Gossamer Fane. You're wonderful.'

Anthony returned, his face drawn in concern. 'Is she all right?' he asked. The night was breaking up, people were leaving. Suddenly the place had an abandoned look. Gossamer answered for herself:

'Yes, thanks Anthony. I'm all right. What was all that about?'

'The reptiles,' Trish said. 'And if they aren't connected to Friend Giles and his escort, who I noticed suddenly weren't there any more, then I'm a suburban matron.'

'But why? Why come here, why did they want to spoil it?'

Trish smiled sadly. 'Oh my dear Gossamer, you are such a sweet fucking innocent. An experienced innocent, but still so innocent. Always were. Gay is dirty to that sort of opinion-former, darling. What you were doing, what most of us here are, it's dirty. Filth. So they expose it. They had a target, you see. All in the public interest, naturally.'

'The man who was dancing, with the blonde girl? The one who was sitting here just now?' Anthony nodded.

'He's a Labour MP, Goss. From a rather muscular part of the North-East. He's paydirt, for them.'

'But that's nonsense, surely. He was with a woman.'

'No he wasn't, Goss,' Anthony said softly.

'What? But – I mean, she . . .'

'Yes. But not a woman. Not on their terms.'

'Oh God.' Gossamer felt tears begin to fall, tears of impotent rage, of sudden hopelessness in the face of good things spoiled by dirty, arbitrary stupidity. Anthony held her hand.

'Don't, Goss,' Trish said. 'No shit, baby. Don't let it spoil everything.'

Gossamer blew her nose on a paper napkin. 'Why not go and have a pee, freshen up, and then we'll go home.'

They watched her go. 'Of course he was a fucking idiot,' Trish said, 'coming here with her. He might have known.'

'Why shouldn't he come?' said Anthony.

'No reason at all. No good reason. Except he shouldn't.'

After a short silence Anthony said: 'Do you think she'll be all right?'

'I'll see she is, dear. So long as she doesn't realise she'll be in those photos, too.'

'She'll see them tomorrow.'

'So? She's still entitled to tonight.'

Anthony looked her in the eyes, and smiled in recognition. 'Sez you.'

'Sez me.'

He kissed her, and when he drew away he had part of

Trish's moustache smudged across his face. Gossamer found them grinning, and laughed with them.

They paid off their taxi in Holland Park Avenue and walked, arm in arm, up from the corner of Addison Avenue. Three skinheads barred their way. One shouted, 'Let's see if this one's got balls,' and they attacked. It was over in seconds. Gossamer saw the glint of a knife in the streetlight and a kick was aimed at Trish. She doubled over in anticipation and then rose, spring-heeling off the pavement.

She heard Trish's umbrella swish through the air and the solid noise of connection with flesh. A man reeled away, his mouth bleeding. Trish faced the others, crouched, encouraging them on.

They came together. With a stream of obscenities Trish sprang at them. One collapsed as if deflated, gasping for air. Trish spun her umbrella and caught it by the point. She wielded it two-handed like a bat, bringing the crook handle upwards between the other's thighs. He fell groaning, clutching his genitals, then turned over, shuffling away on knees and elbows.

Gossamer's shoes were strong and pointed. She swung her foot back and struck between his upraised buttocks, kicking at much more than a thug's testicles. He lay prostrate, spewing into the gutter. She felt a warm glow of complete satisfaction.

Trish shouldered her umbrella, a soldier on triumphant parade. She took Gossamer's arm and they swung, marching, into Addison Place. Trish sang: 'An umbrella is a dyke's best friend.'

They fell into Gossamer's flat, giggling in each other's arms. They staggered through into Gossamer's bedroom, hugging and kissing and laughing. Their clothes fell away from them and they were on Gossamer's bed, naked, caressing and kissing, each urging towards the other.

Her body was beautiful, soft and lithe and knowledgeable. Gossamer was caressed by hands, lips, tongue. Her friend's pointy little breasts brushed her skin and thrilled her. She felt a flame kindle, warm and giving, and she wanted to give back but was shushed into acceptance of pleasure. She uncoiled and lay back, prone and open and trusting.

She relaxed completely. It was like the onset of anaesthetic, sweetly prolonged. Not a word was spoken. She was kissed on the lips, softly and slowly. Their tongues met. Trish kissed her in the corners of her eyes, along the line of her jaw and down across her throat. She kissed her nipples until they were risen. Warmth flowed through her.

The back of Trish's tongue brushed down the flatness of her belly and went down, down. Lips met her parting flesh and again the tongue darted, in and out, up and down, between. Gossamer sighed, closed her eyes, then opened them again on another world.

Trish, her friend, was making love to her and it was wonderful. The ripples began and she lifted in welcome of her kind and clever lover who now caressed the apex of her desire and pleasure.

And she wanted to give it back, to do as she was being done by. Her hand reached out and stroked Trish's hair, then moved down to her neck. She uttered a soft cry of entreaty.

Trish gasped, rose blurry-faced and then was straddling her. Her sex was sweetly bare, a naked budding muskrose. Gossamer gave as she received, and they moved together, rising and falling and rising, rising to release and consummation.

It was like nothing else in any world that she had ever known. It belonged to a world beyond and she was happy to be there, however fleetingly.

And then Trish's face was beside hers on the pillow, her body kissing hers below, their breasts touching, their limbs entwined. Trish smiled and brushed a raven's wing of hair from Gossamer's face. Her eyes were all kindness.

'You're lovely to love, my love,' she murmured.

And Gossamer kissed her.

And when the last lovely ripples had spent themselves, Trish drew up the covers.

It was dark when Gossamer woke, but she saw with

crystal clarity. She saw that she had been to a place where she did not truly belong, a place where she had holidayed but which she could not call home. She saw that homelessness might be the price she paid for this knowledge.

But she recognised that knowledge, however painful, is always preferable to ignorance. And it was painful, that knowledge, and hers alone was the burden of that pain. She accepted it.

Still she could be comforted. She sought comfort then. Her lovely friend lay sleeping by her, turned on her side, her long slender back swooped in sleep, her body warm and living. As Gossamer moulded herself gently to its shape Trish stirred and pressed against her, then relaxed again. They slept.

The night belonged to warmth and ease and comfort, clean and true.

The new day dawned to dirty newspaper.

Gossamer slept late. When Trish woke her with tea she saw her friend had showered and washed her hair. Its fragrant damp fuzz brushed her face as Trish bent to kiss her.

'Morning, princess,' said Trish. 'See, we haven't turned into frogs.'

She was wearing Gossamer's dressing gown and Gossamer saw her breasts, pinkly pointed at the tip. They were very lovely. She held Trish's arm.

'It was lovely, Trish,' she said. 'And you're lovely, a beautiful person. But I know I'm not a lesbian.'

Trish pulled the covers down to her waist and kissed her lightly on each nipple. 'So do I, honey,' she answered. 'But it's okay, it's not compulsory. And who knows, some day your frog may come.' She giggled. 'So to speak. Meanwhile, so long as you're in the woods you might as well do a bit of exploring while you can, and no harm done. Not by me, sweetness.'

Gossamer's eyes moistened. Trish pulled away and turned from her, shucking off the dressing gown. Her body was a delight, trained to fitness and grace. She dressed quickly, pulling on the jeans and top she had arrived in. Gossamer

saw that she had already packed. Then Trish turned back
and she saw that her eyes, too, were wet.

'Do you have to go back today?'

'Yup. Rehearsals, an' 'at. Which is just as well, 'cos if
I stick around here much longer I'm gonna break my
heart over you.' She smiled ruefully. 'Which would do my
reputation a power of no sodding good, eh? See you in the
kitchen, tosh.'

Gossamer would have to accept what Trish had said.
How bitter-sweet it was, so to be offered love where she
could not return it. She wondered what she might become
if she should ever grow used to such adoration. She might
become a monster without knowing it.

Trish had made toast and coffee and had a newspaper
folded back to the racing page. 'Here's a good one, listen:
Queen's Outing, 3.45, Haydock Park. Isn't that great? Worth
a quid each way, too, at eight to one. I think I'll go for you,
buster.' She circled the name.

'You ought to do the gee-gees now and again, Goss,' she
said. 'It takes you out of yourself a bit, keeps you out of
mischief. I generally have a go once or twice a week.'

'Do you win? I mean, make a profit on it?'

'Oh yeah. We-ell. Up to a point, you know. Now then,
you'd better see this while I'm still here to see it with.'

She folded the paper to the front page and put it in
front of her.

'EXPOSED!' she read. 'The gay life of Labour MP
Trevor.'

'He would have to be a Trevor, wouldn't he?' Trish
commented.

It was the MP they were after, of course, but Gossamer
was in the photograph. She looked radiant. She was flanked
by the MP and his friend, whose name was given only as
'Tom'. The caption read: 'Last night's gay ravers at the Queer
Fish.' Trish was in it, too. Not Giles.

'It's only a photo, Goss.' That was true. 'They're not
interested in you, there's no mention of your name.'

'There will be,' said Gossamer.

'Nah, you wait. Tomorrow it'll be I Stand By Him Says Scandal Wife and Twenty Things You Never Knew About Silicone Implants, then he'll get the support of his party, then he'll be booted out. You'll see.'

Trish was wrong, as Gossamer knew she would be. Malling Benedict, in his usual column in one of the serious newspapers, observed that 'charity socialite Gossamer Fane, 19, featured prominently in the photograph of the "regrettable incident at the Queer Fish restaurant." Her presence there was explained by her "close friendship" with Trish, who was described as "a leading artiste in Danse Macabre, foremost exponents of gender-ambivalence" and with Queer Fish waiter Anthony Morland, 21.' He also observed that Danse Macabre were to perform at the Extravaganza, 'the upcoming thrash for the conscience-stricken *beau monde*, which Ms Fane is organising.'

'Ms Fane', he concluded, 'has remained officially unattached since ending her romance with media mogul Carey Lambert, 43, last year.'

There were only two people who could have known about those friendships. Giles Bamburgh, of course. And Carey Lambert.

Ida advised her to think of Ethiopia any time she needed to get things in proportion, and to thank God for work to take her mind off it. She tried to take the advice. Her own concerns apart, it was probably good publicity.

Carey Lambert yawned, stretched luxuriously, and tossed the paper aside. He closed his eyes and, smiling, reflected on what a wonderful world it was, so full of unexpected bonuses for those few who might be bold enough to earn them.

There had been times in his life when, like Edmund in *King Lear*, he had called on God to stand up for bastards. And the wonder and the glory of it was, He really did. God, or the Devil, or whoever. Wasn't it the Gnostics who believed God's creation was the ultimate sick joke, played on all but the very few who were not too dim to see through it? Well, perhaps they had a point there. No wonder they were persecuted! They should have kept their insight to themselves instead of trying to share it with a superstitious public too stupid and fearful even to want to understand. There is nothing the dull world fears and hates so much as the man who has earned the right to play by different rules.

And here was another example. It was like Kevin Germain's accident: it couldn't have worked out better if Carey had planned it himself, right down to the last delicious detail of Trish's hand brushing Gossamer's bum. The camera didn't lie. Only humans could do that; it went with the capacity to believe. More evidence of a God worth worshipping.

It was serendipity, all down the line. Pure chance that he'd been around to see the first editions of the papers, wet from the presses, in the news studio of OffWorld, to see that front page hurriedly cleared for the photo that might be worth a dozen Tory marginals. And the fact that he'd once condescended to attend little Gossamer's concert, that was serendipity too. If he hadn't, he wouldn't have recognised the dyke with the tash.

And it had been like mainlining amphetamine, he couldn't sleep for the buzz of it, the knowing that time and chance had brought him right to the edge of the ultimate thrill. Even so he needn't have gone himself, he could have hired the usual spook to park his car in the street outside Gossamer's flat and kill a few morning hours in it. But a spook might not have noticed the kiss as Trish left, that kiss that was something more than girly friendship. And he'd almost certainly have missed the quality of Trish's smile as she pranced off down the pavement. To the likes of Carey, who had tasted it himself, it screamed of a cat who'd had the cream and knew she could have it again.

It was as if as he'd stood there, on the edge, and asked a silent question. And a voice no one else could have a hope in hell of hearing had answered, loud and clear:

Yes!

But he knew he must move fast. Being one of the elect

himself didn't mean he didn't have a few equals: it never paid to underestimate Malling Benedict. The man might have minions to do his legwork but without his presiding genius that's all they could be: legs. Oh yes, the little monster was a genius, no question. And he'd get there, soon enough, get to the one place Carey Lambert didn't want him to be, not yet. Now was the time for action.

He had no doubts, no qualms, about the main theme, the big plan. It simply couldn't fail, he could read the outcome of it like a map. But there was a sub-plot to script and produce, and without it the whole production would flop. And he'd have to see to it now, make the little cripple perform his part, and that meant taking the biggest gamble he'd ever taken in a lifetime of playing for high stakes.

So let it be. *So let it be*!

He shifted a little, to ease himself. The thought of it had given him an erection.

Malling Benedict had good cause to be satisfied.

It had happened liked this before: two musical themes, one major and one minor, coming together to make unique harmony, strange and new, where each without the other would be merely a forgettable jingle. It had happened before but the thrill was not diminished.

And the upshot of it was, he had placed that delectable little top-drawer tart full in the public spotlight – but only when he chose to turn it on. The MP had been the main attraction, but that would very soon be over; give him a couple of years and he'd pop up again, rehabilitated as Chairman of the Parks and Gardens Committee of Clogsville District Council. Or dead of AIDS in Clogsville District Hospital. Nothing more of interest there, either way.

But the tart was different. The tart was money in the bank. He'd smelt it from the first, that Little Miss Innocent musk. But she'd put him off: he acknowledged that. *Gee whiz, Uncle Kevin*. His lip curled. Oh yes, she'd put one over him there, the clever little screwbag. And he'd respected her for it – respected her, and hated her, and known he had to be revenged. She'd made an enemy for life that day.

And now he had her in his cross-hairs and the beauty of it was, no one else even suspected she could be a target. But it wouldn't stay that way for long, not now she'd come back to ply her old trade among such a juicy clientèle. No, it wouldn't stay that way for long. He'd missed out on Pamella Bordes, and that was the sort of mistake that couldn't be made twice.

But not *too* soon. Now was not the time to monster her. The Extravaganza was only a week away: all the rotten-beautiful people, and all on wall-to-wall television. But the morning after ... Then he'd have her, pinned and wriggling. And then he'd be there to see what maggots might come crawling out of her deliciously corrupt and ruined flesh.

It was all very, very satisfactory. And all gained at the cost of a hundred pounds slipped to a queer waiter who looked like Harold Lloyd. Which of course only went to prove that the look of innocence was never to be trusted, though in his case betrayal had come at bargain-basement prices. The scoop of the year for the cost of a few weeks' supply of poppers! Still, as Walpole said: *All these men have their price*. And who was he to argue with that? Walpole had, after all, been Britain's first Prime Minister. Someone had to keep up that noble tradition of finely-costed betrayal.

Betrayal: ah yes, poor conscience-stricken Giles, half eaten up with guilt because that pretty little shaghole made out she really liked him. Well, he'd soon get over that! In just one week's time, indeed. He'd learn to see through that sort of making-out! That, or give up calling himself a journalist.

His mind played over all the possibilities ... and, a rarity these days, he was aware of his body responding, down there between his withered loins. Tonight, perhaps ... yes, tonight. The usual merchandise from the usual supplier, one to stimulate to action and one to perform the action he could not except in his assisted imagination. And, of course, on subsequent nights, on video. Yes, tonight. Tonight he would be in the mood for it; besides, he had earned himself a little treat.

A telephone rang, his blue one: the private line. Another rarity. He answered it, and Carey Lambert's voice suggested an appointment. Now that was satisfactory beyond imagining: two juicy fish, one on the hook and another on the gaff!

Malling Benedict had never gone fishing in his life, but a really good columnist is never at a loss for a telling metaphor.

It was all work, frantic and frenzied work, and fear: fear of the sort she had once felt at school, waiting in the wings for her entrance in a play and suddenly convinced she'd lost all her lines: that sort of fear, but a hundred times worse. This was not just down to her. After all these weeks of cheerful reassurance almost everybody on whom she, and the Extravaganza, was depending seemed disastrously and lackadaisically behind schedule.

Ida said this was all par for the course. Ida said they always had gone into these things on a wing and a prayer, usually a far less substantial wing and a far more desperate prayer than was the case in this event. But Gossamer was not reassured. This was her first big responsibility and she was horribly aware of it all beginning to slip through her fingers. She had to prove herself but almost everybody seemed to be conspiring, albeit quite unintentionally, to let her down and make her look ridiculous.

Half of her wished she could be as laid-back, as langorous, as all these well-connected and supremely self-confident people. Half of her gave thanks she wasn't: nothing would ever get done.

Costumes were not ready, or if ready had not been fitted, or if fitted had not been tried out in rehearsal. Models promised weeks before had gone to Lanzarote or the Bahamas with boyfriends, families, old school chums. Musicians and caterers – more chums of old chums – were agonisingly vague about what they were going to do and when. Almost everybody seemed to be treating the thing as though it were some sort of lark, a gigantic country house weekend, with herself cast as the Admirable Crichton making everything right for their comfort and enjoyment, a one-woman staff of a hundred. She was ground between the two mills of maddening amateurishness on the part of almost everyone on whom the show depended, and the terrifying hard-nosed professionalism of the DayStar team whose job it was to make the whole thing into an evening's live television. Everything seemed to hinge on her, and the worst of it was that the people who infuriated her most were the ones most conscious of the fact that they were doing it all for nothing, for charity. That meant she had to be unfailingly *nice* to them.

Ida had done this sort of thing for years: how? And what on earth had persuaded her that Gossamer could do it? Letting Ida down was the worst fear of all.

Only complete exhaustion, night after night, kept her from total sleeplessness. In addition to everything else her own outfit was not ready, apparently because it was so special. Everyone told her not to worry, that it would be absolutely ravishing, knockout, showstopping, eye-popping, she'd see, and that she'd know just how to wear it when she had it on. They seemed to think the whole thing was a huge joke. Well, if it wasn't ready she wouldn't go on: that was all there was to it. Really, it seemed the least of her worries.

When, on the day before the show, a replacement model turned out to have a bust three inches too small for her outfit Gossamer had to bite her tongue to stop herself suggesting silicone implants.

After half an hour of trying various fatuously impractical remedies for her deficiency the model suddenly remembered she knew someone called Betty Boob who would die for the chance of wearing it. Gossamer was so relieved she felt like hitting her.

And then it was the morning of the show. DayStar took over, herding all the models and performers off for a long day of rehearsal designed to leave them with nothing but adrenalin and rote-learned discipline to rely on. Matters, so far as the televised part of the proceedings were concerned, were now out of Project Aid's hands: charitable organisation gave way to production values. Everything would just have to be all right. Which, Ida assured her, was bound to mean it would be.

Gossamer's outfit, which she was to wear for fifty seconds on the catwalk, was still not ready although she had been practising a very simple routine to fit the piece of synthesiser-processed slinky-sexy music she had been given to accompany it. The producer's policy was a simple one: if the thing was ready, Gossamer would appear as the last item; if not, the presenter – the female host on the DayStar travel programme *Having A Lovely Time* – would vamp it to cover the gap before the scheduled commercial break.

Of course there was no reason for her to feel anxious at the prospect of appearing for fifty seconds without a costume rehearsal; she had done far more demanding things before. Nonetheless, with the abrupt removal from her responsibility of all the other performers, she found herself nagging away inside at this one remaining uncertainty, and Ida noticed.

'Stop worrying,' she said, 'and have a cheroot.' Gossamer did. It was horrible, but she did stop worrying. There didn't seem much point, at this stage. So she took Ida to the Garnett Arms and bought her a Guinness instead.

On the previous evening two men sat in one of the private alcoves of a dingily respectable London club. It was a club for gentlemen, a place of shadows and muted shufflings, an establishment that placed the highest possible premium on the sanctity of absolute discretion, absolute confidentiality.

Naturally enough in the circumstances, both men secretly recorded their conversation. The fact that each knew the other was doing so did not, of course, make it any less secret.

Carey Lambert eyed Pope Benedict as he shuffled himself to comfort on the studded leather of the *banquette*. The action made the little monster's legs stick out so that he looked even more grotesque, like a word-wearily raddled ventriloquist's dummy. He leered across at the other man, baring yellow teeth.

'You tell me all this now, my dear Lambert. You give me enough dynamite – or ought one to say semtex, these days? – to blow you both so high you'd never fall to earth again. Please don't think I'm not grateful' – he breathed the word as if to give gratitude itself a dirty reputation – 'but a person in my position must ask himself the simple question: *why?*'

Lambert smiled urbanely back, as one man of the world to another. Now for the second roll of the dice. 'It's quite simple, Benedict. I do it in order to ensure you'll never use it.' He made sure his eyes gave nothing away as he spoke the words.

They were received in crepuscular silence which was followed by a noise like the escape of gas from a ditch-drowned carcase. Malling Benedict was laughing.

'Do tell me,' he creaked, 'how you make that out, my dear fellow.'

'Again, it's quite simple, and for the same reason: I've told it you. I know you know. And you know I know. So now I have nothing to conceal from you, nothing for you to find out. Ergo, your occupation's gone.'

Pope laughed again, a carking rasp this time. 'How refreshingly anarcho-philosophical! I don't think I've heard anything quite so rarefied since my student days. But alas, Brother Lambert, the real world dances to a different tune. And I am very much of the real world, you know.'

Lambert remained poker-faced. 'I flatter myself I've got where I am through living in the same real world as you do, Mr Benedict. Perhaps I have not made my meaning quite clear. Let me put it this way: for all your genius and your spy network you still see this girl through a distorting haze of fantasy and rumour. You can't pick out the path that leads to her. What you have is circumstantial evidence, at best: and circumstantial evidence is, as you know, not admissable in Law. And do you not find, as I do, that the great public out there is soon sated on a diet of mere innuendo? Well, they've heard it all before, haven't they? It washes over them. Expose a sex scandal today, like as not its protagonists will pop up on a breakfast TV show the day after tomorrow. It hardly seems worth the effort, does it?'

It was the columnist's turn to put on an act of impassivity. Lambert, scenting victory, continued:

'Let's face it: you could go to press tomorrow with what I've just told you, and what would it achieve? A very bad time indeed, for a week or two, for some poor little bitch nobody's ever heard of. Nothing more, except some Max Clifford type stepping in to, if you'll pardon the expression, make the two of them a few bucks on the back of it. Me? It wouldn't hurt a single hair of my chinny-chin-chin. We had a fling a year ago, then it was over, so what? As for you . . . ! Think how you'd look, my dear Benedict, in these enlightened days. I mean, Cabinet Ministers and Opposition wannabes are one thing, but orphans of the storm, street urchins? Surely a man of your intelligence must draw the line at that!

'Whereas, of course, if ever the lady in question were to be, shall we say, allied to my fortunes in more tangible terms, well . . .' Lambert left the sentence hanging.

Benedict's eyes narrowed. 'Meaning?'

'Meaning, obviously, that she would then be, as they say, in the public domain. By virtue of the fact that I am.'

'You are telling me this is a likelihood, this hypothetical eventuality?'

'I am telling you nothing of the sort. I am merely saying that, if it ever should be a likelihood, I shall make it my business to ensure you'll be the first to know. Exclusively.'

'I am very flattered to hear it, Mr Lambert.'

'Oh I do hope not, Mr Benedict. A genius should never feel flattered. Especially not by another genius who is simply trading one favour for another.'

Benedict bestowed a crooked smile. 'The honour is received and appreciated, Mr Lambert,' he said. 'But not, alas, returned. Oh no, my dear fellow: a genius admits no flaws, and you have admitted one very glaring one. With the best will in the world I really cannot conceive that you are in any position to trade favours. By your own admission, which I shall consider myself obliged to regard as having been made on the record, your involvement with the gorgeous Miss Fane, whatever the future may hold for you both, amounts already to considerably more than a fling. You give me no reason to doubt my ability to blow you out of the water 'ere this day is out. And, forgive me, blowing people like you out of the water is what I have been put upon this earth to do. Do forgive me. I cannot help it: I am what I am.'

'Oh, I'm afraid I could never forgive you. Forgive a fool, Benedict? It's not in my nature. Fools are for screwing and stepping on. Forgetting perhaps, but not forgiving.'

Benedict's expression turned venomous. 'Explain yourself,' he hissed.

'Reluctantly, I will,' Lambert replied smoothly, reaching for the decanter. 'Tell me, please: I believe you are in possession, as they say in old-fashioned novels, of certain photographs of the lady in, ah, certain compromising positions? Yes?' He recharged his glass, ignoring Benedict's.

'Don't play these wanky little games with me, Lambert. You know perfectly well I am: who better?'

'Then, surely her face must have rung a bell for you? A bell that hangs in the chamber of your own personal experience?'

Lambert watched with a raptor's alertness: yes, there was a fleeting consternation there, a momentary puzzlement. Fleeting, but discernable.

'I don't know what you mean,' Benedict replied thinly.

'Ah!' Lambert beat his forehead with the palm of his hand; it was sweaty, he noticed without surprise. But he felt triumph swell in his very balls, a rising exultation. 'Of course you don't! Forgive me, you are quite correct: it is I who am the fool on this occasion.' He skewered the horrid dwarf with his eyes. 'It's not the faces you look at, is it? Down there, going down, under that delightful kneehole desk in your study at home, you can't see their faces, can you, while they're sucking on your little apology for manhood? No, it's the other end you look at: the end that's getting humped to hell and back on your behalf by whatever stud you've hired for the occasion at double the going rate if he spurts his load up her in time with your own little contribution. Silly of me to forget that.'

Benedict's jaundiced devil-doll's face worked wordlessly awhile. One audible syllable at last escaped: 'Her?'

'Yes!' Lambert's voice was a whispered yell of triumph. 'Yes, you sad little pervert: *her!* Her jailbait mouth on your perky cock, down there beneath the Chippendale. Do you record the studs' faces, I wonder? If you do, take another look at what you recorded back in '86. Find one who looks as though his cock's been swallowed by a silky-furred pussycat with a mind all its own, a mind dedicated to giving men pleasure: that's her, Benedict. I speak, you understand, from experience. It's the very best there ever was. And you've been wanking off to it all these years, and never knew! Jesus! Not but what her mouth isn't something else as well, I must admit that – speaking, again, from frequent, unpaid-for experience. But not the same. Oh sweet Jesus no, not the same at all. But, Christ, you had the sweetest little under-age blow job in the whole history of the universe and you never knew who she was, not even when you saw the photos! You poor sad bastard.'

Benedict's face coloured to the hue of bad liver. Lambert wondered idly, in a detached sort of way, if he was going to die. That would be entertaining, if somewhat inconvenient to his purpose. He'd won. That was all that mattered. Benedict's mouth worked. A noise came out:

'How?'

'How? How do I know, you mean? Oh, just listen to yourself! How disappointing to find I've been over-estimating you, after all! Well, that's some sophisticated equipment you have there, my friend – I speak of your very own personal porno studio TV gear, you understand, not your wretched little genitalia. I suppose it's being so small down there that makes you want to be sucked off by girls. You can always kid yourself they don't know any better. So what are we talking about? Cameras mounted to catch all the action, computer-controlled to cut from your face to the fucking so it looks like you're doing it when you mix it all together in that state-of-the-art editing suite – well, I don't need to tell you what you've got there, do I? But you see, I know where it all came from, old chap. I own the firm that supplied it all to you and it has, shall we say, certain modifications fitted as standard. Hence the photographs. Taken from my own personal and – for the moment – very private video library. I'm sure you will understand when I say that I have absolutely no need to watch any of it for my own sexual pleasure. It's a rather different sort of gratification I'm after. And I rather think I've got it, wouldn't you say?'

But Pope Benedict said nothing. His face had now paled to a greyish hue.

'Until, that is, you find yourself in a position to hurt me more than I can hurt you when it comes to matters concerning my very own little Eliza Doolittle. Or—' He paused until he was sure he had his victim's full attention. Then:

'Or, unless by some chance you find yourself in a position to have your revenge on her by using her as a sprat to catch a very different sort of whale, a whale that doesn't go by the name of Carey Lambert. In which event – unlikely I must say, though you never know – you would have my entire blessing to go public with what I told you earlier. But do it to hurt me, my dear Benedict, and I'll have the whole nation laughing at your sad little escapades.'

Lambert rose. 'This evening has been on me, by the way. One of the stewards will be on hand to show you out, when you are ready. Good night, my dear fellow. Sweet dreams. I don't know about you, but I'm in the mood for a bloody good shag. Oh, and see you tomorrow night, of course.'

Carey Lambert walked with lightsome step down The Mall. At the corner of Marlborough Road he was accosted by what he was looking for: a black tart, young and slim and supple. He took her off and had her, swiftly and brutally and to his entire satisfaction.

He left her a very generous tip. He was in a giving mood.

❈ Seventeen ❈

Alec Dayfield watched himself on a TV monitor being interviewed about his contribution to fish farming in Bangladesh. Slowly the camera tracked in until his big features filled the screen. As he watched, a door behind him sighed open and shut, letting in the distant sound of public chatter. A man's voice said:

'She can be very persuasive when she puts her mind to it, can't she?'

The screen dissolved to show two thin dark-skinned boys trawling a large tank with oversized shrimping nets. Alec Dayfield turned.

'Not that a man needs too much persuading to star on one of his own channels, I suppose,' said Carey Lambert. 'Although if I were you I should be very careful about that sort of self-exposure. Look what happened to Robert Maxwell.'

'There is a difference,' Dayfield replied heavily. 'I'm not a crook.'

'Spoken like a true and honest egomaniac,' Lambert riposted urbanely.

Dayfield grunted and turned back to the screen, which was showing a panning shot of the invited audience at the Extravaganza with occasional dissolves to celebrated faces as the commentator, in tones of professionally modulated adoration, muttered of their wonderful behind-the-scenes work for Third World projects. Then a slow zoom picked out Gossamer, a creature of sculpted radiance in safari satin.

Both men caught their breath.

'Oh yes,' said Lambert softly, caressing the close air of

the little private studio with his voice. 'Believe it, Dayfield. She really is something special. A one-off, a unique creation. The innocent mind of Eve, the knowing instincts of Salome – but what you see there did not spring, completed, from the womb of Nature.'

The compère's well-known face now occupied the screen, and Dayfield turned from it to question his interlocutor.

Lambert smiled back with hooded eyes. 'Let me tell you the story of Gossamer Fane,' he said.

Ida's firm hand gripped Gossamer's arm. They stood outside the main auditorium, a little to one side of the stream of arriving guests.

'Well, my dear,' she said, 'Didn't I tell you not to worry?'

'You did,' Gossamer smiled back. 'And I didn't dare believe you. Of course I should have known better, because you knew what you were talking about. You've done it on your own so many times before.'

'Pooh, hardly! This is the first time we've had the cameras here. Now I must go and circulate, inasmuch as my sclerotic old legs will let me. Do let me meet your friend Anthony, won't you dear? If I don't see you again, the best of British.'

'And to you,' said Gossamer, and kissed her cheek.

She set off to find Anthony but, turning to press through the throng, stepped straight into Mike Andersen.

'Hello, Gossamer Fane,' he said. 'You look so different from when we last met.'

Gossamer recovered herself quickly. 'So do you,' she said. 'You're wearing a dinner jacket. And you're smiling at me.'

'Smiles, on these occasions, go with dinner jackets don't you think?'

'I suppose they must do,' she said. 'So, how are you?'

'Very well, thank you. And you too?'

'Mostly, yes, thank you. All the better for being smiled at, of course.' She felt herself beginning to fray with the effort of maintaining this sort of glacial politeness.

It was like acting in a rather poor imitation of an Oscar Wilde play.

'But of course,' Mike said, and smiled again.

She was sure the furious chatter all around them must make it safe for her to risk something. 'Even though I can't know what your smiles might mean,' she added.

He made no reply. The smile faded from his face like winter sunshine. Now he spoke to her with his eyes: but what were they saying to her? Pain? Contempt? Anguish? She plunged on:

'In fact, that always was my problem with you, Mike: every time I thought I was understanding meaning I found all I really had was a series of passing sensations.'

'I remember the sensations, Gossamer. Very well.'

'Oh good,' she said. She couldn't keep the bitterness from her voice. 'How nice for you. I'm so glad you found them pleasant.'

Suddenly he seemed to be standing very close to her. She felt his body, the unique maleness of him, pressing against her atmosphere. His voice came thickly. 'Christ, Sam, you of all people must have seen they were more than that, for me.'

And then she knew anger, hot anger she could control. His words awoke it in her: his use of the name he had given her, first in loathing derision and then in love, a world and a life away; his *you of all people* that probed the wound of *I know what you are*; that self-regarding *for me*, twisting like a knife in her soul, suggesting that he alone had feelings, that he alone had some special aptitude for being hurt. It was the sheer unworthiness of it all that kindled her to anger and made her fury specific. She eased a little apart from him because what she had to say could not be said close in, looking up.

'Oh but I'm afraid I can't speak for 'all people', Mike. I lack your great wisdom and experience, I can only speak for myself. All that time on the road, all through the horror and weariness of it I kept my distance from you, I felt you only condescended to be with me out of some sense of obligation because I was vulnerable and you knew what you were doing. And then I began to feel as though I had to prove myself to you, show myself worthy of your company, make it up to you somehow.'

Now she saw that his eyes registered genuine surprise. It fanned the flame of her eloquence. 'Then came the snake, remember? The snake in the tree. I tried to be calm for you. I believed I was going to die, and that helped. It helped later on, too, helped me through the horror, helped me not to drag you down. That was all that mattered. And then you were hurt and I could be strong for you, I could repay you a little, show I was worthy. Did you notice that, Mike? Did you?'

He seemed to answer from a far country: 'I was grateful.'

'You were grateful! It was all I wanted – no, that's not the whole truth. As much as I wanted my own survival, that was what I wanted. And then I was buried alive, Mike. You buried me alive, to save me. How was that for you, that part of it? You never said. I'll tell you how it was for me: I died. I died in a shallow grave in Africa. And then I was reborn, literally. Born into a paradise garden with you. It happened, didn't it Mike? I didn't dream it all. You were there, weren't you. *You were there.*'

'Oh yes,' Mike replied, very quietly. 'I was there.' She was aware that the crowds about them were thinning. She, too, lowered her voice:

'We were both there, under a waterfall in a cave, a holy place, an enchanted garden. And at last I let go, I accepted it. I tried to speak to you, to offer you the whole of me.'

'I remember your offer. You said you were very young.'

'Yes.' Her eyes brimmed with tears. 'I am.'

His mouth twisted as if with bitterness. 'But experienced. You told me that, too. Do you remember what I said?'

'Yes. Every word of it. You said some experience could get in the way of other experience, and I asked what you meant, how you could know what I knew. And you said—' she had to swallow hard. 'You said you'd walked through hell with me and made love with me, and that was enough to know.'

'Yes, I did say that didn't I. Wasn't that nice of me!'

'Oh, wasn't it just. Such pretty words.'

Now he was mocking her. 'You seemed grateful for them, at the time.'

'Grateful?' she repeated. 'Is that all it seemed like, to you? Oh, I'm so sorry for you Mike Andersen!' Her anger blazed anew, blazed up out of reawakened loss and misery. 'Grateful! That was adoration, Mike. We were equals, yet you were everything to me. I would have done anything for you, anything.'

'Sure. As it was, you did plenty. And it was great, really great. You had me coming back for more and more and there you were, every time, ready to meet me. If we could've gone on living on sex and air and water, we'd still be there. But we aren't. We left. We came back into the real world. And making out in it pretty well, as far as I can see. Trading up, as they say.'

She was cold fire. 'I told myself you must have been hurt by someone,' she said. 'I said to myself, he must have let someone into his very innermost place, trusted her with all his tenderness and vulnerability, and she must have wounded him there, so badly that it hasn't healed. That's what I told myself in my own hurt, in my love. And I wanted to heal it. That's what I meant when I said I would do anything for you. And I blamed myself for not being able to reach you and restore you. I could only meet you with my body, and it felt like failure. My failure.'

His face seemed frozen in a mask of sour contempt.

'After you'd gone, after you slammed the door in my face and left, I wondered if I was wrong. And then I made up my mind you must simply hate all women, for all the brilliance and beauty of your love-making. And then I decided I couldn't know and it would be best not to think about it at all, or about you. And I haven't really, until now. But now I do see that I was wrong. Nobody poisoned you. You make your own poison. It feeds you and justifies you. You'd be helpless without it. You exist only to destroy what you attract.'

He leered at her. 'My word, what a pretty way with metaphors you do have. Well, of course you've grown up a bit since then. Didn't I say to give it a year or so? Better put me down to experience, young Sam. Think of me as a little holiday you once had, out of the world and out of time. You can forget me now you've moved on.' His eyes flicked up and away from her.

'And talking of moving on, hadn't you better be doing just that? There's your little dyke friend doing her stuff, you're on after her aren't you?'

The foyer was deserted except for the two of them. For the first time she noticed the TV monitor. Danse Macabre were on, and she felt a sudden burning annoyance with him for making her miss them. But he was right: she should by now be changed and ready. She ran for the door that led down to the dressing rooms. Then she pulled up and turned back to see him still there, regarding her sardonically.

'How do you know about Trish?' she asked. 'And how do you know I'm supposed to be on soon?' Her voice seemed to slap about the bare walls.

'I read the papers,' he replied laconically. 'And I work for Dayfield. Didn't you know? I'm a sort of troubleshooter.' He passed into the auditorium, his expression woodenly inscrutable.

She fled headlong in a red blindness of anger and panic and bewilderment.

The changing room was a cacophony of raucous voices, a maelstrom of naked and unheeding flesh. She wriggled her way through a clinging tangle of breasts, bellies and thighs. Professional models did their tricks and others imitated them, flicking and squeezing their nipples into pert erection or, in one case, sticking Sellotape over them and ripping it off with yelped curses. Everybody, however frantic the preparations, watched everybody else with half an eye, and she prepared to reveal herself as probably the only woman in the room without shaved or trimmed pudenda. She'd lost that habit in Africa and besides that she hardly needed to, her delta was neat and trim. She remembered Carey used to—

Then she noticed there were men there, too. A muscularly athletic black male drew admiring glances. She saw Anthony, poignantly beautiful in his nakedness. He smiled across at her, speaking 'good luck' with his eyes and blowing her a kiss.

A bell rang, a sharp-breasted girl wriggling out of her panties screamed, 'Fuck me, five minutes,' and a voice nearby said, 'I guess I could at that, honeybabe,' to shrieks of laughter. In the corner of Gossamer's vision two semi-naked women fondled each other with frenetic intensity and drowned in each other's mouths.

She must shut all sensation off. She must be efficient, professional, solitary. A costume box had her name on it; she saw it, and reached to open it, before she noticed Annouska Vane-Venables was there. She had never before noticed how cold, how calculating, that pleasantly-horsey face could look. Fleetingly, and with horrifying absurdity, she thought of female concentration camp commandants.

The woman spoke with a drawl: 'I hope you're heavily into getting things absolutely right first time, Gossamer Fane. There's a bloody sight more at stake here than a few quid for some piddling little charity.'

All sorts of reply welled up into Gossamer's throat, and stuck there. Now was not the time. She undressed quickly and neatly and focused her mind on her performance to come. Naturally she noticed the rubber-necking effect her action had; damn them, she thought, if I can learn to live with my accursed beauty they'll bloody well have to do the same. She stood naked before Annouska Vane-Venables and flicked her hair back, thinking how blissful solitude would feel, after this.

'Right,' Gossamer said briskly. 'Pass me the pants, and is there a bra?'

'No to both,' she drawled. 'This little number is very definitely foundation-free. A one-piece one-off. Made especially, but most especially, for you.'

Annouska glissaded it into Gossamer's hands. The material almost flowed through her fingers. It was not simply soft,

not merely supple. It was sensuous. It was alive. It looked
and felt like living skin.

Her skin.

The woman seemed to read her reeling mind. 'Second
thoughts, honey, you didn't need to try it on. You've been
practising wearing it for years. It even breathes, darling. No
fear of Goldfinger Syndrome with this one. It's your own
bodyskin.'

Gossamer let it flow from hand to hand. It was like
brushing her own ghost with her fingers: the tendons
behind her knees, the particularity of her ankles, her ribs,
her hips. She felt the emptinesses that waited to be filled by
breasts and buttocks, by all the intimacies of her body.

It was unique, as she was. Nobody else could wear it.

Annouska arranged it, rolled down to the crotch. Gossamer winced as though she herself had been skinned. She
saw that she must roll the legs on as if they were tights.

Naked, innocent, she perched on a seat and put on
knowing nudity.

It felt as though her arms and her head were the only parts
of her not uncovered. The rest of her body blazed before the
world in the closest and most intimate of invisible embraces.
Annouska arranged a froth of creamy lace about her neck
and shoulders to conceal the place where Art gave way to
Nature.

'Move, honey. Move about in it.'

Only then did Gossamer hear the silence in the changing
room, a silence merely emphasised by the muttering of the
monitor on the wall. She caught a glimpse of Trish staring
wide-eyed at her from the screen as she performed her very
own *danse macabre* before a silent, awestruck audience.

She moved in a dream of sensuality. Her body in its second
skin exulted in it. She saw herself in a long mirror. She stood
and regarded the reflected dream of herself.

She saw fantasy made real.

It was dark where she was dark, in the little swelling
delta below the flatness of her belly. It blushed where she
blushed, about the firm tips of her breasts. It made her an

image of herself, a picture that could appear to live more vividly than its original.

Yet it was an image in soft focus. A sheen seemed to cling about her like morning mist hovering about the contours of a landscape to make it mysterious and unattainable.

It made her feel langorous, erotically charged, as if she were wearing warm water.

Annouska's reflection joined her image in the looking-glass. 'How does it feel?' she asked.

'Weird,' said Gossamer, speaking to it. 'Weird and wonderful.' She moved, stretched, rippled in it. 'And free. Free and safe.'

Annouska's lips curled in a smile. 'Oh it's certainly safe, my dear. There was a certain amount of latex at its making, among other things. It'll stretch but it won't tear.'

A woman's voice came from somewhere in the room – 'Christ, you could screw all night in that and not get messy!' – and the spell was broken with the release of raucous laughter.

Annouska, laughing with the rest, came up behind Gossamer.

'You see why this had to be made for you, don't you?' she murmured below the renewing din. Her voice was urgently intense as she continued: 'Only you can carry this off, I saw how you were in those Jeans de Nîmes ads and I knew it had to be you. Ida's an old friend and I'm happy to give her cause a boost by showing it here but you do see what else is going to happen, don't you? I can offer any woman who can afford it the most personal, the most intimate and flattering thing they'll ever wear. It'll go under anything, with anything, or just on its own, and it'll be made just for them, just as this one was for you, in every little detail.'

Gossamer froze. Her throat and chest seized and she had to force the word out like a dry cinder:

'How?'

'Computer graphics,' Annouska replied crisply, turning from the mirror. 'Working from photographs, of course.'

Gossamer halted. 'Photographs?' She shot the word out like a bullet at the woman's back.

'Yeah, you know, honey. Photographs. A whole lot of shots of you just as Nature intended.' She saw Gossamer's look of cold horror. 'Aw c'mon, baby! You know the score, surely? You wanted to model their jeans, you had to give them a look at what you had on offer to fill them with, yeah? You did a bit of all sort of business for them, didn't you?'

Gossamer's neck muscles relaxed enough for her to nod. 'Oh yes,' she said hoarsely. 'A bit.'

'As for the rest of it . . .' she shrugged. 'You put things on and took things off, right, along with all the other hopefuls. Well, look at this place, I mean is this a teenage boy's idea of heaven or what? It's like the top shelf at the newsagent's come to life, and those cameras they have all over the place aren't ornaments, you know. Oh, private files, dear, private files. God, I was expecting to have to go down on my knees for those stills, and in more ways than one. As it happened, I didn't. They seemed to have written you off as an asset, my poor love, for reasons I didn't bother going into. So there you are, you see – you could make that go down as one of the biggest mistakes of the century if you wanted to. Okay now?'

'Yes thank you,' said Gossamer. 'I'm okay.'

It hadn't been Carey Lambert's photographs: absurdly, that seemed to make everything all right.

Hers would be the last costume to be modelled. The others would go on seamlessly, one after the other, but before Gossamer's entrance there would be a pause, and the lights would go down until a single spot remained on the performers' entrance. That, and the orchestra playing Handel's *Arrival of the Queen of Sheba* would be her cue.

She would come on wearing a claret-coloured velvet cloak with matching gloves and shoes – 'All snooty and regal, you know, like you've got a plum up your arse.' Gossamer nodded understanding, pulling on the long gloves and working her fingers into them. The music would see her to the point where the catwalk curved to form the out-thrust disc of the stage.

Then the orchestra would 'shiver its strings', as Annouska put it, and a drum would bang to accompany her discarding of the shoes. 'We've got a flunkey coming up behind you to pick them up and look awestruck.'

Then, simultaneously, the orchestra would explode into *Also Sprach Zarathustra* and she would shed the cloak. 'Up to then they'll have been expecting a variation on the little black number,' Annouska giggled. Okay, then you take over, princess. Do what comes, all right? Use all the space. The music'll be with you all the way. Make 'em *feel* you, right? Get under *their* skins, baby. All the way round the stage. Then serenely off. Your flunkey'll have dodged round the back and be there with your cloak, which you'll just whirl round your shoulders as you sashay off. We'll kill the lights and let Richard Strauss do the rest for a few bars.

'And then,' Annouska said, 'if the roof doesn't blow off in appreciation I'll go design oilskins for the cod industry instead. And you can go advertise washing powders. Okay?'

'Yes,' said Gossamer. 'I know what to do.'

'Sure you do.' She gave Gossamer a quick squeezing hug. 'Christ I want to fuck the juice out of you right now, and women don't even turn me on. Oh right, here's your attendant.'

'Hi,' said Anthony. 'Hi Goss. Meet the guy with the brush and shovel. At your service, ma'm.' He gave a ridiculous little bow. He looked like a comedy store waiter, and Gossamer laughed with him.

And, equally absurdly, that too made her feel good about what she was going to do.

The crowd in the room began to thin and the din diminished. Gossamer removed her mind and sat quietly in a state of detached concentration.

Her body told her it knew just what to do.

The images flickered on the monitor. One costumed model

followed another as the commentator breathed enthusiastic intellectualisation over them. There was a girl with a saucepan on her head and another dressed in Westminster City Council bin-liners and wearing a hat made out of condoms.

Carey Lambert yawned hugely. 'Anytime I feel guilty about showing bought-in crud from New Zealand,' he said, 'I'll just remember this, and then I'll know why I do it. What is this in aid of, Dayfield: is it your token Arts contribution, or what?'

'It sold a lot of advertising,' Alec Dayfield growled. He turned to face his adversary. 'I can't believe you told Benedict what you just told me,' he said.

'Why not? It robbed him of the satisfaction of finding out for himself. Take away the spice of discovery, he isn't interested.'

'And why should that matter to you?'

Lambert shrugged and smiled ruefully. 'Call it the creator's protective instinct, if you like. "This thing of darkness I acknowledge mine", you know? It's not as if she asked to be what I made her, after all; I do feel a certain responsibility. Think of it as the dues of paternity, in that sense.'

Alec Dayfield scowled heavily. He was sweating, Lambert noticed.

'She's been in your company twice,' Lambert continued. 'So tell me honestly: did you ever get close to working out what she really was?'

Dayfield considered the question. 'No,' he said. 'She's never behaved the way I was led to expect her to.'

'Quite so. And of course, she isn't what she looks like, is she?'

'No.' Dayfield dropped the word like a lead weight.

'She is a natural . . . performer, so to speak. Born to it. But tutored by a genius, you must admit.'

'I don't know about genius, Lambert. You didn't carry your plan through the first time, did you? It didn't wreck things the way you reckoned it would. We re-shot.'

'Perhaps I was just showing my hand, did that ever occur

to you? After all, you're still here for me to collaborate with aren't you? To my advantage.'

'And mine,' Dayfield replied.

Lambert grinned. 'If that's the way you see it. I must confess your advantage was not exactly my top priority when I put the proposal up to you.'

'You lose more without it,' Dayfield said flatly.

'You're losing enough to want it.'

A pretty girl dressed up to look like a piece of garbage from Cardboard City floated above their heads in close-up. 'Look at that, Dayfield. Look closely, and think about what I've just been telling you. There you see the difference between creative genius and bad art. Genius lies in the art that conceals art. It endures forever. It's power, you see. It writes its name on everything it makes, for those who have the wit to read it. You watch the play, and you believe it must have written itself. And why not? It's what you're meant to believe, after all.'

Alec Dayfield replied slowly: 'You're not Project Aid, Lambert. You didn't put her there. I checked that, of course. The last time I saw her, she was just herself. She has been since, she is now.'

Carey Lambert's eyes narrowed in dangerous derision. 'On the contrary, you bloody fool. She was being more herself the first time. The way she was when she came to you with her plush-lined begging-bowl has my name written across it in neon letters a foot high. Do you still not see that? Well, I can understand your not wanting to. She is irresistible, isn't she? Take my word for it, being with her is like having a willing virgin every night of your life, you simply can't believe anyone else has been there before. You should applaud my strength of will in letting my superb creation loose for a while. Because that's what she is: remember you once offered her the world in exchange for your exclusive and extensive favours, and she turned you down? *She turned you down, Dayfield*. That's what I mean by creative power, my power: the power to let go. You could say I taught her free will, in the perfect knowledge of how she would use it. Once a god, always a god. And no other god but me.'

Dayfield breathed heavily. 'But she left you,' he said. 'Not for anything, or anybody. Straight after that, she left you. And it hurt you.'

Lambert's eyes flicked to the screen, then back to fix his adversary. 'So? She's back now, isn't she? Look at her, Dayfield. Look at her now. Go on, man, feast your eyes: there she is. Living proof of everything I've just been telling you. Flaunting it in front of all your subscription-paying viewers. You don't have to believe me, Dayfield. Just your own eyes. *Look*, Dayfield. Look and learn!'

Dayfield looked; Lambert looked. Each, for his own reason, watched obsessively. Each man saw what he expected to see: a votaress of sensuality. And each drew his own conclusions from what he saw.

The illusion fell from her as the cloak tumbled from her shoulders.

She stood alone, barefoot, unnaturally and grotesquely naked on a public stage and it was cold, so cold, to be so shocked from that dreaming sleep in which she had cast off shoes and cloak in a glory of sustaining self-belief, now evaporated.

She faltered for only an instant, and then she remembered that this was a performance, and she had to give it. She felt her audience press in, voracious for the spectacle of failure and the entertainment of humiliation, smelling her fear. She must push it back, she must put it where she wanted it. She must be professional. Professionals didn't need to believe: they could fake it.

She pretended to be unashamed. She performed only for herself.

The television lights beat down on her pitilessly. Somebody who answered to her name had agreed to do this: now she must carry it off against the voice that screamed inside her head: *no, no, no*.

I'm like one of those cartoon characters, she thought,

running off the edge of a cliff into thin air. Keep running, or you'll fall. All the way down to ruin.

She flaunted the creature whose artificial skin it was her duty to inhabit. She defied the law of gravity. She won her audience, knew she had it on her side, sensed with every nerve its sustaining surge of approval and belief.

She won, at terrible cost: the cost of knowledge. She tasted the fruit of that forbidden tree and saw herself brazenly bare, pretending to be innocently naked. She knew she must face whatever the consequences of it must be, because there could be no going back. How absurd, how absurd and cruel, that it should happen here, now, like this.

She parted her lips in a perfect simulation of ecstasy and the flashlights blazed with a new intensity.

And now, unseen as she turned her back to make for the place where Anthony was waiting to cover her nakedness, she wept with the lost child that was herself.

Anthony's face was a pale shocked blur as she took the cloak from him and swung it round her shoulders. Tears blinded her and her ears were filled with roaring. Only when she was safely backstage did she connect the noise with the image that now filled the monitor screens. It was the audience, frenzied, on its feet, baying for more, baying for her.

Baying like wolves.

Voices spoke in her head:

What have I done, what have I done?

—You know what you have done.

What will I do now, what's going to happen?

—There is nothing you can do. Whatever happens will be what you deserve. All you can do is pray that it will happen soon. And now, here is the dressing room. Perhaps you should compose yourself; up to you, of course but if I were you that's what I should do.

She composed herself and walked blindly in.

The room was empty; there was no one to deceive. Then she remembered that the show was supposed to close with a parade of all the models. They must have been backstage and she never noticed them. There they were now, on the monitor, going through the motions of following her act, without her. She thought they looked resentfully at her, but of course that could not be true.

She clawed at her costume and peeled it off and flung it corpselike on the floor, but the vileness of it clung to her, making her lewdly naked. Her body blazed back at her from the long mirror in all its hateful and pornographic perfection. She must cover her body quickly, hide it away, try to forget it.

Hastily she dragged on her street clothes, pants, socks, jeans, sweater, trainers. With a bit of luck, so far as other people were concerned she might just pass for normal. A normal ordinary girl who was looking forward to her twentieth birthday, with the rest of her life happily in front of her.

She scrunched her pretty dress into a carrier bag and stuffed the shoes in on top. She ground her heels into the horrid mockery on the floor, but failed to damage it. It merely rippled and squirmed. She kicked it brutally into a corner instead. It fell prone, like an invitation to obscenity.

She turned from it in disgust to see if she could find another exit and a voice behind her said, 'Going somewhere, Gossamer?'

Lambert had gone, but Alec Dayfield was not alone in the little room.

'No sign of our star, then?' he asked.

'No,' the other replied shortly. 'Never mind, though. After tonight I'm sure we'll all be seeing a lot more of her.' His lips twisted. 'In a manner of speaking, that is.'

'Oh, I'm sure we shall,' Dayfield replied humourlessly. 'Especially now I gather she's set to rejoin the old firm, as it were. In one capacity or another. Quite a team, I'm sure you will agree.'

The other man briefly registered shock but Dayfield's back was still turned. 'Oh really?' he drawled, quickly recovering. 'Well well. What an evening of surprises this has turned out to be, to be sure. First you and Lambert, now her as well. Quite a *ménage à trois*, indeed.'

'That's enough,' Dayfield snapped. 'Be careful, Andersen.'

Mike Andersen bent over the table and scribbled a note, folded it and sealed it in an envelope. 'Perhaps you'd deliver this to the lady sometime. Or get Lambert to. Would you mind? I'd rather not.'

Dayfield took the envelope and stuffed it in his pocket. 'Painful memories, Andersen?'

The younger man smiled sourly.

'You'll get over it. I'm sure you won't be the last.'

'Oh, so am I.'

'I could give it to him now, come to that. I have every reason to believe it will find its way to her soon enough. And we're on in a minute, bidding against each other for the original of that bloody hilarious cartoon.'

'And which of you is going to get it, may I ask?'

It was Dayfield's turn to make a rueful smile. 'Both of us, as it happens. It's all agreed. We're bidding up to five grand and then calling it quits. Just to show what jolly good chums we are underneath, you see. Sharing the spoils, turn and turn about.'

'What a nice arrangement. But why should you stop short at sharing an expensive picture?'

Suddenly Dayfield was standing very close. Mike could almost smell the brute power of the man, coarse and compelling. 'Like I said, Mike,' he breathed softly, 'be careful. Be very careful what you say.' His little eyes glittered. 'You could find your words come back to hurt you, very badly.'

'Oh, but they do, Alec, believe me, without any assistance from you.'

Alec Dayfield had no reply. He lugged the door open and barged out. Mike Andersen was left alone. His eyes closed and his face contorted. 'Jesus.' He breathed the word like a mantra. 'Jesus Christ Almighty. Jesus . . . fucking . . . *Christ*.' He crashed his fist impotently into the soundproofed wall, again and again until it grew dented and red with blood. He did not feel the pain of it.

'Going somewhere, Gossamer?'

She could not read Annouska's smile. A bubble of air seemed to block her throat. 'Yes. Trying to. Somewhere.'

'You're hot, Gossamer: they want you out there. Know that, do you? You were superb, wonderful. You blew their minds. You were the best, baby, the very very best, and they want you for it.'

'Yes. I don't—' The bubble rose, and choked her off.

Annouska's arm was round her shoulder, her fingers brushing the sensitivity of her hidden breast.

She felt the tip of it begin to rise and stiffen, shaming her and mocking her. She knew herself to be on the edge of being out of control, ready to seek refuge and comfort in anything.

Annouska's eyes met hers knowingly. 'You need somewhere to hole up?'

Gossamer's voice was the merest breath of relief. 'Yes.'

She felt the woman's fingers lightly rake the wool-clad bareness of her back, felt their tips like a breath below. She was all skin.

'This way, honeypot,' Annouska murmured. 'I'll find you somewhere, for the moment. Somewhere safe.'

Annouska Vane-Venables led the way and Gossamer followed, a tired little girl trailing after her, exhausted and trusting.

They rode a lift, and Gossamer said, 'Thank you.'

Annouska blinked. 'You shouldn't thank me. You've made me. And you could make yourself.'

'I don't want to. I don't think I could do it anyway.'

The woman's lips pursed and whitened. 'You will,' she said shortly. 'Once you've got used to the idea of being a grown-up.'

Very briefly, Gossamer felt a fierce resentment. Who was this woman, this creature, to speak to her like that, had she faced death? Then it sank away and she bowed her head. It was true. Tonight she had grown up, or part of her had. The rest of her needed a little time to catch up, and for that she needed a little help.

For the moment, Annouska was giving it.

The lift halted and they stepped out into a grey and silent corridor, dimly lit. It felt like safety. She followed along the corridor, cleaving the warm and silent air. Annouska opened a door at the end and led her into an office. It had a desk, a chair, a small settee and a view over London from a triple-glazed window. Annouska switched on a wall light, warm and dim and restful. Gossamer slumped in the settee and closed her eyes.

'I'm sorry,' she murmured. 'I'm so sorry.'

'Don't be.' The woman's voice was suddenly intense; then it softened again. 'I'm the one who's sorry: sorry I have to leave you. I need to be downstairs, you understand.'

'Yes, yes of course. I'm all right, honestly. I'll be fine here on my own.'

'Sure, honey. Sure you will.' The door clicked shut.

She might have slept. Certainly it seemed like a waking when the door was opened. Gossamer had her back to it. She heard footsteps, two, three, on the muffling carpet. Then they halted.

'Oh, sorry, I didn't know—'

Gossamer had turned at the voice.

'Oh,' she said. 'It's you.'

'And oh, it's you,' said Carey Lambert.

The sconced light from the niche in the wall made him so beautiful.

'I had been looking for you earlier,' he said.

'I saw you. I saw you with Alec Dayfield.'

'Yes. We've just bought a picture. For Ida's great cause.'

'Oh yes,' she said. 'I know. Both of you?'

'Yes,' he said. 'But that's another story.' His hand indicated the desk, the chair behind it. 'Now I'm here . . . may I?'

Almost imperceptibly she nodded assent. He sat. His arms rested on the dark polished surface of the desk.

'Gossamer,' he said. 'You're here. I'm here. There's something I want to, need to say. You see, I—'

She stopped him with her upraised hand. 'Look out of the window,' she said. 'Tell me what you see.'

He obeyed without demur. 'People. Men hanging round, it looks like. Hanging round the side entrance to the building.'

'Oh,' she said. She could not leave, so she might as well stay. 'Go on, then. You were needing to say something to me.' She succeeded in making her voice sound sarcastic. He returned meekly to the desk.

'Yes. I have been aching to say it for a long, long time, Gossamer. I had almost hoped you might ask me to, after I saw you at the Embassy.'

'I've been busy,' she said.

'Yes. Of course you have. But here we are.'

'So you might as well say it.'

'I know who you are, Gossamer Fane.'

She was struck to breathless immobility and silence. The wash of light from the window crisped his hair, turned it to fine-spun wiry fire.

'I know who you are, and you need to hear it from me.'

Her throat made words, her mouth formed them, her lips uttered them across the amplifying silence of the room. 'What do you know of what I need, Carey Lambert?'

'That which I believe is most important to you. Rightly or wrongly.'

'Then I suppose you had better tell me, rightly or wrongly.' She gave a joyless little laugh. 'After all, it doesn't look as though I'm going anywhere just at the moment.'

Gossamer unbent a little, saying this. A siren passed outside, rising and falling. Somewhere out there, someone was getting life-sustaining help. Or being pursued to the ends of existence.

Carey Lambert leaned against the windowsill, his ankles crossed, his arms folded loosely across his chest. He was relaxed and alert, his outline crisp against the flat backwash of the sodium sky, his features softly etched by the soft light of the wall lamp. She could not choose but hear him out.

His voice was tentative at first, vulnerable. 'I'm scared, Gossamer, so scared. I'm terrified to the very roots of me.'

It was the most shocking thing he had ever said to her. And the sudden knowledge burst within her like an epiphany. The whole ground of her being moved shockingly under it. Still her mind steeled her to a response:

'This is something new. Go on.'

'It's going to come out pat, that's what terrifies me. I have rehearsed it so many times, you see, gone over it and over it in my imagination, like a sustaining fantasy, a madness I've created to save me going truly mad. I thought I knew you, knew myself. And then too late I knew that I was wrong. Something I'd been putting from my mind all that time suddenly exposed me, burst upon me like a flare, and I had to follow it, had to test it. And what I found was the truth about you and the much more terrible truth about me. I could only make it good by sharing it with you, but it was too late. Too late. You'd read the corrupted script I gave you, that I wrote for you, and you'd learnt it, and you'd gone. Too late. But I imagined it wasn't, imagined I'd been given one more chance to put things right, and that's what I did, over and over in my head. And now here I am and here you are, and this is my chance to do it, and it's going to come out pat. There's nothing I can do about that, nothing. Except begin.'

Wordlessly and without any conscious signal, Gossamer gave him permission to begin.

'All you know about me is what I've shown you or told you. And all I've revealed to you has been the worst of it. Oh yes, my dear Gossamer, even at the very best you were drinking from a poisoned well. And it still is poisoned. What I have to tell you now is how, and why, it got to be that way. You are down there too, down there in that dark well of my history.'

Gossamer felt a freezing tightness steal over her. She felt it possess her. 'Yes,' Carey continued as if reading her thoughts, 'I know what you're thinking, what you're afraid of. But it's not that. It may be worse than that, but it's not that.'

Gossamer felt a wave of relief. She remembered she had asked him once—

'You said to me once you had been frightened because you thought I was your father. The truth – no, the explanation – is more complicated than that.'

She knew she looked at him then with eyes that brimmed with tears. She could not help it. Reason screamed at her to look away, to look in a different way, but she rejected reason. 'Tell me, Carey,' she said, her voice cracked and husky. 'I promise I won't interrupt.'

He told her, just as he had rehearsed it.

'You never asked me to tell you more than I wanted to show you. Now you do ask me, and I am honoured. I don't deserve it, but I accept it.'

Something changed about him. He did not raise his voice but it was as if he were addressing her as an audience, an intimate multitude. She understood that this was necessary for him, and she accepted it.

'There were two of us, me and my elder sister Connie. Short for Constance. A prophetic name. Our parents were 'unconventional' as they say, and they flaunted it. Our father bedded other women, our mother bedded other men, and women. The terrible thing is, I don't think either of them got much fun out it, in fact I think they were both bloody miserable about it, deep down where it really mattered, but of course they couldn't admit that, could they? They'd have had to divorce if they did, and that was unthinkable because they loved each other. Only they couldn't quite bring themselves to believe in that sort of love. I think that's tragic, don't you?' Gossamer, thinking about it as an old movie she'd just watched on TV, nodded dumbly.

'So that's what we were brought up in, Connie and I. Full frontal nudity all over the place and never quite knowing who we were supposed to be nice to over breakfast: a strange man with a beard or a weird lady who spouted free verse poetry at us, and made us want to giggle. Or cry. Only of course we couldn't.

'We were rich, though, did I tell you that? Well, I hardly need to of course. We were brought up to the knowledge that anything we wanted, we could have – so long as it was something we 'believed in' of course, and provided it was sufficiently unconventional. And not only 'could have' – ought to have. It was our duty, you see.

'Well, we obeyed it. We were unconventional. We kicked against the Establishment – our Establishment, the code we'd been brought up in, the code of rigid 'unconventionality'. Can you guess the rest? Connie ran off to a nunnery and I went tea planting in Kenya. Our parents were appalled, as we intended them to be. As we'd been programmed to make them.'

His face clouded, and he caught his breath. 'And then they died. They were killed in a car crash.' His voice faltered. 'They were off to have a holiday in the West Highlands of Scotland. Just the two of them. They left very early and headed up the A1, and then a lorry crashed into them and they were killed instantly, together. As in Death so not in Life.

'It hit Connie worse than it hit me. I carried on planting tea, but she left her nunnery. A crisis of faithlessness, you could call it. Take away her motivation for being there, she couldn't stay. But she had nowhere to go. Oh, there was family, yes. An aunt and uncle, my mother's sister and her husband. They'd fielded us from time to time, when things got too hot at home. Strait-laced, you could call them, Uncle Albert and Auntie Margaret. Very much the epitome of the sort of thing my parents had reacted against, the same way Connie and I reacted against them. Uncle Albert died but Auntie Margaret continued to do her duty by us. She hated us cordially, needless to say. We were the Devil's Children, but she had to do her duty. It's what she always told us she was doing when we got beaten for showing ourselves naked.'

It was like a fairy story, a fable whose truth lay in its being fantasy. She knew herself to be on the edge of weeping, and somehow it didn't matter.

Carey continued, regardless. He seemed now to be too involved in his own fable to take any regard of her reaction to it. She was grateful for that.

'So my sister Connie came to me. I was doing just about well enough to be able to keep us both.' His mouth twisted. 'And to pay for her passage out; our parents left nothing except debts. Even the house was double-mortgaged. And of course there was no question of my going back, "going home": there was no home to go to. All we came away with was an expensively useless education and an instinctive distrust of what the rest of our generation was calling "freedom".'

He smiled vacuously and held his fingers up in an reversed V. 'Far out! What we knew was that it was just another sort of slavery.

'But I was liberated, Gossamer. Can you understand that? Liberated! It was like coming out of close confinement, one so close I'd never really realised it existed. I began to pursue the self-same things my parents had most despised: ambition, profit, financial reward, worldly success. I suddenly realised that my little rebellion in going out to Kenya had been conducted on their terms: I was merely getting by, marking time, waiting for something to turn up. Then I changed, utterly and irrevocably. And why not? It wasn't as if the things they'd lived by were worth a damn, after all. All they'd ever made was mess and misery. Why shouldn't I turn my back on it all? Turn away from all that corrupting, self-righteous failure?'

The question was thrown out like a challenge. Gossamer realised she was supposed to answer it. 'I can understand why you rejected it,' she said.

'Yes, dear Gossamer, of course you can. You would. But there's something I think you won't accept, can't accept. Not yet.'

She looked at him. Silently she permitted him, commanded him to say what it was.

'Do you know your Philip Larkin?' he asked softly. '"An Arundel Tomb"? "What will survive of us is love", do you know that line? I saw so clearly my parents' greatest failure, their failure to reach out and acknowledge love. So I put that right. I fell deeply and utterly and disastrously in love. You could say love has made me, Gossamer. But it made me all wrong.'

There was a prolonged silence. Then Carey said:

'Her name was Madeline, Madeline Porteous. She was an old school friend of my sister's. She followed Connie out to Kenya for reasons I never guessed at the time. I just thought she was having a bit of fun, seeing the world a bit, moving around.

'I fell in love with her instantly and completely. I made moves and she responded. Oh God, how she responded. It was like a dream.'

He passed a hand slowly over his face as if wiping away cobwebs. The lines on it seemed more deeply etched when his hand fell away.

'I wasn't a virgin, Gossamer. I wasn't inexperienced where women were concerned, but I couldn't have been less prepared for Madeline if I'd spent the whole of my life in a monastery on Mars. Sexually she took me into another universe.

'But it wasn't just sex. Christ no, it wasn't; it would have been so much easier if it had been. It wasn't just "love".' He smiled. 'And it wasn't infatuation either. I adored her, Gossamer. You know what I mean by that?'

'Oh yes,' said Gossamer quietly but unsteadily. 'I know what you mean by that, Carey.'

'Yes. Of course you do.' He lifted his face to her and smiled again. Then his smile faded and he seemed to look through her.

'She was beautiful beyond belief. She was just twenty years old. She had all the physical grace and charm and poise of a mature woman but she combined it with the disingenuousness, the openness and honesty, seeming honesty, of a girl. It was a devastating combination, Gossamer. Irresistible. A guileless sensuality. Eve before the Fall, a dream of Paradise. A dream I believed in.'

His words penetrated her like barbs of ice and fire. A

terrible pattern began to form in her mind, a repeating pattern of adoration and loathing, of purity and corruption. *O rose thou art sick . . .*

His voice broke in harshly. 'She was an erotomaniac. An addict with all the addict's instinctual cunning. She fed on sex, and her mouth was always open. And it was such a very, very beautiful mouth. Who could resist feeding it?

'In particular there was a man called Kenneth Tisolo, an African – of sorts. The result of at least two generations of mixed parentage. But he was an African in mind and soul. Raised as an orphan just like you were. He'd been through mission school and college, and now he was back again, teaching there. He was a lovely man, Gossamer, a fine man. I always knew I would do anything for him, anything I could. I've had very few friends, Gossamer: he was one of them.

'Well, all the time Madeline was accepting my adoration she was screwing Kenneth Tisolo. Or to put it another way: all the time he was adoring her, she was screwing me. Christ only knows how she managed it: still, they say alcoholics are unbelievably ingenious about hiding their booze, don't they? I had my work, of course, and all my remunerative little sidelines, and Kenneth had his teaching. And the one thing Madeline never did was interfere with our work. I was grateful for that, of course; grateful, and smug at the thought that when I wasn't working, there she'd be, when I wanted her. Christ! When I wanted her.'

He screwed his eyes shut. When he recovered to open them again they were hooded. 'And I daresay Kenneth felt the same way.'

Was Gossamer supposed to respond to this? She was dumb with horror.

'She wasn't found out, anyway. All those weeks having the two of us, she was never found out. She told us instead, Kenneth and Connie and me, one cosy evening over dinner. Kenneth had just said grace – he was a devout Roman Catholic, in some ways – and she slipped it in between the "amen" and the soup. "I think you should know I'm pregnant, boys," she said. "And although there's hardly been a day when I haven't fucked you both, I happen to know it's Kenneth's." And then she started eating. What a performer.

'Connie turned grey and rushed out of the room; we all listened to her being sick on the verandah. I'll never forget the way Madeline smiled, listening to that. It was pure, beautiful evil. Then she turned to me and said, "It's probably because Kenny's cock is a good two inches longer than yours actually, darling."

'I wanted to hit her. I should have done. I should have marked her, spoiled her beauty and turned her into the disgusting fuck-hungry slut she always was. I'm being very serious, Gossamer. I've had cause to think long and hard about the man I became after that. Far better I should have maimed her, who deserved it, then and there, and purged my system of it. Instead I let it breed inside me like a poison. I went on to hurt other women instead. You especially, Gossamer, because, God help me, I deceived myself into believing you deserved it in her place.'

Gossamer looked at the floor. The speckled grey carpet seemed to dissolve and re-form, becoming liquid. It heaved and swelled like a viscous mist, clouding her sight and her mind. She shook her head to clear it.

'You don't think so?' said Carey, misunderstanding. 'Then think of Connie. She had been engaged to Kenneth Tisolo. Also she had been Madeline's lover back in England and the bitch seduced her a second time out there. She wrecked all three of us, you see. She liked to destroy where she had devoured. She had to spoil all three of us for anyone else. I'm sure that's why she had the baby; it was easy enough to wound Kenneth and me, simply by facing us with the knowledge that she'd been full of one of us while making love to the other. Hurting Connie required her to go that one step further.

'And succeeded. At the cost of my sister's life, she succeeded.'

Gossamer felt the world lurch away from her, and she believed the unthinkable.

Her voice came slowly. It sounded drugged, death-infected:

'She was my mother. Madeline was my mother.'

'Yes Gossamer. Madeline was your mother.'

She was back in the hollow tree. The puff adder struck, and the world died.

❧ Eighteen ❧

'Yes, Gossamer, Madeline was your mother. She gave birth to you. But that poor good man Kenneth Tisolo was your father. Please, please always remember that as well.'

Her eyes met his. He read the unspoken question in them. Very quietly and gently, and without touching her, he came to sit next to her on the sofa.

'Bear with me a little,' he said. 'I know, it's late and you're trying to take it all in. But the next part at least is soon told. Are you able to hear it now?'

She felt the barrier she had erected against this man and all his works begin to crumble but still without too much difficulty she resisted the temptation to tear it down.

Her voice came faintly husky but it was level. 'What happened to my father?'

'Kenneth walked out of his job and he and Madeline went to Nairobi two days later. A few weeks after that we had a short message from him: "Madeline and I were married today. I am so sorry for the pain but I have to believe it is for the best. I know this to be my child. I pray that time may heal." Poor, good, prayerful Kenneth.

'The morning after the letter arrived I was woken very early by the houseboy. He'd found Connie: she'd hanged herself. There was a note in her pocket. It just said: "I cannot bear the pain."

'I of course had been too wrapped up in my own pain – my own humiliation – to notice Connie's. And when I did it was too late. And of course it was only then I realised she'd been going round like a ghost. And I felt guilty, sickeningly guilty, as many bereaved people do, especially after a suicide. I had a gun. I used to clean it a lot, turning it over and over in my hands, imagining myself into oblivion. That was me, then.'

Gossamer did not break the silence that followed.

'But,' Carey continued, 'people get over it, as they say. They find another channel for all that intensity of feeling. I found I had two channels. One was work. I couldn't just up and leave, so instead I threw myself into all the ventures I was involved in at the time, determined to screw as much money out of them as I could before I cleared off back to England for good, and really made it big.'

He turned to her and she could not help but look at him. It was, her mind told her, like hearing a confession. She had no choice but to go on listening. It was almost as if she were neutral, uninvolved.

'See me now, Gossamer. That's part of how I got to be what you see.'

His mask-like gaze did not alter. 'The other part is hate. Hate, and the urge to revenge. Revenge on Madeline for all the wickedness she had done, to me and to poor Connie and my good friend Kenneth Tisolo and God knows how many others, and for all the evil she personified. Oh, I believed in evil then, Gossamer. I made a study of it. I set out to know my enemy: a dangerous thing to do. Evil is infectious, you see.'

Gossamer heard Marie speaking, a long time ago: *Thermodynamics, Goss. Badness is hot. Bad people are contagious*.

'Yes,' she said dully, 'I know.'

Carey's voice was choked. 'And so her evil lives on. But she cheated me, Madeline Porteous. She escaped before I was quite ready. One day, in February 1972, Kenneth Tisolo turned up again. He'd become another person altogether, a broken man, tired and old before his time, and ill with misery and hopelessness. He had a baby with him, a baby girl. It was so—' He closed his eyes and winced. 'I'm sorry: of course not "it". You, Gossamer, *you* were so beautiful, and barely two months old. And you were his child, no question of that. It wasn't just that your skin was light olive rather than light pink. It was deeper than that. It shone out of you.

And I was glad, Gossamer, so glad for you that it was him, and not me. I always knew he was a better man.'

Gossamer's heart lurched, but she said nothing.

'But he couldn't rear you. All the will to live had gone out of him. Madeline – your mother – had abandoned you after a few weeks, walked out of your life and vanished. Beyond recall, beyond the retribution I'd been hatching all those months. She took up with a Mombasa tramp ship's captain: hitched a ride, you could say. But she never got to wherever she thought she was going. Kenneth showed me the cutting from the *Kenya Star*: the ship sank, and there were no survivors. Sharks, you know.'

He reached out and clasped her hand, and then released it immediately. 'That was the nearest I've ever got to believing in a just God,' he said. Gossamer was aware that her hand, afterwards, felt different from the rest of her.

He continued, talking quietly out into the space beyond them. 'All this Kenneth told me, there on the verandah that fine morning. He said, "My friend, I cannot rear this baby. She does not belong to the world I now inhabit. There is no one else I can say this to." And then he put you in my arms and walked away, and he didn't look back.

'I did not follow him. I could not. All that he had brought with him was his child. And I knew where he was going. He walked away into the bush, and it closed after him, and he was never seen again. He went to meet his destiny and I knew as I watched him go that he would find it there.

'So then there was you, and there was your father's one wish for you. His dying wish for you: that you should inherit a better world.

'I knew I couldn't give it to you. It was an instant decision, Gossamer. A selfish one, perhaps, but the only one I could take, because I simply knew that what had destroyed Connie and your father, and infected me for life, must be kept away from you. And that meant keeping me away from you. Do you understand that?'

Gossamer spoke into the night beyond the window. 'I understand how you felt,' she said.

'Meaning you think I was wrong.'

Gossamer did not answer that. 'You put me in an orphanage, after that? But that wasn't in Kenya. And then there was Shaws. How—?' He cut her short:

'Fate intervened. I acquired an inheritance, that's how. An uncle of my mother's died and I was his only heir. I hardly knew he even existed. I'd made enough on my own account to put my plans for myself into operation and I wasn't looking for assistance from any other quarter, least of all from my family; hadn't I gone out there in the first place to put all that behind me? But here it was with this lifeline, just when I – when *you* – needed it. He was a rich man, Gossamer. He'd pursued wealth the way my mother pursued happiness. His solicitor was a man called Kevin Germain. He became my solicitor, too, now I had all that money. And money, as you probably know, buys discretion, and they don't, or rather didn't, come any discreeter than Kevin Germain. As you certainly do know.'

'Yes, he was very discreet,' Gossamer said. She looked at him. 'And also very concerned that I should have nothing to do with you.'

Carey smiled faintly, making his lips into a hard little line. 'But of course,' he said.

'Why, Carey?'

'Haven't you worked it out, Gossamer?' Suddenly his voice had a cruel edge to it. But he softened his features immediately. 'I'm sorry, Gossamer. I was forgetting what a lot you've had to take in tonight. It's really very simple, my dear: he thought I was your father.'

She still couldn't understand it. 'But he was your solicitor, you must have explained it all to him, why should he think that?'

Carey laughed. 'Oh my dear sweet girl, you're still so trusting!' His look, Gossamer recognised, was desiring as well as humorous. She was suddenly aware of his physical closeness, alert to it. 'Being my solicitor was one thing, believing everything I told him was quite another. I came to him with a story about your being the orphaned daughter of an African friend and an Englishwoman; he assumed you were my by-blow by a native tootsie. It was quite reasonable of him. Nothing was actually said, of course, not then, not ever. But he thought I must be your father, and by the time you met him I had acquired, you might say, a certain reputation. You stirred his conscience, obviously. It must have come as some surprise to him to find he still had one.'

His tone was openly salacious. 'What do you mean?' she said.

'I mean that there's a very discreet club not far from here, dedicated to the entertainment of men who like to pass the time with girls young enough to be their daughters. Or, in some cases, granddaughters. Germain was, so to speak, a full member.'

She saw the man in her mind's eye: immaculate, dapper, proper, pink-skinned, prim, and fussily pedantic; old enough to be her grandfather. A man the girl in her trusted. 'That's horrible,' she said. '*Horrible.*'

His eyes glittered. 'It was his fantasy, Gossamer, his recreation. Reality, as he thought he saw it, was another matter. So he got it wrong, but he did try to save you from what he thought it was. You should give him credit for that. You yourself, at one stage, thought I was your father.'

She met his directness with her own: 'I thought all sorts of things, Carey. And believed others. I trusted you, and believed in you. That turned out to be a mistake, didn't it?'

'Yes,' he said. He looked suddenly haggard. 'I know it. I abused your trust, abused you. I betrayed you, and I know it. I also betrayed myself, not that I expect or deserve any sympathy for that.'

He crossed over to the window. Her eyes followed him as he continued. 'It's late, Gossamer, very late. You must be tired. I'll be as brief as I can.' He gazed out over the city as he spoke. 'I arranged to have you looked after. Timmy, my houseboy, had a sister who'd just lost her own baby, so I employed her as a wetnurse. I flew to London. I met

Kevin Germain and told him everything, withholding only the names. I told him I wanted to provide the best possible upbringing for you out of my inheritance, anonymously and untraceably, and he agreed.

'And he came up with a plan.' He turned from the window and spoke directly to her. 'Or rather, a *fait accompli* Chatteris Choate could bear to be presented with; it wouldn't do for them to be implicated in anything illegal, you understand.

'Lord knows, it was easy enough. I'd got hold of a false Kenyan passport and I flew to Ireland with you as Charlie Laverty, travelling with infant daughter in search of his roots.' His tone warmed, and Gossamer responded to the release of tension.

'People were very kind to me, you know? Single male travelling with small baby. I lapped it up, I'm afraid. I almost had second thoughts about what I was doing.'

They looked at each other very seriously. 'Almost,' Gossamer said quietly.

'Almost.'

Gossamer began to feel the sickness of the evening ebb away from her, all the pain and confusion and hot disquiet of it. She was tempted to believe she didn't have to try any more, didn't have to put on a face to meet the faces that she met. She began to feel safe. She wanted to let go. She said:

'I understand. Go on.'

He shrugged. 'After that it was straightforward. You don't need passports between Britain and Eire. I flew from Dublin to Glasgow as a man with a baby, that's all. And then, not having a forged driving licence, I hired a car in the name of Carey Lambert.'

He swallowed, and his face clouded over. Gossamer's mind raced to remind her of all the injury this man had done her. It prevented her from comforting him in the pain of his reminiscence. It told her she did not owe him that. Or not yet.

'Germain said,' he continued, measuring out the syllables, 'that if a certain baby were to be found abandoned at a certain orphanage that Chatteris Choate had a professional connection with, and if at about the same time Chatteris Choate were to come in the way of an untraceable bequest, say in the form of bearer bonds, in favour of that baby, the firm would be duty bound to put it into operation in that baby's favour. And that, coming from them, the money would talk in certain circles. Official circles, you understand. The sort of official circles responsible for issuing documents that prove you exist, that sort of thing. No questions would be asked. They weren't.'

'I see,' Gossamer said.

'I'm sorry. I'm so sorry I didn't have the guts, the strength of character to bring you up myself. It would have made a better man of me, I know that. As it is I have so much to apologise for, so much to explain. This is just the first thing, the first chance I have to say to you: I'm sorry. Please accept it. Otherwise I can't go on.'

'I accept,' she said. She was not aware of having considered it. The words just came out, and then they were beyond recall.

'Thank you,' he whispered. 'Oh, thank you.' He lifted his head. She saw his eyes were moist.

He cleared his throat. 'So: I drove to a Third Order Franciscan nunnery in Heronsburn on the Scottish Border. The Sisters of the Order of the Tears of Mary.

'I had to do it at night, Gossamer, I couldn't risk being seen, the car licence plate being traced, anything like that. I'm sorry. I rang the bell and left you there, literally on the doorstep. You were asleep. I was terrified you might not be found, might die because of what I'd done. I did wrap you up warm, first.'

She found her voice. 'I'm sure you did, I'm still here.'

His smile spoke of relief and gratitude. 'I returned the car, and then flew to London as Carey Lambert. I shoved a plain envelope through Chatteris Choate's letterbox. My inheritance, your inheritance, was in it, in the form of bearer bonds. I stayed as Charlie Laverty in a cheap hotel. The next morning, early, I took a train for Holyhead and sailed to Lougharne. Then Carey Lambert flew out of Dublin, not by Aer Lingus, and made his way back to Kenya. It took five days. And then I slept, and slept, and slept. And tried to forget.

'But part of me could not forget, and could not forgive. That, too, is at the root of everything: that I could not forgive myself. It's as if I've been expecting punishment for it ever since, retribution without forgiveness. Expecting it and at the same time resenting it, human nature being what it is. Or my nature, anyway.'

She forced herself to allow a little time to pass. She didn't have to think about saying it.

'I forgive you, Carey. For that, I forgive you.'

He crossed the floor and lifted her in his arms and kissed her, lightly and chastely, on the lips. Then he released her; it was all over in a few seconds.

'Thank you,' he said. 'Thank you for that. It is the only thing I shall ask you to forgive, though there is more I should like you to understand. But it'll keep. You've had enough, and I've had more understanding than I dared to hope I might deserve.' He turned away as if suddenly making an effort to be brisk. 'We must see about getting you home,' he said.

He spoke on the telephone to someone called George. 'My chauffeur,' he explained. 'He tells me the coast is clear.' He invited Gossamer to lean on him as they walked to the lift, and she accepted. No advantage was taken.

She asked: 'Why did Kevin Germain tell me my father had set up the trust? He could just have said it was anonymous, an unknown benefactor.'

He paused fractionally before replying. 'Because it was his wish that you be provided for, Gossamer. And because I wanted you to know that, when the inevitable day came that you would ask. I had to do him that honour, that you should simply know that.'

You could respect that wish, Miss Fane. You could do him that much honour. 'Yes,' she said, 'I see.'

They drove out into the chloral early morning light of Central London. 'Gossamer,' he murmured quietly. She opened her eyes. Her head had been resting on his shoulder. 'George needs to know where you live.'

The relief she felt, that he did not know, was inexpressible. She told him. George swung the big, warm, comfortable car around, and she dozed again.

She woke again to find him gently massaging her temple. 'What is it?' she asked.

He smiled. 'Nearly there, my dear. Time to wake up.'

She focused her eyes on the world outside. They were coasting along Holland Park Avenue. Nearly home, her home. Happily, she yearned for it. She was astonished to find herself feeling happy, but she was.

Suddenly Carey's hand was pressing down on her shoulder, hard.

'Get down,' he ordered. 'Down on the floor.' She obeyed unthinkingly. She heard and felt the car swerve and accelerate. The great power of it surged through her.

Still his hand was on her shoulder, then he released it and she came up, gasping in the cleaner air.

'Press,' he said shortly. 'Camped outside your door. I think we got past them quickly enough for them not to make a note of the car.'

She felt something inside dissolve into helplessness.

'It's all right,' he said. 'Do you remember Miranda?'

She nodded. 'Your secretary,' she slurred. She was so tired, so full of sleepiness.

'That's right. We'll go to her flat. She has a spare bedroom.'

'Won't she mind? Being woken up and everything?'

His voice was assured. 'She works for me full time,' he said.

She was past questioning. 'Oh, that's all right then,' she said, believing it.

It was deliciously warm in the car. She closed her eyes and let the smooth power of the engine purr her into slumber.

Time and events passed in a grateful blur. She was being helped across a cold space to a door. She passed inside to a warm place, a safe place. Gentle, competent female hands helped her into nightclothes. Cool clean sheets enveloped her in sanctuary. Carey's voice invited her to sleep, and she slept.

She had no memory of dreaming.

She woke to winter light filtered through dove-grey curtains to give the room an air of cool convalescence, of neutrality. She felt safe in it.

She allowed herself to come slowly and pleasantly to full wakefulness. She was wearing a nightdress of light blue cotton, simple and pretty and comfortable. It was very peaceful in the room, quiet and still. Her clothes were neatly folded on a stool by the window. On the bedside cabinet there was a little stoneware vase with dried flowers in it, and a magazine of some sort. She reached out her hand for it.

It was *The OffWorld Report*, the annual handbook of OffWorld Television. Its cover was a gorgeously enhanced colour photograph of the company's headquarters: what would the architectural description be? Gossamer wondered. It was a fantastical creation, that building and all it represented, yet on it and in it rested the fates and fortunes of so many real, ordinary, flesh-and-blood people. People like Miranda, for instance, Carey's private secretary. She must be very loyal to him, devoted even. She must have reason to be so. She couldn't have been glamoured by him, as Gossamer had been.

Or then again, perhaps she had. A thought said: *Perhaps there's something wrong with you, Gossamer Fane: perhaps you're the one who sees things through a warped window.* She flicked the thought aside as she flicked through the glossy book.

A photograph leaped out and demanded her attention. It was captioned: *Behind the cameras, the Management Team take a hands-on interest in the work of OffWorld*. Carey Lambert was in it, together with a group of power-dressed male and female executives.

One of them was Mike Andersen. He and Carey were pictured sharing some sort of hands-on executive joke.

She flicked back to the title page. The date of publication was given as January 1991, meaning it had gone to press in the autumn of 1990. At which point Mike had been working for Carey, working closely and intimately with him, and Gossamer had been falling deeply in love with him.

And then they'd met, she and Mike. And she had found, had believed she had found, a deeper love with him.

And now, here was this piece of out-of-date glamorising hype, next to her bed in the home of Carey Lambert's loyal female assistant. Had she been meant to find it, look at it, come across that photograph?

Had it been there earlier, when Miranda had put her to bed? Miranda might have put it there deliberately, might know things and wish to make them known to her.

Or it might be pure coincidence. A piece of reading matter put in a spare bedroom by a thoughful hostess and loyal company servant.

But one fact remained: Mike Andersen had been a close associate of Carey Lambert and was now a close associate of Alec Dayfield, Carey's old adversary. He was bound up in every way in her story, her mystery. Her pain and confusion.

She filed this information away for possible future use, then cast the book aside. She lay back on the pillows and closed her eyes.

The door opened softly but not furtively. Opening her eyes she saw Carey Lambert. He stood at the foot of her bed, smiling warmly and amicably.

'You look well rested,' he said. It was a pleasantly neutral remark, safe, like the room. She smiled in kind.

'I am,' she said. 'What's the time?'

'Past noon.'

'Really?' she asked, smiling.

'Really really. Look, please don't be cross with me, but I've been in touch with Annouska Vane-Venables. And good old Ida Spenlowe-Humfrey.'

'Oh?' Her heart tightened.

He continued, though she saw he had registered her

disquiet: 'They're giving out that you've gone away for a holiday. "Gossamer Fane has given freely and unstintingly of all her talents for the benefit of Third World causes and has now gone away for a well-deserved break. All press enquiries should be addressed to Annouska Design Ltd or the Project Aid Foundation." Message ends. I hope you don't mind.'

So now Carey Lambert had broken into her new life. But: 'No, I don't mind,' she said. 'I'm grateful, thank you.'

She looked at him, wide-eyed and penetratingly. 'But I mind about other things,' she said.

'I know,' he replied softly, looking back. His eyes did not glitter, were not hooded. 'That's what I'd like to talk to you about, if you'll let me. Please.' His face appeared to her naked, vulnerable.

'Talk,' she said. 'I'm listening.'

He talked. 'I'll begin at the centre,' he said, 'and work outwards. There was a moment, a defining moment when I dropped my guard and you, as I thought, showed your hand. You will remember it the instant I recall it to you. It was a phone call, me to you. I let slip I knew you were at Shaws. Remember?'

Her voice was the merest disturbance in the still, cool air. 'I remember. I asked you how you knew, and you told me not to be silly, that I'd told you. But I hadn't.'

'No, you hadn't. And I knew you hadn't, and you knew it. But you never followed it up. I have to ask you now, Gossamer: why?'

'I loved you. I was afraid it might spoil everything.'

His voice broke on the quiet rock of her reply. 'Yes. I know that now. The better part of me knew it then, but I denied it. I, Gossamer: the creature I invented, and presented to the world as Carey Lambert. I killed it, that love, that trust. I killed the better part of myself.'

'Why?' She knew the tears were starting and she didn't care. 'My turn, Carey Lambert. Why, why, why?'

His voice, not his eyes, met her question. 'Do you

remember what you said then, Gossamer, after I'd asked why you did not want to tell me you'd been to Shaws?'

'Yes. I told you the true reason.'

'That you had believed, half-believed, I was your father.'

'Yes. I had. It was true. Didn't you believe me?'

'Oh yes,' he said. 'I believed you. Got it wrong.'

'How, Carey? How could you get it wrong?'

'Oh, very simply. I knew who I was, didn't I: the person who stood in place of your father. The lover of your mother. All that.' He groaned. 'Oh Christ, hear me out, let me spill it all out before you!'

She was silent. His voice sawed the air between them:

'It seemed to confirm my worst suspicions about you, it made everything fall into place. It said to me: she knows everything, or thinks she does. She's known all along, and now she's letting you know it, she's got you on the rack where she helped you put yourself and she's going to tighten it, and she's exultant, savouring every moment of it. She is her mother's daughter, after all. She wants to break you up into little pieces, for her own perverted amusement, and then smash the pieces. It's what she's been working up to, all along. It's what she was born for, and she's doing it. So I met like with like. I fought dirty, on your chosen ground. I believed you fully understood what was going on. I respected you for that. I held fast to the knowledge that we both knew exactly what was going on.'

She spoke from the desolation of horror: 'How? How could you believe it?'

'Oh, so very simply: I wanted to. So I found evidence to support it, of course. It's common enough, Gossamer, the self-fulfilling prophecy. Mine was the faith and the revelation, and you played your part to perfection, your part in my sick fantasy. You did, you appeared to do, exactly what was required of you. Like mother, like daughter.'

He choked, gagged. 'There,' he croaked. 'There you have it, the rotten heart of it. Heart of darkness, as you once so rightly put it.'

'But I didn't come looking for you,' Gossamer said helplessly. 'You found me. Didn't you?'

Carey was grim. 'Oh yes, I found you all right. Helen Kepesake told me, as you probably guessed. Lover's talk, Gossamer. You'd guessed that too, that we had been lovers, remember? Something to fill the silence with afterwards, you know, a little conversational offering. "Do let me tell you about this mysterious friend of Jenny's, darling." It was like a bell ringing: something told me it had to be you. All those years I'd deliberately kept myself in total ignorance of your life, and now it was as if you'd reached out to find me, through her. Poor Helen: that was the moment I outgrew her. I knew I had to find you. And so I did. It was no accident, Gossamer. I'd tracked you down and I set it up. I had to see what you looked like, and the minute I saw you I knew it wasn't enough. I had to know everything.'

'So you set that up.'

'Yes. And subsequent meetings. I couldn't leave you alone, you see. I became obsessed. I had to have you. And then I had to go on having you. You were the best, Gossamer, the best ever, right from the first. Your body knew things your mind didn't seem to guess at. And you let me believe I had it all to myself.'

Gossamer's voice was dead. 'Like *she* did.'

'Yes, Gossamer, just like that. Just exactly like that. Except that Madeline wasn't a virgin when I had her, and you were.'

In the same tone she said: 'And except she didn't love you, whereas I did. Loved you completely, adored you, worshipped you, nothing held back. As I said to you once.'

'And as I couldn't believe.'

Tears trickled silently down her cheeks. 'Why, Carey? Why couldn't you?'

'Because you were so good, so gifted, so responsive, so overwhelmingly the skilled and sensual innocent. Too good to be true. For me.'

She felt herself invaded by cruel and hopeless despair.

'For me, you understand, Gossamer. I've tried to do things
right in my life, tried to be open, trusting, accepting, relaxed,
all that. It was the natural way for me to be, once. But it's
been abused so often I've had to unlearn it. What you see,
what the world sees, the ruthlessly successful man the world
knows as Carey Lambert, is the product of that failure. I
couldn't take you at face value, Gossamer, I couldn't handle
it. And so I reacted accordingly to what I convinced myself
must be the truth. And, as Fate would have it, saved my
hardest, most cruel behaviour for the one person I now know
deserved it least. Because, you see, you connived at it. All
unknowingly, you turned my false understanding into what
looked like the naked and brutal truth.'

Now she sobbed freely, wept for the sheer pity and
injustice of it, for the loss of innocence, for the fall from
grace and the expulsion from the garden.

'How did I do that?' she managed to ask. 'How could I?'

'Apart from being what you were, a creature conjured
from my most secret yearning?' He was looking away from
her, haggard, as if he too was wandering alone in his own
country of pain. 'I was being offered everything I'd truly,
secretly wanted and I had to find fault with it, spot the flaw
and exploit it, find my way through the outward show of love
and openness to the devious rottenness that I knew must lie
within. And, of course, I did. Both versions of me got what
they wanted, you see? As that old Chinese proverb says: be
very careful what you wish for lest you be granted it.

'You'd held back on Shaws, you see: there was something
you hadn't been open about. And when I challenged you,
you let fall that you thought, or had thought, I was your
father. That's when the man I wanted to be gave up the
struggle.'

'And after that?' Gossamer whispered hoarsely. 'Are you
saying that after that everything you did was to test me,
prove me false? Revenge yourself? Carey, look at me!' She
struggled up on her elbows like an invalid. '*Everything?*'

His hunted eyes met hers. 'It was at the back of everything. Yes.'

She drew her knees up under the bedclothes and bent over them. She did not want him to see her humiliation, her devastation. Was there no end to this suffering, no breaking this cycle of deadly recurrence? Still his voice continued, implacable, the voice of confession unloading its sins on her soul:

'It informed everything, everything that happened after and everything that had happened before, things you'd said, things you'd done. It was like being given the key to your code, the key I'd been looking for. Things fell into place, Gossamer. Like your friendship with a used-up rent boy, for instance.'

Her head came up and she gasped as if she'd been struck. Her scream was a whispered *no!* But his face, mask-like, continued to move and the words continued to flow:

'One of Daddy Kepesake's hired holes, your friend Anthony, until he got to be too old to be interesting. I know these things, I made it my business to find out. And then there was Trish, the lesbian who screwed men for money, I soon found out you knew all about that, and I got the message, you see: *Remember Madeline, who screwed anything that moved?* Reminding me all the time of my shame and humiliation. So I set up experiments to test my hypothesis. I made you do things with me, things I was used to hiring by the hour from skilled professionals. And you did them, you did them superbly. And I made you do things to yourself, dirty tricks, forbidden things, things men creep into nasty little shops in Old Compton Street to buy pictures of. And you let me photograph them, you flaunted them to the camera like an accomplished performer. But a manipulative one, you see? I was the one you put out to, I was the one who'd taken your virginity. I was your target.'

She found the words to say to him, and flung them at him: 'It hurt, the thing I let you do to me, it was agony, it was like having a stake driven through me and being torn apart by it, I wanted to scream in pain, I almost fainted. And I hated doing those things, it felt filthy, degrading, not just to me but to you as well, to us. But I did it, oh yes, I did it all and let you take pictures of it because you wanted to, I did it because I loved you, I wanted to be everything for you and I didn't want anyone else to do it for you, be it for you, all I wanted was to be the one you wanted. The one you turned to. The one you needed, *me*, Carey, not *it* but *me*. So that you'd stop wanting to do those things, stop needing to do them because love would take the place of that need. That's why I did them, it's why I wanted to. For the same reason I gave you my virginity. I loved you.' She choked on the words, and was overtaken again by sobbing.

He did not move, just sat on the end of the bed as if frozen there. 'I'm letting you into my mind, Gossamer. My mind as it was then. I know it's not nice, I don't expect you to approve of what you find in it. Christ knows I don't. But I want you to understand it, I owe it to you to let you see it all as I so very wrongly saw it, I have to give you the chance to understand the reasons why I acted as I did, no matter what you may think of me afterwards. I won't go on if you don't want me to. Gossamer?'

She closed her eyes. She did not answer. She felt a tissue being pressed gently into her hand. She blew her nose, noisily and messily. Then he continued:

'It was the same, you see. The same with Madeline. The things you said, then and now, the things you did, the lies she told and acted with me. The very same. It felt like a sort of madness, a time-warp hell of my own desires. I couldn't stop myself, didn't want to.'

Outrage fought with misery. 'You're saying I came on like . . . like *she* did?'

Carey's face was impassive, considering. 'I'm saying she put on a convincing act of being as you truly were. Only that's not how it seemed to me, at the time.'

'So you were her first too, were you?' Anger tipped the balance in favour of outrage. 'She was a virgin too. A nymphomaniac virgin whore, just like me.' She heard her own voice sharpened to a wounding edge, didn't care.

He answered calmly, humbly even. 'No, Gossamer. No,

she wasn't a virgin. But she faked herself up to be one, for me. And for Kenneth.'

She was seized with manic hilarity. She shredded the air with savage laughter. She wanted to hurt him with it, and was glad she wanted to. A voice said: *Let him suffer, let him squirm, let him be pinned and wriggling, vulnerable. Stick the knife in, do it now. Enjoy it. Do as you were done by!*

'Oh for Christ's sake, Carey!' she yelled. 'Don't give me all this poor-little-diddums stuff! Faked virginity? Tomato ketchup on your cock afterwards?' The words excited her and the sight of his closed face urged her on. 'Come off it Carey, who do you think you're kidding?'

'Not you, Gossamer Fane. But Madeline was: kidding me, and kidding Kenneth. A little lemon juice and vinegar, a bit of sponge with blood in it, a cry of pain at the right moment.'

Gossamer closed her eyes and wished she could close her ears too, close her mind, disappear, be somewhere else, someone else. Carey's voice reached her again:

'I know, it's grotesque. It's horrible. But it happened, Gossamer, it happened to me. It taught me a lesson, just like Madeline wanted it to. And the real beauty of it, from her point of view, was that all those years later it turned out I hadn't managed to unlearn it. I was very deeply corrupted, as you yourself so rightly pointed out.'

She forced the words out as her screaming mind fought to remove itself: 'You mean, you thought I was faking it? Like mother like daughter?'

'Partly, yes. The part of me that had been busy all those years earning Carey Lambert the bad reputation everyone was so keen to warn you about. It wouldn't let me alone, Gossamer, it wouldn't let me feel the way I wanted to feel about you. It wouldn't let me say, I love you. I love you. It choked the words off.'

Gossamer lay back on the pillows, her eyes closed, those three words echoing in her mind. 'You said once, "What I love about you, Gossamer." Do you remember?'

'Yes, I remember. I fooled it that time, didn't I? I slipped the word past it when it wasn't looking. It punished me for that, Gossamer. It got its revenge on us for that. It started gathering evidence. It made me find what it was looking for.'

Gossamer struggled up, tears streaking her face and blearing her vision. Her hair hung forward in wet strands like beached river-weed. Her breasts strained uncomfortably against the nightdress. 'Evidence? For God's sake Carey, *what* evidence?'

Now he closed his eyes. He rocked gently to and fro. The words came pouring out, a darkly colourless catechism, a lesson learned by rote in pain and cruelty and delivered without intonation:

'Anthony. Trish. Your friends, the sort of people you let me see you liked to have about you. Jeans de Nîmes: your body saying "fuck me" on billboards and TV screens, your lovely tits bared for all to see, your whole body up for sale. You going to Paris with Philippe, young Philippe, handsome Philippe, Philippe the stud. How could such knowledge, such art, reside in innocence? How could it be trusted? When you asked me to help you with Helen's daughter when she got pregnant a voice said to me: See how she reminds you she knows about your past, see how she seeks to torment you with it, leading you on and setting you up. And so I saw. It won.'

Where was she to start? What could she say? It seemed so hopeless. Despair stole through her like an illness and she desired only to yield to it, to cease.

Again, his voice hauled her back. 'I know what you want to say, Gossamer. I said it to myself, back then. And you know the answers, don't you, all those clever persuasive answers, those plausible lies. That's why you're not saying anything. Am I right?'

She understood, perfectly and completely and for the first time, why it was that people could bring themselves to sign confessions to things they had never done and never could have done. It was a matter of survival. They did it for the sake of peace, to make the voices fall silent, to make an end to pain and weariness. They confronted Fate at last, in all its remorseless and unjust cruelty, and gave way to it because there was nothing else to be done. Truth was no shield against Fate. Innocence was no defence. It was a crime, and would be punished. Fate was stronger even than Justice.

All this she knew and understood and, in the wisdom of her engulfing misery, accepted. It wasn't Carey's fault, he was merely its instrument, a weapon fashioned especially for her, for the sole purpose of annihilating her childish illusions. More than that she saw that he, too, was a victim.

She was her mother's daughter. Her inheritance was lust, a feral animal that, once released, could not be destroyed. It accounted for everything, this fatal flaw, this genetic curse of voracious sexuality: it was something she would have to learn to live with, somehow, learn to accommodate and control. Carey had unleashed it, Mike Andersen had been lured and then appalled by it. The knowledge was irresistible. It blew away all the clouds of mystery that before had veiled every episode and every relationship. Everything at last stood clear before her in painful focus. She allowed herself to accept it.

In the exhaustion of her understanding she forgave even herself, which was the hardest thing of all.

Carey had asked: *am I right*? Now she answered with a single whispered word:

'Yes.'

She lay still, her eyes closed, calm in the blessed dark.

'Do you understand me, now?'

'Yes, Carey, I understand. And I forgive you. And Madeline.'

In her darkness there came to her the sound of a sigh: a sigh, as it seemed, of release, of peace, of blessed absolution, the voice of a healed soul. There was one thing she needed to qualify, one misunderstanding to be explained aright before her own healing could properly begin. Quietly, in measured tones, she said:

'Philippe, as you know, is married with three children

and I stayed with them all in Paris. He did ask me to go
to bed with him, but it wasn't there.' She smiled sadly. 'It
was on Hungerford Bridge, of all places. He said why didn't
we go back to his hotel room. I explained about you and he
said, yes, he knew but even so, why couldn't we just make
love as friends, just for fun? And I said no, but I wish now
I'd said yes.' The urge to watch Carey's face as she spoke
was very powerful but she kept her eyes closed because
this was important and she needed to concentrate on it, to
get it right.

'I wish now I'd said yes because it would have been very
enjoyable while we were doing it. I'd have learned all there
is to know about the difference between sex without love,
without adoration and commitment, and sex with it. With
you. I'd have been perfectly friendly and we'd have parted
on perfectly good terms and stayed friends. But I'd have gone
straight to you, wherever you were, whatever you'd been
doing, and I'd have confessed.' She smiled again. 'Gladly
and openly because I should have learned so much, you
see, gained such precious knowledge that it would have
been a greater sin, a greater betrayal, not to share it with
you because there would have been nobody else I ever
wanted to share it with. It would have prevented all the
bad things from happening.' It was as if she spoke about
two other people, mutual acquaintances whom they both
knew intimately: herself as she had been and Carey as he
might have allowed himself to be.

Suddenly, all was silence. She could not even hear his
breathing. The words she needed to say came unbidden
into her mind, and she spoke them: 'I'd have said, "I have
been unfaithful to you, Carey, and now I know that I want
nobody else but you, because I love you."' Now the silence
rang in her ears. '"Please forgive me and take me back, now
that I know I want only to be yours forever."'

He cried out, a terrible shout of rage and pain, a bellow
of terrifying madness. What had she done, what had she
said? His eyes were staring, his face a white rawness: was
he going to strike her? Now he was gasping for breath and

groaning, and she felt frightened. She leaned forward and took his wrists. He was shivering like an epileptic. 'What is it Carey, what's the matter? Are you ill?'

It was true: she had loved him. And she believed what she had said, and she had wanted to share it with him. Surely she had not deceived herself again? It had suddenly seemed such a clean and simple matter to let the light in. Instead she had laid bare another aspect of this man, revealed a wounded animal, at bay. Perhaps a very dangerous animal indeed.

She could think of nothing to do except hold on and be watchful. Slowly his trembling subsided. The colour came back into his face and he blinked and gave her a look of recognition, as if seeing her after an absence. Wherever he had been, to whatever secret and terrible place, he had now returned. She was aware that her breasts were visible below the neckline of her nightdress. She was aware, too, of the tingling in her flesh, of an anticipatory flush of desire as she held him and as he looked at her. Her nipples hardened under the thin cotton.

She kept it, and her voice, under control. 'Are you all right now, Carey?' she asked. 'What was it?'

He smiled, regarding her warmly and appraisingly. 'I am all right now, thank you Gossamer. And what it was, was what you said to me. It hit home.'

She was glad of it, but could not find the words to say so without seeming cruelly triumphant. Yet she was aware too of a tilting in the balance of their relationship, aware that the exercise of control over herself was also an exercise of power over him. She did not let go of his wrists. She looked him in the eyes and said:

'Of course it would have been a great risk, Carey. It might not have happened that way. You might not have been equal to it, after all. You've said yourself you were using me. You might have decided to dispose of me then, scrap me for a new model, rather than carry out your plans for me. It wouldn't have been the first time, would it? You'd have found someone else.'

He did not flinch. He returned her gaze. 'I'd have been a

fool to do that, Gossamer, and you know I'm not a fool.
I could have used you sooner, and to much greater effect.
Who knows what lengths I might have had you go to, what
I might have had you do, to prove your devotion. To make
it up to me. To wipe the slate clean, as it were.'

An image flashed into her mind of Alec Dayfield, naked
and sweaty, bearing down on her, penetrating her offered
sex with harsh thrusts while she angled her body for the
benefit of Carey's hidden camera. Obscene and horrible as
the fantasy was, it differed only in degree from what had
actually taken place, from the plan the man she once loved
had hatched and put into effect, in which her own humiliation
had been a minor but necessary part of the orchestration of
the main theme. There was no need for her to put any of
this into words.

'Who knows, Carey? Why, we do, of course. Don't we.'
She made it a statement that assumed his agreement and
he did not demur. 'Like I say, I should have been running
a great risk but then that's the whole point, isn't it? Would
there have been any point in asking you to meet me and
know me and accept me on the ground of love without
risking everything in the process? And *knowing* what was
being risked?'

This time he spoke the expected answer. Then he said:
'What a terrible pity you did not, after all, take that risk.'

'But then I didn't *know*, did I Carey?'

He could not meet her eyes any longer. 'No, Gossamer.'
The tone was humble, submissive. 'You didn't, and couldn't.
Mea culpa.' Now, she released his wrists. She adjusted her
nightdress so her breasts were fully covered and arranged
her pillows to make herself more comfortable in the bed. Like
a queen granting audience to an errant courtier, she thought.

He looked up, but did not move. 'I was a fool, of course,
a clever one but a fool nonetheless. Also I was a coward. I
knew, but I flinched from the risk. A case of twice bitten,
third time shy. And wrong. So wrong.'

She held her tongue as the implication of his words sank
in. 'Twice?'

'Yes, Gossamer. Twice. It is the last thing I have to tell you.' Now he, too, rearranged himself. He sat at right angles to her on the end of the bed and spoke to a point in the air a little to one side of her.

'There was another. Another woman, Gossamer. After Madeline, and as unlike her as it is possible to be. A good and lovely woman, lovely in every way, brave and beautiful and generous. Her name was Constancia. Constance in English, like my poor sister. An old-fashioned name, an old-fashioned virtue. She had it, and I enjoyed it. And then I lost her.' He paused, and Gossamer felt she knew what he was going to say next. 'She died, Gossamer. My lovely Constancia died and I lost her for ever and ever.'

She gasped with the shock of it though she had known it was coming, but the next shock came without warning. He was looking directly at her now. His face wore an expression of tortured sadness.

'You remind me of her, Gossamer Fane. You remind me of her so much. You could have been the daughter we never had. It wasn't just your appearance, you see, though the resemblance there is very strong. Constancia's parents were refugees from Castro's Cuba and there was very probably some Portuguese in Kenneth's ancestry. And you have her sort of grace and beauty, like liquid sculpture. It was much more than that. It was in your manner, the way you met life, all that freshness and optimism and directness. When I first saw you it was as though she had come back to earth.'

She dragged out the words: 'But you knew I was Madeline's daughter.'

'Yes, Gossamer, I knew you were that as well.'

'And you couldn't forget it.'

A silence. Then, 'No.'

Now he was waiting for her. She found the words came quite coolly and calmly. They might have been discussing a game of chess.

'You wanted your revenge on Madeline, of course, so you looked for the Madeline in me, and you found it. And then you were able to feel you were doing to her what she'd done to you, making her feel as you had felt. Used and corrupted, soiled with betrayal. It was Madeline's body in those photographs, wasn't it?' He nodded assent and she continued:

'She was the one you raped in your office. She was all the women you've been cruel to, all the women you've hurt.' Again, an almost imperceptible nod. 'But none of them reminded you of Constancia, did they?'

His lips barely moved. 'No. That's what made it—'

'Of course,' she said, quietly and matter-of-factly. 'And Alec Dayfield was a business rival who had done you harm in the past, in the other part of your life, so you chose him.'

'He was more than that, Gossamer. My reason for choosing him was much more compelling than that.'

She knew then that she was going to look into the very heart of Carey Lambert's darkness, if he should choose to reveal it.

'We both loved her, Gossamer, Alec and I. It was the same for both of us, exactly the same. He was my boss then, at Rimer Dayfield, remember? I was his media buyer. She worked for his art director. I won't do dirt on him, Gossamer, though you know for yourself what his attitude to women is. But it wasn't like that with Constancia. He really did love her. The trouble was, so did I. He couldn't believe it when she chose me, couldn't understand why, when he had his own genuine love to offer her on top of everything else, she should choose someone who had so much less to give her. When he sacked me I think it was as much to punish her for sheer stupidity and ingratitude as to get his revenge on me for stealing her, as he saw it. He thought she'd come to her senses soon enough, and go to him.

'Only she didn't. She died instead, and somehow he worked it out that I was to blame for it. Me. Christ.' His voice caught, but he recovered himself. 'He reckoned I'd caused it somehow, to get even with him for sacking me. That was the cause of our rivalry, Gossamer. That's why he didn't just sack me, he tried his best to make sure I'd never work in the business again. Then, when I'd boot-strapped my way back, he bought his way into my own agency, and got me kicked out of it. That's the real fucking irony of it. Before Constancia we were a team, Alec and I. Christ, what we couldn't have done between us! We'd have conquered the whole fucking world. But once I'd got going again on my own, there at the back of his mind all the time, in everything he did, was the desire to see me fall down in the dirt and not get up again. Sure, we had to co-operate in a few things, like I told you. That's business. He's DayStar, I'm OffWorld, it wasn't a one-to-one thing. But I was always waiting for the third and fatal blow. Kill or be killed, right? And suddenly I found I had what looked like the perfect weapon of self-defence.'

He laughed harshly, mirthlessly. 'The ultimate pre-emptive strike.' The laugh ended in a groan.

He held his hands out across the bed, palms up. 'Except I had to fight myself first, before I could use it. You know how I did that. You know how you inadvertently helped me do it.' She saw his hands were trembling and put her own hands under the bedclothes lest she be tempted to reach out and take them. He seemed to acknowledge and approve her action.

'It wasn't like that from the beginning, Gossamer. I won't say you have to believe that, I haven't got the right to, but it's true. I didn't even know the fight was going on, at first. But when I did, that was when one side started playing dirty. And all the old poison came out. There was Dayfield, my enemy not my competitor. There were you, Madeline's daughter not Kenneth's. Both of you mocking all my love and loss. Like I said, it was compelling. Revenge and safety and catharsis, all at one stroke.

'It felt like Fate, Gossamer. My own special Fate but I couldn't control it or change it or even know about it. Do you know what that's like, to feel you've been going along all your life like a character in a book that's being written by someone else and that the only way you can possibly cope with it all or perhaps even be happy is just to live in the moment, not look back and not try to guess ahead, just accept it? But that just accepting it is the hardest thing of all to do?'

'Yes,' she cried. 'Oh yes!' She did not restrain herself now. She had thought it was something peculiar to her, this feeling, something nobody else could know or understand. She took his hands in hers, clasped them, felt their warmth and strength as they squeezed hers back. His smile was warm, his eyes crinkled without a hint of mockery. How strange it was, or perhaps how fitting, that Carey Lambert should be the one to know and understand her most secret self, that this should be the ground they met on at last.

And even now he articulated her thoughts: 'Perhaps that's the secret, Gossamer, perhaps that's the answer. Perhaps if we can do that hardest thing of all and give way to it, then we can actually take charge of our destinies a little bit, gain a little control over the flow of life, and then perhaps a little bit more again, slowly. Perhaps that's how we can begin to come off the page and live for real.'

And she said softly: 'Yes.'

Their hands clasped once more, briefly, then parted. Much had altered in the last few moments and much had been explained and understood before then but there was still the chess board, and there had been no victory.

'Your plan didn't come off, Carey.'

'No. And within twenty-four hours I knew how wrong I had been. I couldn't bring myself to contemplate what I'd done. And then, later, I was seized with the most terrible fear for you. I sent Mike Andersen out to find you and protect you. I felt responsible for your safety, I had to know you were all right and that I hadn't driven you away to your death.'

'But there's still Alec Dayfield. He has more reason than ever to harm you now.'

'No Gossamer,' he said gently. 'Bless you for thinking of that, but no. I have made my peace with Alec, you see. We're just business rivals now: ours is a good, clean dirty fight. Forgive me, Gossamer. You should have been the first, after poor Kevin Germain, but you weren't here. I had to tell him.'

'About me? And you, and – everything?'

'He knew about her already, Gossamer. As I say, we were good friends once.' He shrugged. 'Until he convinced himself I'd stolen Constancia off him to get even with men generally, because of what Madeline had been. But he didn't know anything else. Now he knows everything. I'm sorry.'

'It's all right. I'm glad you told him. I'd want you to, if you hadn't.'

'I know,' he said, and smiled his lovely smile again. 'It's one of the things I—' His eyes closed at the sound of her sharply indrawn breath, and his head dropped. 'I'm sorry.'

He stood up and walked to the window, pulling the curtains back to look out on the grey day while her heart stopped racing. He cleared his throat and, without turning, said: 'I sent Mike Andersen after you, after you went to Africa. He worked for me then, Alec poached him after he got back. Fair enough. I had to know you were all right, Gossamer, you see, given what blew up when you were there. I couldn't have your death on my conscience. I don't think I could have made myself hard enough to live with that. I didn't tell him anything, though. That probably accounts for any strangeness you may have noted in his attitude to you.'

Another mystery explained, another knot untied.

His back was still towards her. She could not see whether he knew that she and Mike had been lovers, that he too had had her love, once upon a time. 'You could tell him yourself, of course. I don't have his home address but you could get in touch with him at DayStar. Of course there's always the danger he may think the truth about you is just as bad.' His shoulders hunched. 'I did, for a while, and God knows I ought to have known better.'

'It's all right,' she said. She remembered Mike as he had been last night, his desire and his repugnance. She remembered making love with him, and quickly made herself stop remembering. 'It doesn't matter,' she said, not quite knowing what she meant.

Carey turned but remained where he was. 'It's up to you, of course. It's not my secret any more, thank God. Of course it never should have been a secret at all and if I could go back in time and – but there we are, you can't go back, can you?'

'No,' she said, 'you can't go back, in that sense.'

'I'm sorry, Gossamer.'

'It wasn't all your fault, Carey.'

'Well, no, I admit Madeline wasn't, but—' His voice faltered.

'That wasn't what I meant. I mean that I can see how some of it was my fault, too. I can see now how naïve I was, a dangerous innocent. That night at the French Embassy, for instance – the first night I mean, when you took me – I can see now how it must have looked as if I was flirting with Jean-Luc Frémont. It was just inexperience and immaturity, Carey, and enjoying feeling like an adult, not scared or awkward. And being very lonely, as well as scared and awkward, as a girl. I wanted to be like the people I was with, do you understand that?'

'Oh yes. Protective colouring. Wanting to belong. You don't have to be raised in an orphanage to have a lonely childhood, Gossamer. People with mothers and fathers and brothers and sisters can have those, too. It can make you behave the way you think people want you to.'

'Yes, that's it! And I did it with you, too. When we were – together. I suppose that made it worse.'

'Yes,' he said simply. 'If you mean what I think you mean. I don't mean when we made love, Gossamer. I mean the other things, the bad things. I wanted like hell for you not to let me do them to you.'

'That wasn't just immaturity, Carey. You know it was also because I loved you.'

'I know, Gossamer.'

She grinned weakly. 'A deadly combination.'

He grinned back. 'I ought to have had enough maturity

for both of us,' he said. 'And the capacity to love as you loved me.'

Abruptly, he seemed to change the subject, change gear. He became brisk and impersonal. 'I have to go away for a bit, Gossamer. DayStar and OffWorld are going to co-operate on one or two things – not a merger or anything like that, just a pooling of resources in some areas which is designed to strengthen us both and widen the market for satellite generally. All part of the rapprochement. I expect you'd like to get away for a while, too. Last night's fuss will have died down in a couple of days, I can assure you; meanwhile I've arranged to have your car brought here and if you give Miranda your key she can get you anything you want from your flat. So, you can feel perfectly safe here, all right?'

Gossamer blinked. 'Yes, fine. Thank you.'

'Oh don't thank me, Gossamer. Please. I can tell you that if there's one person I'd be prepared to share my life with it's you. It couldn't be as it was before, of course, but we've both been through a lot to get to where we are now, and we've been through much of it together, one way and another. It seems a pity to waste what we can salvage from that. It is your understanding I crave and not your devotion, which I didn't deserve then and don't now. You couldn't possibly 'reform' me, Gossamer, but you do alter for the better the balance of my personality because you connect as nobody living can connect with the better part of me.

'You could make a good man very happy. I believe there are good men to be found occasionally. I, as you know, am not one of them. This is a proposal of marriage, Gossamer. I don't deserve you and you deserve much better than me, but if you accept, it must be on the basis that we both know and understand what we truly are. I have no hopes that you will accept, but I do hope we can stay friends.'

Dumbfounded, she watched him cross to the bedroom door.

'I shall be thinking of you on your birthday, Gossamer.' He gave her a half-smile. 'They say Florida is very nice at this time of year.'

* * *

When she left London two days later it was not for Florida but for a place that belonged much deeper in her past, to a time when she had no choices to make nor any power to make them, and tomorrow would always be the same as today.

Now, she was staking everything on the unforseeable outcome of one freely chosen action.

❋ Nineteen ❋

Gossamer had taken her lunch in silence under the blessedly unquestioning eyes of the Sisters. She went to her cell afterwards to give Reverend Mother time to return from None. Now she stood outside the door. She raised her hand and knocked on it, and the familiar voice, softly authoritative, bade her enter.

A great calm took possession of her as she stepped into the room. Had she been here before? She supposed she must have been, but it was her expectations that were confirmed rather than her conscious memories: the white walls, the crucifix and the plain wooden furnishings she might have remembered, even perhaps the telephone, but not the fax machine or the PC. Yet they did not look out of place. Perhaps it was the room's human occupant that held all its trappings in harmony, the woman who now smiled and took Gossamer's hand in hers.

'It is very good to see you, my dear. Do sit down. There will be tea in a little while. I hope you had lunch?'

'Yes thank you. I didn't realise how tired I was, last night,' she added.

'It is a long journey,' she said. 'And you have your troubles, my child.'

Gossamer looked up sharply. The words, though gently spoken, were like cold water in her face. 'Is it so obvious?' she asked.

Reverend Mother smiled. 'Oh, yes my dear. It always was. With some children one can never really tell what is going on inside, but with you I always could. You have a window, for those who are fortunate enough to look through it.'

Gossamer blushed. 'You make me feel like a small child again,' she said.

Reverend Mother laughed. 'But of course! We are all the children we once were, though some of us, alas, go to terrible lengths to conceal it. Now, let us talk of other things for a little while, shall we?' Gossamer nodded gratefully and answered questions about the comfort of her room and what she had been doing that morning.

'And do you find it greatly changed, my dear?'

'No, not at all really. I'm amazed how much has come flooding back, how much I'd forgotten I knew. In some ways it's as if I'd never been away,' she said. She smiled. 'You haven't changed a bit, Reverend Mother.'

The woman laughed merrily. 'And why do you suppose that is, my dear? Do you think it's the serene and tranquil life I lead here – or is it because I must have looked very ancient to you fifteen years ago as well?'

Gossamer, happily relaxed, joined in the laughter. A young woman dressed in the habit of a novice brought in tea and for a while they indulged in safe chatter over the cups as the short winter day darkened towards evening. Gossamer learned, among other things, that Sister Agnes was now Head Teacher at a Convent School in Newcastle, and that Sister Bernadette was working at a Mission School in Peru. Gossamer told her about the school in Ethiopia, about Jean Tennant and Father Bernahu, and saw her lips move in silent prayer as the terrible story was told. She said nothing about Mike. Later, perhaps.

At length the other woman spoke a little about herself.

'Life here, as you have observed my dear, has changed very little. And lately, I must confess, it has seemed to me that everything here is indeed going along so smoothly and easily that nothing needs to be disturbed or altered in any way.' She set down her cup. 'And that of course means only one thing.'

'Oh?'

'It means, of course, that it is high time I made way for a new Reverend Mother. The appearance of perfection is a sure sign of failing sight, since the reality is not to be found in this world. I feel it is time for me to go. It is a good thing you came when you did, Gossamer: in a few weeks time I shall have retired. I am greatly looking forward to leading the simpler life once again as Sister Veronica. I daresay the new Reverend Mother will find me work to do in the office, now that I have at last managed to penetrate the mysteries of the modem and the spreadsheet.'

She allowed a little time to pass in silence, then: 'And now my dear it is I think time for you to tell me the purpose of your visit.'

Gossamer met the other woman's kind untroubled eyes. 'I think you could probably tell me,' she said.

'Well, it is not such a very great feat my dear. You're not the first to ask and I'm sure you won't be the last. You have arrived at a place where you find you cannot go forward until you have learned all there is to know about where you have come from. Yes?'

'Yes,' Gossamer breathed. 'Yes, that's exactly it.'

'But not all of it, I think?' She let the question hang between them. 'Well, we may see if I am correct about that. As it is, I fear I may not be in a position to tell you more than you already know.'

Gossamer felt suddenly on the verge of despair. Was Reverend Mother about to tell her, as Kevin Germain had done, that there were things she was not permitted to know, still more hidden keys to unseen locks? But the woman continued:

'I mean only, my dear, that there is very little to tell.'

'Please tell it,' said Gossamer. 'Everything you know. You were Reverend Mother here when I – when I arrived?'

Mother Veronica nodded.

'How – how did it happen.'

'Oh, very much in the usual way, my dear,' Mother Veronica replied, smiling. 'A long ring at the bell, to make sure we heard it, and there you were. We had just finished Compline and were preparing for bed. It was a very cold night, but you were well wrapped up and in perfect health.

About half an hour later there was a telephone call. A man's voice: "There is a baby girl on your doorstep. She has no parents. There is no point in your trying to find out who she is." That was all he said.'

Gossamer tried to imagine the scene, imagine a younger Carey calling to say what he had done. She tried to picture his face as he hung up.

'Can you remember what he sounded like?'

'A young man, obviously an educated one from the words he used. No accent that I could hear, although his voice did sound a little strained even allowing for the fact that he was telephoning from a public call box on the A1.' She smiled again at Gossamer's look of amazement.

'Public telephones made a bleeping noise in those days, until you put your money in, and I could hear the lorries going past in the background. And of course I made sure to notice things and remember them, so I could tell the police.'

'The police?' She had never thought of this aspect before.

'But of course, child. Remember that it is a criminal offence to neglect or abandon a child, or it may even be a case of abduction; we should be breaking the law if we did not notify the police at once. And indeed, in many cases, the police are able to trace the mother, or she is granted the blessing of remorse and comes forward. If not, or if we subsequently become the guardians of the infant in any case, then there are all the formalities of registration to be observed. We are in the world, even if we are not wholly of it.'

'Yes,' Gossamer said. 'Of course. So there was an enquiry.'

'A very extensive one. But at the end of it, all we had was you. And a piece of paper with your date of birth on it.'

'And my name?' Carey had never mentioned that. Nor had he said anything about making a phone-call, just that he had driven away in his hired car, off into the black winter night, alone.

'How did I get my name, Reverend Mother?'

'Think of your Latin, my dear. *Fanum, fani*, a holy sanctuary. Hence Fane. I hope you like it.'

'You chose it?' The Reverend Mother bowed her head. 'Yes, I do like it, it's lovely. Thank you.'

'It was Sister Bernadette who christened you. She said it suited you, so helpless and beautiful and trusting.'

'I should like to thank her, too, one day.'

'Well, perhaps you shall, my dear. I can give you the address of her Mission, and I'd be very surprised if you did not have mutual acquaintances through the work of Project Aid.'

Gossamer's eyes widened. 'You know about that?'

Mother Veronica laughed. 'Why, of course we do! We were your guardians, Gossamer; that is not just a form of words. We followed your progress very closely after you left us, all the way through your schooling until you were eighteen. And we are not a Closed Order; we are allowed to read newspapers, you know.'

Newspapers. They had read about her, this good and moral woman had read about her in the newspapers. Gossamer blushed wretchedly. Malling Benedict. Jeans de Nîmes . . .

'Those advertisements . . . ?'

Mother Veronica nodded, smiling. 'We all agreed you looked very innocent, my dear. Very innocent and lovely, as God made you to be.'

Or naïve and voluptuous, as Carey Lambert had found her. A whore disguised as a virgin, as her mother's blood had condemned her to be . . .

'The world can be a cruel place, Gossamer. So often it exploits and then destroys what it most admires but does not choose to understand.'

'Yes.'

'I am only permitted to imagine how difficult it must be to live in the world with integrity as a young and beautiful woman without the discipline of Faith to sustain her in times of trial and doubt.'

Gossamer seized gratefully on her words. They led back

to the questions she had to ask, the information she had to discover.

'But I don't have the discipline of Faith, I'm not a Roman Catholic. Why not? Why was I treated differently from the others when I was here, if you were my guardians?'

But Mother Veronica was smiling again, and shaking her head. 'I think you may be imagining that we received secret instructions forbidding you to be raised in the Catholic Faith, instructions from your father perhaps? The true explanation is so much simpler than that, Gossamer. When we have instructions from relatives or trustees to raise an orphan as a Catholic, or when we know for certain that a child's parents were Catholics, then we raise the infant as a Catholic and we ensure that this continues afterwards. When we do not, we do not. In your case, as in a fair number of others, we did not.'

'But there weren't any others; I was the only one who was different!'

Again the woman shook her head, but sadly this time. 'So it may have seemed to you, child, but it was not so. Ask Sister Ignatius Loyola, if you like; she has a formidable memory for these things! Ask yourself: how aware were you, the little girl you were then, of all the circumstances of those around you, particularly of those even younger than you or those who did not belong to your own immediate little world of Sister Agnes's group? A child's world, never mind her world-within-a-world, is so very small, isn't it? We often feel lonely and isolated when we are children, when there is so much that we do not and cannot comprehend. But then, after all, we see through a glass darkly, don't we? And then, when at times we have the same feeling as adults, we can see that in reality it was not so, and is not so.'

Gossamer's head swarmed with echoes and voices, her own voice, Carey's voice, the voice of a lonely little girl in a cold winter playground, echoes of all the times when the loveliness of belonging had been taken from her just as she had allowed herself to accept it. She choked down the sob that rose in her, made a great effort to keep her voice under control:

'But I was different, wasn't I, Reverend Mother? None of the other girls at the Convent had a trust fund, did they? Nobody else progressed to Shaws when they left the care of the Sisters of the Order of the Tears of Mary.'

Mother Veronica's face was impassive. 'No, Gossamer, that is so. That was your particular fortune.'

'Please tell me about that.'

Mother Veronica seemed to choose her words with especial care.

'A few weeks after you came into our lives, Gossamer, I had a letter from a firm of solicitors in London, a firm with which for many years the Order has from time to time had dealings. We are not wholly out of the world, you see: there are various matters to be managed, both legal and financial, in the running of a Religious House, and it is vital that they be managed properly. For over fifty years now we have entrusted this to the firm of Chatteris Choate.

'It was to do with . . . a rather unusual bequest, shall we say, that they now contacted us. A Mr Germain wrote to say that an anonymous client wished to bestow a substantial sum of money for what he called "a very specific matter" concerning the orphanage here, and he asked if he could come in person to discuss it with me as it was a matter of the utmost confidentiality. Naturally, I agreed to this request and in due course he came.

'I was soon able to establish that this was not a matter of a will, that the benefactor was someone still living. I must say that I was relieved, Gossamer.' Mother Veronica smiled a little wanly. 'Wills are sometimes contested, I'm afraid, by relatives who find themselves unhappy with the thought of their loved one's money going to a lot of nuns. Mr Germain said that he was permitted to tell me that his client had instructed him to set up a trust whose purpose was to pay for the best education possible for a child in our care, who would upon attaining his or her majority acquire full control of all the assets that were still in it. He gave me to understand that this would be a substantial sum. The he asked me if we had . . . "acquired" was the word he used, "acquired any infant orphans lately". I told him, yes, we had. I did not, at that stage, tell him any more than that. Police enquiries were still continuing, quite apart from any other consideration.

'He said he wished the matter to be arranged as quickly as possible, for two reasons. First, because it would be as well for the trust to be set up soon, so as to get the money to work, and secondly . . .' She paused. 'Secondly, because his client, being unable ever to fulfil personally the function of a natural parent, wished to bestow the maximum possible benefit upon the orphan child in question, anonymously and at a distance. He added that his client had given instructions that the child's name not be made known to him on any account, although of course Chatteris Choate would need to know it. And then he said there was another condition.'

She paused again, and swallowed, collecting her thoughts. Gossamer was desperate to know what this other condition was but she knew she must be patient just a little longer. She knew that, one way or the other, it would lead to what she most needed to find.

'Thank you for bearing with me, my dear. The other condition was that nobody concerned with the welfare and upbringing of the child should ever seek by any means to discover the identity of its benefactor. To do so would immediately and irrevocably invalidate the trust and all payments from it would cease, including those payable to the child upon attaining its majority. Mr Germain was at pains to assure me that if he knowingly allowed such enquiries to be made, by any means whatsoever, and did not immediately cease payments then he himself would be liable for an action in Breach of Trust. As you may imagine, my dear, this was for him by far the gravest aspect of the whole affair.'

Again, Gossamer waited; again, she forebore to ask the question that cried out for an answer. Again, she knew that Mother Veronica read her thoughts and would give it.

'Of course I suspected, Gossamer. That last clause on its own made me suspect that this mysterious individual must be your father; it seemed like a sort of blackmail, especially as Mr Germain gave me to understand – correctly, as it turned out – that the trust wished to make a regular donation to the work of the Convent as a whole, as soon as the other matter was attended to. I asked for time to consider his proposal and he replied that he would be staying overnight in the vicinity. But, as it happened, I only required to go to Vespers and I was able to give him my answer at six o'clock that evening.

'I was tempted, Gossamer, by the argument that even if you were this unknown rich man's daughter it was clearly going to be better for you to be brought up as an orphan if this was how he felt about being your father. I rejected that argument, of course, as the Devil's logic. Two wrongs can never make a right, and it is clear to me that children belong with their parents except in cases of extreme incompetence, or worse. I decided instead to trust equally to Divine and secular judgement.

'I told Mr Germain that we had recently taken into our care a baby girl born on December 20th, well nourished and in good health, with black hair and blue eyes. That was the sum total of my knowledge of you, of course. I told him that, in accordance with the procedure in all such cases, police enquiries were being made with a view to discovering your identity, and I asked him if his client would withdraw his offer if I informed the police that it had been made. He said that provided I told them exactly what he had told me – that he had an anonymous client who wished to provide for an infant orphan in our care – there would be no objection. Indeed, he offered to communicate as much to the police on his return to London. That encouraged me.'

Carey's voice: *Money buys discretion, lots of it, in certain circles*. It would never have occurred to Mother Veronica that Germain's influence could buy off a police enquiry. 'And the Divine judgement?' Gossamer asked.

'Well, it was hardly that, my dear. Divine judgements are

not ours to reach. All we can do is humbly pray for Divine assistance in our own, as I did. I asked him if he believed in God and he said he did; so then I asked him if would be prepared to swear on God's Holy Word that his client was not the father of the baby girl we had taken in.'

So, thought Gossamer, even this wise woman could be as naïve as that. But she was not wholly right.

'He simply said, "No." And then he said, "Neither, and for the same reason, could I take a Bible oath that my client *was* her father."'

Kevin Germain had acted on what Carey Lambert told him, but *He assumed you were my by-blow*.

'That was what decided me, Gossamer. It seemed to me to be an honest answer.'

'Perhaps,' said Gossamer quietly, 'it was just a truthful one.'

The Reverend Mother's pale blue eyes regarded her frankly and piercingly. 'Perhaps you're right, my dear,' she murmured. 'Perhaps that's all it was, after all. In which case what I did was wrong, and you must blame me for it.'

There flashed into Gossamer's mind a vision of how things might have been if Mother Veronica had turned Germain down, of a life lived simply and ordinarily in focus. Of a girl growing naturally to womanhood as others did, with joys and sorrows to share, not condemned to suffer terrifying uncertainty in solitude.

All her life she had been so desperately alone, drifting in an ocean of doubt and loneliness. Now, just as she believed she had come at last to a safe shore, the person who had been the unwitting collaborator in the genesis of all her troubles sat before her, inviting condemnation; saying, as Carey Lambert had said, *mea culpa* and awaiting just punishment at her hands.

It had been a terrible and at times dangerous voyage. Now, surely it was safe to believe that it was over. Now, on her twenty-first birthday, and here, where the journey had begun, was the time and the place to start afresh.

'No,' Gossamer replied, laying her hand on Mother Veronica's. 'No, it wasn't wrong and I don't blame you. I am glad, now, that you decided as you did.'

The old woman smiled. There were tears in her eyes as she enfolded Gossamer's hand in hers. 'Perhaps you would accompany me to Vespers, my dear.' She held Gossamer with her eyes. 'And then, perhaps, you can tell me what you have discovered about your father.'

Gossamer returned her look. 'I should like to do that,' she said.

In the simple beauty of the chapel, amid the sweet praising voices of the Sisters, Gossamer calmly prepared herself also to tell what she had discovered about herself.

When Mother Veronica had said her private prayers after Vespers she asked Gossamer if she would like to take supper in her office, apart from the others, and Gossamer gratefully accepted.

She gave her narrative without interruption, save for the occasional nod or murmur. Time passed outside the room, and in it, but in different ways. Supper was prepared and eaten and cleared away, children were made ready for bed, Compline was sung and the night drew down. Inside, Gossamer wove the strands of her story together with those of all the people whose lives had touched hers and shaped it. She omitted nothing, spared nothing. Mike was in it, and Jean-Luc, and Jenny and Marie; Anthony, Trish, Ida Spenlowe, Philippe, Giles Bamburgh; Jake Carrington and Alec Dayfield; Pope Benedict.

And Carey Lambert, most of all, in all his cruelty and beauty. She spared him nothing and did him no dishonour. To do so would have been to misrepresent herself. She saw, as if for the first time, how each had shaped the other in ways that went far beyond those of conscious action. Fate had made them the way they were, and Fate had bound them together from the very beginning of her life, but the blame would be theirs alone if they chose to make the worst of that destiny. They would both have to learn, one way or another, to accept it and live with it, without delusions.

Carey himself had proposed a way of doing that. That was why she was here, laying the whole of it before the person who had been the earliest influence in her life, a woman who, though not infallible, might see things clearly as no other could. Already, by repeating what Kevin Germain had told her all those years ago, she had confirmed to Gossamer that what Carey had told her was true. It was not this woman's advice she wanted so much as a sign from her, to guide her in one direction or another. And very possibly Mother Veronica would not even know she was giving it. She hoped it was not blasphemous to think of Mother Veronica as a sort of oracle.

All this passed through her mind at the same time as she spoke of DayStar and OffWorld, of Carey Lambert and Alec Dayfield and Mike Andersen, of love and lust, trust and betrayal, desire and loathing. All of them inexplicable, but now perhaps on the brink of being made clear at last.

And as she spoke, her mind gave her the picture of three girls in a red room, the Velvet Girls, of herself dealing the cards, one at a time, from Jenny's Tarot pack. The Page of Wands, all fire and heat, laying out paths and perils to choose between. There was the Moon for delusion and self-deception, and the Devil who stood for thraldom and cruelty. And there were the two powerful older men, the King of Swords and the King of Cups, both attractive, both clever, both combative, both vengeful, both creative and successful, like mirror images of each other.

She blinked and, momentarily, stumbled in her narrative, but Mother Veronica seemed not to notice. *Alec and Carey*. Alec, who pursued Carey out of vengeance for a woman lost to him; Carey, who saw in Gossamer the likeness of that same woman, lost by him to Death and still desired, but who saw also that which he had most cause to loathe and fear and be revenged on. And of course Alec must have seen it too, this resemblance to his lost Constancia, and now he too knew the truth of her origins, knew that she carried in her the genes of the woman who had betrayed his rival and blighted his life. She knew too of her attraction for the man and that it had the potential to run both ways. The three of them were bound up together in the same rope of Fate.

Alec and Carey. Old partners turned to deadly combat, and now perhaps to wary friendship in a business partnership. Both involved with her, in her Fate and in her past life. And which was which of these kings, who was Cups and who was Swords? The Tarot spoke only of possibilities and potentialities, not of proofs or answers.

And what had she, the Page of Wands, got on her side, to guide her and help her? She saw again the two Pentacles that offered financial security and reward for practicality and patience in her work. There seemed little comfort there, little protection with which to weather the great storms the Tarot had held in store for her.

Her voice told Mother Veronica about the night of the Fashion Extravaganza.

And there in the House of Friendship, where comfort ought to be found, stood the hidden figure of the Emperor Reversed. There was the greatest danger of all, the trusted ally revealed, perhaps too late, as the deadliest foe of all. Someone cold and calculating, someone who used his power over her to manipulate her for his own ends. Mike had been a friend first, he had offered her a strong hand out of her difficulty and then she had yielded gladly to him as a lover. And then he had been cold and dead, shutting her out. Mike would be there too, in her life to come, with Carey and Alec if she chose to follow the one clear path that seemed to lie ahead.

But then he might be Alec or Carey, this dangerous Emperor; the Tarot dealt in aspects and personalities, not necessarily in individual human beings. Could he be Jean-Luc, perhaps? Need it be a man at all? Her mind's eye touched on Ida Spenlowe-Humfrey; even, wildly, on Mother Veronica . . .

The thought was shocking, disgraceful. Her mind had been playing games with her, silly superstitious childish games. She glanced at the Reverend Mother as if expecting to see appalled recognition in her eyes, but there was none. She realised that she had stopped talking, and that the woman was waiting patiently for her to continue.

'I'm sorry, where was I?'

'I think, my dear, that you were about to tell me that Mr Lambert has proposed marriage to you.'

'And do you love him?'

The words dropped gently into the still pool of silence.

'I know I did love him,' Gossamer replied slowly. 'But it seems like a long time ago. I'm not sure I know what love means, now. Do you?'

As soon as the words were out she knew she should not have spoken them, not to a nun who had renounced the love of men and women for the adoration of Christ. But the woman appeared unoffended. She answered calmly:

'I know it as a quickening of the spirit and a lifting of the heart. It is like breathing clean fresh air when you have been stifled. It is an understanding, flowing back and forth, something so strong and so deep that it cannot be broken by any small events on the surface of life. I know it as an abandonment to trust, complete and undoubting trust.' She smiled. 'And there are things I remember, too. The thrill of his presence in the same room, or the sight of his handwriting on an envelope. Touching his possessions to call him into being when he was far away from me.'

Gossamer's eyes asked the question.

'He fell at Arromanches, Gossamer. On June 7th 1944.'

'I'm so sorry.' She could find no other words.

'Don't be, my dear. Not for me. Be sorry for him, as I found at last that I could be. I continue to know the meaning of love.'

Gossamer wanted urgently to understand. 'That's why you became a nun, then? Because you lost him?'

She shook her head. 'No, my dear. It is why I thought I wanted to become a nun but it was not the reason I took my Vows. You cannot enter Orders as a means of escaping or hiding. It must be the joyful commitment of a full heart, and not the broken resignation of a despairing one, as mine was at the beginning. And I believe, Gossamer, that the same must be true of marriage, which is also a commitment for life, and for the making of life.'

'Yes,' said Gossamer very quietly.

'Do you feel ready in yourself for such an undertaking, with any man?'

'I feel I must,' said Gossamer bluntly, realising in that instant that in four simple words she had spoken the most important truth about herself. 'I feel I must take myself out of circulation. It's sex, Mother Veronica. I have to acknowledge that my problem is sexual desire, which is a special problem for me because of the way I look. I'm not boasting about that or anything, it's not as if it's an achievement, it's simply a fact.'

Mother Veronica nodded, understanding, accepting.

'Sex is something that's been set free in me, and I can't put it back. But I'm also a romantic, and I think – I'm not blaming anybody, or anything, but it's what I believe – I think that's to do with the way I've been brought up. I've been trained to be innocent, taught to believe in pure romantic love. But I know how I respond sexually and it's no use my pretending I don't. Knowing I'm Madeline's daughter makes it easier to understand this feeling of, of – terrible compulsion, even though it also makes it worse, knowing what she was and what she did. But the other part of me yearns for love and partnership and trust, wants to be clean and happy and secure. Every time I think I've got it I give way to the sexual part of my nature and everything comes crashing down, it's all spoiled.'

Mother Veronica's face showed anguish now, and Gossamer laughed. She felt a little hysterical but felt also that she had it under control.

'I know, I sound like the girl who can't say "no". But I'm not. I said "no" to Jean-Luc because I was terrified of what would happen, but part of me wanted it and wanted him to do it. Oh God, I masturbated after he'd gone, masturbated to orgasm. And then I had sex with Trish because I believed that was safe, somehow, because she wasn't a man, but I know I was just kidding myself. If I don't do something about it, it'll destroy me and ruin other people and I'd give anything not to have that happen.'

Her tongue ran on: 'I know I'm young, but—'. And, shatteringly, she had a vision of Mike, of Mike's face when she had said that to him: sickened, revolted. She fought to wrench back control. 'I really do feel I've learned all I want to learn about it, I can't bear to prove it any more or I'll be—'

She found the right word, one she knew Mother Veronica would fully comprehend. 'I feel that I am in very grave and present danger of being demoralised, Reverend Mother.' And she saw that Mother Veronica understood her perfectly. The woman's hand came gently forward and rested on Gossamer's forehead, and a soft prayer was spoken.

'That is what I want to turn away from. I need to be married to do that, I need to settle down to it and work at it and let it fill my life, be always there in every part of it. And I want the real, hard rewarding work of being a mother. I want to be able to make my fire burn properly, give warmth and comfort. Give life, not destroy it.' She looked beseechingly across the table, imploring Mother Veronica to meet her in understanding.

'It is better to marry than to burn, isn't it?'

'So the Apostle Paul teaches, my dear, although of course that particular piece of wisdom was addressed to men, wasn't it. We can only assume that it was not permitted to him to understand a woman's nature.' A note of acerbity had entered her voice, and Gossamer saw to her surprise that her eyes were twinkling. 'What a pity he cannot be present to discuss the matter with the two of us. It would be such a blessed act of charity to help him over his shock, don't you think?'

Her mouth twitched into a mischievous smile. Gossamer returned it, and they fell to giggling.

Mother Veronica's hand closed on hers again. 'Yes, it is

better to marry than to burn. And I beg you to believe that I, an old virgin woman, have felt those flames and know what it is to yearn as you do.'

'I do believe it.'

'And I believe that you sincerely seek marriage, and to be the mother of your husband's children, and to make that your foundation-stone. And so I have to ask why it is that you consider marriage to this man, this Carey Lambert?'

Gossamer considered calmly: 'I think it's because of what you said about love being understanding. I don't think I'll ever be capable of adoration again, romantic love in that sense, and I don't think I want to be. I feel it's something I've had to grow out of – because of him, of course. I do know I am very attracted to him sexually and I know that's not the most important thing but it is essential. He's a very exciting man, the complete opposite of all the things I couldn't possibly live with. Of course that makes him risky, too.' She thought of Marie choosing the dull safety of Ivor Door as an insurance against risk. Surely it was possible to be rational without being so cynical, so calculating? She continued:

'But it's the understanding most of all, the feeling that I know him and he knows me in ways nobody else could, for either of us. There's so much we don't have to explain to each other, so much we *know*.'

She was reassured to see that Mother Veronica understood what she was saying, even if she might not approve.

'It's as if my life, my ordinary everyday life, is a very small bright circle and outside it, all round it, is darkness. That's how I've always felt, surrounded by dark thickets, all tangled and thorny and full of traps. Every time I try to escape I end up in another little bright circle with the same darkness outside. It's always been part of me although I've never been able to understand what it was. Here I am, with my job and my friends, all day-to-day and superficial, but the darkness outside keeps breaking in, infecting it. And each time the circle gets smaller and I feel more desperate. I feel caught in a web, but it's my own web.'

Mother Veronica spoke: 'Until very recently you have been ignorant of your origins, Gossamer. It has all been a complete mystery to you, a darkness you yourself have filled with all sorts of terrors, like the superstitious pagans of old. It sounds to me a little as though you may be acting out of gratitude to this man simply because he has chosen at last to throw some light on it for you. He could, after all, have done so much earlier, and spared you much pain. Do you not consider that?'

'Yes, but it's his darkness too, it's infected his life as well, worse than mine in some ways. He's explained why he didn't tell me before, and he's explained why he behaved as he did, not fully, not yet, but enough for me to want to go on understanding. We were both victims of it. It's one of the ways we can understand each other. We can see where the paths are through all that undergrowth. I don't – I don't think I can do it on my own. I don't think he can, either. We need each other.'

Gossamer felt suddenly exhausted, as if she were caught in the very thickets she had just described, trapped and alone. She thought again of Marie Hordern-Smith, Marie Ivor-Door, of her frightening resolve to play her life by the law of the jungle and win by whatever methods seemed expedient. It could be worth any sacrifice not to end up like that.

She needed understanding, stability, a sense of proportion. The bright circle of her life was a meaningless place of work and money. There was no love in it, no ease of spirit, no depth or hinterland. At this moment the child in Gossamer needed the Reverend Mother to soothe her and reassure her and let her go to sleep in peace.

But the woman now pursued her like a Devil's Advocate, probing for weakness. She spoke again with a voice that was still gentle, but edged with relentless insistence.

'Nonetheless he remains Carey Lambert. He is what he is. Do you believe you can reform him?'

It was Carey's question, Carey's declaration: *I am what I am*. She settled to answer it.

'If you mean "re-form" him, no. I cannot make him into something else. Nobody can do that for anybody.' Mother Veronica nodded her agreement. 'But "reform" has other meanings, doesn't it? It can mean bringing out the best in something, supporting it and letting it grow. And it can mean amending, reducing the capacity for harm. And in those senses, yes, I believe I can reform him. I can help him become what he can be. And I need it to be done for me, too.'

Mother Veronica nodded again, though this time it seemed more in submission. It was as if something had taken its course, and was over.

'I do so want you to understand,' Gossamer said.

'I understand.'

Gossamer knew there was more to come.

'Also I understand that you don't want me to tell you what to do. But I hope you will allow me to share my thoughts with you.'

'Oh yes, I want you to.'

'I made a comparison, earlier this evening, between the Vows of Sisterhood and the Vows of Marriage. I told you that I had different reasons for taking my Vows than the reasons I had for setting out to become a nun, and I can see very clearly that you are *not* "rushing into marriage" as I once tried to rush into Sisterhood. You take it very seriously.'

'Yes. Yes I do.' She felt a rush of love for this woman, who understood.

'I have known young women who tried to rush into this convent, and I have known some who were every bit as sincere in their intent to enter it as you are to enter marriage. All are told that they must go through a process of affirming their intent, of testing it out until it is fully lived or until it is found to be less than complete, in which case the process is halted before it can go too far. Everything I have seen over the years has confirmed to me that this is a good rule. Some, like me, have been assisted to their vows. Others, very sincere women, have come to realise that sisterhood is not after all for them, or that the right place for them is a different sort of Order.' She smiled.

'But they have all understood why, and that has been a great blessing and strength for them. But Marriage does not have its postulants and novices, as Sisterhood does. Marriage is not something that can be tested out, in stages.'

She rearranged herself slightly and straightened up some papers on her desk. 'I'm not talking about what is popularly, and wrongly, known as "morality", Gossamer. And I'm not talking about "living together", either. Marriage as we understand it is something quite different from that: a sacrament, a binding affirmation of a permanently altered state of life.'

'Yes. That's it, exactly.'

'Then, my dear, all I have to say is that such a marriage is traditionally preceded by a period in which each party to it behaves, separately, as if the affirmation had already been made, and asks the world to behave accordingly. Not for too long, just long enough to test the hypothesis, as it were. Of course many couples 'get engaged', but I don't think many of them consider very closely what the term 'engagement' rightly means. Well, there you are my dear, that is what is in my thoughts.'

'Yes,' said Gossamer. 'I understand what you mean. And thank you, for letting me talk, and for listening. It is what I came here for.'

'Then I am even more glad that you have found it, Gossamer.' Mother Veronica looked at her levelly. 'But it is surely not *all* you came here to find?'

'No, it isn't. I had to make sure that what he'd told me wasn't – I'm sorry. I just couldn't take it completely on trust.'

'There is no need to apologise, my dear. I am sure you may readily be forgiven for that.'

They kissed, and said good night.

Mother Veronica sat on a little, alone, before retiring for the night. She thought of this child whose life span almost equalled her own term in office as Mother Superior. For she was a child, a child grown old before her time, and forced to learn more wisdom than her years ought to bear; wrenched from one state into another. Wrenched by this man, this Carey Lambert.

Well, she had done what she could. She had listened, and answered the girl's questions, and given what advice she could without seeeming to. They was nothing else she could do except pray for her.

She realised as she prepared for bed that she had not told the child quite everything; but still, it was such a trivial thing. It could hardly be worth another meeting merely to say that over two years ago, at the time of poor Mr Germain's accident, she had had another visitor from Chatteris Choate.

She forgot his name now; not Jean-Luc Frémont, certainly. An altogether older man, courteous and businesslike, merely to confirm the dates of Gossamer's birth and the circumstances of her arrival at the Convent and to reassure her, when she had asked, that the donations to the Orphanage would continue, as indeed they had. Apparently Mr Germain had been responsible for more than one such confidential arrangement and although everything was in perfect order his colleagues had felt that a personal visit was required to allay any anxieties on the part of those with whom he had dealt in this way.

No, it could hardly be of relevance to Gossamer Fane. The poor child had enough to think about, surely, without such distractions.

Mother Veronica extinguished her candle and slept, like Gossamer, in dreamless peace.

Gossamer left the next morning, calm in mind and spirit.

She spent Christmas quietly, seeing friends.

She saw Carey again in January.

He was all that she had hoped and expected him to be, only more so.

They met at La Maison Hubert, Carey explaining that it was not the sort of place people went to in order to be seen. It was neither fashionable nor notorious, simply a restaurant that offered good and interesting cuisine and the opportunity to enjoy it in civilised privacy. It catered, he said, for tastes not egos.

They dined at an alcove table screened by plant-trailing partitions, a secluded island in a gently murmuring sea of conversation and laughter. They drank very dry Normandy cider and they talked, easily and naturally. She had no feeling that the unanswered question lay like a void between them while they made uneasy conversation round its rim. Their conversation was general, moving in to matters of shared interest and from them to particulars. He asked after Jenny and she told him that she was just the same, cheerful and optimistic and warmly looking forward to the future.

'Johnny is giving every indication of getting a starred first, so she's even surer than ever he's going to be a disgustingly well-paid professor in the States. In fact he could be offered a research fellowship there, so it'll probably happen. Then she says she'll go straight to the most glamorous specialist she can find and get her back fixed.'

'Oh? What's wrong with her back?'

Gossamer had to remind herself that Carey could not know; it had seemed so natural to be talking about someone they both knew. She also registered that he could not have been in touch with Helen Kepesake. 'Well, she doesn't know, that's the problem. She's tried aspirins and osteopathy and they haven't worked. It gives her quite a lot of pain and she can't sit properly, and she's had to shove a board under her side of the mattress. Actually it is quite worrying, the pain's getting her down and making her tired.'

'That's no state to be in at her age, Gossamer. Hasn't she been referred to a specialist locally?'

'Oh yes – in at least three months' time. You can't do BUPA on a student grant and part-time earnings, Carey. And they won't take help from their parents, either of them. She hasn't told her mother about it and she acts as though there's nothing wrong when she sees her.'

'Then they're foolish,' Carey replied, but not cruelly. 'Money isn't dirty. Tell her – no, I'm sorry. You could tell her, if you like, that I could arrange to have her seen very quickly by one of the best in the field.' He smiled. 'OffWorld does run to BUPA, you see. We'd hire her as a consultant researcher and get her seen under our company scheme. She'd have to do a bit of paid work for us of course,' he added, grinning.

Gossamer was grateful for the offer and the way he had made it. She was sure it was a way of telling how he had changed since the last time he'd helped Jenny. 'Thank you, Carey, that's very kind and thoughtful. I will tell her.'

Whatever you decide, whatever you do, whoever you're with Jenny had told her, *I'll understand, and I'll always be your friend.*

She learned about the new relationship between Carey and Alec: OffWorld and DayStar were going to pool resources on two shared channels, one for films and one for cartoons. Carey explained that it was a simple and sensible expedient to keep costs down and avoid the sort of pointless competition that didn't benefit the viewer. 'No doubt all the usual suspects will yelp and howl and bare their gums at us,' he said, 'but there's no suggestion of any reduction in choice. It just means we'll share one movie channel screening mostly good films instead of having one each showing mostly crap. The only ones to suffer will be the film companies who've been bidding us up against each other for the rights.'

He made it clear he still considered that DayStar was a rotten tree that would fall one day soon, and when it did he intended to be the first on hand to saw up the timbers. 'But that'll be then,' he said. 'This is now. It's a good deal. Good business.'

The two new services were to be called the StarWorld Channels. 'It's got just the right sort of double meaning, hasn't it? StarWorld,' he intoned in a voice that perfectly mimicked the awed, huskily mid-Atlantic tones of the movie trailer voiceover, 'for a *world* of *stars*.'

They laughed together. He was being delightful company.

He drove her back to her flat in his own BMW, and she invited him in.

She knew she was going to sleep with him. Her body knew.

Not a word was spoken that she could remember afterwards. As their clothes fell from them and she felt his hands on her breasts and his penis rising against her belly her body's hunger took over and his responded with a gourmet's appetite.

Her nipples came to warm hardness against his chest and her hand closed round his hard erection. His hands adored her back, her buttocks, her flanks, and the moistening valley where her vulva opened to welcome and receive him. Like homecoming exiles they re-explored each other with caressing hands and lips and tongues, lingeringly urgent, moaning and whimpering in pleasure and anticipation. They turned and rolled together with the weightlessness of mutual desire.

She straddled him and took him inside her. The pleasure was total, terrifying, irresistible. Her flesh opened before him and closed around him, drawing him in as she impaled herself on his sex. She began to ride him as he moved under her, with her, and her mind broke free. She became two women, one a body that hungered as it fed, ferocious, glorying, blazingly exultant, the other a mind that observed herself, not liking what it saw but accepting it.

His warm hands cupped her breasts, his fine lithe body reared between her thighs and the column of his sex swelled and grew inside her, thrusting to the centre of her and returning there, again and again as she moved on him with long, strong strokes. Soon he arched and cried out as he came shudderingly to climax and flooded her with his jetting semen.

Her detached mind knew what she would do next. She

pulled him over on his side, still inside her between her legs, his hands on her, his voice moaning her name. She watched herself do something she had never done before, do it so he could see her doing it. She stroked her fingers down his sweating chest and belly until she found the place were they were wetly joined. She found her clitoris and pleasured it, smiling into his face, squeezing his slightly softened penis with the walls of her vagina.

Smiling, she kissed his face as her fingers moved below. She saw and felt how this excited him, saw the excitement of it in his face and felt him come again to hardness. She clamped him tight inside as the first pulsing ripples of orgasm thrilled through her. Complicit, he lay unmoving as the first climax took her.

Then, as she knew he would, he turned her on her back and came over her to take her in his turn; then, as she knew she must, she spread and offered to him as he took possession of her body. Orgasm after orgasm crashed through her and then he came again, deep and hard.

They lay together, enfolded, washed with the afterglow of desire fulfilled.

'Thank you, Gossamer,' he said, soft and close. 'Thank you, thank you.'

'Yes,' she told him back. 'The answer's yes.'

He said: 'Nothing in my life has ever pleased me more than this moment.' She knew he was sincere.

He readily agreed to a period of close engagement. A few months, he said, would suit him fine. He told the truth.

Her work at Project Aid continued, part-time, separate. Her friends and colleagues were pleased for her. Zara Moberly-Mabbs fixed a date with Humpers on the strength of it. Davina was positively friendly towards her. Ida searchingly observed that she had made a settlement with herself that few others could begin to guess at; then deliberately broke the spell by saying she hoped Gossamer would put the squeeze on her husband-to-be for a good fat donation.

Jenny wrote to say again that she understood, though

she was damned if she knew how, and would she and Carey condescend to visit them even though they weren't going to live in Beverly Hills? She declined Carey's offer on the grounds that people with bog-ordinary NHS ailments shouldn't aspire to private medical complaints.

They did not make a formal announcement. They agreed that it would not be appropriate. Word spread anyway, as newspapers informed their readers that the Bodysuit Girl seemed likely to wed the TV Mogul. She wore a ring of her own on her third finger, nonetheless.

Trish sent a postcard from Aberystwyth: *Guess you know what you're doing, sister. Somebody has to. Me, I'm doing a fortnight in Welsh Arts Centres. Nuff said.*

Carey kept her in touch with his life as he had never done before, in the days when he came to her like Zeus in a shower of gold. In this, as in other things, he treated her as his equal. What had happened between them in the past could never be eradicated, but it could be softened, worn down by new habits, new understanding. She was content with this.

He took her around with him a lot, to theatre, ballet, opera, functions and receptions. In her company he was more than ever witty, urbane and accomplished. She felt the benefit of it, though it was not done to impress her and she was never eclipsed by it. Rather it was as if he drew his energy from her and reflected it back so that she basked in herself and in the two of them, together. At times he was almost triumphant, not as a man showing off a prized possession but as a man who has won the prize of himself, at times she felt as if he had made her his hostage to fortune, the source of his vulnerability as well as of his strength.

Thus she met again Alec Dayfield, and Mike. In Alec she sensed a sort of admiration and respect, in Mike a sort of acknowledgement. His dislike of her was still there, below the surface, like their past, but like his desire for her, it no longer seemed personal or intense. Alec must have told him, then, as Carey had said he would. She was glad not to feel obliged to tell him herself. It would have meant meeting him on a different level. She did not wish to be distracted, as she knew he could distract her, from the settlement she had made with her life. She assumed that he, in his own way and for his own reasons, felt the same.

And Carey always let her know that he was there for her; he listened; he was attentive; he was never patronising. In their love-making he was considerate and responsive, an equal to her needs. He worked on his commitment to her, and it never faltered.

For four months it never faltered, and then it was cut off.

❖ PERU ❖

❧ Twenty ❧

The woman with the cropped hair and the scar on her cheek was scrubbing a wall. It was a fatuous task since the paint would not come off, only leave a paler version of itself behind. The wall would need repainting but that would never happen. All she was doing was creating a pale clean patch to offset the faded pink of the slogan painted on it. She knew all this but it did not bother her.

Shining Path put the slogan there, *Sendero Luminoso*. It read: *¡SOCIALISMO O MUERTE!* It was meant as a threat but it was mild one, it was like *¡VIVA GONZALO!* or *¡VIVA LA GUERRA POPULAR!* It meant: *We are here, we are all around you, do not forget it*.

Gonzalo was their name for Guzman, Abimael Guzman, the leader who was everywhere and nowhere, just like G2, the Army secret police who fought the Shining Path by making people disappear. G2 did not paint slogans, instead they paid people to put up posters asking 'WHO ARE THE TERRORISTS?' and answering, 'DELINQUENTS who do not respect our red and white flag, and want to replace it with a dirty red flag.' They did not give warnings before they made people disappear. G2 did not tell people they were coming to kill them, and they did not kill aid workers. Shining Path did.

'Socialism or death' was really just a figure of speech, but it could be a warning against the enemies of Socialism, like the Church: then it could mean: 'Socialism is what we will have – meanwhile, we will kill those who oppose it.' The woman knew that, she had been taught these subtleties. *¡PARO ARMADO!* was worse, Armed Strike. That meant you were a target for Shining Path, you were on their list. There had been one of those on the gate a year ago, before the woman came here, and the next night they came and shot out all the windows in the schoolroom. Nobody was injured. Then the army made some boys and men disappear in the town.

The worst was ¡*ADVERTENCIA DE MUERTE*!, Death Warning. That meant they were coming to kill you for the sake of their dirty red flag, because Gonzalo had told them to.

Everyone knew the story of how the Shining Path had gone into a village and cut the arms off all the children who'd had vaccinations the day before. There were many such rumours, and the woman did not necessarily believe all of them. In fact she thought it might have been in a film, that story. But foreign aid workers were targeted, that was a fact; they killed women and children for distributing milk and Japanese horticulturalists for showing people how to grow better crops. They killed the deputy mayor of Lima, Maria Elena Moyano, for enslaving the People by setting up soup kitchens. They tried to terrorise people into joining them and the Army tried to terrorise people out of it. It was the way things had been for over ten years in Peru; terror and counter-terror had become a system of government.

She scrubbed and scrubbed, uselessly, her face as blank as the wall. Her fingers were red and raw and the nails broken. Filthy water sprayed back off the wall and over her drab shapeless dress. She did not care. Nobody would mind what she looked like in her dress, least of all the children. Dr Jeffry would not mind. It didn't matter.

People in the Mission said it was the priests in the town who saved them from being killed by the *Sendero*. They passed between the *Sendero* and the Army and made a little space between the two. They couldn't keep everybody safe, of course; sometimes there must be a little price to pay or the priests would compromise their position; nobody acknowledged that it happened at all. But everybody knew that it was thanks to their priest, Fr Montesinos, that the

Mission had not received an *advertencia de muerte*, so far. Perhaps the shooting-out of the schoolroom windows had been a payment on account.

If the *Sendero* sent her an *advertencia*, would it matter? She did not know; that, probably, meant that it would not. It might matter to the children, a little, for a while; but they were used to such things, of course. The little boy she'd helped with his sums that morning had found his parents' bodies in the road with a placard round their necks proclaiming them to be Enemies of the People. He'd got over that; he'd had to. They could not be replaced; she would be.

She knew it would matter to Dr Jeffry, because he loved her. She did not love him, could not, but the thought of his grief would give her pain. She could see that it might well be difficult for him to find someone else.

If she was irreplaceable for Dr Jeffry then that would be one thing he'd have in common with Carey Lambert. The thought gave her a little dull amusement as she moved her brush across the leprous cement.

She wished he did not love her, this good, kind, unhappy man. She wished it could be as uncomplicated for him as she had had to make it for herself. Their affair was quiet, secretive and gentle. The sex was companionable, sometimes memorable. It had begun to heal some wounds; it was nourishing. They might have been a secretly married couple. But she was emotionally numb.

The wounds might be healing but the nerves had been severed. That part of her, she was sure, could never live again. She had told him that and he had said that he understood how she felt. She hoped he did not mean that he thought she would stop feeling that way, one day. He was a good man and she was as happy as she ever wanted to be, knowing she was helping him, giving him comfort and succour while satisfying the needs of her body.

He was a good man and a skilful lover; they had no means of contraception so there were times when they could not make love for fear of pregnancy, and she did not like to when she was heavy with her period. Then, sometimes, they would make love without penetration but often their assignations were to talk, or read together, or listen to the BBC, or simply to be together, quietly in domesticity. In a different lifetime she would have been capable of love for him and he free to declare his love for her. In this lifetime that could never be. Their times together could only be holidays from the separate prisons of their lives.

He had met her in Lima. His first action was to let her know, with great tact, that he did not need to know anything about her. Of her own volition, without mentioning names or incidents, she had told him enough to define herself for him. The second thing he did was to show her photographs of his children, two boys in their early teens and a girl aged eleven. She in turn had understood the need to ask no further questions.

It was some time later, after she had shaved her head and burned her clothes, that he told her about his wife in England. It was later still, after many gentle persuadings and the slow growing of trust, that they first made love and she had known again that detachment, as if her mind and her body coexisted independently in the single organism that went under her name. Now she found it in the embrace of a man who was in every point the opposite of Carey Lambert. Perhaps it had been enough simply to know such a man existed. Finding proof of him, her mind permitted her body to lie down with him and let him enter her, unite with her, and reunite her fractured identity at the timeless moment of orgasm.

She must never promise this man any more than that. More than that was not hers to give, or to know.

On the long journey on a road called the Marginal to Aucayacu and the Mission he had told her about Peru, about the world she had entered and must make her own and about the lessons she must learn in order to survive in it. As if to hammer them home, the pick-up had bumped over filled-in trenches cut by the *Sendero* to hold up Army vehicles at ambush points. For illustration she had only to look at the bodies that floated in the mud-scummy waters of the Huallaga River.

He told her all he knew about the bodies, which was that they had been shot. Perhaps they were victims of a *paro armado*, perhaps of an Army security sweep. Perhaps they were members of the MRTA, the guerrilla rivals of the *Sendero*, who claimed Che Guevara as their mentor and Tupac Amaru, the last Inca king, as their inspiration. Perhaps they were part of a local adjustment in the operation of the cocaine market; half the world's cocaine began in this region where, for every thousand dollars' worth of cocaine processed in Colombia and sold in the West, one dollar fifty went to the farmers who grew the coca leaf. That was twelve times as much as they would earn from any other crop.

Dead bodies in rivers were only to be expected in a country under a permanent State of Emergency. Only under a State of Emergency could the Army fight the *Sendero* and the MRTA, and run the cocaine trade.

'There's a saying in Runasimi,' he told her. 'That's the language of the Indians.' He cleared his throat. '*Yaw, opa, tutayaq wasipi supi moskaq*. Only a fool goes looking for a fart in a dark house. That's how you survive in this country: don't go looking. And hope it doesn't come looking for you.'

Bertha had taught him that, he added. 'She's an Ashaninca who works for the Mission. A very brave and splendid woman. You'll like Bertha, I think.'

Bertha had become her friend. Dr Gabriel Jeffry had become her lover. Survival had become bearable.

But she must keep occupied, stay busy.

Memory rushed in to fill the idle times, the empty spaces.

A gecko crouched by the wall, pulsing in the sun. Its internal organs were visible through the skin, the heart and the liver and the tracery of veins. Its very presence seemed to dare her to destroy it. Only after she had passed did it flick away into the scrubby grass that still failed to conceal its nakedness.

A youth stood by the side of the track opposite the Mission gate, watching. He could have walked in; the gate stood open, people were free to come and go without challenge. But that was not his purpose. His purpose was to stand, and watch, and be seen. Now, as she approached the gateway with her bucket and brush, he watched her.

He stood still, impassive. His face was closed, a mask. Of course he was one of the *Sendero*. He was there to convey the same message as the writing on the wall: *We are here. We see you. We know who you are*. It was just another form of terror.

The Army were in the town but the countryside belonged to the Shining Path, and he was one of them. Besides, he did not have the look of the MRTA, nervy, excitable, hyperactive. She and Gabriel had been stopped by them once, at a roadblock, on their way to a village clinic. They'd said they had no wish to interfere with the work of a doctor who helped poor people; that was what they wanted, to make things better for the people, to stop exploitation, to achieve equality through revolution. Most of them were teenagers with guns and scarves round their faces. The manifesto delivered, they'd been allowed to proceed, waved at as they drove on. Gabriel said the *Sendero* would have killed them, probably tortured them first, but there was little for them to fear from the MRTA provided they were polite and agreed with everything that was said to them.

One of these boy fighters had turned up at the Mission a few weeks later with an infected bullet wound. The others, he'd told them, were all dead. She'd helped Gabriel treat the boy's wound, which was nasty but only superficial. Antibiotics, clean dressings and a few days' rest would heal it. The next morning he'd gone; everybody knew it would be unwise to ask how.

This one, though not much older, was quite different. Quite possibly he had been one of the boy's killers. She recognised his impersonal, focused look of total certainty, total commitment. She had seen it on television, looking out at her from Iran, from Northern Ireland, from studio debates on abortion. She had seen it in the villages, watching her with eyes that missed nothing.

She had seen it, fleetingly, in Carey Lambert, and refused to recognise it.

The next thing for her to do was to help serve the little ones their midday meal. After that she would be giving the older children an English lesson in the schoolroom and later she would be with Gabriel in the clinic.

She turned in at the gate. The drive to the main entrance of the Mission lay in front of her but she was headed to the left, across a stretch of grass and shrubs between the gate and the washrooms.

She entered that empty space.

The television industry reception at the Connaught Rooms: well-known faces and faces of well-known names, a heady, sexy atmosphere of glamour and power, drinking and talking, a boisterous cacophony. Carey achingly handsome in evening dress, Gossamer glowing in a gown of powder blue, a woman at ease with herself. Carey was with a group of men and Gossamer, turning from her group to take another glass, had found Alec Dayfield doing the same, and they had made a little island of conversation together: her job, her plans . . .

And she found herself saying: 'I'm so glad we can be friends.'

And Alec, smiling and bringing his bushy eyebrows down: 'I never thought of you as an enemy, Gossamer Fane. You wouldn't like that.'

'Of course not, you'd eat me for breakfast and spit out the pips!' She laid her hand lightly on his arm, sensing the muscular strength of it beneath the expensive suiting. 'That's not what I meant, Alec, and you know it.'

'Oh?' He took a sip of his drink and the eyes beetled out at her from above his glass. 'So remind me what I know.'

She was quite content to play this game if he wanted it.

'Well, I mean that you and Carey are working together, for a start.'

'That's business.' The words came out emphatically and automatically.

'I know. I can even quote you the rest: "It's a limited fixed-term arrangement to control costs and maximise revenues in the prevailing conditions of the market. Nothing else is implied by it and nothing else should be inferred." It's all right, Alec, I'm not the Monopolies Commission.'

'That's just as well, or I wouldn't be allowed to talk to you in public.'

She laughed again. 'What I mean is, there is a personal element as well, we all know that. That's why I am so glad we can be on friendly terms: because of history. Yours and Carey's, and mine.'

He said quietly, 'Yes.'

'And because we can put that behind us, all three of us.'

'We can.' It was neither a question nor an affirmation. Just the two words repeated.

'All that misunderstanding. All the deceptions and delusions.'

'Oh, I have no delusions, Gossamer. I understand.' Again the smile, again the controlled emphatic voice.

'What makes me happy is that you know about me. Me and Carey. You know my history, you know what I am.'

He was startled; his guard dropped. She saw her words had taken him completely by surprise. He took a little time to find his voice again. 'Yes, I do. I didn't realise you were aware of that.'

'Yes, Alec, I am.' She lay her hand on his arm again, a gesture of fondness and understanding. 'Carey told me he'd spoken to you. And I was so glad he did, because it means I don't have to explain things.'

'As you say, Gossamer. I know your history.'

'And it's cleared the air, hasn't it? We can be friends; you and Carey can do business.'

He smiled slowly, consideringly. 'Oh yes, it's certainly

done that.' He raised his glass to her. 'Here's to breathing, then, Gossamer. Here's to being friends, and doing business.'

'Yes,' she said. They drank.

And then her eyes were dragged across the room and she saw Carey, watching. Calm and still, inscrutable, intense. It made her blood run cold. *What was wrong? She had to know. She crossed the floor to him, trancelike. People drew back to let her through.*

Now she stumbled into the washroom, blinded with tears of humiliation. She had grazed her knuckles on the concrete; she scrubbed them viciously at the sink, to punish herself. *Scrub it out, scrub it out.* She concentrated very hard to stop herself snivelling.

'Carey, what is it? Are you all right?'

Slowly his eyes brought her into focus. His mouth twisted into a smile. 'Hello, Gossamer,' he said.

It sounded like an accusation: she had spent too much time out of his company. She kept her voice light.

'I was just talking to Alec Dayfield,' she said.

'So I observed. He was looking very pleased with himself.'

'He was pleased with – with the way things have worked out, Carey. He didn't realise I knew you'd told him. About everything.'

'So you enlightened him on that score.'

'Yes. Without realising it. I just happened to mention how happy I was, knowing you'd told him.'

'Well, well. And?'

'Well, he seemed a bit taken aback for a moment. I don't know why. I began to wonder if I'd said the wrong thing although I couldn't think of any reason why. Anyway, it obviously wasn't, because he agreed it had cleared the air between us. All three of us.'

'So then you drank a toast.'

'Yes, that's right. To friendship, and doing business.'

He laughed as if at some private joke. At the same time his hand came round her waist and he drew her to him, turning away from the nearest group. 'Oh my dear Gossamer!' He led her a little way off and then lowered his voice, made it gently and amusedly conversational.

'Friendship and business, Gossamer? Hands across the ether? Can you believe that? Mention the business at all, did he?'

'StarWorld? Yes, he did. And he said the same things about it that you say. Used the same words, even.'

'Words, words. Strictly for idiots and children and the DTI, those words.'

'And fiancées, evidently.'

He reacted instantly. His voice was hard, though audible only to her: 'Don't give me that TV drama crap, Gossamer. It's not worthy of you and I don't deserve it. Sure, I gave you the official version but I told you the rest of it as well, remember? Honey, there's only room in the UK market for one satellite operation: he knows it, I know it, everybody in the business knows it. StarWorld's the beginning of the end, for one of us. That's the reality, and it's only a matter of time before events catch up with it. I have told you this.'

She had to acknowledge that was true.

'As for friendship, Gossamer, friends don't dump each other on the garbage. There's only only one prize on offer: one of us gets it, one of us is dead. Right, that's one thing. The other thing, from his point of view, is you, my darling.'

'Me?'

'There's only one Gossamer Fane. You follow? Be careful around him, Gossamer. Be very careful, okay?'

He made as if to move away. 'Carey!' she hissed. 'You can't just—'

His hand gripped her arm, hard. He was smiling. 'Later. Tonight. When we're alone. Okay?'

She nodded. She knew how he'd want to make love to her tonight. She held his hand as they rejoined the company.

It was jealousy, then. Just jealousy, nothing more complicated. It wasn't nice, but she'd have to live with it for a while; until, as Carey put it, events caught up with reality.

His arm came round her and he held her close. 'Gerald! I don't think you've had a chance to congratulate me yet. Gossamer darling, this is Gerald Moncrieff, Paradigm Shift Productions.' *The interval over, the performance recommenced.*

He was married. His wife lived in England, in Cheshire, with their children. Three times a year he went home to some approximation of family life. He was able to be with his children. He lived for those times.

He believed in his work at the Mission although it was demanding and exhausting and at times dangerous. He was no cynic. But, as he said, he need not have come so far from home in order to practise medicine among the deprived and oppressed; it was not necessary to leave one's country to do that. Applying for a post in the southern Huallaga had been part of the settlement necessary to preserve the brittle shell of his marriage.

Helen, his wife, had rejected him sexually after the conception of their third child. It had seemed very sudden, quite unexpected, but, as so often happens in the aftermath of disaster, he soon realised that the signs of it had been present for some time.

'It's not easy to be a doctor's wife,' he said. 'We're all too prone to live up to the cliché of being overworked saints. To be fair, I wasn't a very wonderful thing to share a life with. Taking too much for granted, absent too often – even when I was there, if you see what I mean. Too tired to talk. All that sort of thing. By the time she had to spell it all out to me it was too late.'

And, as is so often the case, he had quickly adapted. He took on more private patients to fund an extension to the house, necessary for the separate bedroom that now became his. Still he had hoped it might not be too late, that they might make a second start; meanwhile he learned the habits that made such a renewal daily more impossible. He told Gossamer that what he'd found most difficult to get the hang of was not touching Helen.

'Living with her, the mother of my children; eating with her, doing the chores with her, still yearning for her love: it felt like having my arms strapped to my sides.' But her own obvious physical distaste soon taught him the instinct to avoid it.

The boys were very young, the girl, Frances, grew up in it; they took it for granted. Other people's parents might be different, but so were other people's houses. Helen and Gabriel were always polite to each other.

For a long time he was sexually numb: sex, for him, had become equated with making love with Helen. As feeling returned and he began to know desire again, the fact that Helen would divorce him if he committed adultery was a more than sufficient disincentive to have affairs. The thought of buying sex he found revolting, the thought of divorce horrifying.

He was a Roman Catholic, but that was not the reason: they both were. They had used contraception in the early years of their marriage. He knew she'd had lovers, after Frances started school. She had not flaunted them, but she had made no secret of them. Sometimes she spent weekends away from home, not pretending to disguise her reason for going. But she always came back. She operated on the basis that there was one code of conduct for her and another for him. He had to accept that.

Divorce was out of the question because he would lose his children. He could not always be there for his children but he must know that he was allowed to go to them, at any time, if they needed him.

He also feared for them. 'I do try very hard to be objective about it, Gossamer. About her. I try to filter out my own resentment. But I believe very strongly that it would be bad for them to be brought up by her, without me at all. If there was another man, a potential stepfather, I'm sure that would be different. I could get to know him. But there's no question of that, Helen's made it quite plain. That's not what Helen's other men are for. She says she doesn't sleep with anyone when I'm away, and I believe her. She only does it when I'm there.'

He had left, by arrangement, when dislike threatened to become outright loathing. He had come to Peru for the same reason he had stayed at home: for the sake of his children. All he desired was to be able to adapt his own life to suit their needs, until they were old enough to stand alone.

'I want to sleep with you, Gossamer,' he'd said. 'I want to hold you and make love with you, and talk, and just be with you. But it would have to be secret, we couldn't share it in public, not even here. I daren't even risk that. And I'm 38 and you're 21; if I asked you to wait until I was free, we'd both be at least ten years older.' He'd smiled.

'I have nothing to offer you, Gossamer, no future. I can't even say, "I love you."'

'Don't say it. I don't want you to. I can't say it to you.'

'I'm being very selfish. I need you, that's all.'

And the woman with the cropped hair and the scar on her cheek said: 'I know. It's all right. Here I am.' And she met his need with a tenderness as great as her detachment from the act of it.

But he did love her, she saw how it weakened his vigilance; saw the look of it in his eyes across a room. She had to be vigilant for him as well as for his sake. She herself had nothing to lose.

Shortly after they first slept together he had gone home on leave. He had sent her a letter full of love, though the word was never used. A lovely letter. She kept it, hidden, in her room.

The first time they made love, he'd cried.

He spread her flesh with his thumbs and entered her from behind all at once. Then he pushed her shoulders down and fucked her hard, almost pulling out between each huge penetration so it was like being taken again and again. Then he squatted low and thrust upward, his hands clamped under her buttocks, the muscle of his penis hard against her clitoris so she came to climax and tightened on him as he moved in her. Now he was crouched above her, his hands on her hips, riding her. Wave after wave of orgasm crashed through her as he dropped to his knees and arched back, thrusting deep; then his own waves broke inside her. He cried out in exultation and fell on her, they rolled over together and he pulled her head round and kissed her furiously, still big inside her. He buried his face in her hair.

'Say you're mine, Gossamer.'

Why should he need her to?

'You're mine, Gossamer.'

She felt him tense up. 'Oh, Carey. You mustn't doubt me. Yes, I'm yours. I am engaged to you. I am going to marry you, I am going to have your children. Do you want me to mention that to Alec Dayfield, remind him next time we meet, drop it into the conversation?' She must get him to lighten up, amuse him out of his stupid fearfulness.

'Yes. That's just what I do want.'

'What, Carey? *What?*'

'Listen, Gossamer. Listen hard while I tell you about Alec Dayfield. Listen while I tell you about yourself.' A cold ocean current of misery welled up inside her where the fire of his possession had been.

'I'm listening,' she said dully. 'I thought all that side of things was over between you, that compulsion of his to hurt you that way.'

'Maybe it is, but he's still Alec Dayfield. A man who's used to getting what he wants and then convincing himself it came of its own free will and should be grateful for the privilege. And he fancies you. He wants you. So you have to be careful.'

'I see. Go on.'

'Maybe he'd get an extra thrill because of what you are to me, maybe not. That's beside the point. The point is, don't encourage him.'

'Do I encourage him, in your opinion?'

'Yes.' He laid a heavy restraining hand on her shoulder.

'Yes, according to his perceptions. He's looking to pick up the signals, Gossamer. He's a one-wavelength receiver. Do you understand what I'm saying?'

'And how am I supposed to be sending these signals?'

He laughed. She could feel it in his chest, in his hand that came down to clasp her breast. 'Oh, Gossamer! You can cause erections just by being in the same room, you know that.'

She hunched into herself. 'Yes, I suppose I do. Well, I'd better not come out with you until I'm visibly pregnant, then.'

'Don't be childish,' he snapped.

She whipped round, blazing anger. 'What am I supposed to do, then? Go on, tell me, what? Wear an old sack? Disfigure myself? Pick my nose? I mean just tell me Carey, okay? Let me know precisely what you need me to do not to give men the come-on and I'll do it for you.'

He studied her for some time in silence.

'You do know that you're more than just attractive. You do know that. Men pick up signals you don't know you're giving. Men like Jake Carrington, for instance. And me, once. That's true, isn't it.'

It wasn't a question. She sighed. 'Yes, it's true.'

'It's not "men", Gossamer, that's not the problem here. Any man who's not been castrated or who isn't gay would want to fuck you, all things being equal, that's not what I'm talking about. The vast majority of our ordinary, non-sexual human contacts with other people have some sort of low-level sexual buzz to them or are influenced by the lack of one; that's true, too, isn't it.'

'Yes,' she said. It was in fact quite interesting. 'Yes, that's true.'

'And it's not that, either. I repeat, darling: Alec Dayfield is Alec Dayfield, testosterone in Savile Row suiting, enough of the stuff to fuel an entire Olympic team of women shot-putters.'

She giggled. 'Not that there isn't a couple of lady discus-throwers' worth in you, Carey Lambert.'

'Tush, woman! I'm just at the upper end of normal, that's all. Seriously, honey: you have to watch out when there's an Alec about. You really do.'

'So what *am* I supposed to do?' She thought about it. 'What you're saying is, that in Alec's case I have to make an extra effort to jam the signals.'

'That's it. Broadcast the message you want him to receive.' He grinned. 'D'you remember the Biloxi Babe?'

She giggled again. 'Wahrl, honey, how cuhd Ah fergit thet dame?' she drawled.

'Quite! Well, word has it that her version of that particular little liaison was that one moment he was offering her a drink and the next moment, dang me if'n Ah wuzn't needin' a coupla Kleenex, an' buhlieve me, screwin' wuz the lahst theng on mah mayund!'

Their laughter seemed to exorcise the other memories of that dreadful evening. She took his shoulders and looked at him steadily, and lovingly, in the face.

'I shall be sure to mention wedding plans, and house-hunting, and school fees, and the problems of finding suitable godparents, at every available opportunity. Is that a good idea?'

'Yes, Gossamer. It's a wonderful idea.'

'I don't want to send those signals, Carey. You do know that? I don't want to put out to anyone except you. I don't want to make you anxious.'

'I do know that. It's why you're so good for me.' They kissed.

He rolled over on his back. 'Fuck me, Gossamer Fane. Yes, yes. Do that. Make me big and hard and then take me inside your wonderful pussy and fuck me.'

And the next time she was in company with Alec she stole a look at Carey and saw on his face the look of serene approval, and she was happy, so happy, to be doing it right.

And Alec Dayfield got the message.

Bertha knew about them. Gossamer's vigilance was not equal to their friendship or Bertha's wisdom.

But Bertha was safe, she could be trusted.

She told Bertha more about herself than she could ever tell Gabriel. Across the phantom divide of history and culture, friendship joined them in acceptance and understanding.

Bertha was the only friend she had, now she had lost Jenny.

Bertha taught her a song in Runasimi, singing it to her softly in the ancient and compelling tongue of her people. When Bertha wrote down the words in English she saw that it was her song:

> *My mother bore me*
> *And my father begot me*
> *In the middle of the rainclouds,*
> *So I would weep like the rain;*
> *In the middle of the storm,*
> *So I would wander like the clouds.*

Bertha was leaving the Mission to work among her own people in the rainforest. Many had been captured by the *Sendero*, Bertha said, and made to do many bad things. Twice the terrorists had burned down the school and hospital the Franciscans had set up, and where Bertha had her first education, but now the Army had special units there, trained by *gringos*; these were good men, men who kept their promises to the people. They called these special units the *Sinchis*, after a hero of Inca legend.

She was full of hope that her people could survive, not as an underclass in the slums and the shantytowns or demoralised in their plundered homelands, but preserving their values and their integrity in a truly modern country. She would help to build a bridge to make it possible.

'I was brought up in the Stone Age, Gossamer, yes? But I have been to Lima, I have worked in an office there. There is ignorance on both sides but it is so easy to overcome; it is not difficult to learn things.' Gossamer thought of Mother Veronica, with her fax machine and her spreadsheets.

'For centuries my people have been exploited. Do you

know, there is no way of speaking of ownership in my language, of things, of property? Now we hear of an exciting new *gringo* concept, one for which my people have a thousand words: it is called a "co-operative"! No two peoples can be poles apart, Gossamer. We are the ends of a broken circle, that is all, and all we have to do is bring the ends together. I will play my part.'

Bertha left in the lurching pick-up, down the dirt road that led to the Marginal. So had an old Merlé tribesman once walked away from her through tall grass, back to his people. Bertha left, and once more she was friendless.

There will be an end to your weeping, Gossamer, she said. *Take care.*

Jenny had said that to her: *Take care, Goss*.

She went to see Father Montesinos.

There were three other beds in the small ward apart from Jenny's. A skeletally thin old woman was asleep in one; the other two were unoccupied. Jenny lay on her side facing the door. Smiling in greeting.

'Hi, Goss. I can't sit up I'm afraid.' One arm rested on her hip, the other was connected by a clear plastic tube to a bag of yellow fluid. She took Jenny's hand, noticing the fingers were swollen. Her arm was pale and puffy where it emerged from the hospital nightie. 'Johnny's told you?'

Gossamer's throat was dry. 'Yes.'

It's Jenny, Gossamer. His voice bleak, neutral with misery. *She's got cancer. She went into hospital last week when her back packed up completely, the doctor got her admitted as an emergency. They're transferring her to the Royal Marsden. She'll get treatment there. When they've decided what's the best thing to do. They'll—*. His voice failed, then rallied. *They'll have to find out more about it first, of course.*

'He told me – what had happened.' She sensed Jenny's recognition of her inablity to say the dreadful word.

'Sorry, could I—' Gossamer released her hand and she scratched her nose. 'Sorry, I can't use my other hand I'm afraid.' Her eyes turned to the bag at the end of the tube.

'What is it?' asked Gossamer.

'Blood-platelets.' Her face was calm but Gossamer saw the fear in her friend's eyes. 'It's the stuff what makes your blood clot, innit. Mine pretty well isn't, you see. Here, pull these down, I'll show you.'

Gossamer pulled the bedclothes down. There were five bruises the shape and colour of black grapes on Jenny's thigh. 'That's where the ambulancemen ever-so-gently lifted me on to the stretcher. The transfusion's to help stabilise so they can operate.'

Painfully, Jenny shifted her position a little. Beneath the scanty nightdress Gossamer saw she was wearing what looked like a disposable nappy. The obscenity of it horrified her, and it must have shown in her face. Jenny said:

'I'm incontinent I'm afraid. The tumour's pressing on my bladder so it just leaks out. So there you go, that's the nearest I'm ever going to get to being an old lady.' Her voice cracked. 'And no babies. Goss, there'll be no babies.'

She twisted her head round, away from Gossamer, her teeth gritting in pain. Her legs flopped apart and Gossamer pulled the bedclothes up to cover her poor nakedness. Jenny began to talk rapidly, fighting back her tears.

'What it is, you see, is a primary cancer in my uterus that's pressing on other bits of me inside. It's not painful, that's the funny thing, I suppose it's because it's not in a part of me that gets any daily wear and tear.' Her voice caught again and Gossamer could tell she was trying even harder to make it matter-of-fact. 'Only of course they're worried about the cancer spreading to other organs, like it has done to my spine. That's bone-marrow cancer, that's why it's affected by blood-clotting mechanism apparently. One of my vertebrae has gone completely, near the bottom, it's fused to the next one, that's what was giving me all the pain. What they're trying to decide now is whether to take the tumour out of my womb first, in which case they'd have to wait quite a few weeks before they could start any chemotherapy or radiotherapy for my back, or whether to start that first in the hope that it'll halt the growth of the tumour or maybe even reduce it a bit. Only they've got to get my blood clotting again before they can operate or I won't heal afterwards. I'll just ... go on bleeding, you see.'

Gossamer swallowed. 'When will they be able to tell, do you know?'

'Dunno. Soon, I hope. Obviously they don't want to hang around. The trouble is, it's so advanced already.'

Jenny's eyes spilled tears. She gripped Gossamer's hand and held it tightly, and Gossamer remembered just in time not to squeeze back. Her voice was small as she said: 'It's my fault, Goss, it's my fault it's got so bad. Johnny's been worried sick for months and trying to get me to nag the doctor about it, and I wouldn't. Your Carey offered to queue-jump me to a specialist and I wouldn't. I kept saying there was nothing really wrong, but I was doing it more and more for my own benefit, you see. I was scared to find out. I gave Johnny a bloody hard time about it, bit his head off. You know me, nothing if not full-frontal. Well, I always did hate being fussed over, that was part of it too. Turns out I must have been walking around with it growing inside me for at least a year, maybe even two. Making plans and looking forward. Christ, you were worried six months ago and I wouldn't even see the bloody doctor!'

Gossamer had to ask: 'Do they – have they suggested any reason for it? The womb cancer?'

She squeezed Gossamer's hand again. 'It's okay, Goss. It wasn't that. That guy of Carey's might have been a patronising smoothie but he wasn't a back-street butcher. There's no reason to believe it's anything other than fucking awful bad luck. Of course, if I'd been one of those Thai prostitutes who smokes cigarettes up her fanny ...'

Gossamer's laughter was dutiful, and she knew Jenny could tell.

'I could pretend I was hanging on till Johnny sat his Finals, putting myself second so he wouldn't be distracted, but it wouldn't be true.' She was seized by gasping sobs and Gossamer could see the pain they were giving her but all she could do was sit dumbly holding her friend's hand, letting her know she was there and remembering all the time not to squeeze it, not to communicate the sort of love that would cause bruising.

What on earth must it be like for Johnny, sitting here, unable to display his love, unable to give way to his pain and grief and helplessness?

Jenny recovered sufficiently to speak again. 'Thank Christ they told us together, Gossamer. I had asked them to tell him everything they were telling me, and not to hold bad news back or give us any false hopes. I think I can fairly say they haven't done that. They've given us an answer to the obvious question.'

Gossamer realised Jenny was inviting her to ask it. 'What did they say about . . . the future?'

'A year to eighteen months if I respond to this first lot of treatment. Three months at the most if I don't, perhaps much less.' Jenny spoke the awful sentence quite calmly – as if, Gossamer thought, she was giving the itinerary for a journey. But of course that was what she was doing.

'They gave us the three-month forecast first. Then when that had sunk in, the possibility of a whole year and a half seemed like the best news we'd ever had. Another two summers, how wonderful! You should have seen how pleased the counsellor was with our positive attitude, Goss!'

And Gossamer, blinking tears, smiled and kissed her friend's cheek.

'Except it isn't true.' She spoke with quiet, bleak certainty. 'I can feel it isn't, you see. I really haven't got very long. And I've got – to tell – somebody.' Her voice was squeezed, almost inaudible.

At last and quite naturally Gossamer found a way to hold her and hug her while the tears flowed. When it was time to part, very calmly Jenny said what she wanted to say:

'I tried to say something to Johnny last night but it was no good. The poor sod, I saw straight away how unfair I was being but I've got to let him know somehow. I've got to let him know from me that he's allowed to be happy again. He's got to fall in love again, marry a lovely wife

and have lots of lovely children, and be happy. He doesn't
just owe it to himself, he owes it to me to be a warm and
lovely memory for him and not a great black empty pain.'

'He's bound to feel it that way, though, Jenny.' Gossamer
was astonished how natural it seemed, suddenly, to be
talking like this. 'He'll be shattered. He'll have to grieve.'
Astonished and a little horrified.

'I should bloody well hope so, too, I don't mean he's
allowed to be *cheerful*!' She grinned at her own outra-
geousness. Then, with quiet intensity: 'You know what I
mean, don't you? It's an aspect of love, not a betrayal. You
understand.'

'Yes,' said Gossamer. She hoped that she and Carey would
achieve that love, win through to this place where Jenny
Kepesake and Johnny Canfield so naturally belonged. 'I
understand,' she said. 'I promise.' And the tired, sad face
of her friend had smiled back, trusting her to do love
honour.

Then a nurse had come to prepare Jenny for another round
of tests, and the visit was over. Johnny would be arriving
afterwards and Gossamer did not wish to intrude on their
time together.

Jenny's last words to her, as she turned at the door to wave
goodbye, were: 'Look after yourself, Gossamer. Take care.'

And Gossamer said: 'I promise.'

She had made two promises. One she kept.

She never saw her friend again.

'Why have you come to tell me this? What is it you seek?'

Fr Montesinos' intelligent ascetic face confronted her
across the table. They were the only occupants of the
room. She knew him more by reputation than by sight,
this priest. She knew he came of mixed parentage, that
his mother had been Scottish; it showed in his saturnine
features, in his black hair and blue eyes. Perhaps he also
owed his reputation as a relentless pursuer of the logical
complexities of his Faith to that Celtic inheritance.

He was held in some awe at the Mission, Gossamer knew.

People wondered why a man of his age – he was still in his early thirties – and potential for advancement should be content to remain in such a dead end as Aucayacu? Why was he not forging a more ambitious course in Lima, or even in Rome? Surely a man of such intellect, of such almost frightening ability, belonged in the capital or the Curia, and not in some blighted cesspit in the Huallaga Valley. Certainly he was no Franciscan, devoting his life to the poor and diseased and oppressed; indeed his distaste for any sort of physical contact, remarkable even for a sworn celibate, was noticeable. Much of his time at the Mission was spent not in ministering to the orphans or the patients, but closeted with the Director in his office.

Rumours, naturally, were rife: that he was a government spy, an intelligence officer for G2, the US Drugs Enforcement Agency, or even perhaps the CIA. The Director, being American and remote from much of the day-to-day business of the Mission, was widely assumed to be a CIA agent. Or perhaps he was one of the secret leaders of the *Sendero*, one of the revolutionary intelligentsia answerable only to the great Gonzalo himself. Such a thing was not unfeasible, after all: was not South America the cradle of the revolutionary priesthood, and did not the *Guevaristas* of the MRTA count priests among their number, fighting Satan with a breviary in one hand and a Kalashnikov in the other? Certainly that would account for a certain fanaticism about him, a tendency to emphasise justice and retribution at the expense of mercy and forgiveness ... Many wondered, but of course nobody asked.

Gossamer saw that he lacked the instinct to offer comfort. Perhaps that was a good thing: she should be made to think, rather than feel. She saw too that his face registered distaste, though whether it was distaste for her as a sexually attractive woman or distaste for her as a person, arising out of some insight into her character, she could not tell. Nor, she told herself, should it matter. It was the priest, not the man, she had asked to see, here in this bare little room at the Mission. But now they were here, and he was listening to her, what had she to say?

'I cannot hear your confession in this place,' he said.

'No, I know that. I'm not a Catholic, by the way, though I was brought up by nuns as a small child. Does that matter?'

He smiled with his mouth. 'Of course not. As God does not turn away any who come to Him with trust and humility, so neither will His priesthood. All are welcome to partake of the Faith.'

Gossamer smiled wanly. 'Does that mean I could become a nun myself?'

There was no smile this time. 'Of course. So long as there was purity of intent on your part.'

Mother Veronica had said much the same, but with more human warmth. Perhaps it was to goad him, because he was a man, that she then said: 'Even though I am not a virgin, and have never been married?'

There was a slight torturing of the flesh about his mouth. 'Then you would be required to undergo a due process of atonement as well as of instruction. Is this what you sought me out to ask?'

She blushed, ashamed of herself. 'No. I'm sorry. I don't know, really. Perhaps it was because I felt so bleak, and in need of some sort of reassurance, some explanation.'

'Concerning the death of your friend Jenny?'

'Yes. Yes, that's what brought it on. And Bertha going away, who reminds me so much of her in many ways.'

'And what is it, concerning her death, that you think requires explanation?'

She shrugged helplessly. 'The cause of it, I suppose. No, I don't quite mean that; I mean the *nature* of it. She was my age, Father: only twenty-one. And so full of warmth, and love, and hope. So *alive* and so lovely to be with. To suffer so horribly and then to die just as life was truly beginning for her, for both of them.' She sighed. 'I know it's not an original question, Father, but *why*? "Not a sparrow falls" – yes? So why did he do that to Jenny?'

'Not a sparrow falls without His knowing it; that is not to say He shoots it from the air. But that is perhaps not what you meant to say; perhaps you intended to ask why God *permits* such suffering, especially to those who, in your view, do not deserve it?'

'Yes.'

'You may as well ask, why does He permit happiness? Do you ever ask that? Do you ever pause to question the justification for your happiness, when you are happy?'

She considered the question. 'I have sometimes wondered if I deserved it.'

'That is a different question entirely. And perhaps that is the question you have truly come to ask me. Not, "did my dear friend Jenny deserve to die?" but, "do I, who lack all her qualities, deserve to live?" Perhaps it is the matter of your own guilt that you wish to address.'

Gossamer gasped and broke out in a cold sweat. She realised in that moment what it was that made Fr Montesinos feared as well as respected. It was as if he had seen through all her protective layers of conceit and self-delusion and stripped her to her bare and despairing soul with that one scalpel-stroke of observation.

She knew what he said was true; and she knew she was not yet ready to meet him on this ground. Now was not the time.

Perhaps he saw it too, for it was as if he offered to let her off the hook. He said:

'However, as I said before, this is not the place for such a question. In the meantime, is there perhaps some little matter, some oversight on your part, that troubles you? Did you speak to him, this Johnny Canfield, as she requested?'

'Yes. Well, as best I could. I saw him a few days after – after Jenny died. It wasn't possible to speak properly, though. The families had gathered when Jenny had the operation, and that in itself was awkward – it doesn't matter why, but there was a lot of tension there one way and another. And of course everyone was shattered by her death, Johnny in particular.' *And Helen Kepesake, who looked at you with such agonised accusation, as if somehow you had killed her, killed everything* ... 'I – I don't know how much he could take in, really. I'm afraid, coming when it did, what I said probably did more harm than good. Perhaps it reminded him of how he hadn't let Jenny say it herself – I don't know. I passed it on, but not the way Jenny wanted me to.' *Of course you couldn't, how can a dupe convey the truth?*

'And was there no opportunity afterwards, later on?'

Gossamer looked down at the table, shook her head, felt a tight sick knot tie itself inside her. 'No. I – I wasn't there for the funeral. It was after I came to Peru.'

'Ah. You had already arranged to come out to the Mission, and it was too late to alter that.'

Her gorge rose; she swallowed. 'No, Father. No, I just ... decided to come, that's all.'

'Something occurred that made you take this sudden decision?'

In a very small, tight voice, she said, 'Yes.'

'I see. Well, let us leave it at that for the present. In the meantime, perhaps you could write to him.' She looked up into his face. He looked as if he were waiting for confirmation of something he already knew to be true – waiting, in the full certainty of finding it out one day.

'Yes,' she said. 'Yes, I could write to him I suppose.' Chatteris Choate could find out where he was; she could send it with a covering letter to Jean-Luc Frémont.

'He might be ready to receive the message now, don't you think? And you would be better able to give it than you were before.'

'Yes. Yes, I'm sure you're right. I'll do that. Thank you, Father.'

He nodded slightly. She did not go yet; something in his attitude told her he was now in charge of the interview, and had something else to say.

'I think that there is more you will wish to tell me, Miss Fane. When the time comes for you to do that, you should find me in my Confessional in Aucayacu.' He drew a card from under his soutane. 'These are the times. Come at the end, if you have much to speak of.'

She took the card. 'Thank you,' she breathed.

She felt his eyes on her as she left the room.

He was right. She found herself able to pass on Jenny's message of hope and comfort and love for Johnny, and she posted it the next day.

The action emphasised her own emptiness. She felt herself begin to spiral down into it. She began to anticipate extinction, a passing from one world into another through the door of a Confessional in Aucayacu.

It was not given to her to know when, or how, or why the transition would occur. She was certain only of what lay on the other side of that door. In this, and only in this, she was entirely wrong.

❖ Twenty-one ❖

Another month passed, another month of comforting drudgery and soothing habit. The raw edges of her mind were further blunted, the unbearable peaks and troughs began to level out to the promise of a gentler emotional landscape, uneventful but habitable. The children came to regard her as part of the furniture of their lives, something to be taken for granted, and she was thankful for it. Even the young *Sendero* who kept his vigil outside the Mission gate became part of the landscape of life, part of a routine that would be more disturbing by its absence than by its daily renewal. People, she reminded herself, could adapt to almost anything. The terrorist at the gate could adapt to the inactive tedium of his watching and those he watched could absorb his potential for terror and grow accustomed to it. Such adaptability was the curse and the blessing of being human, of staying alive and keeping going.

She made love with Gabriel, as before, giving and taking what they needed and expecting nothing, desiring nothing more, in return. Helen had been a silent sexual partner, a passive and unresponsive recipient of his desires and needs. She compensated for this in their love-making. It was not difficult to do. It involved no fakery on her part to show him and tell him her appreciation for what his body did for hers, and it was as rewarding to see his arousal and excitement, and the deep peace that came from its fulfilment, as it was for her when her body's hunger found the food it craved. He was a wonderfully appreciative sexual partner, never cruel or exploitative. If she straddled his face and took him in her mouth it was at her instigation, as a means of reaching each other and meeting their different needs at times when she was at risk of pregnancy. When she took him and guided him, gently and slowly, into her body's other entrance it was to show him he was trusted. And, for a little while, it exorcised the malignant spirit of the man who had abused and ruined her.

These things helped to keep a distance between them. They became habits of their relationship, necessarily restricted as it was. They helped to fix the barrier that they must not, would not cross. She came at last to feel the trust she asked him to believe in.

The Confessional in Aucayacu remained a possibility, a last resort in case of the disaster she began to believe might not happen.

Another month passed, a month of habit interspersed with small events. A journalist arrived, with his camera and tape recorder, and was introduced to them all by the Director. He was an Englishman, a freelance, a middle-aged and rather portly man who clearly suffered in the summer climate. After a few days he, too, merged into the background of the Mission, and they grew used to his presence. It would be good for the Mission to have publicity, even if it was coloured a little to make a better story. Publicity meant funds, and funds meant they could do more work, better work. Nobody could deny being thrilled at the possibility of reading about themselves and knowing they were recognised in the outside world beyond the confines of Aucayacu and the Huallaga; the big bright world that turned remotely and invisibly on this tiny axis, with all its narrow habits of tedium and terror. They might even be in *Time* magazine; the Director, it was said, knew people there.

Gossamer imagined the article being read and used by Pope Benedict. The thought held no terror for her; she was beyond all that now, it couldn't reach her. She was someone else, now; dead to it. Safe.

She was given more responsibility, more personally rewarding work to do with the children. She began to build a new personality on that foundation, a new version of herself. She put down roots; she began to grow and to relax into this new and larger framework. Warmth and hope seeped back into her deadened spirit. A way of being began to shape itself, a future into which she could project the living image of Gossamer Fane. Life, not mere living, was once again a possibility.

So it did not disturb her unduly when someone came into her room one day when she was not there and went through all her possessions.

Nothing was missing: the Béraud Jen-Luc had given her, her books of poetry, a group photograph of all her class at Ryder-Vail, Jenny's photograph, a souvenir of their day on the river, her address book and the one set of clothes she had kept as a sort of talisman, a last slender link with the life she had rejected – all were there. Gabriel's letter was there, his words of honest thankfulness that she read whenever dread threatened to engulf her, in the hiding place under the little chest of drawers. Nothing had been taken, yet she knew someone had been there, violating her space. Things were not quite as she had left them: a drawer was not quite properly shut, her underwear was not folded the way she always did it, her suitcase on top of the wardrobe did not quite match the rectangle of dust that surrounded it. Someone had raped their way into her life, and then withdrawn.

There had been a little rash of pilfering in the Mission lately: nothing serious, not money, not the drugs from the clinic pharmacy. Nobody owned anything valuable except possibly the Director, whose suite of rooms was quite separate from the main building complex and had not, to anyone's knowledge, been entered. But small personal possessions, little mementoes of no intrinsic value, had gone missing and theft was the only explanation. Gossamer checked everything again, but nothing had been taken. It was like the watcher at the gate. Something had announced its presence, its potential, but no more.

She cleaned and rearranged her room to wipe out the stain of intrusion, and tried to put the matter out of her mind.

The weather changed with the turning of the year.

Temperature in this region remained constant at around 70°F all year but in September the humidity rose in advance of rain. The atmosphere became daily more close and stifling as if the warm soupy waters of the Huallaga were infecting it, and the drumming cacophony of the forest beyond the river seemed to draw nearer until the cloying air was filled with thrumming and ticking and pulsing, the invisible hum of a million insects and the manic screeching of unseen parakeets. Gossamer could not grow used to this: daily it increased and became more insistent as the air seemed to wrap itself around her throat and lungs, oppressively insistent, threatening her very sanity.

Her head ached and throbbed, and aspirin did not relieve it. It felt as if it would burst, as if something must break soon. Then the weather broke, and the rain came.

It came as an emptying of the heavy skies, a solid torrent of water, a drowning that was barely, miraculously, dreadfully breathable. Lightning flashed, thunder roared and pealed, and the rain redoubled its force.

Gossamer was outside when it came and suddenly found herself swimming in air. Within seconds she was soaked, her hair plastered to her drenching scalp, her clothes and then her skin saturated with water that poured off her and over her, between her breasts and across her belly, water flooding every part of her body and streaming down her thighs, her calves, over her feet. She was clothed in wetness, naked under the sky. Her body stirred and woke, her nipples hardening and her sex wetly open to the inundation. Her mind, trapped and silent, screamed.

> *So I would weep like the rain*
> *In the middle of the storm . . .*

Tears of rage and anguish filled her eyes, but there could be no resistance. There was no escaping the loop of memory. She joined it at the moment of drowning oblivion and then it played itself over, scene by inescapable scene . . .

*   *   *

Returning under a bruised and wounded sky, the clouds bunched and bleeding overhead; she does not see them.

She was only aware of the accusation in Helen Kepesake's eyes, of Johnny Canfield's stricken face, of her own awareness that the words she had to speak to him could only hurt and not comfort, as they were intended to. She had kept her promise and broken it in the same moment. She had failed, she had let Jenny down. She could not conquer death, as Jenny had by the very conduct of her own dying. She was not worthy of such a feat, such a victory.

And so she had endured the miserable small talk of death's aftermath, heard how the cupboard in Jenny's old bedroom at home still contained her childhood things, her special books and toys and animals that she had put away carefully saying that they were to be kept safe for her own children, one day; she had explained to her the mechanism by which Johnny, proud on her behalf and refusing all offers of assistance, would claim from the Social Fund the thousand pounds it was costing to collect and cremate the body that had once been his beloved Jenny, so warm and lovely and full of joyous life . . .

And then she had fled, desolate and despairing and hating herself. She had come back to Carey, to what she must learn to call home, to what she must work on and make transcendent so that the vows she and Carey were soon to exchange might have validity and not turn to ashes in their mouths as they uttered them.

For richer, for poorer; in sickness and in health . . . Jenny and Canfield had never exchanged them. It had not been necessary.

And Carey is there: attentive, solicitous, concerned . . .

'Oh my dear Gossamer. Was it very awful?'

'Yes. Yes, Carey, it was. Very awful. He's only able to hear echoes of his own grief. It wasn't enough just to pass on Jenny's words. I couldn't be Jenny.' She turned away from him to hang her coat up.

'Poor Gossamer.' He laid his hands lightly on her shoulders.

'Poor Johnny. Poor Jenny. Oh God.' She turned, buried her face in his chest. 'It's so horrible, so horrible.'

'Yes.' His voice boomed against her. 'Yes, it's horrible.' His hands came round her back and held her in to him, comfortingly, caressingly. 'It's horrible for you, and you don't have to be ashamed of showing it.' *And she lets go, then. She gives way to her grief, and his comfort. And when he asks her if she would like to stay home tonight instead of going to the reception to celebrate the launch of StarWorld, when he offers to put in a very brief token appearance and return at once to her, she says no, and means it.*

She did not want to be alone. She did not want to spoil this evening for him. That was not the way things must be. How could she truly believe that he would always be there for her if she could not be there for him, with him?

'No, it's all right, Carey,' she said. 'I'll come, I'll be there, it's important. I see now that it's more important than it ever was before.'

He kissed her. 'Thank you,' he said. 'Thank you, Gossamer. I can't tell you what it means to me.'

She understood him to mean that he felt as she felt and, like her, could not find the words to express it.

'Please don't say anything to anybody, Carey. Not even to Alec Dayfield. I'll be all right, I shan't let you down.'

'I know you won't,' he said. He took her in his arms and kissed her with a passion and intensity that he had never shown before.

It told her that he had invested all his hopes in her. It told her of his gratitude. It gave her the strength she would need, later on, to act the part of herself.

She is wearing a black evening dress, simple and sheer, and playing her part to perfection ...

She knew it was going to be difficult. All the key personnel from DayStar and OffWorld were here, and the lawyers and accountants and bankers. Everyone would have to be on their best behaviour lest tonight's cries and whispers should become tomorrow's published innuendo in City diaries and financial gossip columns. These were fragile times in the City and especially in the media; nervous, jumpy. Valuations could soar or plummet on the whiff of a scandal, the hint of a solecism, a rumour of a rumour of a rumour. Insolvency stalked the Square Mile like the plague; recession hovered overhead like the angel of death, observed but not yet acknowledged. StarWorld was a rational creation, the off-spring of logic and necessity – but it could perish overnight in an atmosphere saturated with superstitious fear.

Gossamer's duty was to be dazzlingly bland, an intelligent and conversible adornment. There was a scattering of bimbos, of course, of both sexes: she must be pleasant to them, too. She was happy to do it, not just for Carey but for herself; she was glad she'd insisted on coming. She was happily aware of Carey's admiration and gratitude, warmly appreciative of the way he never left her side while not seeming to possess her. It showed his trust and sensitivity and it gave her confidence to relax into the rôle she had accepted for tonight.

The drink flowed, the decibel level rose. Smiles became glassier, laughter more raucous, small talk more emphatic. Carey steered her into a group discussing the relative merits of the parties' campaigns in the forthcoming election; someone said John Major on his soapbox reminded him of Norman Wisdom and someone else wondered loudly who Norman Wisdom was; Gossamer said, 'Who's John Major?' and everybody laughed.

Carey squeezed her arm. 'I love you, Gossamer,' he murmured, and she glowed.

'Will you be all right here for a few minutes?' he asked softly. 'Just a couple of things I need to do, okay? Alec's suggesting we have a small private celebration in one of the rooms upstairs, just the three of us. A drink and a toast, and then we can go home. Will you be able to manage that?'

'Of course,' she answered. 'I'm all right, really. Don't worry.'

'Bless you,' he said. 'Keep it up.'

Then he squeezed her arm again. And turned away, still smiling.

She watches him out of sight, this man whose wife she has agreed to be, as he weaves his way across the room. A waitress offers a tray of vol-au-vents and she takes one. When she looks again, he is gone.

Now they are talking about opinion polls and she is not really listening. She feels suddenly weary and a little dizzy; she must not have any more to drink. A gap opens up between two other groups and she sees Alec Dayfield; he seems to be unaccompanied tonight, between babes presumably. He gives a little bow and raises his glass to her and she smiles back, and then the gap closes.

'But of course the Liberals can make any promises they like, can't they? It's not as if they'll ever have to keep them.'

'You don't think there'll be a hung Parliament, then?'

'More like a well-hung one in Ashdown's case!'

'Hello, Gossamer.'

The new voice came from behind her. She wheeled round and he was standing very close, his face flushed, his breathing heavy. She felt intimidated.

'Mike,' she said. 'Hello.'

'Here's to you, Mrs Carey Lambert-to-be.' He drained his glass. Gossamer could see from the way his feet shuffled slightly as his head went back that he had drunk too much. He smiled wetly. 'My, didn't the little girly do well. What a long way she's come, to be sure.'

She wanted to step back, he was just a little too close for her comfort, but the circle had closed behind her and her retreat was blocked. She must not lose her composure, must certainly not give way to any sort of special pleading with him. 'I think you've had a glass too many, Mike,' she said coolly. 'I wouldn't want you to say anything you didn't mean.'

'Oh don't fool yourself, dear Gossamer, I'm saying just *exactly* what I mean.' His speech was not slurred but it was heavy. 'And I'll be the judge of my own excess, if you don't mind. You *don't* mind, do you, Gossamer? After all, you must be a very fine judge of your own. Always were. For all you were *so young*.' The last two words were spoken in crudely breathy parody of her own voice.

Her mind, tired as it was, tried to pick some meaning out of this soup of innuendo. The general offensive tone of it was clear enough and the allusions were also crudely obvious but if there was any particular accusation in it, it eluded her.

'I don't know quite what you're getting at, Mike, but I think you may have the wrong idea about me. I'm not—'

'Oh no, oh dear me no! Oh believe me, I have a very accurate idea *indeed*, the full s. p. as they say in horseflesh circles.' He grinned nastily. Once again she had the feeling he was looking at her as if she was meat. His grin became a slack smile and he raised a hand. 'No offence, okay? No, really. You are what you are, always have been. I was the one who deluded myself. Paid the price, too.'

An interpretation of his words began to suggest itself. It was outrageous and she had every right to be very angry indeed, but she could see he was hurt as well as drunk. Both states had made him clumsy, and she must have tact enough for both of them.

She spoke quietly and kindly, as to an overwrought child: 'I see you've been told about me, then, Mike. About my origins. I don't mind that a bit, but I'm very sorry you should feel this way about it. I don't think it's fair on me, or worthy of you.'

He gaped at her as if in amazement. 'Sorry? You're *sorry?*' His voice was a strangled shout. 'Jesus Christ! Unworthy of me? Unfair on you?' He gave an ugly bark of laughter. 'Well, go on. Do tell me why, I'm fascinated,' he drawled.

'Very well, then.' She made her voice schoolmarmy. 'Because we shouldn't be blamed for things in the past that we had no control over, that's why. It's unfair to be held responsible for them and unfair to be treated as if we should be. Especially if we're trying very hard to overcome them. As I am.'

She detected a note of self-pity in her voice and cursed herself for it. She could feel herself on the edge of a spiralling circle of misery and exhaustion, each fuelling the other. She must shift this horrible, pointless conversation back to an abstract level.

'Or perhaps you don't believe people should do that, come to terms with things like that and try to make the best of themselves. Perhaps you think people can't. Is that it, Mike? You believe in original sin? You despise all these doomed, pathetic efforts to amend and improve?'

'Oh no, Gossamer.' He seemed suddenly sober. He came into focus as he took a small, controlled step back from her. 'That's not what I think at all. Like I said in my note, I congratulate you. I salute you!' He did so, with ironic stageyness.

He raised his glass and performed a pantomime double-take of finding it empty. 'Take the toast as read, Sam. Here's to you. The girl done good. Remember that? Well, here's me returning the compliment. You've done very well.'

His look was piercing. 'You did well enough by me, too. Shame I wasn't up to your standard, that's all. My loss, I'm sure.'

His eyes held her for an instant. Once again he regarded her with an attitude that hovered between loving and loathing. 'Take care, okay?'

He turned and walked heavily away. What note, what was he talking about? She called after him, 'Mike!'

He must have heard her, but he walked away. What was the matter with him, what the hell was it? His whole body was redolent of misery. For a moment she yearned to know, to understand.

Then she hardened her heart against him. To hell with him, to hell with his problems and to hell with his misery, what about hers? And damn him for his compliments and his 'take care'. How dare he, how dare he remind her of the way things used to be, and how dare he use Jenny's words to her!

Her head buzzed with noise and the room swam out of

focus. She shut her eyes against it and told herself not to make a scene. She must go, where was Carey? She wanted to cry, she wanted to sleep, she wanted not to be here any more. What note, did he mean Africa, at the hotel? Forget it, she told herself. Bloody Mike Andersen, damn him for doing this to her. Forget him, what about her? Where was Carey?

She wove blindly through the obstacle course of all the people she didn't want to be with any more, and there he was. Wanted and needed, there he was. Carey.

His eyes were wide with concern. 'Gossamer!' She flung herself forward to him and he took her arm and led her deftly away to an alcove. 'Oh my poor Gossamer.' She pitched into his arms, buried her face in him, let the great wave of her misery break on him.

He held her close, held her still, asked no questions. She was aware of her panic ebbing into him and she knew she was going to be all right, everything would be all right so long as she had him. His calmness flowed into her. So long as she had this, everything would be all right.

She lifted her head and saw she'd smudged his shirt with tears and make-up. 'Oh dear,' she said, touching him there.

'I guess a shirt's gotta do what a shirt's gotta do, darling.'

'Oh, Carey! I'm sorry. People will think I'm drunk, seeing me like this.'

'So what, most of them are. And I'm the one who should be sorry, I shouldn't have made you come.'

'No, Carey, I wanted to, I needed to. And I was all right until just now.' She didn't want to tell him about Mike, not now, perhaps not at all. Let Mike stew in his own peculiar juice, he was nothing to do with her any more. 'It just suddenly got too much for me, that's all, the heat and the noise and everything. I'm all right now.'

'Are you sure? I've got to hang on here for a bit, but—'

'Yes, honestly. I just needed to find you.' They kissed lightly and tenderly. 'I'll have to go and repair my face a bit, though, if your shirt's anything to go by,' she added sheepishly.

'I think you look lovely, smudgy. Okay my darling, you do that. Look, don't come back here, though. So long as you're sure you wouldn't rather go home, why don't you go and have a quiet time upstairs? There's a room they call the small conference suite – in fact, now I come to think about it, it's got its own washroom and everything, too. I booked it for the little private party I was telling you about. Make yourself comfortable there, and we'll join you later. If you're sure you feel up to it?'

'Just you and Alec? Not – anybody else?'

'Is that the way you'd like it?' She nodded. 'I did notice him heading your way earlier. Oh, Gossamer: you didn't want to bother me with it. That was naughty of you. Lovely, but naughty.'

'I'm sorry,' she said.

'Mike is – not, shall we say, the most well-adjusted of men. I think he must have seen something nasty in a woodshed once, and he doesn't seem to show any inclination to get over it. It's why I was glad to see the back of him, in fact, after – well, let's say, after I finally got over my own nasty woodshed experience.'

She kissed him again for that. Everything was all right.

'Gossamer, I don't have a tame monkey like Alec does: that means I'll have to do my own flesh-pressing before I can join you. It also means it's very likely that Alec will join you first. Can I tell him about Jenny, please? I wouldn't want the old bastard to upset you.'

'Bless you. Yes, you tell him. I wouldn't want the old bastard to upset me either.'

He smiled lovingly. 'Also it might encourage him to behave with a little, er, deference. You know?'

'Yes, darling. Don't worry. I shall be perfectly sweet with him, and talk a lot about you.'

He grinned. 'Oh, I'm not sure that would be a good idea, he's jealous enough of me as it is. Just stick to being perfectly sweet until I get there.'

He signalled a waitress over. 'My dear, would you be very kind and show my fiancée to the small conference room.'

His eye caught Gossamer's, and twinkled. 'She's expecting a small conference, you see.'

Gossamer twinkled happily back. 'See you later, darling,' she said.

She saw his face alter swiftly and subtly. It was as though he were looking at her from a great distance, almost with sorrow. He laid his hands lightly on her arms and said:

'Being with you is the nearest I've ever got to being a good man, Gossamer.'

Her heart skipped. 'Carey.'

He smiled. 'I just want you to know how grateful I am, that's all. For everything. Am now, and always will be.' He squeezed her arms gently, then released them. 'Off you go, then. Take care.'

'I will,' she said.

Take care, roared the storm, *take care, take care*. Her hand came up to touch the scar on her cheek that was washed with rain and tears. *Take care*. She opened her mouth to heaven and howled in the storm and the rain, howled her soul out to the drenching sky. Howled in the last scene of all to play itself out behind her blind and streaming eyes.

She washes and restores her face, brushes her hair, straightens her dress, smiles at herself in the mirror and passes into the room. A table and chairs at one end, and at the other end by the window a small settee and easy chairs arranged around a coffee table on which are brandy, champagne on ice and glasses, also a selection of business magazines which she leaves untouched. She sinks into the settee, closes her eyes, calm and relaxed, waiting. She is nearly asleep when the door opens.

'Hello, Alec.' She watched him with eyes half-open as he closed the door, moved past the table and approached her. 'Carey said to expect you.' She smiled up at his neatly massive bulk as he stood over her. 'He told me he'd be up later.'

'Did he now? Well, he told you no lie, then.' He spread his arms. 'Here I am.'

She smiled again. 'I'm afraid I had to leave early, before I made an exhibition of myself. Did Carey explain?'

'Oh yes, Gossamer. He explained. He told me you needed to be on your own for a while. Then he said he'd be about half an hour. Don't worry, Gossamer, he made quite sure I understood the situation.'

She leant back against the cushions. 'Oh, good,' she said. 'I'm so glad. That makes it easier for both of us, doesn't it.'

'Oh, I do hope so, Gossamer.' He crossed to the table, slid his jacket off and hung it over a chair. He removed his tie, loosened his collar, unbuttoned his cuffs, saying: 'He's set the scene for us, hasn't he. Made it all very easy, as you say. Drink?' He raised the brandy bottle.

'No thanks, I won't. You go ahead.'

'Oh, I will.' He poured himself a large measure, drank half of it and set his glass on the coffee table. All the time he never took his eyes off her.

'You know he talks about you a lot, don't you?'

'Does he?' Her voice conveyed a thrill of pleasure.

'Oh yes, Gossamer, he does indeed. Hard to get him off the subject, as often as not. You've really got to him, you know that?'

'I hope so, Alec. I really do hope so.' Of course she knew he would understand why; she could read his understanding in his eyes. 'He talks about you, too, Alec.'

'Really, is that so?' His voice was strained. She must make him, too, understand that it was safe to allude to the past; it couldn't hurt them now.

'Yes, Alec, it really is. And it gives me such pleasure to hear it, after all there's been between the two of you. It means so much to him, the way things are now.'

His lips moved, but she could not catch the words; his hands were balled into fists; what was the matter?

'Alec?'

He focused on her. 'It gives you both pleasure, then. All that.'

'Yes, Alec, it does.'

'And the way he talks about you to me, that gives you pleasure?'

Here was Gossamer's chance to put things beyond any possible misunderstanding. She seized it gladly.

'Yes, Alec. Of course it does. He tried to use me against you once, if you remember. Use me like an instrument to hurt you with and then throw me away afterwards. The fact that it didn't quite work doesn't matter. But that's all in the past now, finished, and what you're telling me proves it. So of course I'm pleased and happy that things can be the way they are now. I'm very happy he's told you how he feels about me, and I'm happy the way he wants me to be with him and the way he shows me off when we're together, because it's his way of telling me, and you, how different things are for him, this time. It means you and I can be here now. I think it's sweet of him, and I love it.'

He laughed warmly, relaxed, came and sat down on the farther arm of the settee. 'Yes, it is rather touching, isn't it? And quite an achievement on your part, I should add. One which I can assure you I appreciate very much indeed. Now I know for certain just exactly how things stand.'

'Thank you,' she said. 'I appreciate your saying that very much. I'm very happy – and,' she grinned, 'a bit relieved. I can relax now.' She leaned back, realising only now how tense she had been. Now it ebbed swiftly away. She hoped Carey would come soon so he could find them like this. It would lay the last little ghosts of his dark fears, break the last of the bonds that still held them to the dead weight of the past.

Alec leant forward to reach his glass, putting his hand on the back of the settee to steady himself. Then he regarded her, legs crossed, glass in hand, smiling into her face. As she smiled back he said:

'Congratulations, my dear, you've done wonderfully well. I salute you.' He raised his glass to her, and drank.

Her smile froze on her lips as her brain recoiled from his words, Mike's words of a few minutes earlier. She made an effort to recover herself, hoping he would not notice.

If Carey came in now he would get the wrong impression. This was just paranoia on her part, stupid and dangerous. Alec couldn't possibly mean anything by it, it was just a pleasant compliment and she should treat it accordingly. As he replaced his glass she said:

'Actually I think I will have that drink now, Alec. Not as big as yours, though.'

'Not now, Gossamer,' he grunted, getting to his feet. 'Later. Afterwards.' He turned. Suddenly he was standing very close to her, his legs bestriding hers. 'Time presses, my dear' he said. 'We don't want to have to rush things, do we?' He took her wrist, not roughly, and pushed the palm of her hand against his crotch.

Time stood still, and she was paralysed in it. It was as if she had been jumped from one existence into another with no possiblity of explaining what had happened in between. It was pointless to try. She must force her frozen faculties to deal with what was happening here and now.

Like an image superimposed on the screen of her vision her mind saw two paths and told her she must choose one. One path began with acquiescence, conscience exchanged for expedience, and led to power, self-respect traded for advantage. She thought of the Biloxi Babe. *One moment he wuz offerin' me a drink and the next moment, dang me if'n Ah wuzn't needin' a coupla Kleenex.* He always made it worth their while.

She chose the other path. *I'm sorry, Carey, you weren't being paranoid.* She must find some way of dealing with this quickly. She would tell Carey about it afterwards.

'Alec,' she managed to say, 'what are you doing?' She spoke gently and reasonably. 'I'm not hearing this, Alec, this isn't happening. Stop it now, and nothing will have happened. Let go of my hand and pour me a drink, please. Carey could come any moment.'

'So could I, ducky, so you'd better hurry up and get your pants off.'

Time unfroze to slow motion. She watched as the muscles and tendons and joints of her arm obeyed her brain's command to pull her hand away from him. She heard the prolonged rasp his zipper made as he pulled it down. She felt the vibration of her vocal cords and the shape of the words in her mouth a slow split second before her voice moaned, *No, no, no, no.*

'Oh but yes,' his hoarse voice countermanded. He forced her hand against him and began to work it up and down against his pants. 'But yes, but yes, but yes.'

His voice assailed her now like the monotonous beating of a club. 'Don't play Miss Innocent with me, you little whore, save it for Auntie Ida who'd be in your pants before you could say "bull dyke" if she knew what you were really made of, like I do.'

As he said this, his hand came round the back of her head and closed agonisingly in her hair, pulling her forward so she could smell the sex of him, rank and urgent. She could see the individual wiry hairs of his forearm and the dark bulge beneath the cotton. She could feel the pulse of it in her hand.

She willed herself not to struggle, not to resist. This must be finished and over very soon. She made herself breathe calmly. She relaxed her stomach, her thighs, her shoulders. She let her head fall forward so her mouth was soft on his wrist as she touched it with her tongue, and he released her hair. He unfastened her dress and his strong fingers slid down and began to massage between her shoulderblades. She slackened her arm and moved her fingers on him, squeezing and caressing. He released his clamping hold on her wrist and she uncurled her fingers and stroked them along his imprisoned sex. He laid the palm of his hand against her cheek and she closed her free hand over it to hold it there. She turned her head to kiss it. She ran the tip of her tongue moistly across his palm, between his fingers. She felt the pulse of his excitement. She heard him begin to moan, deep and soft. He spoke her name. His hand rested, warm and slack, on the bare skin of her back.

She had taken control. Now she must finish it.

She clamped her hand around his scrotum and squeezed

as hard as she could. She sank her teeth into the ball of his thumb while her fingernails dug into the back of his hand. His cry of pain and shock made her do it harder.

She pulled away from him as he sprang back, his face red and contorted. She knew she couldn't go forward, he was filling the space between the wall and the coffee table at her end of the settee. She pulled her legs up, rolled over and crawled to the far end so she could get between him and the door. She could hear her own whimpering as she scrambled to gain safety.

But he recovered swiftly, this time with a yell of arousal and triumph. He crashed on to the settee, started to wriggle over the armrest and pulled her dress up over her back. She felt him grab her pants and yank them down as she fell forward, her hands braced on the carpet.

She was completely vulnerable now, exposed. His fingers forced their way bluntly between her thighs and he turned his hand to prise her open. Her brain whirled in an agony of rapid calculation, telling her she must risk a little not to lose everything.

He was laughing and shouting yes and calling her a wonderful little bitch and telling her she could play all the rough games she wanted. Of course he would always turn things to his use, couldn't exist without getting them his own way and on his terms, must always be justified whatever the cost to others; he was a man, vain and arrogant, he knew he'd always win. And that was her advantage.

She pushed herself back towards him. He'd been expecting to fall on her and have her prone, and it took him by surprise. The flat of his hand skidded painfully across her pubis and then he pulled it away as she flipped over. She was now sitting on the arm of the settee, facing him, her knees drawn up and her pants halfway down her thighs. He was panting, grinning ravenously, idiotically. He sucked the blood from the back of his hand and she saw the bite marks she'd made.

'Come on then,' he rasped. 'Let's see what else you can

do, you classy little bitch. Show me some real tom's tricks, you lovely whore.'

She opened her mouth and ran her tongue over her lips, assured of his aroused and rapt attention. Slowly she raised her stockinged legs higher and watched him through parted thighs. She saw his eyes flick down to her displayed sex, then back again. Good, he was getting the message. She rewarded him for it with the perfect simulation of a sexy chuckle and a sigh of satisfaction and approval as he slid her pants over her knees and down her calves, and off. He knelt before her, on fire with anticipation.

She faked a little moan of entreaty and opened her legs, and as he came forward to go down on her she smashed the ball of her heel into his face, seeing it distort like a rubber mask before the momentum of her savage blow sent head and torso careening back against the other armrest. She brought her foot down a second time into his groin before she too overbalanced and fell over backwards with a numbing thud.

They were up together and met in the middle of the floor. She did not dare to turn her back on him again. They circled, a pair of punchdrunk boxers, stooping towards each other like gunfighters in a corny cowboy movie. The absurdity of it provoked her to hysterical laughter; the danger suppressed it. She made one last attempt to connect with whatever was left of this man's rational mind.

'I'm not a whore.' She caught her breath. 'And I'm not a bitch, Alec. I don't want anything from you. Are you hearing me, Alec, do you understand? *I don't want anything from you*. It's not too late, Alec. It's still not too late. Do your trousers up, Alec, and go and wash your face while I put my pants on and pour us both a drink. It's not too late, you understand? You tried to do a terrible thing but you didn't do it. It didn't happen, I prevented it happening for us both but I can't go on doing it.' She halted. 'Alec?'

He stood still, breathing heavily through his mouth. 'You bet you can't,' he snarled thickly. 'There'll be no more tricks from you, Lambert's whore. You're gonna get screwed, little

Miss Honeytrap. Lambert thought he could use you as bait, reckoned I couldn't resist, made every opportunity to tell me what a sensational lay you were, all the tricks you could turn. I heard it all.'

As he recited the salacious catalogue of body parts she saw to her horror and disgust that he was stimulating himself, bringing himself to maddened self-arousal to block out the last of his inhibition. Before, he had kidded himself he could have her with consent, even reciprocation. Now she knew he intended to rape her.

It was then she realised the mistake she'd made. When she'd stopped circling, he was between her and the door. She found she had nothing to say.

'Oh Christ yes, I've heard all about you, over and over again. I've been tempted to the limit of endurance by Mister Carey Whoremaster Lambert. The way you can always come when he does and make him feel he's the only one who can do it for you.'

'Stop it,' she whispered. 'Please stop it.' She felt sick.

'No,' he shouted back. 'No, I won't stop it, you're fucking well going to listen to it and then you're going to get it. When it comes to your skills as fuckstress, I've had the full treatment. And it's had the desired effect, believe me. I've wanted you for a long time, wanted you all the time. I've fantasised fucking you when I've been fucking someone else.'

She knew about that. Her mind groped towards a hideous conclusion. She said:

'Carey told me that. He – he warned me to be careful.'

'Of course! He was frightened. Listen, sugarplum, I *could* have had you, a dozen times I could have had you and you wouldn't have known it was coming until I was turning you over to give you a second helping. But I haven't, and d'you know why? I haven't because I've always reminded myself Carey must have a reason for telling me all this. You follow? So what could his reason be for telling me all about you, who you are and where you came from?'

'I don't know, Alec. Please explain it to me. I'm so tired, and – and not really feeling very well.'

It was as if he hadn't heard her. And he was still keeping himself erect. 'It's so obvious, isn't it? He wanted me to, of course. And that was the best possible reason for not doing it. But that was then, this is now. Then he was baiting a hook with you; now he's flaunting you. That makes the world of difference, as you should know: you're it.'

'I don't understand, Alec. Why don't you sit down and tell me?'

He shook his head irritably. 'It won't work a third time, ducky, you're gonna get fucked. And forget the protests, you know as well as I do you'll enjoy every minute of it the moment my cock's inside you. But I'll enjoy telling you anyway. *You're* the difference because, like I said before, you've got to him. He's hooked. He actually wants to have you all to himself, he wants to marry you. It hasn't turned out the way he expected at all. He still wants to show off, he still wants to taunt me with you, but now he's shit scared. He worked the trick once, with the photographs, and he thought he'd worked it again sweet-talking you back into his bed. But you're not just a pretty face, are you my dear? You've got a brain and an eye for the main chance. You've pulled the trick back on him. So long as you can keep your hormones in order, you've got him eating out of your hand as well as your pussy. He's haunted by the thought of another man having you. The thought of it being true is torture. The fact of it'll knock him right off his perch. He'll finally know he's lost it.'

His voice came thickly, menacingly intense. 'Do you understand now why I'm going to do it? Business and pleasure – that's why. I'm going to break both his balls at once. You might as well lie down and let it happen, sweetie, because it's going to happen. Right – now.'

'I'll fight,' she said. 'I'll claw and bite and kick. I'll hurt you as much as I can.'

'Fight away, I'll win. Resist and I'll only make it worse for you. I'm bigger and stronger and more determined because

I've been waiting so long for this. Years and years of pain and anger. Your face haunted me long before I met you, you know that? Maybe I'll tell you about it one day. Meanwhile all you have to know is that when I'm fucking you I'll finally be doing to Carey Lambert what he did to me a long, long time ago. And I hope I make you pregnant.' He moved towards her.

Now, too late, she understood why. She calculated her chances and found them non-existent. Despairingly she said: 'You're going to rape me, Alec, you know that. Rape isn't seduction. I'm not Constancia.'

Lust became rage. Cursing, he threw himself on her and she was overwhelmed. She felt her arm twisted up behind her back and his huge hand clamped over her mouth, crushing and suffocating.

'Shut up, you trashy little tart,' he spat. She fought for breath and clawed the back of his hand with her nails as he twisted her arm again until it felt as if it would snap at the elbow. She was certain now that he must be mad. She began to fear for her life.

'Breathe her name again and I'll destroy you, you hear me?' He wrenched her arm again. 'Got that?'

He released his hold but it was only to pull her arms down by her sides and pin them there in a squeezing bear hug. She gasped and moaned and fought for air. Locking her arms with his elbows he wrenched her skirt up to her belly and she felt his penis beat like a truncheon against her buttocks. He wedged his hand between her thighs and brought it savagely up, and a thick blunt finger found its way inside her and forced a passage there. She felt herself grow moist inside.

At the moment of her body's first collaboration with this gross and brutal betrayal her mind at last came free and she found anger, not hot despairing rage but cold calculation. She had been betrayed and set up by a man who was now intent on raping her, perhaps by Carey too but this was not the time to think of that unthinkable thing. But she must think of something quickly because, as he'd said, he was bigger and stronger and utterly determined. His hot breath seemed to envelop her.

She had slipped her shoes off earlier – hours earlier, it seemed. One of them, the right one, lay a little way off, its pointed heel facing her. She calculated swiftly. If she shuffled her foot across she could reach it, hook it towards her, flip it over and get her foot into it. Possibly. It would mean spreading her legs and he would take advantage of that, but perhaps it might delay him a little, too, just for the few precious seconds she needed. It was worth trying. There was nothing else. She must make it seem like a piece of pathetic resistance, not a come-on. She wouldn't get away with that one again.

She put her plan into action and as she had foreseen he took advantage of her new vulnerablity to force a second finger in with a grunt of satisfaction. It hurt, which helped; it concentrated her mind.

Only when mind and body acted together did disaster follow.

She retrieved the shoe and crammed her foot in. He seemed not to notice; his head was in any case level with hers as he had eased his body down and now began butting up between her thighs and taunting her with the anticipation of what was to follow. She must put a stop to this altogether.

She brought her legs together again, clamping him. She felt another buzz and heard him cry out, half in annoyance and half in pleasure. Then she brought her leg up as far as she could and drove her heel down on his foot, and ground it in.

He yelled in pain and in the instant his grip was relaxed she whirled round and flew at him. She was older than she had been last time she'd found herself in this situation (with Carey, with Carey), older and stronger and angrier and wiser in despair. She flew at him with feet and fists and nails, screaming and spitting in his face. She knew even as she did it that she couldn't keep it up for long.

She took her shoe off but at the last moment found herself unable to hit him in the face with it as she'd intended, as if some distracting voice of unwanted conscience had whispered, *Are you sure you want to do this, are you sure it's all his fault?* She threw it at him instead. The heel of it caught him just below the right eye and his head jerked back as it ricocheted off. He reeled backwards and she dashed past him for the door, her dress at last shucking down over her nakedness.

He flung an arm out and grabbed her as she passed, tore her dress as he pulled her round at the limit of his reach. Her breast spilled out as she struggled to get away and his face contorted and she heard him snarl, 'Ah no, ah no you don't!'

He jerked her towards him and then let go and she staggered, neither pitching forward nor falling back. Suddenly everything went into slow motion. She saw his hand draw back and the glint of the lamplight on his chunky gold signet ring. She saw it swing round slowly in a clubbing arc, palm inward. She blinked, and the world exploded.

She was flung backward with the force of the blow and her coccyx met the edge of the heavy table near the door. She heard Miss Manningtree's voice telling her about the conservation of linear momentum as the back of her head met the table top with stunning force. She lost the ability to organise her body, slid off the table and slumped to the floor.

The side of her face felt like a block of wood but something was tickling her chin. He stood over her, panting, hands at his sides. She felt her chin and found wetness, red wetness. She followed the wetness up to her cheek and the pain was so agonising, she screamed and wept, making salt tears to make the pain worse.

She spoke through her weeping: 'What have you done, oh Christ what have you done?'

He laughed. 'I've spoiled you. I've brought you to light. I've scratched through the platinum and shown up the brass, my dear. I've put you back on whore's wages, that's what I've done you silly little bitch!'

'What are talking about? I don't understand, what are you trying to tell me?'

'Shut up, bitch.' He kicked her and she screamed in fear.

'What have I done, why do you keep calling me these things?'

He squatted down over her and she flinched away, banging the back of her head on the table leg. She heard it but did not feel it. His face was a mask of grinning disgust. He looked like a satyr.

'Forgotten what the truth sounds like, have we, after all these years? Forgotten where Carey found you, is that it? Forgotten how you met?'

She struggled to her knees, facing him. There was no escape now, she might as well argue it out while she could. 'What do you mean? Of course I remember.'

'Tell me, then. How did you meet?'

'I was in Hyde Park, a man tried to mug me and Carey was there. He stepped in.'

'And what were you doing in Hyde Park, can you remember that?'

She frowned in concentration. He was clearly mad, but thank God if she could humour him. It would make the time pass. 'Yes, I can. I was running.'

'Running? Surely not for pleasure. Why were you running, were you running away?'

'Yes, in a sense I was. I'd been . . . I was upset. I wanted to get away from things a bit. I was new to London and it was all very strange and threatening.'

'Oh, yes!' He seemed grimly, disgustedly amused. 'I daresay it must have seemed all of that, to you. Nonetheless you were managing to make your way in it all right, weren't you? *Weren't you?*'

'Well, yes, in a sense. I was very young and inexperienced of course, but I did have money and there were people I knew.'

She thought he was going to be sick. 'You had money.' He gagged on the words. 'You knew people, young and inexperienced as you were.'

Mike's words again, why was it always coming back to Mike?

'Jesus Christ,' he muttered thickly. 'Sweet Jesus Christ. Still, it's something you're honest about it. And what then, eh? What happened after that?'

As she came to terms with her pain she was able once again to concentrate on anger, calculated anger. 'You know what came after that, Alec. Just as you know what came before it.'

'Oh, *yes!*' He spat the word at her. 'Oh yes, I know, I know what came after. The Ryder-Vail school of tarty dancing. Baring your tits for the billboards. Playing the nympho in *Dragon Hurst*. Yeah, yeah, I know it all. *And* what nasty old Carey did to you with his camera. And Africa – Mike Andersen included. And Project Aid, and all the rest of it. The BodySkin Girl, oh Jesus yes. But there was something I didn't realise, something I had to be told before I could see through it all.'

Now she covered her breast. He watched her intently as she did it. She couldn't tell if he was still capable of taking her now. She knew that in other circumstances, in circumstances that could never now come about, she could be attracted to this man.

'And what's that, Alec?' she asked. Something in her brain told her Carey was not coming, now. A voice said, *He never was*. 'What is it you didn't realise?'

'That you were a tart all along. A clever little tart but a tart nonetheless. The same hard-bitten little whore you were when Carey found you and took you up.'

'I don't know what you mean. I honestly don't know what you're talking about. You know all about me, you know my origins. Carey was the only man—'

'That's right, sweetie. Your origins. That's right.'

'I didn't choose them, Alec.'

'Society to blame, was it? All the fault of the Tories, no doubt. Still, you must be grateful to Maggie for creating a market for you. All that money just itching to be spent! Especially on a sexy little schoolgirl slut.' He rose quickly to his feet and she saw he was still capable of rape. And still quite insane.

'What was it Carey said? Ah yes: a tenner a fuck, suck you off for a fiver, photography by arrangement, condoms supplied, that was it wasn't it? Of course you did get the odd one who turned nasty but then – along came Carey Lambert.'

She shook her head in disbelief. Was she the one who was mad? 'This is horrible, I can't, it's not—'

He shouted at her, 'Oh for Christ's sake cut the fucking innocent! I *know*, don't you understand? I know everything about you, Lambert told me everything! I know how he found you as a teenager selling your body in the streets and paid to have you smartened up in return for certain favours, *I know all about it*. I know who you reminded him of, that's why he picked you up in the first place, and now I know you're both in this together, you're a team, you set all this up but I'm too clever for both of you and I'm going to screw you both, the bastard and his bitch.'

She had struggled to her feet during this. Now she had to struggle not only against his shouting but also against herself to get the words out. At last she let them go in a screaming torrent of anger and despair as the earth caved in under her and the world came toppling down. She was blinded with tears and she didn't care what happened next.

'It's not true, listen to me, can you hear me? You must hear me, you must hear the truth. I wasn't a teenage prostitute, I was a teenage schoolgirl, I was doing O levels and A levels at Shaws School, you know Shaws? It's where half the women executives at DayStar come from I expect. And before that I was in a nunnery, yes that's right Alec bloody Dayfield, *a nunnery*, a convent orphanage, that's where I grew up. And I met Carey Lambert when I was eighteen, I was in Hyde Park and somebody snatched my bag and he got it back and then later I met him again when I nearly got run over. I was eighteen, I was a virgin, I'd just left school, and I'd just been to see my solicitor. Check it all out, you bastard, go on, check it, Shaws School, the Convent of the Order of the Tears of Mary, it's at Heronsburn in the Borders, get bloody Mike Andersen on to it why don't you, and my solicitors are Chatteris Choate, have you got that? Chatteris Choate, and my guardian there, the man I went to see, was Kevin Germain, he's dead now but you can speak to Jean-Luc Frémont instead, he'll tell you. And that's the truth!'

She screamed the last words so hard it made her faint. She grabbed the table for support and staggered against it, groaning, her eyes shut. There was a terrible silence. 'Well?' she said, streaming tears. '*Well?*'

Nothing. She opened her eyes and saw Alec Dayfield.

His body sagged as if he had just been shot in the chest. His mouth hung open. His colour was terrible, a sort of sweaty purple-grey. His breathing came in thick rasps. He looked through her.

He groaned, he cried out incoherently, he staggered heavily towards her and his hand came up, outstretched.

She screamed. She couldn't take any more. He was going to attack her now. In his madness he was going to fall on and attack her, crush her, strangle her. His hand reached out for her and she screamed again.

She tried to push past him and they got tangled up. He was suddenly a dead weight and she couldn't hold him up. They fell to the floor, she to her knees and him slumped on top of her between them. Now he was calling her name, roaring it out. She screamed, struggled, fell to the floor under him and felt his hands heavy on her shoulders and trying to hold her, pull her up. She screamed again and again and wished she could open her eyes and find it was all over.

And then suddenly it was over. Suddenly the weight was off her and she opened her eyes and a new voice shouted her name.

Enter the Third Murderer. Mike Andersen was there. She sat slumped against the table, blood on her swollen face and her exposed breast, her legs open, her sex on display, and he was there, looking at her. She threw her head back and howled, howled her rage and disgust at this world of men and cruelty and abuse and betrayal and death, howled at the ruins of her blighted and broken life, howled for oblivion.

She heard Mike call Alec a bastard and say he was going to kill him. Good, let him. Let them both fight Carey and all three of them be dead, she didn't care any more.

The two men blundered round the room exchanging swinging, sickening blows and wrestling each other into the furniture. They took no notice of her. She crawled along the floor and found her shoes, scrunched them on. She couldn't go out in this dress, it was torn and ruined and now both her breasts hung out of it and she didn't care but she couldn't go out in it. She hauled herself to her feet and grabbed Alec's jacket off the back of the chair.

As she left the room she turned and saw Mike deal a huge blow to Alec's jaw, saw Alec fall over, heard the crash of his heavy senseless body. She ran, stumbling, down the stairs.

Everybody had gone except for a few of the staff, clearing up. No Carey. Of course.

Outside it was raining as if the world would end. She ran into it, weeping like the rain

It is nearly over for the woman in the rain. Only the last of it remains to inundate her once again, now in the sepia September of the Huallaga as it was then in the orange glare of an April London night of storm and flood. Her body is like the cascading water, a thing of liquid waywardness. She is transfixed in the extensionless present: there is no future.

It is nearly over.

Last scene of all . . .

She ran blind, uncaring and unseen through the sluicing streets. Going nowhere, somewhere, anywhere, past wretched figures huddled in doorways, past hunched and hurrying people with somewhere to go and someone to go to. Past darkling blocks of brick and stone and the fishtank light of shop windows she ran on through the vast indifference of London, gratefully anonymous and waiting only for the moment which must come, the moment when she would dissolve into it and become invisible and be at peace at last.

But her mind will not leave her alone, will not cease its speculations: was Alec lying about what Carey told him or has Carey deceived them both and if so for what purpose unless it is the motivation of pure evil? And Mike, Mike who threatens death on Alec for what he is trying to do to her, Mike who treats her like a lump of dog shit on his shoe, what is she to make of him, of any of them, of herself? Is it that she invites deceit and cruelty, does she seek abuse, is that what she has been made for? In that case let her be unmade, or if not let her be given some sign that it is not so, some reason to hope and to persist with the business of living. But there is no sign.

She turned a corner, another angle of pavement, running between railings, wrought iron to the left where there was the black leafy wetness of a park, aluminium to the right where the cars and taxis hissed meaninglessly by. She turned the corner and her heel broke and she staggered to the sturdy comfort of the park railings, abandoning all pretence of thought.

She pulled her shoes off and flung them away. Hand over hand she made her way along the black iron palings, not caring what would happen when they ran out. She felt her stockings wear through under her feet and she stopped and rolled them off and threw them away and carried on, bare-legged. The rain on her skin and the wet pavement under her bare feet gave her a sort of identity, a connection with the turning earth of yesterdays and tomorrows. She had no other.

She heard feet running on the pavement behind her, shoes pounding on the slabs. Someone going somewhere, someone from another world. She had better be out of the way, she was better left alone.

A gap appeared in the railing where a little gate had been torn off its hinges and dumped in the sour bushes. Beyond was grass and trees and pools of underwater light from lamps in the branches. The running footsteps pounded nearer. She flowed through the gap, seeking to become unobserved, unminded.

The soaking turf was balm to her feet, a little unexpected touch of paradise. Her feet lifted off it and propelled her forward, into the safety of the trees and the dark. A voice behind her shouted her name but of course she was imagining it, it belonged somewhere else and did not apply to her: her unconscious mind told her that, as it sometimes told her that the ringing of her alarm clock was another sort of bell demanding to be heard by another sort of person who did not need to stay asleep.

It called again and she walked on, enjoying the feel of the wet grass between her toes. Then the sound of her name became the heavy warmth of a hand on her shoulder.

She turned, and the voice that was a hand on her shoulder became the presence of Mike Andersen. Its mouth moved, gasping for air. It moved again, and words came out.

'Gossamer. Please. Please don't go. I love you.'

She analysed the sounds. Her name, yes. He wanted her to stop moving. That meant to stay still. Very good. She was. But *I love you*, no, that meant nothing. It connected with nothing. It signified nothing. It was just three lumps of noise.

Now he had put another hand on her. 'Oh Gossamer, I love you and I want you.'

There was something she could understand. She saw he was very wet.

'Oh?' she said. 'Why?'

'I don't know, how should I know? I don't care.'

That made sense. It was reassuring to hear words that did not spin a web to catch her in.

'I'm cold,' she said, noticing it.

He took her in his arms and pressed his body close to hers. Her hands felt his warm skin under wet clothes.

'That's nice,' she said in her head, because it was nice. 'Do it more,' she thought. Now they should be naked; now they were. The wet clothes had been spoiling the dream.

And so they slid to the ground together as they rose and came to meet it.

Their bodies met in the rain and made love in a light-filled waterfall and in the black wet London night, simply wanting each other and wanting this, and taking it together: and so they rode that rolling mindless flooding tide, and broke together in the annihilating crisis of its consummation; and so they found themselves beached on the ebb.

And so it was over, and gone. She was still clothed and wet and shivering in a scruffy little London park, and so was he, the stranger, the man who clung to her and declared his love and made promises of marriage and protection. How could they apply to her?

'Who am I?' she asked.

'Gossamer,' he said. 'Gossamer Fane.'

'And what is she, this Gossamer Fane? You said you knew, once, what she was.'

He looked into her face, blinking in the rain. 'I was wrong,' he said. 'I don't know. And I don't care, I don't care what you are.'

'I know,' she said. 'I don't care either. That's the trouble.' She shivered, chilled to her soul.

She emptied the pockets of Alec Dayfield's sodden jacket, throwing his possessions out: wallet, credit cards, pen, cigarette case. As each one hit the puddled mud it made the sound of a door slamming shut. She was ready.

'Goodbye, Mike Andersen,' she said.

He stumbled toward her, reaching out to her. 'Where are you going? Don't go, I love you, I need you, Gossamer I—'

'*Don't touch me!*' He recoiled, aghast.

'Don't touch me, Mike, I'm fire. Corrupted fire. I burn. I destroy. Don't touch me, don't come near, I'll suck you in and burn you up and when it's all too late you'll loathe me and you'll hate yourself. I could have loved you once but now I'm not for loving. Don't follow me, I can't be found, the thing you need cannot be found in me. Goodbye.'

And so she left him in the night: safe, as she could never be again.

* * *

She wept like the rain in the middle of the storm, and it was over.

She clove the water with her fragile grieving body and passed indoors, and fever took her. So Gabriel found her and took her and gently stripped and dressed her and put her into bed, and so she slept.

And waking in the night she came to him and roused him to meet her different need with his, for hers was to drown her mind in a shallow ocean of forgetful, fleeting pleasure. He yearned for love and she reached out for the remembrance of what could not belong to her.

The night was still and humid so they cast the covers off. Outside the open window lightning flashed and the dry warm thunder rolled as they made love. The light flashed, and sometimes was not lightning.

She parted from him in the morning and resumed the habit of her living, knowing something else was over for them both. For days the dull dread of it was her companion, the unexamined knowledge of it lay like a cold boulder in her soul, waiting to be weighed and quantified even as it drew her down to a deeper drowning, a last annihilation.

The lightning had flashed, and some of it had not been lightning but the camera of the man who was not a journalist but an enquiry agent sent from England to spy on Dr Gabriel Jeffry by his wife, whose suspicions had been roused when their little girl had prattled to her of the letter Daddy wrote to his friend in Peru who had the funny name, a letter now photocopied to its author, along with the photographs.

There were tape recordings too.

He let the obscenities fall on his desk. What it must have cost her, he said, to send a detective all that way. What he must have charged her for his services. Last of all he let fall his wife's letter, a typed paragraph to say she had filed for divorce and taken the children away. She told him he needn't delude himself he'd ever get them back. *See if your little slut will give you some,* she wrote, *or is fornication all she's fit for?*

Their eyes met. 'It's all right, Gossamer,' he said, 'I'm not asking.' She looked down, ashamed at her gratitude.

'What will you do?' she asked.

'Go back to England,' he replied woodenly, 'at the end of the month. I went to see the Director to ask for leave and he said he was about to send for me anyway to dismiss me.' He tapped the filth on the desk. 'He had his own copy. A very upright person, our Director. Very much a dealer in absolutes. Pax Christi, and all that.'

'She's right, of course,' he added. 'I don't delude myself. I've been away too much, for too long. She's been into all this already, she knows the score. She'll get custody and I'll get the odd weekend's access.' His voice faltered. 'Supervised, of course. I wouldn't be trusted not to take them away.' He grimaced piteously. 'Which is a reasonable enough assumption.'

'Oh, Gabriel.' It was a pathetic response. It was all she could say.

'She's quite mad, Gossamer, or so it seems to me. I can't even begin to imagine myself into her mind, understand what goes on in it, or why. That's how society defines madness, isn't it? But she's also intelligent and plausible, and we've kept up such a successful front with other people all these years ... I haven't a hope, Gossamer, nor have they. My poor children. I've failed them.'

Her voice shook, not with self-pity. This was her doing, this good man's misery. 'I'm sorry,' she said. 'I'm so sorry.'

He understood what she meant. 'No, Gossamer. Please, don't say that, I can't bear to hear you say that. It's not your fault, Gossamer. Please, you must understand that: it is not your fault. I asked for everything you gave me, and I'll never be able to express my gratitude for it, for you. My eyes were wide open, and I expect I always knew something like this would happen, in the end.'

She shook her head, dumb with the grief and waste of it.

'She'd have found some way, engineered something in the end even if none of this had ever happened. All I've been doing all these years is delaying it, booming it off while it festered and turned into hate. You mustn't be hurt by it, please. God knows the consequences are bad enough for you as it is.'

She looked at him questioningly. 'I'm sorry, Gossamer: too wrapped up in my own troubles to remember yours. You've got till the end of the week to pack your bags and leave, meanwhile you're not permitted any contact with the children, or with me. We're in breach of that one already, but to hell with it. I had to break it to you before he did.'

Her heart turned to ice, her face to flint. She knew what she must do. It had been an option before, a possibility. Now it was inevitable.

'You'll . . . go back to England, I suppose? Can you afford the fare? I could—'

'Yes,' she said in answer to the second question. 'I bought some travellers' cheques when I came out, enough to cover it.'

'We've got some supplies coming in on Friday, you'll be able to get a lift back to Lima on the truck, stay a night in a hotel . . .' He was finding this unbearable.

'Oh, right,' she croaked. 'That's a good idea, I'll do that then.'

There was a terrible screaming silence.

'Well,' she said at last. 'I think I'd better go before I'm taken away.' They both knew why they must not touch each other now. They stood facing each other, the desk between them. An unbridgeable abyss divided them.

'I could never give you what you need most, Gabriel. I'm sorry.'

'Nor I you, Gossamer. And I'm sorry too.'

She parted from him, but her nerve failed her at the door. She turned to look at him. In three strides he was across the floor and she was in his arms. She felt his tears on her neck.

He pulled away, still holding her, and saw her own tears.

'Don't blame yourself, my dear Gossamer. Don't ever blame yourself for this, I couldn't bear to have that on my conscience, too. Help me to be selfish, Gossamer, please. Think of yourself. Be strong. Look forward.'

'I'll do that,' she said. 'I promise.'

When, for the second time that week and the last time ever, Gossamer had left the Mission on Friday morning she'd sensed something wrong as she passed through the gate.

Of course: the watcher had gone. It felt strange, like a threat.

But the threat was the new slogan on the wall: *ADVERTENCIA DE MUERTE*.

Now she stood at a door in a wall that looked like a slice of mouldy bread, and pulled the bell.

A mangy dog trotted by and a smokily puttering *moto cholo* swerved just in time to avoid it fractionally. Then came an Army patrol who stared at her as they drove slowly past. She turned away from them as the door of the Presbytery was opened, and heard it accelerate away up the street, out of the town, as she walked in. It was followed at speed by a second vehicle whose driver saw only the priest in the doorway, not the woman he was looking for.

She stood aside as Fr Montesinos closed the door.

The first time had been in the church, in the Confessional. There she had confessed her life, omitting nothing: he had extracted the whole of it, probed it to the depths, taken it all in.

There, then, she had declared her intent to accept, to abandon, and to yield.

Now she awaited his decision.

He led her down a gloomy passage, past a study to a door at the end that led to a small chapel, dimly lit from one grubby window and sparsely furnished. Her throat caught on the damp mustiness of it.

He genuflected before the little altar, then stepped aside and motioned her to kneel, to pray. She did not know what words to say. Her mind said: *Into thy hands I commend my life.*

She made to rise but he gestured her curtly to stay on her knees.

She obeyed, knowing that she must learn to practice denial of the will.

She must learn the habit of obedience if she was to assume the habit of a nun.

❧ **Twenty-Two** ❧

She knelt, and the priest stood behind her. He was a voice. The visible world became a strip of red matting, grubby and threadbare. The world was filled with the voice of Father Montesinos. There was nothing else.

'Do you wish to renounce the world?'

There was dirt ingrained between the fibres. 'Yes, I do.'

'For what reason do you wish it?'

The coarse weave of it dug into her knees. 'I am not fit for it.'

'Why are you unfit to live in the world?'

'I am tainted.' Her response required no thought. The knowledge lay in her mind like a bright pebble.

Her answer surprised him. She sensed it in the quality of the short silence that followed; knew that he had expected her to say something very different.

'You? You are tainted, you say, not the world? Why do you say this?'

His tone confirmed her instinct; their dialogue had become a conversation. She shifted her knees into a less uncomfortable position, settled her body and answered:

'Everything goes wrong. Everything I do, every relationship I have. Everything I believe is real turns out to be delusion. It becomes corrupted and causes suffering. I know it's not like this for other people, so I have to believe it's me, it's something in me that does it. It attracts evil. It causes terrible harm to people, good people. It makes me unfit for the world no matter how hard I try to shut it out or put myself in situations where I think it can't operate. It happened in Africa and it's happened again here.

I can't get away from it unless I put myself utterly beyond its reach.'

'In the exclusive society of other women, do you mean?'

'Y-yes. In part, but I—'

'Yet you have willingly had carnal knowledge of a woman.'

Trish. The comfort of her friendship. The tenderness of her lips, the gentle warmth of her body. The consolation of it. A warm and happy memory, nothing more. An episode, merely. But—

'Yes. But—'

'To what do you ascribe this – 'malign fate', as you call it? Do you blame God for it?'

'No! Of course not.'

'Why do you say this 'of course'? You talk of fate, of that which is fore-ordained: I supply the Name of the omniscient deity and you deny He is the origin of your fate. What, then?'

'I was speaking metaphorically, I—'

'And I say let us not speak of what is metaphorical, which is a delusion of the unbelieving mind, but of that which is real. Whence comes this 'fate' that you blame for your tainting, as you put it? Do you blame genetics for it?'

'How can I? I don't know where I came from.'

'Yet you have been told.'

'I was told a story, but how can I believe it? I told you he—'

'Yes, that is precisely the case: *you* told me. I have no corroborating evidence, no proof. Is that not so?'

She hung her head, defeated. 'Yes. It is so.'

'Let us suppose I assume it to be true, what you have told me. Is there another source, then, for this 'fate'? It would seem to me that we have exhausted all the possibilities, real and metaphorical.'

'Yes. You're right.' Where this left matters, she could not imagine.

His tone was softer: 'Let us not then call it 'fate'. Let us call it a 'thing', shall we? A *res vitae*, a thing that seems to govern life. Yes?'

'Yes,' she agreed gratefully.

'So tell me, where is this thing located? What is its source?'

She closed her eyes. Yes, it had to be. This was part of it, an inescapable part of what she had to do. 'In me,' she said. 'It's in me.'

'This thing that you would leave behind you, it is in you? This malignity.'

She saw that he had led her, not to the haven she sought but by a circular path to the same place of hopelessness and anguish. 'Yes,' she whispered. Her head sank lower between her shoulders.

'Now let us name it. It is Lust.'

Silence.

'You do not answer.'

She did not answer.

'You are silent. Very well, I shall fill the silence. I shall consider the phenomenology of this thing that I have identified as Lust, most potent of the Deadly Sins. It led you to yield your virgin body to the man Lambert, a man old enough to be your father and who you believed might be your father, as indeed he may be, according to what you have told me. It led you to perform many acts of unspeakable grossness with this man, who then abused you for it and subsequently raped you. Nonetheless you gave yourself to him again in expectation of the sacrament of marriage only, according to your narration, for him to abuse you further so that you were all but raped by a man whom you know to be his deadliest foe – who, nonetheless, on your own admission, you encouraged, kindling his lust for you in order, according to you, that you might trick him and thereby escape. But you did not escape. You were spared this rape only by the intervention of another man, the man Andersen, who assaulted your attacker. He then followed you to declare his love for you. This was a man whom you had known carnally several times some months earlier. A man who, having known you and taken you, had abhorred you and rejected you, and thereafter insulted you on many occasions.'

She could hear his breathing. She knew it was not over yet.

'You have also been assaulted by a colleague of Lambert's, and you say you believe he was responding to certain signals which – all unknowingly, you insist – you were sending him. You have unashamedly performed an act of forbidden carnality with another woman and, by your own confession, feel no shame for it even now. Most significant of all this – for which, I remind you, your word alone is testimony – is that when you found yourself with a man of decency and honour, your lawyer and guardian Frémont who, you believe, might have offered you the sanctity and haven of lawful union, your body spurned him and you sent him from you.

'Have I spoken anything that is not the truth, the plain truth unadorned by any plea of worldly mitigation?'

She swallowed back choking despair. 'No,' she murmured. No, he had spoken nothing but the literal truth. The rest, she saw, must be nothing: all worldly matter must be repudiated, and this was what was left behind.

'So much for what you have told me, now for what I know. Not from what you have told me of it – which, though not false in substance, is yet false by the greater transgression of omission – but from what I know from the lips of the man who was your partner in it. I speak of Doctor Gabriel Jeffry.'

She gasped aloud, and cried out. *No*, her mind screamed, *not him, too. Not Gabriel. Please God let this not be true.*

'I am his Confessor, of course.' She thought his tone was mocking. Of course Gabriel had not betrayed her. Words uttered in the secrecy of the Confessional could not be betrayal.

Unless, of course, the Confessor himself chose to betray

what was spoken there. Unless he had spoken to the Director, who had written to Helen Jeffry . . .

'For a moment you suspected Dr Jeffry of betraying you, yet again. Now I see you suspect me. Let me disabuse you of this: it was not so.'

It was as if her thoughts had screamed in his ear. She was ashamed.

'You say you are tainted. I could agree. But the word has two interpretations, does it not? The English language is such a rich and wonderful thing, so full of hints and nuances. To be tainted can be to be filthy or to be made filthy. You are not made filthy by the world you wish to reject. Let me pay my respects to the English language and use the word that most exactly fits your case: you are taint.'

The word crushed her and pinned her to the floor.

Now he spoke with open disgust. 'You come to me and you say, I have had a terrible life, I was taken up by a wicked man who made me do wicked things, and since then I have tried so hard to be good but something always goes wrong and now I wish to be a nun so nothing wicked can ever happen to me again and I will not make bad things happen to people.'

It was a travesty of what she had said, but like all travesties it contained a recognisable part of the original truth. Besides, she had neither the strength nor the will to oppose him. She would give him his victory. She must not fail in what she had set out to do, she must succeed in this, her last act of free will before she renounced the right to it forever.

'Is Doctor Jeffry, then, a wicked man?' A crushing silence. '*Is he?*'

She had thought it a rhetorical question. 'No,' she breathed.

'Did he ask you to do these things?'

'No.'

'No doubt you acted out of humanity, is that not so? You had reasons, human reasons – good reasons, as they appeared to you at the time – for this as for all the other things that you have done. This is so?'

'Yes, it is.' She was almost crying now. 'I did.'

'They are chimeras. They are fantasies. They are the veils of venery. You have woven them into a halter that leads you ever deeper into the sin of fornication and from one foul depravity to the next, corrupted and corrupting as you sink into the very sump of sensuality. Yet still you would smear your body with the vile slime of it, this "humanity", as if it were the balm of Gilead!'

She had subsided under the hammer blows of his voice. She had no answer to give him save the spectacle of her body, abject at his feet.

And he regarded her body as it knelt before him, prone in surrender. He regarded every swoop and curve of it through the thin drab dress that covered it.

His voice reached her through a dead haze of misery. 'Yet still I hear the crying of your soul in all that corrupted wilderness of flesh. I hear it, and I will answer it. I will free it from torment and lead it to grace, to the perfect freedom of obedience, to the peace you say you seek. Do you ask me to do this?'

Her voice was very small. 'Yes.'

'Then let us consider your body, this vile body, and let us consider how we may change it. Know you that your body is the temple of your soul? And know you that the sin of fornication, the carnal sin of sensuality, is a sin against your body?'

She knew it: it was Corinthians. Her mind projected a little scene: herself and Mother Veronica having a little joke at the expense of the Apostle Paul. A scene from before the Fall. Then her mind grew dark again. 'Yes,' she said, 'I know it.'

'Then we must first cleanse the temple that it may be sanctified and made fit to be the vessel of your immortal soul. Would you repent the sins of the body and against your body?'

Her response was as swift and automatic as a catechism: 'Yes. I would repent.'

'Consider all that I have said. Are you truly penitent?'

'Yes, I am truly penitent.'

'There can be no true penitance, no absolution without penance. Do you know this?'

Her voice was clearer, stronger. Obedience would set her free, and this was the way of obedience. 'Yes.'

'Then you would do penance? And you would ask it here, and now?'

'Yes.'

'Do so. Ask to be purged of sin.'

'I wish to be purged of sin, and do penance.'

'That will suffice. I will leave you for a little, while I prepare it. Remain where you are, and pray. Pray to God to grant me guidance that I may do what is right.'

She heard his footsteps retreat across the chapel, and the door closed. She did as she had been instructed.

He was not gone long. When he returned it was the door she heard, and the rustle of his robe, but not his footsteps.

'Stand up.' His voice was quieter than before, but more intense. She stood up.

'Take off your sandals.' She bent to remove them, and placed them neatly to one side. The matting was unpleasantly coarse.

'Remove your clothes.'

She hesitated for a fraction. But of course it must be done. She reached below and pulled her dress up over her head and cast it aside. She wore nothing else.

'Turn around and face me.'

She obeyed.

Hard work and a healthy diet had toned her body. He saw her at the peak of youth and in the full flower of womanhood. His eyes took her all in. They lingered on the firm fullness of her breasts, on the ripe swell of her hips, on the trim black triangle of her pubic hair and on the sheer curves of her thighs.

And she saw him. She saw the fervour in his eyes and the resolution in his face. She saw his feet were bare, and that his legs beneath the hem of his robe were dark with hair. Her eyes lingered on the scourge he held across his chest. It had a wooden handle worn smooth where his hand grasped it, and three long leather thongs.

'Your body shall atone for its sin. Turn round and kneel. Place your knees apart. Grasp the altar rail with both your hands. Remain silent.'

Meek and silent, she turned. She knelt, splayed, and braced herself. She closed her eyes and prepared herself for hideous pain. After this there must be peace.

She heard him shift his feet as he positioned himself. She heard him give a little grunt. She heard the whistle of the thongs as they tore through the air.

The first blow fell across the middle of her back from right to left, and she gasped through her nose. As the thongs lashed her something told her that she could bear this pain, that this beating was carefully devised to hurt but not to wound. The stinging became a glowing line. It was not entirely unpleasant.

The second blow fell as before, but this time the thongs curled round and whipped her breast. She glanced down and saw the tip grow red and stiff, and with cool objectivity her mind registered this coincidence between pain and arousal.

He dealt the third blow back-handed and her left breast smarted. Sweat stung her between her shoulder blades. Her mouth opened and she breathed through it. She heard his breathing grow harsh and heavy.

The fourth blow was harder, much harder, and she groaned under the cut of it. Her hands let go their hold as, responding to the instinct to protect herself where she had been hurt, she fell forward to remove her back from range.

He dealt her two savage blows across her buttocks and she cried out loud. He shouted, *Whore!* and *Harlot*! as the seventh and eighth blows lashed her inner thighs, and she screamed. She screamed in pain, and she screamed in terror of more pain, and she screamed for the horror of arousal, for the knowledge of its proven possibility, its hideous reality.

His foot landed on her buttock and propelled her sideways. She rolled over, flinging her hand behind her to support herself. The scourge clattered on the floor as he flung it away. She gasped with the shock of pain as her buttocks ground on the matting, and at what she saw.

He was naked. Sweat streamed from his contorted face and down the thick fur of his chest and stomach. His thighs were bunched and glistening. He was monstrously aroused.

He sprang at her and fell on her, pinning her to the floor. Her head flung back and she closed her eyes. She let her soul out in a great anticipating shout of pain and humiliation. He yelled back and arched over her. His face was transfixed, a glazed grinning grimace of lust.

She knew what must happen.

In one crystallising moment of maturity and insight she understood exactly what was happening. She let her body go limp. It was not her, it was a thing she would reclaim later. Or perhaps she would not bother; perhaps she would will herself to die instead.

She heard two sharp cracks and wondered if he had broken her spine or her pelvis and if so, when would she feel the pain? Then, as in a dream or in a film run backwards, she saw him lift off her body. For a moment he hung upright over her, his mouth open in a soundless shout of fear and rage and incomprehension, then he twisted round. There was another crack, louder and heavier than the others, and he seemed to fly through the air, and was gone. There was a sickening crashing slap, like an egg dropped on a flagstone.

She closed her eyes and opened them again.

Mike Andersen was there.

She must be dead, or mad and in a private fantasy hell of her own.

'Enter the Third Murderer,' she said. It was wildly funny. She laughed and laughed and laughed.

She laughed long and loud and shockingly until Mike bent and slapped her face, and then she stopped. Then she was cold and naked and burning with pain. She was also blubbery with tears.

'Hello, Mike,' she said. 'Here's another fine mess you've found me in. Do you want to fuck me now?'

'Shut up. And for Christ's sake put something on so I can get you out of here.' His mouth was set in a grim line. His eyes betrayed some feeling but she didn't want to know what it was.

'Yes, Mike,' she said humbly. 'Sorry.'

She struggled stiffly and painfully upright. Mike did not offer to help her. She turned to retrieve her dress, and heard the hiss of indrawn breath.

'Sweet Jesus Christ. What the hell was going on here?'

'Penance,' she said. 'Father Montesinos devised a penance to purge the sins of my body. It didn't work, though.'

She spoke in a sing-song voice, like a child. She walked stiffly and splay-leggedly across to where her dress lay crumpled on the floor. A shaft of sunlight from the high window caught the livid weals across her back and buttocks, and Mike swore again. 'Here he is,' she said. 'Father Montesinos, this is Mike Andersen. I told you about him, remember?'

She turned a little girl's face to him. 'He's not saying anything, Mike. He's very still. Have you killed him?'

He joined her and squatted over the fallen priest. He flicked an eyelid back, then let it fall. 'No,' he said. 'He's alive.' He sounded almost regretful. He picked the dress up. 'Is this all?'

She nodded and took it from him, and put it on. He groaned involuntarily at the poignancy of her beauty as she pulled the dress down over her body.

Her eyes widened. 'Oh Mike,' she said softly. 'It's so sore at the back.'

'I'll give you something to help make it better,' he said, his voice choking. He knelt to strap her sandals on. 'Come with me now, Gossamer.'

She put her hand in his and they walked together out of the chapel. 'This is nice,' she said.

'Is this case yours?' he asked. It was by the door, where she had left it.

'Yes.'

'Anything else?' She shook her head, then winced.

'Come along, then.'

Hand in hand they walked down the street. 'Where are we going?'

'Hotel. At least that's what it's called. Bug Hall would be a better name. As soon as you're fit enough we'll go back to Lima.'

'Oh,' she said. 'All right, then.' They walked on.

She stopped as they came out into the Square. It was very quiet, almost deserted. 'How did you find me, Mike?'

'Just now? Some soldiers told me, at your Mission. They'd seen you go in there.'

She became aware of circuits reconnecting in her brain. Her voice lost its childishness. 'What were the soldiers doing at the Mission?'

'There's been trouble. Shining Path. The woman I spoke to there was worried you might have been one of the victims.'

Her brain was fully functional now. She wished it wasn't. 'Who were the other victims, Mike?'

'Heywood, the Director. They hauled him out, made everyone watch while they carved 'CIA' on his forehead with a knife, then shot him. And the doctor, I forget his name, Jeffries? They got him on his way to a clinic. Held him up, tossed a grenade in the back of his pick-up, then waved him on. At least he can't have known anything about it. You'd have known him, of course.'

'Yes,' she said. 'I knew him. Take me to the hotel now, Mike.'

'Yes, we'd be better off the streets. They'll be crawling with military soon.'

The hotel was filthy and infested but Mike's room was a little better; he'd brought bug sprays in his luggage. He undressed her and gently helped her to lie face down on his clean unzipped sleeping bag.

He anointed her with an antiseptic salve that stung horribly, then felt better. He helped her up on one elbow

so she could take some Copraximol painkillers and some
pills he said were called Keflex, to ease the bruising. Her
skin was not broken. He gave her a Temazepam, to help
her sleep, and then he sat quietly with her.

After a while she slept and he left her, locking the
room.

She woke to a muddy light that oozed through filthy glass
and filthier curtains. At first she had no idea where she was,
or why. Then she felt the soreness, and remembered.

She sat up, groggy and nauseous. Where was Mike, what
time was it? She knew she'd be hungry soon, and she was
thirsty now. She needed the bathroom.

Her case was over by the wall, lightly dusted with a fresh
crumble of mouldy plaster. She swung her legs stiffly out
and placed her feet on the hideously greasy scrap of a mat.
Surely it must take quite a lot of time and trouble to make a
place as nasty as this? The air in the room tasted of rotting
vegetables and DDT.

There was a silk dressing gown in her case and she
put it on. Silk against her scourged skin and her feet on
cracked and fetid lino. She must look like something on an
early Seventies rock album sleeve. She felt suddenly dizzy.
It must be the Temazepam, she wasn't used to anything
like that. What time was it? She could try looking out of the
window but somehow she didn't seem to have the energy
to get there.

She made it to the bed and sat on the end of it. A faded
Virgin in a fly-spotted frame gazed down on her in pity, or
on the room with decorous revulsion. Or perhaps did not
gaze at all, perhaps her eyes were shut. Very wise of her,
in that case. The light was too dim, the picture too faded,
the glass too grimy to tell. Perhaps she could have a closer
look . . .

Stop it, she told herself, this is the way people go
mad.

Outside the window there was nothing. Had she heard
something in the night, or afternoon, or whatever it was

she'd just slept through? Engines, tyres, a lot of shouting, screaming . . . Probably a dream, she told herself. Especially the shouting and screaming.

But now there was nothing outside. She let the curtain fall back. It smelt of kippers and dead flies.

Father Montesinos scourged you and would have raped you, but Mike Andersen found you. Like before. Inevitably you will make love with him again. It is ordained. Why? Never mind, it means nothing, will mean nothing, nothing will come of nothing.

Mike Andersen found you and Gabriel Jeffry is dead.

Gabriel Jeffry is dead.

But what time was it? Watch, she had a watch somewhere, where watch, where time, what time?

In the chapel of the Presbytery of Father Montesinos. Of course. He'd keep it as a trophy. Or put it on the altar and smash it. Gone, then. Time gone. Everything gone. Everything over but not over. Everything going on, gone. Everything gone nothing come of nothing evermore time after what time?

A key turned in the lock and the door opened, Mike recoiling at the madness in her voice: '*When is it?*'

'Morning, Gossamer. Saturday morning.' He looked at his watch. 'Seven fifteen on the morning of Saturday September 12th 1992 and all's quiet because the Army hauled half the town off for questioning in the night.'

Her brain absorbed, digested, computed. 'I've been asleep for over eighteen hours!'

'That's right. Congratulations, clever girl. Sleep's the best medicine, as my dear white-haired old mother used to say. How are you, apart from sore?'

'Thirsty. And I need the bathroom, is there one?'

'Up to a point, provided you don't want to wash or clean your teeth. Otherwise it's fine so long as you remember to squat and hover.' He reached in his pocket. 'Here's some tissue.'

She took it. 'Last door on the left, end of the corridor. Follow your nose if you can't remember. It doesn't lock. I'll go and get you a nice bottle of refreshing bilharzia-flavoured InkaCola. Hungry?'

'Probably.'

'Okay, dear. Off you go.'

She went. He called me dear, she thought. Why? All part of humouring me, I suppose. And why not? I quite like it. It's better than being raped and beaten.

When she got back he'd rolled up the sleeping bag and laid out clothes for her to put on. Her own pants and chinos, a big sweatshirt that must be his. It had the DayStar logo tastefully stitched on the left breast. No bra, of course. That was very thoughtful of him. She dressed carefully, like an invalid. That's all right, she thought, I am an invalid.

Mike returned with two bottles of warm sweet fizzy liquid. They sat on the bed and drank them. She looked at him. He seemed very alive, alert and full of energy. She saw how he would look even more craggily handsome in ten, fifteen, twenty years' time. 'You're looking well,' she said.

'Thank you. You're looking more beautiful than ever, but don't say thank you.' He grinned swiftly. 'You can't help it.'

'I cropped my hair with kitchen scissors five months ago and I have a scar on my cheek and I feel like something the tide left behind.'

'True. But you're still more beautiful than ever. Imperfection suits you, but then you never were merely pretty. Lucky you. Is the sweatshirt all right, not rubbing?'

She was growing used to his sudden changes of subject. They went with his palpable physical restlessness. 'No, it's fine thanks. And thank you for thinking of it.'

'Not at all. Anytime you get scourged, just call. Here, take these pills with the last of your gut-rot. Same cocktail as before, without the sleeping pill. You've no broken skin. He beat you very carefully.' He drained his cola. 'Practice, presumably.'

'Presumably, yes.' She swallowed the pills. 'He told me just what I wanted to hear about myself. I talked myself into it. He's a very clever man.'

'Here's to stupidity, then.' He raised his bottle. 'Shucks, empty.'

'Mike,' she said. 'How did you find me? Why did you find me?'

He looked steadily at her. 'I will tell you, Gossamer. But not now. When we get to Lima, I'll tell you then. We'll have dinner and I'll tell you.'

'When are we going to Lima?'

'Now.'

'Mike, I can't! I'm all right just sitting but the journey'd kill me. I'll scream every time we hit a bump in the road.'

'No you won't, because we're flying. You only get to scream between here and the airstrip.'

She did not know what airstrip he was talking about. She knew of none in the vicinity. 'How far is that?'

'Coca Paste International? About fifteen miles, as the truck bumps. We do actually need to hurry, Gossamer. The forecast isn't good, I've fixed to fly out at ten, and I don't want us to be stuck here a minute longer than necessary. The Army are very jumpy, they've obviously got orders from above to be seen to be doing something, and that's always bad news. When an important gringo gets himself assassinated it doesn't do to be po' white trash, never mind a wretched native. And if Shining Path were targeting foreign aid workers at your Mission they won't have forgotten they missed you. Determination and a high bullshit threshold are what it takes to be a really effective terrorist outfit, and if you've ever tried to wade through a volume of Gonzalo Thought you'll appreciate this lot are strong on both. And they're nothing if not thorough.'

Gabriel Jeffry was dead. The thought struck her that for him this had been some sort of solution, and she hated herself for it.

'Okay,' she said. 'I'm ready.' If it hurt like hell it would serve her right.

It wasn't too bad so long as she sat forward in her seat and kept her back straight. She couldn't do anything about the sweat that began to trickle down and sting her underneath, nor the soreness of her body, nor the dull ache inside.

It felt good to be on the road again, good to be leaving Aucayacu, good to be going somewhere. Today she was on the road, going to Lima. Tomorrow she would think about tomorrow.

She was horribly hungry. Mike's food supplies turned out to be a loaf that scarified her gums when she bit into it and a scrawny slimy dead thing which he assured her was a whole cooked chicken. 'Dinner in Lima,' he said cheerfully. 'Keep your mind on that.'

But instead her mind fantasised about what she would like to be eating. A big bowl of cornflakes with white sugar and milk straight out of the fridge. Toast and dark chunky marmalade. Tea, a big strong scalding potful of it. Bacon sandwiches. Baked beans with melted cheese dribbling over them . . .

Jenny's voice. And the food she'd had with them, that time, in their flat. The two of them on the river. Ice creams. Jenny being with her. Jenny cursing the pain in her back. *If it gets to interfere with riding I suppose I'll have to take it seriously.*

Gossamer chewed and swallowed the bolus down.

'Okay?' Mike's voice, here and now.

'Yeah. Okay.'

'It gets to be almost all right after a while, doesn't it?'

'Yes. Almost.'

And then they came to a hole in the road, five feet wide, where a bridge used to be.

There was no official warning sign, only the usual *Sendero* advertisement: ¡*PARO ARMADO!* A rock on the other side of the chasm proclaimed, ¡*VIVA EL PRESIDENTE GONZALO!*

Mike drew the pick-up to a juddering halt. 'Well, well,' he said. 'As political slogans go, it makes a change from "Labour's Tax Bombshell" I suppose.' Gossamer's mind leaped the abyss in her own life, back to the London billboards of that April. It was the first allusion he had made to that time, but now was not the time to pursue it.

Two crudely squared-off tree trunks had been laid across the breach. The gap in between them was slightly wider than the pick-up's wheelbase.

'Do-it-yourself roadworks,' Mike grinned. 'Today the Marginal, tomorrow the M25.' He opened the door and leapt agilely out.

Gossamer watched him heft the end of a trunk and haul it a few inches closer in. Then he strolled across, hands in pockets, to do the same on the other side.

Of course he's putting on an act, Gossamer thought. This nonchalant strolling was an act to convince himself that he wasn't terrified of walking across the swollen Pendencia river in full view of any *Sendero* snipers who might be in the vicinity. And his behaviour generally was an act. He was being warmly companionable, humorous, conversible, considerate, a friend and an ally. She was very grateful to him; he was going out of his way not to make things difficult for her, and she appreciated it. But why? And why was he here at all? He'd said he would answer the second question when they reached Lima; would his behaviour change then, as well?

She couldn't help looking for an ulterior motive. She couldn't help suspecting a trap. Idly she wondered if this was how it would always be for her, after so much deceit and so many disasters and betrayals. Miserably, she supposed it was.

She knew what the world was. She knew what men were. She knew herself. She could have no excuses, now, for not living her life accordingly, making her way as best she could, wary, alert, never going into anything without first being sure of the way out.

Mike returned, let out the handbrake, edged the wheels onto the logs. Eyes fixed ahead, he said: 'If I tell you not to look down, you will. But I wouldn't recommend it.'

She looked. Fifteen feet below them the river boiled angrily, swollen from yesterday's storm. A huge chunk of masonry, part of the blown-up bridge, protruded from it like a jagged fang. She saw what would happen if the

truck were to slip off: it would be torn open on that block
of concrete, and if they survived that they would be drawn
under the roaring muddy flood and drowned instantly.

The tree-trunks were insecure in their altered position.
Before they had been packed into the red earth under the
severed blacktop on either side, no doubt by the army
lorries they had been put there for. Now they wobbled and
shifted, sending shocking vibrations into Mike's clenched
hands on the steering wheel. It was less agonising to look
at the river.

Their front wheels made it to metalled road as the nearside
trunk slewed over to the left. Cursing over the scream of the
engine and a fusillade of spattering stones and mud, Mike
flung the wheel to the right and accelerated. There was a
sickening bang from underneath and a squealing of scorched
rubber, and then they were across. Mike drove a few yards,
stopped, let his breath go, and rested his head on the backs
of his hands. His face was grey and sweaty. Behind them
one of the trunks was canted over and in danger of falling
into the river.

Gossamer touched him lightly on the shoulder. 'Well done,
Mike,' she murmured.

He looked at her sideways and gave an ironic grin. 'Come
on a bit since Ethiopia, then, you reckon?'

Gossamer wondered what the noise was that she was
making. Then she realised it was laughter. 'Either that, or
you didn't have time to lose your temper!'

'Huh, thanks very much! Oh well, thank God for front-
wheel drive, anyway. I have a nasty suspicion that horrible
bang was the sump, so let's hope it can keep going for
another five miles.'

They drove on. Only with the release of tension did
Gossamer realise how much her back hurt.

They turned off the Marginal and drove up a dirt track
that led off to the left in a narrow strip cleared from the
jungle. It was treacherous with mud and ruts and potholes
and as Mike swung the wheel over and the pick-up jounced
and jolted on the slippery cratered surface Gossamer had to

bite her lip to keep from crying out with pain. 'Nearly there,' Mike said, observing this. She smiled back.

But there was another obstacle. Breasting a rise, they almost crashed into a barrier across the track, a wooden pole across two oildrums. A group of men gathered round the truck with guns trained on them. They looked like thugs. They wore a sort of uniform, black shorts and trousers, faded and rusty-looking with dark circles of sweat at the armpits and crotch.

Another man, khaki-shirted and almost clean-shaven, sauntered over from a little hut. 'Got your passport and visa?' Mike asked quietly.

'Yes. In my case.'

'Lift it up on your lap and get them out, very slowly. Let them see everything you're doing.'

'Who are they?'

'Police.' Mike sat very calmly, his elbow out of the cab.

The khaki-shirted man reached in through the open window and switched off the ignition. At once the air was filled with the factory hum and throb of the rainforest and the screech of parakeets. The man clicked his fingers and held his hand out. Mike put his passport in it, and Gossamer passed hers across.

The man turned his back on them and rested his broad bottom heavily against the side of the cab. In the wing mirror Gossamer saw him examine their documents with a pantomime of scrutiny, his face screwed up in concentration as he turned them over and over in his hands as if they were interesting *objects d'art*.

Then he reached behind him and opened the driver's door. 'Sit tight,' Mike muttered. 'Don't worry, it'll be all right.'

He slid out of his seat and one of the fat sweaty men slid in behind the steering wheel and slammed the door. He held a revolver in his lap. He grinned gappily at Gossamer. She smiled tightly back, then looked straight ahead.

Mike and the officer had their backs to her and seemed to be deep in conversation. Mike had his hands in his pockets and she knew he was working very hard to stay calm and relaxed. The officer shot a quick but penetrating glance at her, then looked back at Mike.

The man next to her began to stroke the barrel of his revolver along her thigh. Then, very lightly, he stroked it up to her breast, caressing it, circling her nipple with it.

If this was a trap then she wouldn't bother to struggle. If they raped her from behind, standing up, it wouldn't hurt so much. Perhaps she could take one of their guns while it was going on, then she could kill herself. But kill Mike first.

The officer gave Mike a sharp look that was part anger, part fear. Then he strode over to the pick-up, opened the door, hauled the fat sweaty policeman out and jabbed him in the stomach with his gun. The man's face was a picture of abject puzzlement.

Mike got in, started the engine. Two policemen rushed forward to lift the barrier clear. They drove through.

After they had rounded the next bend Mike looked across to her.

'All right?'

'Yes,' she croaked. 'What did you say to him?'

'I told him my passenger was an English charity worker, a target of the Shining Path and a survivor of the Aucayacu massacre, and that I was taking her to safety. Also that I had an appointment with Commander Alfonso. I have to say I think that was what really did the trick.'

'I see,' she said. She didn't.

He stared straight ahead of him, his hands tight on the juddering wheel. 'You thought I'd set you up, didn't you?' It wasn't a question.

'Yes.'

'That's understandable,' he said. Somehow, that made it worse.

They drove on in unsatisfactory silence. The forest receded on both sides as the cleared strip became wider.

Fifteen minutes later they reached the airfield.

It was a cleared circle of grass and mud, open at one end. At the other end was a single-engined plane, looking absurdly small even in this context. A youth in patched jeans and tee-shirt lounged against one wing, smoking and drinking cola. The only other presence was an armoured personnel carrier parked at the further side of the strip. Mike drove over to it and parked alongside.

'Welcome to Coca Paste International,' he said. 'Out we get. Don't worry. There's nothing to be afraid of, and it's nearly over. Come and meet Commander Alfonso. He's a murderous thug but he won't do us any harm so long as we agree with everything he says, okay?'

'I believe you,' she said.

'Thousands wouldn't. But thousands would be wrong.'

They stepped out into the soupy, chirring heat. A door in the APC opened and a squat male figure waddled out. He wore baggy khaki shorts over his fat legs and his grubby white shirt was drenched in sweat. Two large *mestizo* soldiers alighted after him. They wore fatigues and carried machine pistols.

'Meet Peru's answer to Marlon Brando,' Mike muttered in her ear. 'He thrives on respect, *capisco?*'

The toadlike figure held out a plump hand for Mike to shake. His eyes, piggily appraising, were on Gossamer.

'Señor Andersen, it is you,' he said, his voice slippery with amiability. 'And thees is the precious cargo, si?'

'Gossamer Fane, Commander Alfonso,' Mike said.

'Hello,' said Gossamer, holding out her hand. The Commander bowed and placed a wet kiss on it. 'Señora, I am delightful.' Gossamer smiled demurely. It crossed her mind to curtsey but she wasn't dressed for it. 'And I am enchanting,' she replied, daring Mike to giggle. The Commander visibly preened, and the two heavies, seeing this, grinned hideously.

'You see, Señor Andersen, that our pilot keeps English time, as I promised?'

'I do indeed,' said Mike. 'And I am duly grateful.' He stood to one side and nodded over to the pick-up.

Commander Alfonso waddled over to it, his two protectors in attendance.

'What's going on?' Gossamer hissed. 'What are they doing with your truck?'

Mike replied out of the corner of his mouth, Bogart-style: 'That ain't my truck, toots. That's our plane ticket. Fingers crossed he doesn't look underneath.'

The little fat man looked all round it, kicking the tyres, stroking the wings, rocking it on its springs. The soldiers followed him round like a couple of vaudeville stooges. Gossamer failed to suppress a snort of nasal laughter.

'Just bear in mind,' Mike muttered, 'that he's personally responsible for more deaths than the IRA, okay? That's why he's in the market for a freebie unmarked truck. That's why it matters if he likes it.'

Gossamer's hilarity turned to lead. The air rang heavily with insects and the industrial throb of the meaningless forest.

The Commander unbent, grunting, from his inspection of the radiator grille. 'Ees good,' he said. 'You go now queeckly, okay?'

'I am delightful to go quickly,' Mike answered.

'I bid farewells to your cargo,' said the little murderer, simpering. Gossamer held her hand out and he bent to kiss it, contriving to fondle her breasts as he straightened. 'Safe journeys,' he leered.

Mike put his arm round her waist. 'That's the general idea,' he said, leading her across to the plane.

It was built like a caravan with wings. They had to duck to reach the door. The interior was bare except for two seats at the front, behind the open cockpit. They were covered with greasy red rexine. They both had to stoop to reach them. They took their seats and fastened the threadbare straps.

'It's not a regular passenger service, you understand,' Mike said. 'But it does fly.'

'What is it used for?' Gossamer asked. All the Mission's supplies had to come by road.

'Coca paste,' Mike answered simply. 'This is one end of a trail that goes via Colombia to London, Amsterdam,

Marseilles, New York, you name it. The bucks start here, so to speak.'

'And the Army let it happen.'

'Oh, Gossamer! The Army run it. It's the one significant victory they've scored over the Shining Path in these parts, getting the coca trade sewn up.'

The cockpit door opened and the gangling youth climbed aboard.

'Hi, Señor Andersen,' he said.

'Hi, Loco, meet Gossamer. Gossamer, this is Loco Sanchez, our pilot.'

'Hi, Mees Gossamer.' The youth grinned, broadly and vacuously.

He strapped himself in to the pilot's seat and Gossamer watched as he turned what looked like an ordinary car ignition key in a rather battered dashboard. The engine turned over and coughed into roaring life.

'Loco?' she yelled into Mike's ear.

'Yeah. As in barking mad. You don't have to be loco to fly Alfonso Airways, but it helps.' He squeezed her arm. 'Don't worry, he can fly. It's not that much different from driving a minicab.'

'That's why I prefer black taxis,' Gossamer shouted back. Mike grinned back at her, and squeezed her arm again. The plane jolted violently and bumped along the ground, its wheels squeaking.

Then they stopped, and the engines revved. The plane seemed to crouch, quivering, like a cat about to spring. Then, with a great farting roar, it leaped forward and upward. There were two bone-shaking crumps, and then they were lurchingly airborne.

'Sorry I forgot the boiled sweets,' Mike bawled. The forest dropped away beneath them and Loco turned round, grinning and raising both fists in a thumbs-up salute.

'I also forgot your painkillers,' Mike yelled again. 'Sorry.'

'It's all right,' Gossamer replied above the rattling din. 'I've gone numb.'

Briefly they held hands, then Gossamer took hers back, and closed her eyes.

Yes, she thought, I have gone numb. Today I am flying over the Huallaga Valley next to a man who will probably have sex with me when we get to Peru. That's all right. After that I will go back to England. I'll have sex with other men, from time to time. I'll make my way in the world. But whatever happens I won't share my life with anyone, I won't get hurt again. It won't happen like that again, it can't, I know too much. I'll sleep with men when I want to and because nothing matters any more and because none of it was ever meant to make any sense. It won't mean anything. The part of me that wanted it to is dead.

And so she fell asleep.

They stayed in the Hotel Bolivar in Miraflores, the most fashionable and expensive district in Lima. It was also one of the darkest; Miraflores was taking its turn to have a power cut. There would be running water, though as the rationing took effect on alternate days. The Bolivar had generators, and it stood out like an ocean-liner on a darkened sea.

The hotel was virtually deserted but rooms were at a premium for guests who preferred glass in their windows. Most, like the craters in the road outside, were still unmended three months after a more than usually devastating car bomb.

Mike called it The Laundromat. Only the need to wash dirty money, he said, could explain why a luxury hotel had been built here at a time of zero tourism and 1,700 per cent inflation. But the staff seemed genuinely grateful for their custom, the more so when they saw that they were to be paid in dollar bills. Mike and Gossamer were given adjoining double rooms with minibars the size of small wardrobes.

Gossamer found a crumpled silk dressing gown in her suitcase and took a lukewarm shower. Even so the water stung her back as if she had been sunburned, and drying herself was awkward and uncomfortable. She wrapped a towel round her head and switched on the television.

She felt unreal. She ought to eat but she did not feel

hungry. She ought to rest but she did not feel tired; quite the opposite. She felt like an engine revving in neutral, running on adrenaline. It must be because she felt suspended between two lives, caught in a vacuum of intermission between two acts. As if to heighten the sense of unreality the TV showed pictures of the British minister Kenneth Clarke being jovially earnest with a group of Peruvian politicians who all looked like comedy-show *mafiosi*. The monotonous commentary muttered something about the war against drugs; she wondered which side some of them were on, and flipped channels in search of something more intentionally absurd.

She found a garish game show in which people with tomato-ketchup faces were being made to do humiliating things with fruit and vegetables before an audience who greeted each new travesty with savage hilarity. It looked ideally grotesque and meaningless, and she stretched herself out on the bed, tummy down, watching it as if it were being beamed from another planet.

Mike had said he would explain things when they got to Lima. Now they were here, she almost didn't want him to. She didn't really want to think about anything at all.

There was a knock on the door. 'Gossamer?' Mike.

Briefly and intensely she wished he wasn't there. 'It's okay, come in.'

'Time for your medication, dearie,' he screeched. He put the pill bottles down on her bedside table. 'Christ, what's that? It looks too bad even for the DayWorld Variety Channel. Has that guy got a guava down his trousers or is he just pleased to see us?'

'It's a pomegranate,' said Gossamer, 'and the woman with the blindfold is supposed to find it and guess what it is. I think.'

'Jesus. Kinda makes you hanker for the Hays Amendment, doesn't it? How's your back, et cetera?'

'Sore. I had a very cool shower and it felt like blazing petrol.'

'Could you bear to have me put some cream on?'

'I expect I could grit my teeth and force myself, if you insist.' She caught his eye and returned his smile.

She eased herself up a little and untied the cord of her gown. 'Gently, Mike,' she said.

'Yeah. Ever so, I promise.'

She felt him lift the garment away from her back and helped him slide it off her arms. The air was pleasantly cool on her bare skin. 'What does it look like?'

'Quite angry. Lots of little burst blood vessels near the surface where it's been rubbed on the journey. Actually that's a good sign, it shows things are healing underneath. Honest.'

'I believe you. Will they all go a horrible yellow colour before they heal completely?'

'I'm afraid so, yes. Does that matter a lot?' He sounded genuinely concerned.

'No,' she said, equally genuinely. 'I'm not planning to do any swimwear modelling in the near future.'

'Wrong time of year, in England.' She let the comment pass.

She shivered under the pleasurable shock as he dolloped the cold cream on her tender skin. His hand slid gently between her shoulder blades, down the swoop of her back, over her slightly parted buttocks. She relaxed under it.

'What's in that stuff?'

'Calendula and Hypericum,' he said. 'That's the active part. Ninety per cent of it is bog-ordinary cold cream, of course.'

Bog-ordinary. That was one of Jenny's phrases. It was reassuring to hear it now, to hear Mike use it. It was as if a little light had broken through. She knew it was absurd, of course, to feel like that.

'It's lovely,' she said.

'Oh, good. So are you. You're very beautiful, Gossamer Fane.' His hands did not stray or falter.

'I don't feel beautiful.'

'I know. But that's not your fault, Gossamer. None of that is your fault.'

His words begged a thousand questions but she could not bring herself to ask a single one of them. Instead she simply said, 'Thank you, Mike. You're being very kind and lovely, and I appreciate it.'

His voice, like his hands, was steady. 'And it's lovely of you to say that. I don't deserve it.'

'I don't think any of us gets what they deserve, Mike,' she said. 'Do you?'

'I think it's important to believe that some people do,' he replied. She let that pass, too. She lay in silence for some minutes while he gently smoothed the soothing lotion in. Then he said:

'Darling, do you mind if I use your zapper? I don't think I can bear to watch this woman put a peeled banana down her cleavage.'

Darling. But he had said it with just a saving hint of irony, hadn't he? 'Go on then, spoilsport. Zap away.'

He flipped channels and found a programme with a man in a suit with Brylcreemed hair (or its Peruvian equivalent), a woman with an enormous bust and a tiny waist, and a group of Indians in Tourist Board ponchos.

'Ah, that's better,' Mike enthused. 'DayWorld LiveChat. My God,' he added as the camera lurched and the screen showed a slewing image of people's legs, 'it *is* live, too. Real pioneering Logie Baird stuff.'

'DayStar,' she said.

His hand stopped in mid-stroke. 'What?'

'DayStar, not DayWorld. You're thinking of StarWorld. That's the second time you've said it.' She congratulated herself on being able to say the silly words without it hurting.

'No, Gossamer,' he said gently. 'No, I do mean DayWorld. I thought perhaps you wouldn't know. That's one of the things – well, that's to do with one of the things I've got to—'

But her mind had skidded off the subject and something was happening on the screen: a caption was flashing on and off. 'Mike! Look at the television, look at what it's saying!'

¡*ABIMAEL GUZMAN CAPTURADO*!

'My God, they've got him! They've actually caught him!'

On the television, guests and audience burst into applause and people hugged each other. 'They've really got him!'

It was impossible to resist the transmitted mood of joyous celebration. Mike and Gossamer cheered wildly.

Outside the cars began hooting and there was the sudden crepitation of firecrackers.

'Well, my God,' Mike said. 'The Great Gonzalo's helping police with their enquiries. It's as if they'd finally arrested Jack The Ripper.'

But all Gossamer could think, just at that moment, was: *Why couldn't it have been last week? Why couldn't it have saved Gabriel?* They heard the distant sound of whoops and skirls and the stamping of feet.

'Hey, listen!' Mike said. 'We're not the only people in the hotel after all.'

The television now showed a poor quality picture of the outside of Police Headquarters and a commentator jabbered frantically. 'The poor sod's having to vamp it,' Mike commented.

Still Gossamer said nothing.

'Gossamer?' She remained silent. She couldn't think of anything to say. His hand rested on the back of her neck. 'He meant something to you, didn't he? Doctor Jeffry.'

'Yes,' she replied thickly. 'No. Not like that. He – he was a good man, that's all. A decent man. He'd had such a horrible life. I tried to comfort him, but—' she could not say any more.

Mike spoke quietly. 'Like you say, people don't generally get what they deserve.' He ran his fingertips lightly down her spine, from the nape of her neck to her coccyx. 'There, that's your lot,' he said. 'I'll go and get changed and then we'll eat, yes?'

'Yes. Right. Oh and, Mike.'

'Yes?' He was by the door. She raised herself to look at him. She was showing her breasts but it didn't matter. 'Thank you.'

'You don't have to say it. But thank you for wanting to.'
Then he left her.

It was what she wanted. But she also wanted desperately to make love with him. She recognised the feeling as a weakness, and reproached herself for it.

She rummaged in her suitcase and found her Bella Freud cocktail suit. Beige satin, soft and curvy and short and gorgeous. She remembered buying it at Harvey Nichols. It had earned her status, they'd awarded her a private dressing room, a glass of champagne, a shower, just like Princess Di. She remembered how she couldn't bear to burn it, along with all the other things she'd brought with her in order to destroy them, along with all of her old existence, in the cleansing Puritan flames.

She'd never worn it, perhaps that was the reason. She'd never worn it for Carey Lambert. It wasn't tainted.

It was absurd, ridiculous, but she'd really nothing else to wear. Not on a night like this, when all Lima was in frivolous party mood.

Mike took her took a *chifa* restaurant. *Chifa*, Mike explained, was the Peruvian equivalent of Chinese food, and because it was very fashionable just at the moment it was bound to be very expensive, but very well done. He was right on both counts. They drank rice wine with it.

The restaurant was crowded and the street outside thronged with revellers celebrating the capture of the bogeyman. Mike, she saw, had bribed the restaurateur to give them a table in the furthest corner, where they could talk without shouting.

He raised his glass of *sake*. 'Cheers, Gossamer.'

'Thank you, Mike.' They drank. 'So tell me,' she said, 'what are you this time? Still a writer and journalist, or working for Alec Dayfield, or what?'

'Just a private individual on very generous expenses,' he said. 'But not DayWorld's.'

'You were telling me about that,' she reminded him.

'So I was, but Señor Guzman interrupted me. You

obviously haven't been listening to any BBC news since you've been out here.'

'We – I did listen to the World Service sometimes. Plays, usually. There was a lovely production of *Arsenic and Old Lace.*' She smiled apologetically. 'Sorry, you were saying.'

'Okay, very briefly: OffWorld's finished. Kaput. Carey Lambert did a runner and ALSAT pulled the plugs. Dayfield gobbled it up, renamed it DayWorld, then sold out most of his holding, quit as chief executive, and let the men in suits take over. I now work for them. When I'm not on leave.'

Gossamer's mind scrabbled at this precipice of information and snagged in a fingerhold: 'ALSAT? Who are they?'

'Alliance Société Européenne des Satellites. They own the Astra satellite that OffWorld leased its channels from. Lambert turned out to owe a lot of back rent, and they sent the bailiffs in. Phut, everything went dark.'

A rotten tree. When it falls, I'll be there to saw off the branches.

'What's the joke?' Mike asked.

'Oh, nothing. Go on.'

He chose his words carefully, making minute adjustments to the cutlery and glasses. 'Things happened very quickly after – after you disappeared that night. The next day, Alec cancelled all DayStar's advertising with Lambert's broking agency. That accounted for nearly all its business because over the previous months Alec had been shoving more and more work at them – his own, and stuff for the WorldStar film channel – and it pretty well folded overnight. Then Carey himself turned out to be holed up somewhere, no one could find him, and the market got the jitters. OffWorld shares took a dive, there was still no sign of the man himself, then Alec put out a statement saying the whole WorldStar deal was on ice until "certain irregularities in OffWorld's accounting procedures", as he called them, had been satisfactorarily explained. That really put the cat among the pigeons, as no doubt it was intended to.' Mike grinned, but Gossamer's face was stony.

'You spoke to Alec Dayfield during this period?'

'Yes, Gossamer, I did.'

'Did he say anything about – anything?'

'He never mentioned my nearly knocking his teeth down his throat for trying to rape you, no. But he did say Lambert had gone too far, once too often.'

'I see. That was all?'

'Not quite, no. He ... Look, I can only relay it verbatim, okay?' Gossamer nodded. 'He said, "We were both set up, Gossamer and me. And now the sins of the father must finally be paid for, in full." Just that.'

'The sins of the father.'

'Yes.'

Gossamer pushed her plate away. Mike laid his hand on hers, but she drew it away. It felt as if her own flesh was dead, corrupted.

'Carry on with what you were saying. OffWorld's accounting procedures.'

'Er, yes. Well, Alec himself ducked out of sight after that. The next thing to hit the fan was a leak from the Department of Trade and Industry, who said they were investigating Lambert over allegations of insider dealing just before the announcement of the deal over StarWorld Movies. Apparently one of his cronies had acquired a lot of OffWorld shares and then unloaded them when the price shot up immediately after it became public knowledge, but inside the same dealing period so her name never got to show up on a share register. She'd used his brokers to do it, but it was the sort of sophisticated deal only someone with his knowledge could have set up.'

'She?'

'Yeah. Annouska Vane-Venables. You know her?'

'Oh yes, I know her.' The bodyskin. Annouska very kindly showing her to a quiet room, and then Carey walking in, so humble and solicitous. Annouska triumphant, revelling in the publicity. The press camped out in Addison Place. Oh yes.

'OffWorld shares went belly-up before trading even began

next morning. Then Christ knows what didn't come crawling out of the woodwork. ALSAT went public on the money owing them, MGM and Paramount announced they were tearing up their screening contracts with StarWorld – that was just the morning. At lunchtime they found there was nothing in the OffWorld employees' pension fund except a couple of buttons and an IOU, and share dealings were supended on the stock exchange. Early next morning the SFO raided OffWorld's office and took away a lorryload of documents, and a whole lot of TV screens went blank.'

'The SFO?' It sounded like an orchestra.

'Serious Fraud Office. Theft, false accounting and fraud. They picked up a couple of small fish and put out an international arrest warrant for the shark himself.'

'International?'

'Yeah.' Mike fished in his jacket, pulled out a scrap of newspaper and passed it over. It was a Matt cartoon from the *Daily Telegraph:* an assortment of policemen and officials in an airport concourse with a tannoy saying, *Lucan Airways announce the departure of Carey Lambert from British jurisdiction*.

'Alec bought the original,' Mike said. 'Along with all the controlling shares in OffWorld at a pound a dozen. Then he faded himself out. I haven't seen him for over two months.'

Gossamer registered the sub-text of Mike's last words. He was saying: *Alec didn't send me to find you, the way Carey sent me to Africa. This is different*. Oh yes, she thought, this is different. He is behaving differently, but I am altered. Nothing can ever be the same.

'He must have known, mustn't he?' she said.

'A lot of it, yes. But if he did press any buttons to blow OffWorld up he did it on his own, I'm sure of that. I certainly had no inkling of it.' Their eyes met, and she was sure he was telling the truth. 'I mean,' he continued, 'quite a few of us knew Lambert's methods were rough. The art of coarse entrepreneurship, you know? And worse than that. Me especially, of course. It's why I left him.'

'After Africa.'

'Yes, Gossamer: after Africa. And because of it, to a large extent.'

'You mean, because of me?'

A loudspeaker van drove past the restaurant blaring salsa music.

'Yes, Gossamer, because of you. And me. And him. And all of that.' She let him be silent, let him gather himself for the next part of what he had to say. 'I couldn't reconcile what I felt with what I saw with what I'd been told. It was like being pulled in three directions at once. I just had to walk away from it, and then, when I got back, I had to walk away from Lambert, from his world. I couldn't live in it any more. That just left how I felt, which I tucked away and left, like a sort of appendix in my mind, you know? Like you tuck away scenes from your childhood.'

'Yes,' she said, 'I understand.' This felt like safe neutral territory.

'And then I was told something else, I was told more. God help me, it seemed to make sense.'

'A story about a teenage prostitute who was taken up and turned into something else, or into someone who could give the appearance of being someone else. Me. Alec told you?'

He looked puzzled. 'No. Not Alec. Carey. It's why I sent you that stupid note.'

That note again. 'What note?' She had to shout it above a renewed burst of noise.

He leant in close. 'That note I sent you the night of the BAFTA thing. You remember.'

'I remember the BAFTA thing, but I never got a note. How did you send it? What did it say?'

He looked shame-faced. 'Via Carey Lambert, via Alec. It said something like, "Congratulations baby, you're finally going to get what you worked so hard for." Because he'd told us, you see, Alec and me. Carey had told us. Told us that story about where you came from, how he picked you up and – well, all of that.'

Her head swam. The enormity of Carey's betrayal hit

her like a freezing wind and she blanched before it. 'That night?'

'Yes, while we watched you on the monitor doing your stuff in the bodyskin.'

And after that Carey had come to her, contrite.

'And not just us,' he added.

'Oh?'

'No. Malling Benedict, for one.'

The restaurant dissolved into a messy kaleidoscope of noise and colours that boomed and pulsed behind her eyelids. She felt thin and papery. She heard herself croak out the words, 'Malling Benedict.'

'Yes.' His voice came from very far away. 'He said, Carey said, coming clean was the best way of avoiding dirt.'

Coming clean. And then he had come to her.

The universe shrank to a screaming pin-point.

'I never got your note,' she squeaked out. 'Of course. It would have ruined his plans if he'd passed it on.'

Silence. A silence filled with meaningless cacophony.

'So what is the truth, Gossamer? What's the true story?'

'I don't know.'

They were cocooned in a maelstrom of excited voices.

'I don't know. I was raised in a convent on the Scottish Border as an orphan baby, then I went to Shaws School, then I left and met Carey. I don't know any more. I don't know what the true story is. I'm having to fight very hard to cling to what I think I do know.'

She looked at him. His face sent nothing back. She was drained of all feeling, of all caring about anything.

'Perhaps I don't even know that. Perhaps I've been making it all up. I thought I'd got proof but maybe I made that up as well. Or dreamed it. I don't know.'

Mike offered no assistance. 'I can't say, Gossamer,' he told her.

'Of course you can't,' she replied. 'You don't know me any better than I do.'

He bowed his head in cold and useless acquiescence. She

reminded herself that he, too, had made up stories about himself. Her voice hardened:

'So let's talk about you, Mike Andersen, private individual on large expenses. Who's paying them this time?'

He looked up and replied without hesitation: 'Chatteris Choate.'

She was struck dumb. She could only gawp back at him. He took over.

'After that night, after you'd run off, I went back to see Alec. He was still there. All he could say was that things weren't the way I thought they were but that he couldn't say what the truth was. I was too numb to say or do anything. Then all the OffWorld shit hit the fan. By the time I was able to come looking for you, you'd disappeared.'

'I flew out to Peru the next evening,' she said. She smiled to herself hopelessly, remembering how it had been. Remembering there hadn't even been time to make a significant gesture, like giving her car away, doing a bit of unforeseen good to somebody, leaving a trace behind.

'Yeah,' he said bleakly. 'I went mad, Gossamer. I was desperate to find you, to find some trace of you. I could feel myself beginning to lose belief in what happened in Berkeley Square, in what I said to you there.'

'Is that where it was? Where the nightingale sang?'

'Yes. Didn't you know?'

She shook her head. 'No, I was just running. I found a taxi after that, I just asked it to take me to—. Well, never mind.'

'To Ida Spenlowe-Humfry.'

Her throat contracted. 'Yes. How – how did you— ?'

'I found out, Gossamer. Eventually. She wouldn't say anything at first, nobody would. Or they couldn't. I tried everyone I could think of. All the Project Aid crowd. John Canfield.'

She goggled. 'Oh, yes,' he said. 'And he told me quite a lot of things I didn't know. Things that made me feel very small and stupid and grubby. But not the one thing I wanted to find out. And I spoke to Anthony Morland.'

The name meant nothing to her. 'Who?'

'In your flat. Your gay friend.'

John Canfield. Anthony Morland. People she knew presented to her in disguise, as Mike had known them. 'Oh. Yes.'

'But all he could tell me was that Ida had told him you wanted him to live there and look after it for you. He's a nice chap.'

'Yes, isn't he!' She met his eyes, then looked away.

'He could only refer me to Ida, who was stony-silent. Not for telling the likes of me.'

'Not for telling anyone. I made her promise not to.'

'She kept it, Gossamer. Kept it from me, at any rate. Anyway, after that I gave up. I told myself I had to learn to carry on as if you'd never been. I convinced myself that was what you wanted.'

'Yes,' she said. 'It was. So what happened, Mike?'

'I was contacted. Summoned to Chatteris Choate by Monsieur Jean-Luc Frémont. He's got engaged, by the way. To the daughter of a vineyard. An old family connection, apparently. Anyway, he told me Chatteris Choate were anxious to know where you were because they needed to contact you, and would I please be so very kind as to go to a place called Aucayacu and let you know, and give you all necessary assistance to come back to England, assuming that was agreeable to you.' He spoke the last three words in a humorous parody of Jean-Luc's voice.

'I, er, assumed it was, given the circumstances I found you in. It didn't seem like the right time to ask.'

Gossamer's mind sifted and graded all this information dispassionately, as if it pertained to someone else. 'Ida must have told him,' she said eventually.

'Yes. Which means she must have thought there was a good reason to. I don't know what that is, I didn't ask. It's none of my business. Anyway, I had leave due and DayWorld made no objection. And I had my own reason for wanting to find you.'

'Which was?'

'Which is that I love you. I love you, Gossamer Fane. I want to marry you and have children with you, and bring them up and let them go, and then grow old with you. I want to share the rest of my life with you, but I don't hope for it. I'm only saying it because you have to know it. I don't expect anything to come of it. I told you the last time I saw you that I didn't care what you were. That was inelegantly put, but there's no other way I can say it. I love you the way I find you, that's all. Nothing else matters.'

'It matters to me, Mike.'

'I know. And I know that's why you can't return my love. Mine, or anyone else's. I can't help you there. I hope somebody can, one day. All that matters to me, all I can do anything about, is that the fact that I love you should be one of things you know. You probably don't want to, but it's all right. You do now. It's what motivated me to come out here looking for you, on behalf of your solicitors. Now I've found you and said it you don't have to see me ever again, if you don't want to. I shan't pursue you. Just – just tell me you hear what I'm saying, that's all I ask.'

'I hear you, Mike. That's all. I hear you.'

'Thank you,' he said. 'That's all I hoped for.'

They walked back to the hotel. There was no question of getting a taxi, Lima was given over to the Lord of Misrule, an out-of-season Mardi Gras.

As they neared their destination the night air punched them and sent them reeling into each other. A moment later there was the heavy crump of an explosion and the shrieking of sirens. Two shots rang out and there was the sound of running feet.

Mike recovered first. 'Gonzalo Thought,' he said. 'It lingers on.'

She came to his room and they made love as she had known they must. He laid himself out for her, supine and erect, and she straddled him and took him inside her, body and soul, and rode with him to that climatic meeting-point. And it was as it had been before, with him as with no one else. It was new, and it was known. For a lingering moment of release they were together as one, outside time and space, weightless, dimensionless.

Then they were two bodies, two separate and unknowable existences.

She parted from him, and left him there.

'Goodbye, Mike,' she said.

'Goodbye, Gossamer. Take care.'

'And you,' she said. 'And you.'

Next day they exhibited the Great Gonzalo, caged and humiliated in his cartoon prison suit. He played his part before the cameras, ranting and rattling his bars, accepting his fate and making his settlement with it as his guards stood by, self-consciously grinning and shuffling their feet. They seemed to find the whole thing a great deal more humiliating than he did.

Gossamer caught the midday flight, alone.

She accepted her own fate. *The sins of the father must be paid for in full.* So be it. She was Carey's daughter after all, taint and tainted, conceived in darkness and bred in secret. All her life she had been the instrument of his perverted will, his creature. Now that her creator had removed himself, she was adrift. She had already become all she could ever be.

She knew she should be grateful for the knowledge, knew it was more than many people found in a lifetime of pain and delusion. She had discovered the boundary between order and chaos; now she must be sure never to cross it again, for next time there would be no going back.

She had no future; the dead hand of the past lay across it. She must learn to live continuously in the present, from moment to moment.

She must learn to be herself, alone, unknowable and uninhabited.

❖ LONDON ❖

✳ Twenty-Three ✳

Wind stirred the branches of the sycamore and shook loose a little drift of leaves. One landed on the table between them, brittle-veined and pumpkin-yellow with little islands of exhausted green. Gossamer picked it up by the stalk and twirled it idly between her fingers, then let it fall again.

The sun shone hazily but there was no warmth in the air. It was past the time for sitting outside but both women preferred it out here.

Ida took a long sip of her Guinness, lit another cheroot and smiled compassionately at Gossamer. 'What were you going to say, my dear?'

'You know how it is,' said Gossamer, 'when you're thinking about something and you keep coming across references to it?'

'Oh yes,' said Ida gruffly. 'Happens all the time. Arthur Koestler got very worked up about it a few years ago. And there's a rather good story about it, M.R. James I think or perhaps it was Saki.' She grinned. 'Sorry, dear. Wittering on. Senile decay, I expect. You were saying?'

Gossamer laughed.

'Oh, it was just something to do with a magazine article I read at the hairdresser's, that's all.'

'Ah,' said Ida. 'That great repository of serendipity, the hairdresser. It suits you, by the way. Short but not butch, stylish but you only have to drag a brush through it a couple of times in the morning to get it to look right. And it frames your face beautifully.'

'Thank you,' Gossamer replied gratefully. 'Actually it was

just about the only thing I could have done with it, the state it was in when I got back.'

'Go on, Gossamer, this article,' urged Ida.

'Oh, it was just about this Scottish island, in the Hebrides. The government took it over, in the war I think, to test biological weapons – an anthrax bomb. They evacuated it and set the thing off, and it poisoned the whole island for forty years. No one was allowed to go there because the spores remained active in the soil, although things still grew all right – heather and trees and things. It still looked all right, but it was deadly poisonous. Now they've said it's fit to visit but no one will ever be allowed to live there, even though it is supposed to be safe. I can't remember what it's called.'

'Grunard,' said Ida.

'Gosh, how do you know?'

'My dear girl, I was there! Well, not there exactly, but I was around. I remember them doing it. My grandfather got very worked up about it at the time, poor old devil. Did I ever tell you I had Highland blood in me? So of course this reminded you of you, this article about poor old Grunard.'

'Yes,' Gossamer replied simply. 'It was like being handed the last piece of the jigsaw to fit in. It seemed to sum me up, it – it *defined* me. I look fine but I'm not safe. Visitors only, by appointment.'

Ida's expression was pained. 'Oh my dear. What a terrible thing to say about yourself. It's so bleak and hopeless.'

'Yes, but it doesn't feel like that. Really it doesn't. It's just,' she shrugged, 'well, this is me and here I am. Like the island itself, really. People might get worked up about it, but there it is, it can't be altered and that's that. It's peaceful.'

Ida spoke to her Guinness. 'Peaceful,' she said. 'Dear God. I was married once, you know. A nice chap. Decent, kind, thoughtful, all the rest of it. It was a disaster from the word go, of course. Awful, ghastly. I kept wanting to wake up. In the end he did the decent thing, good chap that he was. Brighton hotel chambermaid, male and female clothing scattered about, that sort of thing. He got married again straight away, blissfully happily, the pair of them. Still alive, see them from time to time. A pair of ugly decrepit old crocks but still in love. Me, I didn't of course. Slept around a lot, women obviously. Fun at the time, mostly, but nothing afterwards. Just couldn't find a partner. Tried to a few times, got badly hurt or did harm, sometimes both at once. Like your nice doctor man, God rest his soul. Not your fault but it feels as if it ought to be. So. Decided it was no go, not for me. Mountain peak, in my case, not an island. Thought of myself as a mountain peak. Reach across to someone else's from time to time, touch hands, say hello, the most I could do or hope for. That's what I've done ever since. Oh, and it's worked all right. Here I am, and all that. Good old Ida, the gruff old upper-class dyke with the hide of a rhinoceros and the heart of gold. She's all right.'

She lifted her face to Gossamer's. There were tears in her eyes. 'But I'm not. I was wrong. I made the wrong decision, and now it's too late. I'm so bloody lonely and there's nothing anyone can do, me least of all. I'm a lonely old hag who drinks too much and smokes too much and doesn't look after herself properly, and who will one day soon be dead, and that's that. And I shouldn't be telling you this, it's not fair on you, but I am, so there.'

She sniffed noisily and re-lit her stinking cheroot. 'God help me, I'd do anything to stop you turning into me. Take my word for it, you won't know it's happening until it's too late. That's all, my dear Gossamer. That's all I want to say. I wish to God you were a lesbian and I'd met you forty years ago, I'd have known what happiness was and I'd still have it. There, now you see what a selfish old bag I am.' Gossamer felt moved to tears but could not respond.

Ida's eyes dried and narrowed. 'Have you been to Chatteris Choate yet, seen young Mister shortly-to-become-a-fully-paid-up-member-of-the-*haute bourgeoisie*-Frémont?'

'No,' Gossamer replied. 'Not yet.'

'I told him, you know. Told him where you were. I broke my promise because he convinced me it was important, important to you. I hope to God I wasn't wrong.'

'I'm sure you weren't,' said Gossamer. 'Actually I have an appointment tomorrow afternoon. I need to see him in any case. I'm about to run out of money.'

'Oh my dear, why didn't you say? I could give you some – no, all right, lend you some, pay me back whenever. If it's just a question of bloody money . . .'

'No, it's not that.' She laid her hand on Ida's arm. 'Really. I need to get it sorted out in any case. It's all mine, now, my trust fund, I never got around to seeing to it before, when I turned twenty-one, because – well, because of the circumstances I was in at the time. That'll be what it's all about, I expect.'

Ida put her own warm, dry hand on Gossamer's. 'I wish Carey Lambert dead and rotting in a ditch, for what he's done to you. I'm so glad you told me all about it, my dear.'

'So am I.' It was true: she was. Ida was the first and only person who had truly understood. And she had no one else. Jenny was dead, Anthony had gone to live with his lover, Trish was out there somewhere, out of touch. Mike was . . . But there was no point in thinking about Mike. It was forbidden.

'What will you do?' Ida asked.

'I don't know, yet. I'd like to act. I know I'm good at it, and it would be good for me to turn myself into other people.' She smiled. 'People with beginnings, middles and ends all properly written down for them. I'd like to join a stage company, though, not do television. Go on tour, move around, immerse myself in it.'

'You're very wise, Gossamer. Wiser than I ever was. You know where to find me, my dear, if that's what you decide to do. Don't forget me, will you?'

'Oh no, Ida. I'll never forget you. I couldn't.'

Ida took a deep breath, flung her arms out, threw her head back. 'Tell you what,' she shouted. 'Let's say, sod this fucking publican!'

A man with a dog, walking past on the pavement, jumped and shot them a look of outraged propriety.

'Sod his shitty little edict that condemns elderly female

smokers to freeze to bloody death in a sodding car park or sit downwind of his customers' pissoir. Gossamer, I know a ruinously expensive French restaurant where they all smoke like chimneys and there's an ashtray on every table. Let's go and indulge ourselves, shall we? And we'll talk about all sorts of other things and drink lots of lovely red wine. My treat, I insist!'

It sounded like the most wonderful thing anyone had ever offered her: simple pleasure in friendship. 'Oh yes, let's!'

'Good-oh!' They rose, stiff from the chill air and from sitting on hard wooden benches; arm in arm, they strode off down to Holland Park Avenue to hail a cab.

That evening, still woozy with the after-effects of lunch, she was visited by Johnny Canfield, who had called to say goodbye before he left for America in a few days' time. She took him through to the kitchen while she made tea.

Gossamer had some difficulty recognising him, not because he had changed in any major way but because all the small details of his appearance seemed to have been subtly redefined, or brought into sharper focus. She had not realised before how handsome he was; a handsome man rather than the nice-looking boy of only a few months before. His face had depth to it and his eyes held a certain wariness as well as pain.

She wondered what changes he noticed in her.

'Oh, Johnny, congratulations on America. I'm really pleased.'

He grinned. 'Thanks, Gossamer. I could hardly not do it, though, could I? Not when it was in the cards.'

'Did – did Jenny do a Tarot?'

A sudden little flood of memory engulfed her, of trapped golden light and the red glow of velvet curtains. Of Jenny saying, *The world awaits us.*

'God, yes, years ago. When she was still at Shaws, in fact. She was very certain about it, as you can imagine.'

'Oh yes!' *You have to believe in it, I do. It really works!* 'She did mine, too.'

'Yes,' he said. 'I know.'

'Did she tell you what it said?' Johnny nodded. There was a small sad silence.

Gossamer squeezed his arm, to lighten the direction of their conversation, and asked him about where he was going in America. They sat at the kitchen table to drink their tea.

'Is, er, Anthony around?' he asked.

'No. He's found himself a partner, a really settled relationship. He's a theatre director. They're living in Hamsptead. I'm terribly pleased for him. Did you meet him?'

'Yes, a few months ago. I called round to see you actually, not knowing you'd gone. I was a bit out of it, really, after the funeral and everything.'

'I'm so sorry, Johnny. About not coming to the funeral.'

'Don't be,' he said shortly. 'You came to see me earlier, and that meant far more. The funeral was ghastly, you were well out of it.'

'Oh, Johnny.' Her heart turned over for him.

'Not just ghastly because it was Jenny's funeral, I mean. Well of course she didn't want a funeral at all, in that sense – we'd sort of talked about it in the past, you know? The way people, couples, do talk about that sort of thing.'

'Yes, yes I know.' She knew about it, though she'd had no experience of it herself. It had never been like that.

'She used to say all she wanted was for her friends to get together at a nice pub and tell each other what a wonderful person she was, and for all the useful bits of her body to go for transplants or research. But that couldn't happen, you see, because – well, because of the state she ended up in. So I got bamboozled into a full-scale bloody funeral-with-baked-meats do. All paid for, naturally. Oh God, it was horrible.' He shuddered.

Gossamer was inarticulate with pity. 'No, it's all right, Gossamer,' he said. 'Really. I mean, it's awful, but it will be all right, eventually. I do know it doesn't mean everything has to be bad, forever. Jenny tried to tell me that.'

'Yes, Johnny. I know.' His eyes asked the question.

'She told me, in hospital,' she said. 'Just after they'd diagnosed it.'

'Oh, I see. Oh Christ, Goss, I feel so *cheated*. All that love I could have shown her, if she'd – well. I could have done it, you know. I could have lived up to it.'

'I know, Johnny dear.' At last she was able to express what she felt. She moved to sit next to him, took his hand in hers. 'I know you could, and wanted to. But you know she had a horror of being a burden on people, of messing people up. People she cared for, and the man she loved. It's why she didn't tell you that time, when she was pregnant. She just wanted to go away and see to it, herself, clear up her own mess, as she saw it. I'm not putting this very well, but – it was partly that she hated being fussed over, and partly that she couldn't bear to think of herself cast in any other role than that of partner, sharer, equal puller of weight.'

He spoke slowly, hesitantly. 'Are you saying you – you think she . . . gave up deliberately?'

'Yes, Johnny. Yes, that is what I'm saying. I'm sure of it.'

He turned his face to her; his eyes were wet. 'Yes, I know,' he said. 'It's what I believe, too. I didn't think anybody else would see it that way, or understand.'

'You meant everything to her, Johnny. You made her complete. She loved you, on her own terms. Right to the end.'

'Yes. Thank you, Gossamer. You – you've settled something for me. Confirmed something I needed to be sure of. Thank you.'

She hugged him. 'Thank you, too, Johnny.'

'Me? What have I done?'

'Oh. Kept me in touch with something outside myself. Something important I needed to be reminded of.'

'I think I see,' he said. They held each other in silence.

'Poor Gossamer,' he said.

'Poor Johnny.'

After a while, Gossamer asked: 'Would you like some supper?'

He dithered in a very male sort of way. 'Oh, well, it's okay, I can get something, I'm sort of all packed up but there's a takeaway just round the—'

'And there's an off-licence just round the corner from here. Scrambled egg on toast and a bottle of Muscadet?'

'Lovely,' he said. 'I'm very fond of Muscadet.'

She made sure she had his address before he left.

Poor Gossamer, she thought. Yes, poor me, impoverished of everything that really matters. You've had too much to drink, she told herself, that's all it is. Yes, her mind replied, I've had too much to drink but that isn't all it is. It's all there will still be tomorrow, when I'm sober. And the day after, and so on forever. All this terrible left-over life to get through somehow, but what's the point of it?

She was not expecting to sleep, but she did: dreamlessly and deeply until bright autumn sunshine brought her to blank and empty wakefulness.

Jean-Luc Frémont telephoned halfway through the morning to cancel Gossamer's appointment at Chatteris Choate. She had planned to see him about money.

'There is much to discuss, and many matters of great significance to be resolved, and for this reason and as it will take some time I suggest the offices of Chatteris Choate would not be the appropriate place,' he said.

'Oh,' she said. 'I see. So – I don't quite see what you mean – not this afternoon, then?'

'Ah no, Gossamer – or rather, yes, this afternoon, but not as was previously arranged. With your permission I will arrange for a car to call for you at, shall we say, two o'clock?'

'Well, yes, I suppose, I – a car? Calling for me?'

His voice was blandly businesslike, pleasant and unruffling. 'Yes, I think that will be the best way. You will of course be shown the driver's credentials.'

'Oh, yes, I see. Of course. I still don't understand why—'

'It was unfortunate that the orginal arrangements were made when I myself was out of the office, otherwise I should not have to ask you to change them at such short notice. I hope this does not cause you any inconvenience? If you have perhaps something already planned for later on, I could of course make fresh arrangements.'

'No, no I've nothing else on. But it does still seem strange. Do you mean you won't actually be seeing me?'

'Oh, but of course I shall be seeing you, very soon! I admit it must sound a little strange to you but I do assure you there is nothing to make you apprehensive in any way. Both as your legal agent and as your friend I have only your best interests in my mind.'

'Yes, I see. I mean, yes of course.'

'That is very good. At two o'clock, then, a car will arrive.'

'Yes. Right. Oh – Jean-Luc?'

'Yes?'

'I'm sorry, I should have said straight away, congratulations on your engagement.'

'Ah, thank you Gossamer. And I also should have said before that Véronique and I would be very pleased and honoured to welcome you as a guest at our marriage next Spring, in Rennes.'

'Oh Jean-Luc, how lovely. Yes, thank you, I'd love to come.'

'Ah, good! Then I will deliver a formal invitation when we meet.' She heard laughter in his voice as he added: 'It is perhaps long notice for a wedding invitation, but we have had to make a certain booking some way in advance.'

'Oh, Jean-Luc! Not the cathedral?'

'*Mais oui*, the cathedral. Well, it is expected, one must say. But also nice.'

'Oh yes, lovely! When next Spring?'

'April the tenth. Please put it your diary right away.'

She laughed. 'I haven't even got a next year's diary yet! But I shall buy one straight away, and write it in.'

'I am so glad. *A bientôt*, then, Gossamer.'

'Yes. *A bientôt*.'

It was only after she had hung up she realised she

had never asked where the car was supposed to be taking her.

It arrived exactly on time. The driver wore a uniform, piped trousers and peaked cap, and called her 'miss'. He reminded her, comfortingly, of Arthur, the day porter at her old flat. Perhaps there was a special employment bureau where men like this came from.

He showed her his credentials, a letter on Chatteris Choate paper:

> *My dear Gossamer,*
> *Please do not be alarmed at the unconventionality of these arrangements, which I assure you are necessary for the securing of your welfare and happiness. You have nothing to fear and much to gain after so much suffering. I am sure Rennes Cathedral in April will as you say be lovely, even if it is not quite as Jean Béraud depicted it!*
> *Encore, a bientôt, J-L.*

'Where are we going?' she asked.

'Sussex, miss. Those are my instructions. Just outside of the village of Balcombe.' The name meant nothing to her. 'I imagine it will take us between an hour and an hour and a half, depending on the traffic. Perhaps you would like to take something to read?'

It was a thoughtful and homely suggestion. She took Donna Tartt's *The Secret History*, which she'd read herself to sleep with the night before.

The car was a Rolls-Royce. She luxuriated in the back as the busy frenzy of London slid silently by outside. Of course you're safe, she told herself. You have Jean-Luc's word for it, your solicitor and your friend, the man whose wedding you have just been invited to; what could be safer than that?

They were passing over Chelsea Bridge. 'Excuse me,' she said, leaning forward, 'do you mind telling me, what's your name?'

'Franklin, Miss. Franklin Smith. Most people call me Frank, actually.'

'Ah.'

As they drove through the dreary awfulness of Croydon, he said: 'Do you smoke, miss?'

'No,' she said. 'Why?'

'Oh, it's just that these days, miss, people often assume they're not allowed to, in this sort of situation.'

She thought of Ida and almost giggled. 'Oh, I see.' Then a thought occurred to her. 'Do you, Frank?'

'Afraid so, miss, yes. I shouldn't of course, but there you are.'

'Please do, if you want to.'

'That's very civil of you, miss. I think I'll have one to celebrate when we reach the M23.'

And, when they reached it, he did. She smelt the perfumed tang of hand-rolling tobacco. 'Thank you again, miss,' he said, opening his quarter-light.

'My name's Gossamer Fane.'

'Very good, Miss Fane. Very nice too, if I may say so.'

She returned to her book, transported sweetly and easily to another strange world as they sped down the motorway. They turned off at a place called Handcross (and there by the village High Street was a carved wooden symbol of a cross and hand) and drove along a twisty road flanked by big beech trees and high hedges of rhododendron. Gossamer closed her book, alert to her surroundings. A water tower passed by at a road junction on their right; fields opened up on the left and then the hedges closed in again, this time red with hips and haws.

The car slowed, passing a little cluster of white-painted cottages. One had wagon wheels propped against it, gaudy in white and yellow and red.

They turned off the road and purred down a narrow gravelled drive, thick with trees on either side. Through the tangled branches she saw the flash of pond water reflecting low autumn sun.

A bend in the drive, and they had arrived. It was 3.15 by the clock on the dashboard.

Bleak House, she thought. Or the country house in *The Secret History*. A place conjured straight out of the imagination into real life; a place she had never been to before but which she had belonged in all her life.

She told herself it was of course a very pleasant-looking place: large and well-kept but not opulently oppressive. It was built of tile-hung mellow brick, with casement windows and tall chimneys, and a lawned garden to the front that disappeared on the edge of the woods in what might well be a ha-ha. At the rear there was a pond and an orchard. A pleasant house that made a pleasant impression: no more than that.

Why, then, this irresistible feeling of *belonging*? Because you keep wanting to belong somewhere, she told herself; so stop it.

The front door opened. 'I expect I shall see you later, Miss Fane,' said Frank.

'Yes. Thank you, Frank.'

A pleasant faced middle-aged woman greeted her. 'Miss Fane? I hope you had a pleasant journey. My name is Mary Turner.'

'Yes, thank you. Very pleasant.'

They were in a hall large enough to contain two Queen Anne chairs and a longcase clock, but not intimidatingly vast. There were beams, and a dark oak staircase.

'There is a cloakroom just there, Miss Fane, and the drawing room is here.' Mary Turner indicated a closed door under the bend of the stairs and an open one on their left. 'I expect you'd like a cup of tea after your journey?'

'Yes, very much. Thank you.'

A log fire flamed and crackled in the hearth, giving life to the warmth of the radiators. Sofas and armchairs looking slightly saggy and very comfortable. Another clock, running two minutes slower than the one on the hall. Oil paintings of landscapes disposed but not displayed about the walls: mostly English pastoral but one of a terraced hillside bright with the sea-reflected light of a Mediterranean sun. Heavy velvet curtains roped back at the windows that gave onto a garden lovely even at this dying season.

The door opened. 'There, now,' said Mary Turner. 'And there's some fruitcake as well, a little warm still from the oven, I'm afraid, so it may be a bit crumbly.' She set the tea tray down on the fireside table. 'It is lovely, isn't it?' she said, joining Gossamer at the window.

'Yes, it is. It must be a lot of work.'

'Enough to keep my husband out of mischief, anyway! He does the gardens mostly, though Frank helps him with the heavy work when he's not wanted for the driving.'

'Frank Smith?'

'That's right, Miss Fane. My brother. I see he's introduced himself. Now then, I'll let you be in peace and have your tea, Miss Fane.'

Gossamer was left alone. She sat by the fire and shucked her shoes off. She sipped her tea, which was strong and tasty, and ate her warm fruitcake. Her chair was comfortable, the fire soothing, the whole atmosphere of the place homely and relaxing, just like Frank Smith and Mary Turner, and her husband who kept himself out of mischief in that lovely garden.

It was all so reassuring that she had quite forgotten to ask awkward questions like *Who do you work for?* and *What am I doing here?*

The logs crackled and hissed, lulling her almost to sleep. Her eyes were closed when the door opened behind her and a man's voice said, 'Hello, Gossamer.'

She did not need to turn around. 'Hello, Alec,' she said.

He entered the room and faced her across the fireplace. He wore a sports jacket and twill trousers, a checked cotton shirt and a soft woollen tie. He stood a little awkwardly, with his hands clasped behind his back like the Duke of Edinburgh. She saw that he had aged. His face had softened.

'I'm so glad you agreed to come,' he said.

'I was not aware of what I was coming to,' she replied, levelly but politely.

'Of course. That is why I am glad you agreed to it. It would have been quite understandable of you not to. Ah good, Mrs Turner.'

'I thought I heard you come down, Mr Dayfield, so I brought another cup and saucer. There's a creak in the stairs,' she explained to Gossamer, 'just over the kitchen, so it saves ringing the bell. Now, is there anything else you'd like?'

'Gossamer? Mrs Turner does lovely crumpets, I can recommend them.'

'No thank you, Mrs Turner. The fruitcake's delicious.'

'Oh good! Now then, could I ask, is Miss Fane staying to dinner?'

'Well, I—'

Alec raised his hand a fraction. 'Could we let you know a little later, Mrs Turner? It's possible Miss Fane may wish to return to London before then.'

'Right,' said Gossamer, smiling to Mrs Turner.

'Miss Fane has been working in Peru, Mrs Turner, with one of the aid organisations. She was there when they captured that terrorist leader, that's right isn't it Gossamer?'

Mike's spoken to him, then. 'Yes, that's right. I was in Lima at the time, it was my last night.'

Mrs Turner said: 'Now is he the one they put in a cage with those silly clothes on? Daft, if you ask me; makes you think regardless of what he's done you can't help feeling sorry for him.'

'Yes,' said Gossamer. 'I think he knew that, too. It was almost as if they were proving his point.'

'Yes, well, there you are, still I don't suppose they go in for fair trials much over there, do they?'

'No,' said Gossamer. 'Not a lot.'

'All as bad as each other then, I daresay. Now then, I'll be in the kitchen, if you need me for anything.'

'Or, of course,' Alec continued as Mrs Turner left the room, 'it could just be that Guzman had cast himself in a particular role and simply had to go on playing it.'

Gossamer considered the point, which was an interesting

one. 'But then you would expect him to adapt it to his circumstances,' she said. 'But instead he just screamed chunks of Gonzalo Thought at the cameras as if he was addressing a cadre meeting. It was like listening to a pre-recorded tape.'

'Yes, I see the distinction.' Alec bent to pour himself another cup. 'Tea?' Gossamer nodded. 'You're saying then that he seems in the end to have become a victim of his own Thought; all he could do was repeat the old formulae, because they'd always done the trick in the past and because he'd actually lost the knack of applying the intellectual processes that had once led up to them.'

'Yes, that's it. That's how it looked: he couldn't bridge the gap between where he was in his head to the situation the rest of him was actually in.' She had thought Alec had started this conversation as small talk for Mrs Turner's benefit; now she was actively enjoying the level on which he had continued it, although she did not forget the bizarre situation she herself was in, nor did she cease to be alert to its potential danger. This man had once before turned nasty on her without warning.

'Well, now,' he was saying, 'that I think could stand as a very useful working definition of madness, couldn't it? Would you say Guzman, then, was mad?'

'I think any sort of hard-line ideological or fundamentalist outlook on things is madness,' Gossamer replied. *Yes*, she thought, *I really do believe that. It's a guiding principle. Anything that believes it's got all the answers – and all the questions – is madness*.

'Ah, well, that's a rather different point – and one I think I'd agree with, but it isn't quite what I meant. I was talking about one man in one particular situation, the way we both see it.'

'I don't know, in that case. He could be. Or he could simply have been doing it for the benefit of his followers, telling them that the fight must go on.'

'The evil that men do lives after them; the good is oft interred with their bones.' He saw her quickly-stifled look of surprise. 'Oh yes, Gossamer; I'm not quite one of those people who thinks "erudite" is a sort of glue.' He grinned, and, very briefly, she saw him in a different aspect. Again she felt a sharp urge to know him better, a sort of attraction that was not sexual but not mere friendliness either, a sort of sharp amity she could not define.

'Which is not to say I haven't also been very stupid sometimes,' he added, his face clouding and closing over again. 'And done great wrong.'

She was silent. If this was an invitation to her to say, *Oh, it's all right*, she wasn't going to accept it. He seemed to take her silence for assent.

'Yes indeed, Gossamer, a very great wrong. And how stupid I was, and also self-destructive. How is the – the hurt on your face? I can see the scar, but only because I know where to look. And why.'

Involuntarily her hand went to it. It had become a sort of companion, a piece of her own history she carried about with her. 'It's all right,' she said. 'I mean, it doesn't hurt. Except when I cry. It still stings then.'

'Oh dear God,' he groaned. His face turned ashen and old, and his head drooped. 'I'm sorry, Gossamer. I'm so, so sorry. You've yet to discover how – how appalled I am by it.'

'I can only hope I do discover. Then perhaps I can understand, and so accept your apology.'

A smile passed swiftly across his face like a paw of wind through grass. 'A fine and honest answer, Gossamer,' he said. He rose and crossed to the window where he stood with his back to her.

'How would you define "evil", Gossamer?'

She sensed that she could take her time to answer. She considered some of the more notable monsters: Stalin, Hitler, Khomeini, Saddam Hussein; Abimael Guzman, perhaps. Idi Amin? Perhaps not; a monster, certainly, but probably mad rather than evil. Madness of course was a word that begged definition, too. And the others were also mad in their way, though not mad in the sense of believing themselves to be Napoleon or mistaking their wives for a hat. They had all behaved perfectly logically on their own terms. Could she find a definition of absolute wrongness in all that?

'Believing that the end always justifies the means,' she said at last.

He did not turn. His voice was quiet, considering. 'Supposing the end, having been achieved, is widely recognised as a good one? There are those who'd simply say that you can't make an omelette without breaking eggs.'

'That depends on what's been used for eggs, doesn't it?'

He laughed. 'Metaphor as the work of the Devil, Gossamer?'

She saw at once what he meant. 'Yes, in the sense of regarding people as ingredients and not as people. Dehumanising people, yes. Seeing them as objects. I call that evil.'

'And so do I, Gossamer. But what do we make of the man who *does* see people as people, and who uses that very insight – into precisely what makes them tick as individual human beings – in order to use them even more effectively, as disposable instruments of his will or his passion. Someone who can tap so deeply into them that they actually *want* to do what he needs them to do. What are we to make of him?'

His tone had altered. 'In short, Gossamer,' he said, his voice louder and clearer, 'what are we to make of Carey Lambert?'

'I don't know,' she said simply. 'I honestly don't know.'

He turned. 'I do, Gossamer. At long last, I think I do. And I reckon I've just about escaped by the skin of my teeth.' He looked at her earnestly, silhouetted against the pale light of the dying autumn day. 'And despite everything that's happened to you, I hope you may think you have, too.'

He drew the curtains, heavy red velvet curtains, warm and sheltering. But there was no warmth trapped behind them, no golden coin of light slanting through as it had upon the Velvet Girls and Jenny's Tarot pack. Instead there was the glow of lamps and the firelight's flicker, turning the room into a cosy-seeming cave. And Alec, bearlike, prowling over to the fireplace.

'He told a lot of stories, didn't he?' he said. 'About you, for instance. Would you mind telling me, please, exactly what he told you about yourself? You know already what he told me – and others.'

'Yes,' she replied. 'All right then.'

She told him. She did not look at him while she spoke, but concentrated instead on the picture that hung on the wall behind and a little to one side of where he sat. It was the Mediterranean one; Greece, she decided. A Greek island, bathed in clear light.

She knew she could not have related Carey's story about Constancia if she had been looking at him. Remembering what had happened the last time she had mentioned her, her mind measured the distance between her chair and the door, and thought of Mrs Turner in the kitchen.

Alec was silent when she had finished. 'There are a thousand reasons to lie,' he murmured eventually, almost to himself, 'and only one reason to tell the truth. Those who tell the truth are not required to account for their choice, but the liar must always ask himself two questions: one, is your lie really necessary? and two, why are you telling it?'

He spoke directly to her now. 'Oh, Gossamer. What he told you has all the ingredients of truth, and very little of it is invention. Some of it is very clever guesswork on his part. Only one part of it is entirely made up. Madeline is true, and Kenneth Tisolo, and Carey's sister. And Constancia. And the consuming hatred that has flowed between us ever since. And of course you know about the Convent. Oh yes, he's been a very clever liar. He answered both questions correctly.'

Gossamer felt herself grow heavy with dread and disappointment. Part of her, she realised, had hoped that Alec would tell her it was all made up.

'How do you know?' she asked.

'How? Well, I was there for a lot of it.' His mouth twisted in a shocking smile. 'And the rest I found out. From a very reliable source. So he told you about your resemblance to Constancia, and what it meant?'

'Yes,' she said woodenly. 'It was to taunt you, when you saw those photographs. He explained it all, he—,' her throat gagged. 'He made a clean breast of it. He said he'd done the same with you.'

'Oh yes, he did. At the same time he told me his other story about your origins.'

'Oh, yes. A cardboard box in Lincoln's Inn Fields, wasn't it?'

'A squat in Somerstown, actually. And that, of course, was a complete lie. That was Carey's fantasy. Part of him probably believed it.'

He looked suddenly helpless, defenceless. His vulnerability was all that kept Gossamer from screaming aloud, smashing the furniture, throwing cushions on the fire, smashing the windows. Rage and despair fought for release, but her urge to help held them in check; that, and the desire to hear all that he might be able to tell her. *Jean-Luc arranged for you to come here*, she reminded herself. *There must be a reason for it.*

She said: 'Perhaps he needed to dupe himself, as well.'

He clutched at her words like a drowning man at a plank. He leant forward, his eyes shining. 'Yes, you're right! I'm sure you're right. And I think it got out of control, Gossamer. He started believing his own lies, and he took his eye off the ball. Thank God, or we wouldn't be here, now. I'd probably be in jail, and you – oh God, I shudder to think how you might have ended up. You've had a bad time, Gossamer, but believe me you've come perilously close to having an infinitely worse one.'

This was unbearable. 'For Christ's sake, Alec,' she shouted at him, 'stop playing games with me! Tell me what you *know*, everything you know about me, now, right now!'

Her words had a shocking effect on him, as if she'd struck him in the face with a whip. His mouth came open and he began to gabble: 'Yes, yes Gossamer, yes you're quite right I must, I've no right, I'll tell you everything, now, I'll ...' He screwed his eyes shut. 'Oh Christ!' he groaned. 'I've been over this scene so many times in my head, planned what I was going to say, worked out how to say it, over and over again for weeks and weeks, and now I – I – oh Christ!'

His eyes opened and he stared at her, desperate. 'Help me, Gossamer. Help me, please. I don't know where to start!'

It was outrageous, but she didn't stop to think about it. 'Madeline,' she blurted, 'tell me about Madeline.'

'Right!' Instantly he seemed to organise himself, as if she had presented him with an agenda to work through, item by item. 'Madeline, right. She's real, or was. She existed. She had Carey like she had pretty well everyone else she came into contact with, irrespective of age or sex. Or race. She certainly had Kenneth Tisolo. But not in Africa, you see. No, that's the bit Carey had to invent, of course – one of the bits.'

Gossamer interrupted, she couldn't help herself. 'Not Africa! You mean none of that was true?'

'Hold on, Gossamer. No, not Africa but no, it's not correct to say that none of that was true. Carey was born in Africa, and his sister. The parents were tea planters, not proto-hippies but not exactly what you might call well-disciplined, either. They led a sort of second-rate Happy Valley life, from what I can gather. But quite well-off, you see, so that when the Mau-Mau did for them – they were both killed in an attack on the plantation – Carey and his sister did have some money behind them. They came to England, and were brought up by an aunt and uncle. Carey became a student at the London School of Economics and his sister, who was a couple of years younger than him, came to London, too, enrolling at a secretarial college. They had a flat together. Carey met Madeline at LSE, and he started screwing her. So did Carey's sister. So did a hell of a lot of other people, of course.'

'Including Kenneth Tisolo?'

'Yes, he was one of the students. A Ghanaian. Then Madeline got pregnant. By somebody.'

Something cold and clammy ran a slimy hand up Gossamer's back. 'How do you know this?' she forced herself to ask. 'Who told you?'

'Carey,' he replied simply. 'Years ago. Before he had any reason to tell me lies.'

'I see.' Her voice was flat. 'Go on, I'm sorry.'

Alec shrugged. 'Madeline was into every sort of sensual gratification, including drugs. She overdosed on a cocktail of Christ-knows-what, and died. Tisolo packed his bags and went off back to Ghana. Carey hit the bottle for a bit. And his sister – well, here we have truth again. His sister did kill herself. Threw herself in front of a tube train. They'd – they'd come to an arrangement over Madeline, you see, the two of them; they shared her. Threesomes. They were both smitten.'

Gossamer's blood ran icy cold. The shadows in the corners of the room seemed to gather in. Her throat opened and words came out, feeble words to beat back the shadows or invite them to rush in on her and engulf her.

'And the baby?'

'What baby?'

As in an nightmare, she knew she was screaming but only a little croak came out. 'Madeline's – baby.'

His voice was very soft, very controlled. 'There was no baby, Gossamer. She was, at the most, two months pregnant. Her name was Madeline Porteous, just as Carey told you. You can look her death certificate up at the National Records Office.'

Gossamer felt herself shaking as if with an ague. She was almost laughing at the absurdity of it. She had got nowhere, she was a nothing. She was alone.

'Gossamer.' His voice called her back from the cold sleepy shadowlands. 'Gossamer, look at this.'

He took a pasteboard rectangle from his wallet and passed it over. With an effort she leaned forward and took it from him.

It was a photograph. It was a photograph of herself, though she did not recognise the dress from the head-and-shoulder image. Her own eyes looked out at her, young and full of hope, and her own lips smiled back, parted in adoration. It was herself, the way she used to be.

'One of Carey's?' she asked. 'I don't remember it being taken.'

'You wouldn't, Gossamer.' His voice shook a little. 'It's not Carey's. It's mine. And it's a little older than you are.'

She gasped. She felt herself grow warm with excitement and alarm. 'Constancia?' she whispered.

'Yes.' His reply was hoarse with suppressed tears. 'Constancia. My lovely Constancia.' He held his hand out, trembling, and she passed the photo back though her eyes lingered on it as he took it and stowed it safely back.

'We both loved her, just as Carey said. I believe him there, Gossamer. He loved her, and he took her, but he couldn't handle it. Perhaps he really did have his demons after all – Madeline's demons, who knows? – and they claimed him, claimed them both. But only for a while.'

Gossamer disciplined herself to say nothing. She knew he was about to tell her of Constancia's death, and she prepared herself to hear it.

'She came back, you see. She left him, and came back to me.'

She felt her eyes widen and her mouth open. Her skin felt stretched and tingling. A cat ran with icy paws up her spine and pressed its cold nose to the nape of her neck.

'She was my wife, Gossamer. My wife when she met Carey. They started an affair. Then he came to work for me, and I found out. I sacked him, and I lost her. But she came back. She came back.'

He was crying now, very quietly. His body shuddered and he gasped for breath. She heard him say he was sorry but she was not sure who he was speaking to.

A decanter and glasses stood on a little sideboard against the far wall. She poured them each a neat whisky. Alec took his and drank it.

'Thank you, Gossamer. No more self-pity, I promise. I'm the least deserving of pity in any case, as you're about to hear. And besides, I'm the one who's still here, aren't I? I didn't die.'

His words were shatteringly reminiscent of Johnny Canfield's.

She could only gape to hear the same sentiments expressed by such a very different man.

'She came back to me, then. She told me Lambert had been very cruel with her, made her do unnatural and nasty things, more and more extreme. She said she was sorrier than she could ever tell me, and that she now knew that she loved me. She would understand if I refused her love, though it would break her heart if I did, because she had done a terrible thing to me. But I had to know, now, that her love for me was real and would endure. Gossamer? God, Gossamer, are you all right?'

She had heard again the words she had used with Carey, when she had suggested that it might have been a good thing if she had been unfaithful to him with Philippe. She saw again Carey's expression when he had heard her use them. Her mind whirled sickeningly around the terrible still centre of Carey's face, his twisted smile, his hooded eyes.

'Yes,' she said faintly. 'I'm all right. Really. Go on.'

'And I took her back. I took her back, young and lovely and so full of love. And a very few weeks later she became pregnant.' He saw her expression and smiled. 'No, I don't mean that. She had one period, Gossamer, between coming back to me and falling pregnant. But. But, but, but.'

He rose, refilled his glass, offered the decanter to Gossamer. She shook her head.

'I was frantically busy for a while, building up the agency. As soon as I could get away, we took a holiday. A little Greek island, off the tourist track, as near unspoiled as you can get. That's it, in that picture. Full of light and simplicity, isn't it? She was seven months pregnant, Gossamer. Seven months. We shouldn't have gone, of course. I've been over it and over it. We shouldn't have gone. But.'

'Was she – at all frail?' Gossamer asked, guessing what was to come.

'No, not visibly. On the contrary, she was full of life, full of hope and joy. But I knew she'd suffered, as a child in Cuba. That's all I knew, though. She wouldn't talk about it at all. She died, Gossamer. She gave birth to a baby daughter, a tiny, perfect baby daughter, and she died two hours afterwards. I don't know why. Heart failure, the doctor said. Well we all die of that, don't we.

'There was a midwife, a local woman, she took care of the baby, organised everything. I buried my wife two days later in the little churchyard on the island, I left money for a headstone, and – and I came home. With the baby. Back to England.'

He drank deeply. 'I hadn't done anything about registering the birth, but I was going to. Believe me, I was going to. But then Carey came. Carey Lambert came to see me.'

He sat down, squared himself, stared straight at her. 'I was in a state, Gossamer, as they say. Clinically ill, I should imagine – mentally, I mean. It was like watching myself, I do remember thinking that. Narrating myself, almost: telling stories about this other person doing things in order to get myself to do them, do you know what I mean?'

'Yes,' she replied, quiet and direct. 'Yes, Alec, I know what you mean.'

'Yes. And then he came. He came, and he said – he said, "Time to wake up, Dayfield. The child's mine."'

'But it – she couldn't have been. You knew that!'

'Oh yes, and I told him so. But he had that one covered, you see. Constancia had this – little habit. I used to tease her about it, call her a prude. After we made love, after we'd finished making love, she always went to the bathroom to clean herself up. No quick wipe under the bedclothes with a tissue or anything like that. She said it was like passing water, something personal. And, well, obviously she'd done the same when she – when she was with him. He said they'd never actually split up. Her coming back to me was a trick, a trick to get revenge on me for the way I'd treated him. Carey had coached her in what she should say when she came back, because he knew exactly what would get in under my defences. To get complete revenge they were going to fool me into thinking she was carrying my baby, then, sometime afterwards, she'd have left me on some pretext, divorced me, taken her share of all my loot and, in due course, she'd have gone back to him. With their child. Their child because on all those little trips to the bathroom she'd taken steps to ensure it couldn't possibly be mine. Washed me out. Daytimes, when I was out at work, she made sure that it would, eventually, be his.'

Gossamer thought she would be sick. She watched him hide his wounded face behind his whisky glass. The thought of the spirit on her lips made her stomach heave. Contemplating what she had just heard was like staring into a pit of maggots.

He spoke hoarsely: 'Can you – can you understand why part of me believed him? Why I couldn't bring myself to disbelieve him?'

'Oh yes,' she said, staring at the maggots, 'I can understand perfectly.'

'I can't – I can't begin to tell you how I felt. Whatever I say is going to sound like a plea in mitigation for something you have every right not to forgive or even want to understand. Disgust, despair, I – they don't even come close. Constancia dead, her baby, and now this, this filth . . . I just wanted to close the book. Reinvent myself, everything, start again, or else end it all. In short, I felt exactly as Lambert wanted me to feel. He'd made a very careful study of me, and he hit the target. Bullseye.'

Down there in the pit the maggots coiled, looped and writhed, loathsome, repulsive. And also fascinating. And strangely, horribly beautiful.

She wrenched her eyes away. 'So what did you do?'

He spoke rapidly, almost in a monotone:

'A girl in my office used to collect money for a Catholic charity. I got an address out of her in return for a donation. I wrapped the baby up warm, drove up to the Borders and left the baby on the doorstep of the Convent of the Sisters of the Order of Tears of Mary. I phoned about half an hour later to make sure they'd found her. As far as I was concerned that was the end of it, but I suppose I had a subconscious desire to confess to somebody, I don't know. Anyway, I told my solicitor, Kevin Germain. He was horrified. In fact he said he would report me if I didn't do something to ensure the baby's welfare. So I got him to set up a trust, I'd just done my first asset-strip and I put all the money into it. In return I extracted the promise that my identity would not, could not, be revealed. Germain kept his promise, I'm sure of that. It was pure chance that put Lambert onto you, that and your striking resemblance to your mother.'

You. Not the baby, but *you*. And *your mother*. Constancia was her mother. Constancia, Alec's wife and Carey's lover. She had seen her mother's photograph. Alec Dayfield was her mother's husband. Alec Dayfield had abandoned her in the convent porch. Alec Dayfield's money had fed and clothed and educated and housed her for nearly twenty-two years. And he had invited her to be his mistress. And tried to rape her. And Carey, Carey had ... *Carey had*—

'I'm sorry,' she said. 'I can't react. I can't take it all in, the implications of it, everything that's ... I can't ... can't speak, I ...'

Alec rose, and took her hand in both of his. He had warm hands, lovely big, dry, warm hands. He did not smile, not with his mouth or his eyes. It was all in the hands, big warm hands, comforting. His voice seemed to speak through them.

'It's all right, Gossamer. Catch your breath. Neither of us has to say anything just yet. Let there be a little silence, a little quiet time.'

He went quietly over to the sideboard. She heard him pick up the decanter. There was the soft knock of the stopper on wood, the clink of glass on glass, the fluttering hum of the fire, a distant and wonderfully comfortable sound of saucepans in the kitchen. He returned and set her glass down with a little solid clonk. He put fresh logs on the fire, and they hissed and crackled and sputtered, perfuming the warm air with the tang of woodsmoke.

Her knots united themselves in all this quiet competence, all these gentle sounds of domestic ordinariness.

It felt like home.

He settled himself in his chair, and they looked at each other. He spoke:

'He never forgave me, you see, for the fact that Constancia came back to me. Perhaps he regarded her as his salvation – I don't know, of course, nobody ever can, but I can see it's possible that part of him saw her as a way out of his own private hell. Perhaps he always had it in him to be ruthless and manipulative and cruel to any woman who ever got involved with him, or perhaps it was Madeline who made him like that, in which case I suppose we would have to say that his behaviour can be explained as taking revenge on other women for what Madeline did to him.'

'And Constance,' she said. He looked blank. 'Connie. His sister.'

'My God,' Alec said quietly. He took a sip of his whisky and set his glass down very carefully. 'His sister's name was Belinda,' he said. '"Stupid little dyke" was always his favourite epithet for her.'

Gossamer's brain whirled. 'Then—'

'Yes. He told you one completely unnecessary lie. But what a revealing one, Gossamer: to make the name so similar. It was necessary to him, it was part of the myth he had to live by, the legend he told himself must be true. The logic of insanity. My God.'

'It could just have been for my benefit,' Gossamer said. 'Knowing me. Knowing what the whole idea of "family" would mean to me.'

'Yes,' he said, 'of course. Hard to tell, isn't it, where rationality ends and insanity begins? Perhaps he blamed me for Constancia's death, for "killing" her by making her pregnant. Whatever the cause, coming to me and telling me what he did, afterwards, was his revenge. And it worked. It made me put you from me. And it has made me ashamed of myself ever since. Made me unable to function, in that sphere of relationships, ever again. You've heard my reputation with women, Gossamer. It's all true. Now you know the reason for it.'

He drank again. 'Time and again since the night I left you I've almost decided to go back and say who I was, who you were. Are. And time and again my nerve failed me. And then as the years passed I convinced myself that it would do more harm than good for you to find out. And then Carey found out, or discovered something, I don't know how, presumably he bribed someone at Chatteris Choate and got some sort of lead, however vague. And then he found you.'

'He once let slip he knew something about me that I hadn't told him. About my school. He said I had told him but I knew I hadn't. I knew, but I convinced myself I didn't.'

'He made you want to convince yourself.'

'Yes.'

'It's the genius of the con artist, Gossamer, to make the punter want to be conned. To know exactly which button to press.'

I pressed your 'on' button, Gossamer. I switched you on.

Alec continued: 'Of course I know why he did it. The same reason I screwed him, back in the eighties when I bought into the company he'd backed himself into and squeezed him off the Board. There were good business reasons for that, of course: we were commercial rivals by then. But I also hated the bastard, I wanted my revenge. I wanted to cut his balls off.'

'He told me about it once. He was full of admiration for you. He blamed his own stupidity in using one of your companies to find the shell he was looking for. He hadn't thought you'd notice.'

'Oh, I noticed! I notice everything, Gossamer. Everything except what's under my nose.'

'You're not the only one.'

He smiled. 'Thanks, my dear. Thank you for that. Oh, my God,' he sighed. 'I didn't know what you looked like, you see! I had, at last, succeded in putting you – it – the whole thing – out of my mind, my conscious mind, anyway. When I saw you it was just coincidence, the way you looked. And then when I saw those bloody photographs, and later when Carey told me about you, I hated you, hated you for daring to resemble her. All exactly as planned. Part of me was going to get revenge on you for looking like her, part of me was going to score a triumph by taking something away from him that I knew he cared about possessing. As he knew perfectly well – as he'd encouraged me to believe. Oh no, it wasn't me who spoiled his plan, Gossamer, oh no. I did exactly as he intended, the perfect dupe. It was you. Twice I let him lead me by the nose right to the edge of the precipice, twice you saved me.'

'I didn't know I was doing it, Alec.'

'No, of course you didn't, you didn't *have* to, don't you see? You were just being you, your true self, the person you knew you were despite the fact that everyone around you, *everyone*, was either telling lies about you or else believing them. You do see, don't you, what it is you saved me from? When I invited you to become my mistress? When I—' his voice grated huskily with self-disgust, 'when I tried to rape you? Incest, Gossamer. The ultimate offence. I came within seconds of committing it. That's what he planned, that was the last of the means he'd chosen to fulfil his purpose of destroying me, utterly and forever.'

Now, at last, Gossamer drank her whisky. As the pure malt spirit stole through her it seemed to reveal everything in perfect and terrible clarity.

'Right from the first, Alec. Right from the very beginning, before that, before he met me. It was the reason he met me, of course. He set up a near rape for me once, did you know that?' He shook his head, startled. 'With a man called Jake Carrington.'

'Jesus Christ. Jesus Christ Almighty. Oh God, yes. It would have to be him.'

'He was testing me, you see. Testing to see if I'd open my legs for another man on request. Then he slipped up, he couldn't resist using the photographs to wreck *Dragon Hurst*. He was greedy for a quick return on his investment and it took his eye off the main plan. But even that didn't work, because you re-shot all my episodes.'

'It still flopped, though. It didn't have you in it.'

She ignored the compliment; it wasn't important. 'But I gave him a second chance, Alec. I may have saved you but I was the one who put you in danger. When I think of what

I said to you that night, how it must have wound you up
... It would have finished you, wouldn't it?'

'Oh yes, Gossamer. It's the last taboo. You fought and
talked just long enough to prevent me breaking it and being
driven from public life. Not to mention how I would have
felt, knowing what I'd done. He'd know that, of course. Part
of the plan. As for how it would have left you ...'

'I was expendable,' she said briskly. 'He wouldn't have
given me a second thought.'

Alec looked at her keenly. 'Wouldn't he, Gossamer? I
wonder. Part of him saw you for what you were, I think.
The same part of him that responded to your mother. It
had the capacity for love, I think.'

'Then it would have been expendable,' she said, 'like me.'
As she spoke the words she knew why it was important to
say them. There must be no room for doubt, not now, not
ever. She spoke the words, and believed them. The belief
made her able to say what she then had to say.

'You would have believed, and the world would have
believed, that you had raped your own daughter, and then
the whole story would have come out: Shaws, the convent,
everything. It would have been the scandal of the year. But
would it have been true, Alec? Constancia was my mother,
but – but how can I know you're my father?' The last words
were a whisper. She knew how they could hurt him, and it
was him, and not her own safety, his hurt and not her own
risk, that she thought about.

He understood. 'Before I answer that, Gossamer, I want
you to know one thing. Whatever you believe, and whatever
the future may hold, I will always regard myself as your
father. And I will behave accordingly. I have already made a
new Will, Gossamer.' He gave her a quick, humorous smile.
'I hope you like this house, Gossamer dear. It'll be yours
one day.'

'Alec,' she said. Her eyes brimmed with tears and she
knew she wanted to love this man as her father, but still it
had to be said. 'I want to, Alec, but I can't. I'm afraid Carey's
poison must have worked too deep. I know I'll never trust

myself to believe it, that's all. However much I want to, I'll never be able to do that. I've lost the gift, Alec. He stole it and broke it and I'll never ...'

It was too much. Finally it was too much. She broke down at last and sobbed, noisily and without restraint.

And then she was in his arms, clinging to him, losing herself in the warmth and solidity of his chest, the smell of his jacket, the strength of him. She wept herself out, and when it was over he gave her an enormous white linen handkerchief and poured her another whisky.

He returned, and sat on the arm of her chair. He put his hand on her shoulder and she rested her head on his arm, and sipped her drink.

'I know how you feel, Gossamer,' he said. 'And I'm grateful for what you've just done. More grateful than I can say. I felt I was giving you a tiny part of what I owe you, as your father. I know what it means not to be able to trust. It's how I've been ever since ... since that. There is a solution to it, though: to this particular problem, I mean. We could find out, once and for all. DNA fingerprinting, Gossamer. We could both go and give a sample of our blood, and have it tested. And that would settle it, one way or the other, once and for all.'

Of course. Of course they could do that. She could find out, at last.

She did not know if she would dare to.

'Yes,' she whispered tentatively. 'We could do that. I – I ...'

'Don't answer, Gossamer. I want you to think about it. Sleep on it, in fact. I could get Frank to run you back, or I could tell Mrs Turner you'll be here for dinner, and you could spend the night here. We have a stock of spare toothbrushes and so on. And nightclothes. A very lovely silk nightdress, in fact, and a gown, and slippers.'

She heard the catch in his voice. 'My mother's?'

'Yes, my dear, hers. Would that bother you?'

'No, Alec. No, it wouldn't bother me at all. Thank you.'

'It is I who am grateful, Gossamer. Always, and more than I'll ever be able to say.'

They talked of other things, and she went to bed early, and slept late. Next morning when she came into the dining room Alec was not there.

But Mike Andersen was.

'Hello, Gossamer.' He kissed her lightly on her cheek and her heart turned over. 'Alec's just popped out to see a man about a herbaceous border. And I'm just going.'

'It's good to see you again, Mike. How are you?'

'I'm fine, Gossamer. Fine. And so are you, I think.'

'Yes,' she smiled. 'Yes, I'm fine. You know, don't you?'

'Yes, Gossamer. Yes, I know.'

'For how long?' Her whole being ached for him to give the answer she wanted to hear.

'For about, er,' he checked his watch, 'forty minutes. Alec called me last night and told me to come down here.'

'Oh good!' Tears sprang in her eyes and she glowed with relief. 'I mean—'

'I know what you mean. And, as I once so wrongly said, I know who you are.'

'Or might be,' she said.

'Or might be.'

'How is – how is Alec?'

'Jumping out of his skin every time he thinks he hears you moving about upstairs. But trying not to show it. Pestering Ted Turner is a sort of therapy.'

'I've made my decision.'

'Good. And that's for Alec to hear, not me. I must be getting back, Gossamer. I have all sorts of boring things to do with my suit on.'

'Yes, of course,' she said. 'I'm so glad I saw you.'

'So am I, Gossamer. As you can probably tell.' He took his jacket off the back of a chair and slipped it on. 'Gossamer, could I ask you something? A very big favour?'

'Yes?'

'When we meet again – if we meet again – could we pretend it's for the first time?'

'Yes, Mike. Yes, we can. I'd like that, too. When we meet.'

They stood still, a few feet apart, and looked at each other, into each other.

Then he kissed her again, as before. 'Cheerio, Goss,' he said, and was gone.

She drove back to London with Alec. Later that day he phoned her to say he had made an appointment for them both with his doctor. Jean-Luc Frémont would be there too, as their solicitor.

⚜ Twenty-Four ⚜

The sun shone, clear and irresistible. Warm air soothed through her as she laid the wild flowers at the foot of the plain white stone that marked the grave of Constancia Dayfield. Their petals, frail and poignant, trembled in the kindly breeze. Her senses were filled with the sensations of this moment, the perfume of the air, the colours of the flowers and the pure whiteness of the stone, the murmur of the balmy wind and the plash of little waves on a white strand.

'God bless you and rest you,' she whispered. The wind took her words and kept them safe.

She stepped back on the short springy turf. The scent of it leapt up and blessed her senses. His arm circled her, protective, undemanding. She trusted herself to it, her eyes closing.

One circle of her life was nearing its completion.

His voice spoke to her, through her, in her: 'Jenny, and Constancia, and very nearly you, suddenly taken. That's what you are thinking, isn't it.'

'Yes,' she said. 'Yes.'

'That life is a walk of indeterminate length on a crust of barely cooled lava, on which is laid a thin layer of vegetation, animal life, civilisation, humanity. At any moment your foot may break through to the unfathomable chaos of oblivion that lies beneath. And the trick of life, the secret of it, is not to be obsessed by that knowledge but to be aware of it, constantly aware of its possibility. So that if you, too, should fall it will be as they fell: full of light, and without whining. Without letting it win.'

'Yes,' she said. 'Yes. God bless you, yes.'

'God bless you for knowing it, and for letting me meet you there.'

They melted into each other. She turned, and their eyes widened, met and melded.

They turned away from the little burial ground.

Arm in arm they trod the path that led to the white strand. A wave that had circled the earth broke gently at their feet. The westering sun shone gold upon them and a seabird mewed plaintively overhead.

'In four weeks it will be Christmas,' she said.

'In twenty-three days it will be your birthday,' he replied.

'Constancia would have been forty-four. My mother.'

'I know,' he said. 'But you are here. We are here.'

'Grow old with me,' she said. 'Please.'

He smiled. 'I'll do my best.'

'I'll settle for that,' she said. 'Happily.'

'Thank God for that.'

'Christmas,' he said, 'Christmas at my dear white-haired old mother's.'

'Who isn't white-haired,' she replied. 'Or old.'

'But who is my mother.'

'And my father will be there.'

'It'll be fine,' he said, 'you'll see.'

'Of course it will. They've got half our genes in common, after all.'

He squeezed her. 'Gossamer Fane, that's awful. You're matchmaking.'

'And why not?'

'She's so much older than him, that's one reason why not. She's fifty-five.'

'That's only twelve years older than he is. The same age difference as us.'

'Quite,' he said. 'My point precisely.'

'Mike Andersen,' she said, her voice scandalised. 'That's an exceedingly sexist remark.'

'No it's not. Our age difference bothers me enormously.

Do you realise, Gossamer, when you're still only seventy, I'll be eighty-two?'

'I know,' she said. 'Awful, isn't it? Just make sure you keep your denture well brushed, dear, that's all. And use a good strong glue so they don't come out when I'm kissing you.'

'Promise you'll be gentle with me?'

'Promise,' she said. 'Up to a point.'

'That's all right, then.'

They kissed.

'Firm as a rock,' she said.

'Epoxy resin. Works wonders.'

They laughed together, happily in love.

She looked at him seriously. 'I know where I am,' she said.

'Of course you do. You're on a Greek island in November, with me.'

'More than that. I could be on a Greek island in November with anybody. But I'm with you, and I'm about to marry you and have your children. Our children. Alec's, my father's, grandchildren. It's all going to happen, Mike. All of it. It's certain. It's fixed, it's a known quantity. It's what I trust and believe in. I think about it, and it's there. It's really there.'

He held her close, and she shivered. A great shudder ran through her, and into him.

'Gossamer?' he said. 'What's wrong?'

'Sorry. Goose walked over my grave.'

Together they looked beyond the breaking surf over the pale beaten gold of the ocean. She clung to him. 'He's out there somewhere, Mike' she said, 'Carey Lambert. I know he's out there, somewhere.'

'Only as a white dwarf,' he replied. She looked at him, inviting him to complete the analogy. 'A burnt-out, shrunken star, Gossamer. Cold and remote. He can't burn you now.'

'They turn into black holes, though, don't they, white dwarfs? And even light gets sucked into black holes. Nothing escapes, in the end.'

'Stop it, Gossamer,' he said, gently but firmly. 'It's too far away to worry about.'

'Like death?'

'Yes, Gossamer. Like death. Too far away to become obsessed with, now. This is now. You and me is now, us. Love and light. And children, lots of children. Our children.'

She felt the glory of the moment, victorious over death. 'I love you, Mike Andersen,' she said.

'Good. Because I love you, Gossamer Fane. Till Death, in its due and natural course, do us part.'

She looked deeply into him. 'I still know so little about you,' she said. 'But I've known you all my life.'

'King of Swords,' he said. 'That's Alec, your father. King of Cups, that's Lambert. That, and the inverted Emperor, and the Devil. But you conquered him, Gossamer. You conquered him, and you saved Alec, and you found me. So what am I? What predicted me, my darling Page of Wands?'

'You were the Ten of Cups, Mike. Long-term happiness.'

'That's a minor card.'

'Yes, but it's my most important one. It was my horizon. The major cards were influences, but you're my destiny.'

'Oh darling,' he crooned with gentle mockery, 'you say the naycest things.' He fluttered his eyelids.

She kicked him playfully on the shin, and they laughed together.

'It's true, though, Mike. I hardly know you. I don't know you nearly as well as I know my father, or Carey Lambert. But I've known you all my life. You've always been there, waiting to happen.'

He brought his eyebrows together and looked at her with mock severity. 'Gossamer Fane,' he said, 'that's a ghastly cliché.'

'I know,' she said happily. 'I've read all those books as well. But I can't help it. It's true.'

They kissed again, and held close to each other until their feet began to sink in the moistening sand.

'Come on,' he said, taking her hand. 'With me. Come on.'

'Mike!' She laughed, clasping his hand and holding him back.

'What?'

'Talk about cliché, Mike!'

'What do you mean?'

'Look where the sun is! The setting sun, for goodness' sake! And we'll get wet, walking into the sea.'

'So? We'll walk into it then. I can't help where the sun is, darling. If it wants to be a cliché, fine. It's nothing to do with us.'

'Oh, I love you!'

'Thank God for that. Well, there we are, aren't we? You did Latin at school? Well then: *amor vincit omnia*, yes? If it's in Latin it must be true: love conquers everything. Including cliché. So come on. Let's conquer it.'

'I love you, Mike Andersen.'

'I love you, Gossamer Fane.'

Together, hand in hand, they walked into their future.